continued . . .

On Secret Service

"A fascinating account of how the Secret Service began and a powerful new perspective on a war the world can't forget."
—Patricia Cornwell

"[With] expert pacing and suspense, [Jakes uses] his signature combination of meticulous research and epic narrative, once again proving himself the foremost historical novelist of our national conflict."
—*Publishers Weekly*

"Deft storytelling . . . full of accurate detail and interesting political insight."
—*The Washington Post*

North and South Trilogy

North and South

"This epic tale will not disappoint."
—*The New York Times*

"A marvelous book [that] should become one of the great novels of American history."
—*Nashville Banner*

Love and War

"Massive, lusty, highly readable."
—*The Washington Post Book World*

"HIS FINEST ACHIEVEMENT TO DATE. . . . Jakes excels himself in this gigantic volume."
—*Publishers Weekly*

Heaven and Hell

"Wonderful! You're going to love *Heaven and Hell*."
—*San Francisco Chronicle*

"Another winner. . . . Dang it, John Jakes! Seven hundred pages is not enough!"
—*The Birmingham News*

American Dreams

"Sparkling family saga."   —*People*

"Exhilarating. Top-notch historical fiction."
                                          —*The Chattanooga Times*

"Realistic detail and period color galore keep this swift-moving
story grounded in the sunset of a largely agrarian America
as . . . WWI arrives to shake the republic out of its golden idyll."
                                              —*Kirkus Reviews*

Homeland

"A new first-rate historical series, chock-full of fascinating period
detail, his captivating story brings to life the sounds, smells, and
tastes of turn-of-the-century America in a manner comparable to
Michener's *Hawaii* and Doctorow's *Ragtime*. An absolute must."
                                            —*Publishers Weekly*

"A powerful tour de force, a rich, sweeping story of America as
only Jakes can tell it. It's been said before, but it can't be said
enough—John Jakes makes history come alive, makes it stir your
blood and excite your senses. *Homeland* . . . is a marvelous blend
of fact and fiction, the stuff of great historical novels. Another
winner from an old pro."   —Nelson DeMille

"Jakes . . . is in top form in this book. . . . From the start
he makes everybody believable and maintains the plot at an
entertaining boil."   —*Chicago Tribune*

"[Jakes] is a master of an old-fashioned sort of novel that
readers still enjoy."   —*The Washington Post Book World*

CALIFORNIA GOLD

JOHN JAKES

A SIGNET BOOK

For Frank Curtis
the best there is

SIGNET
Published by New American Library, a division of
Penguin Putnam Inc., 375 Hudson Street, New York, New York 10014, U.S.A.
Penguin Books Ltd, 27 Wrights Lane, London W8 5TZ, England
Penguin Books Australia Ltd, Ringwood, Victoria, Australia
Penguin Books Canada Ltd, 10 Alcorn Avenue, Toronto, Ontario, Canada M4V 3B2
Penguin Books (N.Z.) Ltd, 182–190 Wairau Road, Auckland 10, New Zealand

Penguin Books Ltd, Registered Offices:
Harmondsworth, Middlesex, England

Published by Signet, an imprint of New American Library,
a division of Penguin Putnam Inc.

First Signet Printing, August 2001
10 9 8 7 6 5 4 3 2 1

Now I wish you to learn one of the strangest matters that has ever been found in writing or in the memory of mankind. . . . Know ye that on the right hand of the Indies there is an island called *California*, very close to the Earthly Paradise . . .

—GARCÍ ORDÓÑEZ DE MONTALVO
Las Sergas de Esplandián
Seville, 1510

In reading the biographies of Californians, I found some recurring themes: restlessness rather than rootedness, innovation instead of tradition, freedom replacing responsibility. . . . I also found an obsession with bigness.

—CAROL DUNLAP
California People

I don't think of California as a place, you see. It is a certain kind of opportunity.

—JAMES D. HOUSTON
Californians

Eastward I go only by force; but westward I go free.

—HENRY DAVID THOREAU

CONTENTS

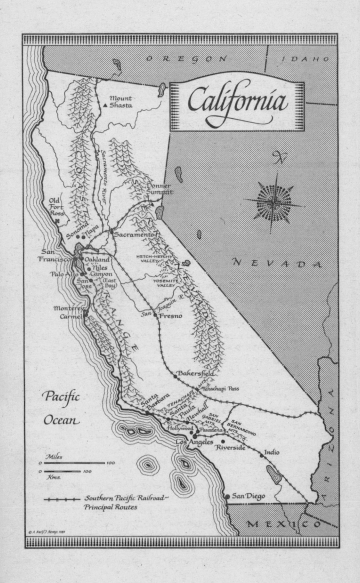

Thirty years after the Gold Rush, men and women of adventurous spirit began to discover the true gold of California. They found it hidden in her soil and her streams, in black oil and golden citrus, in seemingly impractical new inventions such as moving pictures and airplanes.

One such gold seeker set out in 1886, his destination a place steeped in legend, myth, and dreams. She was still a raw frontier, a land of stunning geographic contrasts, of parched savannas and snowy peaks, cold purple valleys and hot yellow deserts. She spilled across 158,700 square miles, and an entire 10 degrees of latitude north to south.

She had already known many cultures. Manila galleons had provisioned in her coastal bays, homebound for Europe with the riches of the Orient. Sir Francis Drake had careened his ship on her shore while searching for the fabled northwest passage to the Indies.

Early Spanish explorers waded her rivers and trekked her deserts in search of mythical cities paved with gold. Like a string of sacred rosary beads, twenty-one Franciscan missions were placed from San Diego to Sonoma. These first European settlers, the soldiers and clerics, practiced what they perceived as a benevolent despotism. In the name of God and civilization they enslaved the first Californians, native Indians whose most warlike activities were digging roots and weaving baskets.

As the years passed, others came to California in pursuit of good fortune or easy living. Mexican descendants of the Spanish soldiers settled on her hills to raise cattle on great ranchos. New England merchantmen sailed in to trade for tallow and hides—"California bank-notes," the Yankees called them. Imperial Russia planted a colony on the northern coast in search of furs and perhaps new territory, only to see it fail after a few decades.

By then a new, menacing breed had appeared: bold mountain men who risked their lives to push through the snow-choked passes of the Sierras. They greedily eyed the sweet rich land sequestered behind the mountain barrier, and soon word of their discoveries filtered east. Many more "Anglos" were shortly on the way.

"Manifest destiny" was a banner the Americans carried from

the Atlantic to the Pacific. In 1846 they seized California, and four years later she was ushered into the Union as the thirty-first state. By 1851 Americans were using the courts to steal the land-grant ranchos from their original owners.

All of this took place against the turmoil of a truly global event. On January 24, 1848, at Captain Sutter's sawmill on the south fork of the American River, a cry went up and echoed around the world: "Gold!"

Hundreds heeded it, then thousands. They walked or rode across the prairies and mountains, or tossed in reeking ships that carried them to California after they trudged through the pestilential heat of the Isthmus of Panama. Other ships voyaged around the Horn, many sinking in its raging storms. By foot and by horse, by wheel and by sail, these modern seekers of the golden fleece, these Argonauts, came. They hailed from farms and cities all over America, from Britain, Germany, France, Switzerland, Russia, China, Hawaii, Brazil, and scores of other places. During the peak of the Gold Rush as many as a hundred thousand of them were swarming into California each year.

A few found gold; most didn't. Those who did failed to keep it. The Gold Rush created not a single millionaire, not one family fortune.

Within ten years, however, other men with different perspectives began to seek and find the real gold of the Golden State. First among them were four shopkeepers, all of ordinary background but extraordinary avarice and energy, who planned, financed, and built the western portion of the first transcontinental railroad.

Other Californians began to strike it rich in silver mines just over the Nevada border. Still others found wealth in vast tracts of land where wheat could be grown bountifully and profitably.

Even by 1886, when she held almost a million people, California had not yet yielded all of her treasures. Despite the disillusionment of many who had already failed there, her shining myth remained undimmed. Her name was still a lodestone for the courageous and hopeful, and she still sang her siren song to young dreamers around the world.

This is the story of one of them . . . and of some of those he met on his journey in search of California gold.

PRELUDE

CALIFORNIA DREAMS

1886

THE THREE HANGED MEN TURNED IN THE WIND AS THE TIMbers of the gibbet creaked and the blizzard covered the shabby coats of the dead with shrouds of white. The boy was frightened of the three, with their closed eyes, fishy white skin, purple throats. He knew them all: O'Murphy, Caslin, and Uncle Dave, Pa's brother. They frightened him nearly as much as this sudden storm.

It came down off Sharp Mountain like a howling wolf, building the drifts an inch higher during the short time he stood by the gibbet. It stung his face, the snow more like pellets of ice, and drove against him so that he resembled a shrunken old man with white hair.

The blue medicine bottle dropped from his numb right hand. Frantic, he pawed in the drift till he found it and then put it in the left pocket of his poor coat, the only one without a hole. The bottle came from the store operated by the mine company—the Pluck-Me Store, Pa called it, because that's what it did to all the miners, plucked them clean.

He started to run through the growing drifts. Hard going; soon his breath was tearing in and out in loud gasps. The storm gripped his bones and made them ache, and he felt he'd never be warm again, never see sunshine again. Stumbling past the last of the hideous frame duplexes where some of the miners lived, he feared he'd never see Pa again, because drifts twice as tall as he was blocked the path home.

He wanted to cry but didn't, because he'd learned that lesson already. Even at seven years old, you didn't cry. If there wasn't enough food—and there never was—you didn't cry. If the winters were endless, freezing, without sun except for a feeble yellow-white glow in the haze now and then, breaking your heart because you longed for warmth and light, you didn't cry. If the mine's hired detectives hanged your uncle for conspiring to strike, you didn't cry. If you were out here, lost, afraid for your life and immortal soul, you still didn't cry.

He ran, slamming through a drift, battering it with both fists, the wind yelling and sobbing and chittering in his ear. His hair was white. Bolting left, he lost his balance and tumbled onto his side. He came up spitting snow and, wild with fright, cupped his hands around his mouth. "Pa? Pa, help me!" Under his nails dark deposits showed; the dirt came from his work, picking and sorting the anthracite with forty other boys. He had Pennsylvania black gold under his nails, but he couldn't spend it.

He feared there'd be no answer. Stumbling, he nearly fell again when he heard a distant voice. "Mack? Mack—son!"

"Pa, where are you? I can't see you. I'm lost."

"Mack, I've been searching for an hour." The voice receded as he ran toward it.

"But where are you?"

"Over here, this way."

This way this way. The sound whirled round and round him, the voices multiplying, echoing, confusing and frightening him more. He screamed for Pa, and swerved to the left, then right, running faster, his cracked old shoes somehow lifting him above the snow, carrying him on between cliffs of snow that formed a steadily narrowing canyon. "Pa! Pa?" he cried, and a hundred answering voices gibbered at him from all directions, the human sounds and the storm's cry a hopeless tangle.

He heard a rumbling, felt it in his feet deep in the drifts. The rumbling grew, and the snow cliffs on both sides shuddered and began to rain down showers of white.

He ran into something solid and cried out. Snapping his head back, he saw the three hanged men. He'd run in a circle. Around the gibbet, ramparts of snow reached up to a sky he was seeing for the last time.

"Help me," he said to the dead men as the snow cliffs burst open; great blocks of white hurtled down. "Somebody help me."

The hanged men opened their eyes and looked down.

He started to scream, but no sound would come. His mouth open, he watched tons of snow descending on him with a roar like the end of creation. Again he tried to force a scream out. Nothing. His throat was silent, dead.

But there was screaming enough. The storm screamed for him, louder, and louder, and—

His eyes flew open. The terrible sound gripped him until he sat up and his mind started to function. There was a thin scrawl of smoke along the horizon. Again the freight train signaled with its whistle, now quickly fading, the train dwindling in the west and leaving nothing but the smoke above the rolling harvested fields. He forced himself to breathe deeply; that slowed the beat of his heart.

The nightmare recurred every few months. It was as familiar

as a friend, but not nearly as welcome. It was compounded of drab memories: the cold, sooty, hopeless world of the coal patch, the little village of Irish and Welsh mining families between Pottsville and Port Carbon, Pennsylvania, where his pa had raised him; and of terrifying ones: He'd been lost for half an hour in just such a snowstorm when he was sent on an errand at age six. He hadn't really been in danger of losing his life, but he might as well have been, so terrified was he before his pa came with a lantern to carry him home.

In the dream he always died, killed by the sunless world of his boyhood, where there was never enough food, never enough firewood, never enough in a miner's bobtail paycheck because of all that the company deducted for rent, groceries, lamp oil, miners' candles.

For most of those who had squandered their few years of health and vigor mining Schuylkill coal, there was never enough hope. In that respect Pa was an exception. Pa had his memories. Pa had his book. Pa had California.

He'd bequeathed all of those things to his son, who now combed a burr out of his hair and stepped over the golden leaves at the base of the tree till he was free of the shadows of the limbs and could lean his head back and let the hot autumn sunshine soak into him. It wasn't as good as the sunshine of California, he was sure, but it was a foretaste.

His name was James Macklin Chance. Macklin was his Irish mother's maiden name. She'd died bearing him, and perhaps his pa had always called him Mack because of his love for her, and his loss. He stood five feet, ten inches, and had a trim, hard frame developed during his years as a mine boy. Though he'd been out in the open almost constantly in recent months, he was only marginally darker than he had been the day he left Schuylkill County forever. He was still a pale easterner.

Mack had inherited his father's straight brown hair and the hazel eyes of the mother he never knew. His beard, which he'd let grow for this journey, was distinctly lighter and redder than the hair above, and it hid a strong chin. He had a broad, likable smile when he felt like displaying it, but his early years in the mines had built a pugnacity into him too.

He relieved himself behind the tree and then hunkered over the big blue bandanna that carried his worldly goods, which consisted of a large clasp knife and the book. He wore corduroy pants and an old jacket of denim, much too heavy for this heat but necessary on the final stage of his journey. He'd set out with no money at all. The settlement after the mine accident was a princely $25, for which he'd signed a paper saying

7

the mining company was absolved of all responsibility. Burying Pa properly had used up the entire sum.

Mack untied the bandanna and debated between the bruised apple and one of the crackers now hard as wood. He chose the cracker and then took out the book, brushing crumbs from its embossed leather cover. Inspecting each corner to make sure none was bent, he then smoothed his palm over the raised lettering, whose feel he knew by heart. The cover said:

THE EMIGRANT'S GUIDE
TO CALIFORNIA
& ITS GOLD FIELDS.

Below this was the author's name, T. Fowler Haines, and a date, 1848.

The book measured six inches by three, and was half an inch thick. Mack opened it to the title page and smiled as if meeting an old friend. BASED UPON PERSONAL EYE-WITNESS EXPERIENCES OF THE AUTHOR. And PUBLISHED AT NEW YORK CITY BY THE CASH BROS. PRINTING CO. PRICE 15 CENTS (WITH MAP). Now leafing through the little book his father had carried all the way to California and back again, his eye touched on a favorite line.

The El Dorado of the early voyagers to America has been discovered at last, giving riches to some, and new hope to all.

His pa had believed that all his life, even though he was one of the thousands of failed Argonauts who came home with nothing but memories of a golden land of sunshine and promise. Mack believed it too, and now that his pa's accident had set him free of responsibility—he'd never had any loyalty to the mine company, or to the cheerless cold land in which it bled its victims of their strength and hope—he was on his way to prove the words of the remote and godlike T. Fowler Haines. In California, he'd never be cold again, or poor.

Mack once more brushed off the book, considered whether the upper right corner might be slightly bent—it was not—and then tied up the bandanna and resumed his walk west through Union County, Iowa, as the morning wore away.

A half hour later he came on two farm boys rolling around and punching each other in the dirt. He jumped in and pulled off the one on top, a stern light in his hazel eyes.

"You let him alone."

"Ain't none of your business," the bigger boy said. "He's my brother."

"I don't care—you're a whole head taller."

"What gives you any right to butt in?"

"Why," Mack said with a touch of a smile, "I just like to stand up for the underdog when he can't stand up for himself. It's something my pa taught me." Then he lost the smile as he pointed his index finger near the bigger one's face. "So you pay attention to what I say. Don't let me catch you bullying again."

"Yes, sir, awright," said the bigger one, now less sure of himself.

"Is there a town anyplace close?"

"Three miles on," said the smaller boy.

"Good. I have to find some work so I can buy some food."

The frame building, the depot of Macedon, Iowa, baked in the midday heat. Rails polished to a dazzle by the sun ran away east and west through the vast fertile prairies, where silos and barns broke the horizon. Mack stepped up into the shade at the east end of the trackside platform, drawn by the sound of a loud, whiny voice. He'd been scrutinizing Macedon's main street around on the other side when he heard the man's singsong speech, or rather, just a tantalizing snatch of it:

". . . never a better time to explore the wonders of California."

The man sheltering in the shade of the platform was old. Actually he was about forty, but to Mack, who was eighteen, that was old. He wore a plaid frock-coat, stand-up paper collar, cravat of peacock blue and green, and a derby. Shirt and collar studs winked like little gold nuggets. Mack saw the flash, not the cheapness. *When I'm rich I'll dress like that.*

The man had set up a folding stand to hold some pamphlets. As Mack drifted closer, he noticed a poster tacked to the depot wall.

"FOR HEALTH—WEALTH—RECREATION"

SEE
CALIFORNIA
NOW!!

EXCURSION FARES
WILL NEVER BE
LOWER!

9

The lecturer was swinging his finger in the air and saying, "And so, my friends . . ." His audience of three jowly farmers in straw hats and bib overalls and the mother of two little girls in ancient gingham sunbonnets didn't exactly look like friends. ". . . do not believe what you may have been told by the envious or the ignorant. Citizens of California have the best of us. Far from living in some kind of rude exile, they enjoy, in fact, the finest climate, the most fertile soil, the loveliest skies, the mildest winters, the most healthful surroundings in the entire United States of America."

Mack had no trouble believing that. He'd heard similar statements from his pa, and had read them in the pages of T. Fowler Haines.

"And now that the Union Pacific and Central Pacific railroad companies have reduced excursion fares to an all-time low, you cannot afford to pass up the opportunity to visit the Golden State, perhaps to discover your new home and—who knows?—the kind of wealth that has drawn the bold and courageous to California ever since the days when the homebound Manila galleons visited her shores, Sir Francis Drake sailed her coastline, and the hardy Spanish conquistadors roamed her valleys and mountain ranges in search of treasure. Step up, my good friends. I have the fare schedules and all pertinent information right here."

The salesman displayed a handful of pamphlets. One farmer leaned over and spat tobacco on the rails. "Too gol-damn far to go. And what for? To be scalped by Injuns or shot by road agents? No thanks." He left.

"Sir—gentlemen—that is a completely unenlightened and unrealistic—"

The salesman stopped. The other farmers were following the first. Then the mother shooed her sunbonneted daughters around the corner after they'd helped themselves to pamphlets. The man watched the girls skip past an old spaniel that lay scratching its fleas in the dust. "Well, I don't suppose those young ladies will be forking out hard cash for train tickets anytime soon. Jesus, what a hick burg." He swept the pamphlets into an open case and started to fold his stand.

Mack stepped forward. "I'd like one of those."

The salesman fanned himself with his derby. "Son, I'm hired by the Central Pacific to travel around and drum up paying passengers. You don't look like you could pay for a ride to the nearest privy."

Mack gave him a level stare. "I can't. But I like to read everything I can about California. That's where I'm headed."

"Is that so?"

Mack nodded.

The man rolled his tongue under his lip. "Then you're smarter than the idiots around here." He gestured west. "Greatest land boom in California history—and a cheap way to get there and take advantage of it—and they don't give a goddamn. Maybe they're not so stupid up in Des Moines."

He flipped a pamphlet at Mack. The cover was a glorious lithograph of a California sunrise over grape arbors and stacked shocks of wheat, with patriotic bunting depicted at the corners, and a grizzly bear strolling in the background.

"Thanks for this," Mack said, slipping the pamphlet into the book, which caught the man's interest.

"What's that?"

"A Gold Rush guidebook."

The salesman wiggled his fingers and Mack reluctantly handed it to him. The man licked a thumb to turn the pages.

"Be careful of that," Mack said. "My pa gave it to me. He carried it all the way to the diggings."

"Oh, he lives in California, does he?"

"No, Pennsylvania. That is, he did till July—he's dead now. He came back when he didn't find any gold."

"Not many did," the man said, now plucking out the tacks that held his poster to the depot wall. Toward the bottom, garish type urged:

SEE!
ORANGE GROVES & OTHER NATURAL WONDERS!
REAL ESTATE & BUSINESS OPPORTUNITIES!
NEW TOWNS FOR RETIREMENT & VACATION!

The glorious promises rolled up out of sight. "And most of those who did," the man continued, "pissed their wealth away on women or cheap spirits or games of chance. In my opinion, my boy, the gold in California's creeks and rivers is pyrites. That's fool's gold."

"I know."

"But do you know this—the real gold out there is in the land." He cast a melancholy eye on the burnished horizon. "Richest, sweetest country a man ever rested his eyes upon."

"I've read that. And there's no snow."

"That's true enough. Unless you live in the Sierras, I suppose."

"Not me," Mack declared. "I'm going to make my way in San Francisco. They call it the Athens of the West."

11

Amused, the man said, "Mighty ambitious. Tell me something. How do you propose to get all the way out there?"

"Same way I got this far. Hitch a ride when I can, walk when I can't."

A board at the end of the platform creaked and a glum middle-aged man with a metal badge on his vest stepped around the corner and folded his arms, eyeing Mack, who was distracted by the salesman's explosive exclamation:

"Walk?"

In the hot stillness he heard Pa say, "The Argonauts knew of the wonders, the bounties, the incredible *possibilities* of California—the wealth waiting to be taken, the freedom to take it with no one to gainsay your methods. Men with that vision wanted to reach California so badly, they sold everything to buy wagons or steerage tickets around the Horn. Those with nothing to sell—I was one—they walked. I saw the prairies black with walkers to California . . ."

"Yes, sir. A lot of people walked all the way in '49 and '50," Mack said.

The salesman laughed, not scornfully so much as with pity. "Son, you're crazy."

"Maybe, but I'm going."

"Then start now," the man with the badge broke in suddenly. "We got an ordinance against loafers and tramps."

Mack felt anger welling up, but he fought it down. "Sheriff—sir—I need work. I need to earn the price of a meal."

"Not in this town."

"Maybe the next one," the salesman said. "Here." He flipped a silver coin with his thumb. It spun through the air, right into Mack's eager cupped hands.

A faraway train whistle sounded and the salesman squinted into the western light. "That's my train to Des Moines. Good luck to you, son. I still say you're crazy, but I'd give a lot to go with you, see California."

"You mean you've never seen it?"

"No. The railroad just pays me to sell it." He smoothed his peacock cravat. "Anyway, I have a wife and nine children in Rock Island . . . I couldn't . . . well . . . I envy you."

It thrilled Mack to have a man so worldly approve of his undertaking, and it took away some of the sting when the sheriff said, "Get moving."

Mack waved to the salesman and stepped from the shade to the blazing light. Watching the Burlington & Missouri local pass him in a cloud of steam and cinders and a *scree* of steel

12

braking on steel, he grinned and waved at two girls in the single passenger car.

Then, whistling, he turned and resumed walking west.

Toward the Missouri River, the Platte. Toward the Rockies and the Sierras. Donner Summit, Emigrant Gap. California.

I

A
THIRSTY
MAN

1886–1887

The first treasure California began to surrender after the Gold Rush was the oldest: her land.

After Mexico had freed itself from Spain in 1821, the new Mexican government in California secularized all the property that had belonged to the missions. The Franciscans returned to Spain, defeated, and the Indians were set adrift.

The first Yankees who reached California perceived the value of the land at once. To obtain their share, some of these Anglos professed Catholicism, married into leading families, and settled down to comfortable lives as owners and masters of rich cattle ranches.

After California came into the Union, other, less principled newcomers also recognized the land's potential worth and set out to acquire it in a somewhat ruder but typically American way: by using the law. The United States Congress had mandated the clarification and settlement of land claims, and a commission was set up to hear the arguments of disputing parties. Unfortunately, not one of its members spoke Spanish.

Further, most of the original land grants had been written in the haziest of language, with claims described and delimited by such landmarks as a tree (perhaps blown down in a recent storm), a stream (its course changed over two or three decades), or a rock (gone completely). And if ill-defined boundaries would not carry the day for the claimant, a forged grant was certain to do so. With the great majority of claims decided by Anglo judges in favor of Anglo clients represented by Anglo lawyers, the Californios—the peaceful, civilized, gentleman-ranchers of Mexican descent—were soon robbed of their land.

As the ranchos disappeared and apocalyptic seasons of drought and flooding rains turned the once-rich beef-cattle trade into a risky and unpopular venture, land baron and small farmer alike turned to wheat, a more stable and profitable crop. Though wheat had been grown at a few of the missions, it was only now that Californians recognized its perfect suitability to the soil of the Central Valley. It would sprout in the short, wet winters, it matured and flourished in the hot, dry summers, it could survive seasons of scant rainfall, and it was hardy enough to withstand long sea voyages to the markets of the East Coast

17

or Europe, where it was soon in great demand. By the 1880s, California was shipping forty million bushels a year.

This new golden crop transformed the flat and featureless Sacramento and San Joaquin valleys into a source of unprecedented wealth. It was the first great agricultural bonanza in one of the greatest agricultural regions on the face of the globe, and it was not to be the last.

But the bonanzas of the future awaited the arrival of something the flat, fertile land could not itself supply in adequate quantity—water.

IN OMAHA, NEBRASKA, MACK CHANCE SWABBED FLOORS **1**
in a saloon for a few days. On the afternoon that he received
his wages, the barkeep's bulldog bit him, and for the next week
he was dizzy with a fever. Limping along a rutted pike leading
west, he tried to convince himself that the salesman was wrong
when he said, "Son, you're crazy."

Outside Kearney, a farmer shot at him with both barrels of
a shotgun. Mack dove over the fence, stolen apples spilling
from his pockets. He despised thieving, and being forced to
be a thief, but the apples provided his only nourishment for
the next four days.

With his mouth dusty-dry, he ignored warnings in the guidebook and sank to his knees beside the sludgy Platte and drank.
The water had a peculiar acidic taste. By nightfall he lay on
the ground, clutching his gut while his bowels boiled. He was
ill for a week.

On the prairie he watched a Union Pacific express flash westward, a long, rattling segmented monster made of mail, freight,
and first- and second-class passenger cars. One of the latter,
packed with pale people in dark clothes, had a canvas banner
nailed to its side.

INDIANA EXCURSION
TO
SOUTHERN CALIFORNIA

The train raised an enormous cloud of dust. A few of the
excursionists spied Mack standing beside the right-of-way and
waved mockingly, and he clenched his teeth and trudged on
after the train, the dust settling like yellow flour on his hair,
his ears, his eyelids.

Camped near Fremont's Ford, where the trail branched away
for lower California, he sat reading T. Fowler Haines by the
light of the full moon.

His father had kept a small shelf of California books, yel-

19

lowing books, mostly secondhand, but full of bright visions, extravagant promises. But T. Fowler Haines was Pa's favorite. Like the other guidebook authors, Haines gave mileage and described landmarks on the old Oregon Trail and, farther west, the California Cutoff. Mack intended to follow this route partway, though he didn't need to rely slavishly on Haines. Almost forty years after Haines had made his trip as an "eye-witness" and written it up, many more hamlets and towns dotted the route, along with railway lines and serviceable roads. Even in the mountains, Mack expected to depend less on Haines than on the transcontinental rails. What he treasured in Haines were the wonders.

So he read again some of Haines's excerpts from the old Spanish novel that had given California its name. The novelist said California was peopled by incredibly strong black women, Amazons, and "their arms were all of gold, and so was the harness of the wild beasts which they tamed and rode . . . There were many griffins, on account of the ruggedness of the country."

That night he dreamed of the griffins and the black women instead of hanged men, snow, death.

Sometimes he sheltered in a barn or a stable, sometimes under a tree in a downpour, unless there was lightning. He saw spectacular things: a cyclone's funnel cloud, a prairie fire burning over an expanse of ten city blocks, a herd of bison grazing—Buffalo Bill hadn't slain them all, evidently.

His clothes tended to stiffen and smell despite conscientious washing whenever he found a suitable stream. He occasionally caught a ride in a wagon, but mostly he stayed on foot. The excruciating pain in his thighs and calves that had tortured and impeded him during the first part of the journey now reduced to a steady ache. He was discovering new muscles all over his body, and he'd not been exactly weak before.

Foraging food was the hardest part. Sometimes he dined on nothing but berries and water. He lost weight, a lot of weight.

Rather than follow the northerly curve of the railroad up through Wyoming and down again to the Salt Lake, he struck more directly westward, for Colorado. Wherever he could, he traded work for food and a bed, or a few cents. He cut and stacked firewood, slopped hogs, whitewashed the interior of a Grange hall.

As the land grew flatter and more desolate, he tended to forget that he lived in a highly civilized country where Grover

Cleveland was president, the great Civil War was more than twenty years in the past, and men once considered young heroes were now garrulous old storytellers.

It was an age of plenty, an age of marvels, with Pullman Palace Cars and steam-driven elevators, public street illumination and incandescent lamps perfected by Mr. Edison, telephone service beginning to link major cities, and three years ago, the new Brooklyn Bridge—an architectural wonder to rival the Pyramids. Although Mack knew about all these things, and a lot more, increasingly they seemed to belong to some other place, some other planet. He tramped for long periods without seeing a tilled field, a freight wagon, telegraph poles, or even a single wandering sheep. He felt that he was approaching the remote border of the civilized world. Once he passed that, and conquered the mountain barriers, he would be in a land beyond all imagining—just as the old Spanish novel said.

There was less daylight every day, and it had a sad, cool cast. He tramped among aspens and alders and sycamores instead of the scraggly cottonwoods of the plains. The beautiful sunlit trees bent in the wind, which stripped them and flung clouds of bonfire-colored leaves around him.

The falling leaves made him sad, reminding him that he had no home.

Except the one that lay ahead.

He stood silently in a roadway that rose at an angle of thirty degrees and shivered. The snow was falling and blowing hard now, already covering the ground. It brought visions of his nightmare. He ran his icy hand through the long beard that reached halfway down his chest, his eyes fixed on the menacing obstacle before him. The Rockies. Black granite and gray ice. Common sense told him to turn back. He listened to other voices.

Never be poor again.

Never be cold again . . .

He stepped out on the snowy, flinty road bordered with boulders and fallen slabs of granite and cried aloud when his weight came down on his left foot, swollen because his mule-ear boots were so tight, the left one especially. He'd cut it open with his clasp knife; now it resembled the ruined shoes he'd thrown away. He'd also ripped up one of the shirts from the roll on his back, and wrapped his foot. The shirting had been clean yesterday. Today it glistened and oozed blood.

He scorned himself for the outcry. Although there wasn't

21

anyone to hear, he thought it unmanly, an admission of weakness.

The wind raked and numbed his face, and fear swirled up as the snow stung his cheeks. He set his mouth and dove his hand into his pocket to clasp the leather cover of T. Fowler Haines, his thumb finding the bold embossed *C* in *California*. Leaving bloody footprints in the snow, he climbed up the steep road toward the peaks.

2 WHITE LIGHT WOKE HIM. HE SAT UP, GRUMBLING, BONE cold.

Hearing voices, he remembered where he was: miles east of Donner Summit and Truckee, in the Sierras, but still on the Nevada side of the border. A late-spring storm had driven him to shelter at sunset inside one of the high-mountain snow sheds built all along the Central Pacific's right-of-way. He'd fallen asleep. Lucky he hadn't slept all night; he might have frozen to death.

Creeping toward the light at the end of the shed, he resembled an upright bear more than a man, a shaggy thing bundled inside several shirts, a filthy buffalo-hide coat, and a fur hat he'd tied tightly under his beard. He wore three pairs of soiled socks, and work shoes he'd bought after cooking for a week for a CP section crew plowing the line in Nevada.

He thrust his gauntleted hands under his arms and peered out. Light snow fell through the brilliant headlight of the locomotive hissing and squirting steam fifty yards down the track. Mack saw a coal tender, a single freight car, and a caboose. The night was vast, cold, forbidding, with a sense of implacable rock all around, and lifeless space.

A lantern swung to and fro between the train and the utility shed of a small coaling station. It belonged to the brakeman, who'd run up from the caboose. The engineer and firemen crunched the snow as they hurried back to join him, their voices carrying clearly in the still night.

"Saw him when he peeked out, Seamus. Hold my lamp while I get my truncheon."

Mack clung in the shadow just inside the shed, squinting against the headlight. The freight car door rolled back noisily.

22

"All right, you. Get out of there. Out, I say. There're three of us, one of you."

That convinced the stowaway; a shadow shape in the steam jumped down. Landing off balance at the edge of the long snowy incline that sloped away from the track, he groped for the freight car to steady himself. The brakeman said, "No free rides on C. P. Huntington's line, mister." Mack blinked at the sound of the truncheon striking the stowaway's bare head.

The man groaned and swayed toward the slope. Laughing, the engineer kicked the man's rear and the brakeman clubbed him again. That pitched him over with a muffled cry. Down the slope he went, rolling, stirring up clouds of snow. Mack heard another strident yell from below, then silence.

The train crew exchanged comments he couldn't hear as they returned to their posts. The brakeman stopped to urinate in the snow, then climbed aboard and waved his lantern. As the locomotive drivers shunted back and forth, the engineer sounded the whistle, and its throaty wail reverberated through the mountain fastness. Now the train came chugging toward Mack, its headlight reflecting on the two steel concaves of the jutting snowplow. For a moment they flashed like mirrors.

As Mack grabbed the beam at the end of the shed and swung around to the outside, his shoe slipped and he nearly fell. Clinging to the outside of the shed, he twisted to look over his shoulder. A chasm. Just a black chasm. *God* . . .

Chugging, rumbling, the work train entered the shed. Mack couldn't help coughing loudly in the thick steam and coal smoke, but the train's noise was so great, no one heard. His nose ran and his teeth chattered. The train passed.

He didn't fancy himself a samaritan, but he couldn't abandon whoever had tumbled down the slope. Carefully he swung himself back around to the track and trotted forward, alone in darkness seven thousand feet above sea level. Some clouds, like gauze veils, parted and revealed the stars and a few last snowflakes settled. The night remained absolutely still. The starlight helped him find the spot where the stowaway had disturbed the snow in jumping from the train. From there, Mack started working his way down the slope. The snow was three to four feet deep and the footing beneath uncertain. He felt the snow soaking his trousers again; he'd spent most of the winter either soaked or drying out. At the bottom, among some boulders, he found more disturbed snow, but no human being. Eyeing the track the man's body had left and where it stopped, he knelt and began to dig with his fringed gauntlets.

He felt something firm in the drift, and sucked in breath. It was an arm, and it was limp. He dug faster.

Mack broke into the utility shed and found a lantern with oil in it. After lighting it, he moved shovels and picks to clear a section of wall, then dragged the man inside, propped him up, shut the door, and turned up the lamp to see him more clearly.

The traveler was about Mack's age, with a delicate, pale face reddened by the weather, and he was clearly emaciated. Yet there was a vigorous and flamboyant handsomeness about him, heightened by thick black eyebrows and shaggy, shiny hair. Light stubble indicated he had shaved not too long ago. He wore a ragged army overcoat, trousers with a large black check on a gray background, and calf-high laced boots.

He groaned and leaned his head back, bumping it on the wall.

"You ought to rest," Mack said. He picked up the man's left wrist. "Anything broken?"

The traveler's eyes flew open; they were blue, innocent and disarming as a child's. He felt Mack's hand on his wrist and, struggling to get upright, he swung a fist at Mack's head.

Mack rocked back on his heels, ducking the punch, then grabbed the man's right arm before he could deliver another. The man's eyes caught the beam of the lantern and changed from blue to an opal blaze, like a cat's reflecting light. For a moment he looked not quite human.

"Listen," Mack said quickly. "I'm not a railroad man. I'm a traveler like you."

"You're—?" Mack felt the tension leave the stranger's arm. He opened his fist and Mack let go.

"I dug you out of the snowdrift down there," Mack went on. He noticed some tiny ruby droplets hiding in the man's snow-dampened hair. "Looks like you've got a cut. Let me see."

Warily, the man bowed his head, while Mack parted his hair. The cut was about two inches long, not deep, but leaching blood and full of dirt.

"I'll wash it out." Mack fetched a handful of snow from outside. Far away, something wild bayed, an angry sound. A wildcat up this high? Or a trick of the wind?

Mack removed the roll of extra shirts from his back. He'd been reducing one shirt piece by piece for rags and bandages, and now he ripped off another section, wet it with snow, and washed the cut. "I don't have anything to clean it better."

"I do." The man fished under his army coat; he seemed

24

surprisingly alert. Handing Mack a small brown bottle, he said, "Don't use too much."

Mack poured a few drops of the strong-smelling whiskey into the cut. The man clenched his teeth but made no sound. He had perfect white teeth to go with his perfect features. Mack had no hope of ever being so handsome.

He opened his bandanna to find a knuckle-sized hunk of goat cheese peppered with blue-green mold spots. "Eat this, you'll feel better."

"I don't want to take a man's last food." But he snatched the cheese and bit it in half, chewing hard.

Mack chuckled. The man shot him a fiery look. Mack waved. "Go on, finish it. I've been walking for five or six months—I haven't starved yet."

Presently the man finished the cheese and wiped his mouth. "Thanks for pulling me out. Suppose I should introduce myself. Wyatt J. Paul. *J* for Junius. I'm from Osage, Kansas. Nobody ever heard of it."

"Chance is my name. James Macklin Chance, but that's too long. I go by Mack."

They shook hands. The young man from Kansas had a powerful grip.

"Where you from, Chance?"

"Pennsylvania. Schuylkill County coal fields."

"Are you bound for California like I am?"

"Yes, San Francisco."

"I'm going down south." Wyatt Paul wiped his nose, showing his white glistening teeth again. "But it's all the same sunshine. Pure gold. I'd say we should get moving and find it—what do you think?"

"In the morning, when there's light. Get some sleep."

"You in the habit of telling other people what to do?" Wyatt Paul's face froze momentarily into ugliness again, then he recovered. "Sorry—I didn't mean that. I've ridden the cars all the way here, and those three are the first who managed to roust me. If I had them here I'd crack their heads."

"Sure, I feel the same way," Mack said, though he didn't. He reached for the lantern and blew it out. The innocent blue eyes simply vanished. It gave him an eerie feeling.

Somewhere the wild animal screamed again.

Snow fell in bleak gray twilight. It had been coming down a long time. Mack's teeth hadn't stopped chattering for hours. Bad as Pennsylvania, he thought.

They had been traveling together for two days, climbing,

25

descending, following great horseshoe curves in the main track. Now Wyatt spied a wooden trackside marker, stumbled to it through the drifts, and brushed off the snow.

CALIFORNIA STATE LINE

Little bits of melting snow fell off his face as he tried to smile. "We ought to whoop it up," he said listlessly.

"Not yet. Keep going."

Wyatt was too spent and starved to show any resentment of the order. Mack trudged by him, back to the center of the track, and together they continued west through the storm.

Two figures broke through the rolling white mist, crunching the shallow mounds of snow, and disturbing half a dozen mountain bluebirds, which shot upward in alarm. The men resembled walking rag heaps, with only the gleam of eyes and the pale flash of bare hands to indicate otherwise.

Mack went faster than Wyatt down the slope. He'd never inhaled such a sweet aroma as that which breathed out from the forest of smooth- and rough-barked trees, giant knobcone pines and tamaracks, white firs and mountain hemlocks.

"My God, Wyatt, just look at that," he shouted, pointing below, where the forest gave way to a field of breaking mist glowing more golden in the sun as he watched. "It's California. The real thing." He flung off the buffalo-hair overcoat, feeling his fatigue, hunger, and pain drop away with it. The tangle of rags and leather scraps on his feet, brown from dried blood, raked a trail in the snow as he raced downward.

"Jesus, Jesus. Feel that sunshine." A dozen yards behind, Wyatt laughed like a boy and turned in a circle, doing a crazy little dance.

They came down from the forested slopes to the low emerald-green foothills while lances of sunshine pierced the mist. Laughing and capering, they flung off more of their stinking rags, here a grimy pile of them, there another. Mack squinted at the sun and turned his face up to it. He felt the warmth, the blessed warmth.

On the breasts of the sweet green hills, yellow blossoms tossed and swayed in a balmy wind. To complement the wild mustard there was fire-colored redbud, purple and pink lupine, deep blue brodiaea, and the white of cow parsnips, a rainbow sea rolling on and on to the west. In the distance, dark specks clustered here and there on a flat tawny-gold plain. Cattle?

Mack stopped among the wildflowers and turned about.

26

Looking back at where they'd come from—the deep green Sierra slopes and, above, the sharp snowy peaks proud against a sky clean and blue like none he'd ever seen before—made his heart surge. He felt new in a way he could not put into words. All of the blind hope of the past was at last made real.

A huge shadow flashed across his upturned face. It was a golden eagle flying back to its mountain home. How wide were its wings? Three feet? Four? He'd never seen such a magnificent bird. Tears sprang to his eyes and, for once, he wasn't ashamed, though it was fortunate Wyatt had run to the next hill. This feeling of exaltation shook Mack profoundly. The mountains and the forests and the golden plain said this place demanded the best of a man.

He'd try to be worthy of that heart-pounding beauty. He was being reborn. He was becoming a Californian.

Three nights later, by a comforting campfire of brush and pinecones, they dined royally on two brown trout Wyatt had caught and cleaned with his clasp knife. Mack was envious; a combination of poverty and cold weather had confined him for eighteen years, and he knew nothing of fishing, hunting, the outdoors. Wyatt knew a lot. He said the wild mustard plants were edible, so they had a small tangy-bitter salad of greens on the side.

They fell to talking about their respective pasts, something they'd been too tired and desperate to do before. Mack described his father, the Argonaut breaking his back day after day in the anthracite mine and living for one thing: to pass on to his son the dream of going to California and making the fortune he'd failed to find.

"Pa had a lot of books about California, but this was his favorite." He showed Wyatt the guidebook. "It's kept me going because it promises that you don't have to be hungry or poor out here. And you don't have to mess with *snow*."

Wyatt's blue eyes regarded him with a mixture of amusement and—perhaps—scorn. He asked to see the book and Mack reluctantly handed it to him. Wyatt leafed through the pages.

" 'As I continued my pere . . . peregrinations'—what's that mean?"

"I don't know."

" '. . . from camp to camp, and saw the hoards of gold, some of it in flakes but the greater part in a coarse dust, it seemed as if the fabled treasures of the Arabian nights had suddenly been realized. Of course those already here expect to be . . .' " Vexed again, he showed Mack the word.

27

Mack sounded it out. "In-un-dated." He shrugged. Wyatt seemed pleased by Mack's ignorance.

" '. . . inundated with emigrants from every part of the globe. But truly, based upon my experiences, I pledge to you that there is gold enough for all.' "

He closed the book and Mack was relieved to take it back. "Do you believe all that stuff?" Wyatt asked. "I mean, the way my old man believed in the Bible?"

Mack shrugged to hide his embarrassment. At a very deep level, beyond words, he did believe. "Don't you?"

Wyatt studied the stars. "I believe I'm going to do things differently than my old man. I believe that I can, out here."

"What do you mean?"

The swarthy young man brushed fish bones and skin from the flat rock at his feet. "My old man never made a dollar that he kept. He was a part-time preacher in Kansas, and of course he was too damn righteous to take any pay for that. He had a trade on the side—rainmaker. He had a whole collection of brass rods and forked sticks, and he said he'd talked to God and God approved of the calling."

"Did he make a lot of rain?"

"Never any that I remember. God didn't either." Wyatt was amused by his own wit, but it made Mack uncomfortable. "My old man earned about as much cash from rainmaking as he did from shouting about Jesus and the Holy Ghost. Of course it didn't make any difference in our house if you prospered, so long as you were righteous." He pronounced the word sarcastically. "That was my mother's attitude. She was worse than the old man. She got my two older sisters to swallow her fairy tales, but I was ten years younger. I guess she was tired out, or I was smart, because I saw it for what it was. A Barnum show. A fucking humbug, you know?"

Just then some deep-throated bird, a horned owl perhaps, made its presence known. The night smelled of sweet grass and the pine forests to the east.

"I'm telling you, my mother was a strange woman," Wyatt went on. "She never served red meat in our house. She said it liberated the base instincts of males. She believed in hydropathy—the water cure. I was a sickly kid, so for a long time I had to sit wrapped up in sheets she soaked in cold water and wrung out. One hour a day, even in winter. You don't know the crazy ideas I grew up with. . . ."

Mack sat silently. Wyatt added, "I came out here to get away from them, and all the rules in our house. Don't drink, don't curse, don't fornicate, and you'll get your reward. Where? Not in Osage, Kansas, that's for goddamn sure. But California—now that's a different story."

More cheerful and animated now, Wyatt hunched forward. "Let me explain what this place means to me. My old man had one big opportunity in his life. His brother from Topeka died and left him forty-five acres of prime land at the edge of town. My old man platted it, laid out a nice little section of houses, and then found out that some of the local ordinances wouldn't allow him to do certain things he planned. Being devout, he couldn't break the law. So he prayed about it all night one night, and next day he sold the whole parcel. And of course the smart bastard who bought it just walked in and bribed the Topeka officials and even a state senator, and developed the section and sold it out at a profit."

Wyatt's sudden smile fooled Mack into expecting easiness, even forgiveness, but Wyatt's words turned bitter again. "You see what kind of fucking fools raised me? Fools hemmed in by the Bible, a conscience—laws. I'll not repeat their mistakes."

"So what do you want to do here?" Mack asked gingerly.

"Buy and develop some land. It was the one sensible thing my old man tried. He just did it wrong."

"And you're going down to Los Angeles?"

"For a start. Big land boom down there. Fewer people, too." He studied Mack. "What's your plan?"

"The same as yours. To make money."

"How much?"

"A fortune."

Wyatt tossed his head back and laughed. "We're alike, Chance. A lot alike. Two gents with high ambitions. It's no wonder we met on the road to California. This state's pretty near brand new. Some parts are still frontier, they say. Not so many rules and laws to bind a man—"

"That's what you think of California? Being free to do whatever you want?" It was an odd new thought.

Wyatt obviously believed it, though, because he responded heatedly. "Damn right. California is Kansas forty years ago. Maybe with those mountains standing up there, keeping out most of the weaklings, it'll stay that way. At least I hope it stays that way till I make my pile. That won't be long."

"You're pretty confident."

Wyatt took the compliment with another toss of his dark head, as if it were routine, nothing but obvious truth.

* * *

With the occasionally foolish enthusiasm and naïveté of young men, they continued exchanging information and philosophies for another half hour. They were arguing the merits of California above and below the Tehachapi Mountains, the state's mythical dividing line, when Mack suddenly stopped and yanked at the dirt-splotched cuff of his trousers. There was some mite of an insect burrowing under his layers of socks, and he killed it between his fingernails. "God, what I'd give for a bar of soap and some hot coffee."

"I can take care of that first thing in the morning," Wyatt said.

"How?"

"Didn't you see that sign we passed at the crossroads—'Good Luck, two miles'? Bet it's an old mining town. I'll go in and get us some supplies."

"You don't have any money, do you?"

Wyatt shook his head.

"Then how?"

Wyatt unfolded his lean body, stretched his arms over his head, and gave Mack that now familiar broad, warm smile. "Why, I'll turn on some charm. I'll just ask them for what we need. They'll take pity on a couple of new Californians. I'm sure of it."

It was a few minutes before 8 A.M. as the old German with white side-whiskers trudged along the alley. He was tired, as played out as the dead and dusty hamlet half a mile from the American River. It had once been a boomtown, but first the placer mining had gone, and then in '84 that damn judge had ruled that the hydraulic mining had to stop because blasting away hillsides with huge hoses poured debris and filth into the rivers and streams, killed fish, and spread poisoned silt on the farms of the Valley. What a damn crime. What good was settling on land if you couldn't strip it of all the wealth *Gott* put there? Since when were trees and fish and water more important than property rights? Some of these Californians, they were crazy. That damn judge, especially. He was the final ruination of Good Luck, whose population had dwindled to 119. The German hung on, operating the only store, too exhausted to start over.

A cat hissed at him from a refuse heap. The German yawned, then suddenly noticed a young, dark-haired man standing by the rear entrance of the store. He was one of the foulest, dirtiest specimens the storekeeper had ever seen.

"*Ja*, what it is you want?"

30

"Need some supplies, sir. Soap, coffee, a tin pot, maybe some hardtack," the stranger said. "You've got those, don't you?" he added with a sunny smile that allayed the old man's suspicions.

"I got them if you got cash."

He'd scarcely uttered it when he found his pudgy neck clamped in the stranger's left hand, and his head flung back against the plank wall. A knife with a five-inch blade hovered a quarter-inch from his Adam's apple.

"I don't think I need a fucking penny. Not if you want to stay alive. Now turn around and unlock this fucking door or you'll be washing that step with your blood."

Wyatt poured steaming coffee from the enamel pot he'd brought back. The American River rushed by with a purling sound, bright in the sunshine.

"I tell you, you're making a mistake heading to Frisco," Wyatt said as he held out one of the tin cups.

Mack tore the small crusty loaf of bread in half and exchanged a piece for the hot cup. "But there isn't any other place in California that can touch it," he said. "That's why they call it the City, capital *C*."

"Just the point," Wyatt nodded. "Too many people there already. Got all the money they need, and they won't want to share it with the likes of us. They'll shut the damn door in your face, Mr. Macklin Chance. When they do, you come on down to Los Angeles and I'll give you a job in the town I'm going to develop."

"But you don't have any money to buy land," Mack said, half teasing.

Wyatt's eyes caught the sun as his head snapped up, the blue changing to that disconcerting opal for a moment. "I'll find it, the same way I found this food. There's always a way if a man has his wits and a good story."

"What story did you tell the storekeeper?"

Wyatt relaxed again. "A smart man doesn't give away all his secrets."

Mack gnawed on the bread. "All right, suppose I travel down south someday. How will I find you?"

"Just ask anyone around Los Angeles for the town with the big arch at the gate. I've already planned that in my head." His slim hands, scrubbed white at last, described a graceful curve in the air. "You'll see the name of the town—I haven't figured that out yet—and then 'The City of Health.' That's what I'm going to call it, The City of Health. Why do you think people are coming out here by the trainload? For the climate.'' He spread his arms to embrace the golden morning. ''The sun shines three hundred days a year in California.'' He dropped his arms and grinned. ''So I've read.''

''I admit the weather's important, but I thought the main reason people came was the chance to get rich.''

''Jesus, Chance, you're dumb. Most people in this world don't know how to get rich. They don't have the brains—or the nerve. Be thankful. It leaves more room for a couple of smart fellows like us.''

Wyatt whipped his cup over, throwing the rest of his coffee on the fire. It hissed and smoked as he jumped up.

''Where are you going?''

''South,'' Wyatt said. ''Time's wasting. You can keep the coffeepot.''

In a few minutes, he was ready to go. ''I appreciate what you did for me in the mountains,'' he said, extending his hand to Mack. ''You come see me in Los Angeles, at The City of Health. Meantime, good luck to you.''

When Wyatt Junius Paul smiled like this, Mack thought, he could charm the angels out of heaven. With a final wave, Wyatt went splashing into the shallow river and soon vanished among the willows and oaks on the other side. Mack stared after him, shaking his head in amazement and not a little relief. Undoubtedly he would never see Wyatt Paul again, and he had to admit he didn't mind. Lighthearted as the Kansan might be sometimes, there was something hard and calculating about him too.

Mack poured the last of the coffee and realized that his brow was sweaty. He rolled up the tattered sleeves of his shirt and squinted at the huge butter-yellow sun in the hazy sky. Hot weather coming. It couldn't get too hot for him. In half an hour, he was moving west.

3 HE PASSED BELOW SACRAMENTO AND INTO WHEAT COUN-try, where fields of tasseled stalks stood two and three feet high in the spring sunshine. In those left fallow for the year, he saw sweating, cursing men behind eight-horse hitches that pulled seven-blade gangplows. In one field he saw ten gangplows moving forward together, like an army, filling the sky with dust. What amazed him most was the openness of the

country. He never climbed over a single fence, or saw one. Did all this land belong to one man?

The morning of his third day in the wheat country, he was trudging along a dirt track leading to a smudgy line of trees. Here the wheat, bleached pale by the sun, grew tall as his head. His mouth felt as dry as the sandy loam in which the wheat was planted, and sweat stuck his smelly shirt to his back—he'd peeled off his rancid suit of long underwear and left it behind. The wheat plain baked. He'd never been so thirsty.

Maybe the trees ahead shaded water. He'd seen several riparian groves on his journey. He started to run but cut it short, his panting making him even thirstier. A pebble or wood chip in his left shoe set him limping, but he was too exhausted to stop and remove it.

Sure enough, where the dirt track snaked through the woods to a ford, he came upon water. It was brown and sluggish, a stream several yards wide in a streambed ten times that width. He staggered through the uncut stand of oaks, sycamores, and willows festooned with wild grapevines and fell on his knees at the edge of the turgid brown water. His face was nearly to the water when a gunshot reverberated across the hot pale wheat fields, and a man came riding toward him at a gallop. On his feet now, his heart thudding, Mack could see two other riders as well, moving at a more leisurely pace behind. He watched the gunman ride down on him and rein his big powerful gray with a cruel yank that pulled the horse's head back and made him whinny.

"You're on my land, drinking my water," the man yelled, poking the air with his gun, a Smith & Wesson Schofield .45. "You got no right, mister." Hatless, his forehead red and peeling from the sun, the man had a peasant's face: small pale eyes, a lump of a nose, a deep dimple on his round chin. A few strands of whitening yellow hair lay flat on his head, combed across to hide baldness. He was dressed too formally, too heavily for the hot day, in a frock coat and large brown cravat. Mack estimated him to be in his late fifties.

The two other riders, a well-dressed man and a very attractive woman, trotted up behind him now and stopped. The gentleman wore a fine white hat, white breeches, and shiny high boots. Beside him, astride a beautiful black horse, the girl was dressed in a white blouse and tight, mannish trousers— definitely not the kind of feminine riding costume he'd seen in magazines. A long gold-colored silk scarf tied in her blond hair trailed down between her large breasts.

"So what have you got to say for yourself?" the gunman

shouted. Standing there stupefied, Mack noticed other details now. The gunman's frock coat showed spots and stains, and under it, the right-hand shirttail was hanging out. He had a belly big as half a watermelon. His small, fierce eyes almost hid in sockets of sunburned skin.

Mack finally screwed up his nerve. "I'm thirsty."

"Yah?" The man snorted; it was hardly a laugh. He lowered the S&W and rested it on one ham of a thigh. With his other hand he scratched his crotch. The young woman didn't see; his back was to her, and she had all of her attention on Mack, as did her companion, whom Mack judged to be somewhat older than he, maybe as much as thirty. He was a well-set-up gentleman with trimmed side-whiskers and a small mustache, and sat easily on his horse, conveying strength and clear contempt for the ragged stranger by the water.

"You wanted a drink, hah? I tell you something, Johnny. This is my ranch. My land, my water. Around here, trespassers get shot."

Mack decided his situation was so bad that cowering was pointless. Besides, the man angered him. He slashed an arm back at the trees, the hidden fields. "I didn't see any signs posted."

"Never mind *signs*," the man yelled, dancing the gray nearer the flat brown stream and Mack. "You come from back that way, you been trespassing on my land for twenty-eight miles."

Mack was speechless a moment. Twenty-eight *miles*?

The man seemed annoyed at his lack of response and shouted, "You damn fool, I'm Hellman."

Mack just stared. The girl leaned forward over the neck of her horse, resting her hands on the high pommel of her silver-studded Mexican saddle and watching the older man, whose anger seemed to amuse her. Then she looked down at Mack with a smile of sympathy. She had a wide mouth, starkly pink but unpainted by cosmetics, and eyes of a deeper blue than Wyatt Paul's.

"Does that name mean nothing to you?" the younger man asked.

"No, sir, not a thing."

The young man stepped his beautifully groomed chestnut nearer the water. "After Mr. Henry Miller of Miller and Lux, Mr. Hellman is the largest private landowner in the state."

"Yah," the gunman snorted, "Otto Hellman—you some kind of bumpkin, some kind of *Scheisskopf*, you never heard of that?"

34

"He's a stranger in California," the girl said. "Anyone can tell that. You can at least be civil."

"Keep out of this, Carla." She didn't like that. She was feisty, certainly the most modern creature Mack had ever seen.

Otto Hellman walked his gray into the water. Mack's eyes blurred with running sweat. He was sure the man could hear his heart hammering. The name Hellman meant nothing to him, but obviously the man was important and not to be fooled with, despite his slovenly, somewhat comic appearance.

"I don't understand why you're sore," Mack said finally. "All I want is a drink. You don't own the water."

Otto Hellman barked rather than laughed. The young man leaned over and whispered something to the girl, who laughed and said, "Shameful, Walter." They were a contrast: her smile large and lusty, his tight and contained. In all of Mack's life, he'd never seen a woman so fair.

"Jesus, Johnny, you don't know much," Hellman said. "Don't own the water? Sure I do. You never heard of riparian rights?"

Mack shook his head.

"This water's mine because I own the land on both sides."

Mack's disbelieving look prodded Hellman to turn to the younger man. "I guess you better explain to him, Walter. He don't know how we do things in California." He swiveled back to address Mack. "Mr. Walter Fairbanks the Third is a lawyer from San Francisco. One of the finest. He's so good, Cholly Crocker and skinflint Huntington and Governor Stanford, they want to hire him for the SP's law department. You tell him, Walter."

"If you think he could understand a principle of law," Fairbanks said, cool and disdainful as he stepped his horse forward again. Mack turned red, then noticed the way the young woman Carla flicked her glance back and forth between them, as if watching duelists.

"The English common-law doctrine of riparian rights says simply that rights to water belong to the man who owns the land through which it flows. Mr. Hellman holds the title to the land on both sides, so he can put up a dam or channel the water in any way he pleases. He can charge for its use in irrigation, if those with land somewhere near the water but not abutting it care to pay the price he sets." The lawyer took off his wide-brimmed white planter's hat and applied a starched handkerchief to his forehead. Sunlight had put several light streaks in his sleek auburn hair. "He can also exclude anyone who won't pay. There's no coercion. They're perfectly free to let their crops go without water.''

"That's the damnedest wickedest thing I ever heard.''

Carla laughed admiringly. "What do you say to that, Swampy?''

"Don't you call me that,'' Hellman retorted. "Your father's entitled to respect.''

"I'm afraid your opinions are immaterial,'' Fairbanks said to Mack as if he were a stupid pupil. "The law is the law.''

"And that damn Assemblyman Wright's trying to change it, but he ain't won yet,'' Hellman burst out. Mack figured he was really yelling at his daughter. "Wright, he's nothing but a thieving radical, him and his water districts with everybody owning a piece—it's communistic. He's trying to rob a man of his God-given right to the fruits of his labor and property.'' Some unseen insect landed on the neck of Hellman's gray, and the horse turned to nip at it and nearly bit the man's left boot. Cursing in German, he slapped the horse's neck, then jerked up the S&W and aimed it at the center of Mack's forehead.

"I guess we wasted enough damn time on you, mister. You understand about the water now. So get moving.''

"The hell,'' Mack said. "I never heard of anything like this—one person refusing a drink of water to another person.''

"Don't make any difference,'' Hellman said. "It's a matter of private property. Besides''—he sniffed, as if smelling pigs— "I don't much like your face.''

"I do, rather,'' Carla said, smiling at Mack, and Fairbank's gray eyes, the color of a metal cashbox, became little slits.

Once again Hellman wrenched his horse around, now to face his daughter. "Sure, you're some judge. Can't find a man who interests you longer than three weeks. I'm surprised you went the six months with Count Boleslaw before you divorced him.''

"Don't shout at me. I married that sot for one reason. You wanted a title in the family, and some respectability with Walter's friends in the City.''

"Never mind, never mind,'' Hellman said. "Don't air our troubles in front of this nobody.''

"Somebody who wants a drink and is going to get it,'' Mack said.

In the middle of the stream, Hellman twisted in his saddle and aimed the S&W at Mack again. "Don't bluff with me, mister. Jesse James used a gun like this and nobody bluffed him. When you own water, you can drink all you want. Not until.''

"You're ridiculous, both of you,'' Carla said, nudging her

horse forward with her boot heels. Her hips were broad, Mack noticed; she had the kind of billowy figure very much in fashion. Despite the heat and tension and the pointed pistol, he felt a distinct physical attraction to the girl. He licked his parched mouth as she walked her black horse between him and her father.

"Go ahead and drink all you want," she said. "He won't shoot me."

As Mack started to thank her, Hellman leaned out and snatched at her bridle. The spirited glossy black shied away. "C'mere, damn you," Hellman yelled, swatting with the S&W. The gunsight nicked the horse's head and it reared unexpectedly. Carla slid off and fell in the water on her billowy rear, letting out a cry.

Whether she was really hurt didn't matter. Mack jumped forward just as Fairbanks dismounted, but Mack reached her first in the dark brown water, splashing Carla's face and partially soaking her shirt; the fabric lay wet and tight on her breasts. Mack leaned down while the lawyer, touching his spotless white trousers, hesitated at the water's edge.

Heedless of the muddy water, Mack swept his arms around Carla. "Hold on." She was delighted to do it. He felt the huge hot pressure of a breast against his shirt. With a stifled grunt—she was not light—he carried her toward the bank. Carla's deep-blue eyes were close to his, watching him intently. He did see a choice opportunity and took advantage of it: He stomped and splashed a lot, and Fairbanks didn't retreat fast enough. Mack set the girl on the loamy bank while Fairbanks stared down mutely at his soiled clothes. Impulsively, Mack leaned down and scooped up water with both hands. He drank so hastily, most of it ran down his chin. The little he swallowed was warm, and full of grit, and wonderful.

Out in the stream, Hellman smirked and grunted, "Well, you don't mind getting a little dirty, I give you that, Johnny." Mack saw Fairbanks redden at the jibe. "And you got nerve," Hellman continued as he caught the bridle of Carla's skittish mount, "but property's property. So I'm through talking about this." Once more he leveled the .45, choosing a larger target, Mack's chest. "You start walking. Right now."

Mack was going to swear at him, but when he saw the humorless determination in Hellman's eyes he stopped himself. He hated these men, hated the feeling of being dirt to be trod on at their pleasure. This humiliation was something he'd remember.

"Which way to San Francisco?"

Fairbanks swooped his hat back in the direction the three had come from. "That way. I'd suggest that you go somewhere else. I don't know why you came to California, but the Gold Rush was over forty years ago, and we don't need penniless trash or inferior specimens like you in the City."

"Oh, you've got some kind of high-toned pedigree, have you?" Mack said.

That amused the lawyer; perhaps he knew he was back in control. "I don't have to explain myself to riffraff. But I don't mind telling you I was born in California. That makes me a native son—something you'll never be."

"Listen, I know what you are. I'd say it, but there's a lady—"

"Damn insolent—" Fairbanks began, but it was Hellman who took the play, kicking his gray to the bank with a lot of splashing. Mack turned in response to the noise, but wasn't prepared for the searing pain as Hellman whipped the end of his rein against Mack's cheek. He jumped away, hearing Carla cry, "Swampy!" in protest, but Hellman managed to hit him a second time.

Blood ran down Mack's right cheek. He wanted to go for Hellman's throat, but Hellman's face had changed from merely hard to ugly. The German brandished the S&W. "That's the road to Frisco," he said. "I find you on my ranch tonight, you're a dead man."

"Swampy, you're a bastard sometimes," Carla said. "You too, Walter."

Fairbanks responded only by glaring at Mack, but Hellman shouted, "Shut up, goddamn it!"

What was it Wyatt Paul had said about a closed door? Mack licked his lips, already dry again, then turned and started walking. He passed the buxom girl, who was standing there muddy and sweaty and beautiful; he didn't miss the look she gave him, hot with admiration.

The attorney didn't miss it either.

4 THAT EVENING MACK RESTED IN A GROVE OF IMMENSE eucalyptus trees. From Hellman's stream he had followed a rutted dirt pike that led toward the coastal mountains, crossing flat land broken by many little waterways with stands of cattail growing along them. At dusk the fog had come down, and though he wasn't sure he was off Hellman's land, he decided to risk stopping for the night. He was almost out of his mind with hunger, a condition he tried to forget by studying the fog. It was soft, white, unbelievably chilly—the thickest he'd ever seen.

Suddenly he heard a horse coming from the east. He dodged behind the trunk of a eucalyptus with the clasp knife in his hand and watched the broad dirt pike, or what he could see of it. His mouth was dusty dry again, now from fear. Was the rider someone sent to make good on Hellman's threat?

The fog swirled, agitated by the horse and rider, who emerged from it like specters. For a moment Mack saw nothing except a dark mass. The rider wore some kind of flapping cape. When he saw long hair, he knew it was no assassin.

"Miss Hellman," he called, stepping from cover.

She reined the black horse sharply and trotted back. The cape hung down over her back, shoulders, and breasts; it was a Mexican serape. "Is that you?"

"Yes, ma'am."

"Good. I knew Swampy's ranch hands would be too lazy to search very hard when the tule fog came down. But I'm not—if I want something. May I dismount?"

There was a certain archness in that question. He knew she was very much more worldly than he was, accustomed to playing games with men—she'd been married to a count, hadn't she? Still, her presence excited him. She flung off the serape and tethered her horse. She wore a clean white shirt and pants and the gold scarf.

"This is the main road west. I thought you still might be on it, and on the ranch."

"Is this a ranch? It looks like a farm."

She laughed. "You have a great deal to learn about California. Farms are ranches out here. See here, I don't know your name."

"James Macklin Chance."

"Jim—"

"No, I go by Mack," he said as she extended her hand. It was a soft feminine hand, yet he felt strength in it. She held his hand longer than necessary.

"Mack, then. May I sit for a little?"

"Why, absolutely. Over here." He led her to where he'd put his bandanna on the ground. "I'm sorry I don't have a blanket."

"No need for one." She spread the serape and sat down

39

easily, gracefully. Mack was sharply aware of their isolation in the still, white fog. She patted the ground and he knelt beside her, leaving a proper space between.

"Your father told me to get off his land but I don't know where it ends." He gestured west. "China?"

She laughed again. "Almost. Would you have gotten off if you knew the boundaries?"

He shook his head.

"I didn't think so. I really do admire you. Papa's a powerful man. And as you saw, he can be dangerous. Frankly, I can't think of another person, young or old, who ever stood up to Swampy quite the way you did. You have remarkable courage."

"I was thirsty—and I just didn't know any better." But he liked the praise, especially from her.

"Walter was very jealous of what you did. Walter would never oppose my father."

"He's your father's lawyer, isn't he?"

"One of them. Walter impresses Swampy because he's very old-line California. Swampy's chasing after respectability in San Francisco like an old bull at stud."

The words brought a hot feeling to Mack's face; young girls didn't talk like that. At least not the daughters of the Welsh and Irish miners back east.

"Swampy isn't a very good father but I'll say this for him— he's a devil of a fine businessman. Henry Miller, another German—his real name's Kreiser—owns a million four hundred thousand acres. But Swampy owns a million two hundred thousand."

Mack whistled. "How did your pa get his nickname?"

"By means of what certain people call the 'swamp scheme.' Too tedious to go into. Both my father and Miller got rich from the scheme, but Papa hates for people to remind him by using his nickname. I goad him with it."

"I noticed. Once or twice he almost made me laugh. But when he aimed his gun, he wasn't funny."

"No. Papa has no sense of humor and no kindness when it comes to money and property. He's cheated and ruined more business rivals than I can tell you about. And he treated you abominably. One of the reasons I came after you was to apologize for him. Make amends. So you'll think less harshly of the Hellmans—"

"Well, I won't soon forget your father." *The son of a bitch.* He cleared his throat. "Is Walter your—uh—beau?"

"He'd like to be." She drew her trouser-clad knees up and

clasped her hands around them. "I don't have a real beau at the moment. I was married to a Polish count—well, you heard. I'm still getting over that." She leaned toward him. "I'd rather talk about you."

Kneeling next to her, he was unprepared when she brought her pink mouth to his and caressed him with it, and then with the tip of her tongue. Her breath smelled of sweet clove and of something not quite hidden by it—gin.

"Is that agreeable, Mr. Chance?"

"Yes. Yes it is, Miss Hellman."

She laughed heartily at his half-strangled answer. Then, softening, she touched his right cheek, careful to keep her fingers away from the dark blood crusted on the edges of the cut.

"Does it hurt terribly?"

"Some. It'll heal."

"Papa was brutal to do that."

"Don't worry, I'll never forget it," he answered with a vague hint of threat.

That amused her all over again. "Good for you." She patted his cheek twice more, a little gesture of condescending approval. It spoiled the headiness of the moment.

The tule fog appeared to be thinning, brightening. The previous night the moon had been full, and perhaps it was up there above the fog, lighting it with a pearly radiance. Carla seized his hand while she got to her feet and then walked off to the black horse. She returned with a large bundle wrapped in a checkered cloth, and a sloshing canteen.

"I brought food and water for the rest of your trip."

"That's very kind."

"Oh, I'll get my reward." Her lightly mocking tone put him off again. Carla Hellman fascinated him, but she began to alarm him a little too. He felt vaguely like a frog spitted on a stick.

She sat down again. "This pike leads you into Wheatville, which is just past the boundary of the ranch. From Wheatville you can catch the railroad to San Francisco, if you can afford it."

"I can't."

"But you're going there."

"Absolutely. I came from Pennsylvania to make my fortune in California."

"Just like that."

"I know it'll take time, but I'll do it."

"I expect you will, Mr. Macklin Chance." Her smile shone. "In fact I suspected you'd go right on to the City in spite of Walter's warning. Walter is no fool, but he can be frightfully

41

stupid about certain things. He believes a lot of tripe about the superiority of Anglo-Saxons and native Californians. I'd advise you to stay out of his way. Not that you'll move in the same circles. But he has powerful friends, and many connections. His father and his uncle started the Fairbanks Trust. A very large bank."

"I'll stay out of his way if he stays out of mine."

"My, you are a truculent fellow. I do like that. Walter's so contained and tight. Every action and utterance carefully considered. Typical lawyer: no blood, no passion." She leaned back against the eucalyptus and rested her head. The golden scarf shimmered in the fog, glowing now with a radiance almost pure white. He saw the line of her breasts silhouetted against the light and he grew stiff, quickly and uncontrollably.

"Tell me about yourself," she said.

"Let's see. My great-grandfather was a traveling tinker in England. My grandfather owned a public house in London but he sold it to come to America—Ohio, where my pa was born. James Ohio Chance was his name. He came out here in the Gold Rush, and met and married a Hibernian lady—not a popular thing for a Protestant to do."

"I went to a Catholic girls' school near Monterey," Carla interrupted. "Saint Ursula's. The nuns taught a number of Protestant girls from good families. I was bored, and I made such a fuss, Swampy took me to Europe when I was eleven. I visited Europe three times before I was sixteen."

"With your father and mother?"

"With a paid companion. Swampy stayed in California. I never knew my mother. She ran off when I was a baby."

"Did you meet that Polish count in Europe?"

"Boleslaw? Yes. He chased me to this country and Papa persuaded me to marry him. It was a ghastly mistake, but Boleslaw was an attractive man, and I couldn't see beneath—" She shivered suddenly. "The fog's chilly. Come keep me warm."

He slid over and hesitantly slipped his arm around her. She murmured and snuggled down, resting her hand on his left knee. The light pressure turned his member so hard it hurt, and he shifted away just a little.

"I've never met a young man quite like you, Mack Chance. You're bold, yet you're very shy."

"No, no—well, I guess. With you. I don't know much about rich girls."

"It's time you learned, and here's your first lesson." She touched him again, and brought her mouth close. He felt the swell of her breast against his shirt as her tongue explored. Then she paused. "Here's the second one. When I can't get something—that's when I want it most. I go after it until I have it." She caressed his hair. "Fair warning?" Another kiss. "Walter Fairbanks would probably commit murder to get where you are now."

"I'm not Walter Fairbanks."

"Thank heaven." She ran her tongue over his cheek. "You can help me forget."

He stroked her face in turn. "Forget what?"

"The past couple of years. Boleslaw, the count, was a handsome man, but he was vicious. I don't mind someone getting drunk, but I discovered that he had worse addictions. Opium. And he didn't care for a husband's duties in the boudoir. But he liked to hire these dreadful depraved people from the streets and watch while—well, I was lucky to get out." Another shiver then. "I didn't think marriage was supposed to leave scars, but mine did."

He was too shocked to speak. Her smile seemed less assured, sad again. "I'll be going to San Francisco soon too. Only a short visit. Some shopping, a couple of social affairs— then I'm going away for a while. I need to be by myself, to get rid of some of the bad memories." She kissed him. "I think you could definitely help." She giggled. "Can you picture Swampy's face if he knew I was making love to someone without a penny?"

That was ice water dashed in his face. He untangled himself and jumped up.

"What's wrong?" she said, getting up too.

"Miss Hellman, don't use me to get back at your father."

She slapped him. He grabbed her arm. To his amazement, she laughed, then flung her other arm around his neck and plunged her tongue in his mouth. His loins shook from the grinding contact of her body.

"I'm not, I'm not, my dear," she said, her hand dropping to squeeze him. He nearly exploded. "Mack, I want to make love. Please, you've gotten me excited. Let's undress. Here, I'll begin . . ." She unfastened the long scarf, spilling her hair, billowy and golden, onto her shoulders. The moon was visible now, blazing behind the shredding veil of tule fog.

He reached for the buttons of her shirt and undid them. Standing close, facing him, she shrugged off the shirt and then the chemise beneath. Her breasts were big and heavy, with dark-brown tips. He bent and kissed them. She threw her head back and exclaimed softly, then hugged him and began kissing his throat, his chest—

She stopped.

"What is it, what did I do?" He could barely keep from pulling at her, couldn't keep his hands still.

"We ought to make this as pleasant as we can. Wait just a minute." She walked slowly, seductively, to her picketed horse, and then brought back a second, larger canteen. "Here. Bathe."

"*What?*"

"Please bathe first. I'm sorry to tell you, but you smell like a barnyard. It isn't very romantic."

He felt stupid, insulted, furious, and went limp, his skin prickling in the chill. He snatched the canteen while she raised her chemise against her breasts with a coquettish false modesty.

He yanked the cork and inverted the canteen with a snap of his wrist. The water ran out noisily, splattering the ground. She watched it, and him, with disbelief. "What in hell—"

"Listen, I may be a clod without much schooling, but I'm not some servant to be ordered around. Put your clothes on and go home."

He kicked the canteen, and it flew past her leg, generating a startled little cry. Moments later, she was heading east at a gallop, repeatedly quirting her luckless black horse. Mack's last glimpse was of the bright banner of her hair streaming out behind her.

Sleepless, he sat with his back against the rough trunk of a eucalyptus. The full moon shed brilliant light over the grove. He wound the gold ribbon of scarf around his left hand, then unwound it and wound it the other way.

He'd thrown away a chance to make love to a spectacular girl. Well, he couldn't help it. She was beautiful, and she'd displayed a certain kindness toward him, but there was another side. She was spoiled, accustomed to having her way, like the old German who'd sired her. The willful streak had suddenly asserted itself, and instead of an eager, generous girl, she was suddenly a queen about to grant her favors for the night. He'd have liked to make love to her. But not on her terms.

With a long sigh, he began to fold the scarf, shortening it until it fit between the pages of T. Fowler Haines, which he put away along with the memory of her hair, eyes, hands, and naked skin. Strange young girl. He didn't doubt that she'd be trouble, a lot of trouble, for any man who involved himself with her.

But why think of that? He'd never see her again.

MACK'S RECENT TROUBLES MADE IT HARD FOR HIM TO **5** appreciate that he was nearing San Francisco. When he arrived in the little town of Wheatville, on the main line to Oakland and San Francisco, his mood didn't improve. There were scruffy blanket men everywhere, wheat-field workers with all of their worldly goods in blanket rolls tied on their backs.

When a crashing rainstorm sent him hunting for shelter in an alley behind the main street, he literally stumbled on a ragged man lying unconscious in the mud between two puddles. It was an old Indian, Mack realized, when he rolled him over and saw the narrow dark face, high forehead, and black hair without a strand of gray despite the man's obvious age. A bloody abrasion marked the Indian's forehead, but he was breathing.

Mack dragged him against the rear wall of a hardware store and, in the slashing rain, managed to wake him up. Hobbling, gripping Mack's arm with an emaciated hand, the old Indian led him back through a warren of packing-case hovels to the one that was his. Solemnly, he gestured Mack in.

The place smelled of offal and rotting meat, but Mack was glad to be out of the rain. The Indian lit a small fire and shared some purple berries and a tasty root that took a long time to chew. Mack helped him wash the bleeding abrasion with water from his canteen.

"Three of the blanket men fell on me to rob me," the Indian said, his black eyes watery. "They found I had nothing and beat me anyway. They would do the same if I were Chinese."

"Why don't you leave? Or is this your home?"

"I am Chumash, from the south. I have no home any longer. I work the fields, up and down. Wherever the white men will allow it," he added for clarification. After studying Mack a moment, the Indian said, "You like California?"

"Yes, I do. I've not been here long, but I'm going to get rich here."

"Hah," said the old man. The joyless laugh showed his brown teeth and ruined gums. "There is a dark side to your

45

dream. My people know. One ancestor, in the mission of San Luis Rey de Francia, was no better than a slave. The friars rented him to the *rancheros* for a profit, and if he protested or disobeyed, they flogged him with knotted ropes 'for the good of his soul.' My father, as a young man, free in the pueblo of Los Angeles after Mexico took back the mission lands, was not much better off. He worked as a ranch hand. He was paid every Friday, with brandy. By Saturday he was drunk, which was the point. He spent Sunday in jail and on Monday morning he was herded out with others of his kind, and his services were auctioned to the ranchers for one more week. By Friday he had worked off his fine and was a few cents ahead. Once more he was paid with brandy . . ." The Indian shrugged. "In California there are only two kinds. Those who take, and those they take from."

"You mean that when I have money, I'll be one of the takers?"

The Indian replied with a grave nod. "You are a good man to help an old Indian beaten and cast aside. But even for you the answer is yes. It is the only way. It is California."

First Hellman and that lawyer tried to darken his dream, now this tragic old man, huddled in this shack with his bitter memories. Silently, with fervor and a little desperation, Mack swore he'd prove them wrong.

In the morning he started off again, following the main line of the railway. Soon the scorching sun dried the countryside, and about midday, he saw through the heat haze a line of forty or fifty men working on the roadbed with picks, shovels, mauls, and tamps.

Mack drank from the canteen, which by now contained just one tepid swallow, then slung it over his shoulder and approached the section gang. Most of the men were bare to the waist and sweating so hard their bodies looked oiled. The work gang included about a dozen Chinese, smaller and more wiry than the whites. He noticed that the two groups didn't speak to each other.

A collie ran up and down the roadbed, frisking and barking. A burly worker swung at it with his pick. "Get outa here, Ruff. O'Malley, control your damn dog or I'll kill him."

Another worker whistled and yelled and the collie lay down in the shade of a flatcar on a spur track. The dog panted for a few seconds, then jumped up and ran off again.

"*Ruffo, ven aquí!*" a man shouted. Mack looked in his direction. Dressed in a heavy black suit, the man was standing beside a mule-drawn wagon. The collie chased over to him and lapped at a pan of water he'd set out. Mack noticed now that the man had a clerical collar, which explained his unusual dress.

The wagon was full of barrels, and Mack guessed they contained water. He walked toward the man, ignoring hostile stares from the track gang. *"Buenos días, desconocido,"* the priest said.

"I don't speak Spanish. Do I look like I should?"

The priest folded his hands. "On the contrary. My assumption is that you're a newcomer."

"What makes you say so?"

With a disarming smile, the man replied, "Your nose. Your cheeks. Pink, and peeling away. Also, your clothes—well, forgive me, but they have a certain, ah, well-traveled look."

"You're exactly right—about them, and me."

The priest nodded agreeably. "I addressed you in Spanish out of habit. It is my native language, and spoken widely in California. If you plan to stay here long—"

"Permanently."

"Excelente. May I humbly suggest that a study of *español* would be courteous, and to your advantage?"

Mack scrutinized the forthright priest. He was perhaps twenty-five, with a massive, square-looking head, a low forehead, and broad nose. His suit showed blacker patches where he'd sweated through. His wide dark eyes reminded Mack of the old Indian's. Mack couldn't decide whether the priest was Mexican, Indian, or *mestizo*—both.

"It's a hot day for traveling," the priest went on. "You're welcome to a drink."

"Thanks, I just ran out." Mack gave a thump to the canteen hanging over his shoulder.

The priest tapped the barrel nearest the wagon's dropped tailgate and handed him the dipper. The water was hot, and after a careful sip, Mack emptied the rest on his head. The priest laughed.

"Thanks very much," Mack said. "I'm on my way to San Francisco."

"From where?"

"Pennsylvania. My name's Macklin Chance."

"Welcome to California, Mr. Chance. I'm Father Marquez. Diego Marquez. Unlike most of these good men sweating for the Southern Pacific, I was born in this state."

Mack started to hand back the dipper, then hesitated. "Wait, I thought this was the Central Pacific."

"Originally. Two years ago the owners formed a holding company to control their various assets. The name of the holding company is Southern Pacific, but now they're calling the railway by that name also. The Big Four, those four outlaws, chartered their holding company in Kentucky because the railway laws are lax there. Almost any outrage against the public or the workingman is permitted."

"And you bring water out to these men?"

"Someone must. The company doesn't consider it their responsibility." He whacked the dipper against the barrel, disgusted. The priest seemed to do everything with sharp, vigorous moves.

"Seems like there isn't a hell—a lot of water in California," Mack observed.

"There is if you search in the right place. Come share what little shade we have." After he scratched the mule's ears, Marquez peeled off his heavy coat, leaving only his collar and black dickey tied at his waist. He wore no shirt, and enormous tufts of hair were visible under his thick arms. He looked like a bull, Mack thought.

Marquez hunkered down on the other side of the wagon, squinting across the simmering plain toward the hazy coast range. Up on the line, picks and tamps *chunk-chunked*, mauls rang on the heads of new spikes, men swore monotonously, and a stubby foreman wearing a side arm paraded, hectoring the workers.

"Water is a fascinating California topic, you know," Marquez said. "One reason is we always have too little because of the short rainy season in the winter. Another is that water's potential benefits remain largely unappreciated. My first ancestor in California was a Castilian soldier. He marched from the Baja with the expedition of Portolá and Father Junípero Serra in 1769 and '70, and left a diary that has come down in my family. My ancestor declared this whole place worthless for farming because of its aridity. Most of the original Indians thought the same. But it isn't worthless. The friars, for all of their other limitations and crimes against freedom, knew that much. With their maize and barley, olives and wine grapes, they saw the miracles water can work in this soil. They taught that lesson to a few Californians who have remembered."

"But there still isn't much water."

"Not here. But have you seen the high country of the Sierras? There, the melting snowpack creates waterfalls and in the spring turns ordinary streams into torrents."

"I wasn't doing much sightseeing when I came through the mountains. There was a blizzard."

Marquez's eyes flickered at the callow sarcasm. "I'll tell you this, my young friend. If that water could somehow flow down to this great Central Valley, this earth would bloom like a garden." His frown sculpted deep lines beside his nose, making him less benign—fierce, even. "But it would be a garden watered with the sweat and blood of those forced to toil for others—for starvation wages."

Without thinking, Mack shook his head, and Marquez reacted quickly. "What do you disagree with, my views about water or those about labor and capital?"

"You took me wrong, Father. I don't know enough to disagree with either one. I shook my head because . . . well, back east, among Irish miners, I saw priests all right. But none like you. Here you are, out in the wilderness alone, serving water like a slave . . . it's kind of puzzling."

"Not at all. I'm from San Francisco, with a roving commission to minister to workingmen. Pope Leo the Thirteenth has been publishing numerous letters to address the concerns of workers around the world and encourage ministries like mine. He even suggests a limited approval of trade unions. The Holy Father does not go far enough, in my opinion, but then my opinions are those of a minority. A tiny minority," he emphasized, smiling. "Tell me," he said after pausing to look at Mack more closely, "why did you come all the way from Pennsylvania?"

Mack didn't want to be taken for greedy. After a moment's thought about phrasing, he said, "To better myself."

"How? With wealth?"

The challenge annoyed him. "Yes."

"Perfectly understandable. This state is blessed by wealth in many forms. Great natural beauty. Tillable land. Even this sunshine, which seems such a curse in the summer. It helps the real estate men sell building lots to shivering tourists. Still, many who search for wealth here never find it." His brown eyes stayed on Mack's. "And some who do are quickly corrupted if the search becomes obsessive."

All at once Mack didn't like the young priest. He knew what he wanted and what he didn't. He didn't want anyone trying to be his conscience. He didn't want the Hellmans, the old Indian, or some Catholic father with strange radical ideas throwing dirt on his dreams.

He was thinking up a suitable reply when a long screaming whistle ripped from the east. Up on the line, the stumpy foreman dragged out a big silver watch. "There she is, there she is, stop everything," he shouted.

The men rushed to form a military line beside the track, hoisting tools to their shoulders as if they were rifles. The train sounded like an avalanche as it approached, churning up towering dust clouds. The whistle blew again and the bell rang. The noise agitated the collie, which raced back and forth yapping.

"Who's on that train, the President?" Mack asked Marquez.

"You would think so. Anywhere on the line in California, men at work have orders to stand at attention when that train passes." To show what he thought of this he spat on the ground between his dusty rope sandals.

Tremors rose from the ground; Mack felt them in the bones of his legs. The collie jumped high in the air, barking. The train was less than half a mile away. It consisted of a single passenger car shimmering with varnish and gilt, a tender, and a Stevens 4-4-0 locomotive with a huge headlight box and balloon smokestack. Eighty-eight tons of wood-fired power, it was a black behemoth, whose passage shook the earth and whipped up a cyclonic cloud of dust and debris.

Ever afterward, Mack saw a series of flashing images.

A jackrabbit, hopping high on the other side of the track. The collie barking and dashing to chase it. The burly man, the one bothered before, angrily swinging his pick down as the dog passed by—a mean-tempered swipe that deeply gashed the dog's flank. Mack heard the yelp above the rising roar. He flashed a look toward the looming train as the dog limped a couple of steps, then fell sideways against the near rail.

"Ruff," the dog's owner shouted, already out of ranks and running toward the fallen animal.

The foreman pulled and cocked his side arm. "Stand fast, O'Malley. You know the governor's order."

"For Christ's sake," Mack yelled, bolting forward, with the priest a step behind. The leviathan was almost on them, rumbling the earth and sucking up great clouds of dust. As O'Malley pulled the collie off the track, he somehow lost his footing and toppled backward. Mack's warning shout went unheard; the cowcatcher struck O'Malley and tossed him into the air in front of the onrushing engine. It sliced his head off, hurled his body aside, and flung a great fan of blood along the trackside. Mack caught a flash of large gilt letters on the side of the engine—EL GOBERNADOR—and a similar decoration on the tender—S.P.R.R. A lacquered coach hurtled by, all windows empty save one. There, an obese man with a chin beard raised

50

a hand to acknowledge the workers at attention. As suddenly as it came, the special train was gone, leaving a settling rush of torrid air.

Mack rocked back on his heels, bug-eyed. It had all happened so fast that he wasn't sure he'd seen it. But the face of the passenger was already seared into his memory, and the red heap on the gravel shoulder was certainly real. It came to him that his face was wet. He rubbed it and stared at his fingers: red. There was also red stippling the faces of the three other men nearest O'Malley. The collie kept whining, trying to rise but unable to.

A worker advanced cautiously to the body. "Jesus, where's his—?" He choked, fell to his knees, and vomited uncontrollably.

Marquez walked up onto the track and eyed the disappearing train, his dark face almost purple. "God curse them—the poor man never even had a chance for last rites." He noticed Mack and threw a bandanna to him. "Wipe off that blood."

Mack scrubbed and scrubbed, feeling he'd never get clean. "Who was that fat bastard?" In the silence, the collie's whine was much louder.

"Governor Leland Stanford. One of the four who built this railroad."

"The damn engineer must have seen that man next to the track."

"Surely. But he was going too fast to stop even if he wanted to."

"Stanford must have seen the blood flying."

"I doubt it, but what if he did? What's it to him if some day laborer loses his life? When he and his partners pushed this railroad through the Sierras, it happened hundreds of times. One more thing: That train never stops—not for anything or anyone." Marquez glanced past Mack's shoulder and covered his mouth a moment. "Do you have the stomach to help me with the body?"

"You going to bury it?"

"No, there's a town about five miles from here. I'll take the remains there and try to locate relatives. I must do it soon, or what's left of him will rot in this heat."

"All right, I'm ready," Mack said with a gargantuan swallow and a prayer that his guts wouldn't come heaving up.

They unloaded the water barrels and laid O'Malley's remains in the wagon under a tarpaulin. Twice Mack almost vomited because of the blood, the buzzing flies, and the smell. Somehow he and the priest got through it, with the white-faced fore-man offering feebly to help at one point. Marquez gave him a withering look and the foreman slunk off to goad his disheartened men back to work. On its feet, the collie whined, limping badly.

The slow-moving wagon started toward a crossroads about half a mile south of the right-of-way. Mack walked along beside it. "Tell me about Stanford and his partners, Father."

"As I said, their construction work in the mountains took the lives of hundreds. If ten died, they hired ten more; human beings were like parts of a machine, replaced without a second thought. Does that make them killers? I don't know. I do know they are men like no others. In this state they are gods. And they didn't build their line as a sweet, altruistic gesture. They were little shopkeepers in Sacramento when they hired poor Theodore Judah, who was a fine, visionary railway engineer. They didn't care about Judah's beautiful patriotic dreams of a country united by steel rails; they merely wanted to control the freight traffic to the Nevada mines. Judah exhausted himself before the scheme was even well started—he, too, died in their behalf. In the course of their magnificent undertaking, for which they took enormous moral credit, the four of them acquired huge land holdings, and repeatedly tricked and cheated the United States and California governments. At the same time, each of the four amassed one of the greatest personal fortunes on the planet. Does that make them criminals, or merely successful businessmen?"

Marquez shook the reins, turned the wagon left into the crossroads, and there reined the mule for a moment. "I know my answer. One day, those four will be found guilty at the bar of history. I am impatient for it. Meanwhile, I'll tell you something a prudent man should keep in mind while in California. There is some doubt as to who wields more power here, Almighty God or the railroad."

Mack stared up at the priest's sunlit face. *Only the takers . . . and those they take from.* He had to keep hoping that wasn't really how it was. He had to keep hoping the gold wasn't the kind his pa found—pyrites, fool's gold.

He raised his hand. "Father Marquez, you've been kind."

The priest's handshake was vigorous and strong. "I hope you find what you are looking for, Señor Chance, and that when you do, it will not disappoint you. Thank you for your assistance back there. I won't forget. Go with God."

He clucked to the mule and the wagon creaked off in a dust cloud. As Mack watched, he heard barking. O'Malley's dog was limping along the dusty road in pursuit of the wagon. The collie fell but got up and kept coming.

Mack whistled to Marquez. The priest turned, saw the dog, and slowed the wagon to a crawl. With a brief smile and a wave, Mack turned west on the crossroad.

A WEEK LATER MACK STOOD ON THE MOLE AT OAKLAND. **6**
It was shortly past noon on a brilliant, cool day. He flung his arms out and his head back and laughed, heedless of the properly dressed passengers hurrying down the wharf in back of him.

God, he was here. Finally *here*. He smelled the sea, sweetly perfumed by salt and fish. Little bright sails of pleasure craft brightened the Bay, and a stiff Pacific breeze put curls of white on the water.

And there it was on the other side, rising in patterns of light and shade on the steep hills: a city of substantial commercial buildings and pastel-and-white residences, pretty as decorations on a cake. On his right, the Bay swept around the land and kissed the sea. In the channel a rusty old steamer equipped with side-wheels as well as masts plowed outward between scurrying fishing boats. That part of the peninsula revealed golden hilltops with a few trees, open spaces not yet heavily built upon.

He lowered his arms, but the intoxication remained. He had no job, no money, and no prospects for either. But he had hope, boundless hope, on this sunny afternoon by the Bay. It banished the doubts and bad memories that had piled up on his journey.

Farther down the two-mile-long wharf, a steam whistle announced the departure of the next Southern Pacific ferry boat, a white floating castle crowded with gentlemen in suits and cravats, ladies with parasols, and a number of shabby poor people who kept to themselves.

Mack strolled down toward a white booth. People eager to catch the boat rushed by, careful not to touch him, for his beard was very long, and he'd last bathed on Wednesday, coming over the coastal hills that were losing their emerald color as summer drew near.

A yellow-and-red sign on the booth said FARE 15¢. Mack

saw the agent in the booth eyeing him, and he turned around and walked the other way, fighting to curb his rising impatience. For an hour he drifted through a commercial section along Railroad Avenue, the western extension of Seventh Street. Then he returned to the mole. Another ferry was departing with hoots of its whistle and chugging of engines. A different man was on duty in the booth, a weak-sighted man with thick silver spectacles.

Mack waited, making an effort to be inconspicuous. The next incoming ferry, *Contra Costa*, docked ten minutes later. She unloaded passengers and prepared to depart again. He waited until the last boarding call, and then darted past the booth while the man inside was squinting to count his receipts.

Brawny sunburned young men secured ropes across the open end of the ferry while others on the wharf uncleated the lines and tossed them aboard. With a fanfare of whistles, *Contra Costa* chugged out of the slip. Mack brushed by a stout woman who looked at him as if she feared rape, and climbed to the upper deck, where he sank down on a bench at the bow. The wind was fierce up here, but still sweet with the sea scent. The light falling on San Francisco's hills and buildings had a mellow, burnished quality unlike anything he had ever seen.

Soon he noticed the ticket collector working his way through the crowd of passengers on the upper deck. Mack held fast to his bundled possessions, screwing up his nerve.

"Ticket," said the little rabbit of a man, his brushy mustache fairly trembling with authority.

"Look here, I don't have one. No money. But I have to get across, because—"

The ticket man turned away with a bored air. "Mix! Portugee!" he called down a companionway. "Another free rider up here."

Mack clutched the rail. Below, the Bay folded back on both sides of the bow, foamy white, eminently dangerous. In Pennsylvania, he'd tried to learn to swim in an old quarry, but never really mastered it.

Mix and Portugee were two of the sailors who manned the ferry. One, dark-haired and cheerily sinister, wore a gold ring in his right ear.

"Damn you, let go," Mack said, trying to shake them off as they hustled him downstairs. He didn't resist too violently, because he didn't want to reach the City beaten and bloody. The ferry was in midchannel. Prolong this a bit and he'd be across. "I tell you I can explain why—"

"The Southern Pacific can't put your stories in the bank, kid," said the seaman with the earring. "No money for a ticket, you swim. It's the rule."

The other one shot a bolt back and opened a gate in the port rail. Passengers watched the little scene with a mixture of curiosity and amusement.

Mack yanked backward, alarmed. "You can't do this. I'll drown, I don't know how to swi—"

A boot against his backside turned the rest of it to a yell. He flew forward into space, the water rushing up at him. He struck, remembering at the last moment to dive his hand into his pocket and seize the guidebook and hold it over his head.

Choking, kicking, he went down, his entire head underwater. He flailed his legs, and that took him back to the surface. Wake from the ferry crashed over him, spuming in his eyes, washing him with brackish water. He held the book high in the sunshine while something slimy brushed against his cheek. The silver eye of a dead fish regarded him. "Shit," he groaned.

On the ferry's stern, behind the rope where the passengers boarded, a father traveling with two children gestured and argued with the ticket taker, protesting their treatment of Mack. It made no difference, though; the ferry *Contra Costa* plowed on toward the wedding-cake city, its whistle blast a mocking good-bye.

He began to kick, treading water simply by instinct. Already he felt tired, heavy. He started to sink again and kicked harder. He'd gambled that they never threw stowaways overboard, but it was a bad wager. He was going to drown.

He didn't see the launch until it was practically upon him. He heard the stutter of its little steam engine, and that caused him to twist around, and there it was, squat in the water, its drab hull showing oozes of black caulk, its single mast minus a sail. At the wheel, frantically signaling to him, was a plump fellow in a quilted green coat from which the sleeves had been cut. The man was Chinese. He wore a black skullcap and a queue wound around his ears and pinned. He looked about thirty, uncommonly fat.

"Hang on, mister, I will pick you up," the Chinese man shouted in clear English. He throttled back almost to a standstill and brought the launch around. Mack saw Oriental characters on the transom, and the name *Heavenly Dragon*. The launch rolled and pitched in the chop, and the man lurched to the port rail. Above the engine's noisy idle and the lap of the Bay, Mack heard him wheezing as he knelt and put down his fat hand.

"Grab hold—throw your leg in."

Instead, Mack flung the guidebook in the boat. The man recoiled. "You crazy?"

"Take care of that," Mack yelled. He hooked his leg on the gunwale and seized the man's hand. He found himself astonishingly weak, but somehow he made it, falling into the launch and landing on a fisherman's net. He banged his head on a bucket full of oysters. The Chinese lurched back to the wheel; another SP ferry was passing on the way to Oakland.

The wake rocked the launch, but the man kept his balance with surprising grace. He had a ready smile that pushed his plump cheeks up, lending him a genial air. Whipping the wheel around, he throttled the engine higher. "I saw them throw you off. I am Bao Kee. I fish these waters."

"My name's Mack. I'd have drowned if you hadn't come along . . ."

The heaving of his middle told him he'd swallowed a lot more of the Bay than he thought. It looked prettier than it tasted. Wet and miserable, he dragged himself over the gunwale and puked. Bao Kee grinned and sent the launch bounding toward Oakland in a series of zigzags, much like a sailboat tacking.

Bao lived in a hovel in a grim Chinese section just above the Inner Harbor near Webster and Eighth streets. The air in the crowded, crooked lanes smelled of cooking oil and something sickly sweet. Mack stripped to his drawers and hung up his soggy clothes while Bao lit a coal fire in an ancient James cookstove with a tin smoke pipe that was wired to a hole in the slat roof. Bao spread mats for them, unrolled a piece of oily paper, and picked up some small fish he proceeded to broil.

"Sand dabs. Local fish. Very delicious." He took off his cap and smoothed his glossy hair. At first Mack had thought him a cheerful but rather witless fellow. Now, noting the way Bao's eyes missed nothing, he changed his mind.

"You know your way around the Bay, I guess . . ."

"Long time Californ'," as the old men say. I was born in this state." Bao explained that the waters of the Bay sustained him in many ways. They yielded fish sold to the restaurants in the City, but he also netted shrimp that a middleman salted and packed for shipment to China, where it was considered a delicacy. Mack had never seen or eaten shellfish. Bao said many Americans considered shellfish to be the fare of barbarians.

Mack told Bao where he'd come from and where he was

going. Bao nodded agreeably. "I will take you over to the City when you want to go. No charge."

A cry in the lane drew them outside. An old Chinese man, matchwood-frail, pointed at a cart with one wheel sunk in a deep rut. The cart carried scavengers' goods: rags, Oakland newspapers, chunks of rough paving block. A fat woman, evidently the old man's wife, screeched protests in Chinese. She pantomimed trying to drag the cart from the rut, and was close to weeping.

"She says it's too heavy for him," Bao called to Mack. He smiled, patted the elderly woman, and with a one-handed tug and a grunt, he freed the cart, which he then pushed down the lane to a nearby shanty, leaving the approving babble of men, women, children, and a few dogs in his wake. Mack once again changed his appraisal of the fisherman. He was obese but far from a weakling.

In the hovel, Bao placed the broiled sand dabs on two tin plates, along with white rice cooked with bits of something black, and filled their small ceramic cups with a strong, fruity wine. While he bustled around, Mack had a chance to study his home. Three irregular pieces of mirror hung on different walls. In a cigar box under the bunk were a collection of dice, playing cards, and hand-carved wooden dominoes with the spots burned in. A lacquered tray on a shelf held a ceramic dish, needles, a small oil lamp, and a long pipe with a ceramic bowl and ornamental ivory bands around the bamboo stem. Mack noticed a black glossy residue coating the lip of the bowl and the ivory mouthpiece.

Bao, aware of Mack's curiosity, took several large polished beads from the cigar box and scattered them on the mat in front of him. *"Chu,"* he said, pointing. "Counters. I like gambling. It's a Chinese passion. It's a gamble making a living on that Bay, too. Most white men hate us." He shook his fist, imitating them. " 'Run run Chinamun!' "

He invited Mack to seat himself on the mat, then, sitting down as well, he picked up a sand dab and bit it in half.

"Have you always been a fisherman?"

Bao shook his head. "I have had many jobs since I was a boy. I was number-one cook on a ranch near Modesto. I carried granite to build a winery in Napa. Scrubbed floors—polished boots—many things. Know what's hardest job?" He dipped the wine cup at his visitor for emphasis. "Staying alive."

"They don't want Chinese here at all, is that it?"

"They want them for certain things. Certain things only." He stated it flatly, but Mack saw the bitterness in his dark eyes.

57

"California's my home. I want no other. But Mr. Kearney over in Frisco, the friend of the laborer, he says, 'The Chinese must go!' So they are always passing laws. I can't become a citizen. I can't own property. I can't even get a business license. If they put me in jail''—he struck his palm against his pinned-up queue—''the Pigtail Law says they can cut this off.'' His mouth twisted. "Thus it is in *Kum Saan*." He toasted Mack with the wine, and drank.

"What's that, *Kum Saan*?"

"Gold Mountain. The men of Canton gave that name to California when they came over the seas in '49. My father came then."

"Your pa was a prospector?"

"Yes."

"So was mine."

"There was no gold waiting for my father, only hard times, and white men who feared we Celestials would work harder, and better. But my father was a man of determination. Religious—that too is Chinese. He drew strength from the invisible forces of life that flow through the universe. When he came down from the gold country empty-handed, he would not quit. He found work over in the City, making cigars. Many Chinese made cigars there. My father earned enough to bring a picture bride from home. I was born in this very town, Oakland. My mother did not like California. The hardship, the hatred . . . she lived but two years more."

He cast a long look at the pipe and other paraphernalia and then turned away with what seemed a visible regret. He picked up a last gob of gluey rice in his fingers and swallowed it, wiping his hands on his old black pants.

"My father took me to the mountains, where he built the railroad for Cholly Crocker. I was small, fit only for menial work. But my father, nimble as a monkey, he was one of those who scaled the rock cliffs to plant the blasting charges. Many coolies fell in the gorges, or were blown to heaven by the nitro. My father missed death many times. It was not until 18 and 69, after the gold spike was driven and all of Crocker's pets were scattering to the winds, that my father died. We were returning from the mountains to San Francisco. We tried to buy a supper in a little town along the San Joaquin, and some white men, very drunk, fell on my father and beat him. He lay nineteen days holding his belly, wasting away, bleeding inside, and then he died. I have made my way since," Bao finished, without self-pity.

"Seems there are a lot of 'keep out' signs posted in this

state," Mack said. "Those bastards on the ferry didn't have to throw me overboard. Hell, I'd have paid back their stinking fifteen cents after I got a job."

"That is not the railroad's way. They have what people call"—he had to struggle for the word—"monopoly. I have studied this octopus." He held out both arms and wriggled his fingers.

"Octopus?" Mack eyed the black bits in the last of his rice. "My God, did we eat . . .?"

Bao laughed loudly. "No, no. Squid. Octopus—that's the name for the railroad. I see it in the papers, I hear it from men on the docks. The railroad runs everything. They have the only trains, so they can charge whatever they wish for goods or passage. They own the coastal ships too, and the Bay ferry—even most of the dock space in Oakland."

He leaned forward. "I listen to what others say. Ordinary people with jobs in the City, they don't like the high price of the ferry. A clever man could turn that fact to advantage. I have been pondering ways."

"Well, I wish you luck. From what I've seen so far, I don't like that damn Southern Pacific line either." Mack rose, stretched, and went over to feel his shirt on Bao's corner clothesline. Almost dry. Out in the lane, someone plucked a stringed instrument that had a strange minor sound.

Bao scraped their tin plates in a bucket, then applied the scraper to the iron sheet on which he'd grilled the fish. Mack noticed the scraper was a large oyster shell.

"You eat those?"

"I harvest them. When it is dark."

"What's the matter with daylight?"

A thin smile. "The oyster beds in the Bay are privately owned."

"Good God. Even under the water." He picked up the guidebook, which had escaped damage except for a few water spots.

"You come with me tomorrow night, I show you an oyster bed," Bao said.

"Would that be a trip for pleasure, or could you use some help?"

"Yes, I could," Bao nodded. "It would be wrong, though, if I did not tell you there might be danger."

Soberly, Mack regarded the fat Chinese, whom he decided he liked. "Fair warning, and thanks. I'll still go."

"You could be a Celestial," Bao said with a beaming grin. "You like gambling too."

The next night Bao Kee's launch ran south in the Bay against an ebbing tide. The villages along both shores gleamed with fairy-tale lights. Mack relished the sweet open calm of the water, the panorama of stars and dimly seen hills. Bao followed a zigzag course through the Bay, which struck Mack as a waste of time. "No," Bao said when asked about it, "the *sha*—the wicked spirits and evil influences that disrupt the flow of the life force—they travel always in straight lines. Straight lines are no good."

Mack smiled to himself. He'd never met someone like Kee—that was his first name, the fisherman had explained with great patience. In China the name of the family always preceded the given name. Whatever name he went by, he was a first-class mixture of practical business sense and religious tenets Mack would never understand. He truly liked the Celestial. He liked that term too.

Bao throttled down; he was operating with a furled sail again tonight. Mack caught the strong odor of the oyster shoals and then he saw them, long and rough-surfaced, like miniature islands flanking what must be a fairly deep channel. Bao shut off the engine, then stood up, studying the shoals while the launch drifted.

"What are you looking for?"

"Watchman. He drinks a lot. Sleeps a lot. Very lazy. Good men can't be hired to work out here. I don't see his light—the flow is with us tonight. Now take this." He handed an oar to Mack. "Close in, the water's very shallow." Mack thrust the oar down into the muddy bottom and they slowly poled the launch ashore. Mack dragged the bow up while Bao dropped a small mushroom anchor. Then the Chinese man pulled some heavy leather sacks out of the bilges.

"There—see?" Bao bobbed his head at a dark rectangle above the reeking beds. Mack read the sign with difficulty.

FITZMORGAN OYSTER CO.
PRIVATE PROPERTY
ALL TRESPASSERS WILL BE
SHOT

Bao was breathing in that wheezy way again. It was a symptom of excitement, maybe, or a problem caused by his weight. He tossed the leather sacks out and passed Mack a pair of greasy stiff gauntlets.

"Do I need these?"

"Yes. Cut your fingers to meat, otherwise." Bao sounded both serious and urgent now; all the good-humored tolerance of the previous night was gone. He jabbed Mack's ribs. "Be quick, be quick. There are sometimes other men here besides the watchman."

Mack's neck prickled. He clambered from the boat and nearly fell. Maneuvering on a bed of oysters was another new experience. It was like walking on cleavers cocked at every conceivable angle.

"What men?"

Bao's round cheeks worked upward but his smile was cold; in the starlight he resembled an ivory Buddha. "Oyster pirates. Like me. They do not like to share their pickings. No more talk now. Work."

He wheezed his way up the shoal, almost to the low summit, then bent over with a grunt and began snatching oysters and flinging them into a sack. Mack felt an increasing sense of danger, though there wasn't another human being anywhere, only the lights on the Bay's eastern shore, and a faint silvery gleam of mud exposed all around the shoal by low tide. Farther south, some big slow vessel, maybe a barge, worked northward. He was angry at Bao for not being more explicit about the risk.

He started picking oysters. They were sharp and slippery and his left glove had rips in the fingers. In a matter of minutes he was cursing under his breath and bleeding from two cuts.

When his sack was nearly full, he picked it up to move it and gasped at its weight. Bao's thick silhouette bobbed up and down, up and down, his movements rhythmically punctuated by his grunts and wheezes. Mack was stunned to see that the Chinese man had already filled one sack, which stood by itself, and was working on a second.

As Mack bent to start picking again, a firefly light winked in the corner of his eye. He straightened, and saw it wink again, perhaps half a mile down the shoal. His hands froze in the gauntlets.

"Bao," he whispered harshly. "There's a lantern. Good God, there's a boat too . . ." He'd been working so strenuously, he'd paid no attention. It had evidently anchored quietly on the opposite side of the shoal. It was different from Bao's little launch—larger, square-sterned, sloop-rigged. It had an ominously professional look.

"I saw it five minutes ago," Bao whispered back.

"But . . . if we can see them, they can see us."

"No talk." Bao spat the words between his teeth. "Bring the sacks."

Easy enough to say, but when Mack tried to heave the nearly full one to his shoulder, the unexpected weight and treacherous footing threw him off balance and the sack slipped from his hands. He hadn't quite secured the drawstring, and oysters spilled out, *clacka-clack-clack*.

Bao cursed him. The noise was ungodly, Mack admitted. He started scooping up the lost oysters, but Bao kicked his arm aside. "Leave them!" Bao squatted, one sack on his shoulder, grasping Mack's sack with a free hand. "Bring my other sack."

"Who the fuck's down there?" someone shouted, and then the firefly light expanded and a beam shot forth from the lantern's full-open shutter. There were men running, three or four, one with the lantern.

"It's that dog-shit Chink," another man yelled.

"Into the boat," Bao cried, pushing Mack. He ran past, and with enormous strength heaved the full sack from his shoulder into the launch. Mack pulled Bao's other sack toward the water as Bao flung the second sack in too. Bao rushed back to help him. As Bao grappled for a hold on the third sack, Mack whipped around to look at the running men and saw a flash of lantern light on bright metal.

Without warning or ceremony, he hit Bao from behind. The Chinese man cursed in surprise, gashing his cheek open on the rocks when he fell. Mack heard the shotgun discharge both barrels and the pellets buzzed by, scattering over the oysters well beyond them, *tick-tack, tick-tack*.

"Hurry," Bao said, struggling up and wiping his bloody cheek. There was no longer any anger in his voice.

"You better run for it, Chinaman," the first man shouted. "We catch you, we'll stuff your queue and your balls up your yellow ass."

"I know him," Bao wheezed, running with Mack, the partial sack abandoned. "Called Redbeard. Bad man."

"This bay's for white men, you fucking dog on two legs," the same voice boomed. Giving a wild look over his shoulder, Mack thought he indeed detected a beard on one of the oyster pirates chasing them.

Another of the pursuers flung a knife, but it fell short. Mack and Bao jumped in the launch from opposite sides, the Chinese man again exhibiting remarkable agility. Mack hauled up the anchor while Bao rummaged in his gear. He startled Mack by producing an antique Colt revolver, which he aimed across his left elbow, firing three rounds.

The explosions rolled and echoed over the Bay, and the white men immediately fell to the ground. Bao uttered a curt laugh and started the engine. It died.

Mack's throat filled with a strange hard lump. "God, come on, get going," he muttered.

On the shoal, the oyster pirates cautiously raised themselves. Hearing no more shots, they proceeded toward the launch, all of them hunched over except Redbeard. Mack realized he was a huge man, six and a half feet or more.

Bao chattered over the controls in Chinese. Mack gripped the gunwale, sweating. Pa had taught him never to run from peril, but Pa also said that men without fear were either fools or crazy, and that if courage had a definition, it meant standing up to peril despite all that fear pumping and churning in you. Maybe he was being courageous now, but it sure as hell wasn't a romp or a pleasure.

Redbeard seemed to be wrestling with his shotgun. Reloading? Suddenly the engine of *Heavenly Dragon* kicked to life. "Aieee!" Bao screeched, shaking his hands at the sky as if in gratitude. He and Mack grabbed the oars and pushed off and the launch shot into the deeper channel between shoals. The pirates peppered them with further curses and warnings, and Redbeard fired both barrels again, some of the shot splattering water against Mack's cheek.

Bao gave a long shuddery sigh and sank down with a hand on the tiller. His face no longer resembled pale ivory, but melting white wax. Mack smelled the Celestial's sweat, and his own.

Bao nudged a leather sack with his foot. "A poor haul." After a silence: "I did not mean to expose you to so much danger."

Mack licked blood from his gashed fingers. "You warned me, but you didn't say we might get killed. I thought it was just dangerous because we were stealing."

Bao remained silent; perhaps that was his way to admit guilt.

For a while neither spoke, the launch racing down the Bay on its zigzag course. The night air cooled Mack's face and settled his nerves somewhat. They passed an iron freighter high as a house, and while they tossed in its bow wake, he watched its lonely lights float by, and its great white name, LIVERPOOL LADY. His anger at Bao faded, but he certainly had a better measure of the man. When he shifted his glance to the passing lights on shore, he thought of T. Fowler Haines. "They sure as hell don't like outsiders around here," he said finally.

"That is true—even though every Californ' was an outsider once."

"The ones who've been around a while, and settled in—they seem like the worst."

Bao nodded. "When I take you over to the City, it would be well to remember that. Assume an attitude of deference and respect. That way, you will survive."

"Hell with that, Mr. Bao Kee. I'm interested in a lot more than surviving. I have as much right to be here as anybody."

Bao Kee the fisherman smoothed his glossy hair with his palm and examined his passenger ruefully, as if thinking that Mack Chance was a naïve, rash, foolish young man.

7 THE VIOLENCE AT THE OYSTER BEDS KEPT MACK AWAKE a good part of the night. Over and over, he experienced the frantic, fearful dash to the launch, heard Redbeard's shotgun and the dark threats. The memory disturbed him, but it couldn't deter him. *Never be poor again. Never be cold again . . .* California was everything.

The day dawned bright and clear. After Mack trimmed his beard to chin length with a pair of Bao Kee's scissors and they ate a breakfast of rice, crackers, and hot tea, they hurried down to the slip.

Bao raised the sail and *Heavenly Dragon* swept over the swells with great speed. White gulls sailed and swooped past. Jauntily-colored ribbons on the masthead tailed out behind in the sparkling air. The city rose up ahead, and Mack began to see particulars: people scurrying, tiny doll-figures; drays and buggies and horse-drawn street trams clogging the steeply in-clined streets. The breathtaking Pacific light painted some walls brightly, left others in shade, the patterns of rectangular shapes, of reflecting windows, reminding him of a painting, with ver-ticals and horizontals creating an enormous grid.

Noting his passenger's expression, Bao said, "You came far to find this place. I am pleased to be the one who carried you on the last mile of your journey."

At the bow, Mack turned to look at him. The wind ruffled and tossed Mack's hair, and he could taste its salt-sweet pun-gency. Suddenly, instead of Bao and the choppy blue water, he saw the image that had been haunting him since he'd arrived in this state: a closed door. He fished the guidebook from his pocket and held it up. "I dreamed of this moment all the years I read this book. It says a lot about the wonders of California, the opportunity, but it doesn't say a word about people closing doors in your face."

And I didn't come this far to be turned away by the likes of Hellman or that Fairbanks. Or by damned thugs who'd beat up an old Indian, or railroad tycoons, or foul-mouthed harbor rats.

"I'll tell you this," Mack continued aloud, shaking the book at Bao. "If they shut the door on me, I'll find the key. Or knock it down. But I'm going through."

The Chinese fisherman looked at the young man brandishing his treasured guidebook. Despite Mack's innocence and the dangers that lay ahead for one so ambitious, Bao could not help recognizing the tenacity in his hazel eyes, the courage suggested by the pugnacious lift and thrust of his chin. Hope surely burned like a fire within him, for no human being walked across a whole continent without hope as a companion.

Bao gestured beyond his passenger. Quietly he said, "Look. We are close now. There is the City."

II

WELCOME TO THE CITY

1887–1888

San Francisco. The commercial, financial, and cultural center of California, she was known as the Athens of the West. So established and so assured, a select group of her residents insisted that she be referred to as the City, capital C.

Before the Gold Rush, Yerba Buena was a tiny, shabby, insignificant port on a splendid bay. But the discovery at Sutter's sawmill changed everything, including her name. Soon thousands of strangers flooded her shores. Not all of them stayed after the gold ran out. One large group that did remain to form the base of San Francisco society was composed of Southerners, some of whom had come for gold, others simply to flee the poverty and political turmoil of Dixie. They fought for control of the local Democratic party, and fought duels over secession and slavery. Harshly conservative, they formed and led the Committees of Vigilance of 1851 and 1856—the infamous San Francisco vigilantes—hanging malefactors indiscriminately to curb crime.

The Nevada silver strike of '59 fueled a second great growth period, for the City was the port of entry for the fabulous Comstock Lode. She soon had quite a cosmopolitan population. Criminal riffraff from Australia had arrived, and penniless Irish. There was a large laboring population, both whites and their formidable competitors, ambitious and energetic Chinese brought in to lay the Central Pacific through the mountains—"Cholly Crocker's Pets," they were called. By the 1880s, San Francisco was home to 290,000 people, prosperous banks, fishing and shipping interests, flourishing theaters, a prolific literary community, and cable cars that had been clanging up and down Nob Hill for over a decade. She boasted many rich and notable families—leaders of a young society who yearned to match the elegance and prestige of Mr. Ward McAllister's New York "Four Hundred."

By this time San Francisco had a distinct and unconcealed arrogance. All those living across the Bay in Oakland, those so unfortunate as to hail from the Central Valley, those residing in the wretched adobes and cow towns south of the Tehachapis—those people simply didn't exist, or if they did, they were scarcely better than savages. This so inflamed the Southern

69

Californians in particular that they tried unsuccessfully to se-cede on several occasions.

Of course, as a practical matter, the elite of the City could do little about the continuing flood of arriving sailors, "Chinks," Irish, Valley parvenus, and the like. Little, that is, but snub them, build invisible walls, and keep the outsiders in their place—on occasion, by force.

LONG AFTERWARD, MACK SPECULATED ABOUT THE DI-**8** rection his life might have taken—how different it might have been—if, on that afternoon, he hadn't followed his nature and acted as he so often did: impulsively.

There was no hint that an impulsive act would be called for as *Heavenly Dragon* chugged up to a ramshackle finger wharf where a number of empty hay scows were moored. Mack jumped to the pier, which was deserted save for a crewman repairing a line on a scow down at water level, and a fisherman, a sickly-looking old man seated on a stool. Neither paid attention to Mack, and the massif of the City, lumber and brick, granite and glass, seemed equally indifferent. Damned if San Francisco would be indifferent to him very long.

He shouted a good-bye, promising to stay in touch, and Bao waved and pushed off. As the launch wake whitened and broadened, Mack studied the busy waterfront curving around toward the northwest. A hundred yards of dark-green water separated this wharf from the next, much larger one; it contained the slips of the SP Central Ferry Terminal.

Passengers streamed in and out of the unattractive wood building, which was little more than a vast dark shed. Ferry officials—the kind who'd kicked him overboard—bustled about. One ferry was coming in across the Bay and another, *Alameda*, was just heading out with a flurry of bells and whistles.

Then Mack saw her.

She was a young woman, poised on the edge of the pier about a hundred feet away. Stylish and very neat, she was wearing a tubular gray skirt, a shirtwaist with vertical stripes of peppermint and white, little white gloves, and a jaunty flat straw hat held in place by a large brass pin. She was slim, with small round breasts and no bustle.

He started walking toward her. She gave the departing ferry a final glance, consulted a small gold watch pinned to her bosom, then clasped her gloved hands together at her waist and matter-of-factly stepped off the pier.

There was a quick flash of her skirt lifting above ankle-high shoes, yellow, with buttons, then Mack heard the splash. He ran toward the spot where she'd jumped. The lone fisherman couldn't help; he was too frail. Mack waved his arms at the ferry churning from its slip. Clearly, the pilot, crew, and excited passengers had seen the girl's suicide leap.

"Save that girl!" Mack yelled across the water. But the ferry engines kept rumbling; *Alameda* did not change course or slow down.

From the edge of the pier, Mack saw the girl's straw hat floating below. Her face was out of the water, her eyes closed, and for some reason she didn't sink.

He shouted at the ferry again. No response. He dropped his bundled possessions, thinking not of his inability to swim but her impending death, and jumped in. As he dropped, he wondered if he could swim well enough to pull her back to the pier. His feet struck, he sank, shot back up sputtering, and reached for the limp girl. His hand found her slippery throat.

Her eyes opened—large eyes, a warm vivid brown.

"Damn you, get away, I can swim."

"Hang on to me," he gasped, splashing, kicking to stay up. "Killing yourself's no answer for anything—"

"Let *go* of me!" Under the surface, her flying feet struck him. He realized she'd been treading water since the moment she went in. One of her white gloves fisted and bashed him. "Idiot. I'm trying to get a story. I'm a reporter."

Mack let go then. And sank.

She hooked an elbow around his neck, wrenching it severely. He struggled a moment, but then realized she must be trying to save *him*. She kicked and paddled, dragging him behind, and in a moment his head knocked against the slimy rungs of a pier ladder.

She climbed up first, dripping water all over him. When they were both on the pier again, he confronted her, angry and mightily confused. He saw a woman his age or a bit older. Her skin was brown from exposure to the sun and she had a wide, determined mouth and a certain strong bluntness to her chin. She looked not at him, but at the SP ferry, now well out in the Bay.

"Those inhuman curs. Their schedules are more important than anything. They probably would have let me drown. Of course, I can hardly prove that now, can I?" Her glance back at him was withering.

Mack snorted to clear his nose and snatched at something sticky on his forehead. Green seaweed. He flung it away. "If that's your attitude, I'm sorry I bothered. Hell, I can't even swim very well."

"Do you mean it?" Her gaze softened now as she turned her attention to him. "I thought you were just clumsy."

"Clumsy. God," he growled, snatching up the bandanna bundle.

"You're furious with me—"

"Why, no, I always expect to be hit and cursed and ridiculed when I try to help somebody. So long, whoever you are."

"Please, don't go. I shouldn't have blown up at you. What you did was generous, and brave. It's just that I hate to lose a story."

"What story? Would you mind telling me what's going on here, Miss . . . ?"

"Ross. Nellie Ross."

"Mack Chance."

He stood there, waiting, and she thought, *What a curious young man. Poor, bedraggled, with a bumpkin look to his clothes.* But he neither acted nor spoke like a bumpkin; he was forceful, and unexpectedly interesting to her. Instead of dismissing him—her first impulse—she pointed to a bench at the head of the pier. "Come rest a minute and I'll explain."

Mack followed the girl; he, too, was doing some appraising. She was about his height, with a quick, assertive stride and a distinct tomboy air. Somehow that didn't make her less feminine.

"It's very simple," she said, patting the bench beside her. He sat, his soaked clothes squishing and leaking water. "Do you read the *Examiner*?"

He shook his head. "I'm new here."

"My employer, Mr. Hearst, took it over just this year from his father, the senator. He's the silver millionaire, the senator. Young Mr. Hearst intends to stop the flood of red ink and make the *Examiner* the best paper in the West. I write for him, under the byline Ramona Sweet. I cover murder trials, train wrecks—the thrill stuff. When there's no real news, we go out and make news. That's Mr. Hearst's way."

Mack was fascinated. The girl had a short, blunt nose—the peasant touch again—and a forthrightness that added an intriguing spice to her. "Is that what you were doing here?"

Nellie Ross nodded. "Staging a stunt. Mr. Hearst hates the Southern Pacific as much as I do. They're indifferent to passenger safety. Last month a boy age seven fell off one of their ferry boats. The crew was slow to stop the engines to pick him up, and he drowned. That's why I jumped in—to see how quickly anyone from the boat or the terminal would rescue me. Or *if* they would."

"And I ruined your stunt."

"Well, never mind—there'll be other opportunities. I was

excited; I just blew up. I'm the one to make amends, I think."
She pressed water from her straight dark hair. "So tell me,
Mr. Chance, what is it that you do—besides interrupt journal-
ists at work?" She smiled, perhaps to soften the gibe.

Water oozed from his squeaky shoes as he flexed his toes.
"Nothing so far. I just arrived in San Francisco. I hail from
Pennsylvania. I need a job."

"I'm afraid we have nothing at the paper, but there's always
a big enamel pot of coffee on the stove. You could warm up
and dry out." She stood, smoothing her soaked shirtwaist. It
clung to her, and he could see clearly that she didn't have the
kind of billowy figure women prized—not Carla Hellman's kind
of figure. But he found her exceedingly attractive.

"I honestly didn't know women wrote for newspapers," he
said.

"Do you disapprove?"

"Well . . ." He looked away at some gulls.

"Mr. Chance, your opinion's written on your face. A woman
belongs in the kitchen, barefoot and pregnant. That's your concept, isn't it? You and a million others."

"Miss Ross, you keep wanting to start a fight."

"You keep inviting it. You're living in the past, you and
every other man I know. There aren't many women in journalism so far. But that's changing—despite the outraged squeals
of my colleagues, most of whom seem threatened by the mere
sight of a skirt in the editorial rooms. But I'm there, and I'll
stay there. I'm what some people call a sob sister . . . Mr.
Chance, do stop gawking at me. Come along."

But he couldn't help gawking; he'd never met any girl like
this Nellie Ross—independent, a trifle hard, pretty in an un-
conventional way. There was something exotic about the shape
and tilt of those warm brown eyes.

He hoisted his bundle and followed her up the pier past the
old fisherman, who kept his guilty gaze on the water. She said,
"If you like, I'll ask around the office about a job. Someone
might know of something. It's the least I can do for my res-
cuer."

"Am I hearing an apology, Miss Ross?"

She seemed to see him, actually see and appraise him, for
the first time. And not unfavorably. The tip of her tongue rolled
inside her cheek a moment.

"Reporters never apologize. It weakens the air of authority.
Follow me, Mr. Chance."

* * *

74

They walked up Market Street, the busiest thoroughfare Mack had ever seen—drays, buggies, horse-drawn trams, impressive buildings, and people everywhere. Above the din, Nellie asked why he'd come to California.

He showed her the guidebook. "Because I've always believed what this says . . . that a man can get rich out here."

A smile flirted over her face, but an innate kindness suppressed it. Bedraggled and poor as he was, he looked so serious, so determined, that laughter would have cruelly insulted him. She found herself admiring his dogged sincerity, in spite of her earlier anger.

"I understand that kind of ambition," she said. "I have it too. My ambition is to write. Not only news stories, but novels one of these days."

"Is that a good way to make a lot of money?"

"Don't be exasperating. Not everyone here worships wealth. I write to tell the truth. To change things. We turn here," she added, striding around the corner two steps ahead of him.

The *San Francisco Examiner*, Monarch of the Dailies, W. R. Hearst editor and proprietor, operated from rooms at 10 Montgomery Street. Mack had never encountered such a place, full of shouting and cigar fumes and boys racing up and down the aisles snatching foolscap pages from the reporters at their desks. He actually saw a man speaking into a wall telephone. He'd seen pictures of the device, but to watch someone using one was a marvel.

Nellie took him to an alcove at the back and poured him some hot coffee. His clothes were already drying stiffly. He sat down at a cheap table, not a little intimidated by this girl and the general air of worldly sophistication in the office. He heard men shouting expletives as casually as other people said goodday.

Nellie took a chair. "That was a good hat that floated away. Oh well." She noticed his expression. "Yes, it's noisy," she added, taking a sip of her coffee, "but in most respects it's a fine place to work. The senator lost over a quarter of a million dollars after he bought the paper, but then Mr. Hearst was thrown out of Harvard, and he came home and asked the senator to let him take over. Mr. Hearst is only twenty-four, but he has wonderful ideas—a real genius for newspapering. He spends money to cover the news. A lot of people don't like him and call him Wasteful Willie, but he's perked up the paper with controversy and much better writing. Our circulation has already passed twenty-five thousand. Two months ago he personally lured Mr. Bierce away from the *Argonaut* to write general news and his 'Prattle' column—a real coup."

A long rail of a young man, in shirtsleeves with garters and natty striped trousers, shot around the corner and dashed to the coffeepot. His center-parted yellow hair, drooping mustache, and pop eyes didn't impress Mack.

"What about the drowning stunt, Nellie?" the man asked, gulping coffee. He had a high-pitched voice.

"It wasn't the right moment, Mr. Hearst. I'll try again tomorrow." Nellie didn't so much as glance at Mack. He warmed to her all over again.

"Well, do—we haven't stuck it to the railroad for a week now. Hello," Hearst said to Mack in an offhand way. He leaped into the aisle to snare the arm of an older man wearing a coat and cravat in the midst of general sartorial disarray. The man had cool, sardonic eyes.

"Bierce, what're you working on?"

"Avoiding colds and drafts. This place is a pest house."

"You can fixate on your health on your own time. Answer my question."

"The story of the moment is Supervisor Smiley and that little tart he's been keeping over in Sausalito," Bierce said. "At taxpayer expense." Thumb in his waistcoat pocket, he studied Mack with lofty curiosity.

"Be careful—Smiley's a thug. If he finds out, he'll be after you," Hearst said.

"Trust in God, but carry Smith and Wesson," Bierce said, patting his coat. Mack saw the outline of a pistol.

Bierce showed Hearst a small leather-covered book. "Also, one of my alcoholic informants got a job as a janitor at Fourth and Townsend. He managed to purloin this."

"What is it?" Nellie asked.

"Southern Pacific cipher book. Copy number seven, one of Crocker's." He licked a fingertip and turned a page. "The word 'bold' means 'cash payments.' 'Concave' means 'do not commit yourself.' 'Gorilla' stands for 'the state legislature.' My favorite is 'adultery.' Translation—'admit nothing.' There's twelve pages of the stuff."

Hearst snatched the book gleefully, and Bierce pressed a handkerchief to his lips and coughed. "Don't excite yourself, Mr. Hearst. It's worthless without copies of the encoded dispatches they use to conduct their rotten business. They'll soon discover this copy missing, change the cipher, and issue eight new books."

"The railroad does business in code?" Mack asked, astonished.

Bierce raised his nose. "Who is this naïve young gentleman, Nellie?"

"Mr. Chance, an acquaintance who put himself out to help me at the ferry terminal."

"Well, Mr. Chance," Bierce said, "the answer is yes. The three surviving members of the Big Four, the Messrs. Crocker, Huntington, and Stanford—Uncle Mark Hopkins died this year, God rest his skinflint soul—are creatures of enormous resource, and even greater cupidity. A large segment of the public is aware of it, and growing more so. Thus a countervailing passion for secrecy has developed within the SP bureaucracy. The man who really cracks the whip, old Collis P., operates from the East—further reason why sensitive management messages are transmitted in cipher."

"Mr. Chance is new here," Nellie said. "He doesn't know a lot about the gentlemen of the SP."

"One of my favorite subjects," Hearst said with a fierce look. "Let me tell you how crooked that bunch is, Mr. Chance. When the line was under construction, they rigged geologic surveys to convince Congress that the Sierras begin forty miles *west* of the commonly accepted point. The per-mile construction subsidy from the government was higher in the mountains than on flat land, you see. Congress swallowed it and the fraud netted those four bandits half a million. That's how they operate. The public is there to be robbed."

The takers and those they take from . . .

"Of course, knowing it and proving it are two different things," Bierce said. "But the *Examiner* does keep trying—" An electric bell rang. "One hour till deadline. Duty calls." He started away.

"Ambrose, just a minute," Nellie said. "Mr. Chance needs work. Have you heard of anything in town?"

"Unskilled, I presume," Bierce said in a way that made Mack boil. "Sorry, no."

Hearst said, "Ned Greenway was looking for a man last week. Could you stand to work for a self-important snob, Mr. Chance?"

"Who is he?"

"Local sales representative for Mumm's champagne. And the arbiter of San Francisco society. Our own, self-appointed Ward McAllister. Delivering for him, you'd get to meet all the best people."

"Look but don't touch," Bierce said. "Charmed, all." After a mock bow, he sauntered off. Hearst shook Mack's hand with vigorous enthusiasm.

"Good luck to you. Nellie, I want to discuss the next exposé, the Receiving Hospital." He shot away into the smoky chaos of the editorial rooms. An unseen press started to rumble; Mack felt it in the floor.

Nellie stood, smoothing her skirt. "Well, Mr. Chance, how do you feel about delivering champagne for a snob?"

"It's work. Will you call me Mack?"

Her chin came up and there was a startled look in her large eyes, as if she hadn't expected that gesture of interest. But she wasn't displeased.

"Why yes, I will. Here, let me write out Greenway's address and you can go straight around while Mr. Hearst and I discuss how I'm going to surrender myself to the abominable conditions at the Receiving Hospital."

9 NED GREENWAY PROVED TO BE ALL THAT HEARST SAID, and considerably more: pompous, posturing, a little whale who strutted or, alternately, minced around his office on tiptoe. He was forty or so, with a magnificent handlebar mustache and the florid complexion of a drunk. He interviewed Mack at half past one in the afternoon, informing him that he'd been up only half an hour. A silver tray bore his breakfast: hard-boiled eggs, a salt cellar, and a bottle of Mumm's Extra Dry. He talked more about himself than about the job. "I have drunk more wine than any man in America"; "Last year I set a new record, twenty-five bottles in one day"; "I am creating in San Francisco a society fully the equal of New York's Four Hundred." He conducted the interview wearing a full suit of evening clothes. He never wore anything else in public.

On the pittance Greenway paid, Mack couldn't afford a good room, or even a good neighborhood. He found a place next door to Major Wells's Salvation Army headquarters, farther up Montgomery in the seething belly of San Francisco's wickedest district, the Barbary Coast. Mack rather liked the raffish array of pawnshops, whorehouses, secondhand-clothing stores, cheap cafés, and concert saloons, where the melodeons cranked away at all hours and barkeeps slipped chloral hydrate to the unwary.

When the victims passed out they were slid through the back door to the crimps; next day they woke up on the ocean, part of a crew bound for the Japans. Mack's pugnacious manner was a good defense against crimps. He was bothered only once, and the crimp crawled away with his balls kicked.

The hours on Greenway's wagon were long and the cases of Mumm's heavy, but the job taught him the layout of the city in a matter of weeks. He spruced up his wardrobe with a plaid suit from a secondhand shop and called at the *Examiner* to see Nellie. The editor informed him she and Bierce and three staff artists had rushed to Sacramento, where a Central Pacific express had derailed and overturned due to a switch failure. Six were dead. Ironically, Hearst had sent his team to the site by special train, over the rails of the line his headlines damned:

BLOODY TRAGEDY ON THE "LINE OF DEATH"!

Horrific Sights! Relatives Seek Loved Ones Among the Corpses!

Absolute Silence from the Rail Moguls Greets Latest Outrage Against Public Safety

---

The byline of the featured dispatch was Ramona Sweet. Mack felt proud; he knew a celebrity, Mr. Hearst's answer to the famed Nellie Bly in New York. He tore out the story and tacked it up in his room next to a city map he studied for a few minutes every night.

When he didn't feel like eating in a café, or ran short of money, the Salvation Army officers next door could always find him a bowl of soup; they did it for anyone who lived in the neighborhood. Mack soon felt at home.

The painted wagon said GREENWAY'S SPIRITS. Mack tied his horse to a trash can in the alley behind the Odd Fellows Hall, then opened the wagon's back doors. He wore his work uniform, a loose white shirt, cord breeches, boots, and a canvas apron. It was eleven o'clock on a Friday evening in September. Infernally hot for San Francisco.

He pulled out cases of Mumm's Extra Dry and stacked them

on the stoop. Noisy conversation flowed out through the hall's back doors, along with the music of Ballenberg's Society Band. One of Mr. Greenway's recently organized Friday-night cotillions was in progress. The dancing had started at ten, and chefs would serve a buffet supper at midnight. Mack's job was to deliver the iced champagne at the last possible moment.

He puzzled at the heavy, almost martial beat of the music, which didn't sound like dance music to him. A police whistle blasted inside and people applauded. He didn't understand the ways of these society types.

He had turned to the wagon, bracing himself to pick up three cases at once, when he heard a man come out, complaining loudly. "Crazy in there. That little fart-face blows his whistle and they all march around like a bunch of tin soldiers. Ain't like any dancing I ever—" The man stopped abruptly as Mack turned to face him.

Mack was just as surprised, and immediately tense. "Good evening, Mr. Hellman."

Hellman scratched the dimple in his chin. His white tie hung crookedly and his formal suit resembled a potato sack. Sucking on a pungent cigar, he keenly studied Mack.

"Move over," he said finally. "I got to sit down."

Mack put down the cases. Carla Hellman's father seemed positively affable—as if he'd never pointed a revolver at Mack and threatened to kill him. And, even more amazing, Mack was actually glad to see him.

"Jesus, hot in there." Hellman yanked at his collar as if it were a noose. He eyed the crates. "So—this is where you got to. You don't need water. You got champagne."

"I don't drink it, I just deliver it."

Hellman shrugged. "Work's work. Ain't nothing disgraceful about it so long as you make money."

"I don't make enough to suit me."

Hellman stabbed the air with cigar. "Now I like that. That's the attitude of somebody who's going to succeed."

Mack tapped one of the champagne cases. "Excuse me, I've got to take these inside."

"Say hello to my daughter if you see her."

"She's here?"

"You don't think I'd put up with this on my own account, do you? Sure she's here. This is a big fancy affair. I got to tell you, Mr.—" He struggled for the name.

"Mack Chance."

"Well, Mr. Mack Chance, my daughter liked you right away

out there at my ranch. She said you're an ambitious *jüngling*—young fella. She liked the way you talked back to me.''

"I wasn't trying to talk back. I was thirsty. One drink wouldn't have cost you anything.''

"Now listen, we discussed that.'' Hellman waved the cigar again. "The law is the law. You got to learn to respect it, and use it, if you want to make money. Hellman's lesson number one.'' He puffed. "Here, take this. It's a dance favor. Crappy, if you ask me, but maybe you can use it.''

He handed Mack an expensive wallet of black-dyed calfskin the elegance of which was spoiled by a garish pasted-on picture of an orange sun setting over rock formations. A lettered ribbon said THE YOSEMITE VALLEY.

Mack thought it was beautiful.

"Thank you, sir.''

"Sure, I got a dozen better. By the way, Carla ain't by herself in there. She came with that lawyer you met, Fairbanks. He just took that big job. Number-two man in the SP legal department.''

Mack's stomach churned in disappointment. "I can understand why he'd want to escort your daughter. She's the most beautiful woman I've ever seen.''

"Like her mother,'' Hellman said with a strange scowl. "That's a big part of Carla's problem, don't you know. Beautiful women are always messed up. When they're spoiled on top of it, you got real trouble. I take the blame for spoiling her. I gave her too much because she's the only child I got. I love my daughter, but I also know all about her, Johnny—''

"My name is Mack, not Johnny.''

Hellman slapped his knee and guffawed. "By God you're all right. Got sand—ain't that what these westerners say? One more little tip before you go.'' He slid closer on the stoop, getting dirt all over his satin-striped formal trousers. "Confidential. Be glad you ain't got the money to hang around with Carla. It's the going after, not the getting, that fires her up. Soon as she gets what she wants—a new hat, a new man—she don't want it anymore; she wants somebody new. On top of that, when she drinks too much she acts wild. I wish somebody could straighten her out, but it's impossible. God pity any man who tries. I'm telling you as a father—you don't want to get mixed up with her.''

Mack nodded. Hellman obviously didn't know about the encounter in the fog, and he wasn't going to inform him.

"Excuse me,'' he said again, stooping and heaving the crates up.

"Sure, Johnny." Hellman sat there squinting into the smoke with a vaguely forlorn expression.

A committee had decorated Odd Fellows Hall with swags of satin and great sprays of flowers. Gaslight rather than electric light illuminated the dancers, who marched four abreast, then split in two and curled back along the opposite side of the floor to the thump of Ballenberg's strident music. In a faultless tail suit, Ned Greenway led the figure, partnered with a homely old woman, who had to be the Mrs. Martin he'd mentioned to Mack. Greenway said Mrs. Martin was a society leader because some relative of hers had founded the local gas works. Together, Greenway and the old woman decided who was invited to these affairs, and who wasn't.

The large room smelled of perfume and pomade. Suddenly Mack saw Carla on the other side, chatting and flirting a fan at half a dozen men clustered around. He almost slipped and dropped the champagne.

"Put that under here and be quick," growled one of the white-hatted chefs arranging the trestle tables with elegant silver dishes of tongue and ham, terrapin and scalloped oysters. Mack slid the crates under the skirted table and unloaded the bottles into boxes full of ice.

With a flourish of snare drums, the dance concluded. Ned Greenway lifted the gold police whistle he wore on a gold chain around his neck and blew a piercing blast. "Supper in twenty minutes, ladies and gentlemen."

The dancers left the floor, filling the room with happy chatter, and Ballenberg's bandsmen left the dais to smoke in the alley. Mack started to carry the empty crates toward the kitchen doorway, but at the end of the long buffet, he stopped.

Carla was hurrying toward him.

He searched for Fairbanks, but didn't find him in the crowd. Then Carla consumed his vision, sailing down on him like a great gorgeous treasure galleon. She wore a gown of dark-green satin with extravagantly high bouffant sleeves. The skirt fell in large folds dusted with gold flecks—little gold stars, he saw as she drew nearer. Her bodice was tight and cut low, showing deep, powdered cleavage. She wore a three-inch-high choker, solid diamonds all the way around, and her earrings too were clusters of diamonds, her tiara a flashing crusty arch of them.

She stood there glittering, breaking his heart with her beauty. "I nearly died when I saw your face," she said. "What a grand surprise. What are you doing here?"

"Working. Delivering champagne."

"May I have some?"

Mack glanced nervously at the chefs arranging the supper. "You'll have to ask one of them." Several guests had noticed them talking, and had begun whispering.

She looked him up and down with a teasing smile. "You're certainly a long way from the Valley, Mr. Chance. And I do believe you took a bath."

"It was always my plan to come here . . ." He let the sentence trail off, feeling more and more awkward, mesmerized by her stunning looks. Her half-revealed breasts were great pushed-up billows of white cream, inviting kisses . . . God, what kind of thought was that? Hellman's daughter could drive a man out of his head.

The teasing smile came back. "You're pursuing me, then."

"I meant San Francisco, Miss Hellman. I have ambitions—"

She rapped his chin with her diamond-studded fan. "Yes, I know. And you still have your saucy tongue. But I like that in a man. It means you won't be defeated easily. I'll tell you, my dear, I was prepared to be royally bored when I told Walter I'd come with him tonight. I'm not bored any longer."

Her tongue touched her lower lip and her dark-blue eyes warmed. Mack felt steamy, and conscious of many eyes on them, but Carla didn't seem to care. "Is there any possibility that you and I could find somewhere to—"

A male voice, quickly growing louder, overlaid hers and made her frown.

"Our forebears were the original Anglo settlers. They bequeathed this state to us as a sacred trust."

Fairbanks. With a trio of equally elegant gentlemen hanging on his words.

"We must use the political process to continually purify California, instead of allowing it to become ever more mongrelized—Carla my dear. I noticed you talking to someone over here. I couldn't imagine who—"

When he finally recognized Mack, surprise gave way to something uglier, though he tried to maintain an air of amusement. "My God, the upstart traveler. Surely you weren't invited here."

"I work for Mr. Greenway."

"You've gone up in the world—or is it down?" Fairbanks wore white gloves. His little mustache glistened with wax.

His companions laughed. One said, "You know this chap, Walter?"

"I do, Tevis. I met him a few months ago at Hellman's place in the Valley. He's one of those newcomers who keep inflicting themselves on us."

"Oh, is California your property?" Mack said.

Fairbanks's gray eyes narrowed a little. "I'd say it's much more mine than yours. We won't debate the issue. I do have certain territorial rights in this hall, however." He pointed to the kitchen. "That's the door for tradesmen. Use it."

"Walter, you needn't be so rude," Carla said. But she was breathing audibly; she couldn't hide a certain excitement over the confrontation.

"I'm simply saying outsiders aren't welcome to mingle with guests at cotillions. How can society be society if there are no rules?"

Mack stood there simmering. They were so stylish, superior, scornful. And they were all men rich enough to possess Hellman's daughter. He felt his face growing hotter. "I'll leave when I'm ready," he said.

"Oh, dear, a ferocious grizzly bear," one of the gentlemen said with a drunken lisp.

Another said, "Looks more like a young thug from the Barbary Coast to me."

Carla linked her arm with Mack's, goading Fairbanks with her glance. "I think you're all behaving like boors."

"Imagine," the fellow with the lisp said, "the daughter of Mr. Swampy Hellman calling us boors."

He and his two friends laughed, though Fairbanks held back. "You bastards shut up," Mack said, stepping in front of Carla. He knew he'd made a mistake—he heard the sudden cavernous silence in the hall—but he was furious and wouldn't retreat.

"I don't like your language, fellow," Fairbanks said.

"I don't give a damn what you like. They should apologize to Miss Hellman."

Fairbanks seized his sleeve. "Get out of here."

And Mack swung.

Fairbanks danced back, and Mack's looping punch missed completely.

Slowly, with relish, Fairbanks drew off one glove, then the other. "Please hold these, Haig." He smiled at Mack. "You shouldn't have tried that. I work out regularly in the boxing ring at my club. Defend yourself."

Mack was just bringing his hands up when Fairbanks's bullet of a fist struck him. He spun to one side. There was an audible gasp as people turned to look, and one woman screamed.

Across the hall, Greenway whirled about, clutching his gold whistle. "What is that commotion—what?" A second punch, coming so fast Mack never saw it, crashed him into a buffet table. He overturned basins of lobster bisque and salvers of smoked sausage, landing among them with blood squirting from his nose.

Greenway pelted up and blew a ferocious blast on the whistle. "What is the reason for this outrageous behavior?"

"This man assaulted Mr. Fairbanks without cause," one of the toadies exclaimed.

"My God, this is mortifying," Greenway cried.

Mack was up now, hair in his eyes, blood on his shirt and apron. He lumbered at Fairbanks. The man was no lily; he danced lightly aside and landed another blow that snapped Mack's chin. Pain lanced his neck and spine, but once more he shambled toward Fairbanks, glimpsing Carla's perspiring face, her shining eyes urging him on. He struck. Fairbanks laughed, and the punch, though strong, glanced off the lawyer's padded shoulder. Then he stepped forward and whipped Mack with a powerful right-left-right combination. Mack staggered back, choking on blood and struggling to stay up. His face resembled a raw piece of tenderloin.

"You're discharged—never darken my door again," Greenway shrieked at Mack. "Mr. Fairbanks, my profound apologies. Shall I summon the police? Will you prefer charges?"

Fairbanks smoothed his temples and flexed his fingers. "There's no need." Smiling, he let Mack see a message in his clear gray eyes: Mack was swept away, because dirt was always swept away.

"Come, my dear." Fairbanks picked up Carla's gloved hand and laid it on his sleeve. "A little champagne would be refreshing just now."

She looked back once, but he couldn't read her expression. Pity? He was furious that he'd lost, been humiliated in front of her.

"Get this vermin out of here," Greenway hissed, dancing up and down in his patent-leather pumps. Three strong men from the kitchen manhandled Mack to the alley and slammed the door.

Mack stood on the corner of Fourth and Townsend. Fog was rolling in, chilling him, but he kept standing there, gazing at a four-story building that had all the charm of a fortress prison. San Franciscans like Mr. Bierce said that Fourth and Townsend, the general offices of the SP, represented more power than the statehouse in Sacramento. "Some say the SP *owns* the statehouse." Mack glanced from window to window, gray rectangles stained with rain. Which belonged to Fairbanks? If the lawyer was his enemy, then so were those who chose to employ him.

10 "SO NOW I NEED ANOTHER JOB," MACK SAID. IT WAS Sunday, late afternoon. He'd called at the *Examiner* in the hope that Nellie would be working on the next morning's edition, and she was. When she finished, they rode a horsecar to the end of the line and walked near the crashing waves along the Presidio seawall. He talked for a long time with barely a pause, telling her about the fight and meeting Hellman for the second time. But he said nothing about encountering Carla at the cotillion, or earlier.

"Maybe what I really need is a boxing instructor," he said at the end.

"I'm terribly sorry that happened to you, Mack."

"I caused it—I swung at him. And I'm not sorry."

"I can understand your reaction. I've met Fairbanks. Do you know much about him?" When he admitted he didn't, she gave him some background.

The Fairbanks brothers were Argonauts from Georgia, some of the many from the cotton South who migrated to California during the Gold Rush. "To this day, members of the family claim to be plantation aristocrats, though if they were, I always wonder why they left."

Shrewder than their counterparts who ran straight to the diggings, the brothers had established a service to handle the dust and money of the miners, the successful ones and the failures alike. "The Dixie Express Company was the forerunner of Fairbanks Trust. Very early, the brothers became active in the Chiv."

"What?"

"The Chivalry. The pro-slavery wing of the Democratic party. It was at its peak before the War. Fairbanks's father also helped form the Vigilance Committees of '51 and '56. Fairbanks himself campaigned hard in Sacramento for the Exclusion Act of '82, to bar Chinese immigration. Now that smugglers have started bringing in more coolies, he's promoting a new law to register all Chinese. No doubt he'd brand them like cattle—and slaughter the weak ones if he could. He's the worst kind of Social Darwinist.''

Nellie went on to explain that the lawyer was also an enthusiastic member of the Native Sons of the Golden West, a private society of white males born in California after the seventh of July, 1846. "That was the day Captain Sloat raised the American flag in Monterey Bay. I consider the Native Sons a bunch of prigs and bigots. There may be some decent members, but Fairbanks certainly isn't one of them. He's a selfish, heartless man.''

"But not stupid.''

"No. That's why he's dangerous.''

"He isn't a weakling either. He knocked me down like a piece of straw.''

She stepped close to him to dodge a plume of spray. As she took his arm, he felt her breast thrusting small and hard against him.

"If you're serious about boxing, I know where you can find a good instructor.''

"Who is it?''

"His name is Jim Corbett. He's an Irish boy whose father owns a livery stable. He's barely twenty, but he's already the middleweight champion of the Olympic Club. Mr. Watson, the Englishman who coaches boxing at the club, thinks he shows enormous promise.''

"Wait,'' he said, laughing. "Women aren't supposed to know about boxing and such things.''

"This woman does. I love sports, and the outdoors. You'll soon feel the same way. It happens to almost every easterner who comes to California. There's something about the climate that turns hothouse plants into sunflowers.''

"Tell me more about this boxer.''

"Originally, the club recruited him to play second base on its baseball team, but a hand injury kept him from it, and his interest shifted to boxing. He isn't like the usual fighter you see at exhibitions in barrooms and barns. He's clean-cut. Bright. A fastidious dresser. Some have laughed at him for that. Then they get a taste of his fists and stop laughing. He has a regular job, but he wants to turn professional. If he does, he could well raise the whole tone of the sport. He works out three times a week at the Olympic Club, and on weekends he gives exhibitions around the area. Billy Delaney's saloon over in Oakland. Terrible dive. Or sometimes, on a barge out in the Bay—''

"Have you been to any of them?"

"I'm afraid not," she said, piqued. "I get my information secondhand, from our sportswriters. Females aren't allowed in the hallowed male confines of the Olympic Club, or at the exhibitions. That's another injustice we'll remedy one of these days."

He grinned and impulsively patted her hand. "You're a fighter too, aren't you?"

"Absolutely. I'm a woman. It's a necessity."

He decided to look up the young prizefighter as soon as he had time and a little money in his pocket. After tramping the streets for a week, he found a job as an assistant cook in a brawling Barbary Coast establishment, the Royal Midway.

The chief cook, a tough, garrulous Filipino named García, taught him a lot in a short time. García occasionally filched a bottle of wine from the owners, and he cheerfully shared it.

"Chardonnay. Charles Krug, Saint Helena. He came over from Prussia, learned viticulture from Haraszthy, and set up his own operation. Krauts make some of the best wine in California. This was a good harvest."

"I don't know anything about wine, García." Mack tasted the dry, tangy, straw-colored wine, then smacked his lips.

García beamed. "Now you know something about wine."

"Yes, and I like it."

He earned enough to put $3 into a deposit account at Wells, Fargo, where a friendly teller with sharply parted hair and keen blue eyes helped him with the paperwork.

He relished the strengthening pull on the back of his legs every time he toiled up a steep street. Never had he seen derelicts so numerous and dirty, women so clean and smart, sunlight so intense and pure. He loved the autumn vistas of cloud and sky, hill and shore, bay and ocean; he rounded a corner, or raised a window, and suddenly there was another, making the throat catch, the breath quicken, ravishing the heart . . .

O California!

Nellie loaned him a copy of *Ramona,* saying it would awaken him to the plight of the California Indians. The author, Helen Jackson, had campaigned for Indian causes before her recent death from cancer, and in her last years she had befriended Nellie. Mack thought of the priest Marquez, and of his own resentment of anyone trying to be his conscience. But he continued to be strongly attracted to Nellie without knowing much about her, so he overlooked his feelings and read the novel, which was all she'd said it would be.

He learned to swallow raw oysters and suck the foam off steam beer. He learned that a nearsighted politician named Buckley—the "Blind Boss"—ran the Democratic machine from his Snug Café next to City Hall, and an Oriental gangster nicknamed Little Pete ran the Chinese underworld. He learned to avoid at all costs the packs of ravenous wild dogs that ran at night. He learned to love Allsop's Ale, and J. A. Folger's coffee, and the candy of Domingo Ghirardelli, "Chocolate King of the West." He learned that San Francisco followed the French eating style; one had "lunch" at noon and "dinner," not supper, at night. He learned that a man could educate himself in the fine library of the Merchants Exchange on Battery Street. He learned not to be bothered by scurryings in the night, for even the best homes were plagued with the gray and black and white rats that had infested the City ever since they jumped ship right along with the Argonauts of '49. He learned that the City's fine gentlemen dined on venison steak and Dungeness crab; that the City's fine ladies bought their gowns at Felix Verdier's Ville de Paris department store; and that after they'd dressed and dined, all the fine people went by carriage to Tom Maguire's Opera House for performances by the world's leading singers and actors. He learned that Sherith Israel Synagogue was orthodox, while Temple Emanu-el was a reform congregation, and he studiously tried to absorb the differences. He learned that Lotta's Pump, the handsome cast-iron fountain and column on Market Street, was a gift of the famous actress Lotta Crabtree, who got her start in San Francisco. He learned that "Alcatraz" meant pelican, and that the fort in the harbor—"The Rock"—housed army prisoners. He learned to love the foghorns, the rattle of ivory counters in the Barbary Coast gaming halls, the sound of accordions in the German beer gardens, the whistles of the great iron steamers of the Pacific Mail Company outbound for China.

He learned to be a child of the City.

A disgruntled patron set a fire in the Royal Midway late one night, forcing it to close indefinitely. So, jobless again, Mack decided he'd neglected his training for revenge long enough. He parted with 15 cents for the hated SP ferry and looked up Bao Kee in Oakland. The following Sunday they went sailing in the Bay to find the young prizefighter.

They located the barge near Oakland's Inner Harbor. Row-boats, small sailboats, and steam launches were tied up to all sides of it. A large crowd of men on the barge shouted and yelled, but there were so many of them Mack couldn't see the fighters.

He stepped onto the barge and immediately found himself staring at the muzzle of a small nickeled pistol in the hand of an Oakland plug-ugly. "No fuckin' Chinks."

"He's my friend."

"I don't care if he's your fuckin' brother, he ain't OK."

From the bobbing launch, Bao said, "It's all right, I'll wait."

Mack nodded reluctantly, glared at the man, and worked his way into the crowd. A very mixed crowd it was, with hounds-tooth sleeve brushing ragged elbow, and scents of hair oil and mustache pomade mingling with sweat, onion, garlic. "Stand up, for Christ's sake, Murphy," a bulb-nosed man screamed, knocking Mack in the head with his brandished fist.

Mack craned on tiptoe and saw the man who was obviously Murphy, a young hulk with a yellow beard and a white gut hanging over his tights. Rivers of red ran all over his face. He had his gloves up, waving them feebly to defend himself, and he threw a sluggish punch. It lazed by the neatly parted hair of Mr. Corbett, whom Mack recognized as the same polite, blue-eyed teller who'd taken his deposit at Wells, Fargo. Corbett wore blue calf-high boots with laces, and tights to match. He looked trim, whippet-lean, as he bounced around the stained mats.

"Finish him off, Jim, this is a goddamn bore," a man said, generating applause and whistles. Murphy eyed the unfriendly crowd and spat a white gob that landed on Corbett's tights, not accidentally. The young bank teller reddened and smacked his gloves together twice, his only display of emotion.

Corbett's handler, a little bald man with hairy ears, cried, "Fight or step down, Murphy."

"Yes, come on," Corbett said, bobbing and shifting with an amazing lightness.

Murphy's head lowered, his dull dark eyes murderous. Someone called a comment to Corbett, who looked briefly in that direction, and Murphy hit him below the waist.

Partisans screamed foul. First Corbett reeled away, with Murphy snuffling and smirking, but then he snapped back, rapped his gloves together once more, and danced in. He stung Murphy with one, two, three blows to the head. Murphy went, "Auugh," staggering backward. He tried to roundhouse Corbett with his right but Corbett wasn't there; he was moving left. Murphy crossed with his left but Corbett had only been feinting. He streaked under Murphy's guard and punished his middle with three more punches. Murphy exhaled, a gaseous sound. His eyes lost focus. Corbett brought his right fist up with a light, airy motion. But the *crunch* in the sudden silence made Mack and everyone else wince.

Murphy was out on his feet; a yellow drool leaked over his lower lip. Someone rapped a hammer on a ship's bell, and seconds later, Murphy was dragged off the mats by his heels, a blood-soaked towel hiding his face.

Corbett donned a robe and toweled off his hair while the banty fellow, Billy Lee Delaney, paraded before the crowd. "Awright, gents, anyone else care to go a round or two with Gentleman Jim?"

There were some jests, coarse remarks, friendly snickers. But no takers.

"Anyone? Awww—no one?"

Mack raised his hand.

"Sympathies to you, lad," said a man nearby. "Like to gimme the name of next of kin?" Laughter.

Mack's heartbeat quickened as he stepped on the mat. Looking down, he saw drops of Murphy's blood gleaming in the sunshine. Jim Corbett was slipping out of his robe. Over his shoulder, he gave the new challenger a swift, dismissive glance. Then he looked again.

He strode forward with a smile and raised a glove. "Wells, Fargo."

"You helped me with my deposit. Chance is my name."

"Jim Corbett." They were about the same age, and something warmed between them there in the bright Sunday air that smelled of sea and fish. Corbett looked him up and down, and not with disapproval.

"Shirt off," Delaney barked. Mack peeled it off and dropped it. Delaney held up gloves one at a time. Mack thrust his hands in and Delaney quickly laced each one. "To your corners," he said with a slashing gesture, then a wink at his protégé. To Mack: "Don't worry, son, I'll stop it if it gets too bad."

Corbett smiled from his corner, a little more cool now as he appraised Mack professionally. Delaney hit the ship's bell. Hitching up his blue tights, Corbett came out with the grace and speed of someone executing a waltz step double-time.

Mack squared up his fists as he'd seen Fairbanks do that night at the Odd Fellows Hall. He never saw Corbett's first punch whiz through his guard, but he felt it slam against his jaw. His eyes blurred. Corbett skipped away.

Somehow he couldn't catch the young fighter. Corbett was too clever and nimble. Finally Mack did corner him, and wound up a ferocious punch and hurled it. Corbett sidestepped easily and Mack's glove merely flicked his ear. Corbett acknowledged the hit with a good-natured blink. Then he sprang away.

By the end of five minutes, Corbett had opened a cut above Mack's left eye and badly bruised his face. Mack's brief popularity as a new challenger was over. Cries of "Another dud" and "Send him down, Jimmy" mingled with boos. Mack stubbornly kept his fists up and stood his ground, shuffling his feet but hardly moving while Corbett got through his guard again and again, punishing his eyes, his jaw, his chest. Corbett's gloves seemed to fly by themselves. He almost looked regretful.

The blows landed faster, sharp leathery smacks. Finally Mack rebelled against the pain, throwing a right that Corbett didn't quite dodge, and the crowd roared with surprise as Gentleman Jim skated back on his heels, nearly toppling. Billy Delaney pushed him from behind to save the moment.

Corbett's face now showed a grudging respect. But not for long. He bore in, determined, and Mack, dazed and hurting, virtually stood there, taking it, blow after blow, till the ship's bell rang.

To Mack's astonishment, he heard some scattered applause for his performance. Corbett snagged a towel for him. "I've fought worse. A lot worse. You have a killer right hand but you don't know how to control it. You don't know how to bob and feint. I had the same problems till Mr. Watson took me on. What's your name again?"

"Mack Chance."

"Well, you're not bad."

"I'd like to be a lot better."

"Serious?"

Mack nodded.

"All right, drop around to the Olympic Club at six any Tuesday, Thursday, or Saturday. We'll go into the arena. I need strong sparring partners."

Mack's puffy eyes glinted with excitement. "I'll be there."

"I'll expect you," Corbett said with a crisp nod and a warm Celtic smile.

Mack didn't get to the Olympic Club immediately, because he found a job with the municipal street department. It wasn't very stimulating, but it paid his meager rent.

After about a week, his supervisor sent him up to the lofty eminence of Nob Hill. Here the City's rich had built mansions even more splendid and spectacular than those at South Park and Rincon Hill. The wind-scoured summit overlooked the financial district, and Mack gazed in awe at wooden castles hurling Gothic towers and spires at the sky in disorderly splendor.

He shoveled dirt from his handcart into a six-inch chuckhole near the corner of California and Mason streets, hardly able to keep his mind on his work for looking at the houses and envying their inhabitants. He didn't know which belonged to whom, but he did know that all four of the Big Four had built residences on Nob Hill, each of the tycoons flinging out more money than the last to please his wife and embarrass the wives of the others. Flood, the Nevada silver king, and other millionaires lived up here too. The cream.

Mack took his tamp and began compacting the dirt in the hole. On the side of the hill facing Oakland, a car of the California Street Cable Railroad clanged its bell coming up. That was the line whose construction had been promoted by Governor Stanford, Nellie said. When he moved up to Nob Hill his bulk made walking to and from home arduous.

Scarcely any other noises disturbed the hushed morning at this rarefied height. Someone rattled milk bottles at an unseen back door. Someone whipped a beater against a rug in an unseen backyard. That was all until a fringed buggy came up the hill from Powell Street and stopped near Mack, who paused to lean on his shovel like any good municipal employee.

In the rear of the buggy sat a handsome older couple, both with the starry look of willing victims. In the front seat, a sharply dressed gentleman put his patent-leather boot on the footboard and pointed his whip.

"I couldn't recommend a better section than this for your new home. Nob Hill is the most exclusive residential address in America."

"Where did they get such an odd name—*Nob*?" the woman asked.

"The great moguls of India, the nabobs. They didn't build small either. I must warn you, folks—there are only a few lots left. And the prices are sky high."

"Oh, that's not a worry," the woman trilled. "Mr. Sineheimer sold the corset factory in Chicago for a lot of money. I mean an enormous amount of money." Her bragging on his behalf made the stoic Mr. Sineheimer inflate and preen.

"Certainly," the broker said with an automatic smile.

"That's why I could sell you any lot up here and assure you of a superb investment. However, if you do build, you can't get away without servants. Plenty of servants."

"I'd like that," said the mogul's wife. Mr. Sineheimer had no opinion.

While Mack observed all this, a middle-aged woman in plain and proper black came out of the enormous mansion on the southwest corner of California and Powell and walked up the hill to Mason. Mack figured she was a servant going on an errand. As she started to cross diagonally through the intersection toward the mansion on the opposite corner, the broker flicked his whip over his bay horse to set the buggy in motion. The woman, peering into her reticule, glanced up belatedly and saw the rattling rig bearing down.

"Get out of the way, woman," the broker shouted, waving his whip. The woman stepped back but dropped her reticule in the street. She would have been safe had she let it lie; instead, she lunged for it.

The broker wildly tugged his rein to the right, but his horse whinnied and didn't respond to the bit. Mack bolted for the woman, who seemed confused or stupefied with fright. He rolled his shoulder against her, flinging his arms around her and hurling her back out of the path of the reckless driver.

They fell hard. Mack jabbed out his left hand, keeping himself from landing on the poor flustered little lady. Meanwhile, the broker shook his whip and the bay trotted away with him and his prospects.

"Ma'am, I'm terribly sorry, I hope I didn't hurt you—"

"No, no," she said, accepting his hand to stand, then brushing off. She was a small woman, dark-haired and stout. Her oval face reminded him of pictures of Queen Victoria, except for her eyes, which were round and protruded, almost pop eyes. "I thought that man would stop. He stunned me when he didn't."

"Sure you're all right?"

"More wounded dignity than anything. Thank you again for your courtesy." She appraised him quickly. "I must say, the street-repair men they send up here are usually little better than derelicts. You don't look like that sort."

"Only job I could get, ma'am. Doubt I'd have taken it, except that it's outdoors."

"You like outdoor work?"

"I do. I love the sunshine."

"Are you a native?"

"I am now."

With a thoughtful look, she said, "My husband keeps race-horses down at his ranch on the peninsula. He always needs alert young men as grooms and general helpers. It's somewhat more interesting work than this, I should think. I'll give you a note to our foreman if you'd care to investigate."

Mack wanted to throw his iron tamp into the air but he feared it might fall back and brain his benefactor. "Yes ma'am, I would. What's the name of the ranch?"

"Palo Alto. It's the Stanford ranch—as in Leland Stanford. I am Jane Lathrop Stanford; the governor is my husband. Come with me, please. My home's just down there. I'll go over to the Crockers' later."

As he followed her back to the turreted house, he saw again the limping collie, the crushed mass that had been the laborer O'Malley, and felt and smelled the sticky blood on his face.

He climbed marble steps to the main entrance. Immediately inside, he found a huge round foyer and saw in the white stone floor a circle of black marble inlays, symbols strange and un-familiar. The signs of the zodiac, Nellie told him later; she knew the house. Everyone knew the house, including those with no hope of being invited in.

A dome of amber glass seventy feet overhead cast an appro-priate golden light. Mrs. Jane Stanford led him past innumer-able rooms whose function he could only guess. He did identify a library, a billiard room, a music room with a grand piano. There were enough paintings, frescoes, and sculptures to fur-nish a museum, and a fountain splashed in a conservatory crowded with hothouse plants. In the next room he spied some-thing even more astonishing: Sitting on the numerous branches of potted trees and shrubs were birds, motionless golden birds.

Mrs. Stanford came back because he'd stopped. "They're metal," she explained. "They move and sing by means of compressed air. The governor loves all things mechanical."

Men and women in black livery trod the halls as quietly as monks and nuns. Mack counted fourteen servants before reaching a fashionably crowded room at the rear, Mrs. Stan-ford's downstairs sitting room.

She invited him to enjoy the spectacular view of the City below the Powell and Pine intersection while she quickly penned the note at a drop-front desk. The opulence left him feeling like he'd done five rounds with Corbett. When she ush-ered him back to the sunshine, he earnestly hoped he'd thanked her—he couldn't remember.

"Nellie isn't here?" Mack said.

"Somewhere," Bierce replied with a shrug. "She's preparing herself to collapse on Market Street, from there to be conveyed into the hands of the cretins and sex fiends who staff the Receiving Hospital. A female patient swears she lost her virginity to one of them."

It was meant as a joke, but Mack didn't like the sound of it. Bierce poured them coffee and sat down at the cheap table. "What brings you here?"

Mack showed him the note.

"My, my. Signed by the great lady herself. Do you plan to take a job at the ranch?"

"Not sure. I saw Stanford once; I didn't like him."

"He'd hate to hear you say that," replied the acidulous Mr. Bierce. Bitter Bierce, his colleagues called him. "Back in the 1860s the governor discovered politics. It carried him in and out of the statehouse and more recently into the U.S. Senate in '85. To this day, 'governor' remains his favorite honorific. The old boy has an abiding desire to be loved by us common folk of California. He kept us in the Union, and all that. His passion for popularity contributed to his split with Huntington, who thinks the only way to run a railroad is to keep to yourself and be a son of a bitch."

"Stanford doesn't run the line anymore?"

Bierce shook his head. "After he and Collis P. got rich, they found they had different styles. Huntington's a money-maker, Stanford's a money-spender. They also had a bitter quarrel over their personal candidates for the other California seat in the Senate. The dear old gov's man lost, so the gov withdrew to his trains, his racehorses, and his other toys. As a Washington politician, he's about as zealous and effective as Humpty-Dumpty."

Nellie sailed in, wearing an appalling dress that looked like it had been put together from gray and copper-green rags. Dirt and a thick layer of rouge smeared her cheeks. She looked altogether cheap and awful.

"You're going out dressed like that?" Mack said.

"Charity cases don't wear gowns by Worth of Paris. Don't worry—I'm taking a little pistol in my garter, in case." He marveled at her casual air. Where did the toughness come from? So far he'd learned little about her, except that she'd been raised near a Valley town called Hanford. She didn't seem to like talking about it.

"You were speaking of our beloved former governor, I believe?'' Nellie picked up the note and read it. ''Mack, surely you're not going to work for him. He's a fat, vain charlatan—a parasite who lives on what the Southern Pacific monopoly extorts from the people.''

''But you told me he's one of the richest men in America.''

''Absolutely,'' said Bierce. ''In any story I write about him, I insist upon paying tribute to that fact in cold type.'' He rummaged among some *Examiners* on the table, then found a headline referring to him as GOVERNOR £ELAND $TANFORD.

''Then working for him might teach me something,'' Mack said.

Bierce laughed. ''God, you're a greedy one.''

''Come on, isn't that what California's all about?''

''That notion may have gotten abroad,'' Nellie said, ''but it's wrong. I'm disappointed in you.''

''Sorry.''

''You mean I don't have any influence on you?'' Underneath the teasing, she was serious. Sometimes he hated that all-too-apparent righteousness.

Now he folded the note and returned it to the pocket of his vest. ''Not this time,'' he said.

Nellie flashed a despairing look at Bierce, who shrugged again.

''Well, my boy,'' he said, ''if you do hire on with the governor, don't tell him you know anyone on this paper. Don't tell a soul at Palo Alto if you want to last beyond the first five minutes.''

MACK STOOD ON THE LOWER RUNG OF THE FENCE, WAV-**11** ing and yelling. ''Come on, Shannon.''

''Stretch out, boy. Run,'' shouted the equally enthusiastic man next to him, a white-haired and bowlegged Basque named Emilio Vasco.

The white fence bordered a one-mile exercise track, one of two maintained on the vast ranch along with a large trotting park. Dust rose as the jockey booted the splendid stallion around the last turn and into the straight, heading for the two cheering in the fading afternoon. It was October and the foothills of the peninsula and the meadows below were golden yellow.

Shannon pounded by, then slowed down, and Vasco waved his silver pocket watch. "Fastest time yet. The governor will be pleased."

The jockey circled back and dismounted, and then Mack led the stallion off through the maze of paddocks to the long stable buildings that housed nearly 100 stallions, some 250 brood mares, and an equal number of fillies and colts. Governor Stanford abhorred gambling, but he was dedicated to improving the world's racing stock.

Vasco walked along, companionably silent for a while. Then he said, "I notice you've gotten good and brown, lad. In a matter of—what is it? Four weeks?"

Mack nodded. "Now if I can just learn to stay up on a horse—"

"You handle them well," the trainer said. "They like you. The riding will come. I watched you in the saddle yesterday—you're learning just fine."

"Thanks, Mr. Vasco," Mack said, glad to be alive on this bright fall afternoon in California. Glad of it even if he was, according to his newspaper friends, on the payroll of a vain parasite, whom he had so far seen only from a distance.

The Palo Alto ranch sprawled over 7,200 acres and employed 150 men, 50 of those Chinese. Except for the senior trainers, they rotated their duties. Some days Mack watered or raked one of the tracks. Other days he cultivated part of the 60 acres devoted to growing carrots for the colts, or planted native redwoods or Japanese cedars in a 300-acre arboretum planned to contain twelve thousand trees. Still other days he did chores around the great oak-shaded manor house that had belonged to a family named Gordon before Stanford bought it. But every day, without exception, he was responsible for exercising several of the ninety colts selected by the governor as especially promising future racers. Each horse worked out for twenty minutes.

One morning he tramped up to the turreted sand-colored house carrying a flat of delicate lady ferns in rich topsoil. He knocked at the shady kitchen door.

"Come in, please."

He'd expected the voice of the chief cook, an enormous Mexican woman, not that of Mrs. Stanford. She was spreading some kind of architect's rendering on a work table. In a drab old gingham dress, she hardly resembled one of the richest women in America.

"Why, it's the young man from the street department—Mack. I saw you the other day. Good morning."

"Morning, ma'am. Your gardener sent me up with these."

"Right there." She pointed to a zinc counter next to a sunlit lace curtain blowing in the breeze. Mack put the flat down and glanced at the rendering, a watercolor of some attractive tan buildings with red tile roofs, reminiscent of a Spanish mission. Jane Stanford penciled a note on the corner.

"This is the university. The one that we're going to build right out there as a memorial to our son." The blowing curtain shifted patterns of light and shade over her lined face. Her eyes, notoriously weak, were redder than usual. "You have undoubtedly heard about our son—?"

"I have, ma'am. Carried off by the typhoid in Italy when he was not yet sixteen. A terrible shame."

"Leland junior was our only child. The governor and I were married years before I was able to bring him into this world. We've named the school for him. We'll make it the finest university in the nation. But we've faced a storm of criticism. The radical newspapers scoff at a new school because the university at Berkeley can't enroll even three hundred students. Mr. Huntington, who is not a kind man, calls this 'Stanford's Circus.'" Her quiet pain touched Mack unexpectedly. "But the governor and I are undeterred. He said it best. Through Leland Stanford Junior University, we will make all of California's children our children. Recompense for the dear boy who . . . who . . . please excuse me."

With her hand at her eyes, she hurried from the kitchen.

"They loved that boy, all right," Vasco said when Mack raised the subject at supper. "They waited so long for a youngster that when he was born, the governor threw this huge dinner party for his friends, and when they sat down, in came two servants with this great big silver platter and dome. Off came the dome, and do you know what was under it? Leland junior, swaddled and powdered and lying there pink on a bed of flowers and ferns. The governor sat proud as you please while they passed the platter around the table for each guest to admire. After they carried the baby out, everyone ate and drank and celebrated. The governor broke down and cried, he was so happy. I wasn't there but cook swears it's true."

The story unsettled Mack's opinion of the governor; he hadn't imagined that a vain parasite could cry.

* * *

Mack finally met the governor in November, when Vasco invited him along to present performance reports on several of the ranch's most promising racers.

While they waited in the library for the governor to arrive, Vasco showed Mack a large book entitled *The Horse in Motion*. It contained a great number of photographic plates—more or less identical, it seemed to Mack.

The door clicked, and Vasco snatched his cap off. There stood the tycoon himself, all 270 ponderous pounds—Amasa Leland Stanford, the governor who had held California in the Union during the Civil War. He moved slowly, and he spoke slowly, dropping enormous pauses like lead weights into the sea of every sentence.

"Does . . . that . . . volume . . . interest . . . you . . . young . . . man?"

"Sir, this is Mack, a new groom," the Basque began.

"I . . . recognize . . . him." Mack silently winced at the labored speech, and began to edit out the pauses in his head.

The man who had turned earth with a silver spade to start construction of the CP and hammered in the last golden spike at Promontory Point to join the oceans, was a massive, elephantine figure, over sixty, with a high, thick crest of hair and a conventionally large, square-trimmed beard. "I financed publication of Dr. Stillman's text and Edward Muybridge's photos," Stanford said. "I commissioned them, to win one of the few wagers I ever made."

"That all four hooves of a trotting horse leave the ground at once," Vasco explained.

"Which they do," the governor said. "Mr. Muybridge, an excellent British photographer now settled in the City, set up a battery of cameras along the track here in 1872. He devised a means to trip the shutters in sequence, and his initial series of studies proved my contention. He has made many such studies since, each more fascinating than the last."

Mack was the opposite of fascinated at the moment. Each of the governor's deliberated sentences lasted an eternity; the Basque's flickering eyes warned Mack not to smile. The governor himself frowned like an intense troubled child, saying, "Let me show you a curiosity. One which has excited the interest of no less a personage than Mr. Edison."

He picked up a stack of equestrian photos similar to those in the book but toned sepia and mounted on thin card stock. "Now—watch." He grasped the stack at the bottom and flipped the pictures at the top. The horse, caught in a slightly different position in each photo, seemed to be running. The effect was crude, jerky, patently artificial, yet the illusion of motion put a sudden smile on Mack's face.

"That's remarkable, sir."

"Yes." Even one word took forever to enunciate.

"There ought to be some way to make money from that—"

"Pictures that appear to move?"

Mack nodded. The Basque's lips pressed together, stifling his scorn of such lunacy. Stanford closed the book and regarded Mack with a heavy, unblinking gaze. Irony crept into his voice. "Well, young man, perhaps you are just the one to do it . . . although . . . experience . . . teaches . . . that . . . many have dreams, but . . . few have the stamina . . . to realize them."

Suddenly he thrust the pictures at Mack and flipped them again, like a child showing a prized toy. Mack never forgot the images: Stanford; and the horse that magically began to run.

Winter came to the meadows of Palo Alto. A miraculous winter, in which sunshine was frequent and temperatures mild. Only occasional rains interfered with work or travel. There was never a snowfall. Mack reveled in it, and grew fit and hard, thanks to the outdoor life. He slept well, in a cozy barracks bunk, despite coyotes that often howled all night. He ate with other grooms at a table where there was always plenty. During a single supper he'd consume a beefsteak and a chop, fresh yeast bread and hot biscuits, six or eight vegetables, three kinds of fruit pie. For a real treat, he would peel and eat a California delicacy never sampled before, a fat, dripping navel orange from the groves in the cow counties, way down south of the Tehachapi Mountains.

Mr. Hearst's *Examiner* was forbidden on the ranch, but Nellie sent him a letter saying her Receiving Hospital exposé was an enormous success. The entire ward staff and three supervising doctors had been fired.

Stanford appeared around the ranch from time to time, shuffling slowly, exhaling in a wheeze between each agonizingly considered word. His presence always called up memories of the bitter priest and the bloody remains of the track-worker. But while Mack knew Stanford was probably the bandit the *Examiner* claimed him to be, he felt a certain sorrow for the man. Rich as he was, the governor seemed earnestly unhappy. Mack found his muddled feelings confusing and troubling; he wished it was more clear-cut.

The Basque foreman liked Mack's work, his intelligence and energy. So when Mack requested a few hours to himself every

Saturday, Vasco, no questions asked, gave him Sunday-afternoon duties to make up the time.

On those winter Saturdays, Mack traveled by train from Menlo Park to Oakland, then took the ferry to the City and rang the bell at the Olympic Club on Post Street. The first time he showed up, Jim Corbett smiled and said he'd all but given up on his new sparring partner. But over the next several Saturdays, in the club's boxing arena, a large hall with bleachers steeply tiered on all four sides, Corbett began to teach him the fundamentals of punching, feinting, and scientific footwork.

On the way home Mack usually looked up Bao Kee and talked for an hour or so. Twice, when the physical need grew intolerable, he visited one of the numerous cribs in Oakland. One time he slept with a cheerful Chinese girl, embarrassingly young, but lusty; the other time, the girl spoke only French, and only what was necessary to make him understand he must pay first and get out fast.

So the winter passed, and he learned, and saved some money, and grew tan and hardy. All that marred his life was impatience; many a night he lay awake in his bunk scorning himself for not moving fast enough toward his dream.

He didn't see Nellie until one fine afternoon in the spring of 1888. He had thought about her a good deal, and, guiltily, about Hellman's daughter too; steamy thoughts of Carla were most common at night. On two different Saturdays in San Francisco, he'd called at the *Examiner* but found Nellie gone on some assignment. The second time, he left a note with a harried and surly reporter. Since he received no reply, he assumed the note had been thrown away or lost in the madhouse of the editorial rooms.

He was exercising a two-year-old stallion named Conquistador by galloping along the edge of an alfalfa field toward Governors Road, the tree-flanked entrance to the ranch. His hair, longer now, stood out like a mane behind him. Suddenly, where the lane of great eucalyptus and walnut trees met the main road, he saw a woman in a buggy. She stood and waved her bonnet.

"Nellie!" He reined Conquistador and trotted straight over. "You'd better beware. Around here, they shoot people from San Francisco papers."

She laughed. "I'm sure of it. I'll take care to stay out of their way. My, you're so brown. The work must agree with you."

"It does." He was thrilled to see her and could hardly keep his thoughts or emotions in order.

"Do you think you could get some time off?" she went on. "A week? Ten days, even? Mr. Hearst gave me a vacation. I'd like to show you some of the real California."

"Well, I can try. The foreman likes me. He wouldn't pay for the time—"

"Is that a problem?"

"No, no. I've been putting money in Wells, Fargo regularly. I'll ask."

"We'd leave Monday. You should bring some warm clothing. I'll arrange for the tent and supplies in Stockton."

"Stockton? Where're we going?"

"Into the Sierras."

His mouth grew dry at the thought of traveling with her. Half facetiously, he said, "Will you supply us a chaperon too?"

"Don't get any ideas, Mr. Chance. A woman in my profession doesn't have much of a reputation to guard, but there will be no threat to what's left. Our trip is for sightseeing only."

Their eyes met and then they looked away almost simultaneously. Had he seen disappointment in her face too? He couldn't be sure.

THE SAN JOAQUIN SHIMMERED, BRIGHT AS A SHEET OF 12
sunlit metal. Mack and Nellie leaned on the steamer's bow rail, the shoulders of their coarse flannel shirts touching.

"I'm Russian," she said. If there'd been no rail, he'd have fallen into the broad, slow river. "My real name is Natalia Rotchev."

Hands clasped, brown eyes on the horizon, she told him about herself. She was a native Californian, and a distant relative of the last leader of the Russian colony. Mack had never heard of Russians in California.

"They had a substantial fort and settlement on the coast north of the City. The experiment failed and they withdrew in 1842, but my father's father stayed. He changed his name to Ross as homage to his ancestry and the settlement, Fort Ross. It was named that after the mother country, *Rossiya.*"

Her father, a competent farmer, had drifted down to the Valley, where she was born. "It was an ideal life in many ways, but Papa was far from an ideal parent. He was extremely old-fashioned. He treated my mother almost like a servant." Nellie swept blowing hair from her eyes and looked at Mack. "Very early, I saw what a terrible life she led. I decided I'd never be trapped that way—dominated by a man."

Near a settlement that became Hanford, Tulare County— "The town was named for a treasurer of the Central Pacific, Mr. Hanford; that's irony for you"—the Ross family settled on land owned by the railroad. "The railroad invited settlement. Their agents promised that eventually farmers like my father could buy his land for two dollars and fifty cents an acre. Years of work, and a lot of improvements like irrigation ditches helped turn what people once called Starvation Valley into profitable farmland. When the railroad realized how the farmers had improved things, they reneged on their promise. They put our land up for sale at seventeen to forty dollars an acre. On the open market."

Hurtful memory hushed her voice. He could barely hear her above the splash of the bow wake.

"Papa couldn't afford that. He had everything tied up in stock, seed, equipment. And he felt cheated. He and other farmers organized a protest group called the Settlers League. One day—it was eight years ago, May 1880—the railroad sent men to claim the land. Armed men, with a marshal. The farmers took out their guns and met them. They say the farmers fired first, but I don't believe it. If they did start it, they were provoked. Seven men died, including Papa. They called it the Battle of Mussel Slough. May of 18 and 80 . . . I was fourteen years old. I saw them carry Papa into our parlor draped in a bloody blanket . . ."

Now her hands were like twisted wires, and drained of blood. "That was bad enough. What came afterward was worse. Railroad men seized the Hanford telegraph office so the story couldn't get out to the newspapers. In the City, Huntington and Charley Crocker went to every editor with their own slanted story, putting all the blame on the farmers. Crocker and Huntington strangled the truth and perverted the idea of freedom of the press. I was just old enough to understand that—and from that moment, there was never any doubt about what I wanted to do with my life. Write. Tell the truth. Destroy the railroad."

Her mother, two brothers, and three sisters had been evicted, as had the families of the other settlers. She left home, changed her first name to Nellie, and plunged into the street life of San Francisco. Telling this, she grew a little more animated.

"I was too young and eager to worry about possible dangers. I had more jobs than I could count. I lived next door to Madam Cora Swett's bordello. The madam fed me and became my friend. I met Emperor Norton the First, a kind of crazy king of the streets. I played with his dogs, Bummer and Lazarus—they were pets of the whole city, practically. I listened to Norton describe his big idea for a bridge to Oakland. Other people jeered, but I thought it perfectly sensible. Finally I had enough money to enroll at the University of California at Berkeley—women were admitted there starting in 1870; it's a very progressive institution. While I was there, I also learned typewriting at night. After I graduated I applied to Mr. Hearst. I showed him sample articles and got a job—probably because I'm a woman. Mr. Hearst is an amorous man. I managed to avoid his embraces while convincing him that I'd do anything, go anywhere, take any risk to be the very best sob sister in town."

The steamer's mate came by. "Stockton in a half hour."

"Now you know everything there is," she finished with a little shrug.

"I understand why you're independent."

"And why I hate the railroad?"

"Yes," he said, "that too."

In Stockton they hired a wagon and filled it with a tent, bedrolls, knapsacks, and provisions. Nellie explained what she called 'division of labor': She rented or bought their supplies and he in return would provide most of the hard physical work. "There'll be plenty, so no argument."

He laughed. You didn't argue with Nellie unless you were ready for war.

They set out southeast, on the Old Sonora Road to the mines of the Mother Lode. "And thence to the Big Oak Flat and Yosemite Toll Road," she said.

"You have to pay to get there?"

"Surely you don't disapprove, Mr. Chance. The local folk are just getting rich like other Californians."

"Ow," he said. They both smiled.

They drove past grape arbors, melon patches, pastures, through wheat fields and tiny towns drowsing in the heat. They crossed the Stanislaus at Knights Ferry and climbed into rolling foothills speckled with red cattle and white egrets. Poppies painted whole hilltops the color of gold. The Sierras grew taller ahead, lower slopes dark green with pines and redwoods, high summits snow-whitened still. He had evil memories of crossing those mountains, but now that was softened by the spectacular beauty—or was it the girl riding beside him on the hard seat, taking her turn and handling the team as competently as any man?

. That evening, he volunteered to help with the meal, peeling and dicing some potatoes they'd brought along, then seasoning them in the skillet with onion and a bit of golden bell pepper. Nellie complimented him on his cooking.

"Pa taught me. If you don't have a lot of food, he said, cooking gives you more time to enjoy what there is."

She laughed.

He thought of something he'd wanted to know for some time, and asked, "That man Hellman, the landowner—how did he get his nickname?"

"That's a strange question."

"No, earlier today I was remembering him from the night Greenway fired me."

Satisfied, she explained that in 1850 the federal government had passed a reclamation act returning millions of acres of worthless land to the western states. "Swampland, marshland—it was that kind of land in other states, but they made a mistake in California. Here the land just looked worthless after a heavy rain. Actually it was some of the richest land anyone could want. But the state went ahead and sold it for something like a dollar and ten cents an acre."

Hellman had been a young immigrant in those days, she said, an apprentice in a Sacramento butcher shop. "I've no idea how he got the capital for his first investment, but he was soon battling Henry Miller for this or that piece of land, and both of them were bribing surveyors and assessors to certify that a given parcel was swampland when it wasn't. Miller and Hellman got rich from the swamp scheme, but Hellman got the nickname."

"Interesting." Mack set his tin plate aside and saw her watching him intently.

"Now it's time for you to talk."

"Yes?"

"Why did you really come to California?"

The cheerful campfire and the camaraderie of a good meal shared with the darkness falling combined to overcome his reticence. Besides, if there was ever a girl to be trusted, Nellie was the one.

"Well, first of all, I came here because in Pennsylvania I

never slept in a clean bed or wore a clean shirt. The air was so dirty around the coal mines, snow turned black an hour after it fell. It was a terrible life. I don't want to tell you anything that'll make you sick—''

She shook her head and gestured him on impatiently.

"I saw my pa's friends from the mines come to supper and cough up blood right on the table. I saw eight- and nine-year-old boys bent like old men from sorting coal twelve, fourteen hours a day. I was bent that way myself for a long time. I watched them go down into the mines about age twelve with nothing to hope for except getting out alive at the end of a day spent driving a mule cart in the dark. I saw special police hired by the mine owners break men's legs with billy clubs because the men wanted to organize for shorter hours or safer work. Jerry Caslin, he was a Molly Maguire—''

"The secret society. I've read of it.''

"The special police clubbed Jerry so hard, he couldn't recognize his wife or kids afterward. All he could do was sit in a chair by the window and drool and piss—excuse me, that slipped out. He couldn't help soiling himself all the time, poor Jerry. Someone finally fed him a tin of rat poison so he could die. Nobody asked who did it, not even the priest. So there are a lot of reasons I came to California, but the biggest reason was my pa. He came out in the Gold Rush, and he failed, and went back, and he was poor all his life. But he still believed in this place. Pa said that if a man couldn't find any hope where he was, he could always find it in California. He believed it in spite of his own sad life, and because of him, I believe it. I always will.''

Moved, Nellie couldn't speak. She reached across the fire to touch his hand a moment. Shyly, he looked away. What a remarkable young man, she thought. Just remarkable.

Next day he observed that she seemed quite familiar with the roads to the high country. She said she'd traveled them often as a little girl. "I went with Uncle Sebastian, who married my mother's sister, Aunt Anya. Sebastian was a Basque sheepherder. Every summer he took his flock to the high pastures, and the whole family went along. Aunt Anya was a rugged woman; she worked as hard as he did, and so did their son, Tomás. I worked too, but it always seemed like a vacation. To this day, Tomás is my favorite among all my cousins.''

At day's end they passed through Chinese Camp, once overflowing with miners, now sparsely populated. A fading sign advertising sturdy work pants by Levi Strauss produced an eerie feeling in Mack. Maybe his pa had trod this same rough road. He often said he'd been all over the Mother Lode country in his search for a rich claim.

They were climbing; Mack could feel it in the sharp thin air. But they must go higher still, she said, to find the secret valley to which her uncle had taken her as a child.

"The Valley of the Yosemite. It's an old Indian name. The original tribe, the Ahwahneechee, named it Ahwahnee: 'Deep Grassy Valley.' White men found it in 18 and 51. The men of the Mariposa Battalion. The militia was out hunting some of Chief Tenaya's Indians, who, they said, were harassing the gold miners. You won't believe the place, Mack. Its beauty will make you weep."

On narrow Jacksonville Hill, Nellie parked in a turnout among the digger pines and explained that many a gold coach had been waylaid up here in the old days. Along the south fork of the Tuolumne, she taught him how to pronounce that strange beautiful word. She detoured down a smaller road to show him the most remarkable trees he'd ever seen. They were cinnamon-colored with incredible height and girth.

"Sequoia. Older than man's memory. They may be the oldest things on earth." It was hushed beneath them, the kind of hush appropriate to a dim church.

Before they left Tuolumne Grove they drove to the Dead Giant, a great tourist attraction, according to Nellie. The topmost section of the sequoia was gone, but some two hundred feet of trunk remained, the upper part jaggedly divided into two towering spires, like horns. The road pierced the center of the mighty trunk.

"Tunneled in 18 and 78," she said. "Drive right through." The wagon just fit. He laughed aloud.

"You mentioned tourists. I don't see any."

"It's early. Summer's the time. Last year twenty-five hundred people came up to Yosemite. One day we're going to be fighting hard to save these places. I have a friend, a Scotsman, a kind of wild, wonderful mountain man I met up here when I was a girl, and he's already fighting."

Shortly he saw why. A caravan of six flatbed wagons, each with eight huge tree trunks chained down, rumbled down past the turnout where they'd stopped.

"Bastards," Nellie said. "They'll strip the high country if we don't stop them."

* * *

He came out of the white dream thrashing his arms and crying, "Pa? Where are you?"

Someone tugged him. "Mack. Wake up . . ."

His eyes flew open. He felt cold night air on his cheeks, smelled the wild grass and pines, saw the high darkness full of blazing stars . . . then Nellie, in her long gray flannel nightgown and barefoot, standing between him and the campfire, which had been reduced to embers that sparked and billowed in the breeze.

He remembered where he was then: in a field near a tiny mountain settlement she called Crane Flat. Across the field, yellow windows checkerboarded the dark, a wooden hotel. He sat up, sleepily rubbing his stubbled chin, his bedroll and extra blanket tangled around him. He'd erected the big fly tent for her, and rolled up on the ground outside.

She sat on a log, neatly tucking the hem of the flannel behind her bare ankles. Only her small white feet showed, but the sight, and the isolation of the night, filled him with painful yearnings.

"You were thrashing and calling out. You almost rolled into the fire. What were you dreaming?"

"A nightmare I've had since I was little. Always the same: snow, darkness, death . . ." He described it in words he felt sure were inadequate.

She sat with her chin in her hands. When he was through, she stood up and leaned over him. With a deeper tenderness and a greater intimacy than propriety would normally allow, she touched his face.

"Maybe the California sun will drive out that bad dream one day."

He gazed at her, then caught her wrist where it lay against his cheek. The campfire embers reflected in her brown eyes. Her small soft mouth opened as she realized what might happen if they allowed it.

He started to rise, but she darted forward and kissed his forehead, a light, sisterly brush of her lips. He felt like an iron had seared him.

"Nellie, I—"

"Good night, Mack. We must make an early start."

She turned and ran to the tent. Before she dropped and tied the flap at the entrance, she looked back, and he saw her eyes saying she wished she could speak the words to invite him into that dark place.

The canvas fell. Confused, elated, wanting to run to the tent, yet afraid to do it, he bundled up in the bedroll and blanket and watched the stars for an hour. He felt young, stupid, inexperienced, hot, angry. In love.

The ascent continued. At Gin Flat, they were seven thousand feet above the sea, she said. Soon the road slanted down again, perilously hacked from a mountain's shoulder. It gave them spectacular vistas of tree-clad valleys and higher granite peaks above and ahead. In shady nooks along the way, pristine snow-banks gleamed.

At Gentry's Hotel and Station, fifty-six hundred feet, they paid their toll for a road Nellie called the Zigzag. "Twelve miles into the valley."

"The morning's for up traffic," the toll collector said. "You have to wait till afternoon."

So they pulled over a short way to another turnout. "Prospect Point—but the teamsters mostly call it Oh My Point."

He understood. Before him lay a vista of great bald rock masses looming over a forested valley. Waterfalls tumbled from the rock summits all the way to the valley floor. Mack marveled as a cloud of birds swept upward past them; there were thousands of them, wings beating. "Passenger pigeons," Nellie cried.

The toll agent put bells on the team to announce their passage down the mountain. Mack drove on the perilous switchbacks carved from the granite. "Italian stonecutters did this," she said. "An incredible feat."

"Don't talk so much," he groaned, aching from hanging on to the reins and maintaining constant pressure on the brake. The wheels smoked, inches from the edge, and the smell of scorched wood rose up through the dust. If they went over they'd never survive.

The scenery no longer existed except as a peripheral blur. The afternoon's descent, at two miles an hour, took nearly six hours. Sweating and brutally tired, he fought the wagon down at last, bringing them into a glade by the fast-flowing Merced. There he looked up.

"God above," he whispered. He wondered if this was how a man felt in biblical times when the Almighty spoke to him in the wilderness.

The sun speared out of the west, low now, lighting peaks and swathes of forest where it touched, leaving dark-blue shade where it did not. They were deep in the glacial valley riven by the white water of the river. Stupendous rock formations towered on the valley's flanks. "That's El Capitan—twice the size of Gibraltar—it goes up three thousand feet from the valley floor. Over there are the Cathedral Rocks and at the far end, Half Dome. The falls of the Yosemite are there on the left, Bridalveil on the right—they're flowing full now because it's spring.'' He watched the awesome waterfalls plunge down in clouds of sunlit mist. Their roar was constant, primitive; something stirred in his loins again.

Nellie hugged herself. ''Did you ever see its like? I'm glad I'm the one showing it to you for the first time.''

''So am I.'' He put one arm around her and kissed her. She slid her arms beneath his and hugged him, giving a little groan of pleasure.

A minute later, patting her hair, then her pink cheek, she whispered, ''That's dangerous. I think you'd better drive on.''

The valley was seven miles long, a mile wide. Beyond the terminal moraine where the last glaciers had stopped twenty thousand years before, the Merced changed to a river of placid green pools and sandbars. They avoided the small raw-frame hotels already busy with a few tourists who sat on the porches in the twilight and made camp in a meadow near thickets of cottonwoods and alders. The trees tossed in a cool wind, their leaves hissing. Nellie could hardly stop showing him things: mistletoe clusters high in the black oak trees, granite lichen darkly staining the great rock formations, glittering eyes that regarded them from the woods.

''Grizzly bear,'' she whispered. ''If one ever comes for food, don't argue—let him have it.''

The blazing eyes vanished.

While the light lingered, Nellie ran out among the red columbines and golden poppies in the meadow and began to dance. She was like a sprite, kicking her bare feet high. Mack clapped his hands to keep time. Her face grew flushed and finally, laughing, she collapsed against him. He held her longer than necessary. She pressed his strong arm with her palm and drew away reluctantly.

The campfire flickered, slices of salt beef sizzling in a heavy iron skillet that Mack held in his gloved hand. He liked the skillet's feel and the smell of the meat.

Standing near him, Nellie said, ''You really do have a talent for that. You'd make a fine chef for the Palace Hotel.''

''Not enough money in it,'' he joked. ''I enjoy cooking. Sometimes it seems like woman's work, though.''

"Mr. Chance, you have very conventional, not to say primitive, attitudes about male and female roles."

"Seems to me that most of the world shares my—"

A halloo interrupted him. Through the dusky meadow, a tall wiry man with nondescript clothes and a knapsack strode toward them. Hair hung to his shoulders and his gray beard was long and thick enough to shelter more than one bird's nest. Nellie waved and started to move toward him.

"You know that man? He looks like a tramp."

"He is, in a way. It's my friend John Muir. I didn't know he was up here."

After Nellie and Muir had embraced warmly, Mack shook Muir's hand, which was brown and strong. He looked about fifty and his eyes were a startling blue. "Pleased to know you," Muir said. It came out *"know ye"*; he spoke with more than a trace of a Scot's burr.

"Can you stay the night, John?"

"Aye." Muir flung his knapsack down, then his brown sugarloaf hat. "There are tourists here a'ready."

She nodded.

Mack said, "Anyone would want to see this place."

"Aye, and we've had our share of visitors since I first came upon the Valley in 18 and 68. I met Jessie Frémont up here, and Susan Anthony."

"Bierstadt painted Yosemite," Nellie said. "Mark Hopkins came before he died. Emerson, and Barnum . . . it's a long list."

Muir sat down and leaned back on both hands, the fire deepening the ruddiness of his weathered skin. "Sometimes the visitors forget to respect what God and nature put here. If enough of them do it, d'ye ken, there'll be nothing left for the next generations."

"John is a staunch protector of the valley," Nellie said.

Muir sighed. "It's a fight. Never ending." He explained to Mack that in 1864, Lincoln, with great foresight, had deeded Yosemite and a nearby stand of big sequoias called the Mariposa Grove to the state of California. "So it's a protected preserve. But the protection's not strong enough. We have jackleg lumbermen up here. And the damned sheep. A quarter million in the high pastures last summer. They leave no grass or foliage; they strip the earth. I herded sheep up here myself until I saw the damage it did."

Mack offered the salt beef. Muir picked up two pieces for his tin plate. "How would you protect the valley, then?"

"Put it under the Interior Department. Name it a national

park, like Yellowstone. Control the tourists, and sequester all these natural treasures so the damned rapacious exploiters can't get to 'em.''

"But look, sir, there are valuable resources up here. I've been told that the mountain snowpack could irrigate the whole Central Valley—maybe even provide water for the coastal cities, if pipelines were built.''

"Pipelines. Great God, son, what else would you allow?''

The scorn irked Mack. "What's wrong with the idea? Water from up here could make the whole state bloom.''

"That idea is hateful,'' Muir said. "If you allow a little to be despoiled, all will be despoiled eventually. Nellie my lass, your friend seems to be one of those apostles of progress who mean to reduce this place to a private preserve for profit.''

"I don't share his ideas, John.''

Mack dropped his plate with a clatter. "And dammit, that isn't what I said.''

"I am opposed to any development that interferes with the ordered state of nature,'' Muir declared.

"So am I,'' Nellie said.

"Are you required to talk that way to play the role of independent female?'' Mack snapped at her.

"You don't like that role, Mr. Chance?''

"Not much.''

"Well, that just demonstrates how perfectly stu—'' She bit it off, then whirled away toward the trees to compose herself. Mack glowered at the fire.

Muir packed his old pipe with tobacco and lit it with a twig from the fire. "I did na' mean to start a row in this camp. A man's entitled to honest views. It's just that I am passionately opposed to the one you expressed, sir.''

"I don't know that I believe every word myself. I'm new to California. Trying to puzzle things out.''

Muir's blue eyes said he'd try to be tolerant, which undoubtedly meant giving Mack a few more years to discover his error and mend his ways.

In ten minutes Nellie was back. "I didn't mean to lose my temper.''

"Nor I.''

Somehow, though, the evening was spoiled, and the travelers passed the rest of it with little conversation and long moody silences.

* * *

Next morning, in bright sunshine, everyone seemed refreshed and forgiving, though Mack felt that forgiving spirit the least. Muir boiled the coffee while Mack fried bacon and Nellie sliced the sourdough and browned it over their fire. Muir freely answered Mack's questions about himself. He'd been born in Dunbar, Scotland, and raised by his immigrant father in Wisconsin. He'd refused to fight in the Civil War on principle; no matter how righteous the cause, he said, war was an abomination.

"I've been a bit of everything, Mr. Chance. A tramp, a guide, a sheepherder, a worker in a carriage-parts factory in Indianapolis. Very fine position, that was. But the outdoors kept calling to me. Now I'm a rancher down below, and husband to my Louise and father to my Wanda and my Helen. But my lassie sets me free to roam because she knows I must." He checked the coffee, then began to fill a new pipe. "Lately I've begun to write articles, and lecture some. Trying to protect places such as this."

While they breakfasted, a great prong-horned elk stepped majestically into the meadow. It had been there only a few moments when a Yosemite hotel stage, an open wagon with canvas top, wheeled into view. On the benches, a gaggle of tourists shouted and pointed. One, drinking from a bottle at this early hour, drained and then flung it. The three at the breakfast fire clearly heard the bottle break on a rock, and the elk bounded away out of sight.

"Y'see the cause of my concern, laddie," Muir said without reproof. Mack had no chance to answer, because one of the sightseers tossed a cigar away as the stage rolled on. Muir leaped up and dashed into the meadow. When he reached the spot where the cigar had fallen, sending up a blue trail, he stamped hard and shouted after the stage. "Stay out of this place if ye can't treat it with respect. Any fool can cut down or burn down a tree, but it takes the Almighty years to make one to replace it."

The shouted sermon went unheard. Laughter drifted from the tan dust cloud hiding the stage, and Muir trudged back.

"More and more people all the time," he said unhappily. "I know we canna set ourselves above others, deciding who is fit to view these wonders and who is not. We canna stop a tidal wave. But we must contain it. Most particularly here. I tell you this. I've tramped the lovely savannas of the Carolinas, and dipped in the blue-green seas of the Floridas. I've climbed Shasta, and come as the first white man into a bay of glaciers, up Alaska way, as cold and quiet as they were in the morning of time. I have seen no place—no place—that is the match of this valley of the Yosemite. It is one of God's crown jewels. That is why I want the national park—and also an organization of dedicated folk who will fight for every wilderness, but especially this one." He slapped his old sugar-loaf hat against his pants. "Would such an organization include you, sir?"

Mack stood up to those fierce blue eyes. "It might. That's the best I can promise."

"Fair enough." But Muir sounded disappointed. "Nellie, I must go. I'm hiking up to the high country to camp and climb and think. Maybe sketch and write a little too. I shall look you up next time I'm in the City."

"Do, John. I want to join that organization."

"Aye. Thought you would." He kissed her cheek, slung his knapsack on his back, and walked away briskly into the brilliant light of the valley.

Nellie sighed. "I really didn't mean to quarrel with you."

He kept a truculent silence.

"Mack, please. We can differ and be friends."

"Not if honest thoughts are somehow made . . . criminal."

"All right, I spoke too sharply last night. It's a bad habit."

"Holding grudges is one of mine." He cleared his throat. "I'm sorry."

"Thank you. It's been a beautiful trip, but we've only this day and tomorrow, and then we must go back. Let's spend the time pleasantly." She held out her hand. "Truce?"

Taking her hand he broke into a smile. "Truce."

She didn't pull her hand back. Instead she squeezed his fingers, giving him a deep, searching look, as if she knew what was inevitable now. He knew too, and he was scared.

They hiked and climbed steep trails and ate a picnic by Mirror Lake in early afternoon. Before they finished, clouds began to come in, thick, gray, and wet, hiding the rock summits. The waterfalls appeared to pour from the beclouded sky. That night he went to sleep wearing the heavy wool coat he'd brought along.

He awoke hours later, freezing and frightened. He knew he wasn't dreaming, yet this was the nightmare. Whiteness everywhere . . . His tongue slid over his lip and tasted ice. Ice melted in his hair. He was blanketed in thick falling snow.

He scooted out of the soaked bedroll and flung off the blanket, shaking down little avalanche clouds of the snow. It slanted in hard, driven by a loud moaning wind, and his teeth clicked as he groped for the log pile. Stirring the dead embers, he shivered all the harder, groaning in the cold.

"Mack?"

He turned toward the tent, but was unable to see it. Somehow he knew the way her face looked, though. Her voice was low, husky with emotion.

"You can't stay out there. Come in. Come in and get warm."

Next day in midafternoon, they went to the base of Yosemite Falls. Crashing and cascading from above, water splashed on great granite boulders and spun off into swirling pools between the rocks. In one of these, well sheltered, and in the lee of tall sunlit mist clouds among the pines and sequoias, they bathed naked and began to make love for the second time.

He kissed her breasts. They were round and firm as fine apples. She broke away, laughing, and crouched to scoop up water and lave her shoulders. He stood over her, so huge and eager he hurt. She touched him.

"What if someone comes, Mack? A stage full of tourists down there on the road . . . ?"

"I don't care. Do you?"

She slid her arms around him, kissing him, and he drew her sideways, directly into the waterfall. He lifted her out of the water and then lowered her again, slid into her wet sable hair, and then into the different wetness beyond. She clasped her legs around him, shuddering. He was part of her, she was part of him, and the beauty of the wilderness was part of them both, arousing them to something like frenzy.

The falls roared. She held fast to his neck as they swayed to and fro under the beating water. At the end, she screamed softly and sank her teeth into him. He held her cold wet shuddering body joined to his, letting the falls pour down on them the raging torrents of the springtime.

The wagon bore them out of the Sierras again. In the foothills, with the golden poppies blowing wild all around, the shattering passion of that encounter with the valley, and each other, kept them silent. Nellie rode with her head leaning against his shoulder, her hand entwined with his. Words weren't necessary; adequate ones couldn't be found.

She had been so different up there. Young, wanting, eager, yielding—not at all the cool, tart, modern girl who'd first intrigued him. She was different people in one person.

Well, wasn't he? He was in love with her. But he hadn't come to California to fall in love; he meant to follow and fulfill the promises of his pa, and the guidebook. How could he reconcile that with this new emotion?

A raucous sound startled the horses, and Nellie sat up, rubbing her eyes. Out of a choking, rolling dust cloud that blanketed the foothills for half a mile in either direction, a honking, shuffling tide of sheep overwhelmed them: rams, ewes, lambs, heading for the high country. The dust and the smell of droppings and the bleats and the suspicious looks of a half a dozen Basque herders kicked Mack headfirst back to reality.

"There must be five thousand sheep," she said, coughing and waving at the dust. Suddenly, clutching his arm, she hid her eyes against his sleeve. "What are we going to do?"

"About the sheep?"

A fist struck lightly at his leg. "Us. About us. I love you. I've never loved anyone before. There was one other before, but he—never mind, he didn't matter. This matters. I have my career with Mr. Hearst, you have your own ambitions—and what happened just—just changes everything."

"How?"

"Complicates it. Unbelievably. I was on a straight, sure course. Now—"

"I was thinking the same." It was scary to utter the words for the first time: "But I love you, Nellie."

"God, what are we going to do? What are we going to do?"

He hugged her to shelter her from the dust. A herder with a crook gave them a stare and trudged on. The world crushed in upon them, full of questions and uncertainties; it was overpowering. He struggled to say what his heart told him. "What does a waterfall do? It goes where it has to go, that's all."

"That's no answer."

"I don't know any other."

Nor did they find one, all the way to the City.

MACK AND JIM CORBETT WALKED OUT OF THE OLYMpic Club together. Mack's left eye was starting to puff and his muscles ached. Since the return from Yosemite, he'd seen Nellie several times. She was affectionate, but there'd been

13

no repetition of what happened in the valley—as if there were some unspoken pact between them.

It was a Saturday in June, cool, with fog creeping in from the western hills. Before leaving the club the young boxer had carefully fastened the horn buttons of his tan broadcloth overcoat and spent a minute adjusting his striped four-in-hand and the tips of his wing collar. His black silk hat sat jauntily, and his tan spats perfectly matched his overcoat; he looked good.

"You're coming right along," he said as they turned east on Post. "If you keep practicing, you'll soon be a pugilist, not just a fighter."

There was something odd about the remark, Mack thought. "I intend to keep practicing, Jim."

"Good. I regret I won't be here to see it. I've left the bank. I'm getting married."

Mack was stunned. "I didn't even know you were engaged."

"Spur-of-the-moment thing, the marriage," Corbett said with a curious look, as if he weren't certain of the step. "She's a nice girl. We're going to live in Utah."

"I wish you the very best. You're not going to give up fighting . . . ?"

"Not if I can help it. Not many contenders in Utah, though."

This disappointing turn of circumstances kept Mack silent for another block or so. Shadows lengthened as they strolled south through the crowds on Powell Street. At Union Square, Mack recognized a stocky man in clerical black standing on a wooden crate surrounded by an audience of seven or eight other men, mostly shabby. After a cable car passed, some of the speaker's words carried to Mack and Corbett.

". . . it is your right to organize stronger trade unions in every sector of commerce. Let no one gainsay you that right. The capitalist masters of this city will try, but I tell you again, you must stand fast. You must not allow . . ."

"I know that man," Mack said to Corbett.

"All of San Francisco knows Father Marquez. His family goes back to the early Spanish explorations of California. Where did you meet him?"

"In the Valley."

"He went out there regularly for a while. Now he's the curate at St. Mary's Cathedral on Van Ness. I don't approve of that radical rot he preaches."

Neither did some other bystanders. One found a stone and

flung it. "Enough of your damn communist cant, you filthy papist."

Marquez turned a calm gaze on the rock thrower. "It's my right under the Constitution, and my duty under God, to say whatever my conscience dictates. Today the voices of my conscience and my church are one. Pope Leo has written that the Church insists on the application of Christian charity and justice to relations between owner and worker."

The objector spat and walked away. Mack noticed a uniformed city policeman nearby, tapping his hickory baton lightly in his palm and watching the priest. One of Marquez's listeners saw him and hastily walked away, and within minutes the priest had no audience except the policeman.

The policeman smiled, touched his forehead with his baton, and left.

"Just a minute while I say hello," Mack said to Corbett. Before he'd reached the other side of the street, though, Marquez had picked up his box and strode away along one of the gravel paths in the square.

In Oakland, Mack found Bao Kee in an excited state.

"Come see something, while there is still light."

He led Mack down to a section of mud flats by the Inner Harbor, and there onto a canted pier with whole sections of rotted planking gone. Tied up near the end of the pier, chains across her gangway and padlocks on her pilothouse, a sixty-foot steam launch bobbed in the swells. The name on the transom was *Grace Barton*. Bao scurried up and down on the pier, admiring her.

"Gambling boat," Bao said. "Two men refitted her for excursions on the Bay. The mahogany bar inside cost two thousand dollars. She made three trips. Then the first partner shot the second partner over money and ran away. She is for sale. Fifteen thousand dollars."

"Looks like she's in good shape," Mack said, noting her paint and brightwork. "But why would you trade *Heavenly Dragon* for this?"

"To have a ferry boat," Bao said. "Take all the customers away from the railroad boats. I have figured a long time on the abacus. With you, me, and one pilot, we can make money charging less than the railroad. Five cents, here to there," he said, gesturing over to the City.

The idea delighted Mack. But not for long. "You don't have pier space."

"We can use the public piers. Here, and over in Frisco."

"The SP has the harbor commission in its pocket . . ."

"They can't keep us out," Bao argued. "We will make money if we buy this boat."

A sharp wind ruffled the water and the sunset etched the hills of the City. "I think I heard you say *we*."

"I need you," Bao said with a sober nod. "Banks won't loan a penny to a heathen Chinee. I am not a person. If I walk in a bank today, and go back tomorrow, they don't know me." The bitterness was deep, and justified. Mack had heard white men at the ranch say Chinese should be registered because you couldn't tell those who'd come in before Exclusion from those smuggled in afterward; all Chinamen looked alike.

"If you help me buy this boat, Mack, I will give you half ownership of my share. Forty percent. The pilot gets the other twenty instead of wages."

Mack felt a surge of hope again, overlooking all the obstacles, delighting in the audacity of it. "I'd love to hold the railroad's feet to the fire. I'll do it. Should we sign some kind of agreement?"

"No, my friend. This is enough."

He held out his hand.

"Ask Mr. Hearst about a loan," Nellie advised when Mack described the scheme.

"Fifteen thousand's a devil of a lot of money."

"One of the fundamental lessons you've got to learn about money is this. If those who have it don't want you to have it, the loan of a dollar will be too much. But if you find someone who wants you to have a loan because he'll make money, you can just as easily get five million as five cents. That's the way money works."

The steam yacht *Aquila* bobbed in her sunny anchorage in the lee of the hills of Marin County. Mack had rowed out from Sausalito harbor and discovered Ambrose Bierce, elegant in a white suit and matching spats, lounging under the awning on the afterdeck. Onshore, Sunday-morning church bells chimed.

"I came out to discuss some story ideas," Bierce said. "But the chief and Tessie are still, ah, resting." He reached for a bottle in a silver stand. "Care for champagne? Excellent stuff. Madrone Vineyard—Senator Hearst's own."

Mack shook his head. Nervous, he sat down in a canvas chair and picked up a copy of the previous day's *Examiner*, which had been discarded on the teak deck.

SPECTACULAR BRAWL ON WATERFRONT!

**Draymen vs. Police!
Blood and Injury
Everywhere!**

Twenty Arrested!
Catholic Priest
Behind Bars!

Mack scanned the story. Sure enough, it was Marquez. "I know him," he said to Bierce.

"Don't worry—officials in the Church already got him out. The riot happened on Friday. Marquez was down on the waterfront at an outdoor rally of draymen. He's urging them to form a union. Some of the warehouse owners got the coppers to break up the party with their clubs."

"Is it a crime for workingmen to organize a union?"

"Not in San Francisco. This has always been a strong labor town. There are plenty of gentlemen here and throughout California who'd like to change that, however." Bierce regarded him over the bubbles in his goblet. "Marquez is a radical. How does it happen that you know him?"

Mack explained. Bierce took it in, then said, "His militance is understandable. The Marquez family owned one of the biggest land-grant *ranchos* south of the Tehachapi. Then the Anglos came in. The family got caught in the flood of land-claim cases and lost all of their holdings except the original adobe. Marquez's father went crazy. Took to the countryside, robbing and murdering Anglos for six or seven years. The duly deputized gentlemen of the posse comitatus finally tracked him and caught up with him back at the adobe outside Los Angeles. They shot him down like a mad dog. Fifty or sixty bullets in his body, as I recall. Splendid tribute to Anglo justice and mercy, don't you think? . . . Chief—good morning."

Willie Hearst blinked and yawned as he came on deck barefoot. The publisher looked especially pale and scrawny in his blue velour robe. Behind him in the doorway, a voluptuous young woman smiled drowsily at the guests. Mack knew her name was Tessie Powers. Hearst had found her waiting on tables in a Cambridge restaurant in his student days.

Champagne and a platter of raw oysters awakened the newspaper proprietor. He listened with birdlike bobs of his head

121

while Mack described the scheme to operate a Bay ferry charging 5 cents instead of 15.

At the end, Hearst sank lower in his chair, his eyes seemingly fixed on a big toe. Tessie glided up behind him and kneaded the back of his neck with both hands, her cleavage showing between the fluffy maribou lapels of her gown. Then Hearst leaned back and closed his eyes.

Mack clenched his sweaty hands between his knees. He must have presented it poorly . . .

Suddenly Hearst's head snapped up. "I like it. A capital scheme. It'll roast those fellows where it hurts most—in their wallets. I can loan you what you need to get started."

Mack thought it over for a few moments. "That's very generous, sir. But if we're to stay in business, and grow, I think we need a good solid banking connection— Something wrong?"

Hearst was shaking his head. "You won't get a dime from the local banks. They're all snugly in bed with the railroad. If you're willing to do business in New York, that's a different matter. I'm on excellent terms with some bankers there. What about the vessel you propose to buy? Is she sound?"

"She looks that way to me. My partner, Mr. Bao, swears she is."

"Good, we've already satisfied one key consideration in a bank loan—collateral."

Mack's heart leaped at that. "Then you think we'd be able to arrange one?"

"If Mr. C. P. Huntington doesn't get wind of your dealings before the vessel's yours. If he does, he'll fight like a mountain lion. He has his own eastern connections. Powerful ones. If I know him, he'd pay many times the cost of that boat just to block your scheme. Huntington hates embarrassment, or any diminishment of the railroad's power. Which is really his power."

Hearst jumped to his feet, startling Tessie, then ran to the rail with his characteristic bobbing stride. There he spun back, stabbing a finger out.

"Our hope lies in moving fast. I'll be back in town this evening and I'll draft a telegraph message. It'll be on the wires by midnight."

On Thursday of that week, Vasco found Mack in one of the paddocks. "Governor's asking for you up at the house."

"I'll go up as soon as I finish with—"

Vasco snatched the pitchfork out of his hand. "Now." Mack

had never seen such a scowl, heard such curtness, from the Basque.

Soon he stood before Leland Stanford in the sitting room. Dust motes danced their slow dance in bars of light falling between the lace curtains. For once the eyes of the governor showed emotion. On a marble table beside him, a file lay open, and Mack saw telegraph flimsies.

"Young man . . ." The voice was as ponderously deep as ever, but anger quickened it a little. "It has been . . . brought to my attention . . . that you, as a principal . . . of something presuming to call itself . . . the Oakland Bay Transportation Line, have applied for a bank loan . . . in New York City . . . for the purpose . . . of buying a steam launch. You were assisted . . . by the offices of that damnable . . . lying puppy William Hearst."

"Sir, how did you learn that?"

Stanford's Buddha eyes regarded him. "Sir, you are not here . . . to interrogate me. Mr. Fairbanks . . . of the company legal department . . . conveyed the information." Thick white fingers tapped the flimsies and the handwritten memoranda peeking out beneath. "He was advised . . . of the loan . . . by Mr. Huntington's staff . . . in the East. What do you have to say?"

Mack straightened his shoulders. Damned if he'd be intimidated.

"That I applied for the loan for a friend, a Chinese the banks won't deal with because the law doesn't permit it. He'll be the one operating the ferry."

"A specious answer, sir. You are involved. Do you . . . or don't you . . . intend to compete . . . with the established ferry service . . . of the Southern Pacific Railroad?"

"Yes, I do. It's just what you say, Governor. Competition. Don't you believe in competition anymore? I guess you don't have to . . . most of the time."

Leland Stanford's hand moved with sudden, astonishing quickness, striking the open file. A tiny vase holding silk flowers fell off the table and broke.

"You are *arrogant*, young man. Arrogant . . . and insulting. I believe in protecting . . . my interests and my property. I gave you . . . a position here . . . in good faith. You have . . . abused my trust."

"I fully intended to come to you, to explain, and resign—"

"Oh, did you? Why do I hear . . . a lie in that pious . . . protestation? You're discharged."

"Don't call me a liar. This is just—just business."

Stanford struggled from the chair like a great whale breaching. Mack thought he heard doors slide open, but he was fixed on the lobster face of the governor. Stanford was no buffoon; there was dangerous strength in his stance, and violence in his eye.

"Get . . . out. Get out with your . . . juvenile threats . . . and your prattle of . . . business. Business . . . indeed. I am . . . the businessman here. You are nothing but . . . a grimy . . . upstart. You'll see . . . who has power . . . in the City . . . my railroad . . . or a piece of . . . trash . . . like you . . ."

Mack's face turned just as red. "I'll go, but we'll break your damned monopoly."

"You . . . young fool. You'll be the one broken."

"Leland," said a woman's voice from the doorway. Mack spun around and walked out past her, leaving Stanford wheezing like a donkey engine. In the hall, the governor's wife rolled the doors shut and followed Mack.

"My husband liked everything he heard about you until this happened. But nothing comes before business."

"Or money. Or property. It's a good lesson," Mack said, cold with fury.

She had some of her husband's toughness. Her poor weak eyes challenged him. "We did give you a job as well as money, food, shelter, generous allowances of time whenever you asked. Faithlessness is not a virtue, Mack. That is another good lesson—if you have the moral character to learn it. Which I now doubt. Be so good as to leave the governor's house."

On the train to Oakland, Mack stared through the dusty glass, miserable with guilt. Some of what Jane Stanford had said was true. He'd betrayed an employer. Maybe the employer inspired, even demanded betrayal. Still, he never wanted to make that mistake again.

Mack moved into Bao's hovel. The seller's attorney readily agreed to let them risk their labor before the loan was approved, so Mack and Bao spent long days scrubbing out the *Grace Barton*, touching up her paint, and checking out her equipment.

In the evenings, Bao taught Mack how to cook Chinese dishes. Mack's favorite was a sweet-sour soup with thin slices of black mushroom floating like anemone in the golden broth. He balked at learning to prepare a favorite delicacy, young dog.

After a meal he usually took a stroll through the neighborhood. He liked the hardy, lively, energetic Chinese. They brightened their squalid huts with festive paper lanterns, and sold an amazing array of goods from wicker baskets and lacquered trays set out in their doorways: dried fish and goose livers, fresh vegetables, opium pipes and silk slippers, packets of face powder and hair combs made out of shells.

One evening, as he was out walking the lanes, savoring the summer air full of buzzing conversation and sweet incense, he heard someone call his name. He saw Nellie running toward him, exuberantly waving an envelope.

"From New York. Good news."

On Monday morning of the third week in July, the newly rechristened *Bay Beauty* accepted her first passengers at the Oakland municipal pier.

At first the pier officials insisted it was illegal. Mack showed them the business license obtained with Hearst's help. Then they objected to a Chinese in the pilothouse, and Mack said Bao was a passenger, not the pilot.

"There's the pilot." He indicated a runty middle-aged man with a weathered face and no teeth.

"That's Bill Barnstable," one official said. "Whiskey Bill. The SP fired him for drunkenness."

"He looks sober to me," Mack said, and went on snugging lines to cleats with a distinct air of defiance. Secretly, he and Bao were worried about Barnstable, who was the only harbor pilot willing to sign on with them.

But the neatly dressed passengers were very willing to ride. Mack and Bao had hired some street boys to hang outside the depot where the SP trains deposited commuters from the outlying areas around the Bay. There the boys passed out handbills advising the commuters of the availability of a 5-cent ferry. By 8 A.M. they had eighteen passengers aboard, and they heard only one complaint. "We'll have benches soon, very soon," Bao promised, smiling.

Barnstable tooted the whistle and Mack cast off. He was exhilarated by the fresh morning, and what seemed like an ambitious start. The wink of a brown flask, hastily stowed out of sight by Captain Barnstable, didn't bother him, but he felt less chipper when he noticed a hulking man with a long red beard watching the departure. The man pointed to Bao and said something to a pair of scruffy companions.

Soon the swift little boat overtook one of the larger railroad ferries, *El Capitán*. Barnstable gave way to port and signaled that he meant to pass. Excited passengers rushed to starboard, waving their hats and shouting at their stunned counterparts on the larger vessel.

"To hell with the railroad! Hurrah for the Oakland Bay Line!"

The new little ferry spread a saucy wake as she passed *El Capitán*. Mack could see the furious faces of her pilot and crew and the amazed and disheartened faces of the SP passengers. He leaned far over the rail, trumpeting through his hands.

"Only five cents on this line."

All of them heard.

That night, in Bao's hovel, they counted coins and currency.

They'd been able to make only five round trips because officials on the San Francisco side had delayed them an hour when they tried to tie up with their second load. Barnstable defied the officials and put the vessel into the pier long enough for Mack to jump off and go running to the *Examiner*. Willie Hearst sent one of his lawyers back to insist that all the licenses were in order, and *Bay Beauty* could not be prevented from docking. The passengers, in bad temper because of the delay, swore they'd never again take a chance on the new line. Even so, at the end of the day, the owners were satisfied. Bao busily ticked off the beads on his abacus, then sat back.

"Nine dollars and forty cents. The mountain begins to yield gold."

Mack felt fine and proud. "Only the beginning, partner." His browned hand clasped the yellow one across the table.

The first full week gave them a sense of their profit potential. *Bay Beauty* made ten round-trip crossings each day. Passenger loads were heaviest going over to the City in the morning and returning at night. On the trips between, with word of the service spreading rapidly, they began to attract women going to San Francisco to shop, and then a whole cross section of those with business on one side of the Bay or the other: domestics, day laborers, messengers, students. For the week, they'd averaged about fifty passengers per round trip.

Bao clicked the abacus beads with astonishing speed. When he finished, his round face shone. "For ten trips, twenty-five dollars. In six days, hundred and fifty dollars. In one month, we will have six hundred dollars."

"Jackpot," Mack cried, clapping his hands. "We'll be able to buy a second boat."

"Yes. Soon we'll have many."

"I expected more fight out of the railroad."

"Only one week has passed. We must be watchful."

That prompted a decision to move their belongings to the ferry, so they could guard her at night. Mack had stored the guidebook in the hovel while he lived there, but there were too many risks of water damage on a boat. He asked Nellie to keep the book safe. She said, "Of course I will. You put such stock in this. I intend to look into your Mr. Haines someday. Discover who he was, what he did."

Bao kept meticulous records. Using a pointed brush he recorded everything—number of trips, passenger count, how much coal bought and consumed—in a small rice-paper book. Soon Chinese characters filled all of its pages and he started a second book.

At the end of their third week in business, the SP began to fight back.

They were on their way to the City, second trip of the morning. Heavy whitecapped waves rolled at them from starboard. Captain Barnstable zigzagged, alternately taking the waves on the bow and the quarter. It allowed for a safer trip, but cost them speed.

Mack stood in the pilothouse with the captain, relishing the sight of the passengers packed on the deck below. Inside the main salon, formerly the card and barroom, he had installed eight hand-built benches, and those too were occupied. *Bay Beauty* rode low in the wave troughs this windy morning.

". . . the night the *Golden Star* blew up and sank, Captain Straws had his whore aboard and wasn't paying no mind to the river. I was his deckhand, a mere tad. I believed Straws when he introduced the tart as his wife."

Barnstable loved to tell stories of the old days, when Sacramento swarmed with paddle-wheel boats carrying the dreamers and the disillusioned up and down the river. The story had temporarily diverted Mack from watching the Bay traffic fore and aft. Suddenly a passenger shouted something and gestured, and Mack turned to the stern.

High as a tall house, an SP ferry loomed. It was the *Santa Clara*. She was close enough for Mack and Barnstable to discern the face of her pilot, fierce and hawkish, pressed to his window.

"What the hell's she doing?" Mack said. "She's too close.""

Barnstable snatched the whistle halyard and blasted her with a warning signal. Lumbering, gigantic, *Santa Clara* bore down. A few passengers watched from her spray-swept decks. Those on *Bay Beauty* were starting to exclaim in alarm.

"She must give way to pass," Barnstable growled. "We stand on. Rules of the road."

"She isn't going to give way."

"By God, I won't." He recognized the SP captain and flourished a fist at him. "What are y'trying to do, Septimus, kill us?"

On the stern deck, Bao Kee wigwagged his arms to warn off the larger vessel, but still she plowed ahead, not fifty yards behind, the battering waves affecting her less than they did the smaller craft. Bao dashed up the pilothouse steps. A wave broke over the starboard bow, soaking passengers there. They yelled and cursed.

"Turn," Bao shouted, practically thrown into the pilothouse by the ferry's sudden rise on the next swell.

"I'll not," Barnstable shouted back, and yanked the halyard. Five short blasts: collision warning.

Bao seized him and threw him aside. He pulled the halyard twice, two short blasts to signal his intent to alter course to port. Then he flung the wheel over.

Mack nearly went through a window headfirst. Captain Barnstable reeled around, screaming, "Mutiny!" Mack heard the roar of *Santa Clara* passing and saw the malicious faces of her master and crew glide by above.

Then the bow wake hit them. *Bay Beauty* nearly broached and a cry went up that a passenger had fallen overboard. Frantic, Mack clambered down the slippery stairs and flung a preserver out to the man. They hauled him aboard safely but he promptly vomited up water. When he left the ferry he promised a lawsuit.

They ran back to Oakland empty except for one Irish housemaid, who huddled on a bench inside, clicking her rosary beads. Barnstable sneaked a fortifying swig from his brown bottle. Bao Kee caught him and took the bottle away. All of them finished out the day in a bad mood.

A hand-inscribed letter arrived at the Oakland First National Gold Bank, where they deposited their daily receipts. It was from Fourth and Townsend, and was addressed to "The Proprietors, Oakland Bay Transportation Line, Gentlemen." A cold legalistic paragraph asked them to name the purchase price of the line and all its assets, stated that the railroad would pay a 5 percent premium for a sale closed within thirty days, and requested the favor of immediate reply. Mack showed Bao the signature: "Walter Fairbanks III, Assistant General Counsel."

Bao's pensive gaze stayed on the fine parchment letterhead

with the railroad's name engraved. "It is war in earnest," he said.

"They lost this round." Mack tore up the letter and threw it into *Bay Beauty*'s galley stove, where the flames disposed of it. "Not for sale," he added with a smile.

When Nellie came aboard for a Saturday-night supper, she confirmed that the war was indeed in earnest.

"Collis P. Huntington registered at the Palace Hotel this afternoon—six weeks ahead of his regular semiannual visit. He's hopping mad about the nickel ferry. In the past, Huntington's never tolerated competition any longer than it's taken him to get rid of it. He hasn't changed."

"We'll worry about that later, Nellie," Mack said. "Sit down, please." He wore a canvas chef's apron. A bottle of dark red merlot from a Saint Helena winery stood on the galley table, already uncorked.

At the stove, Mack checked his skillet. "Just right." Then he served up the fragrant mixture of scrambled eggs, bacon, and fried oysters on three stoneware plates. He poured the wine and took his seat, beaming. "Hangtown fry. Dig in."

"I've heard of it but I've never had it," Nellie said.

"Pa brought the recipe back from the diggings. It's supposed to be the dish a condemned man requested for his last meal. You couldn't get bacon or eggs very easily in the mines, let alone oysters, so the man figured it'd be some time before they hanged him."

Bao laughed and Nellie clucked in a skeptical way. "You're both in a wonderful mood, considering that you've succeeded in bringing the great Huntington, and his wrath, all the way from the Atlantic seaboard."

Mack raised his wine cup. "We're going after a second ferry. We decided this afternoon."

She clicked her cup with his. "My, you are feeling expansive."

He was; he felt jubilant, successful, and brimming with love for this small, bright girl, even though they hadn't made love, and had hardly kissed or embraced, since Yosemite.

He told her about the Fairbanks letter. "Getting that offer is enough to make a man feel like David after he knocked out Goliath."

"I hope your story comes out the same as the biblical one," she said. "This Goliath is far from dead."

She wasn't joking.

* * *

The next week passed with no further harassment by the railroad. Passenger loads remained steady, and they began to carry small freight parcels from businessmen who heard they undercut the SP ferries by 30 percent.

The partners were eager to buy their second boat but could find nothing suitable. Mack was thinking about the problem when he crawled into his bunk late on Friday night. Bao was already snoring in the bed below. Mack lasted about three minutes, and then sleep plucked him away.

About midnight, a sound woke him. At first he couldn't sort it out from the familiar lulling lap of the water on the ferry hull. He raked his hands through his sleep-mussed hair, listening. It sounded like a marine engine throttled back to minimum power. Who could be coming along at this time of night?

He glanced out the porthole beside his head, but could see only the rippling reflections of the red and white port and mast lanterns. He dropped over the side of the bunk and shook Bao's bare shoulder.

"What is wrong?" Bao said, waking slowly.

"Not sure. I think we've some visitors. Or else someone's way off course." No one else ever docked at the half-collapsed pier by the mud flat.

In the dark Mack pulled on his suit of flannel underwear. Now he berated himself for not taking the precaution of keeping at least one pistol aboard *Bay Beauty*. They had simply assumed the SP would compete hard, but fairly.

Bao, having dressed quickly, poked Mack to signal that he was ready. Mack started for the companionway, only to stop again at a sound from above.

A footfall. Then many footfalls. Men jumping aboard.

He felt the other vessel bump their hull. "Who's there?" he shouted, crashing the door open.

He rushed on deck and saw a dark figure swinging a sledge at a window of the pilothouse. Glass burst inward, the shards snatching the green glow of the starboard lantern and winking as they fell.

A quarter-moon shed pale misty light on the scene. Mack counted at least eight men. They'd come from a rust-bucket launch tied up alongside. A tall man with a familiar long beard was in charge, gesturing fore and aft with a crowbar. "Two of you see to the engines and the bilge pumps. Tear this fucking boat apart."

Mack doubled his fists and charged. "Get the hell off this vessel—"

A man he didn't see in time lunged in from his left, striking his legs with a two-handed sweep of a two-by-two. Mack fell and skidded chest-first on the deck. Bao jumped at the man, but he turned and drove the board into Bao's ribs, hammering him back to the rail. Bao held his side, howling in Chinese.

Mack breathed in long wild gulps. Lurching to his feet, he scrambled up the steps to the pilothouse. Redbeard was inside, slipping his crowbar between spokes of the wheel. Quick leverage snapped four of them. Mack made it through the door just as Redbeard shattered the wheel yoke with two blows.

Mack leaped on him, but Redbeard hurled him off and started to bash him with the crowbar.

A piece of tooth flew out of Mack's mouth and blood spurted from his upper lip. Then Redbeard rammed the crowbar into his privates. Mack fell backward out the door. He grabbed for the stair rail and missed, landing on his back on deck, almost knocked out.

Redbeard clambered down and stomped on him. Mack cried out, clutching his middle. "Told you we didn't want Chinks competing with white men in this bay," Redbeard said. "Got it now, have you?" He made a kissing sound, spit on Mack's face, and disappeared.

Mack fought the gut pain, pulling himself up by grasping the rail. He stumbled forward and wrestled an ax from a man savaging the hull. He heard someone's sledge blasting out the last pilothouse window just as he rammed the ax handle under the man's chin and shoved him over the side.

Mack felt dizzy with a mix of fright and rage. All around him, shadow-men wielded crowbars and axes. Bao ran here and there, punching, dodging blows, screeching curses in Chinese. It was futile; there were too many. Mack heard the inside benches splintering and, below, the tortured sound of metal being pried and bent. Down there too, someone was chopping the hull.

He staggered aft and found a man with a knife slashing the new awning he'd hung to protect the open stern deck. Bao rushed the man, grappling him around the waist and crushing him in a savage hug. The knife clacked on the deck. Another man, the one with the two-by-two, now raced at Bao from the dark.

"Bao, behind you!" Mack shouted. He started to run, but time seemed to liquefy and flow too slowly; he couldn't cover the distance fast enough. His arms pumped. His bare feet slapped. *Not fast enough*— The man behind Bao swung the lumber; it seemed slow, so slow. Mack kept running, getting nowhere— The board struck the back of Bao's head and he arched, pitched onto his knees . . . Horrified, Mack watched the blood splatter and spurt from Bao's broken skull.

The man Bao held twisted away, laughing. Bao's unpinned queue writhed like a black-and-red snake. Then Bao screamed, and time flowed again.

Mack leaped on Bao's attacker and tore the two-by-two out of his hands. Then he beat him about the head with it, driving him back, using it like a sword. The man moaned, "Jesus," and vaulted the rail into the water.

Bleeding and sweaty, Mack wiped mucus dripping from his nose. He felt the boat list and heard water gurgling. She was hulled.

Turning, he said, "Well, at least there's one less of the sons of—"

The other man had found his fallen knife. Crouching over Bao, he turned to look at Mack, then rammed the blade into Bao's chest and ran.

"She's finished, boys. Good work. Let's go."

The ferry tilted more sharply, going down on the port side, scraping against the crusted and slimy pier pilings. Men were jumping back aboard the rust bucket, and her engines roared up and carried them away. She bore no running lanterns. Mack watched her white wake spread under the faint misty moon, Redbeard's laughter carrying over the water.

Mack knelt and raised his partner's heavy body in his arms, pulling Bao's fat shoulders onto his knees. "Bao Kee. Oh God, Bao Kee." He didn't dare pull the knife out. "I'll put you down. I'll try not to hurt you. You lie here while I run for help . . ."

Bao's eyes opened. He seemed to recognize who was holding him. His voice was faint and dry as rice-paper pages rustling.

"Kum Saan—Gold Mountain—is dust."

He smiled, as if saying, *That is life's way* and died in Mack's arms.

Mack hoisted Bao Kee onto the pier and laid him under the moon while *Bay Beauty* slowly sank into the flowing high tide. The moon lit his tear-filled eyes. This was not going to be the end. By God, not nearly. He knew the man responsible and he knew where to find him.

THE FOLLOWING EVENING, C. P. HUNTINGTON RE- **14** ceived Walter Fairbanks in the large suite permanently reserved for the railroad chief on the seventh floor of the Palace Hotel. After Huntington's clerk was sent into the next room and the door closed, they sat down for a working supper—oxtail soup, quail under glass, champagne.

The suite offered the same modern amenities found throughout the luxury hotel: fifteen-foot ceilings; call buttons connected with the desk downstairs and with a service pantry on the floor; elaborate multijet gas fixtures (electricity was promised but not yet installed); a completely private chamber equipped with bathtub, washstand, toilet. Such things no longer impressed Mr. Huntington. In his world, he expected them.

Collis Potter Huntington was sixty-seven. A Yankee peddler from Connecticut, he'd made his first substantial money as an Argonaut. On the Isthmus of Panama, he decided he could make some quick money by supplying potatoes, rice, sugar, and similar necessities to others who, like him, had started across the Isthmus on the way to California. To get his goods, Huntington went into the jungles to trade with local people, walking twenty and thirty miles one way on many a trip, defying the fevers and ticks and bad water that weakened and even killed lesser men. In those young days, he was hard as bar iron.

Later, in Sacramento, he went into the hardware business with a partner, forming Huntington Hopkins & Company of K and L streets. He frequently dashed to San Francisco to check incoming ships and temporarily corner the market for blasting powder, shovels, or other items in demand in the gold mines. It was in a room above the hardware store that he and the other men who would become the Big Four first heard the young engineer Theodore Judah propose his transcontinental railroad over the mountains. Huntington was no patriotic visionary; he liked the idea because it could create a monopoly on fast movement of freight to the Nevada silver mines and thus drive a lot of teamsters out of business.

A tall man, he was running to flab now. He maintained that symbol of business respectability, a neat full beard, gray-shot, and was an altogether unassuming and forgettable figure except for the black silk skullcap he wore to hide his humiliating baldness. When he was exercised, however, his keen blue-gray eyes caught fire. Men antagonized him at their peril; his enemies called him "ruthless as a crocodile."

At the moment, supper over and pressing business out of the way, he was expounding some of his philosophy to the smartly dressed attorney.

"I have a broad interpretation of the term *corporate expense*, Walter. Rails and rolling stock are legitimate expenses, but so is the money we spend for a politician's vote in the state legislature or the Congress. I can tell you precisely how much it costs, in either body, to pass a bill favorable to us. I cheerfully disburse money to politicians who have done right by us, friendly newspapers, the local Associated Press man, many others. Spending generates control. Control generates profit."

"That's a breathtaking concept, Mr. Huntington."

Huntington wasn't lulled by the flattery. "It's just the way I operate. You'd better too, if you want to get ahead in this company. You have a lot of promise. You don't let niggling scruples stand in the way of the right deal, the right contract. That's why I wanted to share—"

There was a loud knocking on the door.

"No one else is expected," Huntington said, fire in his eye. "Pedley!" he shouted. "See who's there and send him packing."

As the clerk ran from the adjoining bedroom into the foyer, Huntington waited, seething, while the knocking continued.

On the other side of the double doors, Mack shot looks both ways along the gallery. Below, in the Grand Court, a string trio played, and the hoofs of carriage horses rapped on marble paving. The Montgomery Street entrance was a half-oval that allowed patrons to be driven right into the hotel.

Mack's face bore garish bruises and his chest, thighs, and stomach ached. He'd put on a jeans jacket, clean but shabby, given him that morning by an Oakland harbor mission, along with everything from shirt to shoes. He'd scrubbed up and combed his hair, but even so, no one would ever mistake him for a Palace guest.

Outside the barbershop on the Jessie Street side of the hotel, he'd slipped the shoeshine boy a nickel for the number of Huntington's suite. Then he'd sneaked through a passage next to the billiard parlor and climbed seven flights of a service stair; he didn't dare risk a ride in one of the mirror-paneled elevators.

He knocked again, his eye fixed on the nearby pantry; he hoped he got inside before the butler got back from his errand.

The doors opened.

"I want to see Mr. Huntington."

The whey-faced clerk with round glasses blocked his move forward. Over the man's shoulder, Mack saw a bearded man wearing a skullcap; he recognized him from engravings and photographs.

"Mr. Huntington is not available without prior—"

Mack's hands shot to the clerk's shoulders and he shoved him sideways with no trouble, then stepped inside and kicked the doors shut. As he strode through the foyer to the spacious sitting room, Huntington, who had leaped up, angrily hurled a napkin to the carpet. Mack saw a second man now, and it took him aback: Fairbanks. The lawyer's index finger smoothed his tiny auburn mustache, a nervous motion.

"I'll have your job," Huntington spat at the visitor. "I am a valued patron of this hotel, and no employee dares break in on—"

"Sir, he doesn't work here," Fairbanks said. "This is one of the owners of the nickel ferry."

"What?"

"This is Chance, sir."

"What I own is forty percent of nothing," Mack said. "The ferry's at the bottom of the Inner Harbor."

Huntington came around from behind the table as if loath to use it as a barrier and Fairbanks stepped back quickly out of his way. Huntington confronted Mack eye to eye. He was several inches taller.

"So you had an accident—" he began.

"Which you and your damned railroad arranged and paid for."

"That's ludicrous. An insult. Make sense, young man."

"Try this. Your thugs did a thorough job. They sank our boat and then one of them smashed my partner's head open, stuck a knife in him, and killed him. A decent harmless Chinese who just wanted the right to earn a living. You're a murderer, Huntington."

Fairbanks clamped a suntanned hand on Mack's arm.

"I'll handle this," Huntington exclaimed as Mack flung Fairbanks off.

Fairbanks hesitated, momentarily resentful, but Huntington paid no attention. "By heaven, sir," he said to Mack, "if you think that the Southern Pacific Corporation, or I personally, would ever stoop to employing physical violence of the kind you describe, you're a madman. I will compete with you, or anyone, legitimately. I will employ every business means at my disposal. But I do not condone wanton destruction, or murder—I would never authorize either, and I am outraged to hear you suggest otherwise."

Huntington's combative style and his certitude made Mack less certain. "Someone arranged it," he said.

"Open the door, Pedley," Fairbanks said, knocking aside fronds of a potted palm as he started for the foyer. "I'll get someone to help us remove—"

"I said I would handle this."

Again Fairbanks stopped.

Huntington stepped closer to Mack, never blinking. "I do know your name, Mr. Chance. I have an extensive file on your shabby little ferryboat. I instructed Mr. Fairbanks to make you a substantial offer for the assets of the line—an offer you spurned. Now you come here saying I was forced to resort to hiring thugs. Absurd. Where's your evidence?"

"I . . ." Mack's mouth felt dusty.

Huntington leaped on his hesitation. "I'll tell you where it is. There isn't any evidence, because what you said is a pernicious lie, and you are either beside yourself with emotion, or a criminal lunatic. Get out of here, you gutter scum."

Something flared in Mack's head. He leaped for Huntington with both hands.

"Great God," Huntington cried, reeling sideways and groping behind him. Fairbanks shot between them and threw Mack backward just as Huntington's hand caught the tablecloth and brought down an avalanche of crystal, china, champagne bottles, serving domes, food, and drink.

Mack stumbled against a writing desk, then righted himself. Fists up, Fairbanks ran at him, malicious anticipation in his gray-metal eyes. Mack got his own fists in position in time to deflect the lawyer's whipping right hand.

Mack tried to recall some of what Corbett taught him. He bobbed left and feinted, and Fairbanks's next punch sailed by. The lawyer looked astonished. Mack took the opportunity to jab his jaw—it glanced off—then crossed with his left. That blow was solid. Fairbanks's eyes glazed a moment and he retreated.

Mack didn't press. He felt a fool, trying to box in the middle of a sitting room. Huntington ran by, throwing him the kind of look he might give a plague rat. "Damn you, Pedley, stand aside." Doors crashed open; cello music and a faint hum of

Grand Court activity drifted in. Huntington's voice had a hollow quality as he shouted down seven floors.

"Police! Get the police up here! This is Huntington—I've been assaulted!"

Mack scanned the four doorways that opened off the sitting room. Could he escape through any of them? Which one? He'd been stupid to let his grief and rage goad him into this. What had he expected—that Huntington would fall to his knees and babble a confession?

In the corner of his eye he caught blurred motion. Mack spun toward Fairbanks, whipping up his guard. But the lawyer was faster, his punch well aimed and powerfully delivered. Mack's head snapped back and he went down. He flopped on the thick carpet and watched the gas nozzles of the ceiling fixture go round and round like a carousel. The floor spun under him. *Damn fool, when will you learn?*

Dazed, he heard the elevator stop, and then the police came charging along the gallery.

Mack lay on his back on the stone floor. It was the only space he could find. Five men were squeezed into a holding cell at the Kearny Street jail that was designed for two. The cell had no lights and it reeked of a full waste bucket in the corner.

A pickpocket had claimed the iron bunk. Two drunks maundered and bickered. The bull-like figure of Diego Marquez occupied the only stool. When the police threw Mack in the holding cell, he'd been astonished to discover Marquez among the prisoners. The priest had listened attentively while Mack told of his misadventures with the ferry, and his accusation of Huntington. Now Marquez sat perfectly still, powerful hands folded in his lap, while lying on the floor, Mack tried to sort out the truth from suppositions and outright fantasies generated by his anger. He slipped his hands under his head, thinking aloud.

"Maybe Huntington was telling the truth. Plenty of white men on the waterfront hate the Chinese, especially a successful one. Bao poached on Redbeard's oyster beds, and I saw Redbeard watching us the first morning we ran the ferry . . ." He changed position, resting his crossed wrists on his forehead. "I don't know what to think."

"I think you ought to shut up," one of the drunks muttered.

"Go to hell."

The pickpocket lurched from the bunk, and pissed noisily into the waste pail. Marquez unfolded his hands and turned slightly on the stool. The gaslight that came through the barred doors at the end of the corridor of cells revealed dark bruises around both eyes, stigmata of a recent beating.

"I think I would agree with you about Huntington," the priest said. "He probably wasn't responsible. He hires politicians to drive out his competitors, not criminals. It's too bad that you'll never have a positive answer, but you won't. You know the railroad's passion for secrecy."

"I know," Mack sighed. He rolled over and looked up at the priest. "You didn't say why you're in here again."

"Tonight I spoke to another public gathering. The police objected, I refused to step down—here I am." A bitter smile. "Last time I was charged with disturbing the peace. This time it's more serious—criminal syndicalism. It's nonsense. But there are men in this city and this state who believe that the slightest improvement in the lot of the workingman is somehow a direct threat to their property. That's so misguided. A worker's right to join a union is his by his very nature as a man. The Holy Father himself proclaimed it so. But the men who hate the idea have great influence and many friends in city government—"

"So I'm learning. I still don't understand why a priest has to go to jail. Can't your superiors raise bail?"

"They can, they do. It takes a little time. My work causes controversy within the archdiocese. Archbishop Riordan is lenient with me. But he's a fair man, so he listens to all factions—the relative few who support me, and a much larger number who do not. I can't despise those priests who oppose me. They are my brothers in Christ, men of conservative mind but sincere conviction. They are sure that the owners are right, and the labor movement a dangerous, satanic force."

He clasped his hands again, now under his chin. "They don't see the one-sided nature of the battle. The poor and downtrodden have few resources. Their rights must be upheld—militantly, if necessary—and all the more so because the richer classes have the wealth and the influence to defend and promote themselves more than adequately. That precept shapes my ministry. Sometimes, though, a strong inner voice says I'd be more effective—less restricted—if I didn't wear this collar, or have to deal with my enemies with Christian restraint. When I saw what they did to my father—shot him down for the murderous outlaw he became after he lost everything—I was grieved and angry, but overcome by the futility of his last years. I chose the Church because I thought God's glory could effect more change than my father's gun ever did. So here I am, not punishing those who oppose me, but praying for their enlightenment."

"I'd pray for their defeat."

Marquez chuckled wryly. "Yes, I expect you would, Mr. Chance." It was a compliment.

The iron door at the end of the corridor opened and a cretinous guard shuffled in and unlocked the holding cell. He waved his truncheon.

"Chance."

Mack pushed up with both hands, elated, almost forgetting his various aches and bruises. "Did someone put up bail?" The *Examiner*, probably; their police reporter routinely scanned the blotter for new arrivals.

The guard said, "Oh, sure, sure, all arranged."

"Good news," Marquez said as Mack stepped outside. Then the guard whipped his truncheon into Mack's kidneys from behind, and Mack slammed face-first into the bars of the empty cell opposite. He spun around, blood oozing from his nose. The guard grinned, tapping his truncheon on his fingers, a sadistic little invitation.

"Bail for you? Not hardly. One of the detectives is waiting to have a word. Lon Coglan—Old Silver Tooth. Hardest man on the force, Silver Tooth. You're in for a fine time."

Detective Lon Coglan wore a natty striped vest and a heavy silver watch chain that matched his hair and his tooth. All of his upper front teeth protruded, the silver right incisor most prominently. It had a rodentlike sharp point.

Coglan wore his silver hair long, beautifully combed, but years of cheap whiskey were written on his red cucumber nose. He was half a head shorter than Mack, whom he'd shoved into a chair under a sputtering gas fixture trimmed to its dimmest level.

The room smelled damp, and there was the faint sound of water trickling somewhere. Chunks of plaster lay crumbling amid rat droppings; no one had patched the small craters left when the plaster fell. Another detective stood by the door with arms folded. Coglan walked round and round Mack's chair while he talked.

"Somebody from the Hearst rag knows you're in here. So we'll be letting you go soon. Mr. Huntington won't file charges."

Mack couldn't believe such good luck. And he didn't—not just yet.

Coglan's silver tooth gleamed, reflecting the flames of the

gas. "I talked to the arresting officer who collared you at the Palace. I understand you accused Mr. Huntington of sinking your boat and killing your partner." The detective leaned down, smiling. "Did you really do such a thing, laddie buck?"

"You already know."

Coglan hit him.

The blow, unexpected and powerful, caught him below the breastbone. He jerked backward, choking on vomit. He didn't fall out of the chair because Coglan had tied his hands in back.

"I do, and it's a damn outrage, because Mr. Collis Huntington is an honest, patriotic, law-abiding gentleman. That's my personal opinion, I want you to know. He didn't put me up to saying it. But I'm the detective assigned to this case, so I reckon you have to listen to my opinions, eh?"

Mack blinked, gasping for air. "I—guess I do."

Coglan hit him.

"Louder, laddie buck. I had trouble hearing that."

"I said . . ." Red drool ran down Mack's chin. A lower canine tooth wobbled in his gum. "I'll listen."

"That's a lot better."

Coglan was amiable again. Mack felt tight as a twisted wire. The detective resumed his walk around the chair.

"You're a nobody in this town, Chance, and you're an asshole, too, if you think you can sling mud at the SP and get away with it. Two cousins of mine work for the railroad—decent fellas, Christian men, with big families—and I'll tell you, if they heard your accusations against Mr. Huntington, they'd tear you apart. When Mr. Huntington and his partners built their railroad, they united this great country of ours. The railroad's done more for businessmen and farmers—more for the state of California—than you and all your thieving slant-eyed pals could do if you lived a hundred years." Coglan paused, letting his words sink in. "Something else, too. The jailer told Jackie here"—Coglan indicated the other detective—"that you were chummy with that communist priest. Is it true?"

"I know him. Is it against the law?"

Coglan hit him.

The blow knocked him over, chair and all. He bit his lip to stifle a yell. Coglan sucked his silver tooth noisily and signaled Jackie forward to help him right the chair.

"Don't give me lip, laddie buck. You're not the one with the authority to ask questions."

Mack glared. Coglan chuckled; he liked that.

"If you know Marquez, that tells me a lot about you. We

140

don't want your kind in the City. I'm here to make sure you're absolutely clear on that.''

The softness of those words made Mack's scalp crawl.

''I want to impress on you that we don't want and won't tolerate radicals like you stirring things up, threatening and insulting our civic leaders. I want to demonstrate that to you so you'll never forget.''

He extended his right hand, palm up. A big paste diamond in a pinky ring glittered.

''Jackie, give me the knucks.''

He slipped them on his right hand. Mack stared at the ridges of yellow metal.

''This will just be a light lesson, Chance. I sense that you're a smart enough fella to learn it right off. After we let you out, you'll have twenty-four hours to leave San Francisco. Mr. Fairbanks persuaded Mr. Huntington to drop charges—avoid a lot of useless bad publicity—in exchange for assurance from headquarters that we'd get rid of you.''

He grabbed Mack's hair with his left hand and yanked. Mack clenched his teeth and slitted his eyes. Pain seemed to come from all parts of his body, consuming him.

''After midnight tomorrow, if a member of the force spots you anywhere in the City, you'll come back to this room for another visit. After that one, you won't be in any shape to walk anyplace.''

''You fucking ape,'' Mack gasped. ''If I ever catch you by yourself in a fair fight I'll kill you.''

His words reverberated and died. When Coglan got over his surprise, he put on a pious face.

''That was nasty, laddie buck. Rash and nasty. That'll prolong your lesson a bit.'' And Coglan hit him.

Blood glistened on the metal knuckles. Coglan's merry eyes belied his soft tone. By the door, Jackie scratched his groin and watched with a smile.

Sit up, Mack shouted in the silence of his ringing head. *Don't make a sound. He wants crying and screaming.*

Coglan hit him again.

Mack rose with the blow, taking the chair six inches up and slamming it down again. Coglan's gold-plated fist rose and fell, rose and fell, administering his lesson.

''Beginning to catch my drift, are you?'' Coglan was breathing hard. Mack's eyelids were almost swollen shut. The detective was a shimmering blur that divided into two Coglans, then fused again.

''I don't hear you, laddie buck.''

Mack spat at him. It landed between his own feet, blood-red.

And Coglan hit him again.

Two policemen carried him out and flung him on the curb. There was a glitter of blue-white as rain obscured buildings and haloed lights. Mack groped for a purchase on the curbstone, missed, and slid into the gutter face-first.

He jerked his head up, sputtering, and water sluiced some of the dried blood from his face. A lightning bolt excited a horse harnessed to a hack across the street, and it neighed wildly and pawed the air.

The hack door flew open, and a woman jumped out, then a man. They splashed through puddles while Mack floundered, rain dripping from his brows and nose and chin. In another burst of lightning, Mack recognized Bierce.

"Christ. This town is a moral leper colony."

"Stop your posturing and help me, Ambrose." Nellie tugged Mack's arm out of the gutter. They got him into the hack and away while the policemen watched from the shelter of the jail doorway, amused.

"They broke your nose," said the elderly doctor Nellie had awakened at 2 A.M. Mack sat gingerly on a chair under the gas in the doctor's surgery. He was bare to the waist. His torso was a landscape of purple and yellow, and he could barely see through his slitted eyes.

"As to internal injuries, I detect nothing, but we'll have to wait and reexamine you to be certain."

Mack thought of Coglan's deadline.

"The physical damage will take plenty of time to heal," the doctor continued. "For a month or so, you're going to look as though you boxed thirty rounds with Jim Corbett."

"And lost," Mack said. Only Bierce smiled, leaning against the wall next to a hanging skeleton.

"Send the bill to the *Examiner*," Nellie said.

"I want to see him again in three days."

"Sure," Mack said through his cut and swollen lips. "Thanks for your help."

He woke in the sitting room of Nellie's flat, which was located, fittingly enough, on the slope of Russian Hill. The gray light of day fell through a huge bay window awash with wind-blown rain. It cast strange moving shadows on Mack's ruined face. Every limb, every joint hurt in some fashion.

He'd been sleeping on a pallet of furs, sables and sea otters. Nellie didn't believe in killing wild animals. Where, he wondered, did these pelts come from? The sitting room had other unusual features. Contrary to fashion, it contained very little furniture beyond four plain, solid-backed chairs, a table, and a sideboard, all of which looked old, handmade. Three framed photographs of stern dark-eyed men hung over the mantel. One man wore a huge round fur hat. No carpets covered the beautifully finished floor, just the scattered furs. A four-foot silver samovar decorated with elaborate filigree dominated one corner. Nellie had once told him vehemently that she was American, her Russian ancestors existing only as memories. He wondered.

Nellie brought him a bowl of golden broth. "You look horrible."

"I can thank Walter Fairbanks."

"At least you're not going to prison." She sat while he spooned up some broth. He had trouble swallowing. "I have a valise for you in the bedroom, and clean clothes."

"Nellie, I won't run."

"You haven't any choice. They own the police force. I'm not saying any money changes hands. It's just that the SP is such a power, such a presence. Mr. Hearst wouldn't dare oppose them if he didn't have the senator's fortune and prestige behind him, and the newspaper."

"Those people are too damn powerful. They're nothing but dictators."

"A lot of Californians agree. Mr. Huntington and his partners have had almost twenty-five years to entrench themselves. But you can't kill the Octopus by yourself, nor can I. Not even Mr. Hearst can do it alone. If it's ever to happen, it will take time, thought, and a great deal of courageous effort from people in every part of this state. Meantime, the railroad runs things. At the moment they're running you. I don't want you to leave, but you won't be safe unless you do."

"It's cowardly."

"It's good sense."

Under her prodding, he told her of things that needed to be done when he left. Captain Barnstable was owed money from the receipts on deposit in Oakland. "Bluedorn's Coal Yard too."

"I'll see that both are paid."

"I have twenty-one dollars on deposit at Wells, Fargo . . ."

"Leave it. Anything else?"

"No. Everything I owned sank with the *Bay Beauty*."

"Except this." From the mantel she brought T. Fowler Haines. She brushed the cover with her palm. "I thought you'd want to take it. I've also been curious about this." She drew Carla's gold scarf from between the pages. "It's expensive."

He thought quickly; she still didn't know about Carla. "My mother's."

"Indeed. Unusual. I would have guessed it belonged to a younger woman. From the color."

At another time, he might have been amused, flattered by the jealousy of some unknown rival, but he was relieved when she didn't pursue it. She replaced the scarf and gave him the guidebook.

Mack turned the book in his hands, riffled the pages, and read a few sentences. *A more beautiful, hospitable country never spread its panorama to the human gaze!* He shook his head.

"I was going to get rich in a year or so. Walk right through the golden doorway . . ." His hand clenched the spine of T. Fowler Haines. "Swampy Hellman was the first one who shut the door in my face. Then there was Fairbanks. The scum from the Oakland piers. Coglan . . ." Something hard, gnarled, grew within him. He sat up straighter on the pallet of furs. "They slammed the door this time, but it won't stay shut forever. They can bolt their goddamn door and hammer in a hundred nails. I'll still come back and kick it down and break it up for kindling. I'll tell you something else . . ."

He struggled to his knees, alarming her. "Be careful, Mack, you're not—"

"Next time," he interrupted, taking hold of her shoulders, "next time, Nellie, I won't come sneaking into San Francisco aboard some little fishing skiff. I'll sail right up to the SP pier in the biggest, longest steam yacht you've ever—"

"Stop." She whispered it, pressing her hand to his lips. Her eyes shone wet as the rain that slashed the bay window and hid the hills of Marin. "Please stop. You'll only make yourself feel worse."

"You don't believe I can do it."

"I believe you should get out of San Francisco before midnight. Do you have anyplace to go?"

"No. I guess I'd better try the other city—Los Angeles. A man I met said there was a land boom down in the cow counties."

He rested his hands lightly on his legs, kneeling there while she walked to the window. She crossed and uncrossed her arms in a restless, troubled way.

144

"Nellie."

She looked at him.

"Any possibility that you'd come along?"

She caught her breath, trying to hide her emotions, but a huskiness in her voice gave her away. "No."

He knew she meant yes, there was a possibility, she wanted to go. She was slim and fragile and yet, gazing at her, Mack thought her perhaps the toughest person he had ever met. It made her all the more desirable.

"No," she repeated more strongly. "I have work to do here. I have a place where I can be heard. Maybe make a difference."

"You're damn near as ambitious as I am."

She didn't deny it.

He went to her in the window, slowly, hurting, and touched her hair. "I hate to leave you. I don't altogether understand you, and I don't think too much of your ideas about women or what they should do with their lives, but ever since Yosemite— maybe since that day I jumped in the water and ruined your stunt—you've meant a lot to me." He curved his bruised hand, nestling her chin in his palm, caressing her cheek with the inside of his fingers. He felt tears. "You still do."

Some fierce storm raged in her dark eyes then. He saw the turmoil without fully understanding it. She reached up and clasped his hand against her face.

"Oh God, Mack. I think I'd have been better off if I'd never met you."

"Maybe I should say the same but I can't. It's like the falls where we loved each other. They go over the edge because there's no other way. No way to stop the force—"

"You're a strange, complex young man. Driven."

"You're not driven?"

"Yes, but not into the shackles of matrimony. I have too much to do with my life."

"Who ever said . . . ?"

She tore away, crossing her arms again. "It comes to mind when two people lo— When they have feelings for one another. You have to know what I am, that's all. Then, if you know and you still want me . . ."

Their eyes held. The rainy light cast its moving shadows on them. "I'll be here if you come back," she added.

"I will. To open that door."

"I believe you, I believe you."

He flung his arms around her, but it was questionable as to which of them came more eagerly into the embrace. Nellie's

145

kisses were hungry and sad at the same time. He held her as tightly as he could, ignoring his injuries. When they fell to the furs, rolling back and forth and kissing, he knew making love would bring exquisite pain. She stopped it.

"It would hurt you too much."

He heard what she really meant. It would hurt her too, in a different way. Her voice was soft steel when she said it; he didn't argue.

Later, saying little, she sat with her legs drawn up and her hands locked around her skirt. She watched him pack and latch the valise, and then she watched him go. She heard his footsteps fading on the outside steps, the rain soon muffling them altogether. She bowed her head and cried.

15

AS A SHARP WIND FROM THE NORTHWEST CHILLED THE summer evening, the clouds blew away, revealing a sky ablaze with stars. Dots of blue and white and yellow sparkled on the hills of San Francisco.

Mack limped along the rutted road leading south over the peninsula. Every now and then he shifted the valise to his other hand. About half past eleven, he paused to rest.

He gazed at the City again. Hurrying through San Francisco's first elite residential districts south of Market, he'd felt small and worthless. The splendor of the lights enhanced the feeling, as did his pain and the wild, unreasonable emotions whipped up by Bao's death, Fairbanks's felling him, the police edict.

He felt both disappointment and wrath. But then he thought of the familiar nightmare, all the years in the cold white winters of Pennsylvania. He thought of Pa, and the promises, the hope that this state represented for hundreds of thousands, and for him.

They had defeated him in the City, but there was a lot of California left. In the south he'd start over. There he'd make the dream come true. And then he'd come back.

"Never be cold again. Never be poor again." He recited it like a church litany, let it buoy him. Giving the City a last look, he picked up the valise. His body still protested, but his spirit felt refreshed. He grasped the guidebook in his pocket and hobbled into the dark.

III

LIFE AMONG
THE ESCROW
INDIANS

1888–1889

*El Pueblo de Nuestra Señora la Reina de los Angeles de Por-
ciúncula—Our Lady the Queen of Angels.*

In 1781 Spanish governor Felipe de Neve established a pueblo
on the Los Angeles River to produce crops for missions and
presidios along the coast. A determined band of settlers from
the state of Sinaloa—thirty-four married soldiers and twenty-
four married settlers, including some Indians and blacks—were
the first residents.

Growth was slow; in 1820 Los Angeles still had only 650
inhabitants. She was a quiet, unsophisticated, not to say rustic
queen in those days. But the influx of Anglos during the Gold
Rush transformed her, and she became a haven for the desperate and violent, with fights, robberies, murders, and lynchings
a way of life. San Franciscans derided her as the City of Fallen
Angels.

In 1871 two members of the city's small Chinese population
quarreled, and when a policeman stepped in to mediate, he
was killed. Over four hundred Angelinos rose up and ran riot,
claiming nineteen victims in and around the Chinese district at
Sanchez Street. This did nothing to improve the Queen's tough
and tawdry reputation.

A number of businessmen were concerned about the lawless-
ness, and perhaps even more, about the declining cattle trade,
and felt that bringing in the railroad would establish stronger
links with the more civilized outside world. The Southern Pacific was quite willing to lay track to Los Angeles, but demanded payment of an appropriate subsidy. Using this simple
plan, the railroad had built southward through the San Joaquin
Valley. Communities that appreciated the railroad's benevo-
lence and remunerated it accordingly soon saw the rails coming over the horizon. Los Angeles paid a subsidy, in the form
of special assessments, totaling $600,000. Other, less enlight-
ened communities like San Bernardino saw the railroad choose
an alternate route, often miles away.

A second, simultaneous force helped civilize and populate
Southern California. In 1872 a New York journalist named
Charles Nordhoff published California: For Health, Pleasure,
and Residence. *This hymn to climate and opportunity stam-*

149

peded hundreds onto the westbound cars. No other book on the Golden State was so influential.

A torrent of similar promotions poured out; there had been nothing like it since the heyday of Gold Rush literature. Meanwhile, the Southern Pacific finished its tracks to Los Angeles in 1876. Always spinning its own elaborate web, the railroad soon determined that allowing a second line—a competitor—to enter Southern California would serve its devious ends. In 1885 the SP sold its Mojave-Needles division to the Atchison, Topeka & Santa Fe, in exchange receiving assurances of no competition in certain other places. Everyone, from railroad mogul to small merchant, wanted and needed to generate more business. They needed tourists, but permanent population too. So the SP slashed passenger fares, and the Santa Fe retaliated. Seventy dollars from the heartland to the Pacific. Then fifty dollars. Then fifteen. Then five. Then, for a few dizzying days, one dollar, Kansas City to Los Angeles.

Each railroad's promotion department worked as never before, organizing special state or group excursions from the East, churning out ads and literature that extolled the California way of life. The Los Angeles city fathers supplemented these efforts with advertising of their own. Each citizen became a booster, taking every opportunity to tell a newcomer about Southern California. Soon the excursion trains were rolling over the Sierras by day and by night, spilling hundreds of wide-eyed passengers into the Los Angeles sunshine. Hundreds every month, then hundreds every week, then thousands. Eager real estate dealers awaited them; the breakup of the great ranchos had made land available.

The Los Angeles boom was on. The Queen threw off her shabby past and confidently faced the future. No one dared call her rough, lazy, or backward any longer. She was wide awake; she was modern; she was a booster.

MACK ARRIVED IN LOS ANGELES ON A HOT AUTUMN **16**
day, the second Monday of October, 1888.

He came from the direction of the sundown sea, riding west to east on an old pack mule he'd earned by working three weeks in Monterey. The owner was ready to shoot the mule so Mack took it in lieu of half his wages.

He found that the mule had plenty of miles left in it, plus a determination to prove it was not yet ready to die. Mack liked that kind of determination.

From Monterey, he passed along a wild, spectacular coast where mighty waves struck and exploded on giant rocks beneath sheer cliffs. Some days he saw one traveler, some days none. Little towns cropped up occasionally; otherwise, the coast was a beautiful wilderness.

In San Luis Obispo a tavern keeper told him Charles Crocker had died in August, taken by a diabetic seizure at the railroad's own Del Monte Hotel in Monterey. Two of the Big Four were gone. An age was passing.

Yet as Mack jogged south, he felt himself journeying back in time. The occasional *ranchos* or frame cottages reminded him not of modern, civilized San Francisco but of the West he'd crossed on foot. This was frontier, lonely and grand.

At the same time, around thriving Santa Barbara, he began to notice differences in the land. The sun seemed brighter. The plant life wasn't the same as in Northern California; here grew towering palms, and cactus, and many fernlike pepper trees. He rode by lemon groves with villas of white-painted adobe drowsing shyly deep within.

He followed a trail over the Santa Monica Mountains and down to the Pacific. His hair was long, to his shoulders now, and his hazel eyes were clear and full of hope again. He felt strong and fit. His nose was healing, the clogged, painful breathing cleared up, but he bore a permanent souvenir of the beatings: a ridge, like a tiny earthwork on a sun-browned hillside.

When he reached the shore, he whooped with delight and ran up and down the sparkling sand, turning somersaults and walking on his hands. He stripped naked and raced into the surf, yelling for joy when the foaming waves picked him up and rolled him back. The defeats in the City were forgotten. He loved this sunshine, this ocean, this new fresh face of California.

After camping overnight, he rode east toward the town that lay in the bow curve of the Los Angeles River. He saw workers cultivating pea fields and extensive fig orchards. In the foothills of the mountains he came on a sign of the land boom Wyatt Paul had described. A large, flat tract had been laid out with small pepper trees marking the blocks. One lonely manor house rose in the distance. A whitewashed sign said the subdivision was HOLLY WOOD.

Through the haze of the autumn afternoon, he first saw the city as an unlovely hodgepodge of frame and brick buildings jutting above the flat coastal plain. Drawing closer, he saw single-story adobes, tan or brown, spread around the central district. To the northeast of town, beyond the river, the land rose in a series of low plateaus. Distant white cottages, tiny as dollhouses, marked other subdivisions. Behind it all was the breathtaking loom of the San Gabriels.

He nudged his mule, which he'd named Railroad, and the old beast dutifully jogged a little faster. Mack felt himself an experienced, not to say worldly-wise Californian.

He was twenty years old.

The citizens of San Francisco scorned Los Angeles as a primitive cow town, and there was something to be said for that. Almost immediately, Mack found himself pushing against an oncoming herd of cattle and the fierce-looking *vaqueros* driving them. Next he came on a spring wagon with a rear wheel mired in a black hole that gave off a tarry stench. A burly citizen stepped in the black ooze in order to push the wheel with his shoulder.

"Goddamn *brea*. Why don't they fill these holes?"

"*Brea,*" Mack said. What was it? Did it have value? He tucked the word away in memory. He'd seen other tarry holes in the area, he recalled.

Starting at the outskirts, there was evidence of frenzied real estate activity. Mack saw signs nailed on fence posts, jutting up in weed patches, crudely painted on adobe walls.

SUBURBAN EXCURSIONS!
LOTS! LOTS!! LOTS!!!
CORNER LOTS—INSIDE LOTS!

Agents pleaded for immediate attention and promised affordable El Dorados and Xanadus in mystical, musical-sounding places—Santa Monica, South Pasadena, Monrovia, Riverside.

Bemused by this excessive promotion, he soon arrived on Los Angeles Street, an ugly thoroughfare flanked by uglier commission warehouses where farmers were unloading produce wagons. He turned left one block to a parallel street, the main business artery, named, with scant imagination, Main Street.

It was a street of jarring contrasts. Men in cowman's garb told time from two elaborately modern clock towers in the business district. Chinese people scurried on errands, and Mexican women walked sedately, their heads covered by black shawls. There was a great deal of horse and wagon traffic, every sort of conveyance, from buckboards to two-wheeled ox-drawn *carretas*. He saw horsecars on the tracks in the middle of the street, kerosene lights, and silk dresses, and many more side arms, worn openly, than he'd ever seen up north.

Most evident and visible, however, were the tourists: men, women, and children of every age and physical type, easily spotted by their excited expressions, pale faces, and dark, heavy clothing. They rode in bunting-draped wagons, haggled at storefronts advertising real estate, sat on their luggage outside the St. Charles Hotel contemplating its NO VACANCY sign. The tourists reminded Mack of the people he'd met on his walk through the states of the Midwest. Their numbers astounded him.

At the corner of Main and the town plaza, he passed an imposing three-story stucco hotel with rows of tall arches fronting both sides of its corner site. Two stone pediments, one overlooking each street, proclaimed it the PICO HOUSE.

In the plaza he dismounted and drank from a trickling fountain under the shade of a cypress. Suddenly four distant gunshots disturbed the afternoon, and there was a sound of horses galloping away. Railroad perked up his ears, but no one else paid much attention. An unseen guitarist resumed his music.

A hooting train whistle lured Mack past an unprepossessing chapel with a bell tower, the Church of Nuestra Señora la Reina de los Angeles, to the railway depot. An SP passenger train was arriving, spouting smoke from its beehive stack and steam

153

from under its cars. Pop-eyed visitors leaned from the windows, pointing, exclaiming, inhaling the air.

A ratty youth ran along the train waving a placard on a stick: REAL ESTATE OPPORTUNITIES! "Right here, folks," the tout called. "Talk to me first."

Mack was encouraged. "Looks like the boom's still on, doesn't it?" he said to Railroad.

The mule was anxious to please, but couldn't manage a reply.

On his way back to the plaza, Mack noticed more touts accosting tourists. And real estate offices crammed into the most unlikely locations: ground-floor rooms partitioned by blankets, shanties, even a covered wagon. Surely, with all this promotional frenzy, he should be able to make some money.

At the Pico House, he watched the arrival of a six-horse stage covered with desert dust. While porters unloaded luggage, he slipped inside and discovered a central court with a splashing fountain, banks of fresh flowers, and caged birds twittering. Guests coming and going tipped their hats or paused to greet a distinguished man of eighty or more who sat in an alcove that suggested a place of honor. The man was burly, square-headed, with bronzed skin and pure white hair cropped close. Despite the warm day he wore a frilled shirt, large cravat, and an old coatee with velvet collar and cuffs. Mack counted six silver finger rings of varying design. The old man had an air of dignity and power, his face reminding Mack of a schoolbook engraving of Victor Hugo. To each person who addressed him, the man replied courteously and gravely in Spanish.

A porter bore down. "No loitering here."

"That's no way to treat a stranger," said a gentleman on his way out of the hotel. The man was slim as a reed and swarthy, with a Mongol mustache and snapping dark eyes. He wore a frock coat and flat hat, and carried a pile of legal documents. The porter scowled and left.

"Lo más justo y honrado," the stranger said with a nod at the white-haired man.

"The just and—what?" Mack said, following him toward the street. "My Spanish isn't that good yet."

"The most just and honest man. Pío Pico, the last Mexican governor of California. He's a revered figure. He built this hotel. Unfortunately he managed his investments poorly. He no longer owns it, but everyone pretends he does."

They reached the outdoor arcade beneath the arches, and

154

Mack untied his mount. "Fine-looking mule," the stranger said. "What's his name?"

"Railroad. I named him that because he gives a better ride than the SP, his price is fair, and you never have to worry about him cheating you."

The stranger laughed. "You have a nice sense of humor, sir."

Mack hadn't thought about it, but he guessed it was coming back after his bad time in the City.

"You're a newcomer," the man added.

"I am."

"We have many. When I came up to Los Angeles five years ago from the state of Durango, the town had a population of twelve or thirteen thousand. Last summer, perhaps fifty-five or sixty thousand, a good two thousand of them Escrow Indians."

"Escrow what?"

"It's the local name for real estate promoters and developers. A greedy and ruthless tribe, the Escrows," he said, flashing another smile. "They lie in wait for the unwary visitor, incited by our civic boosters such as Colonel Otis of the *Times* newspaper, who yearns to give our town some of the luster and prosperity of San Francisco. Three to five excursion trains cross the border into California every day. Very good for the Escrows, very bad for the rest of us who live here. However, it won't last. Too much of everything inevitably bursts the bubble. It's already starting to happen."

"The town looks crowded."

"Nothing compared to '87. That was the peak. Come, I'll show you."

What he showed was an Escrow Indian's notice board, with prices and locations erased and reerased so that the latest postings seemed to peep from a chalky cloud.

LOVELY SALOON-FREE
ONTARIO!
VILLA ACRES CUT TO $125
HORTICULTURAL LOTS SLASHED TO $95
OTHER DRASTIC REDUCTIONS IN
MONROVIA—ALOSTA—GARWANZA—
SYCAMORE GROVE
INQUIRE HERE!

Mack's earlier optimism began to wane. "Are there jobs?"

"Again, not so many as last year."

"I know a local promoter who might have something. He

told me to look him up if I ever got here. His name is Wyatt Paul.''

"I've heard of him: The northern part of the county . . . ? I'm not sure. I'm a lawyer, but I don't do all that much real estate. I can take you to the office of someone with better information.''

"That's kind of you.''

"De nada," the lawyer shrugged. "Not all Angelenos hate the tourists, you must understand. Most of us here were tourists once.''

The lawyer led Mack back along Main Street, past the commercial blocks to a section less prosperous. "Here we are.''

Mack peered into a long, narrow sales office, dusty and full of shadows. On a plank counter, show cards and untidy piles of pamphlets competed for the attention of customers. Above the door, a sign with a gorgeous golden sun rising over a pyramid of oranges identified SOUTHWOOD'S SO-CAL REAL ESTATE.

"If you ever need legal services, call on me." the lawyer said, offering a card. "Enrique Potter. In the Baker Block, Main and Acadia.''

"Macklin Chance. Thank you. I'll need a lawyer one day. I'm going to make money here.''

Potter gave him an appraising look. "I believe you, sir." He tipped his hat and excused himself, citing business at the courthouse on nearby Spring Street.

Mack's stomach was snarling. He took a piece of biscuit from a saddlebag he'd improvised from a burlap sack. While he wolfed it he examined the flyblown window. Various pieces of paper had been pasted up helter-skelter, until not one inch of clear glass remained. Suddenly, from all the gaudy clutter, one advertisement leaped out.

A handbill, black type on orange stock. The headline promised A FREE RIDE AND A FREE LUNCH! TRIPS DAILY BY EXPRESS RAIL AND COMFORTABLE COACH! ABSOLUTELY NO OBLIGATION! What arrested him was the illustration, an engraving of an impressive gateway arch, crowned by a huge sun with flaring arms. Between the scrolled top and bottom of the arch, cutout letters proclaimed the name.

SAN SOLARO
"THE CITY OF HEALTH"

He'd found the man he rescued in the mountains.

* * *

He dashed inside, rousing the real estate agent from contemplation of a peeling wall. The agent rocketed to the counter, shooting his hand over.

"How do you do, Southwood's my name, Newton Southwood, Swifty to my friends. See Swifty for the fastest deals in— Oh."

He saw Mack more clearly—the length of his hair, the poverty of his wardrobe, his youth. The agent smoothed the part in his oiled hair. He was a sleek Escrow brave, with canny darting eyes.

"I'm interested in a real estate development," Mack said.

"We got sixty-five, seventy of those platted around here. On the ocean, down south, up in the hills—you can take your pick. If you got any money," he added with a suspicious eye.

Mack pointed to the San Solaro handbill. "That's the one— The City of Health."

"Out in the Santa Clarita Valley. The excursion only leaves in the morning. You take the SP local to Newhall, then a wagon. The developer picks up the thirty-five-cent round-trip rail fare."

"In the window it says you go by express train and a comfortable coach."

Southwood handed Mack a pamphlet with the arch on the front. "Developers say a lot of things. Where you from?"

"Not here." Mack disliked Mr. Swifty Southwood.

"In Los Angeles you can say that about damn near everybody but the Injuns and the greasers up in the Sonora barrio. Me, I came out from Cleveland two years ago. I'm not making the money I expected to make." He gestured to the array of posters and literature. Mack saw more boxes of material piled all the way to the rear of the shotgun office.

"Pie's cut too thin. Too many offerings. It's the same all up and down the coast, here to San Diego. The railroads cut fares too far. They hired too many hacks to write books. We get the lookers but not the buyers." Mack obviously belonged to the former class. "You got to excuse me."

He trudged back to his desk to resume whatever Escrow Indians did when they had no victims to waylay.

"Are there any cheap restaurants here?" Mack asked a gentleman in a white sombrero and string tie.

"How should I know? I'm from Wisconsin."

He asked several other people and was finally directed to a noxious little slum near the plaza, bluntly referred to as Nigger Alley. There he saw mostly villainous-looking white derelicts, cowboys, and a few ragged *mestizos*.

157

He had a dollar left. At a cantina he bought a plate of beans and a glass of clear, hot tequila, a drink he'd sampled before and liked. He sat in a corner reading Wyatt Paul's pamphlet. It promised marvelous amenities in San Solaro, a new town founded on the benefits of Southern California's healthful climate.

Persons suffering from almost any medical malady will find San Solaro a useful aid in restoring them to health. The overworked and overworried soon regain their lost energy and equilibrium. Consumptives declared past all help have come here and in a few weeks have shaken off that eastern ice-born curse. Our valley is safe for anyone whose heart condition might be threatened at higher altitude. In short, we may assert that death here is a remarkable event. Any physician depending on his practice will soon starve to death!

On succeeding pages, one engraving depicted a street flanked by buildings taller and more substantial than most in Los Angeles, and others showed model cottages, orange groves, a steam packet docked at a pier in a broad stream. Mack was amazed.

Twenty cents bought him a place in a stable loft, and a stall and a feedbag for Railroad. In the morning he purchased a ticket on the 8 A.M. SP local bound north to Santa Barbara and intermediate points. He could hardly wait to see the new town of San Solaro.

17 "I DON'T BELIEVE THIS," MACK WHISPERED. HE RE-called Swifty Southwood's remark: "Developers say a lot of things."

He stood beneath the gateway arch, which was black wrought iron, huge, and splendid. The great sunburst dominated, powerful and faintly menacing, like some primitive icon. The arch was exactly as the pamphlet showed it.

Nothing else was. The arch opened on a large tract of dry, treeless land at the head of a small valley. Flanking the valley were steep hillsides with the characteristic parched golden hue of the dry season. A rutted wagon road ran through the property, and beyond the arch, cardboard nailed to a stick identified the road: GRANDE BOULEVARD DE SAN SOLARO.

Sweat ran down Mack's neck. The temperature was ninety or better. Hot gritty wind rattled the boulevard sign. He walked through the arch and noted similar signs all over the tract, which appeared to run to the far end of the valley, where the golden hills converged. The signs within reading distance made profligate use of words such as *Royal, Imperial, Elysian, Paradise.* Flagged stakes marked out the building lots. Other large signs on certain parcels identified the SAN SOLARO OPERA HOUSE; W. J. PAUL COMMERCIAL BLOCK; SANITARIUM AND HEALTH SPA; PROPOSED SITE OF 100-ROOM LUXURY HOTEL. There were no cottages, no buildings save one, farther down the main road, a single-story structure of unpainted wood with trusses framed in above and a partially finished roof.

The hot wind blew in gusts, snapping the brave yellow, red, and blue marker flags. Along Grande Boulevard Mack saw five lots tagged as sold. He turned down a cross street, following an arrow pointing to SAN SOLARO CANAL. This proved to be a wide and shallow creek bed. The mud in the bottom was hard from days of baking in the sun.

Mack walked along the bank until he reached the site of the FUTURE BOAT DOCK. Not a little depressed, he gazed down the parched watercourse, following it as it twisted and disappeared in the folds of the hills. He was seized by a strong urge to leave. Only his desperate need for work held him.

He cut back to the boulevard and the raw wooden building. A painted board on the end proclaimed RAILWAY DEPOT. No rails could be seen. Near the door hung a sign identifying it as the TEMPORARY SALES OFFICE. He stepped up on the depot platform and raised his hand to knock.

Music startled him—low belches of a tuba, a cornetist practicing a run. He stepped past the end of the building and saw, about fifty feet distant, an open-sided circus tent of heavily soiled yellow-and-white striped canvas. FREE LUNCH HERE!!

Inside, a stooped woman with gray hair pottered behind trestle tables, where cheesecloth covers protected the food. Mack saw wooden beer kegs, galvanized tubs for ice, and a row of glass pitchers waiting to be filled. Four men in garish scarlet uniforms heavy with gold braid sat on rickety, wooden chairs, one reading a magazine, one smoking a cigar, and two tuning up.

The bald cornetist noticed Mack and returned his stare. Despite all, the audacity of this outlay—the pretense that something existed when it didn't—brought a grudging smile. He knocked on the depot door and said, "Wyatt Paul?"

From the desk against the wall of the waiting room, Wyatt stared at his visitor with annoyance and no recognition. He wore white duck pants and a white shirt, sleeves rolled up, the pale color dramatizing his dark skin. His bright-blue eyes struggled with memories and at last found the right one.

"Chance. Mack Chance. My benefactor from the Sierras." He jumped up. "How the devil did you get here?"

"Took the local to Newhall and walked."

"That's four miles. Oh, but I forgot—you walked from Pennsylvania. But what about San Francisco? Didn't you get there?"

"Things didn't work out. Too many closed doors."

"I warned you."

"You did. You also said that if I got to Los Angeles, I should look you up."

"Sure, certainly—I don't know what to say—I'm still astonished. But glad to see you. Yes indeed. Here, take a chair."

He threw a stack of pamphlets into a nearby crate and brushed off the dusty seat. Then he sat down again, and Mack took his chair a little nervously. Wyatt Paul was handsome as ever, yet there was a rasp to his breathing. Maybe he needed the healthful climate more than any of his prospects did.

"You managed to find your land—"

"Eighteen hundred acres. All the way up the valley. It was a distress sale. I got a bargain." Even so, Mack wondered how a penniless traveler stealing rides on freight trains had come up with the necessary funds.

"It's impressive." He could think of nothing more positive.

"Not yet, but you wait," Wyatt said with enthusiasm. The cornet player ran up the scale, shrill bright sounds. A profusion of site plans, conceptual cottage sketches, and sales documents were tacked up all over the walls. Directly behind Wyatt hung an artist's drawing of fruit-laden trees crowding a hillside. FUTURE CITRUS GROVES—TOWN OF SAN SOLARO.

Wyatt leaned back and ran both hands over the temples of his black hair. "Are you in this part of the world permanently now?"

"I'm here for a while. I'm going back to San Francisco after I make some money. You said I should come around if I ever needed work . . ."

The last word raised a wall in Wyatt's eyes. He picked up a

pen and studied the nib blackened with dried ink. "So I did. Trouble is, right now I have all the people I need."

Mack grasped the arms of his chair, prepared to rise. "Then I'd better—"

"No, sit right there—let me think. We'll work out something. I'm making money here." He swept his hand in a curve that embraced all the visionary plans and drawings on the unfinished pine walls. "Big money."

That sounded the first genuinely wrong note. Through the depot's open ticket window, Mack could see a large adjoining room with a small iron stove, and a skillet full of souring grease. An unmade bed was in the corner, a block of wood propping one leg.

Wyatt saw him staring and instantly jumped up and yanked down the milky glass ticket window. A trick of the light put that strange opal blaze in his eyes for a moment.

Mack wondered if he really wanted to stay. Then he thought of probable alternatives in Los Angeles: unloading produce, sweeping someone's sidewalk. Here there was nothing but parched earth and treeless lots—for the moment. There might be money to be made in the future. He'd stay if he could.

Wyatt clapped Mack's shoulder now, having recovered his good humor. "I've sold thirty-nine lots so far. Today's load of prospects is due around noon. I have a greaser kid who collects them from the hotels and agencies in town, rides with them on the nine-thirty local, and drives them from Newhall in our wagon. Come on, I'll show you around till they get here."

Mack nodded, then noticed one of the pamphlets in the crate. It wasn't the same piece of literature he'd picked up in town. "May I have one?"

"Absolutely, old friend," Wyatt said with high enthusiasm. "I'm beginning to have a very good feeling about this reunion."

Outside the sales office Mack examined the pamphlet.

MIRACLES OF THE CALIFORNIA CLIMATE
AMAZING BENEFITS AND CURES
IN "THE CITY OF HEALTH"

On the cover, the artist-engraver had repeated the gateway arch, but in this version, a radiant sun peeped over the hill behind. A healthy family of four stood beneath the arch, admiring the vista.

They began walking toward the head of the valley. Mack

161

scanned the inside of the pamphlet. His mouth fell open and then he laughed aloud.

"Catch your fancy, does it?" Wyatt asked.

"Well, it—Wyatt, you're promising that the climate in your town will cure everything from nerves and dyspepsia to the fantods and marital disorders."

"Right. I decided to leave out cancer."

"What about these photographs? Where did you get this one? You look like you're ready for the grave."

Mack pointed to a matching pair of stiff portraits. In the right-hand one, "After," Wyatt looked normal, but the "Before" shot depicted him with deep, dark eye sockets and wasted cheeks above a beard longer than a Civil War general's.

"An artist in town doctored that one for me. I told him to make me look as bad as possible."

"It says California completely cured your consumption. I didn't know you had consumption."

Wyatt laughed as they cut past the end of the tent. Neither the woman nor the four bandsmen gave their employer friendly looks or a greeting. In fact they were all sullen.

They walked along Grande Boulevard. "I noticed you're going to build a sanitarium."

"Absolutely. Have to have one to attract the one-lung crowd. That's why I faked the picture."

Ahead, on the hillside to their left, Mack saw a cluster of half a dozen twenty-foot trees with globular orange fruit. They looked decidedly peculiar, their leaves high above the ground and clustered at the ends of thick branches.

Wyatt spoke in a reflective way. "Mack, I owe you a considerable debt. So I'd like to find a place for you. But if I do, you'll have to understand how things work. Easterners come out here with their noses dripping snot, their lungs sloshing with blood, their bowels stopped up with glue, their cocks dead since last Fourth of July, their cunts full of cobwebs and fairly quivering for a second coming. One drink from the California grail, they think—one drink. Bang! A fucking miracle."

Mack's smile hardened in place and his skin crawled.

Wyatt gestured in that grand way of his. "They step off the train. The sun dazzles them. The balmy air. They're in a beautiful daze. They see what they want to see—a warm, bright place, free from sickness, away from the cold—where anything's possible—even the redemption of their corrupt white flesh . . ."

His gaze fixed on thunderheads in a sky whiting out with heat haze. Mack saw the opal flash of his eyes.

"I hated my parents, but I learned something useful from them, stupid as they were. My mother taught me there are always fools panting after miraculous cures. And you remember my talking about my old man?"

"That he tried real estate, and failed—yes."

"Two things whipped him: a conscience, and too many laws hemming him in. I don't think I was ever bothered with a conscience, and out here I don't have to bother with laws. That's the beauty of California: the freedom. That's the lure. That's why we're all here."

"Wyatt, there are plenty of laws in California."

"I'm not talking about the petty stuff. A legal hack in Newhall handles that for me. I'm talking about forgetting higher laws. Thou shalt not deceive thy prospects. Thou shalt not cheat, thereby remaining poor. Higher laws," he repeated, with such charming good cheer that Mack was almost persuaded that what he said was perfectly all right.

Almost.

"Anyway, my prospects deceive themselves. They've read Charley Nordhoff's book or the SP advertising in their railway depot back home. They *know* that they're going to live better—feel better—in California. I just say to them, 'Certainly, help yourself to the miracles.' Even if they are manufactured."

With a merry expression, he crooked a finger, summoning Mack to a path leading up the nearby hill. He lifted a rope hung with KEEP OUT signs. They ducked under and scrambled up the slope.

"Still carry a clasp knife?"

Mack handed it to him. Wyatt reached to a high branch of the nearest tree and cut through twine. An orange dropped from the twisted tree limb. Every orange was hung that way, on all the trees.

"The pride of the South," Wyatt said, balancing it aloft on his fingertips. "The California navel." He tossed it to Mack. "These are Joshua trees from the Mojave. The trick isn't original with me; I picked it up from a developer down in Riverside, where you find the real groves. I keep that rope up, and I keep the prospects down on the boulevard, and it works." He clapped his hands and flung them over his head. "Miracles. Goddamn miracles!"

Mack was alternately fascinated and repelled. He didn't know what to say. Music saved him, a snare drum and the horns, striking up a march. Wyatt shielded his eyes.

Dust boiled around the gateway arch. From the tan haze a

large wagon emerged, rigged with a canvas top on poles. Someone with a dark face under a straw hat drove the wagon.

"That's the crowd from the nine-thirty local." He counted aloud. Two men, three women, plus a couple of youngsters seated on the wagon floor. "Shit. I should get rid of that kid who rounds 'em up. Too young. No push. Besides, he's a greaser. Porters and waiters in the good hotels won't give him the time of— Wait a minute." He snapped his fingers and pointed at Mack like a prosecutor. "You know how to drive a wagon, don't you?"

Wyatt conducted the prospects on a walking tour and Mack trailed along behind, admiring the performance. Wyatt had a fine command of words and the persuasive, emotion-charged delivery of a preacher. The group was cross from the heat and dust of the trip, but Wyatt's jokes and line of chatter soon charmed them out of that—all except one.

Soder and Edna Erickson hailed from Minnesota. The two young girls, one shy and silent, the other maddeningly forward and noisy, belonged to them. Soder Erickson said he raised corn. He was overweight, red-faced, and perspiring, but he refused to remove his heavy coat of black alpaca, and he greeted Wyatt's every claim with a suspicious mutter or a sideways sneer at Edna. Mack felt uneasy.

There were also a Mr. and Mrs. Cato Purvis, Danville, Illinois, colorless people traveling with the wife's equally drab sister.

The baking white sky seemed to generate hellish heat, and Wyatt's face glistened as though washed in oil. The children complained, the ladies fanned themselves with hankies, but nothing diminished Wyatt's energy. He only stopped his sales talk when someone asked a question.

". . . in answer to that, Mr. Purvis, yes, the prime lots are going fast. I sold four yesterday. But I can show you a couple of beauties up here at the town square. A hundred and fifty dollars each—and each lot comes with full water rights."

Soder Erickson swabbed his sweaty triple chin with a bandanna. "What water?"

Wife Edna clucked. "Now, Soder, we accepted Mr. Paul's hospitality, we mustn't be rude."

"What is rude? In Norway, where I was born, a question is a question, water is water. I don't see any water."

"And it's a good question," Wyatt said. "A very good question, sir. I like astute customers." Of course he didn't, and Mack saw that behind the clenched smile, heard it beneath the

164

forced friendliness. "Step this way and I'll show you the answer."

They straggled down a cross street toward the dry watercourse. The obnoxious daughter pulled up one of the lot stakes. "Please put that back," Wyatt said. Edna Erickson had to reprimand the brat before she would obey.

"At present," Wyatt went on, "this property is served by a water well. Not adequate for a town, of course. The town's supply will flow in here, through the San Solaro Canal." His sweeping hand painted a rushing blue torrent in the air. "Each individual lot will be irrigated by a *zanja*, one of those highly efficient wooden ditches you see throughout the Los Angeles basin. The San Solaro Development Company intends to widen and deepen this channel to assure every owner a full and constant supply of fresh pure water for household and agricultural use."

Mack stood back, smiling despite himself. My, how it flowed: the charm, the persuasion, the invisible water . . .

Soder Erickson folded his arms. "I ask you again, Paul. Where does this water come from?"

"Why, sir, from the greatest free supply of water on the continent." He raised his hands to embrace the hills. "The rains from the mountains, delivered to us by nature's dependable force of gravity."

"You say that's how it's going to be. I see how it is right now. No water."

Wyatt gritted out his reply. "Of course not. Technically this is still summer. The rains don't fall in California until the winter months. We are building reservoirs."

"Show me."

"I'll show you the blueprints. Construction has not yet started. By next year, however, the first one will be finished, along with our primary irrigation system."

"How do I know?"

Wyatt stared him down, ice in his smile. "You have my personal assurance, Mr. Erickson. My pledge and my promise." Erickson's snort declared his opinion of that. "I'll also be happy to put it as a rider in your sales contract."

"Won't be any contract. I'm not buying anything."

"Oh, Soder, I like this pretty little valley," his wife said. "Can't we at least consider—"

"No."

Everyone else remained silent, embarrassed by the enmity in the air. The walking tour continued, the prospects now subdued.

At a spot near the rope with the KEEP OUT signs, the obnoxious little girl exclaimed, "Mama, look. Real orange trees." She dashed toward the rope. Wyatt shot out a hand to hold her back.

"Orange trees are delicate, miss. You must obey the signs."

Soder Erickson pulled his daughter away from Wyatt. "I've never seen an orange tree close up." His stare challenged Wyatt to restrain him. Mack thought, *This is getting bad.*

"You'll see hundreds soon, Mr. Erickson. The San Solaro groves will be a source of beauty and natural wealth for all those who live here."

"Soon? I thought it took five, six, seven years for an orange tree to bear. What kind of tricks are you pulling? I'm going up to see those trees."

Wyatt stepped in front and pushed him back. "Listen, pilgrim, I told you . . ."

Erickson snarled and scuffled with him, while his wife clutched the girls against her skirt. Mack saw the bursting rage in Wyatt's eyes and ran between the men.

His pale shadow fell across Erickson's face. The farmer blinked, startled. Mack gave him a friendly clap on the shoulder and a sunny smile.

"Look, sir. Any good town has rules for the citizens. San Solaro has rules, and one of them is this: No one, resident or visitor, disturbs the orange trees. That's clear and fair, isn't it?"

"What's clear is that this whole operation is a damned fraud, and I'm wasting my time. When does the wagon leave?"

Wyatt shouted, "When I say so."

"Wyatt," Mack began, turning to him, away from the others, trying to calm him with grimaces of warning. He heard Erickson's wife pleading, Erickson saying, "No, no," the obnoxious girl whining. Finally, Soder Erickson stumped away up the street. His family followed, and then the confused and embarrassed Purvises. Wyatt watched them, trembling so hard it scared Mack.

"Goddamn that fat fucker—"

"Wyatt, stop. Calm down. Let me take care of it. Stay here. Stay right here."

Wyatt seemed too overwrought to do anything else. He dragged a handkerchief from his pocket and rubbed at the sweat on his face. His eyes remained on Erickson. They were venomous.

Mack dashed after the prospects. Band music drifted through

the still air and he exhaled, relieved. He spread his arms like a shepherd behind a flock.

"That music means they have the buffet ready, ladies and gentlemen. You'll be more comfortable back at the tent, in the shade. There are cold drinks too. Please step right along."

Obediently, the Purvis trio shuffled in the direction Mack suggested. Edna Erickson clutched her husband's arm to restrain further outbursts. When their obnoxious daughter whined that she wanted sweets, he yelled, "Be quiet or I'll tan you."

Mack let them get well started and then turned back to Wyatt, who stood at a corner with an air of embittered defeat. He was no longer trembling, Mack was happy to see.

"Thanks for that," Wyatt said.

"I had to prove that I could be of some use when you hire me."

Wyatt managed a smile. "*When.* You're pretty certain."

"You need a helper. I need work. Come on now, you have to stay with those people till they leave."

Wyatt started to argue but changed his mind. Apparently his crazy violent mood had passed. He fell in step. "Wasted effort. I won't sell anything today. One bad apple sours the whole basket. I'd like to kill that sneering son of a bitch."

Mack shot a quick sideways look at Wyatt Paul. He sounded ready to do it.

Moths flew through the open window of the depot's back room and fluttered at the chimneys of two feeble kerosene lamps. Wyatt picked up a pork chop from his plate and gnawed at it. Mack put a boot heel on the scarred table and gazed at the lamps. Out in the dark hills, wild dogs barked.

"Wyatt, how are you going to get gas illumination out here?"

"I don't know yet."

"How will you get the water in?"

"I don't know. Hire an expert. A *zanjero*—a water commissioner. Do you want to be the commissioner? What the hell does it matter? Even if no town is ever built, anyone who buys a lot in San Solaro is making a prime investment. Land is always a prime investment."

"Granted. But you're selling a town. On promises."

"I can take you to a dozen tracts doing exactly the same thing. What brought you to California? Promises."

Wyatt gnawed the last meat off the pork-chop bone. "You're a damn good cook." He tossed the bone on the stained plank floor. Then he picked up a lamp and prowled past the ticket window into the office half. As soon as Wyatt's back was

167

turned, Mack threw the bone out the window. Then he walked into the other room. Wyatt had just finished inking his pen, and now turned to a sheet on the wall headed DAILY SALES. He scratched a large zero in the box under the day's date. Single digits filled a few other boxes.

Suddenly Wyatt stabbed the pen into the tally sheet, tearing and spotting the paper with ink. Mack held his breath.

"Might have closed that Purvis couple. Erickson bastard ruined it."

Mack said nothing. Wyatt stalked to the open door and leaned there against his raised forearm, staring out at the night. Mack tried to lower the emotional temperature by sitting again and putting his feet up. "I wouldn't take it so hard. I don't think the Purvises were enthusiastic. I heard in town that people aren't buying the way they were last year."

"That's right. Competition's fierce. You have to work and scheme that much harder." Wyatt came back and found a bottle of red wine in a desk drawer. He held it out to Mack, who shook his head. Wyatt uncorked the bottle and took three long swallows.

"Let's talk business," he said then. "You could be a big help to me. Having another honest face out front is important. And sometimes my temper gets away from me. It did today. You stepped in, and if that farmer hadn't been such a complete shit, we might have closed the Purvises. So I'd like to hire you. But there are considerations. Every sale on that tally sheet involves a contract. In other words, the cash down payments are small. Sometimes no more than five percent. That money gets eaten up by overhead—the food, the musicians, thirty-five cents a head on the train. What I'm saying is, I can't afford to pay you a salary."

"I don't work for nothing, Wyatt. Never have, never will."

"I don't expect you to work for nothing. I'm just telling you a salary's out of the question." He paused, whether to think or induce a response, a concession, Mack wasn't sure. Wyatt's brilliant blue eyes were as blank as a newborn's. Grease glistened on his delicate, almost girlish mouth. Mack waited him out.

"I'll give you an equity position in San Solaro, an interest in all unsold lots, common property, everything."

Mack fought to hide his excitement. This was a big step—a huge step. And unexpected. "What kind of position? What percent?"

Another prolonged pause. Wyatt toyed with one of his bushy eyebrows. "Twenty."

"With full water rights?"

He could see Wyatt thinking that over. Mack struggled to keep a straight face. His eyes gave it away. Wyatt's laughter boomed.

"Damn right. I hereby appoint you water commissioner of San Solaro." He uncorked the bottle and drank again. "How do you feel about living in a tent, commissioner? Best I can offer."

"It's no problem. I like the outdoors."

Wyatt's chameleon face changed again. The blue eyes became like a child's, guileless. But Mack now understood that it was deliberate, a protective ruse.

"If I give you a stake in this place, I want to be sure you stick around a while. I don't know you very well yet so I think we need something on paper. I'll write up a little agreement that says if you no longer work here, I'm entitled to buy back your equity for a dollar and you have nothing to say about it."

Mack played Wyatt's game, waiting a moment. "An agreement like that should work two ways."

That surprised Wyatt. "You mean that if I leave, I forfeit—?" This time his laugh was derisive. "Not likely. Not damn likely." Grudging respect flickered on his face. "But if those are your terms . . ."

Mack looked at him steadily. "Yes."

"All right." Wyatt held out his hand. "Deal."

They shook. Wyatt pushed the wine bottle at him. This time Mack drank, sparingly, of the heavy, acidic wine. Wyatt slugged away the rest and brushed his palms back over his sleek shining temples. "I'll have the hack in Newhall draw up the paper. In the meantime— What is it?"

Mack had bent over, spying something white under the corner of the desk. It was a woman's handkerchief, fine linen and lace, smelling faintly of lemon. "One of the prospects leave this?"

Wyatt took the handkerchief with a sly smile. "It belongs to a lady I met this summer. Now and then she drives over from her ranch on the Santa Clara. Ventura County. Wish I wasn't so damn busy with this place—I'd see her more often." He tucked the handkerchief in a drawer. "She usually comes for supper and spends the night. Never thought I'd meet a woman who could keep up with me in bed, but I have."

Mack laughed in a good-natured way, though Wyatt's boast made him feel a keen loneliness for Nellie. "You were about to say something—'in the meantime'?"

"Yes. While the hack draws up our agreement, you can start

169

learning how things are done in The City of Health. First lesson: The suckers don't fall off the trees. We've got to reach up and pluck 'em. In Los Angeles. From now on, that's your primary job. I fired the greaser kid after he got back from depositing our guests at Newhall.''

"But I wasn't hired yet."

Again Wyatt laughed. He tilted his head and touched Mack's arm. Mack could feel some invisible apparatus switch on.

"I knew you'd say yes. People do what I want."

"Erickson didn't. What if I said no?"

"You wouldn't, because that would make me angry. Very angry."

He was still smiling.

They pulled a canvas tent from a storage shed and, working by lantern light, set it up on a lot beside the dry streambed. The tent was large and comfortable, and Wyatt located some blankets for Mack to use until they could buy a cot. Mack asked to borrow paper and pen. Around midnight, he wrote a long letter to Nellie. He found himself describing Wyatt.

He's crooked, though I suppose no more so than the other "Escrow Indians." He's wily, and nervy, and he can charm almost anyone. But he isn't straight. I mean in his head. I don't really understand him, but I recognize a bad, dangerous combination—no conscience, and a temper like a flask of nitro. A lot worse than mine.

I want to make money. A lot of money. But my pa raised me to believe a man has to give thought not only to what he does but how he does it. I don't feel altogether good about what I've got myself into . . .

He signed it "Yrs. affectionately" and settled down to uneasy sleep while the wild dogs barked.

18 THE WOMAN WHO PREPARED THE FREE LUNCHES found Mack a serviceable suit of dark-brown broadcloth. Wyatt told him how the Mexican boy had operated in town, gave him $10 cash for bribes, and put him on his own. Mack's first three trips into Los Angeles yielded no pros-

pects. When he returned empty-handed the second time, Wyatt had already started drinking—it was not yet noon—and cursed him like a deranged man. Mack turned and left.

About the only thing he accomplished on those early trips was bringing Railroad from town on one of them. The ride took almost all day, but it presented some interesting sights. Up a steep-sided canyon near Newhall, he spied a rickety oil derrick. He followed the canyon a short distance and found three more, their little steam engines chuffing away. He knew of the oil bonanza in Titusville, Pennsylvania, of course, but he wasn't aware of similar drilling out here. Another item to file away.

He asked Wyatt about the derricks.

"They've been hauling that tar out of Pico Canyon for years. Reason I know is, the old still's near Newhall. It was a scheme of General Andreas Pico and his brother, the governor. Lamp oil, medicine oil, axle grease—you see how successful that was, don't you? Pío Pico's a pauper. People with money to waste have drilled wells near here, but there's nothing in them but sand, water, and grief. Forget it."

By the start of his third week Mack was acquainted with town. He introduced himself to some of the agents and called on Southwood again. He familiarized himself with the commercial hotels and those working there who could be paid off for leads.

On one of his train trips he fell into conversation with a man who knew something about oil. The man expanded on what Wyatt said. Yes, there were wells throughout this part of Southern California—Tar Canyon, Sespe Canyon, Ojai—some drilled for practically nothing by the old Chinese spring-pole method. Lyman Stewart, a wildcatter from Titusville, was pumping oil from Star No. 1 in Pico Canyon, and early in the year he and his partner had brought in a genuine gusher, Adams Canyon No. 16, above Santa Paula, over in Ventura County. The well produced five hundred barrels a day, but Stewart and his partner had yet to see a substantial profit. Many failures canceled out the occasional success. And if the oil business was chancy everywhere, it was more so in Southern California. The man explained that the geology of the region, the underground faults and rock formations, ran every which way, making drilling more difficult than in the East. A strike was virtually a matter of blind luck.

It was something to keep in mind.

* * *

Autumn was settling on Los Angeles. Days were still warm but the evenings cooled, and the sun fell toward the Pacific a little earlier each afternoon. There were a few prospects, but the supply was definitely drying up. A baggage man at the depot reported some trains completely empty of visitors. On a siding, Mack saw an excursion flatcar decorated with flags and bunting, the kind used to haul prospects out to remote tracts. The car had been standing unused for a week.

Still, he was determined and willing to work long hours—to exhaustion, if need be. On Wednesday of the third week, he caught a 5 A.M. train for town and went first to the Pico House.

In the busy lobby, he noticed that the double doors of the banquet room were open. Waiters were clearing breakfast dishes for a sizable crowd of well-dressed men. He looked in the door, thinking that his contact, Reilley, might be working in there. On the dais under a banner reading PROMOTE A GREATER LOS ANGELES, a man in military blue decorated with shoulder straps and medals addressed the gathering. He was about fifty, with a gray soup-strainer mustache and imperial. As he spoke, he beat the podium with his fist or chopped the air with slashing saber strokes, fairly radiating energy and spleen. Curious, Mack lounged in the doorway and listened.

". . . the boom is clearly over, my good friends. While we may not care to admit that in public, it is a fact. Our enemy, an economic slump, is advancing to overwhelm us. What, then, should be our strategy?"

Glancing around the meeting room, Mack spied Reilley, a burly Irishman with thick spectacles, carrying a tray of dishes. Reilley caught Mack's signal and nodded before he vanished in the kitchen.

"My experience in the field during the Civil War taught me the answer to that question. When life and property are threatened, if you hope to save them and defeat your enemy, you do not surrender to him. No." He hit the podium again. "You attack. To offset the rapidly declining real estate market, I propose an all-out campaign. First, I urge the formation of a chamber of commerce to promote this city, and the region. We can offer cheap land and cheap labor. Why be modest about it? Second, I urge each of you—indeed, every responsible businessman—to follow the lead of my newspaper and proclaim Los Angeles as a unique safe haven for business."

There was an unpleasant shrillness in the man's voice. If he owned a newspaper, Mack wondered, why did he wear an old army uniform?

"Proclaim it as nothing less than the city of the open shop.

172

The city untainted—as San Francisco is tainted—by the foul muck and slime of trade unionism. That is the enemy, gentlemen—unionism. The outrider of radical foreign governments and foreign ideologies. We shall not have that pustulant cancer growing here. No! We shall turn back the malignant enemy at our borders. Kill it forever. How say you, then? Will you join me in this great crusade?"

Men jumped to their feet, stamping and applauding. Mack thought of Diego Marquez and decided he didn't like this man much. Someone tugged his sleeve.

"Reilley. Didn't see you—"

"Came around the back way." Reilley hooked his thumb and stepped behind one of the floral banks to screen them from chance observance by the desk. Reilley's eyes darted to the roll of notes Mack pulled from his pocket.

"Who's that speaking?" Mack asked.

"Lieutenant Colonel Otis. Owner of the *Times*. He's a big booster of Los Angeles."

"Why does he wear a uniform?"

"Guess he liked soldiering in the War. Ohio fella. Wounded twice. Scouted behind Confederate lines, he claims. Came down here from Santa Barbara some years back, dead broke after running another paper. Went to work on the *Times*, bought in, and later scraped up enough to buy out Boyce, his partner. They didn't get along."

"I don't imagine he'd get along with anybody."

The waiter offered no opinion. "Really wasn't much of a paper when he took over. Then the boom hit. Now Colonel Otis and that circulation manager of his, Harry Chandler—they're on top. We should all have such luck," he added with another greedy glance at the cash.

"Doesn't sound like Otis cares for working people."

"You noticed that," the old waiter said bitterly. He cleaned his spectacles on an apron stained by eggs and coffee. He looked whipped, his eyes watery and red.

Mack fingered the roll of money. "What have you got for me today?"

"Something good, for a change. The Santa Fe brought in two carloads of Iowa Hawkeyes last night." He pronounced it Santa *Fee*. "Half of them are staying here. These are the names and room numbers."

Reilley showed a crumpled slip of paper. With another swift look around the lobby, he handed it to Mack and Mack gave him a bill in exchange.

"And another for Chauncey, on the desk. He made out the list."

Mack paid him and hurried to the stairs.

After a cautious look around, Mack tapped softly at room 323. The hall smelled of cigars and dust. He knocked again, trying not to sneeze.

"Yes, I'm coming," said a foggy voice.

The door was opened by a middle-aged woman who was fatter than Soder Erickson, with freckled white skin and round brown eyes dulled by sleep. She wore a feathered gown much too delicate and feminine for someone of her years and girth.

Mack smiled. "Mrs. Hoover?" Before she could speak, he whipped two squares of cardboard into her hand. "Your tickets, ma'am."

"My—?"

"Tickets for a free sightseeing excursion to San Solaro, The City of Health. A free band concert and a buffet luncheon are included. See the beautiful California countryside—no obligation whatsoever. You'll be back in town by nightfall, and you'll thank me. You're traveling with your husband, are you not?"

"Yes, he—" A querulous gobble interrupted her; it was the husband, asking what was happening.

"May I have his name, please?"

"Why—Oswald. Oswald Hoover. I'm Rheba," she added with midwestern candor.

Mack wrote in a small notebook and then beamed again. "I'll meet you right in front of the hotel in one hour. The Southern Pacific local to Newhall leaves at nine-thirty sharp. Don't be late."

"No," said Mrs. Hoover, as though she wouldn't even entertain the thought. She waved her ticket. "No!"

Mack checked off the room number and tipped his hat.

Eleven Iowans clustered in the mellow sunshine. Wyatt was at his peak—friendly, glib, alternately laughing like a boy and pondering like an economic sage before he answered questions. The bright autumn day and this unexpectedly eager crowd restored his spirits.

Of all the Iowans, Mrs. Rheba Hoover was the most enthusiastic. Her husband, a wan, arthritic man, had nothing to say. When Mrs. Hoover marched, he fell in line. On the train from town, she had rushed to make sure she got the seat next to Mack. Her bulk crushed him to the wall, but he kept smiling. She hung on his words, her eyes growing more adoring every minute. By the time they arrived in Newhall, she was leaning into Mack's arm with her whaleboned bosom. There was no doubt that her interest did not lie solely in real estate.

Now, in sunshine interrupted only occasionally by fat floating clouds, Rheba Hoover was still in a state of excitement—frenzied to buy.

"Oswald's arthritis demands a change. Is there any medical opinion about the climate here?"

"For health purposes it's the best, my dear woman," Wyatt boomed. "The very best in the United States. I like to put it this way. San Solaro is God's own remedy for the consumptive, the dyspeptic, and the broken-down. I must also mention my cousin. He is a professor of surgery at Harvard. He says all the leading eastern medical men agree."

Mack stood back, hands in his pockets, suppressing a smile. Wyatt was amazing. What did he know about eastern medical men? Nothing.

"Oh, good. I've fallen in love with this corner lot. *Love*—that's the only word for it." Her eyes rolled feverishly and came to rest on Mack. He pretended to examine his shoes.

"We would have to build a cottage, Oswald," she said as the group walked on. "Mr. Paul, when did you say the irrigation system will be finished?"

"He didn't say," a man answered. A sour, prune-mouthed man, he was the only skeptic in the lot.

Wyatt's blue eyes changed, as though shadowed by a floating cloud. *God, don't let his temper spoil this,* Mack thought. But Wyatt remained smooth and smiling.

"The flume system and the first reservoir will be finished before the rainy season ends. To a man, the board of directors of the San Solaro Development Company is pledged to that. It's something we've promised to the many good people who have already declared their intention to make this town their permanent home. We'll have water for you."

The crowd was moving in a leisurely way. Dividing now, they flowed around both sides of a depression in the street that Mack hadn't noticed before. Shiny black ooze filled the sinkhole.

The prune-mouthed man said: "Well, if you don't, you already got liquid of some sort. 'Course, it's black as a nigger."

Several people laughed. Not Mrs. Hoover: "What is that vile stuff, Mr. Paul?"

"All the grease—our Mexican friends call it *brea*. Tar. There are pits and pools of it all over the region."

"You even see them in the streets of Los Angeles," Mack said. Mrs. Hoover bathed him with her adoring gaze.

Prune Mouth dipped his fingertip in the ooze and grimaced. "What a stink. Petroleum, is it?"

"A form of it. That's all I know, except that it's worthless, and a nuisance."

"My wife almost stepped in it and ruined her shoes," Prune Mouth said. His tone hinted that he might hold Wyatt liable.

"We'll take care of it immediately." Wyatt snapped his fingers. "Chance, find a shovel and fill that in." Band music floated on the breeze. Wyatt seemed to surge up on his toes, spreading his arms to embrace them with his good feeling. "Ladies and gentlemen, that's the signal that our buffet is ready. Mr. and Mrs. Hoover, please join me at my table in the pavilion. Now where are the other two couples who expressed interest in the terms of our sales contract?"

Hands went up.

"Fine, marvelous, I'd like to invite you to my table also."

Off they went, chattering, happy as youngsters let out of school in fine weather. Mack gazed after them with unconcealed resentment. He didn't like the way Wyatt had turned on him, ordering him like some serf.

Then he saw Mrs. Hoover, clutching her husband's arm but looking back at him. She waved her kerchief. Mack was immediately grateful to Wyatt for setting him a task.

He looked at the black mirror surface of the sinkhole. Squatting he sampled the ooze on his fingertips and sniffed. Tarry, all right. He rubbed his fingers together thoughtfully.

Wyatt dismissed things he didn't understand or care about. Mack considered that foolish; a man should be open to every possibility. If Pennsylvania wildcatters were hunting oil in these valleys and canyons, then might not this ooze be a sign? The sign of California gold of another kind?

At the Newhall station, Mack persuaded the prospects to publish a card of thanks in a Los Angeles paper of their choice. It was a standard technique of developers, good publicity. Mack was prepared with copy.

We, the San Solaro excursionists of the above date, take this opportunity to express our sincere thanks to the management for its kind care of us throughout the trip. Especially are thanks due to Mr. Paul for fatherly and considerate attention. We feel that with such a man at the head, San

Solaro is on a firm basis, and is certain to have a bright future.

Mrs. Hoover insisted on embracing Mack before she left. As the train pulled out, she stayed on the platform of her car, waving her kerchief and giving him intense looks he didn't fully understand until a few minutes later. Then he found a metal key in his pocket, and a scrawled message.

Adored one—
   Oswald retires early. A cyclone will not wake him. I await you.

                                                    R.

Mack drove the wagon along the road toward the sunburst arch. Last week he'd fitted the wagon with a canvas top, of the kind he'd seen in Yosemite, and painted the bed a pleasing sunshine gold. It looked new and fine. He felt old and exhausted.

Towering cumulus above the western hills created a spectacular sunset, bright gold changing to scarlet and shot through with deepening blue-purple, but he couldn't enjoy it.

As he guided the plodding team up the road, he thought San Solaro had a lost, lonely look. The flagged sticks marking the lots threw long shadows. But the kerosene lights glimmering in the depot seemed to welcome him. If he didn't precisely love this place, he was growing used to it. And he never lost his love of the California countryside.

As the wagon approached, Wyatt burst out the door, waving papers and cutting a little dance figure in the dust of Grande Boulevard.

"Signed contracts. Three of them. Best day I've had since April. I practically bought out the crossroads store. Wash up, we're going to celebrate."

"Wyatt, I'm pretty tired—"

"Wash up," Wyatt insisted. "I've invited company."

Twenty minutes later, with water dripping from his new-combed hair, Mack walked into the depot's back room. He couldn't believe what he saw spread out on the old white tablecloth.

Six bottles of cabernet wine. A tin pail of oysters. A jug of cream. Half a wheel of Gouda cheese. Loaves of sourdough and salt-rising bread. Six roasted quail nestled in a box of precious melting ice. A gooseberry pie, an apple pie, a grape pie. Every cracked saucer and tin lid in the place had been set out to hold the various foods. The extravagance stunned him.

"How did you get all this? Did one of the buyers put down some cash?"

"Not a penny—not yet. I talked the storekeeper into credit." Wyatt held his palm over the stove. "Stove's almost hot. That's cream in the jug. How about stewing the oysters?"

"How about telling me why we're eating up our profits? Hell, with this feast maybe our overhead for the rest of the year."

"Mack, you'll never be a good Californian unless you quit being a goddamn puritan." There was an edge in his voice.

"I'm a puritan about seeing profit go into our bellies."

"Well, I closed the sales; it's my celebration." It was an open challenge. Mack's temper boiled but he held it in. He put his palm near the stove top and counted silently. At eight, when his hand hurt, he yanked it back. A count of eight to twelve was the standard test of adequate stove heat.

Noisily, he flung a pot on the stove, dumped in the oysters, and uncorked the cream jug. "Where's the damn salt and pepper?"

"Will you stop, for Christ's sake? Up on the shelf." Wyatt crouched before a triangle of mirror set inside the ticket window, combing his hair and fussing with his cravat.

Mack heard a carriage coming. With a boyish nervousness, Wyatt exclaimed, "That's our company. Wait till you meet her."

"Her?" The cream jug nearly slipped from his hands.

Wyatt ran through the office to the front door, Mack following. Against an evening sky the color of fire and smoke, a snappy little phaeton with yellow-painted wheels careened through the arch and banged along the road at reckless speed. A portmanteau bounced on the seat beside the woman holding the reins. So this was the one who stayed the night . . .

Mack's face whitened suddenly.

The woman driving the phaeton was Carla Hellman.

CARLA SKIDDED THE PHAETON INTO A CURVE IN FRONT **19** of the depot, reined the horse, and braked with her riding boot. Dust clouded up and she fanned it away with a gray glove. As she turned to the two men waiting for her and saw Mack, her face froze.

"Chance, what are you doing here?"

It was Wyatt's turn to be surprised. He glanced from one to the other. "You know each other?"

"Yes, we're well acquainted," Carla said. She was deliciously pleased. And beautiful as ever.

"I met Miss Hellman and her father up north," Mack said to Wyatt.

She extended her hand for help in alighting. Mack hurried forward and she jumped down into his arms. She laughed and straightened her rakish black felt hat. It had a rolled brim and curling gold-dyed ostrich plume that matched her hair, as did the tailored waistcoat of gold silk worn beneath her smart French gray suit. A golden girl, he thought. The effect was surely deliberate, but it fit her marvelously.

Carla slipped her arm through his, letting him feel the swell of her bosom. "June told me he'd taken on a partner. I never imagined it was you. Why did you leave San Francisco?"

"I couldn't get a drink there either."

She laughed.

"I'll explain it all later," Mack said. "We have a regular feast inside. Who's June?"

"Why, our host."

"Junius is my middle name," Wyatt said.

"That's right, I forgot. But June is usually a woman's name."

"So? Sometimes it suits me." He was standing in profile, his delicate face limned by the last bonfire light of the day. For a moment, the tilt of his head, the set of his lips, did create the illusion of a woman. Mack realized again that he simply didn't understand his employer-partner, or all the sides to his nature.

Wyatt tied up Carla's horse while Mack fetched down her portmanteau. To Wyatt she said, "That trombone player you sent over with the invitation didn't arrive until half past four. He got lost."

"He better not have," Wyatt said. "I paid him fifty cents and loaned him Mack's mule." Mack had the feeling Wyatt was angry because Carla was not only acquainted with him, but warmly cordial.

She kicked at her accordion-pleated skirt and went inside the depot. When she saw the table, she clapped her hands. "It *is* a feast."

"I wondered if you'd bother to notice," Wyatt said, glaring at Mack.

She responded with a chilly smile. "Jealousy bores me, June. I don't linger around boring men. Open some wine, please." She tugged her left glove off one finger at a time.

Wyatt used a waiter's corkscrew. As Mack stepped in front of Carla to reach the stove, those well-remembered dark-blue eyes locked with his.

Carla's eyes said that nothing had changed; she found him far from boring.

Mack seasoned and stewed the oysters. He was glad to keep his back turned. Carla and Wyatt, whom she insisted on calling June, fell to drinking and chatting, and at times their conversation had an unfriendly bite. It made him tense.

Seeing Carla again generated strong and even disturbing reactions in Mack. Though he could recognize some of her less desirable traits, he was still strongly attracted—and jealous of Wyatt's success with her. Carla aroused him. He stood close to the stove to conceal that when it became pronounced.

Two and a half hours later, with the roast quail gone, and all the stew, and half the bread, and four of the bottles of heavy red wine, Mack's head was buzzing. His overstuffed stomach ached and gurgled. He felt more relaxed, though. Thank God for wine.

Carla had undone the white silk tie of her blouse; the ends hung outside her open gold waistcoat. The blouse itself was unbuttoned far enough to show the first golden-brown curves of her cleavage. A light sheen of sweat polished her upper lip.

As Wyatt snaffled up the last of the grape pie, Carla held the wine bottle over Mack's glass. He shook his head. Smiling in a vaguely taunting way, she poured more for herself.

Conversation had rambled during the course of the gluttonous meal. Carla heard how Mack and Wyatt first met. Mack learned that she'd left San Francisco a week after the cotillion, and had been relaxing in Southern California ever since.

"Then you'll stay around here for a while?" Mack had asked.

"I might. In many ways I prefer it to the City. The climate's glorious. I can't say that about the men. Pack of boring farmers. With a few exceptions."

The subject of oil came up now. Mack was interested to hear that there were tar pools on Swampy Hellman's ranch in the Santa Clara Valley. He'd given a development lease to the Pennsylvania wildcatter Stewart.

"Oil's filthy stuff, and it attracts filthy people," Carla said. "Go into Santa Paula and you might think you were in the wildest part of the West. Shootings every night. The men are all dirty and illiterate, with the look of desperadoes—"

"Whereas in San Solaro," Wyatt said, waving his glass and spilling some, "we are genteel."

"And drunk," she said.

"Drunk," he agreed.

She refilled her glass. To the top.

The kerosene lamps were trimmed low, lending the room and the three diners a forgiving softness. It was impossible for Mack to keep his eyes away from Carla. She was rounder and heavier than he remembered—an erotic heaviness, broad-hipped, big-breasted. A perfect Victorian woman, at least physically. The more she drank, though, the more she behaved like a dockhand. She matched Wyatt/June glass for glass.

"If the country around here is so rough," Mack said, "is it safe for you to drive here alone?"

"If anyone bothers me, I tell them I'm Hellman's daughter. If that should ever fail, I have something in my travel bag that won't. A Remington vest-pocket twenty-two-caliber. I'm an expert shot. Papa taught me. So be careful, Chance."

Gazing at Mack in a way that unsettled him, she toasted him, then gulped her wine. Red droplets dotted her gold waistcoat like bloodstains. She sighed and leaned back.

"God, too much food. A positive orgy."

"It was a big day," Wyatt said. He staggered to the ticket window and took a cigar box from the drawer. "Three lots. Got to sell the rest by the end of the year. Stick the suckers with the deeds, take the cash down payments, and get out."

Mack pressed his palms on his knees under the table, trying not to get upset. Wyatt fumbled with the box lid. "Boom's about to hit bottom."

Carla licked the rim of her goblet and glanced at Mack. It aroused him all over again.

"In town they say it already has, June."

Wyatt blinked at her, shrugged, produced an enormous dark-green cigar, and struck a match on the stove. He blew a cloud of smoke over the table and dropped the burning match. Mack stepped on it.

"June, that is absolutely vile," Carla said.

Wyatt scratched his groin. A bit of food still clung to a corner of his mouth. "Cuban. The finest."

"It still smells like burning grass and dog shit."

Mack's face tightened. Carla was speaking more and more sloppily, like Wyatt. It was hard to tell who was drunker. Hellman had said alcohol made her crazy.

"Put it out," she said.

Wyatt's anger boiled up, but only for a moment. He gave her a low bow—he nearly fell over—and stabbed the cigar into the glass she'd just refilled for herself. "Anything for you, sweet." He caressed her arm, his knuckles pressing into the swell of her breast. "Anything at all."

"June, you prick, you're sodden." She turned her glass over and poured the whole mess on his littered plate. Wine ran onto the table and dripped to the floor. Mack had never heard such language from a woman. Perhaps rich girls were excepted from the rules. But, strangely, it made her more desirable—at least when he was full of wine.

Wyatt bent to nuzzle her neck. "Carla, be nice. This is a special evening."

Her lips pursed, as if tasting something bad. She pushed him away. "Don't do that. I'm tired."

She slipped out of her chair, avoiding his hand, and went to the open window with a rolling, tipsy step, the whole withdrawal conveying not anger so much as boredom. There was emotional white water churning up, and maybe a storm. Mack squelched his jealousy and cleared his throat.

"I've got to be up early to catch the train to town. Thanks for the dinner, Wyatt. Glad we had a successful day."

Wyatt fell into his chair, cravat undone, strings of raven hair falling over his forehead. He kicked out his lanky legs and gave Mack the barest of nods, his eyes staying on the guest indifferently gazing out the window.

"Miss Hellman—a pleasure. Good night. Perhaps I'll see you again . . ."

She turned quickly, all her drunken sloppiness seeming to slough away. Above Wyatt's nodding head, her eyes seized Mack's again. Wide, dark blue, ardent . . . Nellie was forgotten.

"I'm certain of it, Mack. Dream sweetly."

Outside, he closed the door and leaned against it, exhaling with relief. He hated leaving Carla, but he was glad to be out of that drunken scene. As he rubbed his sleepy eyes, he heard their voices.

"Would you leave your hands off me, June? My head's spinning. I'm tired."

"Tired, tired—is that how you repay your kind host? '

"Don't whine, June. Whining bores me to death."

"You're a fucking stuck-up bitch sometimes."

"Shut up. I want to go to bed."

"By yourself?"

A long silence. "Pour me the rest of that lovely wine. Then we'll see."

Deeply troubled, Mack stumbled away into the dark.

IN SPITE OF THE DEPRESSED MARKET, THEY SIGNED **20** their agreement in Newhall. The legal hack said:

"Bear in mind, Chance, this document gives you no rights except as stipulated. You have no voice in decisions affecting San Solaro. No access to the books and other confidential papers of the corporation. No bank privileges. If we're clear on that, please sign here."

Twenty percent of nothing is still nothing, Mack thought. He signed anyway.

After selling three lots in one day, Wyatt couldn't close on any more, couldn't even come near.

Prospects grew scarcer. Mack doubled his effort in Los Angeles, calling on twice the number of agents, offering twice the number of tips to porters and waiters. But fewer tourists arrived on the trains, and those who came didn't buy real estate, even at distress prices. Platted towns and subdivisions began to disappear, along with their developers. Prices continued to fall. Wyatt's outbursts of temper were directly proportional to the number of visitors Mack brought back. On days when there were none, he cursed and drank and broke things, and Mack stayed away from him.

Nightmares plagued Mack again: the blizzard dream, and another, of Bao Kee lying dead in his arms while *Bay Beauty* sank. The wounds of his humiliation and defeat had healed, but the scars would stay forever.

He slept four hours a night. An ambitious person couldn't afford to lose more time than that. From 10 P.M. until 1 A.M., he studied all the San Solaro sales contracts; Wyatt had given him permission. He read chapters of a book on real estate law Wyatt kept on his desk but never opened. He wanted to know what the law required of a man who bought and sold property. He wanted to know some of the pitfalls. He learned.

One bright October morning, Mack spied Swampy Hellman driving a buggy along Main Street in Los Angeles. On an impulse he hailed the old German, and Hellman nearly ran over three pedestrians in his haste to turn the buggy around.

"Well, Johnny, what a surprise. I got a while till my appointment. I ain't looking forward to it. Lawyers, phooey. To them and to most, I'm just a vein of gold waiting to be mined. Hop in, I'll treat you to a lager."

"Mr. Hellman, it's nine-thirty in the morning."

"So what? Beer in the morning aids digestion. I been drinking it for breakfast since I was seven. Don't argue—get in."

At the uncrowded bar of Noonan's Bird Cage, Hellman blew foam off his stein and scrutinized Mack. "They ran you out."

"Yes, but not permanently."

"Good for you, Johnny. You making any money down here?"

"A little," he lied.

Hellman sighed. "Well, it's good to be ambitious, but I'll tell you, some problems money won't touch. It won't relieve gas or reform a daughter. Carla's in Southern California, did you know?"

"Yes, I heard that," Mack said carefully.

"I wish she'd leave."

"Why?"

"Oh, she's got herself in another mess. She's running around with two, maybe three men."

Mack paled.

"I don't know who they are, except one, but he's the one I worry about," Swampy said. "Buddy Beavis. Lionel Beavis, the lumber king. Know him?"

Mack shook his head.

"He's got a face like a flounder, but downstairs—the part that keeps the ladies happy—they say he's a regular *Schwert Kämpfer*. A Mr. Swordsman, if you get the drift. Buddy wouldn't give Carla a tumble at first. So naturally she had to chase him. Damn little fool—Buddy Beavis is a married man.

They went off to some backwoods lodge for a few nights but they weren't careful and somebody saw 'em. It was a rotten scandal. Still simmering."

"He's in lumber, you said. Where—Oregon?"

"Nah, just his trees are up there. His papa's trees. Buddy lazes around in San Diego. They say he's still loony about her. She can have that effect on gents."

Mack stared into his beer.

"Of course by now Carla's had her fun," Swampy went on, "so she cares for Buddy about as much as a squashed bug. If you see my daughter, do yourself a favor. Cross the street. Quick."

On an afternoon in November he retreated to the San Solaro orange grove to answer Nellie's latest letter. As the shadows lengthened, he sat with his back against a Joshua tree, and from time to time glanced up to watch Wyatt leading three prospects through the tract. Wyatt was walking slowly, without his usual energy. Earlier, Mack had listened to part of Wyatt's sales talk. He droned on by rote, and his own indifference fed that of the prospects, who were a sad, cheap lot to start with. Another bad day.

Frowning, Mack concentrated on writing his letter.

I keep coming back to one bothersome question. This land isn't worth much, but obviously it cost something. Where did he find the money?

The sound of thudding hooves and rattling wheels snapped his head up again. There came Carla's phaeton, billowing dust behind.

She drove fast, as usual. She spied Mack sitting up among the Joshua trees, waved, and slowed down. Mack hid the unfinished letter in his shirt.

Carla tied the horse to a lot stake, ducked under the rope, and ran up the hill. She wore a smart riding habit, white cambric trousers and jacket with full sleeves. Her hair was swept back inside a gold scarf, a duplicate of the one he kept in the guidebook. Deep shadows beneath her eyes suggested nights without sleep.

But she was spirited and smiling as she hurried toward him. He felt both excited and wary—Carla had a way of mixing him up like that.

"What are you doing here? Wyatt said you never came over during the day."

"I made up an errand. I ate lunch in the tent. You weren't there." It was pointed, heavy with sexual intent.

"I was doing an extra chore—repairing a hole in the depot roof. It rains in whether or not we have prospects."

"Well, your partner is positively sullen today," she went on.

"And every day. Business is terrible."

Her eyes darted past him, checking for something. He turned. Wyatt and the prospects were walking the bank of the canal, almost out of sight. Carla relaxed and stepped into the scanty shade of a tree.

"Since you're so reticent, Mr. Chance, I'm forced to be forward. I made up an errand for a daytime visit because I can't exactly slip out to your tent when I'm here at night. If Wyatt found out, it would cause a dreadful row."

"Are you sparing me, or yourself?"

She liked the retort. "Both of us, my sweet," she said merrily. "It's time you and I were alone together. Where can we do it safely?"

Mack's heart raced off like one of Stanford's blooded horses. "Carla—"

"Let's choose a day." Her voice was husky all at once. "Instead of going to Los Angeles you can drive over to Ventura County. You can say you didn't find any prospects."

Had she acted like this with Beavis, the lumber king? He snapped at her. "Carla, no. Forget it."

She reacted with surprise, then gave him a vicious smile. "Oh, did I misjudge you? Have you been playacting all this time? Do you have a hidden aversion to women?"

Mack's expression indicated the remark was a mistake. Hastily she stepped back, then held out an appeasing hand. "I'm sorry—that was cheap. That was awful of me. I just don't understand this . . . reluctance, when I've come here virtually pleading . . ." Her voice trailed away.

Mack said, "I can explain my *reluctance*, as you call it." He reached for an orange. It was wrinkled, and had lost its vivid color. Time to replace it—another of his jobs. He tapped the fruit. "This belongs to Wyatt. As far as I can tell, right now so do you."

"That's for me to say, thank you."

"No, you're lovers. You don't keep it secret."

"Occasional lovers. I'm tired of him. He can be charming, but he's very irresponsible. Lately he's been a boor. He seems to feel he's never obliged to control his temper, not under any circumstances."

Again she looked toward the distant figures by the canal. Screened by a Joshua tree, she stepped to Mack, her breasts touching him through the white cambric. "Whereas you, my dear, are a man in almost perfect control. I intend to break that control. It won't be unpleasant, I promise . . ."

He wanted to kiss her but somehow found it in himself to push her away. "If I'm going to poach on another man's territory, I'll decide when and where."

"You don't want me as badly as I want you?"

"Not under these conditions, no."

She colored suddenly, and pulled her right hand back as if to hit him. But she didn't deliver the blow, instead forcing a chilly smile. "You have a very peculiar and old-fashioned code of honor, Mr. Chance. I put you on notice—it'll do you no good. I admire you intensely. You may be poor now, but you won't be forever, because you go after what you want."

He searched for signs of coquetry, insincerity, but saw none. Now she pressed the attack. "I'm like you: I go after what I want. And if someone denies it to me, that only redoubles my determination to get it. And I always do get it, my love." She caressed his cheek. "Always. Fair warning?"

She ran down the hill to the phaeton, and Mack watched it speed away. *Stupid damn fool, turning down a woman that beautiful. A woman who doesn't scorn a man's ambition . . .*

He couldn't do anything else—that was the problem. With a curse, he seized one of the oranges on the Joshua tree and yanked it so hard the cord broke.

Daybreak. December. Yellowish light was seeping into the gray over the eastern hills. Mack's breath plumed as he checked the horse's bit. The secondhand wool coat he'd bought in town was too light.

The depot door opened and Wyatt stumbled out barefoot, hugging himself. His two-day-old beard, black stubble, marred his good looks, and his purple satin robe, its elbows worn through, hung on his narrow frame. At least he didn't seem truculent. It was too early.

"God, winter's in the air." He slapped his ribs and hugged himself again.

Mack climbed to the wagon seat. "I thought it never got this cold in Southern California. Never any danger of frost to kill the oranges and lemons—"

"You've been reading that book again. You should know better." Wyatt grinned, sleep-bleary but cheerful. Mack thought the mood propitious for questions, but he didn't ask the important one immediately.

"Wyatt, I've always wondered—how much did you pay for this land?"

"Sixteen dollars an acre."

"Eighteen hundred acres—that's close to thirty thousand dollars. Where'd you get that kind of money?"

Wyatt sniffled and wiped his nose with his sleeve. "Borrowed it from Carla's father."

"Otto Hellman? You never mentioned that."

"For a reason. A lot of people despise Hellman. Having his name associated with San Solaro could hurt the project. Hellman's a reasonable man, though. When I stated the situation, he understood, and we agreed to keep his interest quiet. If it ever does get out, I'll just deny it." Though still friendly, his tone sharpened. "That satisfy you, partner?"

"Sure," Mack said, though he was still puzzling over it. The sweetly reasonable Hellman just described didn't sound like the Swampy he knew. Was Wyatt really so persuasive?

"Get going or you'll miss the train." Wyatt slapped the snorting horse lightly. "Bring back some warm bodies."

"If there are any to be had."

Mack drove the canvas-topped wagon toward the arch. Light streaming across the eastern hills struck the wrought-iron sunburst, igniting a show of fiery color. His eye lingered on it.

That sun isn't rising, it's sinking. Fast.

In the deserted lobby of the Pico House, a Mexican boy on a ladder was hanging small tempera-painted *piñatas* from the beams. Christmas—Mack had forgotten.

He found Reilley in the steamy kitchen.

"Nobody," Reilley said. "Not for three days now."

"That's bad."

"You think I don't know it?" the old waiter said, sadly polishing his spectacles.

"The waiter called it," Mr. Swifty Southwood said, squaring a stack of pamphlets on the counter and blowing dust from another stack. "I can't give these things away. The golden bubble's burst—" A *pouf* with his fingers demonstrated.

"Thanks anyway, Swifty." Mack put on his broad-brimmed hat and started out.

"Don't bother coming around next week. I'm taking the wife and heading up to Vancouver. We'll feed on my brother a while. I'm starving to death in this town."

Mack tramped Main Street as the December sky lost its pale lemon hue and lowered like a slab of slate. How empty the street looked compared to that bright day in October. Most of the people abroad were residents. The clots of tourists outside the hotels and real estate offices were gone. He passed an agent's storefront with its sign hanging crookedly, the chain broken at one end. It rattled to and fro in a rising wind. White-washed letters on the grime-coated window said FOR LEASE. At the SP depot he found the platform empty except for a baggage man. Cold rain began to fall, and Mack shivered, stepping along the platform to shelter, turning up the collar of his coat.

Monday of the following week—two weeks before Christmas—he again returned from Los Angeles with no prospects. The gray weather had been unrelenting, but today the wind increased the discomfort, blowing in from the east. It was a strangely warm wind, full of grit, and howled down the canyons and raked across the hills, a breath of the high desert. It roiled and spun the dust along San Solaro's deserted streets, flapping the canvas of the striped tent and making the stays whine. It tormented the ear and rubbed on the nerves.

Mack sat on a wooden chair inside the yellow tent, wondering what to do. He'd come back at half past one and reported to Wyatt, who already had a bottle of wine open in his office. Wyatt wasn't paying attention to his appearance anymore; he used his straight razor every four or five days at best. He'd said nothing in response to Mack's terse report, only given him an accusing look and then started riffling through a ledger, muttering about expenses.

The four musicians were playing a silent game of whist. Mrs. Brill, the woman in charge of the food, sat like a statue behind the trestle tables. Yesterday the leg of mutton had a purple-green cast. Today he could smell it. The wind caught one of the cheesecloth domes and sailed it away. Mack looked at her. She looked at him. Nobody moved.

Suddenly Mrs. Brill's eyes snapped wide, fixing on something outside. Mack turned to see Wyatt reel out of the dust clouds. His paper collar was attached only at one end, waving in the wind, and his shirttail hung out. He carried the expense ledger and some small envelopes.

Just inside the tent, he stopped. "I'm letting the band go. You too, Mrs. Brill. I have your wages in these envelopes. One day's pay."

Mack felt as though the earth had opened. Mrs. Brill burst into tears. The bandsmen dropped their cards and knocked over their instruments getting to their feet. The leader, the tuba player, a portly man with out-of-date burnside whiskers, ran over to Wyatt.

"You gotta do better than one day's pay and one day's notice."

"No I don't, Edelman, I can't afford it." He held out the envelopes. Edelman glared, refusing them, and Wyatt dropped four envelopes in the dirt. "Hell with you," he muttered, and lurched on to Mrs. Brill, who took her envelope.

Wyatt rummaged under one of the tables and pulled out a bottle of wine. The bald cornet player counted his money and waved the envelope angrily.

"Listen here, Mr. Paul, us four had an agreement with you. Reg'lar work six days a week, till January first."

"Where the hell's the corkscrew?" Wyatt said to Mrs. Brill.

Still crying, she fumbled her hands over the table. "Here somewhere. Oh, I'm so upset—"

Impatient, Wyatt broke the neck of the wine bottle against the central tent pole.

"Mr. Paul, we had an agreement," the cornetist repeated.

Wyatt drank sloppily from the shattered bottle. "A verbal agreement," he said after a few swallows. "Show me something in writing."

"I'll show you something, you goddamn chiseler," the cornetist yelled, bolting at him. Mack jumped in and wrestled him back.

"Leon, talk to him," Mack shouted to the leader, while the cornetist tried to pummel his stomach. Mack pressed the man's forehead to hold him away. The bandsman was no match; Mack was much stronger, and soon had a tight grip on the man's wrists. He didn't admire Wyatt's tactics, but fighting solved nothing.

The cornetist stopped struggling and dropped his hands, deflated. Mack released him. Leon Edelman stumped back and forth, fretfully tugging his burnsides. Mack said, "Look, Leon, I always deal straight with you—"

"Yeah, I know."

"I can't find prospects in town. That means no sales—no money. Wyatt's right. We can't meet expenses. The boom's over."

The musicians were decent men, not brawlers; the cornetist swore and slumped back to his chair and Edelman settled his braided scarlet cap on his head. Wyatt was wandering around the tent with a glazed expression. Edelman glanced at him, then addressed Mack in a low voice.

"Awright, Mr. Chance, but I gotta say this to you. You seem like a smart young fella. Honest too. So I don't know what you're doin' wastin' time with a lyin' shyster like him. I could have told you there's never gonna be a town here. This land is trash. He's trash."

Mack stared at him, dismally thinking the bandsman was right. He'd known it almost since the first day, hadn't he?

Muttering recriminations and lugging their cases, the musicians were gone within five minutes, Mrs. Brill with them, still sobbing. Mack stood in the center of the empty tent, while Wyatt, at the western side, stared out, emptying the bottle. He hadn't looked at those leaving, hadn't offered so much as a word of thanks or good-bye.

The tent poles creaked and the striped canvas gave off cracking pistol-shot sounds. Uprooted shrubs sailed by in clouds of dust. It seemed to Mack that the hot, dry wind was lifting away the soil of San Solaro before his eyes. He could believe the old bandsman. This was trash land . . .

A clink of glass brought him around. Wyatt was groping in the wine crate.

"Jesus, will you stop that?"

The shout snapped Wyatt's head up. His eyes weren't innocent now; they were the eyes of some baleful beast. His beard showed black, heavy, a dirty growth. He wrinkled his nose like a sniffing dog, then suddenly lifted the buffet table with both hands and threw it over.

Cheesecloth domes sailed away and crocks and plates of stale food spilled and broke. "I'm not aware of any laws in California saying a man can't drink whenever he goddamn pleases," Wyatt screamed, swinging his fists from side to side like some demented preacher. "I'm not aware of any fucking laws like that."·

"If there was a law, you sure as hell wouldn't obey it," Mack shouted back. The wind howled. Wyatt crouched and plucked out another bottle.

"Look, this doesn't help," Mack said, struggling for calm, for patience. "This place is folding. The question is, what are we going to do to cut our losses?"

"*My* losses. *Mine*," Wyatt cried, thumping his shirt bosom. "What we're going to do is forget about it. Just forget about it for a while."

He wandered from the tent and, blind to an overturned chair in his path, nearly fell over headfirst. Yelling obscenities, he picked up the chair in his free hand and hurled it high and far. The chair landed on a big cardboard sign skating along the ground, and the sign flapped noisily.

"Forget it," Wyatt said with a wave of his bottle. He spoke to the wind. Mack didn't exist. Wyatt went into the depot and slammed the door. Then came the loud whack of the bolt shooting home.

The next day Mack didn't bother with the trip into town, instead riding Railroad to Newhall for supplies. At the post office he found a letter waiting from Nellie, a long one this time.

Mr. Hearst had raised her salary, at the same time instructing her to surrender herself to an alleged ring of white slavers operating in the City. She was to pass herself off as an innocent new arrival from the remote Mount Shasta district. Nellie was elated at the opportunity to write another sensational exposé, and Mack knew better than to warn her of possible dangers.

He didn't see Wyatt that day. After dark, he lay in his tent, writing to Nellie. The wind still blew hard from the mountains, rattling the canvas and fluttering the flame of the lamp beside him.

All I do is break up his fights. What the devil am I doing for myself—except learning the wrong way to develop and sell a town—?

"Mack?"

The voice outside made him bolt up. Just as he identified the speaker, Carla lifted the flap and walked in.

She wrinkled her nose at the cramped interior and the few shabby furnishings. Mack had taken off his shirt but had kept his trousers on, thank God. He combed his hair with his fingers.

"I'm here because Wyatt and I arranged it last week. Where is he?"

"Inside the depot, I suppose."

"Both doors are bolted. I called and called. I got no answer."

"Then he's still sleeping it off. We had a bad day yesterday. He drank way too much. Again."

Disgusted, she sank down on a stool near the foot of the cot. She wore the white cambric riding outfit, but no gold scarf, her hair in disarray from the wind.

Mack straightened the blanket, all too conscious of their iso-

192

lation, the night. "Wyatt's in bad shape, Carla. He's fine when he closes a sale, but he hasn't closed one since the day we celebrated. San Solaro is all but out of business. Your father may have to take the land when the corporation defaults on the loan."

"What loan?"

He frowned. "The loan your father made to Wyatt. So he could buy this property."

"Papa's never been near San Solaro."

"But Wyatt told me—"

"Papa doesn't know this place exists. Or Wyatt either. And I'm certainly not going to tell him."

Mack didn't know what to think. Hours of the whining wind had worn away his nerves. He swore and strode past her, his bare feet scuffing up puffs of dust. Yanking up the tent flap, he saw nothing but blowing dust.

"God, this wind could drive you crazy."

"You're not the first one to say that. It's the wind from the desert. The *santan*."

"The what?"

"*Santan*. It starts in the mountains, but the desert sucks and burns all the moisture from it. That's why it's so hot and dry. Usually it doesn't come this late in the year, but now and then it does. The Indians call it the wind of evil spirits. When it blows, people do terrible things. Sometimes they kill each other."

Mack looked into the Stygian dark, trying to plumb it with his eyes. He couldn't see beyond the rolling dust. The wind sounds changed constantly, one moment a high keen, the next a moaning growl. Then he heard soft noises of movement behind him and suddenly felt Carla's hands slip around him and press his bare belly.

"But mostly, when the *santan* blows, people go out of control in other ways." Her right hand began slowly moving in a small circle. She ground her breasts into his back, and then her hips.

"All of us live with wild creatures inside. The *santan* lets them loose . . ."

Her mouth pressed his shoulder blade, her tongue licking his flesh. He wanted to turn and take her, on the cot, on the floor, it didn't matter so long as he had her. He hurt from wanting that. But he fought the need for the same reason he'd fought it before, and lifted her hands away when they dropped beneath his waistband.

She stepped back.

"San Solaro's still Wyatt's property," he said. "So are you."

"When are you going to stop this stupid, priggish—"

"Go home, Carla. Just go home."

He patted her shoulder but she wrenched away. He sighed and walked to the cot, missing the reaction on her face—anger, and then a steel determination.

She started to say something sharp, but before she could, her eye fell on the crate he used as a bedside table. She snatched up T. Fowler Haines and pulled out the gold scarf.

"This is mine. You saved it."

"What of it?"

She crushed the silky material in her hand. "It means that your protests are just talk. It means you really want the same thing I want, and one day you'll stop all your idiot prattle about respecting Wyatt's rights. He hasn't any rights. That's simple enough. So is this: I want you and you want me. Here's the proof."

She lifted the scarf and kissed it seductively. Her deep-blue eyes held his while her tongue tasted the fabric a moment. Then she laughed, a little laugh of victory, flinging the scarf on the mussed cot. He stood staring at it after the tent flap fell in place behind her. The *santan* howled like some wild beast baying in a cave.

21 THE *SANTAN* FLUNG DUST CLOUDS THROUGH THE streets of Los Angeles and Mack held tightly to his hat outside Southwood's So-Cal agency. Boards nailed over the door said Swifty Southwood's vacation in Vancouver was permanent.

He trudged up toward the plaza. Christmas bunting and greens decorated the hotels and the windows of stores. In a season of hope, he searched for hope within himself and couldn't find any. That had never happened before.

He wasn't a religious person. Not formally, anyway. He knew nothing of Catholicism. Still, almost unconsciously, he was led to the studded doors of the church on the plaza, Nuestra Señora la Reina. He sank down in a back row, rested his folded hands on the pew ahead, and gazed at the glittering altar, the candles in tiny red glasses, the melancholy Christ gazing down from the cross. He sat there more than an hour, a drab figure, noticed but not bothered by the elderly priests who walked through occasionally. He searched deep in himself for the hope that had always been there to lift and renew him in bad times.

Presently the noise of the wind fell off outside, and the solitude and reassuring strength of this holy place restored him. Christmas without a home made a man feel a crushing loneliness, but he'd survive that, and he'd survive San Solaro, and move on. Moving on was imperative. There was no longer any doubt.

Muted voices interrupted then, and a door squeaked open at the head of the left aisle. A priest in a white surplice shook hands with a man wearing a dark sheepman's coat. The priest vanished through the door and the other man walked up the aisle toward the plaza entrance, carrying an old leather valise. Mack recognized the broad nose, heavy features, bull-like body, and scrambled from the pew.

"Father Marquez."

"Mr. Chance. *Que placer encontrarlo*. Totally unexpected." They stepped outside. The wind had calmed, and westward over the Pacific, evening light was breaking through rents in the clouds. The stocky priest had a fatigued look; he lacked the energy Mack remembered.

"How long have you been in Los Angeles?" Mack asked.

"One hour."

"Are you transferring here?"

The priest shook his head. "There has been a bitter dispute between the owners of the three morning newspapers and their union typographers and printers. Because times are growing hard again, the owners want to cut wages ten or twenty percent. I understand there have been lockouts, and negotiated settlements on the *Tribune* and the *Herald*. But the *Times* men are still out. A strike may be a worthy and necessary endeavor, but it can't fill the empty bellies of a family. The men will need encouragement."

"And you came for that?"

"Yes." Gravely, he added, "Without sanction by my superiors. Indeed, they expressed disapproval."

"Father . . ." Mack approached the subject hesitantly. "All three of the morning papers are still being published. I read the *Times* today."

"How can that be? The telegraph message I received said the printers were still out. I must go to headquarters—"

"I have my wagon at a stable close by. Come along, I'll drive you."

* * *

195

The wagon bumped south along Spring Street. Gaslights in stores and cottages made the dusk even more lonely. They passed an adobe with a candle-decked holiday tree in the window and heard a family lustily singing "O Little Town of Bethlehem."

"It has been a long while since we met in the jail in San Francisco."

"And a lot's happened," Mack replied.

"Change rolls on like the sea. But some things—injustice, the greed of those who control property—they do not change." Marquez chuckled. "You perhaps understand why my reputation grows steadily worse within the Church, and my position more untenable."

"But you came here anyway."

"There is a call. One answers," the priest said with a solemn shrug. "Actually, this is both duty and a holiday of sorts. When my family lost most of its grant lands, they managed to save the main building, the original heart of the *rancho*. I am its temporary custodian. When my only nephew, Gonsalvo, is grown, I am hoping he will marry and take the place over. Until then, it stands empty. It's a beautiful spot, down the coast, overlooking the sea. I was going to hire a horse and have a look. Would you like to go along? I'd welcome the company."

Mack started to say no, then asked himself why. Wyatt spent all his time drinking. He'd been asleep when Mack left that morning to dutifully check the station and the hotels for prospects he knew he wouldn't find. In the lonesome December dark, the priest's invitation cheered him.

"Yes, Father, I'd like to go. I have the time, and I've never seen one of the original *ranchos*."

"Please—not 'Father' any longer. Diego."

Mack grinned and shook hands on it.

The small frame building on South Spring housed the Los Angeles local of the International Typographers' Union. Half a dozen men were gathered in the office amid a litter of literature, handbills, and copies of the *Times*. There was a dispirited air about the printers, though they welcomed Marquez warmly.

The priest shucked off his sheepman's coat; underneath he wore a white shirt with his clerical collar. He pointed to a stained bandage on the head of one of the typesetters. "Is that a result of the trouble?"

"Aye. Otis brung in some plug-uglies from San Diego and

Sacramento. They're scabbing for him. I got this from one of 'em. The scabs are the reason the *Times* is still being printed. 'Course, the colonel, he lauds 'em to heaven . . .''

He gave Marquez a handbill. After scanning it, he passed it to Mack. The florid prose referred to the strikebreakers as "Liberty-loving immigrants. Pioneers of sound, selected stock, who vow to defeat the cancerous foreign-inspired plague of trade unionism.''

"They're a rough bunch, Father,'' another printer said. "No need for a godly man to mix it up with the likes of them.''

"But there is every need,'' Marquez said. "Are you manning a picket line?''

"Yes, sir.''

"I want to see it.''

Three pickets walked wearily back and forth outside the *Times* office on the northeast corner of First and Fort streets. It was a substantial building of brick and granite, dominated by a three-story turret at the corner. A bronze eagle with spread wings stood guard atop the turret, and a bronze plaque proclaimed the credo of the proprietor.

STAND FAST. STAND FIRM.
STAND SURE. STAND TRUE.

Mack tied up the wagon horse while Marquez introduced himself to the pickets. Presses grumbled inside the building, shaking the sidewalk. A guard on a stool in the gaslit foyer glowered at the new arrivals.

Marquez laughed at something a picket said, then walked to the doorway. The guard stepped up to bar the priest with his arm.

"What do you want?''

"I want to speak to the men in your pressroom.''

"No unauthorized visitors permitted. Orders of the colonel.''

"Then get the colonel down here so I can speak to him.'' The guard didn't move. "Summon him. I insist.''

The guard slammed and latched the door. A few moments later, Otis marched out, garters on his sleeves, ink on his thumb, lightning in his eye. Three hulking pressmen in stained aprons followed, though they stayed in the foyer, eyeing the pickets. Otis drew up at attention in front of Marquez.

"Who are you, sir?''

"Father Diego Marquez of the Archdiocese of San Francisco."

"Here in what official capacity?" Otis sounded like a sergeant hectoring a private.

"None. I come as an individual, the messenger of my own conscience. I want to speak to your new printers."

"Why?"

Marquez stood up to the hostile stare, the intimidating tone. "To tell them what they're doing is wrong. They're abetting an unjust cause."

"Ah, so that's it. That's what you are—some communist. Well, sir, you may mount your filthy attacks in San Francisco and suffer no opposition—that town is a moral sinkhole, a nest of radical Democrats. But try it here and every decent citizen will mobilize against you. Stand away from my door."

Marquez drew a breath. He looked strong as a great rock, braced there on his short heavy legs. "I will not be moved. I intend to go in."

"Men!" Otis shouted, swinging an invisible saber, and the hulks in the foyer jumped out to the sidewalk. Marquez turned sideways and tried to slip between two of them. Mack yelled a warning, too late; one man pounded a fist in the priest's gut, doubling him over and sending him to his knees.

Otis kept shouting oaths and incoherent orders, and another pressman ran over to kick Marquez from behind. Mack threw himself on the man's neck and dragged him around. Astonished, the man put up his fists to defend himself. Mack feinted, drew the man off balance, then slipped past his guard with a left-right combination taught him by Corbett. The man's eyes crossed, then he leaned over the gutter, cupping the blood spurting from his nose.

The pickets swarmed around Mack and Marquez to protect them. Mack shot his hand out to the priest and Marquez clasped it and hoisted himself up.

"Had enough?" Otis roared.

Marquez said, "No, I'll be back, walking this line."

"At your peril, sir. At your peril. Men, if any of them attempt to breach our defenses and invade the building, retaliate with force." He pointed at Marquez. "I've memorized your face. Foment anarchy in Los Angeles and we'll muster the entire town against you. You'll be jailed, maimed, or worse—and that papist collar won't protect you."

"We'll peel your brown greaser hide and hang it out to dry," one of the pressmen added. He leaned over and blew spit in Marquez's face.

Marquez's fists flew up, but he fought them down and with visible effort contained his fury. The pressman laughed and went inside.

The priest turned and squeezed Mack's arm. "Thank you for pulling that man off. Bravely done."

The pickets decided to abandon their vigil for the night. "I'll be back here standing with you the day after tomorrow," the priest promised them as they crowded into the wagon.

"That would be Christmas Eve, Father."

"What day more fitting? Our blessed Lord was Himself a just and militant man. Often at odds with entrenched powers. We'll carry on in that spirit on His birthday."

Someone else said, "It's a damn disgusting mess. Here's that Otis, a card-carrying union typographer and printer ever since he was a boy in Marietta, Ohio—and he locks us out, and pits thugs against us. Why does a man do that?"

"Money," Marquez replied. "The alchemy of money and property. It debases the gold of character. It destroys all but the strongest."

In the back room of the local, Mack and the priest talked until after midnight. Marquez carried three well-thumbed books in his valise: a Douay Bible, Marx's *Capital*, and a work called *Progress and Poverty* by Henry George.

"George was an editor on the *Oakland Transcript*. One day, in the hills, he had a vision, something like St. Paul's on the Damascus road. It came to him that the principal cause of the gulf between rich and poor in California, indeed everywhere, is land monopoly. The person who works the land pays a high physical and financial price for mere survival. The person who owns the land amasses wealth without labor—at the expense of others. To redress that, George proposed a single tax on what he calls the unearned increment—the wealth created by rents, and the inevitable increase in land value."

"I don't like that idea very much," Mack said. "I own an interest in some land, and I work hard at the same time."

"Then perhaps you're an exception. Whether you will be all your life . . . time alone will answer that."

"I wouldn't want some radical taxing me—"

"Don't talk like Otis. And don't condemn what you don't understand. Read the book. It appeared in '79 and it has never been out of print. George is in the East now. He has many followers."

Mack fixed the title in his mind, said good-night, and rolled up in a blanket. As he drifted off, the priest was still sitting in the corner, studying his Bible by the light of a candle.

Early next morning, the two men drove toward the Pacific under a clearing sky. They crossed the new Santa Fe branch line to Redondo. As the wind freshened and the temperature soared, both shed their coats.

"I've brought some simple provisions, and two bottles from Buena Vista," Marquez said. "Haraszthy's own vineyard. We'll celebrate the Christmas season like the outcasts we are." He was jocular about it.

The two talked easily, acquaintance beginning to edge toward friendship. Mack described his enforced departure from San Francisco and his misadventures in Los Angeles real estate. The priest brooded aloud on his cause, and the increasing problems it created for him within the Church.

"Ah, well. So be it," he concluded. "I wouldn't be anywhere else but standing beside my brothers in Los Angeles."

"The printers were right—things could get ugly there," Mack said. "Otis thinks the open shop will attract a lot of new business and be the making of the city."

"And never mind that workingmen must starve to build his metropolis." They reached a crossroads. Marquez signaled the way: the coast road, south.

Dead or dying real estate developments rolled by one by one. LA BALLONA CREEK ESTATES: HOMES ON THE PROUD NEW HARBOR OF THE SOUTH! They crossed a bridge over a flowing tidal creek and Mack pointed seaward. "They dredged out there, serious about developing a harbor to replace Wilmington. The plans were good, but they failed anyway."

They passed through Walteria, where two Chinese men were chopping up signs advertising a SACRIFICE PROPERTY AUCTION. They rode along the perimeter of the abandoned New Market Tract. They cut a corner of an apple orchard planted with five thousand young trees for settlers who would never pluck their fruit or savor their shade.

Late in the morning they passed a white boundary stone with a Spanish inscription. Mack heard the Pacific surf beyond thickets of palms and sea grape on his right. The late-season *santan* had blown out, replaced by an invigorating sea wind. Soon the wagon bumped southwest on a peninsula, and started over a series of low hills. When they surmounted the last, Mack reined up, awed by the breathtaking view.

The peninsula jutted into the Pacific, where a million needles of light bobbed on the blue water. Scattered about the peninsula, half hidden among the scrubs, Mack saw tiny wooden cottages. Squatters—perhaps fishermen. The end of the peninsula was dominated by a large adobe ranch house on a rise of ground that gave a commanding view of the land side as well as the sea.

"There it is," the priest said. "Rancho de los Palos Verdes del Pacífico." His dark callused hand swept in an arc, right to left, more than 180 degrees. "You see before you and around you the land of the Marquez family of Spain and Mexico. We have been passing through other sections for almost an hour."

"How much of this peninsula did you own, Diego?"

Memory haunted the priest's eyes.

"All of it."

The rambling ranch house of gray adobe, unpainted oak, and redwood was an enormous *U*, two stories high. The arms of the *U* pointed inland and a veranda ran around the entire house on both floors.

Marquez showed Mack through. There were twenty-eight rooms, this one equipped with six clay ovens for baking, that one filled with silent looms that had once woven blankets and carpets, another for cellaring hundreds of bottles of wine, several for general storage, and the remainder living quarters for a large family. In most of the rooms, spiders spun in the ceiling corners and rodent droppings littered the hard-packed earth floor. The spartan kitchen, the parlor, and one bedroom with three commodious beds were less dusty.

"This was a self-contained world," Marquez explained as they walked. "You get some hint of that from the extent of the house. There were many other outbuildings, however. Stables and barns, sheep-shearing pens, a tannery and rendering plant, an underground cave for storing ice from the mountains. At one time, before the Anglo revolution, the adobe supported ten thousand longhorns, three thousand sheep, and a herd of one thousand blooded horses. New England ships put in along the coast, and we did a brisk trade in tallow and hides—California bank notes, they were called in those days. To the east, in the fields, we raised corn, beans, peas, lentils—everything the adobe required. The well in the quadrangle brimmed with sweet water. Now it's cloudy and stinks of salt."

A short distance from the adobe, Marquez rigged a snare. Within an hour a fat jackrabbit hung upside down by his rear leg. Marquez killed and slaughtered the rabbit without apology, then set Mack to work at the chopping block, dicing onions and yellow peppers from his provision bag.

While the sun set on the Pacific, the two men sat in sturdy wooden chairs on the second-floor veranda, resting their heels on the rail as the unseen surf below the bluff boomed rhythmically. Marquez uncorked the first bottle of Buena Vista white. The wine was warm, but crisp and delicious.

The priest rolled the barrel-shaped glass between his palms. His eye roved to the red horizon, where a steam packet churned north against the half-circle of the sun.

"My grandfather entertained the young sailor from Harvard Richard Henry Dana on this porch. My father died at this house. When the Anglos and their courts and judges stole our land, something twisted in his head."

"A friend in San Francisco told me the story."

"That he became an outlaw? Terrorized the southern counties for six years, killing gringos?"

"Yes."

Bloody light tinted Marquez's face. "They cornered him here. The house was built on this rise of ground so that strangers riding up the road were completely visible. They cleared trees and brush from the roadside for that reason. My father saw the posse coming and put his silver pistols away after he counted forty riders. He went into the courtyard bareheaded, unarmed, to face them. He stood shouting at them as they rode up. He said this was our family's home—our family's land—he would never surrender it . . ."

Marquez's voice fell so low, Mack almost couldn't hear it above the surf.

"They counted sixty-one bullets in his body before they buried him."

"Where were you when it happened?"

"At first I was in my room. I was ordered to hide, but I crept out. I saw the Anglos wheel their horses around him. I saw them shoot. They laughed; they were enjoying themselves. I saw my father fall, while the bullets kept striking. His body leaped and twitched on the ground . . ." He swallowed. "I saw everything."

A great condor wheeled and swooped out of sight below the bluff. Mack was so moved by the emotion in the priest's voice he couldn't speak.

Marquez sat with the untasted glass tight between his palms, watching the steamer diminish and disappear. The sun was down and the water flashed with sulfurous reflections from the clouds.

"There is so much cruelty in the world. So much injustice.

I have faith that the ways of our Lord Jesus Christ are the right ways. And yet—sometimes—often—they do not prevail. At such times, to my shame, my wrath rises up to defeat my reason, and my faith wavers. I waver—''

His voice broke. Mack saw the tracks of tears on the priest's broad dark cheeks. Marquez sensed the scrutiny, turned his head away, and quickly drank his wine.

Marquez opened the kitchen shutters. They squeaked and creaked and one rusty cast-iron hinge tore out of the adobe. He gazed sadly at the shutter a moment, then let it hang.

Dusk gave way to night. The air was mild, the sound of the Pacific soothing. The second bottle of white wine stood between them on the hand-hewn plank table. Marquez was more relaxed now, the sharp edges of memory dulled by the wine.

"Delicious," Mack said. He forked up some of the rabbit the priest had stewed with the onions and peppers, some flour, and seasonings. "I have a friend in San Francisco, a news reporter, who wouldn't approve of me enjoying this. She hates the slaughter of animals."

Marquez wasn't offended. "I learned to hunt before I learned to read."

Mack brought up the priest's favorite subject again, the labor situation in California. Marquez said, "It isn't ideal, not even in San Francisco, a town people think of as a workingman's bastion. The truth is, class strife has split San Francisco for decades."

He spoke of a Jim D'Arcy and his followers, called Sandlotters because they held rallies in vacant lots. He mentioned Denis Kearney of the Workingmen's party. "Both of them purported to speak for the laboring man, but both were bigots, and their organizations protectionist. They wanted jobs secured at the expense of those they considered beneath them. Kearney's slogan minced no words: 'The Chinese Must Go.' Despicable," he said with a shake of his head. "But perhaps I expect too much of people. Perhaps that's why I'm so uncertain about my course. What it is, what it should be . . .''

He sighed and poured wine. "What of you, my friend? Are you still certain of your direction? To better yourself with wealth—wasn't that how you put it when we met?"

"Absolutely. I want some of that money and property that 'debases the gold of character'—isn't that how you put it?" He saw Marquez smile. "In fact I want a lot of it," he went on. "When I have it, I won't be stingy with it. I grew up poor. I remember what it's like."

"Laudable," Marquez murmured, "if somewhat unrealistic."

"You don't believe a man can be rich and decent too?"

"If you are, you will be one of the rare ones, Mack. One of the very rare ones."

His eyes said he really didn't think it possible.

Mack slept that night in one of the three beds, in a corner. On one wall above him hung a pair of huge Mexican spurs, handmade of silver, with sharply pointed rowels and silver *conchas* decorating the old faded leather. From a niche in the other wall, a Madonna with gentle hand upraised beheld the room. A nice pair of symbols of the priest, Mack thought.

In the morning Marquez repaired the shutter and they drove back to Los Angeles. It scarcely seemed like Christmas Eve, with the temperature so warm and the wind picking up again, fierce and gritty from the mountains.

Mack squinted into the blowing dust that revealed and then hid Los Angeles on the plain. "I thought we were through with the *santan*."

"But nature is never through with us. Perhaps it won't last long. It certainly isn't usual this time of year. One would say it's a bad omen—if one were a native, given to traditional superstitions."

Marquez was smiling as he poked fun at his own background. Mack smiled too. He liked the priest, except for his tendency to establish himself as a conscience for others.

"Thank you for accompanying me," Marquez said when they neared town. "I need to check on the property occasionally. You made the trip less onerous."

"Thanks for that excellent dinner. Even if you did kill a rabbit."

"I am nothing if not a Californian. Merry Christmas, my friend."

"Merry Christmas, Father Diego."

The *santan* howled. The men leaned forward on the seat, trying to protect their faces from the worst of it. The air filled with debris and dust, dark as some evil twilight.

That same afternoon, Wyatt woke on the floor of the office, and retched at the smell. Suddenly it came back, all of the wine drunk up the previous night . . . and then falling, rubber-legged, face-first, into his own vomit.

The runty owner of the Newhall mercantile store had started him on this latest binge, riding out late yesterday with a deputy

204

and insisting that the San Solaro account be cleared up. It was several months, in arrears. Wyatt had smothered the visitors with charm, but it hadn't worked. The storekeeper said he would file a lien. *Bastard.*

Wyatt staggered to his feet and leaned against the wall, his raven hair hanging to his eyebrows, his shirt out again. He could still smell the wine fumes. Perhaps they were real, perhaps imaginary. On the desk he saw all the damned papers and letters demanding things; they weren't imaginary. On the wall he saw the mocking record of his failure. He ran at the tally sheet and tore it down, shredding it to tiny snowflake scraps that fell around him.

A bottle gleamed under the desk. It still had two inches of dark red fluid in the bottom, and he drank it greedily. The ticking wall clock showed half past three.

Wyatt's eye fell on the desk again, and the letters itemizing supplies purchased months ago, requesting payment, then insisting, then threatening legal action. He swept them off the desk in one motion.

It was all over. He knew it was all over. It had been failing for weeks—months—and he knew that too. He'd concealed it from everyone. From his sanctimonious partner, whom he sometimes admired, sometimes hated. From Carla Hellman. From himself, with the aid of drink . . .

Wyatt's mind began to slip back and forth from the present to the past. Flickering scenes from Osage, Kansas, blurred over the vista of San Solaro he saw when he opened the office door.

God, the *santan* was blowing again, turning the day to night. Pathetic marker flags snapped in the gale wind. He walked around the corner of the depot and let out a cry. Inside the tent, motionless, he saw Mother. Pale, pious, dumbly affectionate—

"Get away," he screamed. She vanished.

He went wandering the streets of his dying dream. Ghost towns, that's what the Escrow Indians called these failed tracts. He saw Mother standing by a lot marker, and he shouted at her again. She vanished. *Oh yes, ghost towns,* he thought.

Sand began to accumulate in his hair, settle on his eyelids, crust on his mouth. At the intersection of two streets, he discovered another bottle. Joyfully, he ran and snatched it up. Empty. He smashed it on the ground.

A large square of cardboard skated up behind him and nuzzled his legs: SAN SOLARO OPERA HOUSE. He fell on it and ripped it apart, and the wind took the pieces, flung them aloft, sailed them away. Suddenly he was sitting in a corner, snow-drifts outside the window, with Mother wrapping his naked scrawny body in wet sheets. *"Leave me alone."*

She wouldn't. He felt Mother's hands on his head, exploring the phrenological configurations: the bumps of intelligence, moral firmness, sin, bad character. He kept screaming at her, and everything blurred, but this time she only retreated to the orange grove, where she stood among the Joshua trees, regarding him with her Christian solemnity . . .

The past flickered behind his eyes again. He was doubled over with pain in the privy, shitting out his insides, shitting so hard he couldn't stop, because of all the stuff she'd forced into him—pepsin syrup, calomel, bitter castor oil . . .

"Health and cleanliness are pleasing to God, Wyatt. I pray nightly that your body will be clean and healthy forever, my sweet boy. Swallow this."

She was calling to him from the orange grove, and snarling, he went over the rope, scrabbled and clawed his way up to the Joshua trees. Mack hadn't changed the oranges, goddamn him. The fruit was brown and withered.

Wyatt tore the oranges from the trees, hurling them every which way. Most of them rolled toward the street, and soon the slope was covered with oranges bouncing and caroming downhill.

"Wasted my time on this place. Too many problems. Too many rules. Got to be easier ways. Not here, though. Not here," he shouted to all those who'd conspired to defeat him: Mack, Mother, Carla, creditors. "Not here—the hell with this place."

When he came to his senses again, he was standing in the middle of the dry canal. Snakes of wind-driven sand and soil writhed past his feet. Mother appeared farther down the canal, a bottle of milky calomel in her hand. She held it out to him with the tenderness and pride of someone serving a fine meal. Mother was right: Health was everything. You could sell health in California, but not here. San Solaro was unhealthy.

"The hell with this place. The hell with you." Strange echoes of his cries threaded through the wind's keen—or were they in his head? He reached for the wind to choke and silence it, silence his enemies, silence his failure. Covered with dirt, wine stains, and vomit, he beat back the heavens with his fists, screaming: "The hell with you! *The hell with you!* THE HELL WITH YOU!"

* * *

Toward three o'clock the next afternoon, Christmas, the windstorm ended as abruptly as it had begun. Mack felt very much in need of a bath as he drove slowly to the arch and in beneath the pagan sunburst of The City of Health.

San Solaro had a strange quiet air. It was more than stillness after the blow. It was a sense of deadness. And something else, alarming—

Someone had trespassed.

The cardboard signs were not merely ripped down by the wind, but lay in torn bits. The flagged stakes had been pulled up and broken in two and three pieces. With sharpening anxiety, he drove along Grande Boulevard. On lot after lot, parcel after parcel, someone had destroyed the marks of a platted town.

"Wyatt?"

The shout drew no response but an echo.

Mack saw the circus tent then—collapsed, folded on itself, the white-and-yellow stripes running in all directions. *"Wyatt?"* He drove faster through the litter of signs and markers.

At the tent, he found two ends of a guy rope; they had been slashed with a knife. So had the other ropes.

He ran to the depot, and pulled up short at the sight of a paper tacked on the door. He tore it down, unable to believe the words crudely inked on it. Had Wyatt gone crazy?

IT'S ALL YOURS.

It was unmistakably his partner's hand.

Mack's stunned eyes jumped from the paper to the fallen tent, the building lots beyond. Not a sign or stake remained standing anywhere.

ALL YOURS.

"On Christmas," Mack said, his face reflecting his astonishment and dismay.

PAPERS LAY ON THE DESK IN NEAT PILES, EACH ONE **22** surmounted by a stone, a brass weight, or a child's handmade trinket. The law books on the shelves looked well used. Enrique Potter's third-floor office in the Baker Block was sunny, with an air of prosperity and efficiency. Displayed on a side table behind orderly rows of briefs, letters, and contracts, a framed ambrotype captured the good cheer of a stout Latin woman and five youngsters, dark-eyed as their mother, beaming for the photographer.

Potter puffed on a long cigar as he tapped the paper centered in front of him.

"Perfectly legal, Mr. Chance. You're entitled to your partner's share in return for one dollar."

"Provided he doesn't come back."

"Think it's likely?"

"No. Wyatt agreed contractually to hold all the down payments in escrow, but it turns out he didn't. He deposited them in a regular personal account at the Farmer's and Merchant's Bank. What percent of the escrow funds he skimmed off, I don't know. I suspect it wasn't small. I'll bet he bled us dry, because the cash drawer was always empty—we could never meet our bills."

"You knew nothing about this private account until now?"

"Nothing. Wyatt kept details like that secret. I stopped at the bank before I came here. They wouldn't divulge the last balance in the account, but they verified that Wyatt took it down to zero the first morning the bank opened after the Christmas holiday."

"They had no idea the funds of San Solaro Development were legally required to be in escrow?"

"I can't answer that. Maybe they looked the other way."

"Were the down payments in cash?"

"About half the time."

"And the other half? Checks, were they? Written how? To the corporation? Its escrow account?"

"I never saw any written either way. They were always made out to Wyatt personally."

"Didn't you think that peculiar?"

"I didn't know enough to think so, Mr. Potter. Now that it's too late, I do."

"I must say, you take embezzlement calmly."

Mack's hazel eyes fixed on his. "I can't undo it. All I can do is learn from it."

The lawyer from Durango regarded his visitor with a growing respect. Mr. Macklin Chance was poorly dressed and unpolished, but he was no bumpkin. He had a driven air about him, and he was unquestionably intelligent. Potter suspected no one would have to make an important point to him more than once.

"How many lots did the development company sell?" Potter asked.

"Only thirty-eight."

"At what price?"

"It varied according to location in the tract. The lowest interior lot went for two hundred forty-five dollars. A corner lot, along the canal, cost five fifty."

"What was the usual down payment?"

"Wyatt asked twenty percent, but in some cases he had to drop that to ten or even five to sign the deal."

"So with a full down payment on the highest-priced lot, we're only talking about a loss to the buyer of a hundred and ten dollars. Your partner didn't get away with all that much cash."

"Any is too much," Mack said, giving him a bleak look. "But he stole more than down payments. Wyatt closed on seventeen of the lots at full price. He insisted on cash at closing. He said banks tended to snoop and regulate too much."

Potter flashed a cynical smile. "Those seventeen buyers won't be a great threat. They received deeds for real property which does exist. The primary worry are the customers who lost their deposits. The sums are relatively small, but that is no guarantee you'll get off the hook. People are emotional about their money. So this is the first issue. If you want the tract, you also get the responsibility."

"I want it," Mack said without hesitation.

The lawyer flicked ash into a spittoon under his desk, then brushed a speck of it from his trousers. "The transfer should be properly recorded at the courthouse. I'll handle it, if you wish."

"For how much?"

Potter laughed. "Now there's a smart client. Ask a lawyer about his fees first, not after the work's done—when the fee is liable to quadruple. Ten dollars, plus the county recording charge."

Mack nodded to signal assent. He sat holding his hat between his knees, still unsettled by the shock of Wyatt's disappearance. It was three days after Christmas; he'd ridden Railroad all the way into Los Angeles to find some answers. The most important one eluded him: What to do next?

The question had occurred to Potter. "Your creditors . . ." he began.

"I ran the total last night. Eleven hundred seventy-three dollars, twenty-five cents."

"It's an honest man who counts the pennies."

"And someone who grew up poor. When pennies are scarce, you learn to count, Mr. Potter. Carefully. Most of the debt is owed to the surveying firm. I'll pay off all of it as soon as I can. I don't want anyone taking the land."

"How many creditors are involved?"

"Five or six."

"Give me a list. I'll work it out." Potter smiled at Mack's reaction. "Calm yourself—I won't charge. Sometimes I work for nothing if I think there's more business to be had in the future. You strike me as a client with that sort of potential."

"Well, thank you. I'm not sure your faith's justified—"

"False modesty. Of course you do."

Mack reddened, caught. He laughed and then so did the lawyer.

Potter grew serious again. "I don't know what you intend to do with San Solaro, Mr. Chance. Indeed, I don't know what you can do. It was a viable piece of property in fat times, even though, from what you tell me, your partner had only the vaguest idea of what's actually necessary to develop a town. Some of our Escrow Indians are like that. They're gone now. Times are lean. I have a client in Newhall, so I've seen your property. Given San Solaro's remote location, I'd say the land's largely worthless except as pasture."

The quiet assertion hit Mack hard. Potter handed back the agreement. From his pocket Mack took T. Fowler Haines. Why he'd brought it along he couldn't clearly say; he needed it with him, that was all. Enrique Potter looked at the guidebook with frank curiosity, but Mack didn't explain. He slipped the folded paper in beside Carla's scarf and put the book away.

A faraway drum roll of thunder drew his eye to Potter's window. Over the roofs of nearby commercial buildings, the pale winter sunshine had been eclipsed by a threatening gray sky.

"There's one possible asset on the land," Mack said. "Deposits of tar. *Brea*—"

"Ah, that's interesting. You might be sitting on oil. Do you know anything about getting it out of the ground?"

"Nothing."

"Given your present straits, Mr. Chance, it might be a good time to learn."

Mack rode Railroad over to the *Times* building. A block away, he passed a delivery wagon stacked with freshly printed copies. Reporters and others on business bustled in and out of the newspaper office unimpeded. Four weary pickets carrying placards trudged their circular path in front. Mack recognized one man from the first visit.

"Afternoon. Have you seen Father Marquez?"

"He was here till noon. There's been some trouble."

Uneasy, Mack resettled his feet in the stirrups. Railroad flicked his ears forward. "What kind of trouble?"

Another picket spat out a stream of tobacco. "The day after Christmas, Father Diego had another face-down with Otis. The father tried to stop him from going inside. The words got pretty hot, and Otis called out more of his plug-uglies. They told him a priest had no right to get down from the pulpit and mix in a labor scrap. They pushed Marquez around, he pushed back—"

"Looked like it might get real bloody, but it didn't," a third picket put in. "Just a scuffle, mostly. But a lot of threats."

"Somebody made good on 'em," said the first man.

"Yeah, but you'll never prove Otis had anything to do with it."

"What are you talking about?" Mack said.

The first picket's face grew bleak. "A rider came hightailin' in here this morning. Last night, somebody burned the Marquez family adobe. Father Diego left an hour ago."

He saw the smoke long before he saw the *rancho*. Long thin plumes drifted up at forty-five degrees against a sky turning as black as the granite lichen on the great rock faces of Yosemite.

Mack wore no spurs, but he worked Railroad hard with his boot heels, and the mule was lathering badly, almost spent from the long ride. There would be rain any minute, the storm right behind the dust plume Mack's passage had raised on the peninsula.

He wasn't concerned with that, only with the terrible message of the smoke rising above Rancho de los Palos Verdes del Pacífico. The mule climbed the last hill and then Mack halted, aghast at what he saw. Not the adobe where he'd spent the night, but its remains: fallen rubble, a few black beams at wildly canted angles. The central chimney stood alone, like a graveyard monument. The thick sour smell of burning was everywhere.

He saw a saddle horse tied to the crumbling well, but not the priest. He booted Railroad down the hill. Behind him, a lightning bolt clove the sky and forked over the mountains, appearing to strike them in three places. The wind rose, spreading the stink of the fire.

"Diego?" He shouted as he rode up to the well. "Diego, where are you?"

Raindrops fell, fat, widely separated drops that splatted the dust, leaving dark spots. He leaned on his saddle pommel, scanning the ruins. Nothing moved except the smoke tendrils rising all around the quadrangle. The raindrops blew in gusts, then, abruptly, the brief shower ended. Thunder pealed to the east.

"Diego?" he called again, choking it off when the priest stepped from behind the chimney and clambered over heaps of rubble, one hand stretched out as though he might fall any moment. His thick black hair tossed in the wind.

Mack jumped off the mule and rushed to meet his friend. "I heard about this in town. I thought you might need someone to help with—" Then he saw Marquez's eyes. Living hell. "My God, Diego, who did this?"

"Not anyone I will ever be able to find, or prosecute," the priest said with bitter fury.

"You don't think Otis ordered it?"

"Of course not. Colonel Otis is a Pilate. No need to incriminate himself. He can wash his hands—the mob will act for him."

"What can I do?"

Marquez waved him off, then lurched past him, muttering. "This is how they punish those with the temerity to speak against them. They can never be defeated fairly. The fight can't be won by turning the other cheek. It can only be won by men who fight as they do. I can't fight confined like this." His hand flew to his clerical collar and pulled, but the fabric was strong. Ropy muscles rose up on the back of his hand, and then the collar tore. His clenched hand fell to his side, the ends of the collar fluttering in the wind. Marquez stared at Mack with an ugly curl on his thick-lipped mouth, as if daring him to criticize or condemn.

Mack shivered, because he recognized something new in the priest's eyes. They no longer reflected an inner civility and compassion, only brute anger.

"What are you talking about, Diego? What are you going to do?"

"*Do?*" Marquez repeated with a thick poisonous sarcasm. He threw the collar in the ashes, and in a moment a thread of smoke arose. "From this hour, I am going to fight them on their terms, not the Lord's. I am going to war."

The winter rain began to fall again, this time in earnest. The downpour soon smothered the embers, and when the charred beams cooled sufficiently, Mack used them to put together a crude shelter, with his saddle blanket for the roof. Marquez paid no attention, wandering disconsolately along the bluff.

For a while Mack feared he might throw himself onto the rocks below.

After a bit the priest returned. Mack offered him some hard-tack from his saddlebag, but Marquez wouldn't touch it. He hardly spoke, and Mack passed a miserable night trying to sleep under scant cover. Marquez squatted in the open, soaked, staring at nothing.

In the morning, he was calmer. He pressed Mack's hand and clasped his shivering shoulder. "I appreciate your kindness. But I'd like you to leave me now."

"I can't just ride off and abandon—" Mack sneezed.

The priest almost smiled. "Come, do what I ask. I don't want your death on my conscience. I have other things to deal with."

Rain dripped off Mack's soaked hat brim. He peered into Marquez's eyes, trying to fathom his intent. What did he mean about war? Where would he go? How would he survive?

"Leave me," the priest said again. It was emphatic and cold.

Mack growled something and put his boot in Railroad's stirrup.

At the head of the first rise, he glanced back. Marquez was kneeling in the rain amidst the canted beams and rubble, hands clasped, head bowed. Somehow, Mack didn't think he was praying to a kind or forgiving God.

IN THE DEPOT OFFICE THE FOLLOWING NIGHT, MACK **23** began to rifle through Wyatt's desk.

He pulled out everything: ledgers, unopened letters, notes Wyatt had written to himself. As he sifted through them, he began to see how complex a man Wyatt was. Some of the notes bristled with ideas for promoting San Solaro—"moonlight excursion?" "champagne supper?"—things Wyatt had never followed up. The ledgers were blotted, sloppily kept in a poor hand, with significant gaps between the dates of the entries. Many of the letters were creditor demands that Wyatt had ignored. In the stacks and stacks of paper, a portrait grew of a man brilliant, unscrupulous, and erratic. Mack had known that about Wyatt in some deep well of wordless understanding. He hadn't wanted to admit to himself that his partner was a criminal as well as dangerously unstable.

The sound of a horse and rig came to him over the pelting of the rain. He picked up a kerosene lamp and held it high in the door.

The phaeton with yellow wheels rolled out of the night. Carla jumped down with a dripping parasol that hadn't protected her from the rain; her hair was darker and plastered flat to her head. She was mussed and excited.

"I came the instant I heard. It's all over Ventura County, I gather. Wyatt's absconded."

"That's right. Come in."

Streams of rain sluiced noisily down the roof. Carla shook her parasol and plucked her wet blouse away from her breasts. As soon as she let it go it clung again.

"You don't look like you've slept . . ." she began.

"I haven't, much. I've been plowing through all these." He indicated the paper stacks. "Trying to find out who he cheated." He struck the desk with his fist. "Who put up the money? That's the big question. How the hell did he get thirty thousand dollars to buy this land?"

"Well, you certainly won't find out by exhausting yourself and ranting." She perched her parasol in a corner and smoothed her riding skirt. "Are you going to be polite and offer me a chair?"

He pointed to it. She sighed and sat.

"What's the real upshot of all this, Mack? Are you saddled with his debts?"

"I have a good lawyer working on that—Potter, in Los Angeles. I want to pay off the debts if the creditors will permit it." He sat at the desk, feeling the weariness settle into him at last; wild energy generated by repeated shocks had staved it off, but couldn't any longer. He rubbed his forehead. "I'm sorry I don't have some wine to offer you. Not much food, either."

Carla touched her hair, an unconscious feminine gesture. "I didn't come here for food or wine." Uncomfortably, he saw her dark-blue eyes finishing the statement.

"If Wyatt's gone," she said after a moment, "what happens to the title to San Solaro?"

He explained the agreement, and she clapped her hands. "Then you're the owner. Everything is solved. I knew you'd be successful."

"Certainly," he said with a bitter look. "I now own a hundred percent of nothing instead of twenty percent."

She leaned forward. "Whatever money you need to right the

situation here, pay your creditors—I have it. More than enough. It's yours.''

"Carla, the money I pay to the creditors has to be money I make myself.''

Her eyes flashed with reflections of the kerosene lamps. "I'd be angry with you if you weren't so crashingly upright to the point of being ridiculous.'' She leaned over him and kissed him lightly on the lips. Damp hair fell against his cheek. He smelled the wet-musky odor of her skin. "You're as stubborn as old Swampy. We can discuss that later. There's a more urgent problem. One that has needed a resolution for many a week.''

Again she kissed him. This time it was longer, firmer, with a sinuous little caress of the tip of her tongue. Despite his exhaustion, his body responded.

"I really came over because I knew you'd be alone. Finally. I never belonged to Wyatt, but you seemed to think I did . . .''

Her tongue touched his cheek, a slow, tantalizing lick. "So now I'll remind you . . .''

Her hand dropped into his lap. She laughed low over what she found.

"Wyatt is gone. There's no one to disturb us. Those papers will wait. We can be together all night long.''

"Carla—"

"No, Mack. No more protests. I get what I want. What I want is you.''

Her hand down there between them caressed and pressed, and he broke. He seized her face in both hands and kissed her with all the violence of emotion finally released.

He blew out one of the two lamps. Hoisting her in his arms, he kissed her face, her ear, the corner of her mouth.

"Not here," he said. "This was his. The tent.''

"No, I can't wait. I can't wait.''

Carla held on to his chest. She was astride him, and her thighs and flanks shone from the exertion of rising and falling. Mack's left hand gripped her waist and his right held her breast. He felt her hard nipple on his palm.

The passion wracked them. Carla threw her head back. She began to bite her lips and toss her unbound hair.

Suddenly he took hold of her waist, lifted, and rolled her over. She tumbled on her back on Wyatt's bed with a cry of mingled surprise and excitement, and he flung his leg across her thighs. She was browned evenly by the sun on every part of her body.

With a gasp, he heaved himself on top, kissing her hard to forestall argument. She groped for him, guided him, her blue eyes huge with a bewilderment soon replaced by foggy understanding.

She cried out, eyes shut. Mack drowned in her scent, her softness, kissing her throat. She kneaded his shoulders and beat the backs of his legs with her heels. The passion was so intense it hurt. He thrust harder and deeper. They rode that way, up to the peak.

Shattered, he slept with Carla in his arms.

Much later, the storm intensified. Heavy rain slammed the roof, leaking through some crack out in the office. Lightning washed the streaming windows. Unseen faults in the earth seemed to shudder with every thunderclap.

He gently touched her round, voluptuous body, brushed her shoulder with a kiss. She woke, muttering, then felt his hand touching her and laughed.

"Wait, though—" She struggled away.

He propped up on his elbows. "What for?"

"Do you have the gold scarf? The one you saved? This time I want to wear it for you."

Entering her again, he found her slick and fever-hot. The rain slackened a little. He could hear the bed creaking fast beneath them. She was incredible—soft, pillowlike, with no prudish restraint. She bit him and petted him and whispered into his ears shocking words that made him love her the more furiously.

A new sound brushed at the edge of awareness while they rode up toward the climax again, a rushing roar. Then he guessed its source: water in the canal, water streaming off the steep hillsides, crashing through the dry channel in a torrent.

"God, God, I love you," she cried over the roar.

The gray sky boiled with clouds of darker gray and a light shower speckled the overflowing canal. The water was still draining from the hillsides, rushing along to spread in huge pools out where the banks of the streambed flattened, three quarters of a mile beyond the gate.

The air was cool and refreshed. They walked along the canal bank, Carla clinging to his arm affectionately. She'd pulled her hair back and tied it with the scarf and her cheeks had a scrubbed shiny look, free of rouge and mascara. Mack had never seen this woman before: satiated, quiet, meek.

He watched the flowing water, pondering.

"What are you thinking?"

"You'd be insulted."

"No, tell me."

"I'm thinking about this." He jumped off the bank, landing knee-deep in the swift brown flow. The canal actually almost resembled the dishonest illustration in Wyatt's brochure. "Water," he shouted, flinging his arms out. He strode upstream, splashing, his glance flying back and forth from the black-clouded peaks to the dry thirsty shores of the canal. He remembered Marquez talking about the importance of water. The old Indian in Wheatville too.

Carla watched him with amused surprise as Mack splashed up fans of water with his hands. "If we had this much water all the time—in a reservoir, behind a dam—this land wouldn't be worthless. Wyatt promised it to buyers but he didn't have a notion of how to deliver. I'm going to find out."

Exhilarated and soaked, he came back and clambered up beside her. "There, I told you what I was thinking. You're insulted, aren't you?"

Still amused, she said, "Only a little. I got what I wanted. Finally." Quite unexpectedly, she caressed his face. Her eyes grew strangely anxious. "Did you like it, Mack? Please tell me you did. I'm not good for much else."

Unbidden, Nellie's face came to mind. What would Nellie say about a woman who thought so little of herself? She would erupt. Maybe Carla couldn't help her feelings. She seemed so unsure all at once, vulnerable as a child.

Reassuring her wasn't hard.

"I liked it." He smiled. "Very much."

"Then let's go back and—"

"No, Carla. No more today. I have to plow through the rest of those blasted papers. I have to figure out what I'm going to do with this place."

"I said you needn't worry. I have enough money for both of us."

"I've taken all I can from you."

His firmness destroyed her docility, and the old familiar Carla came back, a puzzling conspirator's smile fleeting over her face.

"For the moment," she said, kissing him.

They walked back toward the depot along the rushing canal. "When will I see you, Mack?"

"I don't know. Maybe when this is all straightened out."

After she left, he realized with some annoyance that she had still been wearing the golden scarf.

On New Year's Eve, 1888, he found a news clipping.

It was in a large tattered envelope, one of the last desk items he examined. With it were a lock of dark hair wrapped in a cheap woman's handkerchief, a certificate of birth from Osage County, Kansas, and a small oval daguerreotype of a tired young woman with light eyes and a smile so strained it was obviously supplied just for the photographer. The clipping was from the *San Diego Bee*, dated November 1887.

SENSATIONAL MURDER!

Remains of Don Ysidor Sterns Discovered at His Residence

The battered corpse of the wealthy and respected Don Ysidor Sterns, a longtime resident of this area, was found Monday morning in the main house of Rancho de la Bahía, the Sterns family home for ninety years.

Authorities report Don Ysidor was bludgeoned to death in a most brutal manner. The Don, a widower whose numerous children and grandchildren reside in other parts of California, lived alone. He was faithful in attendance at Sunday mass at his church. When he failed to appear on Sunday, Fr. Anselm Gruder, fearing illness, rode to the Don's residence early Monday morning. Fr. Gruder discovered the grisly corpse.

There were no signs of forced intrusion. However, authorities discovered a large metal cashbox, which showed dents and scratches. Its lock was broken, the contents removed. Don Ysidor was considered a man of means, with substantial investments in San Diego street railways, and also in Elisha Babcock's land syndicate, which constructed the sumptuous Coronado Hotel and developed the Coronado Heights and South Coronado tracts.

Mack laid the yellowed cutting on the desk with an unsteady hand. "Damn you, Wyatt. God damn you."

Now he knew where the money had come from, even if he'd never know how Wyatt had charmed his way into the house, and the presence, of the man he murdered.

On the first business day of 1889, Mack returned to Los Angeles and called on Potter. He handed the lawyer the old envelope, sealed with blobs of wax.

"Will you keep this in your safe?"

"Certainly. What is it?"

"Some personal papers. Nothing important."

Enrique Potter bobbed his head and squared the envelope in front of him. He regarded Mack with a pleased smile.

"Happy New Year, then. It certainly looks more auspicious than the last one."

"I don't know how you can say that. San Solaro Development owes all those people their down payments—"

"Yes, but as a practical matter, how many of them reside anywhere nearby?"

Mack had often seen the list. "Not a one."

"Then they will have to come out here again, or at least engage California attorneys, to institute proceedings against you as owner. Considering the relatively small sums involved that may never come to pass. But if it should, I can maneuver and gain you some time."

"All right, do it. I'll pay those people back, every one. With interest. But there's still the eleven hundred and seventy-three dollars locally—"

"No, those six creditors are paid. There are no immediate encumbrances on San Solaro."

Mack assumed he'd misheard. "No—?"

"Debt. For the moment, the property is yours to do with as you wish."

"Potter, what the hell's going on?"

The lawyer slid a drawer out. "A young woman called on me late on New Year's Eve. A very attractive young woman, from Ventura County. She said she was your partner. She gave me eleven hundred and seventy-three dollars in cash. I didn't mention the twenty-five cents."

Mack missed the gentle joke, blurting, "I don't have any partner besides Wyatt."

"So I thought. However, she was quite insistent about helping you. To protect you, I wrote a short agreement. It merely

219

states that a loan was made to you at no interest, with no due date, and no other contingencies. In other words, you may pay her back tomorrow, or never. I didn't expect her to be willing to sign such an agreement.''

He drew it from the desk, rolled up and tied with the gold scarf.

Mack snatched the paper and tore the scarf away. Carla's large signature was slashed at the bottom of a short paragraph.

"Otto Hellman's daughter," Potter said. "Very impressive."

"Damn it, she can't do this."

"I'm sorry—I thought you'd be pleased. I've already paid the creditors. I can hardly go back to them and say you'd like to renege and assume your debt again. I think they'll prefer to keep the cash. Frankly, I don't understand this reaction."

"Personal. Never mind." Mack stood up so quickly his chair almost turned over. "Please have someone keep watch on San Solaro. I'm going away for a while to get money to return the down payments and then develop the property. I'll pay you for all your trouble."

"No trouble. Consider it another investment in the future. How will we communicate?"

"I'll be in touch as soon as possible."

"Very good, Mr. Chance."

"If you're my lawyer, it's Mack."

Potter was pleased. "May I ask where you intend to go?"

"To follow your suggestion about oil."

"Be careful. The oil towns are some of the roughest in the West. Carrying a side arm might be advisable—"

His client was already out the door.

Mack hammered up hasps on the two depot doors, ran a chain through each, and then secured them with padlocks. He stood back and surveyed the building, clean-washed by January sunshine falling through broken clouds. Patterns of light and shade lay on the steep hillsides and the air had a refreshing sharpness.

He patted Railroad as he tied a small carpetbag to his saddle. "Come on, old son. We're going prospecting again."

The mule flicked its ears forward and back. Mack climbed up and jogged toward the arch, looking behind him once. A shaft of sun illuminated the sham orange grove.

He'd gotten over some of his anger, but he despised Wyatt for involving him in a project financed by murder. There was no concrete evidence that Wyatt had killed and robbed the San Diego businessman. But why else would he preserve the news cutting with his other personal treasures, except as a reminder of his prowess?

Of course Wyatt hadn't exactly begged Mack to join in; he had knocked at the door. Well, nothing to be done now. San Solaro existed above and apart from the circumstances of its purchase. And he owned it. He didn't like Carla's intervention, but he couldn't change that either. Not for a while.

His spirits were lifting again. The canal was dry, but he'd seen it flowing with water that could transform this arid valley. He owned the canal, and eighteen hundred acres besides. And despite the debt to all those Wyatt had robbed, he was encouraged. He was a man of property.

He was on his way.

He passed by a sunken pool of *brea*—a good omen. Recalling what Potter had said about carrying a pistol in the oil towns, he decided he'd buy one first chance he got. He rode out beneath the iron arch and turned west.

The crooked sign on the crooked post said HELLMAN.

The malevolent black sky threatened rain and raw wind blew from the Pacific. Mack tugged his hat lower against the dust, wondering if he had the right place. A dirt track left the main road at this point, meandering out of sight over a hill where cattle grazed. They looked well fed, and that persuaded him to try the road.

From the hill's summit he saw the ranch beside the Santa Clara River. The house was substantial but not opulent; it spread in several wings and was constructed of tawny stucco, with red half-round roof tiles. A few *vaqueros* worked around the barns and outbuildings.

A broad-shouldered woman with black braids answered the fall of the enormous ring knocker. Mack worked out the words in his head before he addressed her.

"Hablo con Señorita Hellman, por favor."

"¿Señorita Hellman?"

He nodded.

"Pero ella no está aquí." The Indian woman took pity on his Spanish and repeated in English, "Not here."

"Will she be back soon?"

"No, she packed everything. She has gone to Paris."

"Paris, France?"

"Is there another?"

He felt a stab of disappointment. For days he'd thought of Carla. Every night, too. She was a craving, like a drug. He'd repeatedly been tempted to ride over here to Ventura County, but had kept from it by telling himself what he already knew: She was beautiful, but she was willful and dangerous.

Instead, he'd decided on this kind of visit—to cut it off with a polite good-bye, tell her he'd repay the loan and that would be it between them. She'd stolen a march. He turned the brim of his hat in his hands. The Indian woman started to shut the great carved door.

"Wait. I came to say good-bye to Señorita Hellman. Please write my name down—Macklin Chance."

Indifference gave way to politeness. "Ah, Chance. Señor Chance. For you she left a message."

"What is it?"

"She said to tell you it was necessary for her to leave for a while—"

"Necessary? Why?"

The woman ignored his question. "She said she would see you again, you are to be assured of it."

She bid him good-day and closed the door. As he mounted the mule, he saw the dark-gray clouds boiling from the west, full of storm. He turned the mule's head out into the bitter wind, mightily confused about Carla's sudden departure, and his own reaction to it.

Two days later, waiting in a barbershop in Newhall, he picked up a Los Angeles paper from the week before.

DOMESTIC VIOLENCE IN SAN DIEGO!

Police Summoned to Beavis Mansion! Tycoon Hospitalized with Stab Wounds!

Wife Files Alienation of Affection Suit; Heiress Named

A rotten scandal, Hellman said. Now Mack understood. He also knew Carla's disposition. She might flee the trouble, but not forever . . .

You are to be assured of it.

He was overjoyed, and at the same time he dreaded the moment of reunion. He was angry about his confusion and helpless to get rid of it. The one certainty was that she'd be back.

IV

ROUGHNECKS

1889–1895

They called it la brea, *the tarry stuff in Southern California that congealed in pools, hinting at huge deposits of petroleum lying below.*

For a long time, hardly anyone cared. To the early coastal Indians, brea *was a common brown-black substance useful for waterproofing canoes and baskets, cementing bundles of yucca fibers to make brushes, or setting ornamental inlays of shells. Now and then an enterprising member of the Chumash or Yokut tribe hauled some of the stuff inland and bartered it to other tribes for spearheads and furs. It was not considered particularly remarkable—not by the tribes, and not by the early settlers. Coming down from the mountains into California, newcomers saw oil seeps hellishly aflame on the plain, and glimpsed similar fires far up in narrow canyons. Later, a few of their brighter counterparts collected buckets of this pitch, as they called it, using it to grease the hubs of their wagons and the moving parts of their farm machinery.*

It wasn't until the 1850s, however, that Californians made a serious attempt to dig out the tarry material for commercial purposes. Even then, those wanting to sell or lease land to prospective wildcatters found that they needed promotional help, and hired the inevitable consultants. One such was the famous and distinguished chemist Professor Benjamin Silliman of Yale. Silliman wrote enthusiastic endorsements of the riches lurking under the ground in California, including several tracts he never visited. He analyzed and lauded the quality of certain samples of California oil, but when some rival academicians, perhaps jealous of the professor's high consulting fees, proved that the samples were enhanced with Devoe's Kerosene, an eastern product widely available in California stores, Silliman's reputation was ruined.

Still, even honest promotion couldn't make California oil better than it was. Back in 1859, Colonel E. L. Drake had sunk his famous well at Oil Creek, Pennsylvania, and touched off an oil boom there. Pennsylvania crude was high-grade stuff; it could be refined into superior lubricating and illuminating oils. It yielded grease of a fine, thick consistency and lamp oil that burned clean, bright, and hot, virtually without smoke. No such claims could be made for the lubricants and oils haphazardly produced in California a few years later.

The state's pioneer oil industry was a pygmy, and a weak pygmy at that. Nevertheless, California oil attracted men from Pennsylvania and elsewhere who migrated west late in the century, eager for the wealth that had eluded them back home. When they arrived, the familiar pattern repeated once again: It was the outsider, the newcomer with more greed than geology, who would suck California's black gold out of the earth and make it pay.

In the spring of 1889, in Ventura County, **24**
Mack Chance worked for a driller named Mulroy.
Mulroy had a lean purse; he hunted for oil the two-thousand-year-old Chinese way, using a drilling tool attached to a spring pole. Hour after hour, Mack pulled the pole down on its fulcrum, then released it to slam the tool into the ground. Mindless, grueling work, it paid only $1.50 a day. Mulroy's shallow holes were all sunk on the south side of the Santa Clara River, and every one was a duster. After Mulroy abandoned the sixth, Mack decided he could learn nothing more, and quit.

Up north of the river, in the foothills of the San Rafaels, oil sands promised a profit, but the slopes were too steep for conventional derricks. Hardison & Stewart Oil, out of Santa Paula, designed horizontal tunnels for the hillsides. When complete, and infused with water, the tunnels allowed seeping oil to float out on top of the water and then, by gravity, trickle through a system of wooden ditches down to large open collection tanks.

Mack worked the rest of 1889 on the crew digging the tunnels into Sulphur Mountain. Some were sixteen hundred feet, longer than most deep wells. To provide the diggers with light, mirrors were set up and properly angled at the tunnel entrance, reflecting sunshine into the shaft. It was an ingenious system. Someone told Mack that Africans had invented it long ago.

Mack earned $3 a day for the tunnel work and sent most of the money to Potter in Los Angeles for the taxes on San Solaro; the lawyer had promised to advance him any shortfall sum for the year, and wrote to say that, thus far, there had been only one threat of legal action by a purchaser. Deep in the tunnel, awash in his own briny sweat, Mack struck all the harder with his pick whenever he thought of Enrique Potter. If the lawyer had such faith in him, he had to justify it.

After hours, he asked questions of the older men, the supervisors, about the nature of the underground oil formations (unpredictable), and the characteristics of California crude (in one word, poor).

In December an explosion in a tunnel killed four men. As Mack watched the pine coffins being loaded on a wagon, he decided he'd learned all he could from the Sulphur Mountain operation.

He rode Railroad to San Solaro. The gateway arch was rusting and weeds and scrub vegetation stood knee-high, but the padlocks on the depot remained secure. In Los Angeles he paid a call on Potter, who was now fending off three purchasers with legalistic letters containing vague promises of repayment.

Then Mack left the city and rode over the mountains to the flatlands of Kern County, where he discovered work was scarce. In a month, he found nothing in the oil business and was soon down to eating one meal a day. Finally, he took the first job that came along, a bad one, in a godforsaken spot called Asphalto.

Lying in the western part of Kern County, Asphalto produced what its name suggested: asphalt for roofing and street paving. Huge kettles boiled the raw asphalt for twelve hours, putting a permanent stench in the air, then the hot asphalt was poured from the sediment into forms of sand, for shaping, hardening, and eventual shipment.

To get the asphalt, miners worked in large open pits. Because the stuff quickly destroyed clothes, they worked naked. At the end of a twelve-hour tour—in the oil fields, this word was pronounced to rhyme with *hour*, for no reason ever satisfactorily explained to Mack—a corps of boys with wooden horse-scrapers swarmed over the miners, scraping off the tarry stuff and a lot of skin too. Mack and the others then washed down in stinging petroleum distillate. They sat naked in the mess tent, their chests and flanks still shining from the distillate, as if lacquered. Mack discovered you never got totally clean. The management insisted on covering the mess benches with newspaper, and at the end of his very first meal, he stood up and found big sheets of paper stuck to his ass.

The work paid $3 a day because it was mindless, filthy, and lonely. A few coarse whores hung around Asphalto, but even they expressed distaste for the smelly, sticky miners. In the dark of the bunk tents, men made love to each other. Mack often lay awake, forearm on his forehead, hand clenched, listening, longing for Nellie, struggling against the urges of a young man's body.

A new man came to work, a man of intimidating bulk. He wore a wide belt with a studded buckle and he often used it as a weapon, so others called him Strap. One night, outside the bunk tent, Mack found Strap Vigory grappling with one of the scraper boys, a timid lad named Homer.

"Look, Vigory, leave the boy alone," Mack said.

"You interferin' with a man's pleasure?" Vigory said, touching his studded buckle.

"Never. So long as it's Homer's pleasure too. Doesn't appear that it is. Homer, scoot out of here."

"Yeah, Homer, I see you later. This gent an' me, we got business."

Mack and Strap Vigory squared off, buck naked, in a ring of miners excitedly making bets. Strap used his belt while Mack fought bare-knuckled. Strap lashed him and flayed him around the head and shoulders, drawing blood, but Mack waded in, and in ten minutes his deft punching wore through the bigger man's defenses and put him down. The fourth time Strap fell, he didn't get up. Mack left him snorting and thrashing.

Next morning, in the wagon stable where he quartered Railroad, Mack found the mule lying motionless—bludgeoned to death by some kind of blunt instrument. Strap Vigory had already disappeared. Deciding he'd had a bellyful of Asphalto, Mack quit at the end of that week.

By early autumn he was back in Santa Paula. It was a small place, about three hundred in the permanent population, but that was swelled by a constantly changing troupe of wildcatters, roughnecks, gamblers, and other parasites who fed on the oilmen. There were also some characters with no discernible reason for their presence unless it was a desire to hide out from civilization, and maybe the law. A lot of the transients lived in tents or packing-box hovels, which lent the town an even more temporary air. Santa Paula's rough element boasted that they had a saloon for every seven families. Shootings were a common occurrence.

Mack signed on as a roughneck with Hardison & Stewart Oil, which soon was to merge with two others, Sespe Canyon Oil and Torrey Canyon Oil, into a larger and stronger firm called Union. With some of his wages Mack finally bought a pistol, a secondhand Model '73 Peacemaker Colt, six-shot, .45-caliber. It was a popular frontier weapon, simple and well built, with walnut stocks and a blued finish. Mack chose the more citified snub-nosed version, the so-called Shopkeeper's model. He packed it in a holster riding behind him, at the top of his right buttock.

Hardison & Stewart sent him to a crew working in the hills north of the river. On the fourth day of spudding in a new well, the bit cocked in the hole and couldn't be dislodged. Mack volunteered to go down after it, not out of any bravado, but to see whether human strength could solve such a problem. The lost bit, which roughnecks called the fish, was stuck at a depth of 245 feet.

Mack stripped off his shirt. They tied a hemp line under his arms—he stuffed rags into his armpits first—and after lowering a lantern to be sure there was breathable air, he stepped into the narrow hole.

Down he went in the dark, suspended on the sand line from the sand reel. The sand line normally lowered the bailer that brought out the slurry of rock broken up by the drilling tool, which worked on a separate line. Very shortly, Mack regretted volunteering. He could hardly move in the well, its diameter roughly 2 feet. About 150 feet of heavy sheet-iron casing had been put in, and it scraped his shoulders till they bled. The air grew heavy, rank, almost impossible to breathe. Down he went, and down, until the light above no longer revealed his own hands in front of his face. The sense of confinement, of being buried alive in a small grave, worsened every moment.

Finally he was just above the jammed tool. He had no room to bend and reach it with his hands but could only draw his legs up slightly, then kick. He kicked for ten minutes, sweat pouring over his face. He thought he would die from lack of air. Finally he raised one hand to yank the line and signal the crew to pull him up. He didn't like being defeated but it seemed impossible to free the tool. He vented his disgust in one last clumsy kick.

The tool dislodged from the slate ridge where it had stuck. Mack gasped—he was ready to faint—and yanked hard on the line. The steam engine rewound the hemp line on the sand wheel. He was brought up into the sunlight a hero.

The firm's senior partner, Lyman Stewart, personally rewarded him with two tours off, at full pay; cable tool drills were expensive items.

Stewart was about fifty, a small-boned, natty man with a beard, pince-nez, and the demeanor of a Presbyterian deacon. He walked among the foul-mouthed roughnecks like a schoolmaster among rowdy but promising pupils. Stewart was currently raising money to build a new chapel in Santa Paula.

At the end of a little speech of commendation, Stewart said, "Be prudent with the extra money, Chance. To squander it on drinking or chewing is to play the Devil's game." A good Presbyterian, all right.

* * *

Mack's trip down the hole earned him a reputation in Santa Paula. Another wildcatter sought him out, a man with offices in a crude one-story wood box of a building located directly across the main street from the crude one-story wood box Stewart and his partner shared with Mission Transfer, a pipeline company.

Jason Preston Danvers, a Pennsylvanian, headed Keystone Oil. The company had leases up in the foothills, but no producing wells so far. Danvers was a heavy man with large spectacles, a high pompadour, and an air of being oppressed, and depressed, by circumstance. Like Enrique Potter, he kept a photograph of his family on his desk. Mack counted eight children, the oldest but ten or eleven.

"Thank you, Mr. Danvers, but I've got a job like that," Mack said after he heard the man's offer.

Jace Danvers sighed. Another defeat. "What is it you want, then?"

"To learn more about the business. I figure the only way I can do that is to move up to tool dresser." A tool dresser was number two on a two-man drill crew, responsible for sharpening the tools to the required diameter and keeping them sharp at the derrick forge. A tool dresser also did whatever else the driller told him to do.

"Oil is something that interests you? I mean, as more than temporary work?"

Mack nodded. "But I've got to be honest. I don't know much about petroleum geology."

"Hell, neither do nine tenths of the men punching holes around here. What good would it do? The surface signs, the standing pools, aren't reliable. You'd think oil up above would mean oil right below, but no. The strata are tilted every which way. You can't pierce them straight and clean, the way you can in Pennsylvania. Even if you get the crude out, it's inferior. Paraffin content's low . . . California lubricating oils and axle grease flow like water. The key is refining—better refining. I've discussed that with Stewart. He's working on it."

"I appreciate that there are problems, but—"

"You can't imagine how many," Danvers interrupted. "One of the biggest is the railroad."

"Then I'll learn about those too, when I get the right kind of job."

He sat waiting, sensing that Danvers could be prodded. Presently Danvers shot him a look from under his dour brow.

233

"I have a new driller working up in Salt Marsh Canyon. Derrick's just being built. He might take you on."

"As a tool dresser? Four dollars a day? That's standard—"

"Chance, I'm hard-pressed for cash."

"If I do the work, I want the pay."

"All right, all right," Danvers said wearily. "You've got a good reputation. I'll hire you if the driller says yes. Go see him. I'll write the directions."

He rummaged for paper on a desk overflowing with it, in the process knocking a stack off the edge. "God, sometimes I wonder why I stay in this rotten business."

Out in Salt Marsh Canyon, the derrick floor was down and the rig-building crew was dragging four peeled tree trunks from a wagon. The logs would be the lower legs of the derrick.

"Where's the boss?" Mack asked one of the rig men. He was referred to a tall, lank, homely fellow in his mid-to-late thirties, with a long, strong-looking jaw and crinkly hair already showing a lot of gray. He wore tooled boots, tight jeans, a work shirt cut off at the shoulders, and a large flowing yellow bandanna. Holstered on his left hip was a longer, more expensive version of Mack's Peacemaker Colt.

Mack went over to introduce himself. "Macklin Chance is my name." He held out his hand. The older man didn't shake. He was sunburned, his face as rough and full of gullies as the land roundabout, and his eyes were pale green, the color of new leaves on a cottonwood.

"Johnson. Fella from town said yesterday Jace was sending you out. Know anything about worrying down an oil well?" There was a thick slice of the South in the man's speech.

"I've worked in parts of the business almost two years," Mack said.

"That's no damn answer. I need an experienced tool dresser."

Mack didn't care for his bluntness. "I don't have experience but I can learn. You tell me once, it'll be done."

Johnson snorted. "Cocky cuss, ain't you? Well, why not? I don't see any other candidates lined up around here." He calculated silently. "Three-fifty a day and your keep."

"Four dollars. Regular tool dresser's wage."

"You got no experience. You said so."

"I'll work that much harder to make up for it. Give you double effort on every tour." He rhymed it with *hour*. He could tell Johnson caught that.

"Let's discuss it up at my palatial ranch house yonder." He

indicated a shanty a short way up the slope from the well site. The company's financial condition was clear from its sign: just an amateurish keystone and a large *14* painted in whitewash.

"I got a few swigs of popskull in a bottle," Johnson added. "Mighty hot out here, and these boys can get along for a while. Follow me."

Mack followed.

Johnson put wooden chairs against the front of the shanty. From there he could watch the rig builders setting spikes into braces between the first pair of derrick legs. These spikes would be hammered the rest of the way when the legs were raised in position.

Johnson brought out his brown bottle but Mack passed on it. The driller set it under his own chair, tilted back, and began to worry invisible specks off the barrel of his Peacemaker with a clean rag.

The gun was a beautiful weapon, its silvered metal elaborately engraved, each of its mother-of-pearl handgrips embossed with a large lone star. The front half of the trigger guard was cut away, for faster shooting. The Colt did not look like an amateur's piece.

"Fine gun," Johnson said when he noticed Mack's interest. "A hundred dollars, new, in Fort Worth."

"That's where you're from?"

"There and elsewhere. First name's Hugh, H-U-G-H. Hell of a name for a Texas boy, ain't it? My mama hoped I'd grow up to be a gentleman. I sure-God disappointed the dear woman."

"When did you come to California?"

Johnson's expression grew guarded. "Oh, some years back. I used to be a cowboy. Then the big ranch combines from New York started buying up all the spreads I worked for, one after another, and cutting wages, and soon I couldn't earn a dime. So I drifted over the mountains and learned a new trade." He gestured to the derrick site.

"So now you're an oilman—"

"Till something better shows up. I never stick long at any one thing. Somehow or other I was born with an urge to drift. I reckon I can't drift until I punch this hole for Jace Danvers. Lord, that man travels with a cloud of pain and woe thicker'n a blue norther."

"I noticed."

"Jace is a decent sort, I'll give him that. Loves his family. Wants to provide. It flogs him something awful." Johnson idly scraped at a nostril with his thumbnail. "It's a reason I never married. Among many."

"I'm single too."

"What are you doing in this part of the world?"

Mack gave him a level look, the two of them seated there with chairs tilted back in the scant shade. A foot-long chuckwalla lizard with a broad fat head wandered by in the shale below. Apparently unafraid of daylight or human beings, it stuck out its tongue at the men. Johnson stuck out his tongue at the lizard, and it ran.

"What I'm trying to do is get rich," Mack said.

"How?"

"Any way I can. I'm from Pennsylvania, like Danvers. I already own some land over in Los Angeles County."

"And I'm 'sposed to learn you what I know about oil, huh?"

"I guess you'd better." Mack swung a hand to encompass the steep narrow canyon and the derrick site. "I don't see any other candidates lined up here."

"By God you're a pert cuss, Mr. Chance. Pertness says to me that a man's got sand. I like that. I dunno, though. I'm out here to work, not run a school."

A long silence told Mack he was in trouble. Impulsively, he said, "I'll take care of the grub too. Bear steak, fancy omelets, hangtown fry—I'm a damn good cook."

"You're hired."

25 MACK HAD SEEN OPERATING WELLS AND KNEW something about their components, but he'd never had his hands on a standard tool rig or helped spud in a new hole. This equipment was modern, a far cry from Mulroy's spring poles.

The basic tool string consisted of a chisel-like bit hooked to the stem, an iron bar connected to a long two-and-a-quarter-inch Manila line. A coal-fired boiler generated steam for the little twenty-horsepower engine. The engine spun the band wheel, and the band wheel and its pitman rod tipped a walking beam up and down over the hole. Pulling the tool string up and dropping it by means of the walking-beam action dug the well.

Johnson was a brusque, impatient teacher, but a good one.

There was no job on the rig Mack didn't learn. He sharpened tools at the coal forge, and clambered to the top of the derrick to free a drill line fouled on the crown block pulley. He and Johnson sweated to make casing out of columns of steel pipe, one wedged inside the other; to Mack fell the task of pounding the casing with a sledge to indent it, thus creating a strong bond without rivets. The casing, heavier than the tools, had its own special block-and-tackle support system, running off the calf wheel.

Mack learned the nine-strand splice and soon repaired broken line so well that the original break was invisible. He ran the bailer to pull up drill cuttings. He cleaned scale from the inside of the boiler. He did the cooking.

Johnson kept the logbook: how many feet drilled per day; how many feet cased. And he knew tricks. "If you have a good day, go short on what you report in the log. That way, when you get a bad day, and you will, you got leeway. Some extra feet to make up for your mistakes."

The Texan handled another important job around the well. Mack discovered this one afternoon when the little steam engine quit. Johnson peeled off his shirt, revealing a long hook-shaped knife scar, deep once but healed now, running down the left side of his back. Then he attacked the engine with wrench, pliers, and a crowbar and sweated and swore over it for half an hour, at the end of which time it sputtered once and died.

"Damn modern machines," Johnson said heavily, then started working again.

Looking on, Mack said, "I'm glad you're mechanical, because I'm not."

Johnson spat a stream of his plug tobacco. "I ain't mechanical, just available. On the range I always got stuck repairin' the chuck wagon because nobody else would . . ." After another adjustment he started the engine. In ten seconds it started to die again. Disgusted, he whacked it with the crowbar. The engine went *whump-thump* and then settled down, running smoothly.

They broke one tool in the crazy tilted strata of Salt Marsh Canyon. Then they punched through a layer of hard rock into sand, and the new tool went too fast and stuck. It took three days to free the fish and recover it.

At 605 feet, sulfur water gushed up. They hooked up a pump and ran it for a week, pumping water but no oil. Jace Danvers rode out and gloomily inspected the well and then the log, and authorized another 100 feet. They hit more slate. The drill line

237

broke, the sides of the well caved in, and fishing couldn't recover the tool. Jace Danvers returned, grimmer than ever.

"I'm pressed on every side, men. Pressed and stretched thin. The railroad rates are killing me. Keystone Nine's producing marginally—forty to fifty barrels a day—but I can't afford to ship the crude to a coastal port. I'm closing down this well. We'll start Keystone Fifteen farther up the canyon."

Mack and Johnson exchanged looks; Danvers wore the expression of a man dying a lingering death.

Johnson liked Mack's cooking, and he approved of his uncomplaining hard work. A friendship began to grow, though it had its limitations. One Sunday night, eating supper, Mack said, "Tell me some more about your cowboy days, Hugh."

"Don't use that name. I hate it."

"Then you should get a nickname."

"Got to have a reason for a nickname. I got no reason."

"Nothing from your time in Texas?"

Johnson's green eyes had a defensive, hooded look. "Nothin' to talk about. Just a lot of long hours and saddle-sore butts. Quit palavering. Let's eat."

Every other Saturday night the two men rode into Santa Paula. Both wore their side arms, as did most of the other drinkers, diners, and card players in the Ventura Bar & Grill, which became their refuge of choice. Upstairs, a little Mexican girl named Angel took Mack's mind off Nellie and Carla for half an hour. Johnson preferred heavy women; his regular weighed 270.

Shortly after midnight one Saturday in March, Mack and Johnson were leaning on the Ventura's scarred mahogany bar, a half-consumed plate of oysters on the wet wood between them, along with several glasses that had contained whiskey or hot clam juice. They were jawing away about the dim prospects of Jace Danvers when loud whacking sounds upstairs were followed by a scream. Then a door banged open.

"Get out, don't you touch me! He whipped me, Gert," a hysterical whore cried.

A huge man stormed down the stairs. Mack's hazel eyes opened wide at the sight of his face and the red-stippled belt with the studded buckle dangling from his fist.

Poker games suspended abruptly, and the fiddler too. The man with the belt lurched toward the swinging doors, looking straight ahead, the sobs and screamed accusations continuing from upstairs.

As he went by, Mack yanked the belt out of his hand.

"Strap Vigory, you son of a bitch—you killed my mule back in Asphalto."

Vigory swung around with a snort, and as he grabbed for his belt Mack flung it behind the bar. He'd been a fool to confront Vigory impulsively, but it was too late to change things. He reached behind for his Shopkeeper's Colt.

"I'll kill you too, you fucker," Vigory said then, crashing a knee into Mack's groin.

Pain flashed up Mack's trunk and down his legs. It loosened his grip, and Vigory snatched the Colt and leaped back. The round unblinking eye of the muzzle looked at Mack at chest level. *Lord, I've done it now.*

Vigory snickered and the knuckle of his trigger finger whitened.

Hugh Johnson swept his silvered Peacemaker off his left hip so gracefully that hardly a patron saw it. The first bullet drilled Vigory's breastbone and knocked him down. Vigory shot from a convulsing hand; the bullet plowed into the ceiling. Behind him, poker players yelped and ducked under their tables as Johnson put a bullet in Vigory's left shoulder, another in his right, one in each of his knees, and the last through the center of his forehead. The back of Vigory's head exploded against the floor.

The crashing thunder of Johnson's .45 rolled away to silence. Vigory's convulsing body came to rest. A sticky red pool spread all around his head. Mack snagged his piece off the blood-spattered floor, unable to avoid the sight of Vigory's corpse. Vomit rose up into his throat.

A card player eyed Johnson fearfully. "You put six slugs in him. Five after he went down."

"He was out to kill my friend. You heard him say so. Someone like that, you take him at his word—you don't ask him if he's serious or allow him time to show you. It was self-defense. Nobody disagrees, do they?"

Johnson's clear, cold eyes, leaf-green, generated a chorus of nos. Vigory's body had relaxed and his bowels let go. The stench was too much. Mack reeled for the door and puked in the street.

Inside he heard Johnson say, "Somebody fetch the law. I can't stay in this town all night."

They rode homeward at daybreak, released without charges.

The world felt sweet and fresh, the owls hooting their last and the small birds waking—kingbirds, linnets, orioles, and canaries in the alders and willows along the road to Salt Marsh Canyon. As the mauve sky changed to flaming orange, red cattle tinkled their bells on a hillside and a sleepy farmer waved from among the outdoor hives on his bee ranch. Swallows began to fly, and a hawk plummeted to catch a meal in a dewy field, the mountains rising up in blue haze behind. Mack was thrilled with the beauty of California once again, beauty that made the dirty death of Vigory almost unreal.

He was plagued by curiosity too. Finally, as they jogged through a cathedral arch of shaggy eucalyptus with blue-white spring leaves, he couldn't contain it..

"Just a cowhand, that's all? Stop fooling. Your story may explain why you're a good rider, but it doesn't explain how you placed six shots so perfectly. You've had experience."

"Well, some," Johnson said, and then was silent. Mack's eyes prodded him. "Listen, if it's all the same, I'm damn tired, I'd rather not—"

"Hugh, come on. You saved my life. That's a special thing. No more secrets."

Their horses plodded along. The hawk soared into the orange sky with something in its beak. Johnson appraised his partner with those green eyes, then the chill left them and he slumped. His beard was showing, stubbly gray.

"Ah, shit. I 'spose we're too far from Texas for it to matter much." He sniffed and eyed the blue hills with a queer cramped expression, as though ashamed of what he was going to say.

"When the jobs ran out, I joined up with three of my friends—every one of us dead busted. We robbed a little piss-ant bank at a wide spot in the road. Driscoll, Nueces County."

Mack couldn't help looking surprised. Johnson squinted at him, hunting for signs of accusation as well. He saw none, but nevertheless went on emphatically.

"Didn't hurt a living soul, and you better by God believe that." He snorted, all the laugh he could manage. "Do you know how much we split between us? Ninety-seven dollars and twenty-four cents. Should of picked a bigger bank. I rode over the border four hours ahead of a posse. Hid out in the state of Coahuila the best part of a year. It was too much change, too fast. 'Bout broke me . . ."

He reared up and inhaled the sweet air, as if trying to restore his soul with a few cool breaths. "This ain't the same United States I knew as a boy, Mack. Not the same country at all. Those big cattle corporations just swallowed all the family spreads back home. They pushed fellas like me into peculiar new trades. Wildcatting. Banditry . . ."

"Build a railroad like the SP, you can steal millions and get away with it."

"Guess that's the truth. Just too much crazy change goin' on to suit me."

He scanned the tranquil blue hills. "Right here, I could almost believe it hasn't touched California. But you go in those oil towns, full of hard cases and starry-eyed greenhorns hoping for a strike—or you ride around Los Angeles and bump into hop-headed hustlers selling every crazy thing from dope to a new-design windmill, and you know that California's where the change cuts deeper and faster than anyplace. This here's the knife edge, and sometimes I don't like it. But I dunno where else to run 'less it's into the Pacific."

"Don't run anyplace. Your secret's safe."

"Better be. I got lots more ammunition."

Hugh Johnson's smile said they were finally friends.

A week later, Mack said, "You know, Hugh, there's *brea* showing all over the land I own in the next county. Maybe we should stop working for Danvers and put our own rig together. As partners."

"A string of tools costs money."

"How much?"

"Maybe forty thousand dollars for a complete one, good quality. That's secondhand, mind."

"Interested?"

Johnson worried the cleaning rag along the engraved barrel of his Peacemaker. "Not right now. I'm getting the urge to drift. Won't be long 'fore I can. My nose tells me Keystone Fifteen is another dry hole."

So it was, and so was Keystone 16. By the summer of 1891, Jason Preston Danvers faced a crisis.

"Your charges to ship me the coal are more than the coal itself," Danvers shouted into the trumpet-shaped mouthpiece of the wall phone. Mack sat tensely in a side chair and Johnson leaned against the wall, his dusty hat crushed under his arm. Bars of light swarming with dust motes lit up the Santa Paula office.

Fascinated, Mack listened to the tinny voice issuing from the box on the wall; he'd seen the instruments but never talked on one. Danvers reddened and pounded the wall. "No, no, I don't believe you. This is just one more case of the SP strangling small business. If I were a big-volume shipper, you'd come around fast enough. You'd give me the same rebates you slip under the counter to your—"

A protesting squawk and a loud rattle interrupted him. "Wait, wait!" Danvers shouted. The rattle continued. He hung up the earpiece, beaten.

"Four of my crew quit yesterday," he said.

"Then I'm sorry we picked today to ride in with the bad news on Sixteen," Johnson said. "You want us to keep on there?"

Danvers fell into his chair and held his head with both hands. "No, no. Abandon it. Tear down the derrick. Salvage all the timber you can."

The oilman had lost weight. His eyes were haggard and his speech slow. On the sweaty sleeve of his shirt he wore a black velvet armband. His son Bernard, second from the youngest, had died of diphtheria the preceding Wednesday.

"The bank won't carry my equipment loan any longer. I have to make a payment. That means I have to defer wages."

"Is that why the other men quit?" Mack asked.

Danvers replied with a ponderous nod. He held his head again.

"It's OK with me," Mack said, "so long as we get the money eventually."

"Sure," Johnson said, shrugging.

"You're good men, both of you."

"One problem," Johnson said. "I don't do so good when I defer eatin'."

"Mrs. Danvers will fix food twice a week. She'll bring it out to Salt Marsh Canyon in the wagon."

"That's a lonesome trip for a woman," Mack said. "Not too safe, either."

"There's no other way," Danvers said. "I'm up against the wall."

Danvers's troubles compounded. Keystone 19, which another crew punched in, began producing crude in the autumn, but Danvers couldn't afford to ship it. He was deeply in debt to the rig builder, who threatened liens, and available money went to pay that obligation.

Danvers owned no tank cars and no one would lease him cars on credit. Though Hardison & Stewart's pipeline from Newhall to Ventura, a four-inch metal snake suspended on cables, had capacity available, again, it was only for cash up front. Danvers appealed to every bank in the county, and two in Los Angeles; they all rebuffed him—no more loans.

On a hot gray afternoon in November, Danvers summoned all his roughnecks to a meeting in his office. Mack and Johnson had discussed in advance the certain outcome of the meeting and they weren't wrong.

"I'm folding," Danvers announced. "Everything's being attached. I'll meet payroll this coming Friday, but not afterward."

"You talkin' about back pay too?" said a bald man with a beard. "As of last Friday, you owed me for seven weeks."

"Eight here," another said. Nineteen men jammed into the office were all in approximately the same fix. Mack noticed a rectangle on the wall, lighter than the surrounding area, where the telephone had been connected.

Danvers had lost at least thirty pounds. His pompadour, once shiny-dark, was a crest of gray. From deep-sunk eyes, he surveyed the unhappy men. "I can't pay anything but the current week."

"Jesus," Hugh Johnson said. His slitted eyes looked dark as emeralds.

Mack stepped out from the others. "We trusted you, Mr. Danvers. Carried you and trusted you to pay up."

"I'm aware of it, Mack. Believe me, it rips me apart to default. There's just no money."

"There was," Johnson bit out. "Sounds to me like you didn't know how to handle it."

Most of them growled agreement. There was no more tolerance in that room, no more kindness—just hungry, angry, cheated men.

Danvers rose and spread his hands, his voice shaky. "I'm an honest businessman. I gave this enterprise everything. The cards are stacked. You want to blame someone, blame the banks and their friends at the goddamned gouging SP."

"Ah, shove it, Danvers," a man said with a weary wave, heading for the door.

Another shook his fist. "You better have money for us Friday or we're liable to find us a coil of rope and take your case to Judge Lynch."

Danvers sat down again, sweating.

"Come on," Johnson growled to Mack. "It ain't decent to stick knives in a dying dog."

In the street, a big round four-hitch oil wagon rolled by. Hardison & Stewart. The driver wore a brand-new fawn vest, and Mack eyed it with bitter envy.

Johnson leaned against the rack where they'd tied their horses. "Well, that's it, *amigo*."

"What are you going to do?"

"Drift a while. I was gettin' tired of the job anyway."

"Where will you go?"

"Maybe over to Kern County. Anything there?"

After a shrug Mack said, "Bean fields, asphalt plants, some mighty pretty Indian girls, too much hot weather. What about my offer—partners in our own outfit?"

"Going to swing that with the cash you get from Mr. Danvers, are you?"

Johnson's sarcasm left Mack groping for a reply. His boasts to Nellie and Marquez and others about making a fortune came back to taunt him. Hell, he couldn't make enough money to repay even one of Wyatt's victims. He hadn't opened T. Fowler Haines in months—with good reason.

When several seconds of glum silence had gone by, Johnson eyed Mack, shrugged, and muttered, "Sorry I ragged you that way. But I'm drifting."

"All right, but if you change your mind, get in touch. Leave a message with Potter, the lawyer, in the Baker Block, Los Angeles."

"You'll be around, will you? Hanging on?"

"Absolutely," Mack said without conviction. He was lying to Hugh Johnson; he was probably finished in California.

The friends parted Friday night, after the pay was disbursed at the office. Mrs. Danvers handed around the little envelopes, explaining that her husband was indisposed. "Indisposed with shame, I don't doubt," Johnson muttered to Mack outside. It wasn't a condemnation, merely a statement.

Mack and the Texan shook hands by their horses. "You taught me a lot, Hugh. One day I'll repay you."

"Sure, when we all get rich." Johnson stepped into his stirrup and mounted. "You ever gonna quit using that name I hate?"

"Not till you get another. Remember, now—Potter, in the Baker Block. I'll get the message."

Hugh Johnson touched his hat brim and turned his horse's head. Mack watched the Texan ride out and dwindle to a speck against the fiery rampart of the sunset hills. He couldn't remember feeling this low since the night he left San Francisco.

In San Solaro he found no significant change, except the weeds were higher. He took a job washing dishes in Newhall. A week before Christmas, a time in which his feelings of loneliness and defeat seemed particularly keen, he picked up a copy of the *Times*, and a story on the front page caught him.

SHORE SUICIDE?

Mysterious Drowning Claims Oilman!

A day earlier, a body had washed up on the beach at Santa Monica. It was Jace Danvers. The story described him as an "oil-company proprietor recently caught in severe financial straits." The preceding Sunday, he'd taken his wife and seven children to the ocean. While they spread their picnic, Danvers stepped behind a rock and donned his bathing costume. He left his clothes with his wife, neatly folded. He walked into the Pacific, waved at the children, and began to swim. No one saw him again until a fisherman watched the surf float his body ashore.

"Poor bastard," Mack said, putting the paper on the shelf above the tub of rancid dishwater. He knew Jason Preston Danvers hadn't been the best of managers, but he was well intentioned, industrious, honest.

Not good enough. Circumstances had undone him—and the railroad too. For Danvers, the California dream had failed.

Mack immersed a plate sticky with pork-chop grease. Two waiters burst into the kitchen, quarreling and threatening each other in Spanish. Cheap tinsel letters hung over the doors to the restaurant. FELIZ NAVIDAD! Mack stared at them and thought, *Am I another Danvers?*

HE DRIFTED FROM JOB TO JOB IN THE FIRST HALF **26** of 1892, managing to save $28. He no longer opened the guidebook; sometimes he loathed the very sight of it. A suspicion took hold and grew into conviction that he was repeating the pattern of his pa's failed life.

Once a month he wrote Potter's office with a current address, asking for mail. In July the lawyer forwarded a letter from Nellie. She planned to be in Los Angeles early in August to prepare a story about the harbor fight, which had been simmering for a couple of years. The city of Los Angeles wanted a permanent deep-water port at San Pedro. The SP, with its customary heavy-handed attention to self-interest, was campaigning locally and in Sacramento to locate the port at Santa Monica—where, of course, SP owned most of the available harborside land.

"It's the first time I've found myself on the same side as that damned Otis," Mack said to Nellie on the buggy ride out to the Pacific. He had hardly stopped talking since he picked her up; he was excited about seeing her after so long, but a little sad and envious too. She was doing well. He'd borrowed $15 from Potter to hire the rig and buy a picnic basket from a caterer. The last dollar went to a tailor to repair a tear in the sleeve of his brown broadcloth. He still felt dirt poor in her presence.

He'd called for her at the Pico House, where she was installed in a suite at Hearst's expense. Brown and slim and vibrant as ever, she was the picture of a successful city girl, in a smart yachting costume of white linen with a navy belt and foulard with white polka dots. Her cap was white with a navy bill, her shoes small white oxfords. She said the outfit was French.

Full of news, she was as talkative as Mack; they laughed about it. She told him that Muir had organized his conservation society, the Sierra Club, in San Francisco. Leland Stanford Junior University was open in Palo Alto, with a smart young president from Indiana, David Starr Jordan, in charge. Of Diego Marquez she knew only one thing; "He quarreled with the hierarchy, issued some inflammatory statements, then left the Church and disappeared out in the Valley. Some of his superiors called him a dangerous anarchist. It was in the headlines for nearly a week."

Rancho Topanga Malibu Sequit was a twenty-two-mile tract of choice ocean property stretching south from Ventura. The present owner and prospective developer, a man called Rindge, kept it heavily fenced and peppered with signs that warned, NO TRESPASSING—VIOLATORS PROSECUTED!, though the public ignored them. Mack knew an isolated ranch road that took them to a wild beach not far from Santa Monica. Here he spread blankets, then the contents of the hamper. It was a blowing, sparkling day, with huge white combers roaring in. The invigorating air smelled of salt. But everything seemed to remind him of Danvers and his sad end.

He poured glasses of cheap white wine. The restaurant had

246

packed thick, starchy sandwiches in waxed paper: bologna and peppered sausage, layered with slices of strong cheese. Nellie took off her hat and shook out her dark hair, chattering on.

"The harbor fight looks fierce. Huntington is pulling every string in Washington that he can. He has the *Post* in his pocket, so he can float a favorable story whenever he wants. Your friend Fairbanks is handling the campaign in California. He's a vice president of the corporation now and runs the political bureau—otherwise known as the legal department. Not to be confused with the SP Literary Bureau."

"What's that?"

"A sardonic name for their propaganda machine. They bribe editors and writers to treat them favorably. Pay them off with cash, passes, weekends at the Del Monte in Monterey—in San Francisco, I know for certain that the *Bulletin* and the *Call* take their money. If you consider that, and all the state legislators they control, plus their own railroad managers—sometimes a ward boss, sometimes a freight agent—in every county in California—you'd have to say that Walter Fairbanks wields more power than the governor."

Mack's face showed a cynical disgust. "At least that keeps his mind off me."

She laughed. "I don't want to insult you, but I think they forgot you and the nickel ferry long ago. Running you out of the City satisfied Huntington. Fairbanks too, presumably. I expect you could go back anytime you want."

Mack's hazel eyes raked the ocean horizon. He saw phantom images of Danvers, swimming to his death. "I'll go back. But not till I have enough money to be a serious player in their game."

"So you haven't lost a whit of your ambition—"

"Have you?"

"No." She unwrapped a sandwich. "When I have a spare hour, I write stories. No one's published any so far. But they will."

"You're still happy in San Francisco?"

"Yes, but Mr. Hearst has plans to send me somewhere else."

Mack sat up abruptly.

"He's doing wonderfully with the *Examiner*," she went on, "but he wants to expand to New York. If he can start or buy a paper there, he wants me to work for him. It's the most important city in America, Mack. I doubt I could turn him down."

"And that's what you want? To spend the rest of your life in an office?"

"Lord, you're such a mossback. I thought you might have changed."

"I'm a man. What can I change?"

"Your attitude, sir. Your primitive attitude. What would you have me do?"

His dark hair blew in the sea wind. "What about marrying someone?"

"Who?"

"Me, for instance."

"You want a wife who stays home and contents herself with raising fat babies. . . . Well, don't you?"

"Yes, I do."

"Then let's change the subject." Her voice was sharp, even a touch angry. "How are you getting on down here? Making any money?"

"Plenty." Now he was curt.

"Mr. Chance, why do I get the distinct impression that you're not being truthful?" She touched his work-scarred knuckles. "Please. You know I care about you—"

"Let's eat."

"You're impossible."

"Nellie, I love you—"

Instantly she lost color, and her self-assurance. "What? What did you say?"

He took her hands in his. "I said I love you. I always have. But I can't be anything except what I am."

Now the color rushed back into her face, and she pulled her hands away with an angry "Oh!" She wiped her palms against her eyes. "You are what you are—is that a fact, or an excuse?"

"I don't want to quarrel, Nellie. I've waited months to be with you again—"

"If you don't want to quarrel," she said in an unsteady voice, "you'd better give me another sandwich, because I'm about to throw this one right in your face."

The rest of the outing was polite but strained, with no physical contact save her quick peck on his cheek when he delivered her to the arcade of the Pico House.

"Good-bye, Nellie, take care of yourself."

"Mack, wait—"

"No, I've got to get this rig back to the stable. I'm already late."

"Will I see you again before I leave Los Angeles?"

"Yes, I'll try," he said, knowing he wouldn't. Nellie was

248

going up in the world. He was standing still, if not sinking. And sometimes she didn't seem to like what he was—not at all.

She let the curtain fall but stayed at the suite's window, the fading sunlight through the old lace patterning her cheeks. The street below was almost deserted, but she'd stood there for many minutes, expecting–no, hoping—to see him come racing back in the buggy. He didn't, of course, and she was left with a grab-bag of emotions.

Sadness, first, because he was tense, and gaunt, no longer the energetic, brash young man who'd jumped into the Bay to save her. Despite his pretensions, his confidence was gone.

She felt a lovely warmth when she remembered the stunning moment when he said "I love you," but she hated her own foolish, prickly responses. She loved him too—loved him even though he was far from perfect.

Nor are you, Miss Ross. Shall I cite some specifics? You've struggled so hard competing with all those tough cynical male reporters, you talk and act like them. Brusque. Blunt. Worse than that, your so-called standards are too damned high. You treat a lover the way you treat old Huntington . . . as a candidate for your reforming zeal.

It was true. But what could she do? Could she change now, even if she wanted? The real trouble was, she didn't want to, at least not all of the time, and whenever she faced that fact instead of fleeing from it, as now, the pain and confusion tore her apart.

Nellie kept standing there while the twilight settled, a sun-browned hand touching the old lace as if it were some memento of love. The angled beams of the setting sun made her tear-washed cheeks glow.

Late in September, Enrique Potter invited Mack to Sunday dinner at his home. The large, pleasant stucco house stood among willow trees out on the west side of town. It was part of another unsuccessful subdivision, the Wilshire Tract, planned by one H. Gaylord Wilshire, a Harvard dropout, walnut and grapefruit grower, and socialist entrepreneur.

The Potter home was cool and spacious, with a lemon tree flourishing in the front yard. Dinner was at two, after the Potters returned from mass, and Elena Potter served an enormous meal, the best Mack had eaten in a year. The lawyer with the ferocious Mongol mustache was a kind but firm father, keeping his five children in their seats until he was ready to dismiss them for play. "Pick up that crumb under your chair, Felipe," he said as they dashed out. Felipe returned without a murmur. Potter gave the boy a smile and pat, sending him out happy.

Potter lit one of his stupendously long cigars. "Mack, I must say, you look terrible."

Mack folded his napkin. "I've had one rotten job after another. I've spent five years playing what amounts to penny poker. If I can't play for big stakes, I'm going back east."

"I'm sorry to hear that. I know how much you've always wanted to make California your home."

"Maybe it was never meant to be." Visions of the Pennsylvania blizzard flashed before his inner eye; the nightmare came frequently of late. "Either I change my own luck—and soon— or I'm through."

Potter rolled his cigar back and forth between thumb and fingers. "I admit the situation isn't good. I wanted to discuss it with you. Do you recall Loren and Estelle Hutto?"

"Hutto," Mack said, rubbing the center of his forehead; a sharp ache had started there. "It's familiar, but I can't . . . wait. The buyer list."

"Yes. Mr. and Mrs. Hutto, Elyria, Ohio. On Friday they filed suit against the corporation to recover their down payment. I'm fairly confident that I can slow things down with a demurrer—a technical objection to the sufficiency of their pleading. If the court agrees the pleading's insufficient, the Huttos will have to start all over again, and we'll gain time. Even so Mack, I'd be less than honest if I didn't tell you there's going to be a reckoning eventually. If the worst happened, you might even face a jail term. Unless, of course, you find some cash—soon."

"And where am I going to do that, Enrique? I look and I look, but there's no damn gold in the rivers anymore. Maybe there never was."

"I could attempt to settle with the Huttos out of court, then put San Solaro up for sale."

Mack was tempted, mightily so. But something made him say, "No, I'm not quite ready for that. The property is all I've got."

They stared at each other through the slow-twisting smoke of Potter's cigar. From the arched window came the bright sounds of children playing on the lawn, and the music of a bird warbling in the Sunday sunshine. California music . . .

Mack didn't hear.

His spirits sank further in the following weeks. He quit his dishwashing job and hired on at a lumberyard, menial work again, but at least it kept him outdoors a good part of the time. One night in early October, he stopped for a drink at the El Dorado on lower Main Street. He settled at the bar next to a wiry, tough-looking citizen in his mid-thirties, with fair, lightly freckled skin, a thick mustache, and an enormous scar on his cheek. Mack noticed a Catholic medal around his neck and a pistol riding on his hip.

After Mack ordered a lager, he saw the pistol toter showing a companion something in the day's *Tribune*. "Excuse me," Mack said. "Is there anything in there yet about the championship?"

"Right here." The man pointed to a dispatch from New Orleans.

"By God, he won," Mack exclaimed. He scanned the article for details. "A knockout in the twenty-first round." It filled him with pride that his friend Gentleman Jim had defeated John L. Sullivan for the heavyweight title.

"Yeah, and with gloves, in three-minute rounds. What do they call those new rules?"

"Marquis of Queensbury." Mack took a swallow of his beer. "Corbett's a friend of mine—he taught me to box."

"That right?" The tough, shrewd eyes of the pistol toter swept him up and down, including the holstered Shopkeeper's Colt. "You a Californian, then?"

In spite of recent doubts Mack found it natural to say yes.

"Know anything about the tar pits around here? *Brea*, asphaltum—whatever they call it?"

"Matter of fact I do. *Brea* is a seep of oil that's thickened in contact with air."

"My guess exactly. First day I got to town, I saw a wagon carrying a load of it. I asked some questions. The local people burn it."

"Instead of coal, because coal costs ten to fifteen dollars a ton in Los Angeles. Couple of hundred years ago, the Indians were waterproofing baskets and caulking canoes with *brea*."

"How do you know all this?"

"I've worked in the oil business for two years."

"Charley, pay attention," the pistol toter said, nudging his partner. Then he extended his hand. "My name's Ed Doheny. This gentleman's Charley Canfield."

"Macklin Chance. Call me Mack. Where are you from, Mr. Doheny?"

"At the moment, right here. I was in New Mexico a while, gold prospecting. That's no way to get rich."

"You interested in work?" Canfield asked. "We need one more man."

"To do what?"

"Hunt for oil," Doheny said. "With so many tar pits all over town, I figure we must be standing on top of a lake of oil." Mack refrained from telling him that the surface signs were often deceiving. "I bought a lot and I'm going to sink a well."

"Where's your lot?"

"Not far. Out on Second Street. The area they call Westlake Park."

"You mean you're going to drill in Los Angeles?"

Doheny bristled. "I'm going to dig, my friend. The same kind of hole farmers put down for a water well in Wisconsin, where I grew up. I can't afford fancy equipment, and I wouldn't know how to run it if I could. Charley and I paid four hundred dollars for the lot. We're almost dead broke. You want to swing a pick and shovel for a percentage, we can talk."

Mack drained his beer to give himself time to think. The idea of hunting oil in town, ludicrous at first, didn't seem so after a little reflection. He'd seen the tar pits on his very first day in Los Angeles. Why couldn't a well produce here as easily as in open country? What was California all about if not risk, and hope, and the fulfillment of crazy dreams? And what did he have to lose? Nothing.

Maybe it was the beer, or Doheny's cocksure toughness, but Mack's confidence, so low at Potter's dinner table, surged up for the first time in months.

"Twenty percent."

Doheny fixed him with those hard eyes. "Ten."

"Fifteen."

"Charley?" Canfield nodded. "When can you start?"

"Five minutes after I quit the lumberyard in the morning."

On November 4, 1892, a mile west of downtown, Ed Doheny, Charley Canfield, and Mack Chance started to dig a common miner's shaft, four feet by six, with pick, shovel, and the expenditure of their own strength. Doheny hired a boy with a horse and cart to haul away the dirt and shale.

After a few days, they attracted spectators, most of them joking at the expense of the three men sweating in the pit. It infuriated Doheny but somehow it only excited Mack.

Seven feet below the ground, Mack suddenly saw a glistening ooze on the shaft wall. "Ed, Charley, get down here," he shouted.

As they clambered down the ladder, Mack swiped his fingers over the crumbly shale. They glistened black. "Oil seep," he said, grinning.

"It's here," Doheny breathed. "By God. I smell it—don't you boys smell it?"

"I smell money," Mack said.

The next night, after hours of exhausting work, Mack dragged himself off to prowl the neighborhood. As the days passed he went off alone at every opportunity, keeping his purpose to himself. A surging certainty told him that he and his partners were onto something incredible.

Doheny and Canfield moved out of their hotel and into a tent on the lot. The following evening, Mack trudged back to his rented room to find his flint-faced landlady waiting for him. "You in some kind of trouble, young man? There was a process server here with a legal paper."

"Trouble?" Mack's heart pounded. "Nothing that I know of, ma'am."

"Well, he's coming back tomorrow. Meanwhile, I want next week's rent—in advance."

"Yes, sure, I'll get it first thing in the morning."

An hour later, with his few belongings in a bundle, he slid out the window of his second-floor room and dropped. The noise roused the landlady, who fired a shotgun, but luckily she missed him. He vaulted the high back fence and fled through the night. A few minutes before midnight, he moved in with his startled partners.

A few nights later, they heard sounds near the well site. The three ran out to discover a man carrying off picks and shovels. Doheny raised his revolver and dropped the thief with a bullet through his left calf.

"You're good with that, Ed," Mack said later, while Doheny cleaned the piece.

"I've used it a considerable amount," the Irishman said in that guarded way of his. "Used it on a mountain lion that attacked me down in New Mexico. Cat almost got me." He touched the disfiguring scar. "Used it once on a man out to kill me."

"And?"

Doheny snapped the hammer down and sighted along the barrel.

"He didn't," he said.

* * *

As November wore on the shaft deepened steadily and the shored-up walls began to exude a poisonous odor of gas. At around 150 feet, the odor grew so strong, Mack warned them off.

"If there's a spark we'll all go sky-high. We can't stay down here digging."

"Good, because I can't breathe," Canfield said, choking. "What do we do now?"

"Drill."

"You know we can't afford a string of tools," Doheny exploded.

Mack swiped his sweaty face with an oily forearm. "Then we drill with something else."

What they found was a fallen eucalyptus tree on a neighboring lot. They hauled it to the well, sharpened a point on it, rigged a supporting frame, hooked it to a donkey engine, and slammed it into the hole. Their new drill.

Spectators continued to gather and jeer, but a plain, stoutly built woman turned up almost every day and watched their progress with avid interest. Mack was intrigued because the woman sat on a packing box for hours, peering into the well with all the devotion of someone admiring a new lover. He drew her into conversation.

"I'm Mrs. Emma Summers. I live just over there. I'm from Kentucky but I trained at the New England Conservatory, a piano teacher. I've never seen anything as exciting as this."

Mack joked with her. "There are plenty of tar pits around here. Maybe there's oil in your own backyard."

Not smiling, she replied, "That's exactly what I'm thinking, young man."

Mack increased the frequency of his nocturnal trips through the neighborhood, while keeping a wary eye out for the sheriff's men, who might somehow stumble on him. He wrote notes on scraps of paper and soon had a pocket stuffed with them. The eucalyptus drill went up and down, up and down, with a persistent monotonous rhythm. Doheny constantly bombarded Mack with questions.

"If we hit oil, how much will we get for it?"

"About a dollar a barrel right now."

"The market's pretty small, isn't it?"

"Not as big as it should be," Mack agreed. He pointed at the tent's kerosene lamp. The dull, dim flame sent a constant twist of dirty smoke up to the tent's vent hole. "There's one reason. Too much carbon in the crude. Better refining could fix that. But improving the kerosene won't expand the market much."

"What will?"

"Using oil for fuel. Mostly it's poor people who use it now. But think of the SP. I don't like those bastards, but suppose their locomotives burned oil instead of coal? The wells couldn't pump fast enough."

They dug forty days and forty nights. On the forty-first day, a potent gush of gas was followed by a gurgle of oil in the bottom of the pit. In five minutes, the sharpened tip of the eucalyptus trunk was submerged.

In ten minutes, the oil was fifteen feet deep.

"We're millionaires!" Doheny shouted, running down a bucket to bail some oil.

"Millionaires!" Canfield echoed. "May I have this dance?" He caught Mack's waist and they waltzed all over the vacant lot, singing and whooping. Doheny ran at them with a bucket of crude.

"Merry Christmas!" he cried, and emptied it on them. Canfield spat and sputtered, while Mack collapsed with laughter, black crude plastering his hair, oozing into his ears, dripping off his nose, whitening his eyes in the middle of a minstrel-man face.

They bailed all day and managed to draw off seven barrels. The well remained as full as before; the level kept rising in the shaft.

Mack took the night's last horsecar to the western suburbs and then walked from the end of the line. At half past two he pounded on Enrique Potter's door.

Potter answered with a lamp in one hand, shotgun in the other. "I thought it was a burglar. My God, you stink."

"I spent a dime for a bath. I can't get rid of the smell."

"Where the hell have you been, Mack? I thought you'd died, or fled the state. I've been going crazy with the authorities. There's a bench warrant out for you, and a lien against San Solaro—"

"Enrique, Enrique, listen. It doesn't make any difference. None of that makes any difference. We'll settle with those people—all of them. Just get me a little more time." He seized the lawyer's shoulders and shook him. "Enrique, there's *oil* in Los Angeles. Now let me in."

At the kitchen table, while Potter watched with sleepy displeasure and Elena's distant voice quieted children awakened by the knocking, Mack sorted the wadded notes from his pocket.

"There are building lots for sale in Westlake Park. Those are descriptions of five of them—lots with *brea* showing close by. None costs more than five hundred and seventy-five dollars. Tomorrow morning, I want you to buy them for me. All five. Put a mortgage on San Solaro."

"Are you joking? You can't mortgage property that's tied up in a court proceeding."

"Then take out a loan yourself. Your credit's good, isn't it? I'll give you an IOU for two—no, three thousand dollars, to be paid as a bonus."

"From where, prison? I could wind up there if I'm not careful . . . my God, you've got nerve. I'm in awe."

"Enrique, I know this will work. I know it! You said you thought I'd amount to something—well, I will. But only if you help me."

"Wait, I don't understand, you're talking too fast."

Trying to control his giddy excitement, Mack spoke more slowly. He explained the events of the day to the lawyer, who knew nothing of his involvement with Doheny and his partner.

Potter listened with increasing skepticism. "Are you going to sink wells on all those lots?"

"No. I'm going to hold them sixty or ninety days and sell them to other people who want to sink wells."

"What if this well of yours is a fluke? What if it goes dry tomorrow?"

"Then I lose my collateral."

"Mack, the risk's too great. I advise against—"

"Buy the lots, Enrique. I know I'm right."

Never be poor again . . .

Enrique Potter gave him a long, speculative look. But he picked up the oil-stained notes one by one.

Mack leaned back, his head spinning with a strange drunken exhilaration. Every sense seemed sharper. He heard night insects outside with an amazing clarity. The glint of lamplight on the beautifully painted tiles of the kitchen hearth made a picture he'd never forget. Potter's old robe, scrawny chest, sleep-baggy eyes—those, too, he'd remember forever.

This is the night, he thought, riding the wave of emotion. *This is the night it begins. The night of the day I struck gold.*

Mack bought all five lots. By February 1893 he'd sold them all, the lowest for $1,850, the highest for $2,775. He repaid the Huttos and two other buyers, with ten percent interest to each, and Potter got the warrant voided and the charges against him dismissed. Mack inked a line through the three names on the master list of buyers, then with his remaining cash bought more lots and held them. Prices were escalating rapidly despite counterbalancing shocks from the national economy.

On February 24, the great Philadelphia & Reading Railroad filed for bankruptcy. All through 1892 there had been faint drum taps warning of a panic and now they became a thousand kettledrums, beating doom. On March 4 Grover Cleveland took office as the nation's twenty-fourth president, and he and his vice president, Adlai Stevenson, confronted a nation, and a world, on the brink of monetary chaos.

Belmont, Morgan, and other financiers warned the new president of impending ruin, blaming the Sherman Silver Purchase Act of 1890, a friendly gesture to the nation's mine owners that now threatened to push America off the stable gold standard. But the warnings came too late. When the World's Columbian Exposition opened in Chicago on May 1, the crowds rushed in to forget what was going on outside: more railroads failing, brokerages closing, runs on banks, federal gold reserves dropping below $100 million, European investors dumping huge quantities of U.S. stocks and bonds.

It was a full-fledged panic.

Reacting to it, Los Angeles crude-oil prices dropped as low as 45 cents a barrel. But the rush to buy land and sink wells slowed only slightly.

Mack set up a desk in a tiny room rented in the Chalmers Block. He bought and sold more lots, doubling the value of his original investment, then doubling it again. He also paid back nine more San Solaro buyers. Potter shook his head, admitted he'd been too cautious, and now executed Mack's orders with alacrity and enthusiasm. In spite of economic disaster stalking across America like a cowled specter, Los Angeles boomed.

Daily, in Westlake Park, Mack watched crews uprooting palm trees, digging up yards, tearing down cottages, and hauling away the rubble that derricks soon replaced. The smell of gas thickened on residential streets. An oily film quickly settled on hands, necks, and faces everywhere in the neighborhood.

Wagons plowed up and down carrying pipe, drilling tools, lumber, their wheels chewing the streets to rutted ruins. Other wagons hauling out barrels of crude from the new wells dripped their poorly sealed contents into the same streets, softening horses' hooves and filling ruts and holes that caught fire from careless sparks. Often half a dozen pools burned through the night, turning Westlake Park into a weird landscape of red-lit smoke. It was hell on earth in Southern California.

The piano teacher, Mrs. Summers, bought lots and put up derricks. Farmers and storekeepers and pensioners put up derricks. There were nearly a hundred derricks by the end of 1893, polluting the eye with their rickety sprawl, the ear with their incessant noise. Some too timid to sink wells huddled in their cottages surrounded by derricks. Oil slicked the leaves of cabbages growing in garden plots, and anyone rash enough to hang out laundry found it polka-dotted with oil mist.

The kind of people inevitably attracted by a boom soon showed up along Santa Monica Boulevard. They erected their shanties, boasting pool tables, faro banks, and tobacco counters, and their tents, where women sold themselves and didn't object to oil on a man's hands if the hands held cash.

Mack sank no wells. The bankers all at once had confidence in him, and they treated him cordially, calling him by his first name when he walked in in a new suit to arrange a new deal. He paid off the remaining buyers, inked lines through every name on the list, paid Potter the promised bonus, and banked his remaining money, nearly $38,000 of it.

One night almost a year after the start of digging on the Doheny well, Mack rode out to Westlake Park at dusk. He was mounted not on a horse but a smart new $18 contraption from Singer, the sewing-machine company. Like many other firms, Singer had started a new sideline in response to the craze for the bicycle. The *wheel*, Americans called it. Mack's featured the new triangular safety frame and pneumatic rubber tires of equal size; gone were the hard rubber tires and the huge five-foot wheel in front. The improved design had touched off the craze.

Mack liked riding his wheel, which was finished with bright

yellow-gold paint. Pedaling strengthened his legs. He wore a townsman's derby and spring clips on his trousers to keep them from tangling in the chain-and-sprocket drive.

He pedaled along through the bedlam of thudding tool strings, pumping engines, cursing roughnecks, children playing, Mrs. Summers giving piano lessons. The cratered streets were afloat with standing oil and the usual noxious haze clouded the air. The derricks loomed dimly against the stars like crouching beasts from prehistory. Several times Mack nearly fell off his wheel. The streets were unfit for bicycles. Wheelmen all across the nation were demanding better pavements, in town and countryside.

When he reached the site of the original well, he discovered that Doheny had a new crew working, men he didn't know. Doheny himself had moved on to other wells. He and Mack had parted friends, and Mack's royalty was deposited every week in a special account he kept for that purpose at Los Angeles National. He parked his yellow-gold wheel and visited with the new men for ten minutes. All was going well.

He was striding back to his wheel when a voice out of the dark said, "Hey."

He spun around, surprised and alarmed. There at the edge of the lot was a tall man, standing still. *Strap Vigory*—

Even as he shot his hand under the tail of his coat, he thought, *No, absurd.* That was fortunate; there was no holster riding on his hip. He didn't carry the Shopkeeper's Colt when he dressed like a businessman.

The man in the dark stepped forward. He wore a black hat and long frock coat the same color with a brilliant green bandanna streaming out in the hot night wind. Lanterns on the well illuminated his face.

"Johnson. God almighty. Don't sneak up on a man that way."

"That's the way I come and go. Quick. Saves trouble with sheriffs an' jealous husbands."

"You scared me. For a minute you looked like the Reaper himself standing there—"

"Sorry," Hugh Johnson said; it was his entire apology. "Potter told me you was out here. I hear you're doin' good."

"Doing fine."

"I wore out Kern County. I could use a square meal. Nobody cooks as good as you."

Mack smiled. "You back to stay?"

"Till the itch to drift comes again. I'm ready to go partners if you are."

259

"San Solaro?"

"San Solaro."

"Yes, sir!" Mack said, breaking into a grin. "Let's have a drink and talk about it. Got a horse?"

" 'Course I got a horse. You don't think I'd ride a sissy thing like that, d'you? My God, you're gettin' as crazy for new gadgets as the rest of these Californians."

Mack packed away his city clothes and put on dungarees, strapped on his pistol, and together with Johnson rode over the mountains to Bakersfield. Johnson had seen a secondhand water-well rig in storage at the Harron-Rickard Supply Company. They bought it and hauled it back to San Solaro.

At the Newhall lumberyard they put in their order for rig timber, having decided to save money by building the derrick themselves. They located two thousand feet of drilling cable and sand line in Los Angeles and a supply of casing pipe in several sizes at an iron merchant's. Then, with Mack's cash almost depleted, they called at the Vines Coal Company.

Vines, a rabbit-toothed man with a defensive air, showed them a price sheet. "Right there, same for everybody. In town here, twenty-two dollars and fifty cents a ton. Delivered to your site it's thirty-two dollars."

"Jesus J. Christ," Johnson said, smacking the price sheet on the counter. "Is this here a coal yard or the headquarters of road agents?"

Offended, Vines said, "It's the freight charges. You don't think the SP will cart to Newhall for nothing, do you?"

Mack said, "I don't know a lot about your business, but I know your price is too high. You've got more in the freight than you do in the coal."

"Is that a surprise?" Vines said with a sneer. "You run a big company, the SP gives you preferential rates. Small operations like this"—he tapped the price sheet—"the customer pays."

Johnson picked a fleck of tobacco from the corner of his mouth, then wiped his hand on his long sea-blue bandanna. He had a whole rainbow wardrobe of them, Mack had discovered; it was Johnson's only vanity.

"What y'think?" Johnson asked.

Mack figured in his head. "We can afford two, maybe three loads." To Vines: "We'll haul from here and save the extra. We have a wagon."

"Loading hopper's out back."

The partners left the office. Mack thought of C. P. Huntington dining in the opulence of his Palace suite. He thought of Leland Stanford's vast ranch; it had passed to his widow when he died in June. He thought of Walter Fairbanks's fine clothes and fine airs. All of it infuriated him all over again.

"You know," he said as they climbed up opposite front wheels of the wagon, "I calculate that over the next couple of months, three big loads of coal will run us clean out of cash. My royalties don't mount up fast enough to cover big outlays."

"Potter'll advance you something, won't he?"

"Potter carried me once. I don't want to ask again."

"The banks—"

"The panic's dried up loan money. Especially loans for wildcatting. I went to Los Angeles National last week. Went to Security Loan too. They weren't so friendly. When we burn the last load of coal, there won't be any more."

"Somebody ought to fix those railroad gougers."

"One of these days we will. Drive."

In the light of a cool misty morning—January 1, 1894—they finished nailing down the derrick floor and framed in the belt house. They had sited the well at the bottom of a hill where a ten-foot pool of *brea* showed. Lumber, pipe, coils of line, and the tarp-covered coal wagon littered the work area. Johnson sawed a board and Mack painted the black letters.

CHANCE-JOHNSON NO. I

They nailed it to a post and stood back. Winter sun pierced the mist and brightened the steep hillsides of the dead, silent valley. Most of the lot markers had rotted or blown away and except for the distant depot where they lived, there was no sign of human habitation.

"Mighty impressive," Johnson said of the sign. "Name has a fine, proper ring to it."

Mack grinned. "That it does. Since it's New Year's Day, I suggest we open a jug, fry up some oysters, and celebrate. We won't be taking holidays once we start spudding in."

"One thing I feel bad about," Johnson said as they walked toward the depot. "I ain't putting much into this deal."

"Your experience. Your sweat. Your company. You don't think I'd stay out here and do all this alone, do you?"

"Listen, just so's you understand—I'll take wages if we hit, but I don't expect anything more."

"I don't care what you expect, you get one third of anything

261

the oil company earns. I'm a big man with percentages. That's how I got this place, on percentage.''

"You're a crazy bastard. Maybe that's why I like you.''

This time Mack kept the logbook.

Jan. 9—8⁵/₈" casing—down 88 ft.

Winter rain streamed over the page and blurred the words as fast as he wrote them. He crouched in the lee of the belt house, eyed the turbulent sky, and shivered.

Jan. 22—376 ft. cased—hard drilling—many crooked holes.

Hours dissolved into days, days into weeks, darkness into daylight, sunshine into cloud and back to sun again. Unspoken between the partners was the need for a roughneck to spell them, but they couldn't afford an extra man, so instead of quitting at the end of a tour, they worked until their eyelids fell shut, or their muscles burned with blowtorch pain, or they began to forget details and stagger into things when they walked. Many a night they never returned to the depot, simply fell under a blanket on the derrick floor and snored.

Feb. 13—1,338 ft.—through the oil rock—sulfur water showing.

The little steam engine broke down; Johnson repaired it.

Feb. 27—pumping 5th day. Still sulfur water but also 2 bbls. oil.

At 1,672 feet, Southern California's unpredictable geology undid them again. They drilled into another black slate layer, punched on through 100 feet of it, 200 feet, 300— The cable broke, the tool disappearing into the depths. After three days of fishing, they snarled and yelled at each other for half an hour, walked off in opposite directions to sulk, walked back when they calmed down, offered awkward apologies, and thought about what to do next.

March 10, 1894. Chance-Johnson 1 abandoned.

Filthy with grease and mud, the partners manhandled a suspended bit over a new hole, Chance-Johnson No. 2, half a mile from the first site. It had taken two weeks to salvage timber and erect a new derrick. Then some muscle in Mack's back seized up. Working now, he was in constant, exquisite pain.

Johnson grimaced as they struggled. "I got a feeling about this one, a good feeling.''

Apr. 9 '94—abandoned. Lost 200 ft. 8⁵/₈" casing.

* * *

Mack looked up from the logbook as Johnson returned from the coal wagon. The walking beam shunted the No. 3 tool string up and down, up and down. Spurred by the balmy spring weather, both men had taken most of their clothes off; they worked in greasy long underwear unbuttoned to the navel.

Johnson tossed something that glittered in the sunshine. Mack dropped the logbook to catch it. It was a lump of coal.

"Last load's more'n half gone. Our luck damn well better improve. Quick."

May 1 '94. Another dry hole. Abandoned.

Mack had a strong feeling about No. 4, punched down near the canal. It was the same kind of feeling Johnson had had about the second duster: a baseless confidence that this time, they'd hit. Only a quarter of the original load of coal remained. But Mack was wildly confident—maybe because they were desperate.

May 17—1,055 ft. Water—some oil. Have not seen anybody but H.J. for 3 wks.

"Don't think this one's going to pay out," Johnson said at half past ten the following night. They'd worked since five in the morning.

"Shut up," Mack said. He was splicing sand line.

Johnson stiffened, glared, then folded his arms and left.

May 18—1,106 ft.—rock again. SON OF A BITCH.

He scratched out the intemperate note. But he'd written it large, and it stayed visible under the horizontal slashes, accusing and further discouraging him. It was 10:40 P.M.

Six hours later, under the feeble glow of lanterns on the derrick, Johnson mopped the sweat accumulated in his scraggling beard. Neither partner had touched a razor for days; both smelled to heaven. The night was still, every chuff and squeak and thud of the well machinery magnified. A sticky evil haze blurred the stars. Johnson stared unhappily at his bandanna, one of his good ones, buttercup yellow, ruined by oil and sweat.

With an oath, he threw it in his hat lying nearby. "These damn underground slate beds got us whipped. Ain't an oilman west of the Divide who can tell where they are, 'cept by bustin' or losin' tools." He yawned, then groggily sat down on a barrel, getting an oil stain on the drop seat of his union suit. "It must be almost morning. Let's give it up and sleep. This here's just another dry hole."

Mack stared at the well with a fixed, almost fanatic expression. "No. We've been drawing some oil for the past two hours. I have a hunch about this one."

"Lord you're persistent. Must be because we're starvin' to death out here."

Dawn came, pale and still. The gas smell had thickened steadily. The walking beam lifted and dropped the drill line. Lifted and dropped it. Mack and Johnson sat watching the equipment, fatigue-glazed eyes not really seeing anything but some inner vision of failure.

Suddenly, a different sound at the well head brought Mack to his feet. Mud-brown water burbled from the casing.

"Johnson," he whispered without looking around. The little engine chugged with maddening persistence, then, deep in the earth, he heard another sound. A subterranean rushing. Mack gigged his partner with his bare toe. "Johnson."

Filthy dirty and complaining, Hugh Johnson finally struggled up. He heard it too—the rushing that deepened to a rumble. He stared at Mack, his green eyes full of warring hope and skepticism.

"I wouldn't want to get too excited, because if it ain't—"

Liquid spurted from the well head, quickly rising under pressure to a three-foot column. The muddy brown flow changed to black, the rumbling becoming a roar. It shot up to a six-foot column, and then exploded at the sky, rising like the black barrel of some enormous howitzer aiming at God. Above the derrick's crown block the oil spread in a great fan, and fell back.

"Gusher!" Mack shouted. "We got a gusher, Hugh!"

"Jesus God, I think so!" Johnson shouted over the roar of the hundred-foot-high column of oil. It slicked the boards under their feet, dotted and then blackened their union suits. Johnson ran his hands through his hair and stared at them. Black as patent leather.

He threw his head back and crowed like a rooster. Mack tilted his head and opened his mouth and spread his hands and let the oil soak his skin, his forehead, his eyelids, his tongue.

May 19, 1894—No. 4 pumped 27 bbls. crude.

May 20—62 bbls. crude.

May 21—114 bbls.

Next day the steam engine stopped and the pump fell silent. The coal was gone.

The single lump Johnson had brought in lay between them on the depot desk, seeming to mock them with its rough, glistening beauty. Johnson speculated aloud.

"We can sell the crude in the storage tanks and buy more—"

"No." Mack jumped up, pounding the desk. "Not another

264

penny. We buy coal from Vines, we're pouring cash into the railroad's pocket. I'm tired of enriching those bastards."

"Well, I reckon we can always lift the oil out by hand, a teaspoon at a time—"

Mack ignored him. "There's got to be a better way."

"Good luck, then. I'm going to catch a snooze."

Johnson wandered off to his cot in the back room. Mack flung the front door open and leaned there, chewing his knuckle, staring at the lemon-colored evening sky above the steep hills. He stared at the silent derrick farther back in the tract. Stared at it, and through it, to the larger problem.

All at once his brow puckered up. "Johnson," he said in a tentative voice. "Hugh Johnson. Come here a minute."

Grumbling and scratching, Johnson shuffled from the back.

Mack spoke slowly, testing the idea that had hit him. "Maybe we're overlooking the obvious. I told Ed Doheny that poor people around here burned *brea* because it was cheap. I told him the oil market had to be expanded with a product other than kerosene and axle grease." He paused. "Fuel. What we're pumping in that well is fuel, just like coal. Why the hell can't we burn it instead of coal?"

"Yes, sir. Why not? I'll tell you why not. Got to have some contraption to make it ignite proper. A special—I dunno—special-design firebox, maybe?"

"Well, you're the mechanic," Mack said. "Build it."

Johnson talked a Newhall hardware merchant into selling him a kerosene burner on credit. Quickly finding that the heavy crude clogged it too badly for combustion, he rigged a metal pan with rocks in the bottom, and a nozzle to drip a steady flow of oil onto them, but that didn't work either. Next he snipped and hammered and jerry-rigged a special nozzle, wide and flat, which diffused the crude into something approximating a spray. There was a momentary flame when Johnson touched a match to it, then it fizzled out.

He was ebullient. "If I can get a spray under pressure, don't y'see—a steady fine spray—I think we can get a flame in that there kerosene burner. I need tools and more coal. You got to ask Potter for a loan."

Mack hated doing that, but he did, and he ate some more of his pride and bought enough coal to run the engine for a short period. On June 12, Johnson was ready. Mack fired up the boiler and started the little engine. Apprehensively, Johnson crouched over his contraption. He struck a match, then turned a valve and oil hissed through a line into the special nozzle, now concealed within the housing of the cleaned-out kerosene burner. When Johnson slipped the match to the burner ring, a loud bang and spurting flame threw him back on his heels.

"Valve it down," Mack exclaimed.

"Thanks, never would have thought of that," Johnson snarled, fingering his left eyebrow, which the blowback had burned away almost totally. He twisted the valve.

The flame settled to a constant level above the burner ports. Johnson jumped to his feet and covered the burner with a ventilated housing of battered metal, then stepped back, awaiting congratulations.

"You did it, Hugh," Mack said with an enormous grin. "That's a hell of a burner."

The pale-green eyes danced. "Say. That's a hell of a name too."

Mack didn't get it.

"Hell-burner Johnson. Hello, Hellburner. So long, Hugh." He certified his approval with a rebel yell.

Chance-Johnson No. 4 pumped 825 barrels a day. Soon all the wooden storage tanks were full, and Mack signed a temporary agreement with Lyman Stewart's 14,000-barrel-capacity refinery in Santa Paula to take all the crude. Stewart personally inspected the burner Johnson built. Enthusiastic, he dickered with Mack for two hours over a licensing agreement before they came to terms.

The following week, Stewart's machine shop started construction of forty burners, Mack taking ten as part of the payment to Chance-Johnson. Stewart was elated over the burners and visited San Solaro again to report that he had his shop draftsman working to modify the principle for a locomotive firebox. "I'm going to install one aboard a Southern Pacific locomotive to show those gentlemen they never need coal again. Think of the market if that happens."

"I've thought of it," Mack said.

"Will you go with me to sell them?"

"No, I won't." He didn't explain and Lyman Stewart didn't press. Macklin Chance had a reputation as a peculiar hermit-like maverick. Of course, now, with No. 4 a gusher and the capital coming in to punch new holes all over San Solaro, overnight Macklin Chance had become a man with money and prospects. The foibles of a man like that could be forgiven.

"Hold still," cried the photographer.

Wearing their best, they posed on the derrick floor of No. 4

while the well pumped away. The photographer raised the flashlight holder and the powder exploded. Mack and Johnson bear-hugged each other while the reporter from the Los Angeles *Tribune* hastily finished his notes.

"Uh, gentlemen, one thing. Ours is a family organ, you know. I'm not sure my editor will allow the words 'hell burner.' "

Johnson daggered him with those leaf-green eyes. "One word: 'Hellburner.' You tell him he better allow it or I'll pay him an unfriendly call. Hellburner's my name, boy. I'm proud of it."

They bought tanker wagons and teams, hired drivers, drillers, tool dressers, roughnecks, a cook, built new storage tanks and shored up the old, put up dormitory tents, opened a machine shop, punched down new holes, put fresh paint on the depot, and enlarged one side for a bigger office. They deepened Wyatt's original water well, started framing in a cottage, a permanent house for the owners. Mack sited it on the canal, with the porch beside the dry bed. Putting it there was an act of faith. One day, the sounds of flowing water would soothe whoever sat on that porch.

Mack had never been so busy, never felt so good. Everything was going well. Then came a letter soaked in orange-blossom scent.

> I'm back, my dear.
> Yours,
> Carla

A MAN HAD DAYS OF GOOD LUCK AND BAD. THE DAY **28** he thought of burning their own crude for fuel was one of the good ones. Long afterward, he counted the day Nellie visited as one of the worst. And it had started auspiciously.

It was October: cool, bright, pleasant. Nellie drove her buggy through the iron arch shortly before noon, having taken the train out to Newhall and hired the rig there. Reining the horse by the large signboard erected on Grande Boulevard, she smiled at the gaudy lettering, though she was impressed by what it represented:

CHANCE-JOHNSON OIL CO.
SAN SOLARO FIELD

Seven wells were scattered through the tract, all pumping noisily, and the number of workers swarming on the property amazed her.

"Mack?" She knocked at the office door.

He was cranking up a wall telephone. "Nellie. What are you doing here?" Slapping the earpiece on its hook, he ran to hug her. He looked fit and prosperous in a checkered vest and clean white shirt with cuffs turned up. A thick gold chain hung from the watch pocket of his trousers.

Breathless, she threw her arms around him. He lifted her five inches from the floor and set her down. "More harbor hearings," she said. "I planned to skip them till I saw a copy of the *Tribune* in San Francisco. An article about you and your new partner and your gusher. There is one—?"

"Yes indeed. Number Four." Mack was unexpectedly emotional at the sight of her. "You must meet Johnson. He's in Santa Paula this morning. Rode over with a caravan of tank wagons. Here, sit down . . ."

She took the chair he dusted for her and inspected the office. Thick ledgers, files, and papers were stacked everywhere. Two walls were covered with tacked-up maps, charts, reports, and plats. One huge schematic showed all of San Solaro, with various points labeled PRODUCING WELLS and others marked NEW WELLS. She counted eleven of the latter.

"You've done so splendidly . . ." she began. Then, on a corner of his desk, she recognized the embossed cover of *The Emigrant's Guide to California & Its Gold Fields*. She smiled. "You finally struck it, didn't you?"

"Yes. Promised you I would."

"I'm happy for you—happy and proud." She covered the sudden surge of emotion by taking off her lavender gloves and fussily folding them in her lap.

Mack sat back in his walnut chair. He couldn't get enough of gazing at her, realizing now how much he'd missed her, how much he cared for her.

"Are you staying in town?"

"The Pico House, as usual."

"Let me go back with you and we'll have dinner." *And afterward?* he thought with longing, and a sudden consuming

268

fear of rejection. Afterward, could there be something more? He hoped so. Now that affairs at Chance-Johnson Oil were settling down—he and Hellburner Johnson worked a mere twelve, fourteen hours a day—he should be thinking about things other than money. Starting a family, for instance.

"There's a hearing scheduled for tonight," she said.

"Important?"

"I'm not sure."

"Then forget it."

She saw his intent and blushed, breathing a little more quickly. "All right." Again, with effort, she composed herself. "I have a piece of news about Diego Marquez. He's turned up in the Valley. He left the Church, as you know, but he's still preaching—to the field-workers. This time it's a different gospel, much more militant."

Mack unlocked a drawer with a small key. From a cashbox he took a packet of bills and counted off ten of them. "Can you get that to him?" he asked, handing them to her. "As a donation?"

"I'll certainly find a way." She counted the money. "Five hundred dollars. Mack, can you afford this with so much overhead?"

"Let me worry about that."

She put the money in her reticule. "You're a generous man. It's a side I've never seen before."

"Never had the wherewithal to be generous before. My pa used to say that if you were lucky enough to get rich, you ought to give some back by way of appreciation."

"Not all your ideas are mossbacked, Mr. Chance."

"Thanks, ma'am," he said with mock politeness. Suddenly he thought of Yosemite, and the memories overwhelmed him, as did the warm brown eyes that found his, and held.

Mack flung himself out of the chair and reached for her. He pulled her up to his chest and she raised her strong chin and waited with a frightened-doe expression.

He tilted his head, put his mouth lightly on hers, and felt the rush of her warm breath, the uncontrolled trembling of her slim body—

Then he heard a buggy drive up.

Nellie drew back with mingled dismay and relief, patting her hair with nervous little motions. "Visitors, Mack?"

Mack went to the door and was stunned at what he saw: the phaeton with yellow wheels. A man Mack had never seen before helped Carla Hellman alight.

* * *

"Darling, darling." Carla threw herself on him with hugs and squeezes and breathless exclamations. Mack dutifully embraced her in return, all the while watching Nellie. Her reaction to Carla's show of emotion was not good.

"How marvelous you look. After I came back from the Continent I spent six weeks in San Francisco. They were talking of nothing but your success down here."

"I doubt that." He wondered about her high spirits, given the circumstances under which she'd left the country. Beavis had recovered from his stab wounds, and at the behest of family members, pressed no charges against his wife. Her lawsuit had mysteriously dropped from view, and she and her husband were reported on a second honeymoon in the Greek islands.

"Oh yes, even Walter mentioned how well you're doing," she said.

"Fairbanks? Do you see him a lot?"

"Of course. At social functions. He won't leave me alone. It's a beastly bore."

The mention of Fairbanks pricked him with irrational jealousy. He knew Carla's gushing must be for Nellie's benefit.

"I want to see all these oil wells that are making you so much money. I want a personal tour. I have a proprietary interest, don't forget."

Mack's mouth drew tight. "I'd have settled the debt before this, but I didn't know where to find you."

"What a dear man. Promise you'll show me everything."

"Yes, certainly," he said, resigned.

"And my friend too. This is Clive Henley. Clive, Macklin Chance."

At last Mack had a proper look at Carla's companion. He was Mack's height, and about the same age, but a little heavier. His skin was the color of fresh milk, though relieved by a facial ruddiness that suggested an active life outdoors. His hair was yellow and combed straight back, flat to his head, his eyes a mild gray. He carried himself in a relaxed way and the immediate impression was of affability and good manners.

He was stylish too. His flannel coat and trousers fit perfectly. He wore a straw boater with a band striped in burgundy and white. His bow tie matched, as did the ribbon on his lapel, at the end of which dangled a monocle.

"Very fine to meet you, sir," Henley said, with a marked accent. His handshake was firm; it surprised Mack because of the man's paleness.

"Mr. Henley. You're an Englishman—"

"I am, sir, though a permanent resident of California now."

"Clive grows citrus," Carla said. "Down in Riverside—The area they call the Great Orange Belt and Sanitarium."

"Actually, I— Oh, excuse me," Henley said, almost in a stammer. His eye rested on Nellie, whose cheeks were nearly as red as his. Mack rushed to her.

"Nellie, I apologize for the confusion. Miss Hellman, Mr. Henley—Miss Ross, from San Francisco."

Henley tipped his boater, bowed, and murmured the right pleasantries. "I know Miss Hellman by reputation," Nellie said with perfect politeness and unmistakable double meaning. She extended her hand. She'd put her gloves on again. Carla clasped the hand and held it briefly while they took each other's measure. Their eyes exchanged secret messages; each had instantly sensed the other as a rival.

Mack offered chairs, but no one moved. In the strained silence, the pounding of the derricks seemed louder, and the emotional temperature of the room shot up several more degrees.

Mack said to the visitors, "Miss Ross is a journalist. She writes for the *Examiner* under the name Ramona Sweet."

"Of course—the sob sister," Carla said. "I've read a few of those sensational stories. What an unusual way to spend one's time. Mingling with the dregs, so to speak."

"All in the job," Nellie said. She was simmering.

Henley tried to turn the conversation onto an innocuous tack. "What I started to say was that I don't actually raise oranges, I merely own the groves. Mexicans do all the hard labor. When my father sent me over here five years ago, I discovered that a man could be an orchardist and a gentleman at the same time."

Henley beamed. Mack suspected the man didn't mean to sound like a pompous idiot, but he did.

Carla swept off her little tweed hat. In her matching full skirt and jacket, high-collared silk shirtwaist, and smart buttoned forest-green gaiters adorning brown oxfords, she was very much in the French mode, and very much more stylish than Nellie.

"Clive's father is a baronet," Carla said to Mack. "Fourteenth of his line. Where is it again, dear?"

Henley was tolerant of her flippancy. "Fontana Hall. Oxfordshire."

"Oh yes." She gave Nellie a sweet smile. "But it's you who fascinate me, Miss Ross. Frankly, I've never met a woman who is—how should I put it—in trade."

"Put it . . . however you choose, Miss Hellman. I'm sure you will anyway."

Carla flashed her a hot look. "Do you like this—crude sort of life?"

"I wouldn't do anything else. Except perhaps write novels."

"Even more bohemian! I'm just overcome. I've simply never known a member of our sex who worked for a living, though I've heard of some, who get arrested regularly . . ."

Equally hot now, Nellie said, "Prostitutes and journalists, it's all the same to you, is that it? Well, for your information, Miss Hellman, you'll see more and more women, respectable women, working in the future. You will, that is, if you ever care to spend a few minutes in the world of real people."

This was going all wrong. Mack couldn't stand by and let them spit at one another like cats with their fur up. He stepped in and grasped Nellie's arm. "If you'd just excuse us a moment." A slight pressure got her moving toward the door, though her eyes flashed angrily. She was not merely unhappy with Carla. "I want to discuss . . . dinner . . ." Mack added.

By then they were outside. He said the word "dinner" quietly, but Carla had chased them to the door, and overheard. "Yes, we must have dinner, and get even better acquainted," she said with venomous sweetness. "There's a charming little inn that opened recently on the road to the coast. The chef is Belgian. We could all drive over and—"

"Thank you so much," Nellie said with a poison smile of her own. "I'm afraid I can't. I have to cover a hearing in town. Just a common working girl of the streets . . ."

Carla reddened and vanished from the doorway. "You said the hearing wasn't important," Mack growled under his breath.

"It wasn't, until I saw that I was keeping you from your company."

"You were pretty nasty to Carla—"

"*I* was nasty? Good God, what's got into you? Unfortunately, I'm afraid I know."

"Nellie—"

She pulled her arm from his hand, her brown eyes brimming with hurt and anger. "Good-bye, Mack." She hurried to her buggy. Snatching the long whip from its socket, she switched the withers of the horse three times, and then she was gone.

Damn you, he thought. *If that's how much you care—yes, good-bye.*

The buggy's dust plume rose slowly and elegantly in front of the new signboard for Chance-Johnson. Mack squinted at it a moment, then spun and stomped into the office. Clive Henley had gone out the other door and could be seen walking up and down and fanning himself with his boater while he surveyed

Mack's property. Carla was removing her gloves and straightening her high white-silk collar. She didn't look at him. There was no need; they both understood how the contest had come out.

"Oh, Mack, it's lovely to see you again. Did you get my note?"

"I did. It took me by surprise. What exactly happened with the Beavis lawsuit?"

Before she could answer, pink-cheeked Henley returned and immediately began to chatter. "I say, old fellow, this does look like a going enterprise. Carla wasn't exaggerating; half of California is talking about you. The young Midas of the oil fields. They speak of you in the same breath with that Irishman Doheny."

"And you're much better-looking," Carla teased. She slipped her arm through his, on the side away from Henley, and pressed him with her bosom, her dark-blue eyes conveying invitation. "Papa says Mr. Doheny has a reputation. There are whispers that he killed a man in the Southwest."

"I don't know anything about that."

"You sound cross. Is it Miss Ross? Did I interrupt something important?"

"I haven't seen her for a while, that's all."

"You've not seen me either, my dear," she said tartly.

"I tell you," Henley put in, "if you're looking for a place to invest your oil profits, you couldn't do better than citrus. Come down to Riverside and I'll show you."

"Thanks—I might. I have some problems to solve first. We're freighting our crude to the Santa Paula refinery on a temporary basis, but I'd like to ship it all the way to Ventura on my own. If I sold it there, I'd make a bigger profit."

Carla swept between them, seizing the arm of each. "Tell us about it, my dear." A heated look flushed her face. Nellie was gone; she'd won the day. She was reveling in it.

Johnson returned at half past four, and they drove to the inn Carla had mentioned. Everyone drank too much wine, but Carla drank the most.

The Englishman and the Texan spent almost the entire meal talking to one another. The faster the merlot flowed, the more boisterous and incoherent their conversation became. At the end of the meal, while the two new friends continued to shout genially at one another, Mack and Carla had a chance to talk with a degree of privacy. Again Mack raised the question of the Beavis lawsuit. Carla was matter-of-fact.

"After Swampy got through cursing me up and down, he hired Stephen White's law firm in Los Angeles. One of White's young attorneys, a genuinely tough little fellow named Earl Rogers, persuaded Gladys Beavis to drop the suit. Gladys had her own string of lovers in years past; and Rogers promised that would come out. She withdrew the suit, Mr. White cabled the news, and I came home. Of course I felt terrible about Buddy being hurt that way. I suppose he said something about me to start the quarrel. But the truth is, we'd broken off months before."

Her shrug struck him as callous. "Carla, the man nearly died because he fell in love with you—"

"Who said that? Swampy?"

"Calm down, everybody who's read about the lawsuit knows it. I just don't understand how you can get rid of a sense of responsibility so easily."

She glared. "I can't. Why do you think I go through the days with a glass in my hand?"

"Well, you shouldn't. It isn't good for you."

"Oh shut up. Just shut up and put something in this glass."

Reluctantly he poured more wine. She took a sip, then leaned against his arm, her brief anger passed. "I want to sleep with you so badly," she mouthed silently.

Mack stared into the dark-blue eyes. Her beauty was overpowering as ever . . .

Clive Henley whooped and rocked back in his chair. "That's rich, Hellburner. Oh my dear fellow, that's choice."

Mack poured a little wine in his own glass as Carla carelessly drank the rest of hers. Some of the wine ran down her chin, like the flow from a wound. Under the table, she began to caress his hand. His head was buzzing. *Hell with you, Nellie,* he thought, and reached for the bottle.

With a headache, a churning gut, and a bitter remorse born of sobriety, Mack took the train to Los Angeles next day. He'd been a fool. He meant to undo it, but he got no farther than the desk of the Pico House.

"No, sir, Miss Ross is no longer here. She left for San Francisco early this morning."

The following day Mack rode over to the Hellman ranch on the Santa Clara River and gave Carla a bank draft for $1,173. She pleaded with him to spend the night, but though he wanted to, he invented a problem with one of the wells. Their visit consisted of a sumptuous luncheon, full of her lively chatter, any number of double entendres that made him chuckle, frequent praise for his accomplishments, and several references to Walter Fairbanks. These were intended to remind him that he had competition, that if he wanted her, he must be aggressive. He was in awe of her feminine skills; in pursuing him, she goaded him into the role of pursuer. But he stuck by his determination to leave. As he cantered from under the portico, a stronger inner voice said, *You'd be better off staying away from that woman.*

On the road to San Solaro he tried to analyze the reason for his feeling. He decided a part of him wanted Carla badly because she was so womanly and warm, and many other men would have sacrificed almost anything to have her; Beavis had almost died because he couldn't. But another, perhaps deeper and saner side of his nature clung to Nellie. She had walked out, though. He might win her back as a friend but he wasn't so certain about winning her as a wife. Their ideas were too different, their natures too conflicting, their ambitions too strong. At any rate, she was gone again, and without her he felt vulnerable. And now he harbored a deep fear that at some weak or impulsive moment he might give in to Carla completely.

MR. EZRA PLASSMAN WORE A STIFF COLLAR AND A **29** stiffer expression. As the Newhall freight agent for the Southern Pacific, he recognized his own importance.

"Our price to ship from our depot to Ventura is one dollar a barrel, gentlemen."

It was November and still balmy and dry. The *creak-thunk* of the wells drifted into the office. Johnson reacted to Plassman's statement with an outpouring of obscenities. The freight agent was righteously shocked—he was a church elder—but he wasn't intimidated.

"That is the published rate, approved by the railroad commissioners."

Johnson propelled some dark fluid into a spittoon. "Three crooks in Sacramento. All in your pocket, I don't doubt."

Plassman sneered at the remark.

Mack cleared some papers encroaching on the corner of his desk reserved for T. Fowler Haines. He wanted to punch Plassman's oatmeal face, but in the most reasonable tone he could manage, he said, "It doesn't cost this company anything like a dollar to get one barrel out of the ground."

Plassman shrugged. "I can do nothing about that. However, businessman to businessman, I certainly don't want to be unreasonable. Occasionally we do grant more favorable rates in the form of rebates."

"Occasionally? I thought it was standard practice."

"You're astute, Mr. Chance. As astute as your partner is rude. Yes, rebates are certainly standard for any shipper whose volume is large enough."

"Large enough by whose measurement?"

"Ours. I can easily determine whether yours is sufficiently large by examining your books."

"My—?" Mack couldn't finish. Johnson's boot heel fell off the corner of the desk and hit the floor.

"Books," Plassman repeated. "I'd have to take them with me. I will return them in a day or so."

"The books of the Chance-Johnson Oil Company are private."

"The information will be treated confidentially. But we must see the figures before we discuss any rebate. That's standard SP procedure. Many other shippers, larger and more prestigious than you, have willingly and gratefully allowed us to—"

Like a snake rising to strike, Mack came out of the chair. "Get the hell out of this office. Get off our property."

Plassman snatched up the file he'd brought from Newhall. "You may get satisfaction from displaying your temper, Mr. Chance, but you'll get nothing else. Not from us. The railroad is friendly to those who treat it as friends."

Johnson slid the Peacemaker from its holster. "You heard my partner. You better run 'fore I put a bullet in your ass."

Something, at last, shattered the composure of Mr. Plassman. He nearly fell retreating down the office steps. From the safety of his wagon he called, "I certainly wish you luck in your search for another rail line to handle your oil."

The buggy raced away.

Johnson seethed. "I should of plugged that toad. The goddamn gall—demandin' our books—"

"I heard they do it all the time. I didn't believe it."

"Just like I said at the coal yard. Pack of road agents."

"They're worse than that. The law can catch up with road agents. The SP owns the law in California. It's also an unbreakable monopoly. But Mr. Plassman isn't unbreakable. I'm going

276

to figure out some way to make him eat his rate schedule."
He kicked the desk. "Wait and see."

The wind blew across the open porch and lifted dust in the
bottom of the canal. Daylight was fading in a brilliant display
of red radiance and purple cloud.

Johnson worked at the eternal job of removing invisible rust
from the silvered barrel of his gun. Mack sat in a rocker and
gazed out at the dry canal. Issues of a scientific journal were
stacked up beside him. One lay open in his lap.

"Must be a fascinatin' magazine," Johnson remarked.
"You're ready to fall asleep."

"No, thinking."

"What is that rag?"

Mack showed him. The masthead said THE IRRIGATION AGE.

"Looks about as excitin' as watchin' my grandma darn
socks."

"It's a pretty influential journal in the West. A man named
William Smythe publishes it. Smythe's convinced that scientific
irrigation could make the land in this state bloom like Eden.
So are a whole lot of stockmen and farmers and engineers and
town-builders. Several hundred of them held a congress at the
Opera House in Los Angeles last December. I didn't know a
thing about it."

"We was otherwise occupied."

"Here's an article about irrigation development in Kern
County, for instance. Here's an advertisement for a tour of
model communities around Redlands. And here's the piece that
interests me."

He handed Johnson the magazine, open to an article full of
schematic diagrams.

"Pipelines, huh?"

"For water. Maybe that's our answer for the oil. It works
for Stewart—why not for us?" He jumped up. "You can handle
things here for a week. I think I'll take a little prospecting
trip."

The capitol rotunda in Sacramento was a fine airy space,
flooded with sunshine and ringed by massive marble columns,
and buzzing with the voices of legislators, clerks, lobbyists, farmers, and ranchers coming and going. Discreetly shielded behind a column, Walter Fairbanks III conducted a conversation
on behalf of the SP political bureau.

Fairbanks's auburn hair was precisely parted and his mustache neatly trimmed. He wore a sedate black suit with a gray

cravat and gray spats over black shoes. His gray eyes veiled his contempt for the legislator from Zamora, Yolo County, a man with greed written all over his lumpy face.

"I'm glad to know you look favorably on Santa Monica for the harbor site, Senator LeMoyne."

"That's my present thinking, yes, sir."

"You'll continue to be under tremendous pressure to change your mind."

"Already am."

"Stand fast, and Mr. Huntington, Mr. Herrin, and all the rest of us at the SP will be most appreciative. By the way—" He drew some plain sealed envelopes from an inside pocket. "Here's your annual pass. Good on any of our routes."

LeMoyne snatched his prize. "I noticed envelopes like this here on all the desks in the House. Wondered when I'd get mine."

The wretched provincial was fairly slavering over his bribe. Fairbanks smiled. "Because of your seniority and your record of friendship, you get a little something extra. There's a letter in the envelope presenting you and your family with a complimentary week at the Del Monte Hotel. It's a splendid resort—"

"I know, I know. Nothing but the best people—"

"Quite right. We built it originally to help fill our southbound trains from San Francisco. Now we use it to reward friends."

"Count me one of those, Mr. Fairbanks. Yes, sir." LeMoyne jammed the envelope in a side pocket and held his hand over it, as though fearful of meeting someone as dishonest as himself.

They shook hands and LeMoyne left. Fairbanks wiped his fingers on his trousers and stepped from behind the pillar.

And stopped.

Like a rock in an eddying sea, Macklin Chance was standing in the center of the rotunda.

Despite the noise and bustle, Mack saw Fairbanks immediately. The lawyer looked hale and prosperous as he sauntered over. Although Mack had put on broadcloth, neat and respectable, it was rag compared to Fairbanks's superbly cut black suit.

"Well, Chance. What a surprise to see you." Fairbanks didn't offer his hand.

"I'm trying to locate Otto Hellman."

"He's here. The railroad commission rate hearing." He gestured to some chamber behind Mack. "I hear you're handling oil instead of champagne these days. Well settled in Los Angeles, too."

"Not permanently. I have business in San Francisco one of these days. A few accounts to settle. There's a detective in the police department, for instance. Coglan's his name."

Fairbanks showed not a ripple of surprise or recognition. The self-possession probably made him a good lawyer.

"There's Hellman," he said, raising a hand to signal. Hellman saw him and changed course. A young clerk got in his way and Hellman shoved him aside with a curse. He was as large, untidy, and bumptious as ever. Unexpectedly, Mack was glad to see him.

Fairbanks fiddled with his pearl-gray cravat. Nervous? Mack wondered. Then he guessed the reason: Hellman's daughter.

"Hello, Walter. My God, look here. It's the champagne man. Now he's the oilman. How are you, Johnny?" Hellman pumped Mack's hand with genuine warmth.

"Fine, Swampy."

"I don't like that name."

"I don't like *Johnny*."

"That's right, that's right, I forgot. Ha-ha." His raucous laugh disturbed the rotunda, where any crime was tolerated so long as the perpetrators maintained decorum. Hellman slapped Mack on the back like a lodge brother. Under his wrinkled jacket Mack was astonished to see the holstered Smith & Wesson.

Fairbanks said, "Otto, how is Carla?"

"How should I know? She don't tell me much, she just wires for money."

"She was fine when I saw her two weeks ago," Mack said. "Shall I give her your regards?"

"You see her often?" Fairbanks asked coldly.

Mack stared him down. "Often."

"Then please do. Otto. Your servant." Fairbanks stalked off, livid. Mack permitted himself a smile.

Hellman drew him to the side of the rotunda. "Is that true, Johnny? You see my daughter a lot down there in Ventura County?"

"Some," Mack hedged. There hadn't been another encounter since his ride to the river ranch. "She has a regular friend, a Britisher. He owns citrus groves in Riverside."

"Oh, that one." Hellman plucked a cigar from his jacket. With a look to see whether anyone was watching, he bit off the end, leaned over, and spat it behind the pillar.

"You know Henley?"

"Yah, sure, I met him. Remittance man."

"What's that?"

"Somebody whose family sends him regular checks. Either they don't want him back or he can't go back. Henley's old man, Lord Whoozis-Something, he packed him over here a while back. Maybe Clive put his *Schwanz* in the wrong little girlie, maybe he insulted the queen, maybe he killed somebody. Who knows and who cares? We all got our little secrets. There's a whole bunch of limeys like him down Riverside way."

"He and Carla seem to like each other."

Hellman waved his cigar. "Won't last. Carla's still got a yen for you. But like I said before—you hook up with her, you're in trouble. Well, Johnny, nice to see you. Guess we both better tend to business."

"You're the reason I'm here."

"What? How's that?"

"I telegraphed your San Francisco office and they said you were in Sacramento, so I took the train up here to see you."

"Make it fast, Johnny. I got to get back to the hearing. Sometimes those three idiots on the railroad commission forget who their friends are. If I ain't careful, they're liable to give everybody who ships wheat the same rate I get as a favored customer. Then who'd be dealing with me because I sell cheaper? Nobody. I got to look after my interests here." He chewed his cigar. "What is it you want?"

"Money."

Hellman's eyes lost their geniality, and he scratched his pot belly. Two undone shirt buttons showed his fish-white chest.

"From everything I hear, you got plenty."

"Yes, but I have a big overhead. I have a seventy-man payroll. I've built new storage tanks, bought a fleet of tank wagons—I'll pay them off soon, but I need capital right now."

Hellman chuckled. "Impatient cuss."

"All my crude oil is going to Lyman Stewart for refining. He's tough. He does no favors on price. I can get a better deal selling on the pier at Ventura. The problem is moving the oil to the coast. I want to build a pipeline, San Solaro to Ventura. Forty-seven miles, eight-inch line. Bigger than Stewart's."

"You got faith in the oil business down south, hah?"

"I have faith in everything I do. Sometimes it gets a little worn around the edges but I never lose it."

Hellman chewed his cigar harder. "What's the matter with the railroad to Ventura?"

"Screw the railroad. They want to crucify me with their

highest rate. Look, Swampy, you loan me the money to build the line, I'll give you a royalty on every barrel I move through it for five years."

"Ten years."

Mack drew a long breath. "Maybe."

"You want the cash, there's no maybe. Anything else?"

"I'm going to trench and bury the line. Stewart's line is suspended above ground. Looks like hell. Ruins the landscape."

"Sensitive, ain't you?"

"This is a beautiful state. If we rip it to pieces, we'll never be able to repair it."

"You got some damn radical ideas, you know that?" Mack kept quiet. "How much you need?"

"At least two hundred and fifty thousand."

"I keep that around in shoe boxes." The rap of a gavel in some distant room started a rush in the rotunda. "Send me a proposal."

"Where do I find you?"

"Here, there, someplace—you're hungry enough, you'll find me." He waved the cigar and waddled off, leaving Mack with mingled amusement and exasperation.

Suddenly Hellman thought of something and turned back. "And remember what I said. Stay away from you-know-who."

By the end of 1894, the Chance-Johnson Pipeline Company had acquired its right-of-way by purchase or lease and sent survey crews through the hills to the coastal plain.

Ezra Plassman of the Southern Pacific paid a hasty visit to San Solaro. "We're informed that you're building a pipeline to Ventura, Mr. Chance."

"True."

"You know, that's a completely unnecessary outlay of capital. The SP's special pricing committee discussed your situation only last week. Even without—ah—access to your corporate books, it's evident that Chance-Johnson is rising fast. A potential power in the oil business. Enormous volume. The pricing committee reviewed the matter thoroughly and I'm happy to say the SP has granted you substantial rate concessions."

Mack leaned back and touched his fingertips together. He smiled like a small boy with a new jackknife or pet frog.

"I thought they would, Mr. Plassman."

Then Mack threw him out.

* * *

281

Through his lawyers and bankers, Swampy Hellman handed Mack money the way lesser men handed out change for a daily newspaper. Mack quickly learned the simple but astonishing lesson Nellie had tried to teach him in San Francisco: The problems in obtaining and handling $10 or $1 million were essentially no different; only the numbers were different. He finally believed it, and he knew he'd taken an enormous step forward.

In 1895 Chance-Johnson started the pipeline. A crew of 125 men would trench it and a follow-up crew of the same size would then lay the pipe sections and connect them with threaded collars. Still other crews would build the pumping stations along the line, where steam would heat the crude and reduce its viscosity to keep it flowing.

On an auspiciously clear and sparkling day in February, Mack and Hellburner Johnson took part in a brief ceremony outside the gateway arch. Together with the follow-up crew, they gathered beside an open trench that contained pipe stenciled CHANCE-JOHNSON COAST LINE.

Mack held a bottle of Mumm's aloft. Sunlight flashed from the green glass. With a smile at his partner, he wound up and hurled the bottle into the trench with the speed of a fast baseball pitch. As the bottle smashed, champagne foamed and ran down over the pipe. Johnson tore his Peacemaker from the holster and emptied it in the air, howling his familiar rebel yell. The crew yelled and whistled and waved small American flags and pennants decorated with the company initials.

"Cover it up," Mack said.

The shovels flew and the dirt poured in. Mack felt like a man in a small boat teetering at the summit of a great falls. Things were moving fast, faster than he'd ever dreamed.

In terms of property, if not cash, James Macklin Chance was a rich man. He was twenty-six years old.

The partners traveled down to Wilmington, on San Pedro Bay. At a pier head they inspected *La Jolla de San Diego*, a small coastal steamer with a chain across her gangway and padlocks on her cabins. Gulls sailed lazily in the sultry spring sky. A fishing smack chugged by, laden with mounds of mackerel and rock cod shiny as coins.

"I brung you down here 'cause it seems to me we're already in the business with both feet," Johnson said. "So we shouldn't ought to be at the mercy of the damn shipping companies if we take a notion to send our crude to San Francisco or San Diego—even 'round the Horn. We need our own vessel. I ain't much for numbers, but I'm learnin'. I did a rough work-up . . ."

The paper was yellow foolscap, scribbled in pencil. Mack took it. "How much will she carry?"

"I had some engineers figure it. Once she's refitted, about seven thousand barrels."

"How much for refitting?"

"About fifty thousand."

"How much for the steamer?"

"Askin' seventy-five. Lawyer says they'll take sixty. We should do it, Mack. Honest to God, we should."

Mack was amused. "You really like this business."

"What I like is gettin' rich without stickin' my pistol in someone's face."

Mack took about two minutes to survey the abandoned *La Jolla de San Diego*. Her decks were warped and, in places, rotted out. Hatches gaped without covers. He saw barnacles on her hull and cracked glass in every pane of the wheelhouse.

"Buy her."

The breathless promoter gestured to the map.

"The land's currently in wheat. That doesn't mean you'd be restricted to that crop. Without hesitation, Mr. Chance, this is the finest ranch in the San Joaquin."

"I read the prospectus. Go on."

"The foreman, a top man, agrees to stay on for two years . . ."

He hovered expectantly.

Mack waved. "Draw up the contract for my attorney in town."

Mack and Enrique Potter drove out to inspect a nine-hundred-acre tract in the Cahuenga Valley. They passed a few homes, neat and solid as midwestern burghers yet with an air of sunlit destitution for all that. But the citrus groves and the fields of watermelon and bell peppers were thriving.

In the shade of a huge pepper tree, they stopped and peeled off their coats and Mack said, "I came by here when I first rode into Los Angeles. I remember the Holly Wood tract. It's never taken off as it should. It seems logical to me that as Los Angeles grows, it'll certainly grow this direction, toward the ocean. This tract has everything. Flatland down here for cottages and farms. Up there—" He indicated the mass of the Santa Monicas, where a few isolated small houses clung to the foothills. "Spectacular sites, and there's access to Cahuenga

Pass over to the San Fernando." He picked up the reins and turned to Potter, who looked more affluent these days. "Buy it. Buy yourself another new suit while you're at it. Buy Elena a silver bracelet. Buy those youngsters a sack of toys. Put it all on this bill."

Enrique Potter fussed with his perfectly tied cravat and indicated it would be a pleasure.

"You've studied scientific geology?" Mack said.

"Yes, sir. At Yale," said the young man in the visitor's chair, a fresh-faced, bespectacled fellow with red hair full of cowlicks. "With a name like mine, you have to go in for something unusual, wouldn't you say, sir?"

"I would." Mack felt ancient compared to the applicant, Mr. Haven Ogg of Stamford, Connecticut. Haven Ogg was a mere twenty-one according to a reference letter in the file on the desk.

Ogg was nervous, anxious to please, and kept clasping and unclasping his hands. Mack reached under some ledgers for a square of cardboard. "We need to put this company on a scientific footing. I sketched this . . ." He showed a crude layout for an advertisement:

CHANCE-JOHNSON
Gas—Oil—Asphaltum
Finest Machine & Illuminating Oils

"This isn't the company I'm running, it's the company I want to run. Any comments?"

"Yes, sir. Illuminating oils. The days of water-white kerosene as a significant product are finished. It's all electricity now."

Mack slashed a line through the offending words and tossed the cardboard in Ogg's lap. "Think you could do the rest of it? Set up a refinery? Everything?"

Ogg clutched the cardboard to his chest like a precious possession. "Yes, sir. What I don't know—and I'm sure there's a great deal—I'll learn. Developing the company might take ten years, but with capital for the proper equipment I'm certain it can be accomplished."

A lot more hope than experience in this young man, Mack thought. He liked him. "Not ten years, Mr. Ogg. I'll give you five."

"I'll take it, Mr. Chance."

On horseback, Mack, Johnson, Clive Henley, and an agent climbed a gentle road to Arlington Heights. Mack was hatless and his forehead had developed a dark mahogany patina. He wore fine riding trousers, English boots, and the Shopkeeper's Colt on his hip.

It was a glorious morning, the air smelling of oranges and eucalyptus. The agent's name was Moses Marwick. He never stopped talking.

"Riverside is a fine, prosperous community devoted almost exclusively to citrus. Colonel North, the man who founded the colony in 1870, bought up large sections of the old Rubidoux and Jurupa *ranchos*. He envisioned a thriving silk industry. It didn't work out but now we have something much better."

Henley threw an amused glance at Mack, as if to apologize for the agent's enthusiasm. A flat, sunny mesa stretched behind them, running past the Santa Ana River to the mountain barrier in the north. From the shade of groves on either side of the road, sweating Mexicans and *mestizos* in dark smocks and flat sun hats watched the quartet of well-dressed riders pass in a cloud of dust.

"There was a certain rage for citrus even before the Tibbetses planted the original navel cuttings from Bahia, Brazil. The cuttings were sent out here by someone from the Agriculture Department. That's why we call them Washington navels. Old-timers will tell you that Mrs. Tibbets watered the young trees with her dishwater."

They rounded a bend and came upon a FOR SALE sign bearing Marwick's name. Rows of trees with lustrous dark-green leaves rolled away up the hillsides of the property.

The agent swept off his white sombrero. "There you are, gentlemen. Two hundred acres of the finest citrus in the new subdivision. All from the original Washington cuttings, and guaranteed to be completely above the frost belt. The soil is largely decomposed granite, with excellent drainage. A progressive mutual water company sees to your irrigation needs. What's more, this grove is established and producing. No waiting five, six, seven years for the first crop."

Mack leaned over to an exceedingly sour-faced Johnson, who was mopping sweat with an orange bandanna.

"What do you think?"

"I think you can do anything you want. But I ain't tendin' no fruit."

Mack reared back, laughing. "Don't worry, I'll hire someone else.'' He turned his frisky saddle horse off the road onto a dirt track. "Show us around, Marwick. I'm interested.'

An hour later, he signed the offer to purchase.

The agent left them and rushed back to other appointments while the three men rode to the far southern limit of the property. Here the land rose to a magnificent round hill bleached golden brown by the summer sun. Up on the windy summit Mack dismounted.

"What a beautiful place. The air's as sweet as a perfume shop.''

"Old chap, we'll be delighted to welcome you as a new resident.'' Clive Henley dropped gracefully from his saddle and popped his monocle out of his eye. "We have two clubs you'll enjoy, and you must be my guest at both. There are a number of British chaps in the membership, but many of your countrymen also. Gentleman orchardists, every one.''

Henley had grown chummy very quickly. Mack didn't mind. He liked the polished yet puppylike remittance man. It was hard to envision him committing a crime serious enough to get him banished—or handling Carla, whom he referred to as "a friend.''

"If you enjoy horseback riding, at the Riverside Golf and Polo Club I can introduce you to a fast, rough game some of our lads brought from India.''

"What game's that?" Johnson asked.

"Why, exactly what the club name suggests, H.B.'' Henley's monocle flashed as he waved it. "Polo.''

"Never heard of it.''

"Perhaps not, but your seat's excellent, I've noticed. We might enlist you as a player.''

"So long as I don't have to tend no damn fruit.''

Mack laughed again. "Before I start doing that, I'll have to design and build a house. A big house.'' He strode across the golden summit with the orchards below, the California sky above, other hills and orchards sweeping into the hazy distance. At the hill's highest point he raised his arms.

"Right about here, I'd say.''

They stayed overnight in Riverside, completed the papers, and returned by train to Los Angeles and then Newhall the next day. They were nearly at San Solaro by dusk. Mack felt well rested and excited about his purchase, and looked forward to settling in Riverside County at least part of the year, building a new, California-style residence, learning about citrus. Maybe he'd even investigate that game Henley mentioned. A grand, opulent house in Riverside, and a life-style to go with it, might lure Nellie away from her busy life with Hearst and especially from the temptation of New York. He wanted that; he hadn't heard from her in some months, and he missed her constantly.

Johnson was dour as they rode along, scarcely saying a word. Perhaps things were moving too fast for him. Or maybe he wanted to go roaming again. Mack didn't ask. He was enjoying the balmy evening, the panorama of the busy derricks with their winking lights and rhythmic machinery, sights and sounds he'd grown to love.

They turned from Grande Boulevard into a side street leading to the cottage beside the canal. From two blocks away, Mack spied a man sitting on the rear stoop, smoking. A block from the cottage, he stood in the stirrups, hoping the twilight had tricked him. But no. The man rose laconically. He was thin as a stick, clearly undernourished, and shabbily dressed. There was a familiar cockiness to his wave.

Johnson scowled. "Who in hell's that?"

"My former partner. Wyatt Paul."

A bleak wintry feeling settled over Mack. They rode up to the back stoop and reined their horses.

Wyatt's raven hair had a dirty, dull cast, his clothes little better than a tramp's. But his blue eyes blazed with that familiar merry innocence that charmed so many, and masked so much.

"Hello, Mack. I heard you were making a pile of money from San Solaro. I came back for my share."

MACK INTRODUCED WYATT AND JOHNSON. THEN **30** he asked Johnson to vacate the cottage for the night. "Wyatt and I are going to be talking business."

Johnson, visibly unhappy, protested that it was his cottage too. He had heard a few stories about Wyatt, most uncomplimentary, and he didn't like being dismissed.

"Wyatt's part-owner of the land leased to Chance-Johnson. We have a lot to discuss. It's personal." Mack fairly barked it; he could tell Wyatt was enjoying his visible discomfort. "Do me a favor. Don't argue. Bunk somewhere else."

Johnson stared at his partner. "Shit," he said, and squirted some spit between his teeth. He turned his horse back up the road.

"Inside, Wyatt," Mack said. "You aren't staying long."

Wyatt put a match to a cigarette, a form of tobacco Mack never touched. He flipped the match into the yard, amused. "We'll see." He held the back door. "After you. Partner."

Mack could barely contain his anger. Just when you held four high cards, and your luck was running, and the pot was the biggest ever, the dealer handed you a losing trey. He wanted to take hold of Wyatt's grimy collar and toss him out. Only conscience restrained him—conscience and a certain animal wariness. Wyatt Paul wasn't like other men. He couldn't be counted on to act rationally most of the time. Usually Mack took off his holster when he came home; tonight he didn't.

Wyatt said he was thirsty and Mack uncorked a large jug of red table wine. It was a mistake. An hour later, with darkness settling, Wyatt was guzzling from the jug and they were still going round and round, the same arguments.

"I'm telling you again, Wyatt. I stuck by the bargain. My lawyer in Los Angeles is holding the paper. And the dollar I owe you."

"I disappeared, but it was only temporary. Partner."

"Stop chattering that word like a damn monkey." Mack stormed to the end of the porch and pointed to the derrick lights. "You didn't contribute anything to all that. Not one dime, and not one ounce of sweat."

"Did that ignorant cowboy contribute?"

"A lot."

"What's he get out of it?"

"His fair share."

Wyatt tilted the jug over the back of his arm, dribbling wine into his mouth, then wiping his chin on his sleeve. "I contributed. Whose land are those wells built on, Mack?"

"How many times do you have to hear it? You disappeared. You abandoned San Solaro. You took cash belonging to buyers who trusted you, and you damn near landed me in jail because of it. Now you walk in again as if it never happened. And you won't even say where you've been, for God's sake."

"Mexicali. Catalina. Hawaii. Nowhere important."

Light in the neatly furnished parlor struck Wyatt's eyes, giving them that opaque sheen. "I have a bad impression from this conversation, Mack. An impression that you want to push me out. I guess I had the wrong idea about you." A pause. "I once thought you had a conscience."

Mack bolted at him, then checked himself.

Wyatt stood his ground, laughing. "Thought that'd get you." He slapped his thigh.

Mack stalked off the porch and walked over to the edge of the canal. Rubbing his palms over his face, he could feel the grit of the long day's travel, the frustration, the anger. He quelled it and thought hard. Would the original agreement with Wyatt hold up? Yes. Potter had assured him it would. Then there was an answer, an old and trusted one: percentages.

"All right," he said in a hoarse voice, approaching the porch again. "I'll cut you a new deal. I'll give you ten percent of the net profit of Chance-Johnson."

"Don't insult me, partner." Wyatt swigged.

"Twelve and a half, goddamn it."

"Am I upsetting you, partner? You're cursing a lot. No deal."

"Fifteen," Mack said with pained reluctance.

Wyatt thought it over, then smiled. "Seventeen and a half."

"All right. On one condition. You collect your checks at a bank in Los Angeles. You stay away from here."

The silence was enormous. Wyatt set the jug on the porch with a loud thud, then stumbled down the steps into the starlight. His voice, much lower, carried real enmity.

"Why?"

"Because this is a business. A profitable and well-run business. If I keep it that way, we'll both make money."

"Are you saying I wouldn't keep it that way?"

"Drop it, Wyatt."

"No, get it all out."

Silence.

"Get it all out, Mack."

They stared each other down.

"San Solaro is producing income now, big income. It's going to produce something else if I can bring water in here—the water you lied about to our real estate customers. It's going to produce a town. A *real* town, not the one you dreamed up on paper. No steamboats on a bogus canal. Stores, homes, schools, churches, real streets, real people. It's called progress, Wyatt. It's entirely unrelated to a free ride, a free lunch, or a fast dollar. But it won't happen if you're around here to beat up any banker who says no to a loan, or any contractor who happens to question an order."

"I didn't know you had such a low opinion of me."

"For God's sake stop it. You have a lot of talent and charm. But you let it run wild, you don't harness it."

Wyatt ran to the porch, seized the jug, and smashed it to

289

pieces against a porch pillar. "When are you going to understand? I didn't come to California to climb into a fucking *harness.*"

"Shut up—dammit, you're ranting."

"No, sir, no—I'm going to say this. You've been pretty fucking candid tonight. Well, you listen to this, Mack. Candor can be dangerous. Sometimes it poisons a friendship. Poisons it forever. You understand me?"

"If that's some kind of threat, the hell with you. Do you want the seventeen and a half percent or not?"

"I want it. I'm entitled to it."

"Then collect it in Los Angeles. My attorney's name is Potter. He'll settle the arrangements."

"We'll settle it together. I'm staying right here."

Mack was shaking. He wanted to pull his Peacemaker, but pulled something from memory instead.

"What does the name Sterns mean to you? Don Ysidor Sterns, Rancho de la Bahía?"

Wyatt stood absolutely still. His voice became reasonable again, and very faint.

"I don't know the name Sterns."

"That's peculiar. After you left, I found a long news cutting about Don Ysidor Sterns in your desk. About his murder down near San Diego. Someone killed and robbed him of a lot of money." Mack swallowed, dry-mouthed. He toed an invisible cliff that would either hold, or crumble and carry him into an abyss. "About as much money," he continued, "as it took to buy this land, I figure. They never found the murderer. Damn funny that you'd keep a clipping about a man you didn't know."

"Are you saying—"

"I'm saying it's funny, Wyatt. And I'm saying you didn't get the money from Otto Hellman. That was a lie—never mind how I know. That's all I'm saying—right now."

Ten seconds passed. The night breeze carried the rhythmic pumping of the wells and an owl hooted back in the hills.

Without warning, Wyatt started for Mack and Mack instantly snatched the Colt off his hip and cocked it. "Don't make this any worse."

"I want the clipping."

"No. It's locked up in a bank vault."

"What do you want, then?"

"I want you to get out. Potter will take care of you. Just don't come back here."

Wyatt stood so that the lamplight from inside fell on half his face. Mack watched the charming grin slide back, the charming, smarmy, insincere grin. There was no humor in his eyes, only china-blue malevolence.

"Whatever you say, partner. I'll sleep on your couch and in the morning—"

"I want you off the property now. I'll find a man to drive you into Newhall."

Wyatt thought it over, then lifted one shoulder casually to consent. It was so easily done, so relaxed and pleasant. Somehow it frightened Mack more than Wyatt's ranting.

"Sure—I'll go. I don't expect we've seen the last of each other, though. In fact you can count on it. Let's find that driver. Partner."

THE SOUTHBOUND OVERLAND EXPRESS SLOWED **31** down.

Mack snapped back the lid of his gold pocket watch. A few minutes after 1 A.M. on a Friday in June 1895. He put his tablet aside and leaned toward the window. Black out there—not a light showing.

He sat back and reflected on the irony of traveling on the line he hated. The accommodations were comfortable enough. He was riding in a first-class Silver Palace sleeper similar to those of Pullman's. A powerful ninety-ton 2-8-0 pulled the train. He'd observed the locomotive carefully before he boarded. It was one of those manufactured in company shops at Sacramento and had a straight stack—coal-burning—and the name RED FOX handsomely painted on. Too bad the men who financed *Red Fox* lacked the plain solid honesty of their engine.

The elderly conductor came tiptoeing through. The other passengers had retired into curtained berths, but Mack had asked the porter not to make up his space, two seats facing each other, into a berth. He didn't plan to sleep.

The conductor was a paunchy man with yellowing bags under his eyes. He noticed Mack peering out the window.

"There's heavy fog tonight. We slowed down for the Tehachapi Loop."

Mack nodded and the conductor passed into the dark. The Loop was one of California's engineering marvels. Ten miles north of the four-thousand-foot pass, and the start of the descent to the Mojave, the line twisted through the mountains on five levels. At one point a train chugged into the tunnel for which the Loop was named and came out directly below the point of entry. If the train was long enough, passengers could watch part of the same train going the opposite way.

Mack's shirt collar was open, his vest unbuttoned. On the seat opposite lay his reading material: John Muir's new book, *The Mountains of California*; several issues of *The Irrigation Age*; the latest number of *Land of Sunshine*, a new illustrated magazine promoting Southern California; *Overland Monthly*, a literary journal Mr. Bitter Bierce called the "warmed-overland monthly"; the *Fresno Morning Republican*, headlining the Supreme Court's decision upholding injunctions against Eugene Debs, the railway labor leader who'd brought America's rail traffic to a halt the previous year until federal troops broke the strike.

Mack had laid them all out and hadn't picked up one. He was struggling with a letter. He tore his sixth attempt off the tablet and applied his pencil to a clean sheet.

Dear Nellie,
     Writing to you on the trip south from the Central Valley. Just bought more farmland there, a fine tract of 14,000 acres near Fresno. The promises of that old guidebook are finally coming true. I am striking more kinds of gold than I ever imagined—

Air brakes hissed and iron squealed on iron. The passenger train was slowing again, perhaps for the station. A series of stop-and-start lurches shook the car. Behind an upper-berth curtain, someone muttered fretfully.

but what I really want to tell you is that I am sorry your last visit ended the way it did. I am not involved with that woman you met—

Frown lines cut into his brow. He hated lying. Was Nellie worth it? Yes.

and never have been in any serious way. Can you please get away from Mr. H. for a few days, come down and discuss it? I want to show you a certain place I have picked out to build a new—

More lurches and—rattles. The train crawled forward. He scowled and peered out. A few distant lights sprinkled the dark diffuse, misty lights. The fog was soupy, all right.

Suddenly a ferocious lurch fluttered the low-trimmed wicks of the kerosene lamps mounted above him. Other passengers awakened and began to ask questions of each other. The car smelled of dusty carpet, bed linen, the kerosene in the lamps.

From the shadows of the vestibule the conductor called out softly, "Tehachapi Summit. The station is Tehachapi."

Mack decided to stretch and take the air. On his way out he passed the berth of a Scandinavian couple, who were traveling with their daughter. He heard the wife. "What do you see, Nels?"

"Blasted fog, dat's all."

Yawning, Mack clambered down the steps to the platform of a spartan passenger station. Electric lights inside were muted by the cold wet fog, the thickest he'd ever seen. The station was empty. He gazed through the pane at the silent telegraph key. Why was no agent on duty?

The baggy-eyed conductor trudged back from the engine swinging his bull's-eye lantern, its tilting beam slicing the fog like a broadsword.

"Can't proceed till this fog thins out," he said. "It's a real hazard up in these mountains. The engineer hopes it will clear in an hour or so."

Passengers in robes or rumpled clothing poked their heads from the first- and second-class cars. One man climbed down and cornered the conductor. "We're on the main line, aren't we? Shouldn't we wait on a spur?"

"Only one line through here. There are no other trains this time of night."

Mack spied something at the end of the train, something that sent a nasty tickle of worry up his spine. Beside the track, the lens of a two-sided signal lantern shone green.

"Conductor, even with no trains, shouldn't that signal be red?"

The Scandinavian couple appeared, the stocky wife wearing a hairnet heavy enough to catch trout and the husband attired in a fine satin robe, nightshirt, and pointed Turkish slippers.

Mack was watching the conductor. Something was wrong and the man knew it. He tried to cover it with hasty assurances. "Oh, it's some mechanical problem, that's all. I'll have the brakeman see about—"

A train whistled in the dark. Loudly, stridently. Mack's heart hammered. The train was behind them, chugging rapidly down the grade.

"Jesus and Mary," the conductor whispered, crossing himself. The passengers began to mill about and exclaim, consternation soon changing to panic.

"That's a down-bound train—"

"On this track. Scatter!"

"Kirstin," cried the wife. "Nels, Kirstin's asleep—"

Her husband's thick Scandinavian speech lapped hers. "Others, too—"

"Get them out of there, conductor," Mack yelled. Pop-eyed, the conductor raised his lantern and stared at Mack, his mouth working soundlessly. The roar and chuff of the unseen train grew louder.

Nels, the husband, ran toward the rear, waving his arms. "Stop, hold up—" He lost one slipper, then the other. "Stop!"

A broad white beam slashed around the last curve before the station. Intensified by its mirrored reflector, the headlight flooded the platform and the standing train with a glare as brilliant as a burst of lightning. The train itself appeared with a crescendo roar. Mack had a glimpse of the balloon stack of a woodburner. Shoving the paralyzed conductor aside, he ran up the steps and kicked open the door of the Silver Palace car.

"Everybody get out—right now!"

The engineer of the down-bound train signaled the impending calamity with a screaming whistle. Mack ran along the car, shaking curtains, shouting. "Wake up, there isn't a minute to—"

Impact. Crushing, crashing, hurling the car and the train forward with a violent motion. The lamps over Mack's seat shattered. Hot oil splashed from the broken reservoirs and ignited. A woman poked her head from her berth, saw the fire, and began screaming. Mack struck her with an open hand. "Be quiet, get out, save yourself—"

He heard another terrified yell behind him. Then he felt the car start to tilt off the rails. Everything was leaping flame, writhing shadow, the snap of breaking timbers, the yelp of bending metal. And above all, there were the screams.

The shrillest came from the berth of the Scandinavian girl. Evidently she was trapped. He fought toward that end of the car, a hopeless effort because the car was falling over. He lost his balance and tumbled into the open seat he'd occupied. Muir's book and all his other reading were afire.

Mack smashed down against the outer wall, now the bottom of the car settling on its side. His head slammed the frame of the broken window and he almost slashed his throat on jagged glass.

Flame from the burning cushions ignited a shirt cuff and his vest. He fought to stand up, slapping out the fire. Passengers, bloodied and screaming, crawled or stumbled toward the ends of the car. Up and down the train, the screams multiplied.

The worst was still the girl's. What was her name . . . ?

He roared it. "Kirstin!"

"Here! Who's that? I'm caught—help me!"

He had trouble reaching her. Choking smoke filled the aisle. He had to crawl and clamber over the berths that now formed a floor for the car. Tearing the curtains off the girl's berth, he found her huddled in tangled bedding, hands jammed to her throat, blue eyes round and wild. He yanked the covers until he unsnarled them, freeing her. What had really imprisoned her was her own fright.

"Reach up. Arms around my neck. Quick."

She obeyed. Coughing, he lifted the girl out of the berth and teetered there, trying to decide. The end of the car? No, fire from his seat had leaped across the aisle. He found the partition separating the girl's berth from the next. "Kirstin, hold on to this wall."

"Don't leave me here, oh please don't."

"I won't—be quiet." He ripped down the curtains of the berth across the aisle; it was now above him. He braced himself, then crawled up into the berth and beat at the window with his elbow. Turbulent red smoke almost hid the girl beneath him. He struck the glass again.

Again.

Again—

The window broke and he shielded his eyes and face, but not in time, the glass slashing his cheek and opening a long cut on his forehead. A fleck lodged under his left lid, a needlepoint of incredible pain. "Oh, Christ." He blinked and blinked, felt tears well in the eye. Then, mercifully, the needle was gone.

Fire spread rapidly now, brightening the car's interior. "Kirstin, take hold. I'm going to pull you up and boost you through this window." She saw the ragged glass all around the window frame and cowered.

"Come on," he yelled, and grabbed her wrist too hard, hurting her. Never mind a broken bone; this was a question of her life. He wedged himself in the berth and somehow dragged her up. Then he put a hand under her hip and shoved.

"Somebody out there help this girl!"

Voices, then heavy footfalls, a man running along the side of the overturned car. "Yes, coming. Here, girl—"

In a moment Kirstin was safely in the man's arms out there

in the firelit murk. Mack gulped sweet damp air, listening to a bedlam of questions, the crackle of fire, the wailing of the frightened or injured. He reached through the dangerous glass-toothed opening to find a hold and lift himself to safety—

He heard a voice, a feeble male voice. Someone else trapped. *Save yourself,* something said to him, but he didn't listen. He dropped back inside. The smoke was acrid, almost opaque. Covering his nose and mouth with his handkerchief, he heard the faint plaintive voice again.

"I can't move. I think my leg's broken."

Mack's face poured off sweat. The cry came from the other end of the car, from a berth beyond the flames that created a hot bright barrier across the aisle, just where he'd been sitting. *I don't want to do this,* he thought.

He knuckled his eyes, dragged a blanket from a berth, folded it, and wrapped it over his head for protection.

Then he held his breath and ran toward the fire barrier, and through.

Mack rested in his double bed in the cottage. He'd designed the room with a wide window beside the bed; that way he could always wake to the sight of the derricks pumping money from the ground.

His arms and shoulders were dressed with cotton batting over a paste of oxide of zinc and ground acetate of morphine, the latter for pain relief. Roller bandages held the batting in place. He'd been lucky—no burns worse than first-degree, and those over a limited area. A smart young doctor up in the mountains had minimized the burn damage by soaking him in cold water in a horse trough, then applying household molasses.

His eyelids tended to droop; that was the opium tincture the local doctor prescribed for pain. Mack was ashamed to lie helpless in front of visitors. Sickness was unmanly.

Nellie sat on a chair, Bierce behind her. They'd shown up with no advance warning. Nellie looked tired and uncharacteristically pale, but Bierce was his elegant self in a spotless ivory suit and vest and a flowing bow tie.

Bierce laid a small book on the coverlet. "That might amuse you while you recuperate."

Mack picked it up: *Tales of Soldiers and Civilians.* "Yours?"

"Yes. The usual portions of grue and vitriol. Read it when you hate the world."

"Not right now," Mack said. His tongue felt thick and clumsy. "I'm thankful to be alive."

"You're a hero," Nellie said. He'd rescued the girl Kirstin, and then the man trapped in his berth. Nellie's tone conveyed her pride.

"If you don't think so, Uncle Willie's minions will make sure," Bierce added.

"Are you two down here to write about the wreck?"

"Naturally," Bierce said. "Rushed to the scene by another special train from the beloved SP. Frankly, it's a relief. For weeks I've been flogging the Crime of the Century, as our proprietor christened it: A sleazy little Sunday-school superintendent at Emanuel Baptist did away with two of his female pupils. I can find nothing else sensational or titillating to say about the undergarments of the deceased. We came on from Tehachapi to see how you were. Tenderhearted Nell insisted."

She reddened, embarrassed. Bierce ignored her. "That was an unscheduled work train, you know, with an inexperienced engineer. Further, when word of the train passed down the line by telegraph there was no one at Tehachapi to receive it. The agent was malingering in some deadfall."

Mack hitched higher against the bolster. "I noticed the station was empty. I also saw a green signal that should have been red."

"They still don't give a damn about the safety of passengers. We'll roast them with our usual crusading verve."

"Not that it'll do a lot of good," Nellie said. "Fairbanks is already paying off the passengers. The one man who was killed worked for them."

"The conductor," Mack said.

"Yes. He was crushed when the cars overturned. His widow filed a damage suit in San Francisco, but we had a telegraph message this morning saying she's withdrawn it."

"Why would she do that?"

Bierce sighed. "What a naïf you are, Mack. I expect she realized that silence and a pension are superior to justice and poverty."

"Bastards." Mack stretched to take Nellie's hand. "I've said it before: I'll help you nail them one of these days."

She kept her hand just out of reach. After a nervous glance at Bierce she cleared her throat. "I hope to be able to do a much better job of that in New York."

Mack's stomach twisted. "You're going?"

"Not immediately. But I've made the decision. Mr. Hearst is off in Europe with Tessie. Before he left, he sent our business manager, Charley Palmer, to New York for preliminary negotiations. There are four newspapers for sale. The *Times*, *Ad-*

vertiser, *Recorder*, and the *Morning Journal*. Mr. Hearst plans to buy art objects in Europe, and then come back and buy one of those failing papers.''

"Oh, the *Journal*, by all means," Bierce declared. "It's so cheap and racy. They call it the chambermaid's delight. Onward and upward with the bright banners of journalism.''

"When is this likely to happen?''

Nellie said, "Before the end of the year, I should think. Mr. Hearst wants me to be the sob sister. And keep an eye on Mr. Huntington's tricks. At the moment, Huntington's other priority besides the harbor is the railroad's debt to the government. It goes back to the days of construction in the sixties. Huntington wants Congress to cancel the debt, or reduce it drastically. That would be fraud on a mammoth scale. It's disgusting.''

"It's the dear old Southern Pacific.'' Bierce patted his various pockets one by one. "Here a legislator, there a legislator—soon you have exactly what you want.''

"Ambrose," Mack said, "would you leave us alone?''

Surprise erased his sardonic smile. "I beg your pardon?''

"I need to speak to Nellie privately.''

"Certainly. If I hear any sounds of unbridled lust, trust me to remain discreet.''

He turned away. Nellie watched the back of his jacket with visible desperation. She didn't want to be alone with Mack.

Humming, Bierce closed the door.

Mack wasted no time on polite preliminaries. "Nellie, forget New York.''

She dabbed at her stubby little nose—a nervous, unnecessary gesture. She wasn't a woman given to showing anxiety. But he saw it in her eyes now.

"And do what, Mack?''

"Marry me. I've bought a fine piece of land in Riverside—''

"More property?'' She laughed in a hollow way. "You've become a spendthrift.''

"I'm rich. I'm making investments. Don't change the subject. The property is beautiful, up on a hill in a subdivision called Arlington Heights. Orange groves cover most of the acreage. I'll show it to you when the doctor lets me out of this damn bed.''

She folded her hands and sat still, gaining control.

"What is it?'' he said. "Carla Hellman? Would I be proposing if she meant anything to me?''

Nellie shook her head. "Afterward, I was so ashamed of what I did. I only flared and walked out because I do care for you. Deeply. Your proposal is tender, and lovely—"

"A man covered with white goo and doped with opium isn't tender or lovely." A pause. "But he means it."

She struggled for her next words. "I know what I'm about to say will offend you. No, stronger—you'll probably despise me. I'm truly sorry. I have to be honest. When you ask me to marry you, you're asking me to be less than what I can be with Mr. Hearst."

"I'm offering you my life, damn it."

"Yes, but in exchange for taking mine."

"That's a hell of a way to look at love."

"I think—" Her eyes flooded with tears of confusion, something else completely unlike her. "Oh, I think if you really understood me—if that was part of your love—you wouldn't even ask."

"My God—no, I don't understand your crazy ideas. Who put them in your head? Who?"

The shout brought her to her feet, red-cheeked. "The world, Mack—the world. This is almost the twentieth century, not the Dark Ages."

He fought his temper. "Stop it. All that matters is this: I don't love anyone else; I never will love anyone else."

"Nor I. But you love your own ideas too. They're grotesquely old-fashioned. You love what's in that wretched little book you worship. Look at you, running wildly up and down the state snatching up farms, orchards, spending as if you're going to die tomorrow morning . . ."

He sat up straight in bed. It hurt, but no more than his anger over the way this was degenerating. "What the hell's wrong with ambition? I know people who admire it in a man." *Carla, for one.*

"Nothing's wrong with it, Mack, unless it comes before everything else—unless it builds a wall."

"What about *your* ambition? What about New York?"

Her rueful smile said he'd hit a fair target. "Two walls." She gave a sad little shake of her head. "I don't know, Mack. We're right for each other—absolutely right—and at the same time, all wrong."

"Nellie, don't do this."

She rushed to the bedside and bent to give him a kiss. The moment their mouths touched, he seized her shoulders. She fell sideways, her hip on the bed, bracing her leg and surrendering to the embrace. "Oh, you'll hurt yourself . . ." As he kissed her more fiercely, she shuddered and closed her eyes.

The deliriously emotional kiss went on, sweeping away all the arguments and objections.

But not for long. As Nellie pulled back for air, Mack saw the lifted chin and determined eyes he remembered from that first day on the pier. He released her and let his hands fall.

"I'm sorry, Mack. The city desk . . ." She rose. "They're expecting telegraphed copy tonight. Ambrose and I have a meeting with the sketch artist. Come see me in New York."

Mack's hazel eyes held hers, and the stoniness of his stare said it would never happen.

"Mack, please . . ."

Nothing. Nothing but that stare. She left the room quietly, and he heard her murmuring with Bierce, then the front door. Shortly the *clip-clop* and rattle of the buggy faded away beneath the familiar sound of the pumping derricks. He turned to the sunlit window, blind now to the sight of the wells. He'd never felt so unwanted, miserable, furious, defeated.

32 EARLY IN JULY, HELLBURNER JOHNSON RETURNED from a month of roaming the Baja down in Mexico. He rode in through the arch and found his partner in the expanded office section of the depot. Amid the usual desk litter of ledgers, reports, contracts, and memoranda stood an open bottle of Kentucky whiskey. An inch of the liquor shimmered in a shot glass.

Johnson slapped dust from his striped pants, staring from the whiskey to his partner. "This time of day?"

"This or any other time of day, what about it?"

Johnson clicked his tongue and left. In talking to a few men around the field, foremen and roughnecks, he found there was no secret about it. Ever since Mack had gotten out of bed, he'd been at the bottle. Heavily.

Lieutenant Colonel Harrison Gray Otis paid a call.

Mack received him in the office in the afternoon. Otis carried a malacca swagger stick, and in his lapel he wore a military rosette of some kind. Some years before he'd edited the

G.A.R. journal, and he was still active in that organization of Civil War veterans.

The colonel was disconcerted by Mack's unshaven, unkempt appearance. To someone accustomed to alertness and discipline, such a foggy expression was displeasing.

"Unexpected pleasure, Colonel."

"You are a long way from Los Angeles, sir. A difficult man to find. Have we perhaps met before? There's a certain familiarity—"

"It's possible." Mack wasn't yet so drunk that he'd forgotten the altercation when he drove Marquez to the *Times* office. "Join me in a drink?"

"No, sir. But you have one if you wish."

"Yes, I'll have another." He opened a drawer and uncorked the bottle. Otis tapped his knee with his swagger stick, a march cadence, and Mack regarded him blearily. "I don't always drink in the daytime, you understand. Only when I feel like hell."

The heavy humor failed to move Otis to smile. "You were injured in the Tehachapi wreck. I hope you have recovered."

Mack raised a full glass. "Works wonders."

"Mr. Chance, if this is an inconvenient time . . ." Mack's wave said no. Some of the whiskey spilled on papers on the desk. Otis's disapproval grew more apparent. "I traveled out here, sir, because you have made an impression upon the Los Angeles business community. You are proving yourself one of the most astute entrepreneurs in the region. Further, from what I read in Mr. Hearst's execrable San Francisco rag, you comported yourself heroically at Tehachapi, though you are no partisan of the railroad."

"Almost everywhere in California, the SP has a monopoly. I don't like that kind of stranglehold."

"Precisely. The very reason I'm here. I want to enlist your support, personal and financial, for our continuing war against the railroad's machinations to secure the harbor for Santa Monica. I invite you to join the ranks of the chamber of commerce. I ask you to lend your energy to the creation of a greater Los Angeles—a greater Southern California—free of the stinking infection of communist trade unionism."

Mack set his glass down. His eyes seemed to clear, and his speech too. "I'm not opposed to all trade unions. Owners and workers should support and encourage each other, not exploit each other. That way, everyone makes money."

Otis stiffened as though Mack had whipped his face with a glove, Prussian style. "I find those sentiments repugnant, sir. Look at the riot and rebellion last year during the Pullman strike. The minions of Gene Debs subjected Sacramento to mob rule. Governor Pardee had to send regiments of militia up the river on steamboats to prevent anarchy, arson, and mass murder.''

"Come on, Colonel, it wasn't that bad." Bad enough, though, Mack had to admit; the strikers had weakened a railroad bridge and a train had plunged off, killing the engineer and four soldiers of the 5th Artillery.

"Bad, sir? It was heinous. It was treason against the principles of free commerce. Any man who employs union labor—deals with union labor—or even sympathizes with union labor, as you apparently do, is an enemy of the decent citizens of Los Angeles.''

Mack was just drunk enough to forget this man's power. He leaned on the desk corner, squinting in what he hoped was a truculent way.

"I have a friend, Colonel. Marquez is his name. Diego Marquez. Is he your enemy?''

Otis acted as though Mack had invoked Satan. "Marquez the priest? Marquez is nothing but a mangy yellow dog of a socialist. He betrayed his sacred oaths—his church—the Almighty Himself. A few years ago, he attempted to infiltrate the citadel of the *Times,* but I repelled . . .'' Otis sucked in a breath. "Wait. That's where I saw you. That night with Marquez.''

"Correct, Colonel.'' With a smirk and another toast with the shot glass, Mack drank down the whiskey.

Otis snapped to his feet. "Your reputation deceived the business community. I'll set them straight.''

"Before we leave the subject of Marquez—who burned down his *rancho* when he supported the printers? Friends of yours?''

Otis flung up the swagger stick.

"I wouldn't try that, Colonel.''

The stick shook, as did the freckled, veined hand grasping it. Harrison Gray Otis fought the stick down to his side. "I withdraw my invitations, Mr. Chance.''

"And I withdraw my tolerance of you. Get out of here.''

"Happily. Happily!''

Otis quick-marched to the door. A moment later his buggy rattled away. *Well*, Mack thought, *now I have enemies in Los Angeles too*. He slopped another full measure of booze into the glass.

That afternoon the wind shifted, blowing from the east, hot and parched, and by evening the sky was red as the heart of a steel furnace. Mack sat on the cottage porch with a fresh bottle at his feet. He stared inward, at the certainty that Nellie was lost to him, at a growing awareness of what little was left.

About half past seven, Johnson strode around the corner of the house. He gave Mack and his bottle a disgusted look as he stomped up the porch steps. A clump of uprooted weeds sailed by.

"*Santan,*" Johnson said.

Mack drained his glass. The wind reached inside him, rubbed and grated and bloodied his nerves. The *santan* was the wind of murder and madness. When it blew, people lost control. He was losing control.

The Texan sniffed. "I don't smell supper."

"Fix it yourself." Mack threw the empty glass in the yard and started for the road. Johnson grabbed him.

"Where you goin'?"

He flung Johnson's hand away.

"Where I belong."

MACK'S HORSE TORE ALONG THE ROAD WITH ITS **33** mane standing out, lather streaming off its flanks and thighs.

When Mack pulled the reins hard to the right, the horse balked and almost threw him. But after an impatient kick, it lunged up the dirt track past the crooked sign saying HELL-MAN.

Dust clouds blurred the outbuildings. A *vaquero* ran for shelter with both hands clutching his sombrero to his head. The wind tore a spinning weather vane from the roof of a barn, spiraling it upward into the heart of the cloud, where it vanished. In the same barn maddened horses neighed and kicked their stalls while *vaqueros* shrieked curses in Spanish.

Under the portico Mack jumped down, the wind snapping his coattails and tossing his hair while little veils of sand trailed from his trouser cuffs. He didn't bother to tie the horse; the stallion was too frightened to run off.

He hammered the huge ring knocker down twice, then kicked the doors open.

"Carla?"

He slammed both doors. One failed to catch and crashed

against the wall. Cyclonic wind rushed through the high, dim hall, causing an ornamental gourd to fly off its peg and break on the tiles, loud as a rifle shot.

"Carla, where are you?"

He climbed three stairs to an arch, which led to a huge living room. A jutting adobe fireplace dominated one wall, with colorful broadly striped blankets decorating the others. Dark polished chairs stood along the walls like straight-backed soldiers, and leather cushions and an enormous divan created a horseshoe near the fireplace.

In a second archway opposite the entrance, the Indian woman hovered, wide-eyed, taking in Mack's disheveled state. Whatever she meant to say died in her throat, and she fled.

He overturned one of the chairs, a ferocious clattering.

"Carla, answer me!"

The wind roared through the open front door and he could feel it whipping and eddying in the room. Every shutter in the house was closed against the storm.

Appearing in a third arched entrance, this one opening into the wall opposite the dark hearth, she took in his agitated state, and her smile tightened.

"I hardly expected you, my dear," she said.

"So I surprised you. What have you got to drink?"

"From the sound of it, you've had quite a lot already."

"Does that mean I'm not welcome?"

She came down the short stair slowly and licked her lower lip. Although she wore no lipstick, it was red, as though bitten.

"I didn't say that."

He staggered to the divan and sprawled, arms spread to either side, head lolling. Carla watched from the foot of the stair. She wore a translucent wrapper of white silk and, beneath it, her corset, pink-brocaded and frilled with lace along the scooped bodice line. The corset fit over a chemise of linen with the hem trimmed in lace; the rolled tops of black stockings showed below. Her blond hair tumbled over her shoulders.

She touched the silk. "I was undressing for my bath, hardly prepared for visitors."

"You look fine. Gorgeous as a fifty-cent whore."

"God, you're stinking drunk." She was amused, though. "I'll not quibble. I've finally got you where I've wanted you. All to myself."

He waved toward the other arch. "I saw your Indian woman—"

"I'll take care of her." She glided over the cool tan tiles in her stocking feet. "What would you like?"

"Champagne."

"I have it. Dom Pérignon. I have a cellarful." Carla smoothed her hands down the underside of her bosom. "I have enough to last all night."

Soon she returned with the champagne and two crystal flutes. "I sent Ynez to her quarters. She's happy to lock herself in for the night. The wind's frightful. You can scarcely see three feet outside."

She held out the bottle. "Will you open it?"

Mack took it from her and struggled with the cork. He couldn't loosen it. Pushing her back, he stepped to the jutting corner of the fireplace and smashed the neck against it. Champagne foamed over his hand and dripped to the floor.

"That's one way," Carla said. She held out the flutes.

He filled both, then, seizing his glass, he drained it before she finished a first sip. He was weaving on his feet, his hazel eyes crawling over the deep round cleavage her corset made.

Carla licked the rim of her glass. "My. It isn't difficult to tell what's on your mind."

"You don't like it?"

She licked the goblet again slowly, tongue sliding to one side, then sliding back, leaving wet traces. "Did I say that?"

Mack threw his flute in the hearth and pushed against her. One hand circled her waist, the other closed on the swell of her lace-covered breast. She dropped her glass and sagged in his arms and said, "Oh my God," in a voice both excited and frightened. He kissed her. She opened her mouth and he tasted her frenzied darting tongue.

Up above them, outside, the *santan* tore away red roof tiles. It sounded as if someone were shooting at the house. The wind spun the tiles away to smash on the baked earth. Barn siding ripped loose and sailed away. Trees surrounding the *rancho* creaked and bent and lashed their branches, limbs snapping and flying aloft like missiles from a crossbow. A sharp one gored a mare loose from the barn. She tumbled over, wailing and howling in the wind and darkness. No one heard her die.

Carla undressed herself quickly and fell on her back in her enormous bed. Her boudoir was dark, every shutter rattling and leaking windblown dust. Mack groped for her, and she guided him. The *santan* screamed, a wind of craziness. They were both crazed with lust. She struggled and writhed in her haste to take him into her.

* * *

305

Carla woke.

Her eyes flickered open, drowsy and momentarily bewildered. A bedside candle fluttered on a small table. Next to it was a disorderly mountain of books, a peak in a littered sea of unread newspapers.

With a start, she saw Mack's hazel eyes. The bleariness had cleared. He sprawled naked beside her, the bedclothes shoved together in mussed ridges and valleys. On his left shoulder she noticed the imprint of her teeth, and this made her smile.

The wind was as loud as ever. Carla brushed a plump forearm across her eyes. Her body glistened, pink and moist from the lovemaking. "What time is it, love?"

"Almost midnight." He reached down beside the bed and produced another bottle of champagne, this one uncorked. "Still thirsty?"

She made a little animal sound indicating she was.

"Here," he said. "Don't take too long." She looked down. He was erect again.

She pushed a spill of blond curls off her forehead. Smiling, she clasped hands on the bottle and greedily sucked at it, then trickled the liquid on her nipples and into the golden nest of her sex.

He took the bottle from her and upset it trying to stand it on the floor beside the bed. There was the sound of the wind, the sound of champagne running out, then the louder sound of the bed creaking and shaking.

A match scraped in the dark. He relit the stubby candle a gust of wind had extinguished. Carla woke after a moment, muttering and making soft complaining sounds, her eyes still closed. He left the bed and returned with a fresh bottle of champagne. She drank, then he drank. She grasped the bottle's neck again, caressing it.

He laughed, drunk. Somewhere down inside, a little flame of sanity blew out, like the candle. He took this bottle away from her too. She felt him and uttered a sleepy erotic laugh. "You're insatiable."

She slid beneath him.

Out in the dark, a horse neighed and kicked a stall.

The night smelled of the dead mare's blood.

And the wind went on . . .

He woke, tasting a cotton layer inside his mouth, smelling champagne and sweat.

Carla was sleeping. He touched her breast. Cool. He rolled over as quietly as he could. Slitted light patterned the floor.

The bedroom was a mess. Broken glassware, flung bedding, overturned furniture—the disorder of a battleground. A fine old Spanish chair with a thick leather seat was pulled against the foot of the bed. He dimly recalled that one of the times they'd made love, it had been in that chair.

He scratched his belly and carefully stood on the cool tiles. His legs wobbled, incredibly weak. There were empty green bottles all over the room. Finding one with a half-inch of stale champagne in it, he drank.

He padded to the nearest shutter, careful to avoid broken glass, lifted the metal latch, and pulled the shutter inward. Ruddy light struck his eyes, driving him back with a groan. He slammed the shutter and latched it.

In the bed, Carla stirred. He fought off a rush of dizziness. Her deep-blue eyes opened with a strange catlike solemnity. Her skin looked raw from all the kissing and embracing.

He touched the shutter. "It's morning."

"No—afternoon."

"What? Are you sure?"

"I was up a while this morning. We've been here nearly a whole day. It's five or six in the afternoon."

She sat up, folding her arms over her bosom. She was heavy as a classical nude in a painting: great golden thighs, a waist growing plump. The breasts would be heavy with matronly sag before many more years. She was the ideal woman, big and billowy like Lillian Russell. The whole world loved Lillian Russell . . .

Carla rubbed her legs and shivered. "I've never had love like that. Never." She was profoundly shaken.

"I haven't either."

He wandered through the room till he found a full champagne bottle, then tugged at the cork till it blew, *pop*, ricocheting off a ceiling beam. He offered the bottle.

"No, I don't want any more. All I want is you. The two of us together, always." The dark-blue eyes seemed to grow huge, and draw him in. "Marry me, Mack."

He was silent. Stunned. Outside the shutters, the light was fading. There was no wind.

"Mack, did you hear me?"

He thought of Nellie. But she was gone. He swallowed, then thrust the bottle to his mouth and gulped.

With a strange, vulnerable softness in her face, she said, "The least you can do is answer me."

"All right, Carla, yes. A man needs a wife. Any man would be proud to have a beautiful wife like you. I'll build a fine new home for us down in Riverside . . ."

Triumph flooded her face like a breaking dawn and her eyes danced. "I never thought I'd hear you say it. I never thought I'd get what I wanted most in the world. Come here, come here . . ."

She opened her arms and wriggled her fingers. He swigged again, then put the bottle aside and walked to the bed. As his bare foot touched one of the newspapers, he glanced down and saw the masthead MONARCH OF THE DAILIES. A three-column headline snatched his eye.

THE TEHACHAPI TRAGEDY!

Southern Pacific Negligence Claims New Victim!

Exclusive Dispatches by Our Roving Correspondents Mr. BIERCE & Miss SWEET

Forget her. She's gone. He muttered an oath under his breath.

"Mack? Sweetheart? What is it?"

"Nothing." He put his foot on the paper and twisted it. The paper tore. Kneeling on the edge of the bed, he braced both hands above Carla's shoulders, leaned down, and kissed her.

Her wet mouth pressed hard against his. "Once more, darling—can you? To seal the bargain?"

Nellie, why isn't it you? he thought. An invisible cliff loomed, and he was at the edge.

"Mack? My darling husband? Please?"

Her eyes were closed again and she made small whimpering sounds of anticipation. Tired as he was, his body responded. Seizing Carla's billowy nakedness, he pulled her against him. As she raised her legs straight up for him to enter, he was gripped by a wild sensation of falling.

On July 30, 1895, James Macklin Chance married Carla Marie Hellman in a civil ceremony in Los Angeles. Hugh Johnson stood up for his friend and partner. The Texan was polite to the bride, but oddly reserved.

The state's second-largest landowner gave the bride away. Afterward, at the reception in a hotel parlor, Hellman said, "One more word of advice, Johnny, and this time you better take it. Stay a hundred miles away from your wife when she's drinking. She got started too young. My fault, I let her, I was too busy to notice what was happening. When she drinks too much, it makes her a crazy person."

"Well," Mack said with a strange smile, "she isn't alone in that." He raised his champagne glass in a toast that puzzled his father-in-law.

V

GENTLEMEN
OF RIVERSIDE

1895–1899

The orange was blessed with a rich and mystical heritage long before it came to California. Somewhere in the cradle of civilization, legend said, it flourished in a lush garden. Someone named it the golden apple of the Hesperides: the golden apple of the sun.

Bedouin princes savored the orange, imperial Romans sucked its juice at their banquets, and medieval Spaniards planted and cultivated the trees. Columbus carried the fruit to the New World on his second voyage, and the conquistadors spread it and propagated it. By 1750, most of the Jesuit fathers in California grew oranges on Church lands.

In this early period, the California orange was thick-skinned, generally sour, and full of seeds. Its enormous value would not be perceived until it had caught the eye of venturesome newcomers. The fruit itself had to change as well.

In 1841, a former trapper from Kentucky, William Wolfskill, set out two acres of Mediterranean Sweet oranges on some land at Central Avenue and East Fifth Street, Los Angeles. Though his neighbors ridiculed his agricultural adventure, Wolfskill steadily expanded his grove to seventy acres, and by the 1870s the old trapper began to boast of profits of $1,000 an acre. That was enough to attract other farmers. New groves started to appear, and then new varieties, more suited to popular taste.

But the true watershed was 1873. That year, cuttings from sweet seedless oranges from Brazil arrived in California via the U.S. Department of Agriculture. A Riverside couple, Luther and Eliza Tibbets, planted and nurtured the cuttings. Like so many Californians, the Tibbets had started out elsewhere, but they found their home, and their life's reward, on the Pacific slope. Before long, everyone wanted "Washington navel" cuttings. Luther Tibbets could ask $5 for every bud and get it.

In 1876, America's centennial year, Valencia oranges came to the state from Spain. Valencias ripened in the summer, navels in winter, so citrus could become a year-round industry.

All that was needed was a year-round market, and old Wolfskill helped create it. In 1877, he loaded an entire freight car with his oranges and dispatched it to St. Louis. The car was a month in transit, but when it arrived, midwesterners rolled back the doors and stood in awe before the bounty it contained:

fruit as bright as sunshine, from trees ever green, in a land where snow never fell. Even after a month, the fruit was still edible and flavorsome.

Older sour varieties were improved, and the groves multiplied. The Riverside-Redlands area proved the ideal location for navels, while Valencias grew best in parts of the new Orange County. But Southern California was equally hospitable to bright-yellow lemons from Sicily and Spain, which did especially well in sections of Santa Barbara, Ventura, and San Diego counties.

In 1887, the first California oranges reached New York City, arriving in ventilated boxcars, and by 1889, refrigerated cars were being developed. The railroad, cursed by so many, quickly transformed a local industry into a national one. By 1890, there were more than a million orange trees in Southern California; five years later there were at least three or four million, and tourists were taking special excursion trains to Riverside, Redlands, and the other new citrus towns just to admire and photograph the groves.

Gentlemen who never would have dreamed of owning pigs or potato fields found the cultivation of oranges an entirely suitable occupation. They established great tracts and great homes and a tradition summed up by the slogan "Oranges for health—California for wealth."

Thus, once again, the golden apples of the Hesperides grew in a magical garden in the West.

ON THE HILLTOP, THE GENTLEMAN ORCHARDIST **34**
built a mansion of twenty-six thousand square feet.

The house crossed a Tuscan villa with a California mission, and was designed by the San Francisco firm of Arthur Page Brown in the fall of 1895. Brown was the high priest of Mission Revival, the neo-Franciscan style that looked to California's roots for inspiration, having given the style its most perfect and popular realization in the California State Building at the World's Columbian Exposition in Chicago. When complete, the new Southern Pacific Ferry Terminal in San Francisco would be another. Charles Lummis, editor of *Land of Sunshine*, promoted the style vigorously. The SP was designing many of its local depots to resemble missions, and individual homeowners followed the trend, building their own personal shrines to California's past. Mack joined them enthusiastically.

The thirty-eight-room house would command a magnificent view of the heights, the town, Mount Rubidoux, the Santa Ana, and the flatland groves of lemon trees and hardier, more frost-resistant Valencia oranges. Mack and Carla's bedroom was to measure forty by sixty, Mack's office, with its various storage crannies and book spaces, twenty feet more in each dimension.

The plan blended warm tan masonry with exposed beams, decorative tiling, and a red roof to create a structure with a distinct aura of lightness. Even on the rare gray day in winter, the house would appear sunlit, the architects promised. There would be lavish touches throughout. Mack insisted on solid masonry arches, not hollow ones of plaster and lath. For an additional $22,000 he proposed to bring electrification to the hilltop. The architects specified decorative tiles imported from Mexico and Italy, not imitations manufactured in Los Angeles. They protested his demand for an outside rear staircase; it would spoil the design and serve no purpose, they said. But Mack felt that among people of wealth and station, no home could be considered a mansion without an outside staircase. The staircase was added, with a lot of joking behind his back.

An iron gate inspired by the one at San Solaro would welcome the visitor to a winding foothill drive, a full three quarters of a mile long. For the gate as well as the house Mack designed an oval cartouche framing the initials *JMC*. He conceived it as a way to show his pride in his accomplishments and could see nothing vain or foolish about this, though Hellburner Johnson dismissed it as just another cattle brand.

"Sometimes you're too blasted frank, H.B."

"You don't like it, I can always mosey."

"You will anyway when you get ready."

"That's true. Just stay away from me with your damn brand, hear?"

In Charles Dudley Warner's best-selling book on California, Mack read these words:

It lies there, our Mediterranean region, on a blue ocean, protected by barriers of granite from the Northern influences . . . our Italy.

Taken with the comparison, he decided to name his new house Villa Mediterranean. He didn't consult Carla or anyone else, simply presented her and the world with the accomplished fact. He was by now determined that he would make only his own mistakes, no one else's.

The mansion was a huge, ambitious undertaking, and it went up slowly. Until it was ready, projected to be the autumn of '96, Mack and Carla occupied a gingerbread castle they rented at the end of Magnolia Avenue—Riverside's fashionable address. At this home on Magnolia Avenue, Mack drank a little California wine with evening meals. He had touched nothing stronger since the hour he proposed to Carla.

It was a happy period, those early months following their honeymoon in Hawaii. Carla was ardent in bed, affectionate at other times, and laughed often. Except for an occasional and guilty memory of Nellie, Mack had no cause to regret his marriage.

He had many interests that moved forward on parallel tracks. Dealing with all of them cost him enormous energy and hours of work, but he didn't mind, and he assumed Carla didn't either; she'd encouraged his ambition.

Once again the guidebook occupied a special corner of his desk. He believed in its promises more strongly than ever, and felt that minute by minute, task by task, he was giving life to the dream that had brought him to California. Indeed, there were many more dreams than one to be realized, he discovered. As soon as one hope was fulfilled, one goal reached, another revealed itself. Coupled with Carla's warmth and good cheer, this gave life a magnificent zest.

Mack never lost sight of his intention to return to San Francisco. To this end, he kept track of the political situation there and throughout the state.

In the City, some strong anti-railroad alliances had formed. Claus Spreckels, the sugar magnate, joined with Adolph Sutro, the populist who had been elected mayor in '94 on an anti-SP ticket, and together they spearheaded organization of a new railroad, the San Francisco & San Joaquin. This was the so-called People's Road, free of the control of Huntington and his henchmen. Construction began at Stockton in 1895. Mack bought $250,000 worth of shares.

Down on the flatland, he picked up forty-five hundred acres of established Valencia orange trees. Since they ripened in summer, and the Washington navels in winter, the purchase put him in the citrus business year-round. He needed two work forces, one for the orchards, the other to brush, wash, sort, pack, and box the oranges in his packing sheds.

In this connection, late in 1895, he received a visit in his office from a Mexican gentleman. On the desk lay an end panel from an orange crate, which bore a crude black stencil:

WASHINGTON NAVELS
CHANCE ORCHARDS
RIVERSIDE, CAL.

Mack didn't find this too imaginative and was struggling for something better. Little sketches and scratched-out names covered a tablet lying under the stenciled wood.

His caller was slender, deeply sunburned, and unctuous. He introduced himself as Alfonso Vicente Blas.

"Es un gran honor conocerlo," he said.

"Igualmente," Mack said. His Spanish was by this time serviceable.

Blas sat down without invitation. He crossed his sharply creased trouser legs—he wore a white suit, some sort of statement about his importance—and informed Mack that he might call him 'Fonso.

In reply, Mack said, "What can I do for you?"

"I hear you are in need of men to work in your groves."

"Yes. I've hired a few, but I can use many more."

"I am your *padrón*," Blas exclaimed with enormous good

317

humor. "*Comprador. Mr. Boss. You deal with me—I will get you all the men you need.*"

"I'm doing my own hiring, Señor Blas."

"No, no—'Fonso." His smile was a little stiffer. "You deal with me. One contract—no trouble."

"Why should I expect trouble?"

"You hire the wrong kind of men, it happens."

Mack had heard about these labor contractors. Crooked, most of them. They charged the growers too much, paid the labor too little, and pocketed the difference.

"Do you mean to say someone *makes* it happen, Señor Blas?"

"There were fires in '93, you know. Much rioting in anger. Now we have Mexican labor that takes care of itself. Goes home to Mexico in the off-season—you never have to worry."

"I'm not worried about anything except my time, which you are wasting. Excuse me."

Blas uncrossed his legs. His smile hadn't disappeared, but now it had a fixed, hard quality. "This is foolish of you. I am an important man."

"Get off my property," Mack said.

To find the workers he needed, Mack went personally to Riverside's small Chinatown. Blas had referred to the troubles of '93, when white men had driven the Chinese out of many of the groves. The Chinese in Riverside were eager to come back—especially when they heard what Mack was offering to pay.

Johnson had agreed to act as temporary foreman. He and Mack learned the business together. To his surprise Johnson found that he liked citrus growing. It was hard, demanding work, but it kept him outside, and the Valencia and the Washington navel were the aristocrats of trees; orchardists were the aristocrats of the agricultural world. If this wasn't so, why did so many tourists ride the Santa Fe to Riverside to view the groves?

After six months of marriage, Mack and Carla's relationship began to change. Their lovemaking grew less frequent, and her ardor diminished. She smiled less often, becoming increasingly remote. When she did address him she was usually cross, complaining about his long absences from Magnolia Avenue.

On one such occasion, he flared. "You're the one who praised ambition and encouraged me to work hard."

Her smile had a faintly nasty air. "Do you always believe

everything I say, Mack?'' She kicked her skirt behind her and walked out of the room.

The word "bored" reentered her conversation. She showed no interest in running the household; her earlier attempts had been a pretense, he decided. The staff fended for itself, following his general orders.

To escape the rising tension, he worked even longer hours and she went off on shopping expeditions, with never an advance word or note of explanation. He was aware of the servants replenishing the liquor supply more often.

When they dined together she was listless, uncommunicative, sometimes openly sullen. He began to actively seek ways to occupy himself elsewhere. If there was a pause in the work in the groves, he filled the spare hours by closing himself in his office and going through stacks of newspapers and periodicals, both popular and technical, hunting for bits of information he might use. He was aware of the cycle that was perpetuating itself: He was busy, Carla grew bored and drank; the more difficult she became, the more he sought to absent himself. It was a disturbing trend, and one he felt he couldn't discuss with anyone, not even Johnson. He harbored a melancholy and unreasonable hope that if he didn't acknowledge what was happening, it would go away.

But he saw evidence of Carla's malaise everywhere, even in situations that should have been pleasant. Clive Henley's good offices gained the two of them immediate entrée to the social life of the "British colony," as Riverside was sometimes called. Accepting an invitation to join the Casa Blanca Tennis Club, Carla tried to learn the game but didn't play well. The stoutness that made her attractive to men hampered her, and she soon gave up, preferring to sit in the canvas pavilion at courtside, gossiping and drinking the fine English tea served between matches. Mack tried not to recall her father's repeated warnings. But given the sudden veer and drift of the marriage, he didn't have much success.

Clive Henley sponsored Mack for the Riverside Golf and Polo Club. Initiation dues for a polo membership were $10. Henley taught Mack and Johnson rudiments of the ancient game, and was impressed by Johnson's horsemanship and innate ability to hit the ball. Something to do with hitting a man with a bullet?

Johnson told Mack that he was as taken with polo as he was with the orange groves; he was surprised that he liked what had struck him at first as a sissy sport. Clive Henley revealed that back east, on Long Island, certain teams were already paying experienced riders. "I have heard they also do it up north at the Burlingame club," Henley added. Johnson pondered this for a couple of days, then demanded a small salary.

"But my dear H.B.," Henley said, "we only play games amongst ourselves. We have yet to challenge another club. Fact is, there aren't many in California."

"Don't matter—I'm a professional; I don't ride a horse for free 'less I'm going somewheres. One dollar a month."

The club members agreed, took a collection of small change, and laughed about it. Soon it became a matter of some pride that Riverside's team included a genuine Texas cowboy.

Gradually Mack acquired six polo ponies, the minimum a rider needed for a six-chukker game. One of them, Fireball, was fifteen years old and couldn't live up to his name. Another, Jubilee, was Mack's pride. She was a small Spanish horse, fourteen and a half hands high, fast, strong, and smart. She cost $4,500 at the breeder's in Pasadena, while the other ponies had gone for less than $500 each.

The club agreed to provide Johnson with ponies, but he bought two of his own, Full-O'-Gin and a fleet, wicked-tempered little black horse he named Sam Houston.

Mack joined the Southern California Fruit Exchange, a non-profit cooperative that had sprung from earlier groups and had been organized to get around independent agents who charged gouging prices for packing and shipping oranges and lemons. The Exchange provided services at cost, and maintained offices in Los Angeles and Riverside. Because it shipped in volume, the SP and Santa Fe gave it favorable low rates. Growers such as Henley made no secret of their enthusiasm for the railroads. Rail shipment to the East had dramatically expanded the citrus market and enabled California growers to compete with Florida.

Mack also attended meetings of the Riverside Horticultural Club, and donated several hundred dollars to the club's research into the problem of orchard heating.

Busy as he was, however, there was time for a relaxed social life, and he tried to interest Carla in it. Once a week they dined at the Anchorage Hotel, or at Frank Miller's Glenwood Inn. At the Loring Opera House, Mack took a season box. They saw a traveling troupe perform *The Gondoliers*—Gilbert and Sullivan were idols in the British colony—and a production of *Camille* starring Helena Modjeska, the Polish expatriate who'd fallen in love with California and lived for a time at the artists' colony at Anaheim. When James O'Neill came to town in his signature production of *The Count of Monte Cristo*, Mack arranged a postperformance reception at the house on Magnolia Avenue. O'Neill favored the guests with a ringing recitation of Poe's "Raven." Only Carla drank more than the actor.

In March of every year, Riverside held a citrus fair in the pavilion at Main and Seventh streets. It was here, in 1896, that Carla told Mack she was pregnant.

He remembered the moment exactly. They were standing in the broad aisle beside the booth where Clive Henley was exhibiting his fine Eureka and winter-maturing Lisbon lemons. Carla told Mack, then, wildly excited, hugged and kissed him in front of dozens of fair-goers.

At the start of her third month she miscarried. "Oh, Mack, I'm sorry," she said when the doctor first allowed him to see her. "I know it disappoints you."

"Doesn't it disappoint you?"

"Yes, I suppose." She was wan, and her voice weak. It strengthened when she clutched his hand and said, "I hurt. I hurt terribly. I don't like that."

Perhaps she wasn't so sorry after all, Mack thought, and was instantly stricken with guilt for thinking it.

The doctor insisted that Carla rest in bed for fifteen days. Hellman paid a visit to see how she was getting along, and that evening, after dinner, he said to Mack, "Listen, I got a question. Does Carla ever talk about me?"

Mack was silent.

"Come on, tell me. This ain't no street peddler asking. I'm your father-in-law, family. Well?"

"Yes, she does talk about you. She says she wishes you loved her. She says it goes back to her mother . . ." He stopped, frowning.

"Go on, go on," Hellman demanded.

Mack didn't have an easy time telling him. "She says you thought her mother was . . . immoral."

"You mean a whore. That's what she said, isn't it—whore?"

Mack didn't deny it. "She says you think she inherited a lot of her mother's disposition. Look, I didn't want to say this—"

"Never mind," Hellman snarled, and then his brows pulled together and his voice dropped so low that Mack could barely hear him. "I don't discuss Carla's mother. Far as I'm concerned, she don't exist. You want to stay friends, never bring up the subject."

"You asked the question, for God's sake."

"So I excuse you this time. This time only. I'm going to bed." Hellman stood up and left the room.

Mack sat a while, wondering about the old man's strange reaction to discussing the mother Carla seldom talked about. Hellman was surely suppressing some bad feelings about the woman, and they carried over to his daughter—or so she thought. Perhaps it was a clue to Carla's behavior. He didn't fully understand it, but it prompted him to be as tender and attentive as possible during her recovery.

But Carla didn't respond. She seemed completely indifferent, and when she was on her feet again, she no longer bothered to conceal how she felt about Riverside.

"The place is contemptible," she said one night at dinner. She was at the far end of the enormous refectory table, her wineglass in hand as usual. "Contemptible, provincial, and dull as a church. Take away Clive's accent and what is he? A farmer. The same goes for the rest of them."

"And me?" Mack growled.

She shot him a look as she drank.

Red-faced, he pushed his plate away. "Carla, you've made it clear a hundred times that you'd be happier somewhere else. But what the hell am I supposed to do, leave?"

"Why, of course not, my dear," she said with a sweet smile. "You have your *business*. But maybe one day I'll leave."

"Christ, spare me the cheap threats," he said, and walked out.

The young geologist Haven Ogg did a superior job with Chance-Johnson Oil. The assets under his management now included 192 miles of pipeline; large storage tanks at Newhall, Santa Paula, and Ventura; a small refinery at Ventura; three tanker steamers; ninety railroad tank cars; and thirty-five six-mule tank wagons for local delivery. Chance-Johnson owned producing wells not only at San Solaro, but in the newer Summerland field southeast of Santa Barbara, in Whittier, and in Coalinga, Fresno County, in the shadow of the Diablo Range. Soon Ogg would personally lead an exploration crew into the low hills near the Kern River at the eastern edge of the San Joaquin.

Mack read the company's profit figures with amazement, and in mid-1896 he promoted Haven Ogg to general manager, giving him a munificent salary increase that allowed Ogg to marry and build a house in Newhall.

Oil fever still consumed Los Angeles. The derricks of more than five hundred wells made the town dirty, noisy, and ugly, but those getting rich didn't mind. One of these was Mrs. Emma Summers, who now drilled her own wells and had expanded into brokering crude oil, her piano pupils long since forgotten. People called her the Oil Queen.

The petroleum market was growing. Smooth black asphalt paved many Los Angeles streets. Lyman Stewart had convinced the SP that oil was the fuel of choice, and its locomotive fleet was undergoing gradual conversion from coal and wood. As a result, Mack was selling refined fuel oil to the railroad. He felt that he was dealing with the Devil, and compensated for it by purchasing more shares in the People's Road.

Oil was important to Mack, but citrus was his job. He spent hours with the orchardist's Bible, *The California Fruits and How to Grow Them*, by Professor Wickson of the University of California at Berkeley. Mack annotated the book so heavily that some pages grew illegible and he had to buy a second copy.

He educated himself about bud stock and refrigerator cars, climbed ladders along with his Chinese workmen to prune his windbreak trees, and learned to watch his trees for signs of cottony cushion scale, the terrible insect accidentally introduced from Australia in the late sixties. The egg sacs of the insect had once covered whole groves with a snowy mantle that yellowed leaves, shriveled fruit, and ultimately killed the stock. In the 1880s the scale had threatened to wipe out the industry. Then in '89 a Department of Agriculture scientist sent to study the problem in Australia made a serendipitous discovery. A ladybird beetle, *Vedalia cardinalis*, devoured the scale insect. Imported beetles saved California citrus, though the scale was only held at bay, not eliminated.

And then there was frost.

Up on the hillsides, the so-called frost-proof belt, the oranges were supposed to be safe. Clive Henley and others warned Mack not to be caught short, however. If a subfreezing night arrived and heat was needed, there was no time to order equipment and fuel. Mack bought and warehoused hundreds of two-and-a-half-gallon sheet-metal heaters, storing barrels of Chance-Johnson crude oil to burn in them. It was an enormous, wasteful expense, but it couldn't be avoided if a grower was realistic about the improbable but not impossible night of cold that could kill.

One morning before it was light, Mack slipped from bed without waking Carla, put on old clothes, thrust a clasp knife and a wad of cash in his pocket, and left the house on Magnolia Avenue. He had an early breakfast meeting with several growers at a café; a drummer passing through town was going to demonstrate a new-design orchard heater.

Outside the rented house, he paused to look at its mass of turrets and gables black against the first radiance of dawn. He'd never imagined he would live in such a handsome house, let alone the one he was building. He didn't often stop to relish some of the rewards all of his work, and his money, were bringing him.

In the cool, sweet air, he strode on down the avenue with his thoughts turning to the subject of his own life; of the amazing things that had happened to him since he met Doheny that night, and of all the numbers—sums—wealth—that followed as a consequence of his determination, and that accidental meeting.

How much was he worth now? He spent some time turning pages of a ledger he kept in his head—one page for San Solaro (red ink), one page for Chance-Johnson, pages for real estate, citrus, stock and bond investments, and so on. He'd always been quick with figures so he had no trouble arriving at a total. At present he was worth five and a half million, give or take a few hundred thousand. But it kept growing, which raised another question. How much was enough? Money was the yardstick with which he measured his success. So how much *was* enough? The question had a bearing on the rest of life.

He was pondering this when he realized he was within a block of the café, whose windows gleamed yellow in the dawn. Nearer, on his side of the street, the marvelous yeasty aroma of warm bread came from the open doorway of Frontière's Bakery. A little girl with her head covered in a ragged shawl stood there, her face pressed to the window.

She heard Mack's boots on the walk, turned, scrutinized him warily, then smiled. He was taken aback, not solely because the girl was just seven or eight, and ragged as they come, but because she was striking. She had perfect Oriental features, but skin the color of dark chocolate. He had never seen a person with that kind of mixed parentage. It lent her an exotic and fragile beauty, which would probably be scoured away by years of poverty and toil.

But this morning she was smiling, hugging herself, and inhaling the yeasty odors coming out Frontière's open door.

"It smells so good," she said to Mack, who had stopped. "Like heaven must smell, don't you think?"

He nodded and pointed to some of the fresh loaves already heaped in the window. "I like Mr. Frontière's rye bread best."

She studied the dark-brown loaves. "I've never had any of that. I've never had anything from this shop."

"Why not?"

"I haven't any father; he died. There's only my mother and older brother working for the six of us."

Impulsively, Mack pulled the roll of cash from his pocket and peeled off the top bill. "Buy yourself some bread for breakfast," he said, handing it to her.

The girl smoothed the crinkled bill between two fingers. She was a little less sure of him all at once. "Why are you giving this to me?"

"Because I get pleasure out of it."

"But I know how much it is. Ten dollars . . ."

He smiled at her misreading of the $100 on the bill. "That's all right, take it." A thought came suddenly. "Money's like bread. I can always make more."

Wonderment broke over her face then, and she rushed into the bake shop before he could change his mind.

A buggy rattled into view and stopped at a hitch rail in front of the café on the other side. The grower emerging from it waved, and Mack cut across the street. He was satisfied that he'd answered the question that had occurred to him—maybe not in the happiest way, but certainly in the inevitable way. How much was enough? For a man like him, enough would never be enough . . .

Mack and Carla moved from Magnolia Avenue to the hilltop early in November 1896. On Thanksgiving Day they invited three hundred people from Riverside and the outlying area to an enormous buffet feast.

Japanese nurserymen who had no special feeling for the American holiday were planting palm trees and Italian pines along the winding drive as the guests arrived in their coaches and carriages. Mack thought the marriage of palms and pine trees a curious one, but the landscape architect assured him the effect was "completely Californian."

Villa Mediterranean was an enormous success from the first moment. The owners themselves were enormous successes. They were rich, and Mr. Chance was a popular and enthusiastic gentleman orchardist. Ladies enviously examined the silver plates embossed with the *JMC* cartouche; on the linen Mack had allowed a smaller cartouche with the initials *CHC*. Gentlemen with monocles pumped his hand and told him it was all jolly good.

So it was, from the standpoint of the table. The guests sampled blue points and green-turtle soup, boiled California salmon and sliced wild turkey roasted with chestnuts. There was goose, quail, and venison, sweetbreads smothered with mushrooms, orange fritters, and croquettes of oyster. There was celery and lettuce from some of Mack's own fields in the Central Valley. There were five varieties of potato, and giant bowls of starchy vegetables. There were French champagnes and California wines, Edam and Roquefort cheese, Málaga grapes, mince and pumpkin pie, charlotte russe, and of course English plum pudding with brandy sauce, as well as heaps of fresh oranges.

Mack had had no time to cook lately, and he longed for that. He wished the sprawling, noisy house contained a few friends today, instead of all these acquaintances. Johnson mingled for a while, eating and saying little. Then he struck up a conversation with a buxom young widow. She left soon, smiling. Twenty minutes later Johnson followed.

Mack and Carla circulated separately. She was flirtatious with several of the Englishmen, and it irked Mack, but he said nothing. He noticed she drank large quantities of champagne, and then equally large quantities of claret. At half past three in the afternoon she disappeared. He didn't bother to look for her; he knew she was drunk in their bedroom suite. He hoped she was asleep.

That night, after the guests had driven away down the hill and the only sounds in the mansion were those of the household staff clearing and cleaning, Mack found Carla in her silk wrapper, muzzy from her nap and a fresh glass of claret in her hand.

"Why did you do it, today of all days?"

"Because I was bored. Those silly, vapid people bore me to death. Riverside bores me. This stinking huge house bores me."

"This new house? This bores you?"

"Yes, yes, completely."

Over the raised glass, her deep-blue eyes defied him. She drank all the claret in gulps.

* * *

So, with interwoven strands, the tapestry of the first year and a half of their marriage completed itself on the Riverside loom. Mack felt that he grasped and manipulated the individual threads but had no sense of a larger pattern. He continued to fill his hours with work, reading, physical sport. He saddled Jubilee and galloped up and down the polo field on Jefferson Street, practicing back and tail shots with his mallet and the cork ball. He hiked alone in his groves for hours. He shadow-boxed, remembering his friend Corbett, the heavyweight champion. He wondered what to do about Carla's ennui, expressed in increasingly strong, blunt language. He tried not to recall that Swampy, who seldom visited, had predicted exactly this outcome.

Matters came to a head on New Year's Eve, 1896.

A NORTH WIND BLEW ALL DAY. EVEN AT NOON IT **35** breathed out cold air, shaking the lustrous leaves and ripening fruit of the groves on Arlington Heights.

The temperature had been falling for twenty-four hours. In the hilltop grove, Mack worked alongside Chinese in coolie hats and heavy quilted coats. They all shivered as they hauled the sheet-metal burners from mule-drawn wagons parked in the lanes. Johnson was down in the flatland groves, supervising the same work.

Teams of workers filled burners from a barrel of crude. Two seized each burner and ran with it, placing it according to a regular pattern, one between every two trees. In the cold shade, their eyes glistened white as they cast anxious looks upward. A few thin cirrus clouds trailed away east. Otherwise the sky was clear, blue-white, like new pond ice.

Mack tried to forget his obligation for that evening, but it nagged him as he stalked up and down the lanes, helping wherever he was needed. Where he saw a weak point, he told the men to set out additional wire baskets filled with soft coal or kindling. Freeze damage meant more than the loss of the season's crop. If severe enough, the freeze would destroy the stock. Trees worth hundreds of thousands of dollars could be lost, requiring a wait of five, six, or seven years until new stock bore for the first time.

Throughout the afternoon he drove himself, and the workers

too. By five o'clock all the burners and baskets were lit. Mack dragged himself into the saddle of his Morgan and walked the horse up the winding road to Villa Mediterranean.

Winter's pale light was slanting from the west. Long sharp shadows lay on the heights. He overtook two wagons laboring uphill, stacked high with oil barrels. Would the fuel last? How low would the temperature fall?

Mack had made his decision about the evening, and he was braced for trouble.

He changed clothes in the wardrobe adjoining his office. At his desk, he tried to study the December cost and production reports. It was impossible; he couldn't concentrate.

He heard the wind gusting over the roof tiles and raised his head and stared at the dark ceiling beams. Although Mack was not yet thirty, horizontal streaks of gray showed in the hair over his ears. Tonight his eyes had a sunken, fatigued look.

He heard her coming, her pumps rapping the floor in the hallway. It was hardwood, not the soft fir of the homes of poorer people.

She swept in without knocking. He had to admit she was breathtaking. Why not? She'd spent the afternoon bathing and dressing. Her princess gown was black satin and favored her golden complexion, with decorative ribbons of gold velvet falling from either side of the bodice all the way to the hem. Black aigrettes adorned her hair and black suede gloves reached above her elbows to puffed sleeves of black lace net over satin. She carried a painted and tasseled fan in her left hand, and on the fourth finger of her right hand, outside her glove, she wore a $15,000 emerald, rectangular and scissors-cut, in a gold mounting—his wedding gift.

"Mack, is it necessary for me to remind you that it's New Year's Eve? Supper starts at seven. We must leave in half an hour. Maria laid out your evening suit."

"I wish she hadn't gone to the trouble."

Carla kicked her voluminous skirt behind her and the garments under her dress rustled in a way he found very feminine and seductive. "What do you mean by that remark?" she asked.

"I mean I can't go. I have to stay in the groves. We're going to have a bad freeze. Those oranges are my livelihood."

"Ridiculous. You can buy ten more orange groves tomorrow."

"It's the livelihood of the men too. I need to be there, not abandon them."

"This is the best country-club dance of the year. Clive told me so. Everyone will be there—"

"The only people who'll be there are a few who have no investment in citrus. And the chefs, the waiters, and the orchestra. You won't have many partners."

"I'll find a *man* to dance with—don't worry." It implied that he, perhaps, was not a man.

Frowning, he crossed in front of her. He caught her heavy orange-blossom scent and then, underneath, whiskey. He switched on the two elaborate ceiling fixtures with trumpet-flower glass shading the electric lamps and, above them, gas mantles, necessary because the power company often shut down without warning.

"Are you going to ignore me completely, Mack?"

Remaining angrily silent, he unlatched the shutters on the windows overlooking Riverside. The sky was a cold dark blue. Lights winked below, lovely jeweled patterns. How strange that millions could be lost on such a pretty night.

Wind pushed at the windows, setting up a humming vibration. The windows were the finest antique glass obtainable, full of visible waves. Each had a decorative border of leaded red glass rectangles. That was yet another sign of wealth; red glass was made with ground gold.

"Mack, I'm waiting. I insist you take me to the club."

"No. I'm staying."

"My feelings aren't important to you?"

"Of course, but—"

"If I'd known when I married you that you'd act like this—"

"You knew exactly what I was. If you wanted some other kind of man, why did you want to marry me?"

A sweet smile. "You screwed me into it, darling."

"My God." He fell into his favorite leather chair and tossed a scarred boot onto the ottoman. "You're a beautiful woman, Carla. But sometimes you're a foul-minded drunk too."

"Oh, aren't we righteous." She kicked her skirt again, stalking him. "Aren't we good . . ."

A blood vessel stood out in his left temple and he closed his hand on the chair arm. "I'd still like to know—why did you marry me?"

She leaned forward, spat the words. "It was something to do."

He glared. "I believe you."

"Why did you decide to marry me? Because you couldn't get a tumble from that little newspaper slut?" He jumped up.

"Oh, I saw how you looked at her. I've no illusions. And you have none about me. A foul-minded drunk—isn't that what you said?"

"Carla, I'm sorry . . ." He tried to appease her with outstretched hands. He felt helpless; she was mercurial and unreasonable when she drank. ". . . I'm sorry I lost my temper. Please go ahead to the dance."

"How generous."

"Ah Sing will drive you and bring you home."

"I don't want a damn ignorant Chink for my escort; I want my husband."

The blood vessel rose up thick as a rope. Outside he heard a horse on the winding road. "I'll watch for the coach coming back. We'll open a bottle of champagne." He walked toward her. "Please have a good time if you can. I'll make it up to you some way."

He started to kiss her cheek but she pulled back, withholding herself. The whiskey odor engulfed him. She gave him another of those sweet, vicious smiles.

"Good night, darling," she said.

"See you next year, then."

"Who knows? Let's hope so."

She kicked her skirt back a third time and sailed out, her dancing pumps rat-tatting on the hardwood.

Then that faded beneath other, heavier footsteps. Johnson's boots. He walked in with uncharacteristic long strides that spoke of agitation. He wore dirty jeans, a leather vest, his usual long bandanna. This one, ironically, was bright orange.

"All your burners going?" Mack asked.

"Yep, every one we got. There ain't enough by half to take care of the Valencias."

"What's the temperature?"

" 'Round thirty. Falling."

Mack snatched his broad-brimmed brown hat from the desk and Johnson trailed him down the faintly lit hall. "Something wrong here, Mack? Carla was dressed up prettier'n a queen, but she looked like she could spit bullets."

"Nothing's wrong. She's going to the dance alone."

"Listen, it ain't gonna warm up just 'cause you hang around. Climb into your fancy suit and go with her."

"I can't do it. Not tonight."

He clattered down the hardwood stair. Johnson followed, an even deeper frown carving the deep lines of his face.

* * *

The north wind blew relentlessly and constellations sparkled, the veils of cirrus gone. As they tethered their horses Johnson took notice.

"Not a cloud. Not a blasted one." A cloud blanket would have moderated the effect of this wind that felt frigid as the North Pole.

In the hilltop grove, groups of Chinese huddled near the burners. Mack could smell the strong crude oil as he and Johnson walked under the trees. He checked every burner and adjusted the drafts of some.

To supplement the burners the men had lit torches, sooty smudge pots, and more soft coal and kindling in the wire baskets. Smoke drifted and stung the eyes.

"Wind's too strong," Mack said. "It'll dissipate the heat."

"Not much we can do about that," Johnson said.

Mack jammed his hands in the pockets of his sheepskin coat and eyed the winter sky.

By eleven, he was stretched out beneath a tree, Johnson dozing next to him. All across the horizon in the foothill belt you could see the glow of burners and coal baskets—the watch fires of the gentleman orchardists . . .

Mack wondered if Carla was having a good time. In another hour a new year would begin. Would their relationship be better? Not unless he did something about it. Something other than pleading for understanding; she was incapable of that.

Johnson woke, checked a tin pail by his side, then held it out. *"Cerveza?"*

Mack drank some. "Hell, the beer's the only thing warm tonight. What's the temperature?"

Johnson consulted a thermometer tied to a branch. "Twenty-six."

"Wind's down, though." It was true. The smudge-pot and coal-basket smoke no longer dispersed immediately. The burner could be felt.

"It'll go hardest with the lemons down yonder," Johnson said, squatting again. "Up here, maybe we'll make it. You should of gone to that shindig."

Mack didn't respond. They heard some workers arguing softly and then the click of gambling tiles. Mack thought of Bao Kee. It made him feel worse.

Johnson finished the beer. "Tell me somethin'. You been married most of a year and a half now. You happy or not?"

Mack's hazel eyes caught the blue-white flicker of the flame in a burner. "I should tell you it's none of your damn business."

"Just askin' as your friend."

Mack blew on his hands. "If being happy is making money, then I'm happy."

"Not exactly what I meant."

"Anything else I'm too busy to notice."

The pale-green eyes fixed on him. "I can understand you frettin' about the oranges. Still, women do take some noticin' now and then. I ain't ever been tied up in matrimony, but I learned that much."

"Sure, I know, but . . ."

Suddenly he was tired of dissembling. He needed to confide in a friend. He sat up straight.

"It's more than a fight over a dance. Carla's slipping back into her old ways. She was fine for a few months. Now when I try making up to her with little gestures, suggestions—a horseback ride in the country, a picnic—she isn't interested. She's bored. She wants something else—a party, a trip, always something else. Swampy warned me."

"Seems pretty clear all she wanted tonight was what both of you'd planned on."

"And I was the one who balked?"

"Uh-huh. You got reasons for what you did. Pretty good ones. But you still stayed home. Don't put all the burden on Carla."

"Thanks for the lecture."

Johnson sighed. "You can be a mean bastard when you're riled. That's good in a fight, but it don't do much for marriage." He paused a while. "Listen here. We get through this night, I got somethin' to say to you."

"Something else? Say it now."

Johnson ignored the sarcasm. "In the mornin'. If we ain't wiped out. 'Scuse me."

He sank down on his haunches, his back to the tree, snapped his hat low over his eyes, and went to sleep.

Mack watched patterns in the coiling smoke. He stood and held his hands near the burner. It warmed his flesh but not his soul. He didn't know how to handle a rich, spoiled woman like Carla. His intentions were good, but his temper, and her whims, canceled that out.

At midnight someone in a distant grove fired a volley to welcome 1897. That was the extent of the celebration. He expected Ah Sing would bring Carla home in an hour or two.

The cold lonely night chastened him. Johnson was right:

Carla's bad behavior didn't excuse his own; he bore half the responsibility. In the morning, he'd try to make it up to her.

Mack woke. The ground was frigid under his legs, the tree trunk hard on his spine. He didn't remember falling asleep.

The rasp of Johnson's snoring penetrated his sleepiness. Johnson hadn't budged from the tree, though his hat had fallen off. In the east, the morning light was breaking.

Mack's breath plumed when he exhaled, mingling with the burner smoke rising in scores of straight columns, as though the grove hid a whole subdivision of row houses with fuming chimneys. One of Mack's best men, a young Chinese named Kim Loo, opened the door of a burner to check the oil supply.

"Almos' gone, Mist Chance."

"Better refill them. Feels like another cold day."

Kim Loo nodded and hurried away. Mack stood up, stretching and flexing out the stiffness in his knee joints. He checked the thermometer. Twenty-four degrees. He plucked down an orange, wiped it, pierced the skin with his thumbnail, and sucked the juice.

He nudged Johnson with his boot. "I think we made it."

Johnson yawned and complained. After a few minutes, Mack decided his foreman was sufficiently awake.

"Now, what was it you wanted to tell me this morning?"

"Gettin' restless, that's all."

"You mean you want to traipse off again?"

"Think so. In the spring, maybe."

"The polo club won't be happy. We need you. I'll never play as well as you. You're our strongest rider." They were still making up teams exclusively from their membership. Mack looked forward to playing another club someday.

Johnson chuckled. "Yeah, and I got to admit I like the applause from the ladies on the sidelines. Like gettin' paid, too. Just never figured a dirt-poor Texas boy would take to a fancy-pants game like that. Still, I do get these hankerings—"

"You know I depend on you," Mack said. "But it's always been conditional. You've always been free to go. Still are."

"What about all this?"

"I'll promote Billy Biggerstaff till you get back."

"Will you get along all right if I go off a while?"

"Sure—absolutely," Mack said with a quick nod. Could his friend tell that he was lying?

Half an hour later Mack trudged up the hill to Villa Mediterranean. The great house was still and chilly. He felt grubby and exhausted as he climbed the stairs to the master suite. He took care to open the carved door quietly.

The huge room was dark, all the shutters closed. He listened.

Silence.

Anxiously, he walked toward the bed. The pegged flooring gave off small creaks.

"Carla?" he whispered. "Happy New Year—"

No breathing. Nothing.

At her side of the bed, he ran his hand over the spread. The bed was perfectly made. Empty.

He went downstairs for a cup of coffee. In the kitchen, the household majordomo, an old haughty Mexican named Rodolfo Armendariz, showed him a bottle of Mumm's standing in a silver bucket. Water filled the bucket to a depth of six inches.

"Here is the champagne, Señor. I set it out at midnight, as you requested."

Mack had completely forgotten. He'd spoken to Rodolfo before going to the groves—preparing for a little celebration when Carla came back.

"The ice is melted, Señor."

"I see. Someone else can drink it. Anyone. There won't be a celebration this morning."

Mack slept for three hours, then ate breakfast. It was another clear, cloudless day. But the wind had died and the cold felt less severe.

He checked his pocket watch. Quarter past ten. Walking down to the lower limit of his property, he inspected the new barracks. Two stories, closed in and roofed but not yet painted, the building was tucked out of sight behind a windbreak. He'd built it to provide clean, comfortable quarters for some of his workers, the young bachelors like Kim Loo who could not yet afford a bride from one of the Chinatowns or the home country.

He walked the groves a while, talking with the tired men refilling the burners. There was some defoliation from yesterday's wind, but no sign of the split bark caused by sap freezing in the cambium layer.

He leaned against a tree. It felt like the end of the afternoon. He pulled out his watch again. Half past twelve.

Looking down the winding road, he saw only two of his Chinese on foot.

He wandered aimlessly for more than an hour. Finally, up on the summit, he walked into the dirt yard in front of the carriage house. A Chinese boy with greasy hands was using a wrench to tighten the front hub of Mack's new safety bicycle. He saw the owner and smiled.

"Got her all fixed, Mr. Mack. Wheel run good now."

"Thanks. The cycling club's going on a twenty-mile ride on Sunday, and—" The rattle of a coach on the hill interrupted him. "Thanks," he shouted, enthusiastically this time, and ran.

Ah Sing halted the team, avoiding Mack's eyes. When Mack opened the coach door with the gold-leaf *JMC* cartouche blazoned on it, Carla regarded him with puffy eyes. She was still in her New Year's Eve finery.

"Long party. It's after two o'clock."

"I got a little drunk. Some friends put me up."

"What friends?"

"Oh, I'm now accountable to you, am I?"

Her clothing looked mussed and all her lipstick was worn away. He fought a jealous anger. "No, Carla, and you never have been."

She jerked the door shut and thumped the front of the compartment. "Ah Sing, goddamn you, go on." Ah Sing shook the reins. The sudden forward lurch of the coach flung her against the cushion with a pained cry. She pressed her palms to her temples, eyes squeezed shut.

The coach passed and left him standing in dust.

After dark the temperature dropped below thirty-two again, but the night was windless. Mack stayed in the grove until midnight, then made a bed on the couch in his office. In the morning he saddled up and rode down to the flats. Damage was spotty, and most of his oranges were unharmed.

Clive Henley's lemon grove was different. It had the blasted, wasted look of a war zone. Work crews wielded axes and saws, cutting off defoliated limbs, in some cases all the way back to the trunk. Teams of dray horses with chains pulled other trees right out of the ground.

Mack hated to see it. He hated for living things to die. Besides, the grove struck him as a suitable picture of his marriage.

36HE SLEPT IN THE OFFICE AGAIN THAT NIGHT. NEXT day Carla offered a half-hearted apology and asked him to come back to their bed. He did, but she refused his good-night embrace, and he slept on his side, turned away from her. At the end of the following week she packed and left to visit her father for several days.

Meanwhile, Mack took the Santa Fe into Los Angeles. In his suite at the Pico House, he talked business with Potter. Then, on the second afternoon, he walked briskly to the Phillips Block at Spring and Franklin, where the Southern California Fruit Exchange kept offices in rooms 77 and 78.

On the way he saw sign painters putting up new shingles for three doctors. He'd read an editorial in the *Citrograph* proudly proclaiming that California already had more doctors in proportion to its population than any other state—quite a contrast to Wyatt's claim that doctors were few because no one sickened or died. Doctors wanted to practice here because they had so many patients; Otis and his cronies at the chamber of commerce brought them in by hawking the climate like a patent medicine. To potential new residents the chamber advertised Los Angeles as "the world's greatest sanitarium for years to come."

In the rooms of the Exchange, about two dozen growers from the region gathered for a meeting. The only one Mack knew well was Clive Henley, who'd taken an early-morning train. The hottest topic of the afternoon was the cost of a citrus crate. The price had risen from 11 cents to 12 in the past year. Total production price of a crate of oranges from most groves, including Mack's, was about 50 cents. If crate costs went higher, so would that figure, and no grower could afford it.

"It's the cost of box shook," one grower said. "We're helpless. We have to pay what the market demands."

"We wouldn't if we had our own timber," Mack said.

"You mean the Exchange should go into lumbering?"

"Exactly. We should own everything that's necessary to produce a finished product." There were mutters and scornful exclamations, almost universal disapproval of the radical idea. Mack shrugged. "Well, you gentlemen think whatever you want. This morning I authorized my attorney to buy ten thousand acres of prime timber up in Lassen County. I'll have my own shook supply in a year.''

After the meeting, they crowded around him, wanting to know how the Exchange could make an arrangement.

Mack and Clive Henley rode the early-evening local back to Riverside, discussing the new president-elect, McKinley. Mack and Clive were Republicans, and had voted for McKinley over Bryan; Clive and most other Riverside Republicans thought Mack far too liberal, however.

Mack speculated about the coming title fight between Corbett and Bob Fitzsimmons, a serious contender; it was scheduled for March, at Carson City, Nevada. They talked also about Cuba and the nationalist revolt against Spain; both Hearst and his New York rival, Joe Pulitzer, were ardent supporters of the rebels. Many critics flayed Hearst for war-mongering for the sake of circulation.

And inevitably, being Californians, they discussed the railroad. Only a few days earlier, Congress had settled the debt issue, actually handing Huntington a huge defeat by refusing cancellation or remission of the debt. Governor Jim Budd, a Democrat, had declared a state holiday in celebration.

Clive, always more friendly to the SP and Santa Fe, resented this. He brought up the familiar arguments about the railroads creating prosperity for citrus growers by opening eastern markets.

"But what does it have to do with the debt, Clive? Or the holiday? I sent Budd a telegram congratulating him.''

Through all the talk, Mack had a feeling that Clive had something else on his mind. The Englishman wasn't his usual relaxed and affable self. His mild gray eyes had a guarded look.

The conductor announced Colton. Mack said, "We'll be in Riverside soon. I think you'd better get down to the real topic.''

The red rose straight up in Clive's face. "Oh, God, I'm a terrible dissembler, aren't I?''

Mack smiled. "Yes, you are. Come on, what is it?''

"Well, ah, I was asked—appointed, actually—to speak to you. Because we're friends. Teammates—''

"You said *appointed*. By whom?''

"Oh, some of the other chaps—growers . . . Riverside.'' It had a strangled sound. Clive popped his monocle out and polished it furiously on his white-linen sleeve.

"What are you supposed to discuss?''

"Your, ah, labor force.''

Now Mack began to understand. "My Chinese?"

"Yes, old fellow, exactly. You know of the, ah, trouble four years ago?"

"I know that mobs of fruit tramps—white men—threatened and intimidated a lot of the Chinese in the groves because they wanted their jobs."

"Indeed, but it was worse than that. Celestials were robbed in the streets, beaten, driven out of their little houses and shops. A mob burned the Chinatown in Redlands. We had state militia on patrol, and two hundred special deputies. We don't want to go back to that sort of thing."

"No," Mack said. And waited.

Clive coughed and wriggled in his seat. "But Mack—it's the consensus that white men deserve the jobs in your groves also."

"Because they're white, or because they'll work for half of what a Chinese worker demands?"

"Yes, there's that—seventy-five cents a day and board against a dollar forty or fifty is a significant difference, old boy. The greasers and those half-breed Indian blokes, they'll accept the lower wages too."

"I want the best workers, not the cheapest. The Chinese and Japanese are born agriculturists. Look at the Orange County boglands a few years ago—nothing there but drifter camps and poor people digging tule roots because they couldn't afford potatoes. Then a couple of enterprising farmers hired some Chinese to experiment with celery growing. Now they ship thousands of carloads of celery out of the bogs every year. Land that was fifteen dollars an acre goes for five hundred and six hundred dollars. The Japanese worked the same kind of miracles with California asparagus, cantaloupes, lettuce, sugar beets. Orientals have a touch, a feel for the earth and for growing things. I want workers with that touch."

"But when you pay high wages, it's bad for the rest of us. It leads to agitation and unrest. Perhaps we will be forced to pay more . . ."

"Hire anyone you want, Clive, and pay them anything you can get away with. I'll stick with the men I've got."

"But my friend, I told you that this isn't merely my position. I'm stating it for the entire community of Riverside orchardists."

"You mean I'm out there alone?"

"Yes, nearly," Clive said with a hangdog smile.

"Tell me this. If I refuse to change my ways, will it cost me your friendship?"

This released a gush. "Oh, my dear chap, no. I only spoke

with the utmost reluctance, at the insistence of the group. We remain friends always. Actually, I thought I might be doing you a service. There are still fruit tramps in the district from time to time—"

"Yes, I've seen them camped along the roads."

"They're hungry. They might not be inclined to accept your position peaceably. Then of course there's Blas."

" 'Fonso Blas, the contractor?"

"Yes, he called on me."

"And me. It was over a year ago. I threw him out."

"Blas called on me last week. He's very intolerant of you. He suggested that matters might, ah, degenerate into a renewal of the trouble of '93."

Clive Henley was pleading with his eyes, his posture, his whole earnest gentlemanly demeanor.

God, I don't need this, Mack thought. "Sorry, Clive—the answer's no. As for Blas—I don't like him. Nobody threatens me."

In his office on a Saturday in late February, Mack wrote an enthusiastic letter to the president of the Los Angeles Litho Company, praising the company's art department and placing an order for a crate label, to be printed by chromolithography, from stone plates, in six colors. After struggling to find a name for his citrus and an illustration idea, and rejecting everything that came to mind, he'd woken with an idea at 3 A.M. two weeks before. He'd had a terrible, loud fight with Carla over her drinking and general indifference before bed and in the middle of that miserable night, the perfect label design had popped into his head.

A gaudy watercolor rendering of it lay near the guidebook. It showed an old California prospector, bearded, tough, and slyly smiling, offering succulent oranges in a miner's pan. The label said:

CALGOLD

BRAND

WASHINGTON NAVELS

How often did good ideas come out of bad times? He didn't know. But the label was perfect.

He quickly finished the letter. Later, he was expecting Swampy for one of his rare overnight visits.

* * *

Hellman came down by train from the ranch on the Santa Clara. A hired rig awaited him at the Riverside depot. His son-in-law had offered to meet him but Swampy said no; wealth conferred the benefit of independence, and Swampy enjoyed it. He did, however, always travel with his S&W, his Jesse James pistol, in his gladstone bag. California was still full of wild cowboys, sinister greasers, yahoos, and other undesirables.

A beautiful white cattleman's hat shaded Swampy's eyes against the winter sunshine. His white suit, custom-made and brand new last Thursday, already showed stains and wrinkles. He slowed the buggy horse to a walk as he approached Mack's boundary stone on the left side of the road. A lot of Chinese were hard at work in the groves. Industrious little buggers, Swampy thought. He relished the sight of industry, especially industry that enriched an owner.

About fifty yards ahead, on some wooded land to the right side, he saw something less pleasing: a bunch of yahoos, twenty or thirty of them, camped among eucalyptus trees. A scrawl of smoke from their cook fire stained the sky. Lounging by the fire or sleeping under dirty blankets, they all had the same ragged, unshaven appearance.

As Swampy's rig approached, three of them strolled down to the road shoulder. Directly opposite, at the end of a windbreak, several Chinese were putting up ladders to prune the trees.

Swampy itched his lumpy nose. He didn't like the look of these yahoos, especially the three pointing and making remarks about the Chinese. The workers paid no attention, two of them scrambling up ladders with pruning saws.

As he clucked to the nag to speed up the buggy, one of the tramps by the road picked up a stone and lobbed it to the other side, hard. It whacked a ladder and startled the Chinese climbing up. The man almost fell, but caught himself.

"Go ahead, jump, you little bastard," one of the tramps yelled. "Maybe you'll break your neck."

His two companions laughed. One of them pulled out a big clasp knife and, after unfolding its four-inch blade, began to scrape under his nails, in a way the Chinese couldn't miss. Swampy's buggy drew abreast and he gave the yahoos a stare. He could smell their dirty clothes. Phew.

The tramp with the knife said, "What the hell are you looking at, grandpa?" The long blade caught the sun and flashed.

Swampy halted the buggy abruptly. "You, mister. Stay away from my son-in-law's property."

"You mean that grove? We ain't on it. We're over here. This is free land."

Hearing the exchange, other tramps drifted toward them. Swampy pulled his gladstone closer with his boot. But they made no further move toward him and he shook the reins. Soon he was through the iron gate and into the winding drive.

When Swampy arrived, Mack wanted to show him the label. But the old German had other things on his mind: a glass of peppermint schnapps, and the fruit tramps.

"Ugly-looking bunch, Johnny."

"They've been camped there for three days." Mack crossed the living room and found the schnapps. He hated the stuff but he kept it for his father-in-law.

"What the hell they want?"

"One of them came over and asked for work. I told him I had all the men I needed. He made some threats. Until they move on, I keep a man on guard by the main road every night. With a rifle, to sound an alarm."

"Coming out of Riverside, I seen a bunch of guards in the groves. No rifles, though."

"Those are posted to keep the tourists out, so they don't steal souvenirs from the trees. The tourists are worse than a plague of locusts. I don't have that problem up here in Arlington Heights. Not yet."

"Those yahoos got some special reason to pick on you?"

"They hate the Chinese. And I had a run-in with a labor contractor whose services I wouldn't use. I expect he spoke a word or two when this bunch drifted into town. Let's forget about it. Bring your drink to the kitchen."

"What's for supper?"

"Bonito."

"That's a mackerel, ain't it?"

"Tuna. Brought up from the coast yesterday."

"Will I like it?"

"You better. I'm going to cook it."

Swampy chuckled and waddled after him, sloshing the schnapps around in his glass. Some of it stained his white suit cuff, but he didn't notice.

"Where's Carla?"

"Napping."

"She going to eat with us?"

"I don't know," Mack replied in a flat voice. Swampy sniffed. He smelled trouble on another front. In this case it didn't surprise him.

They dined at the long refectory table, Mack at the head, Swampy at the foot, Carla between them. Overhead thirty-six candles burned in a great ring chandelier of hammered iron suspended by chains. It was a hundred years old, and the only fixture in the house not equipped for gas and electricity. Mack liked its mellow light; it gave the vast cool room the air of an ancient cloister.

Carla drank claret from a long-stemmed glass, but left her food untasted. Her father, on the other hand, ripped through his plate of fish in a few lip-smacking bites.

"Good, Johnny. Carla, you should take a cooking lesson from your husband."

His daughter regarded him with scornful amusement. "Really? Why? We have servants."

"Yah, but it's a woman's duty to cook."

"Leave me alone, Swampy."

The nickname goaded him. He leaned toward Mack. "She never wanted to learn. Can't even break eggs, can she?"

Mack didn't answer. Looking venomous, Carla pushed her chair back and walked to the sideboard, draining the contents of her glass before she got there.

Mack rapped his knife on his plate. "Don't you think four's enough?" His voice was controlled—not angry, just tight.

"I'll decide what's enough, thanks." She helped herself.

Swampy gave Mack a dismayed look, then sat back while one of the Mexican girls glided up to serve another piece of the grilled fish.

"You know, Johnny, I'm worried about those yahoos. They look mean. A businessman like you, he don't need that kind of trouble. Wouldn't it be easier to hire a few, give 'em some dirty work, and calm things down? You could make room by firing some of the Chinks."

"My men don't like that word. I don't use it."

"Oh, sorry," Swampy said, rolling his eyes. He grabbed his mug of beer and swigged noisily, then wiped foam off his mouth. "I don't get you sometimes. Why do you mess with those little yellow buggers if everybody hates 'em?"

Mack tried to control his annoyance. "I mess with them, Otto, because they're fine workers. I'm not going to replace them with white riffraff just because someone tells me to. The groves would go to hell. Besides, it wouldn't be right."

Mack was all too aware of Carla still at the sideboard, drinking with her back to them.

"I still don't get it," Swampy said, slurping more beer. "Why are you all the time so worried about the underdog?"

"I guess because I was born one. Weren't you?"

"Yah, sure, but I come up in the world. That changes things."

They were saved from argument by a distracting noise outside. A second later Mack recognized it as Hellburner Johnson, shouting. The Texan burst into the room. Mack saw his Peacemaker tied on his leg, a sheen of panicky sweat on his face.

"Tramps all over the place, Mack. They set fire to the barracks."

The Shopkeeper's Colt hung on a peg in his office. He ran there, snatched it from the holster, and stuffed it in his shirt.

Out in front of the house, Johnson was already in the saddle. Mack jumped up behind him and Johnson booted the horse down the steep road. Mack smelled the sweetness of the trees, and the sharper tang of smoke. He clutched Johnson's waist and cursed when he saw the distant firelight.

"Why wasn't there a warning shot?"

"I don't know."

"What happened to the guard?"

"Quit yelling at me. I don't know. Hang on."

Johnson reined the horse into a turn. They galloped along a side road, a dirt road beside the windbreak. At the road's end Mack saw milling men silhouetted against a huge fire. Flames already consumed half of the two-story barracks.

From the end of the building not yet burning, the fruit tramps dragged struggling Chinese into the yard. Jolting along the road, Mack watched two tramps shove a Chinese to his knees. The one behind held him and cut off his queue, while the other kicked him in the belly and groin. He cried out, and the tramp behind kicked him three times in the small of his back. The Chinese toppled over.

Mack pulled the Colt from his shirt. All over the yard, the tramps had the workers outnumbered and at their mercy. They beat and kicked them. Other white men dashed from the barracks with the workers' belongings and flung them into the fire.

Johnson reined the horse so sharply Mack almost fell off. A Chinese man ran out of the burning section with his quilted coat afire, disappearing toward the road, blazing in the dark like an earthbound comet. Mack jumped down and hit the ground running.

He headed for a tramp holding a worker's throat with one hand while he stabbed him with the other. Mack stepped side-

343

ways for a better shot, aimed hastily, and fired. The tramp screamed and grabbed his leg. The Chinese man ran away yelling, the black thorn of the knife bobbing in his arm.

Mack didn't risk another shot. Men were running, shouting, cursing, struggling all around him; the glare and the thick smoke made it hard to tell attackers from victims. Johnson understood this. He waded into the melee with the barrel of his Peacemaker in his left hand and swung savagely to right and left, clubbing any tramp within reach. He hit one man's jaw and the man raked his hand down across Johnson's eyes. He jumped back but the tramp's nails had torn his cheek open. Then the man tried to throttle Johnson with his own bandanna. Johnson broke the tramp's nose with a blow of the gun butt.

Someone grabbed Mack's arm, jerking it hard. Before he could pivot to fend off the attacker, a rock bashed his temple. He reeled back and sat down hard. The tramp laughed and lunged in, sweat drops shining in his yellow beard. Mack heard a distant guttural shout but had no time to wonder about it. Before the tramp could brain him again, he fired a bullet into the man's thigh.

The tramp's right leg collapsed like a snapped stick and he crawled away. Mack struggled up, the heat scorching his face. All around, the Chinese were running with whatever possessions they could salvage. A few resisted, but most refused to confront the hate-crazed attackers.

Johnson's wild clubbing soon drove all the tramps away from him and he stood in an open space with his head lowered and blood dripping from his chin. There was a brute gleam in his firelit eyes. From the direction of the windbreak, the shouts grew louder. It wasn't English. Mack recognized Swampy's German.

Suddenly he spied someone familiar on the ground: the young bachelor Kim Loo, rolling from side to side and holding his gut. Bruises and bleeding cuts marked his cheeks and forehead. Mack ran over and leaned down to drag him out of the center of the yard.

Bending, he heard Johnson shout, "Watch your left side!" Turning, he stumbled on Kim Loo's outstretched leg and as he fell across the young Chinese the Colt flipped out of his hand. A tramp landed on Mack's back with both knees and Mack's jaw slammed in the dirt, jarring and dazing him.

The tramp raised his right hand like some prophet at a sacrificial altar and light flashed off the rippled blade of a fish-cleaning knife. The tramp's hand whitened and the knife started its descent—

Johnson's bullet hit the tramp between the shoulders. The fish knife flew out of his hand. The tramp fell, and Mack crawled away, retrieved his revolver, and staggered to his feet. As he did, he saw Kim Loo push to his feet and run for the dark road, his queue flying behind.

Swampy Hellman pelted across the yard, red with exertion. He brandished his S&W .45. "You goddamn bums—you trash—get off this land." He veered to the nearest tramp and blew him off his feet. For a moment the man actually appeared to fly against the background of the fire.

Many of the tramps saw that, heard the man's wild scream as he went down, and it broke their nerve. They tossed away stones and bloody two-by-fours and ran for the windbreak, and the darkness. Johnson collared one but the man bit his hand and escaped.

Mack hurried to Swampy, who was pivoting this way and that, hunting a target. "You shouldn't have come here—"

"Don't get the wrong idea, Johnny." The old man was gasping. "I did it for you, not them Chinks."

"Sit down before you fall down." There was an ominous purple tinge rushing into Swampy's cheeks. "Sit!" Mack yelled, pushing him. Swampy was suddenly short of breath, and pop-eyed with fright because of it; he sat down without protest.

Mack stared at the burning building hopelessly. There was no water at hand—the pump platform was burning too, the pump itself already engulfed—and the nearest storage tank was a quarter of a mile away. Mack ran toward the high bright wall of fire, as if he could somehow extinguish it by the sheer force of his anger.

Johnson's arm slammed across his chest. "Stay back. The barracks is done for."

"Goddamn it, I'm not going to stand by and—"

"Yes you are." Johnson stepped in front of him. "Can't do anything else."

Much of the noise was dying out—the shouting, the hurt cries—leaving the hoarse roar of the fire. It consumed the entire building now. Mack's shoulders sagged. Johnson stepped away and shoved his Peacemaker into its holster.

" 'Least there's no wind. Fire'll just burn itself out. It won't damage the trees."

It was true. Spark-laden flames shot straight up, and the large cleared area all around would keep them from spreading.

Mack searched for Swampy. Relieved, he saw him sitting

345

like a fat-legged infant, right there in the dust in his fine white suit, the S&W resting on his thigh. He was still panting.

Movement near the windbreak drew his eye. He saw three Chinese huddled together, watching the fire. Mack rushed toward them.

"You can come back, they're all gone. Come back, you're safe . . ."

When the Chinese saw him, they fled into the windbreak and disappeared.

Mack stopped in the middle of the dirt road, all the strength and fight having left him. The fire roared, overlaid with a new and louder grinding sound. He didn't turn around until after the upper floor crashed down.

After Mack had posted men to watch in case a sudden wind shift fanned the fire, Johnson came to tell him the picket had been found. Mack trudged after the Texan and gazed down at the young Chinese who lay near the roadside boundary stone, his rifle gone, an empty plum-wine jug in his lap. Perhaps he'd fallen asleep; they'd never know, because someone had smashed open the side of his head. Mack had never seen the human brain before. He walked off with vomit in his throat and tears of fury in his eyes.

In the morning a deputy took Mack's statement. Grimy and exhausted, Mack saw the man to the door as Johnson returned. The Texan looked equally tired and dirty.

Mack poured two cups of coffee and Johnson sank down on his spine in a deep chair. "I got Billy Biggerstaff cleanin' up down there. He took some of the houseboys."

"What about the tramps?"

"They either crawled off or got carried off. The camp across the road's empty. The tramp I shot was left behind. He had this in his pocket." He handed Mack a folded and stained scrap of paper.

Mack's mouth turned to a grim slit as he read the terse message. "Someone promised him a cash reward if he got rid of me. Someone who signed himself with the initial *F*. As in 'Fonso.''

Swampy walked in with his usual mug of morning beer, his color normal again. Mack nodded to acknowledge him and said to Johnson, "How many of our Chinese are left?"

"Not one. They all lit out and I expect they're still runnin'. You blame 'em? It makes me sick. They were good boys."

Mack pounded the desk so hard that papers and the guide-book fell off.

Swampy took a chair and blew into the beer foam. "Johnny, I got some advice you don't want. You got the wrong attitude for a man of property. You care about the wrong people. Gonna keep getting you in Dutch." After a considered pause he added, "Could get you killed one of these days."

Mack simply stared at him defiantly.

Johnson sipped coffee and stretched his legs. "I think it's time I got out of here for a while."

Later that day he gathered his gear, saddled a horse, and disappeared.

Carla had slept through the night's commotion. Drunk, Mack assumed. Not that it mattered much. When she woke, her regrets about the barracks were perfunctory. So was his thank-you.

That afternoon he strapped on his snub-nosed Colt and rode down to Riverside. There he asked for some directions and then rode west to a small adobe house in a dusty bight of the Santa Ana. He pounded on the plank door of the house. A stout Mexican, middle-aged, answered, and then quickly stepped back, recognizing him.

Mack asked in Spanish, "Where can I find Alfonso Vicente Blas, sir?"

"Gone," blurted the other, as if relieved. "Gone to see his relatives in Mexico City."

"He lives here, though."

"He does, sir. I am his cousin Carlos."

"Can you get a message to 'Fonso?"

The heavy man took his hand off the door frame he'd been gripping so tightly. "Ah," he said with an unctuous smile. "You want to hire some men?"

"I want to tell your cousin not to come back to Riverside. If he does, I'll put a bullet in him."

'Fonso Blas never returned to the district.

A week later, cantering into town again, Mack came upon half a dozen ragged tents at the roadside. Without thought he dropped his hand to his belt. But of course he usually didn't wear his pistol. His mouth set in a tight line as he rode toward the seedy camp. All at once he spied two children rolling a hoop back and forth, and the tension left him.

An emaciated old man, beard like snow, skin like milk, shuffled to the roadside and waved a feeble greeting. Mack nodded.

The man started to cough. Not a light cough, but deep and phlegmy. He coughed some kind of glistening lump into the weeds.

Silent as phantoms, other squatters stepped from their tents. The old man grabbed his belly and kept coughing. The hoop fell over and the children let it lie. They stood quiet and sad-eyed like the older people. Even a yellow hound that padded into sight looked feeble. Till now Mack had only heard of these tent camps, full of people sick with consumption who had come to California for its curative climate but couldn't afford a sanitarium or a boardinghouse. How many of them would die, disillusioned and still diseased?

The consumptives stood for a long time, silently watching the healthy man ride away.

Mack trotted past the boundary stone and up the foothill road. In the groves to either side, new men, white and brown, worked in the sunshine. Billy Biggerstaff had recruited quickly, efficiently, and cheaply. Mack booted his horse into a gallop, his face stony, his eyes straight ahead.

Mack traveled to Carson City with Clive Henley for the championship fight on March 17. Clive was generous with his expressions of sympathy about the fire. "I must confess that your new, ah, labor arrangement pleases the other chaps."

"Fine, but I don't really care. I'm in business to make money, not friends."

Clive covered his dismay by clipping a new cigar.

The outdoor arena, against a spectacular backdrop of snowy mountains, held more than twenty thousand. They sat behind Gentleman Jim's corner. Mack was excited about the fight, and nearly as excited over three boxy cameras set up outside the ring. "Veriscopes," he told Clive. "I read about this."

"What the deuce is a Veriscope?"

"A camera that takes pictures on a moving strip of film. For the first time, they're going to photograph a prizefight." He pointed to the ring. Along the edge facing the cameras, bold painted letters announced: COPYRIGHTED BY THE VERISCOPE COMPANY.

Clive popped his monocle out and shined it. "Wait a moment. They'll be taking still pictures?"

"Yes and no."

"Come on, my dear chap, which is it?"

"The camera takes a series of still frames in sequence. But when the film's developed and run through a peep-show machine like Edison's Kinetoscope, you see the action. The pictures move—or appear to move. I saw Governor Stanford demonstrate the principle years ago—"

"Scope this, scope that. Sounds ridiculous, old boy. Ridiculous and useless."

The opponents paraded into the ring amid great applause. Corbett had weighed in at 180, Fitzsimmons at 172. Gentleman Jim was favored 10–7 over the Cornishman, and just from appearances, it was understandable. Fitzsimmons was balding, knock-kneed, freckled as a schoolboy. While Corbett danced lightly around the ring, Fitzsimmons lurched and shambled. In the first two rounds he hardly touched Corbett, who kept hitting him with jabs.

By the end of five, Fitzsimmons's face was cut and bleeding badly. When he slumped in his corner after the bell, his wife, Rose, could be heard urging him, "Hit him in the slats, Bob." In the opposite corner, Corbett's manager, old Delaney from Oakland, was smiling and whispering to his man in a smug way.

In the sixth, Corbett knocked Fitzsimmons down, but the Cornishman clutched Corbett's legs and the referee didn't start the count immediately. Rose Fitzsimmons screeched, "Get up, Bob!" and finally Fitzsimmons lumbered to his feet on the count of nine. Furious, Corbett shouted that he'd been down for a count of fifteen. The referee ignored him and the fight went on.

By the end of the thirteenth round Fitzsimmons was clearly desperate, flinging clumsy punches at Corbett's head and torso, few landing. But in the fourteenth, Gentleman Jim grew careless for a moment, and Fitzsimmons suddenly unleashed a left hook to the midsection. It flung Corbett to his knees for the ten-count, ending the fight. A solar-plexus blow, Delaney called it afterward. Corbett's partisans left the arena shaking their heads. Their man had clearly outpointed his opponent, and had scarcely been touched until the last round.

The hotel party, meant to be a celebration, became a wake. Corbett and his second wife, a fair and buxom young woman named Vera, wandered through the crowd like people suffering a sudden bereavement. When the defeated champion saw Mack, he gave him a quick squeeze of the shoulder. "Thanks for being here. It meant a lot to me. I'm just sorry it came out the wrong way."

"You gave it everything, Jim."

Corbett averted his eyes as if to say otherwise.

"Look, when you're rested and feel up to it, I want you and your wife to come for a visit in Riverside."

"We'll see," Corbett murmured without enthusiasm. "Thanks again." He moved on, a beaten man. Mack recognized the signs because, lately, he shared the feeling.

37

HELLBURNER JOHNSON STAYED AWAY TWO MONTHS. "Went out to Death Valley," he said the afternoon he returned. "Plenty of gold fever out there—Randsburg, Joburg, Atolia. But my God, the desolation. Big spires of this stuff they call *tufa*. You'd think you was on the Moon. Cross it off the list of places you think you need to visit, 'cause you don't."

"I hadn't planned to go there, actually."

Johnson digested the curt, almost dismissive reply. "How's the wife?"

"About the same. She's up in San Luis Obispo this week, beautifying herself in the mud and sulfur baths at Newcomb's Spa. You anxious to go back to work?"

"Not so's you'd notice. Anxious to play a little polo, though."

"Good—the team needs you: We have an interclub game Saturday. Carla should be back for it, and my friend Jim Corbett's finally coming down for a few days."

"With his missus?"

"No, she can't make it; she's packing. She and Jim are going to try New York for a while. He doesn't know what to do with himself since Fitzsimmons beat him."

Johnson slipped a plug of tobacco under his lip and worked it around. "Losin' the title must be damn hard on him."

"Losing anything you care about is hard." In his imagination, with keen guilt, he saw Nellie.

Mack galloped down the polo field in a melee of noise and dust. From the bleachers he heard the shouts of the partisans of the red and blue teams. He paid no attention, reaching down, straining down with his mallet. He caught the speeding cork ball squarely and hammered the ball toward the red goal. In the sixth and last chukker, reds and blues were tied at four goals apiece.

Mack's dirty face streamed with sweat, the field on Jefferson Street a sunlit blur, with shadows of horses and ponies flickering in the corners of his eyes. How much time left? Only seconds, surely. He booted Jubilee. Always the best horse in the last chukker.

The ball rocketed on over the trampled sod. Then, with a neat reverse of his mount, Eric Portfield of the blues hit it the other way. It shot past Mack and Johnson and Clive Henley and Bunny Bunthorne, the reds, toward the blue goal.

Mack whipped Jubilee's head around and galloped. He passed Johnson, who'd donned a red bandanna for the occasion; the rest sorted themselves out with colored armbands. "Come on, Jubilee!" he shouted over the pony's neck. Jeremy Fripp of the blues advanced the ball and then looked back. He saw Mack gaining and his brows shot up. Mack was a feared player, not so much because of skill as because of a deep-gutted recklessness, especially in tight spots.

Mack shouldered Jubilee into Jeremy's horse, a rideoff, and Jeremy and his mount lurched away. Mack now caught up with the ball and windmilled his mallet arm in a mighty back shot that reversed the ball toward the other goal. The red partisans cheered.

Johnson, Clive, and Mack all raced neck and neck for the ball. Bunthorne was more timid, lagging. The eyes of the ponies bulged and their manes streamed. Hot wind rushed over Mack's face and sweat ran out from under his canvas helmet, his only safety protection. Suddenly Chitwoode of the blues bore down on him like a juggernaut. Mack had to yank Jubilee's head right and veer off; Chitwoode, not controlling his pony well, would have run over him.

Cursing, Mack rode away from the line of the ball, and Johnson drilled it between the goalposts. Then he stood in his saddle, raised his mallet, and let out a cheer. Mack slowed Jubilee and the whistle blew. Clive Henley yelled, "Hip-hip."

Chitwoode trotted over, apologetic. "Bloody horse was running out of control. I wasn't trying to foul you, old chap."

"Just kill me?" Chitwoode looked dismayed. "Forget it." Mack clapped Chitwoode's shoulder. He excused the near collision because the other man was a poor rider.

Mack tore off the helmet, which he couldn't stand, and shoved it in his belt as the eight players trotted toward the chalked sideline, exchanging congratulations and jibes. Clive shot out his hand to shake. "Bloody good riding, old friend."

The players reached the sideline, where the fashionable ladies and gentlemen of the audience were spilling down from the bleachers into the pavilion of striped canvas. There, other ladies prepared the tea service.

"Mighty polite game," Johnson remarked. "We oughta play nasty once in a while. You hear about them clubs in the East, they've been goin' twenty years and better—some with a lot of hired players who know plenty of dirty tricks. We ought to be ready for that kind of stuff."

"Oh, I say, H.B., you're not really suggesting we lower ourselves to that level and practice fouling?" The speaker was Portfield, who was a young grower with a starchy disposition but great riding skill. "We're gentlemen. We play polo for sport."

"What if we meet a club that doesn't?" Mack asked. "Hell-burner's right—we're novices when it comes to rough tactics."

"We'll never be in that sort of game," Jeremy Fripp said.

"And if we are, we're ready," Clive said. "Grit will always win out, old boy."

Mack doubted it, but he didn't argue. He'd heard tales of vicious rivalries on the field, deliberate fouls intended to maim a horse or rider. There were stories of fatalities too. From the sidelines, polo appeared to be a game of stamina and speed, but little danger. Playing it, Mack found it exciting, but also dangerous, full of stunning physical shocks as players deliberately ran their horses into each other to control or steal the ball. So far there'd been no mishaps at the Riverside club, but that didn't preclude them.

No reason to worry about it this afternoon, he supposed. The reds had won and it was time for socializing. He saw Carla escorting Jim Corbett into the pavilion and he noticed that she held tightly to his arm—so tightly that Corbett couldn't help but feel her bosom.

Frowning, he dismounted and patted Jubilee affectionately. She was beautiful, fleet, and brave. He'd rub her down after he enjoyed a cup of tea.

Some of the gentlemen were still explaining the game or its history to their female companions, most of whom fluttered their eyelashes and pleaded bewilderment. Nellie would never playact so inanely, Mack thought, then reproved himself for thinking of her again.

". . . goes back all the way to the Persians, m'dear. They played it to train their fastest cavalry. Why, they say even old Ghengis Khan's Mongols played it—using the severed heads of prisoners for balls. Har-har."

Mack unwrapped his mallet strap and walked into the pavilion ahead of Johnson and Portfield. They were discussing the club's new grounds at Van Buren and Victoria avenues. There the club had temporarily leased two fine large lots, but they were having trouble financing a clubhouse and bleachers. Members argued about whether to raise money by charging higher dues or by expanding membership, which some of the club snobs like Portfield resisted.

Carla's blue eyes sparkled as she brought Corbett his tea. She looked fresh and crisp in a skirt and blouse of white lawn. The blouse had a stiff high collar and a jabot embroidered with tiny orange blossoms. She'd abandoned her straw hat, her pleated summer cape, elbow-length gloves, and silk umbrella, all of them white too. White became her, flattering her sun-browned skin.

Mack worked his way toward his wife and his guest, pausing to smile and acknowledge compliments on the victory. Clive reached Carla and Corbett first. "Mr. Corbett, it is indeed an honor to have the world's heavyweight champion witness one of our practice matches."

Corbett looked uncomfortable with the fragile teacup. "I'm pleased that my friend Mack Chance invited me. But it's *former* champion, remember."

"Congratulations, darling," Carla said to Mack. It was her brittle good cheer intended for others, not him.

"Thanks." Mack squeezed Corbett's sleeve to buck him up. It had been a sad and difficult weekend thus far. Corbett wasn't the ebullient young man Mack remembered. He was depressed, withdrawn. Mack kept trying to find ways to get him to talk. "Tell us honestly, Jim. What did you think of what you saw?"

"I thought it was fine. You should have a match with a Bay Area team. There's an excellent one at the Burlingame Country Club."

"Is the club part of that new real estate development in the South Bay?" Carla asked.

"Yes, Burlingame Park. Mighty expensive place. Expensive and exclusive. The members brag that their polo field is better than the one in Newport. The team carries two or three paid players."

"Surely none as good as our original Texas cowhand," someone said, slapping Johnson's back.

"Jim, it's infernally hot in here," Carla said. "Might we stroll while you tell me more about Burlingame?" She lifted the teacup from his hand, then curled her arm through his again.

Corbett wasn't sophisticated, but he sensed the deep currents here, especially when he saw his host's wife watching her husband with a smile so sweetly generous it approached a smirk. He stammered his answer.

"I think—maybe—I'd better see about a train. Don't want to leave all the packing to Vera—"

"Oh, I'm disappointed. Can't you spare me a few minutes? Of course you can. My father's mentioned Burlingame, and a gentleman I know, Mr. Fairbanks, belongs to the club. I must hear everything . . ."

She swept Gentleman Jim out of the pavilion on her arm, teasing his cheek with her fingertips while she whispered something. The champion blushed.

Bunthorne's wife, Mavis, a notorious gossip, rattled her cup on her saucer to attract the attention of the ladies around her. Mack overheard her say, "To whom is she married, my dears? Mack or Mr. Corbett? A stranger might wonder."

"What a performance," he said, livid. "You practically threw yourself at him."

"I did not. You're boorish to say I did."

He'd drawn her away from the pavilion, down past the bleachers. The other players and spectators were moving to their buggies and coaches as swift gray clouds darkened the sun.

"I don't care—I don't like you flirting that way. Everyone saw it. At least they did once Mavis announced it in her megaphone voice. Jim was embarrassed."

"He didn't say so."

"He's too polite." Corbett had left ten minutes earlier, driven to the Santa Fe depot by Johnson.

"You've been fretting about your friend's state of mind all weekend," Carla said. "I was only trying to cheer him up."

"It looked like a lot more than that. Jim's a married man. You don't throw yourself at a married man. You were all over him, whispering and touching him—"

She laughed. Loose fluffy strands of her hair fluttered in the gusty wind. "You're such a dreadful prude sometimes. I didn't think you'd notice. You hardly notice me any other time."

"Is that why you did it? To get back at me for some imaginary slight?"

"My. Such wounded innocence."

"For God's sake, Carla, stop this stupid game."

"Who's playing a game? You're jealous. Jealous and nasty."

Mack seized her wrist. "Carla—"

"Go to hell," she said, tearing free and dashing past him

354

along the chalked sideline. "Clive," she called. "Clive dear, wait—I must speak to you."

At half past ten that evening, Mack left his office. Villa Mediterranean was hushed, the electricity off for the night, the gas mantles trimmed low. At the polo field, while he rubbed down Jubilee and tended to his other ponies, Carla had persuaded Clive Henley to drive her home. She'd been absent for supper. Sleeping, her maid said.

Mack walked along the dim upstairs hall to the double doors of their suite. He took his hand from the pocket of his purple silk dressing gown and turned the knob.

The door wouldn't open.

He tapped softly. "Carla?"

Silence.

He knocked again, louder. "Will you please unlock this? I was tired after the game. I lost my temper. I know it was just harmless flirtation. I want to apologize."

Dresses, shoes, undergarments strewed the bed and the carpet. Trunks and portmanteaus, empty or half-packed, stood about the room. Carla sat on the bed watching the bolted door. Her hair hung in golden tangles, her bed gown of silk and lace pulled apart to show the heaviness of her thighs. With an unsteady hand she spilled more bourbon into her glass.

A little late, aren't you? You're always so damned wrapped up in yourself. In your polo ponies, your oil, your orange trees—every goddamned thing that touches your life but me. How can I get you to notice?

"A harmless flirtation, did you say?" She swallowed bourbon. Some of it ran down her chin, between her breasts. "Don't be too sure, sweetheart."

Her voice came through hoarse and thick. He felt sick; she was drinking again. He heard the bottle clink. "Don't be too damn sure," she repeated.

He grabbed the door handle and rattled it. "Carla, this is childish."

For an answer he got another extended silence. It produced a rush of heat in his face. "I said open the door, damn it." He didn't knock this time; he pounded.

Huge silent tears washed the blacking off her eyelashes and it trickled down her face. *You bastard. Why can't you love me? Am I so worthless? Is she so much better?*

355

He pounded again. "You want me to kick it down?"

Crying, she lunged up and flung the glass at the door. It burst so explosively that a tiny splinter flew all the way back to her cheek. She gasped and pressed her skin. A perfect jewel of blood formed between two fingers as the last pieces of glass tinkled on the floor and bourbon ran down the carved wood door.

At the sound of the glass breaking, he jumped back. Then he slammed his palms against the doors. *"Carla."*

Nothing.

He pressed his ear to the wood and heard what might have been a mutter or a muted sob. That and the broken glass defeated him, and putting his hands back in the pockets of his dressing gown, he walked away down the dark hall.

In his office, he lit the gas in the reading nook, a square alcove lined with ceiling-high bookshelves. It was his burrow, his lair, his retreat and place of inspiration.

Surrounding the large, deep chair were books of every kind, periodicals, all of the Los Angeles papers for the past four days, and copies of the *San Francisco Examiner* delivered by post twice a week.

In one corner he'd collected articles about steam yachts, descriptions of some of the greatest pleasure vessels in America. William Vanderbilt's *Alva*. Morgan's *Corsair II*. *Namouna*, the 227-foot beauty built and sailed by Gordon Bennett, the newspaper publisher. He had a whole file of engravings of *Namouna*'s period furniture, fireplaces, and elegant carvings and ornamentation; she was a mansion afloat. The descriptions and pictures were slowly shaping his own dream yacht. He'd made sketches and voluminous notes.

Another corner overflowed with his collection of stories and pictures about horseless carriages. They were the coming thing, no doubt of it. But inventors and designers still argued about the best motive power. Gasoline? Electric battery? Steam? And what did you call such a vehicle? There was endless dispute in the press—and no accepted name. Sometimes it was *automaton*, sometimes *petrocar*. *Motorig*. *Mobe*. Or *motocycle*.

Mack knew only that he wanted one. One of his favorite pastimes was rereading a long news account of the great race held in Chicago over Thanksgiving in '95. Just one day after a bitter blizzard, six courageous drivers had raced their vehicles through rutted drifts from Jackson Park all the way up the shore to Waukegan and back. An Electrobat and a Sturges Electric competed against the "motor wagon" of the Duryea brothers and three German-built Benz cars. After more than eight hours at an average speed of seven miles per hour, the Duryea won. Mack sometimes shut his eyes and imagined himself careening along icy roads, gloved hand firm on the steering tiller, his other hand alternately sounding the foghorn or the brass trumpet. He wanted a horseless carriage; new inventions excited him. He yearned to be first to try them, own them, show them off. And he was beginning to have enough money to make it possible.

No dreaming of horseless carriages tonight, alas. A dreary but important legal document lay on the leather chair seat. He turned up the gaslight and sat down to read seventy-seven pages of by-laws and articles of incorporation for San Solaro Irrigation, Inc., a mutual water company formed under the Wright Bill. Mack planned to develop the town site eventually; the articles drawn up by Potter established a community water district to be owned by future residents—ten shares of stock per building lot.

He slogged through the dry paragraphs, his mind constantly slipping away, returning to Carla. Around half past one, he heard footsteps in the corridor. He jumped up, but his expectant smile vanished in a moment. The stride was too heavy—one of the servants?

Following a soft knock, Johnson stuck his head in. "Saw the lights. What's the matter? Can't sleep?"

"Work to do," Mack said. Johnson yawned as he ambled in, bowlegged as ever. His knee joints creaked and his beard stubble showed, gray as his crinkly hair and ready for the morning razor.

"I was twistin' and jumpin' a bit m'self. Decided to stroll a while." He poured two fingers of Mack's best Tennessee whiskey. No permissions necessary; they were friends.

"Drag up a chair." He did, gratefully, then slipped off his boots and sampled the whiskey. Mack poured some for himself; it was his first hard liquor in a long while.

"What was you readin'?"

"The water-company charter. Have to get through it. But I'd rather be drawing up designs for the yacht."

Johnson chuckled. The gaslight put a convivial gleam in his green eyes. "Swear to God, Mack, I never seen anybody with such an appetite for tryin' out new gadgets."

Mack relaxed and put his feet on a stack of books. "Seems to go with the climate out here." He sipped the whiskey. It warmed his belly but not his heart.

Johnson watched him. Finally: "You're not feelin' so hot these days."

Mack concentrated on his glass. "Ever since the fire—"

"Oh, it ain't the fire. We got that licked. Your pride took a whippin' when you had to hire some of them slow-witted white boys, but Biggerstaff and me, we're bringin' 'em along. It's somethin' else." A pause. "What?"

Mack shook his head. "You know me a little too well, Hugh." He spoke slowly, uncomfortably. "Ever since the day I walked down from the Sierras and looked around and said, By God, I've made it, I'm in California—ever since then I've lacked for plenty of things. Sometimes a night's shelter. Sometimes food. There was even a day here and there when I feared for my life. But I never lacked for hope. I kept opening that guidebook and I never lacked for hope. Not until lately."

The office clock ticked loudly. Johnson slowly rolled the tumbler back and forth between his hard palms. He figured it would be good for Mack to get it all out. If he would.

"Things are bad with Carla . . ." Mack began.

"That's no surprise, I'm sorry to say."

"No, but I can't seem to untangle them, either. Every time I try, I blunder."

"Maybe that's why you been so sore lately. Like a high-strung yearling feelin' a saddle the first time."

"You're a candid bastard."

Johnson shrugged a lanky shoulder. "If all you want is violins and geraniums, I'll go back to bed."

"No—stay. It's just that—well, it's tough to look at yourself and admit you're failing."

"Maybe it ain't entirely your fault, Mack. You said Hellman warned you she wouldn't take to marriage. Not very long, anyhow."

"That's true. She gets bored. I saw it start six months after the honeymoon."

"That the reason she set the house girls to packin' her baggage right after the game this afternoon—she's bored?"

Mack sat up, alarmed. "She's packing?"

"I had a cup of coffee in the kitchen 'fore I moseyed up here. 'Twas that bosomy little one told me. Nuncia—the one I keep tryin' to bed. Nuncia said the señora is goin' into Los Angeles in the mornin'. Plans to be there an' shop for a few days."

"That's the first I've heard of it." Mack felt a rush of relief; for a moment he'd feared she was walking out for good. But the relief was quickly replaced by a feeling of insult, because

358

she'd told the servants and not him. Given the scene at the polo field, he supposed he couldn't blame her.

"Reckon you could hightail upstairs and put a stop to it."

He considered it, then said, "No, I'd probably make matters worse. A few days on her own may do her good, calm her down. I'll wait and then go in town and patch it up. Pour me another drink."

ON A MORNING FIVE DAYS LATER, MACK TOOK THE **38** Santa Fe to the city. He went first to the Los An- geles Litho Company, where the foreman brought in press proofs of the Calgold crate label featuring the old prospector. There were proofs of the separate plates—red, pink, dark blue, light blue, yellow, and black—and a composite proof of all six colors.

They discussed corrections, then Mack, voicing his enthu- siasm, signed off on the changes and hurried to the Baker Block. There he spent two hours with Enrique Potter and the water-company papers.

When they finished, the lawyer said: "That priest you know opened an office in town. Only he's no longer a priest. The Church excommunicated him. He's got a girl with him."

Mack asked for the address. It was a bad block in the south of town. Walking there in the mellow sunshine, he marveled again at the changes since the day he first saw Los Angeles. Most of the adobes and false fronts were gone, razed to make way for taller buildings of granite and brick. Trim electric trol- leys with overhead poles shot along shiny rails in the center of asphalt streets. The look was that of a thriving city, not a cow town. It could have been mistaken for an eastern city, were it not for the mountains and, against their sunlit splendor, all of the hundreds of oil derricks pumping away north and west of the business district. They were ugly, Mack had long ago de- cided. But he liked the derricks—maybe because their gangly presence symbolized enterprise, money, taking risks: every- thing California meant to him.

Soon he left the more crowded streets with their eternal wan- dering flocks of tourists, most of them pale, some of them sniffling and wheezing. He was in the bad section; Anglo and Mexican riffraff eyed him from the *cantinas*. He took note but didn't worry. The sawed-off Colt rode on his hip, under his coattails. He didn't need it; his eyes and his demeanor kept the sidewalk clear in front of him.

Up a rancid stair and down a dark corridor where bugs scurried in the dirt, he found a solid door with a card tacked to it: LABOR LEAGUE OF LOS ANGELES.

He tried the handle, but it was locked. He rapped on the door.

"*¿Quién es?*" It was Marquez's voice.

"*Es el señor Mack Chance, Diego.*"

He heard footsteps, then the bolt shooting back.

"My friend," Marquez exclaimed, and flung his arms around Mack. They hugged and slapped each other, Mack getting a noseful of sweat, garlic, and the stale musty smell of clothes worn too long.

The girl had been hovering behind the ex-priest. She was barefoot, a small-breasted, timid waif with a starved look. She had straight stringy hair, brown with streaks of yellow, and luminous brown eyes that regarded him with hesitancy or perhaps fear. Her appearance shocked him as much as the sordid little office: two rooms, the outer one crowded by a huge cheap desk. An unwashed window overlooked a yard where two cats prowled a refuse heap. Through a half-open door Mack glimpsed a gas ring, stacks of pamphlets, and a floor pallet big enough for two.

Mack smiled to hide his dismay. Diego Marquez, always a burly man, had gained thirty or forty pounds, most of it in the belly that rolled over his belt and strained the buttons of his threadbare white shirt. Red wine stains spotted the shirt front. He had also let his beard grow. It was huge, fan-shaped, and shiny-black, tipped with white. He wore rope sandals; his toes were dirty.

"It's good to see you, Diego."

"And you." Marquez grinned widely. "What a sight. What clothes. *El millonario.*"

"Not quite." He glanced at the girl.

"Ah, forgive me." To the girl, in Spanish, he said, "Felicia, this is Señor James Macklin Chance. A good man, a decent man—despite his capitalist disguise. Will you run to the corner and get us a bottle of red?" He gave her a coin and she slipped out like an obedient puppy. Marquez carefully bolted the door after her.

Mack dropped his cream-colored rancher's hat on the desk strewn with scribbled notes and some printed sheets headed MANIFESTO! On the wall hung a state map. Dots, arrows, and cryptic inscriptions in different colors covered the Central Valley and the regions around Los Angeles.

"Where did you meet that girl, Diego?"

"In the Valley, near Fresno. I was organizing the stoop labor. Her stepfather grows melons and treats his workers like serfs. Worse than serfs—swine. Felicia is nineteen years old. The man married her mother nine years ago and corrupted Felicia herself shortly after. He promised a posse would lynch me if she associated with me, but it was all bluff. She helps me in my work, and she has a better life now than she ever had before. Besides, I was chaste for many years; I have a lot to make up for."

A flash of his eyes under his bristly brows carried a warning: *I've said all I have to say, so don't ask more.*

Marquez offered him the only chair, and out of courtesy Mack sat down. The former priest said he moved his headquarters often, going wherever he felt needed, organizing workers whenever they were courageous enough to risk the firings, threats, and violence of their employers. "I have another roving commission, but a less popular one than before. And you—you're doing well—"

"Reasonably. I'm married—did you know that?"

"Oh, yes, I heard. Los Angeles is still a small town, and you are a large figure in the landscape."

"I own some orange groves—"

"Riverside," Marquez nodded. "So now the gold drops into your lap from the trees while at the same time it flows out black from your oil wells. Remarkable. The day we met you said that your goal was riches. I congratulate you." There was no mockery or reproof in his tone.

Felicia returned with a clay jug of wine. She placed it on the table, put her hand on Marquez's shoulder, and raised on tiptoe to kiss his cheek. With a smile and a murmur to Mack, she went to the inner room and closed the door.

Mack didn't want wine at this hour but he took half a cup and held it. "My lawyer told me you'd set up shop in Los Angeles."

Marquez studied the cats prowling in the garbage. "Not a very impressive headquarters for a war, is it? But we don't have much money—by 'we' I mean the movement—and what we have is better spent on handbills and meeting halls."

"Why Los Angeles right now?"

The ex-priest snatched up a copy of the *Times*. "Because in Southern California, there is no greater Satan than Otis. He is the Antichrist of workingmen. Scarcely a day goes by without some attack, usually gratuitous—'' He turned the pages, found what he wanted, and read aloud: " 'The scabrous scum and degraded desperadoes of the communist conspiracy skulk among us again.' "

Mack laughed. "He can turn a phrase, anyway."

"It would be funny if it weren't so despicable, not to say dangerous. He's winning the battle here. Do you know what they're starting to call this bastion of the open shop? Otis-town.'' Marquez ripped the paper and flung the pieces on the floor.

Felicia was softly singing a lullaby in Spanish. Glancing at the inner door, Marquez's face gentled. Mack put his wine cup on the desk and reached inside his coat. "I'd like to give you a bank draft. A contribution to your work."

"Why? I'm not in the business of selling absolution to rich men anymore."

"That's damned insulting." Mack stood up as if to leave.

"Yes," Marquez said, frowning. "Yes, I suppose it is. I apologize. I am so used to every encounter being a confrontation, or becoming one, I've lost my churchly manners.'' He laid a big hand on Mack's shoulder. "I'll be happy to accept a donation. Anonymous or otherwise."

"I'd prefer it to be anonymous."

That seemed to disappoint Marquez, but he said nothing. Mack wrote the draft for a thousand dollars.

"Thank you," Marquez said quietly as he took it. Then he read the amount. "Thank you—*madre de Dios*. What a blessing. Be assured it will be put to good use." He folded the draft quickly and thrust it in his shirt pocket, as though the miracle might vanish. "You are a good man, Mack. I apologize again for the slur of a moment ago. I heard that you defended your Chinese workmen bravely.''

"I guess I was stupid to do it. All the growers were against me because I paid a living wage, and 1893 just repeated itself. I couldn't hire so much as one Chinese after the fire."

Marquez locked his hands behind his back and eyed the colored map thoughtfully. "This is a noble state in many ways, full of shining hope and opportunity. But some do not want to share California once they have carved out their portion of it. They especially do not want to share it with people whose color or speech is different from their own—"

"Diego, I must go."

Marquez regarded him with unblinking intensity. It was an eerie moment; the priest had come back to life. "You look haggard and tired, my friend. All is not well with you?"

He wanted to lie but somehow the man inspired honesty. "No. I'm losing a small battle of my own." Pain and embarrassment overwhelmed him. "I came to Los Angeles to find my wife. We've been having difficulties—"

"There's no difficulty finding her. I saw her yesterday, in fact. A handsome woman. Everyone knows her. I believe she's stopping at the Pico House." Again he put his massive hand on Mack's shoulder, to commiserate and wish him a successful quest.

"Thanks, Diego. Take care of yourself."

"And you also. May the Almighty save us from meeting on some field of battle."

"You're expecting more battles."

"Many more. God go with you."

"Yes, sir, she certainly is in the hotel," said the clerk at the Pico House. "She went to the dining room not ten minutes ago."

Mack found himself walking quickly, eagerly, toward the elegant headwaiter stationed near the doorway. Hearing string music, his spirits lifted. He set his mind on pleasing and complimenting Carla, on making her feel good about seeing him and going home to Riverside. Maybe he'd try to interest her in plans for the yacht. She could help with the interiors, choose the furnishings, travel to Europe for them, spend whatever she liked—

"Yes, sir, good day," said the headwaiter, bowing.

"I'm Macklin Chance. I believe my wife's here?"

The darting eyes should have warned him. "Quite so, Señor Chance. Will you step this way?"

A nervous little cough accompanied his smart pivot, and he marched away between the crowded tables, no longer blocking Mack's view of a cozy table in a corner. Carla sat there, but not by herself. She was dining and chatting with Walter Fairbanks.

Mack was immediately less cheerful, but more determined. Carla saw him first. Her annoyance showed only a moment.

"Mack, dear. I had no idea you were coming to Los Angeles today."

"I had business with Potter." He took off his hat and gave Carla's companion a cool stare. "Fairbanks." He found himself turning the hat brim in his hands, a betrayal of his tense, angry state.

"Hello, Chance." Reluctantly, Fairbanks caught the waiter's eye. "Another chair."

The waiter brought it from a nearby table but Mack remained standing. He noticed a dark-green wine bottle in a silver stand. Empty. So were their glasses. It explained Carla's high color.

"Well, do sit down," she said.

"I certainly don't want to interrupt . . ."

The lawyer's cold gray eyes said yes, he was doing exactly that. Mack sat.

Walter Fairbanks was as fit and elegant as ever, his mustache so neat and perfect, it might have been painted on. His dove-gray hat, matching gloves, and silver-knobbed stick lay on a narrow ledge beside the table.

Carla's eyes darted between the two, as if she expected antagonism, perhaps hoped for it. Fairbanks snapped his fingers and ordered up another bottle of Chardonnay and a third glass. The string trio sawed away at "The Emperor Waltz."

"I'm in town on business," Fairbanks said to Mack. "I didn't expect to bump into any old friends." He transferred his perfunctory smile to Carla and infused it with warmth. "We met on Main Street, quite by accident. Your wife was coming from a dress shop. Followed by two nigger boys with their arms laden up to here." He raised his hand above his head.

Carla touched Mack's sleeve. "You'll scold me when you see all the boxes from Mademoiselle Claudine's. But not too hard—please?"

The waiter opened the wine, presented the cork, and poured a little for Fairbanks, who sampled it and shrugged. "It's satisfactory." Mack studied his wife, so unexpectedly bright and cordial. It was friendliness for Walter's benefit, brittle and false.

The waiter filled the glasses and left. Each of them took a swallow, Carla a larger one than the men. Fairbanks said, "I understand you're still throwing money into that foolish railway in the Valley."

"What's foolish about competition?"

"In sports, nothing. I relish it. But—"

"When the San Francisco and San Joaquin is finished," Mack interrupted, "farmers and small businessmen won't be stuck paying anything your board of directors demands. They'll have a choice—your road or the People's Road."

Fairbanks reacted with a superior smile. "What a grandiose name that is. I can understand a crazy foreigner like Adolph Sutro backing such a scheme, but not Claus Spreckels. He's thoroughly Americanized. He has some pretensions to respectability in San Francisco.''

Mack laughed. "By God, Walter, you want a hell of a lot. You and your bosses already own three fourths of the state legislators, and your tame dogs in Washington. Now you're saying every rich man in California has to kowtow?''

"It's hardly a matter of *kowtowing*, as you put it. I would expect intelligent self-interest and cooperation from men of a certain class—that's all. Men of substance, and good breeding . . .''

Fairbanks blurted it. *Got him*, Mack thought, delighted. He slouched in his chair, grabbed the wine bottle—the waiter darted forward, too late—and refilled his own glass. He contrived to spill some.

"Well, as you've known for a long time, I don't meet your qualifications. Never have, never will. In your eye, Walter.''

And he knocked back the wine, all of it, like a thirsty miner in a Mother Lode saloon.

While Fairbanks fumed, Carla's excitement made her lean into the table, her bosom crushed against the edge, her eyes large as a spellbound child's. What was it—the excitement of pitting one man against the other?

The waiter brought Carla and the lawyer their food, sweeping the silver domes off roasted capons and holding the domes aloft.

"Splendid,'' Fairbanks said without enthusiasm.

"Eat—don't let it get cold,'' Mack said.

Carla picked up knife and fork but Fairbanks didn't touch his. "Carla tells me you play polo.''

"I do.''

"With a team that includes a Texas cowboy and some limeys living on remittances.'' He sighed. "God preserve us, and the noble game.''

"My teammates are damn good riders.''

"Never so good as our Burlingame team, though.''

"Do you ride for Burlingame?''

"Yes.''

"We'd be glad to put your proposition to a test anytime you say.''

"What a good idea,'' Carla exclaimed. "Riverside has only played interclub matches so far. They're eager for a regular game.''

Fairbanks leaned back, unconsciously smoothing his auburn hair. There was no need; like his mustache, it was sleek and perfect. "It might be amusing to bring our ponies down here to the cow counties and show you fellows how the game should be played."

Deep color flooded Carla's face. "Oh, you must arrange it. The Riverside team's really quite raffish, Walter. My dear sweet husband has a strange fondness for people of that sort."

"Why, Chance? Do you feel guilty about your newfound wealth? Or are you still a bit uncomfortable among gentlemen?"

Mack's carefully maintained politeness blew away. He pushed back, stood, and shoved the chair to the unoccupied table it had come from.

"When you're ready to go, Carla, I'll call a cab to take us to the train."

"I'd like to finish my meal, please."

There was a characteristic edge in that. He reminded himself of his resolve to make things better. "Of course. Take as long as you want. I'll wait in the saloon bar."

His unexpected mildness seemed to please her.

Fairbanks produced a leather case, plucked out an engraved card, and offered it between his index and middle finger. "This is the club address in Burlingame. Have your team secretary write ours to set a date."

"You can get your ponies down here?"

"Oh, I think a special freight car can be arranged," Fairbanks said, as if Mack were a dunce.

He wanted to bash the lawyer's face. "I'll look forward to seeing you on the field, then."

"No more than I." Fairbanks's voice was ice.

Mack donned and tilted his big rancher's hat with deliberate swagger. "I'm anxious to have you home again, Carla. I've been lonesome. Fairbanks."

A curt nod completed his good-bye.

Fairbanks glared after him. Mack saw it when he tipped the headwaiter at the door.

Well, why shouldn't the bastard glare? The table talk had carried an unspoken but clear declaration of war. Carla recognized it; she came rushing out of the dining room in ten minutes—without Fairbanks. She was gay and affectionate, as if they'd never quarreled.

A bellman brought down her luggage and all her purchases— sixteen boxes. At home that night, she said she was sorry for her behavior at the polo game. He offered the same apology and they made love twice in an hour.

366

Afterward, while she slept in the curve of his arm, Mack wondered if she was ardent and agreeable because he was willing to challenge another man, with her admiration as the prize.

WITH A THUNDER OF DRIVERS, SCREECH OF WHEELS, **39** spurting of sparks, neighing of unseen horses, Burlingame came to town.

A switch engine shunted two SP livestock cars onto a siding. Mack and Johnson watched the ponies come down the ramps and stamp, swirling the golden dust.

"Holy shit," Johnson muttered. "How many'd they bring?"

More ponies clattered down the ramps. There were twenty-six in all.

"I knew Fairbanks wanted to win," Mack said. "I didn't know how badly."

At a Friday-night reception before the Saturday game, the hosts entertained their opponents. Fairbanks mingled easily and affably with the local people but the other members of his team weren't as social, ill at ease in their suits and stiff collars. There was Billy Rodeen, a white-haired, pug-faced little fellow with a tough air. There was Petticlerq, a stringy young man with patent-leather hair parted in the center and a face heavily pitted by some childhood disease. The third was Roscoe Eagle, a huge bowlegged man with a broad broken nose. He looked like a cross between a cowpuncher and a Plains Indian. He said he hailed from Oklahoma, but that was all he said.

"Old fellow, I smell some rotten fish here," Jeremy Fripp whispered to Mack. "That's to say, I smell the odor of cash."

"What do you mean?"

"If those three chaps are clubmen, I'm dear old Queen Victoria. Your chum brought three paid players."

Six Burlingame people—three couples—arrived on the Saturday-morning train. It was a perfect autumn day, fair and warm. The club erected two open canvas pavilions, and about noon the spectators began arriving with portable tables, luncheon hampers, silver wine buckets, fresh-cut flowers, and sun parasols. The field swirled with the smells of dust and dung, perfume and tinned lobster.

The twenty-four Riverside ponies—exactly enough as long as there were no mishaps—filled temporary rope corrals behind one set of goalposts. Burlingame used similar corrals on the other side of the field. Mack donned his canvas helmet with a sense of trepidation. The hired opponents were an unfriendly, unsmiling lot.

Fairbanks walked over before the opening ceremonies, swinging his mallet jauntily. Mack tightened the girth on Fireball, his first-chukker pony.

"Splendid new pony, Mack. Real beauty. I don't know how we'll fare against a team like yours."

He delivered the mockery with a straight face. *Hold back,* Mack warned himself. *Anger is what he wants.*

"I'm sure you'll find a way, Walter. Those friends of yours look like real polo blue bloods."

"Well, they're keen for the game."

"Are they keenest before or after they get their pay?"

Fairbanks gave him a startled look, then a hostile one. "You smarmy little upstart."

After the ceremony of welcome and introductions, the two mounted umpires took the field, then the teams. Eric Portfield rode at the number one position, Mack at two, Johnson three, and Clive four. Their opposites at Burlingame were Petticlerq, Eagle, Fairbanks, and Rodeen. At the strong-rider positions, Johnson and Fairbanks were presumably the best players.

The ponies snorted and fretted, eager to run, and when the whistle blew the spectators cheered. The sideline referee threw in the cork ball and the opposing teams charged it. With horses and men clustered so close, the rules dictated a half-swing to knock the ball free. Fairbanks took a looping full swing, missed, and struck Clive's right knee. Clive cursed and clenched his jaw manfully.

The umpires missed the foul. Pock-marked Petticlerq cut the ball loose with a shot under his pony's neck, right to Roscoe Eagle, who drilled it 160 yards down the field with a forward shot from his off side.

So that was how it was going to be, Mack thought as he galloped Fireball in the pursuing pack. Win at any cost. All right—he was warned.

The Burlingame men were hard riders, and cool and deliberate about their insults and attempted fouls. A minute from the end of the first seven-minute chukker, Eagle dashed past Clive and Eric Portfield. With an artful back shot from his near, or left, side, he put the ball through the twenty-four-foot

368

opening between the goals. The chukker ended with Burlingame up 1–0.

They rested the customary four minutes. The crowd was quieter; Burlingame's skill and aggressive play were apparent to the Riverside folk, and they were not sanguine about the outcome. Johnson looked grim as the team trotted out on fresh ponies.

The teams changed goals as they did in every chukker. For the first couple of minutes they raced up and down the three-hundred-yard field with neither gaining an advantage. Fairbanks was a fast rider and a good player—Mack couldn't deny that.

Mack captured the ball and sent it toward his goal with two precise fore shots. The rider following the line of the ball had precedence over the others and could not be interfered with. Theoretically. Fairbanks was no respecter of theory. As Johnson took the ball, Fairbanks cut back and forth ten feet ahead of him, much too close with horses traveling full speed. Johnson shouted for him to veer off, but Fairbanks kept riding directly ahead. Suddenly Fairbanks pulled his pony up, causing Johnson's pony to plow into him.

Clive shouted an outraged warning. Johnson's mount lost its front feet and started to go down. Instantly, Mack saw that the falling pony would throw Johnson forward, then crash on top of him while Fairbanks galloped away unharmed. But Johnson leaned back and savagely reined the falling pony, literally pulling its head up by physical force, and he kept it up until the pony regained its footing. All of it happened in seconds, and Mack gasped and wondered if he'd really seen it.

Johnson's furious face proved that he had. The Texan cursed at Fairbanks, while the umpire called a foul at last.

"Dastardly," Clive said to Mack. Then he repeated it to Rodeen trotting by. "Dastardly—that's the most dangerous kind of fall in the game, and you know it."

White-haired Billy Rodeen grinned and said, "Fuck yourself, limey." He trotted on.

The officials awarded Riverside a free shot at their goal from thirty yards out. Eric Portfield missed the shot and play resumed. Fairbanks hectored his teammates like a general in the field. This was no game, but a grudge match, with prestige, reputation, God knew what else, at stake.

The chukker ended with the score unchanged.

* * *

Third chukker.

The afternoon sun broiled the field and the dust swirled thick. Riverside rode hard, but somehow they couldn't break through and score. Fairbanks's sweaty face showed a faint smile at last. The game was flowing his way.

Clive forwarded the ball with a powerful shot, then Johnson hit it. Riding a rangy little sorrel named Soubrette, Mack came pounding back from the goal for a shot that could put the ball over. He rode with his legs sticking out and away from his mount. Fairbanks charged from the left, his pony shouldering into Mack in a hard rideoff. Mack reeled from the impact. Then the lawyer snapped his right leg out of the stirrup and hooked it under Mack's left leg, giving him a hard elbow in the ribs. It broke his concentration and put him off balance.

Suddenly Fairbanks raised his right leg to tip Mack and throw him off his pony. The sky, the field, Fairbanks's glittering eyes, tilted crazily, and Mack grabbed the saddle with his left hand to abort the fall. Shaking himself free of Fairbanks's leg, he watched the ground speed by underneath; he was hanging off Soubrette at something like a forty-five-degree angle. Then he saw the ball. Furious at the foul, he struck downward and back, making hard, solid contact. The ball rose in the air and sailed between the posts.

In the largest pavilion, Carla jumped to her feet so precipitously that she upset her fifth glass of wine. She applauded wildly, perspiration bleeding through her heavy rouge. Behind her hand, Mavis Bunthorne wondered aloud to her intimates about Carla's applause. Was it for her husband's goal or for the foul by the handsome lawyer that had almost unhorsed him?

The chukker ended in another forty seconds, tied at one goal apiece.

They rested for ten minutes at the half. Riverside's grooms offered the usual encouraging clichés, but none of the riders took them seriously. They had the full measure of Burlingame now; it was the kind of team Johnson had warned against earlier in the season, the kind that would do anything to win.

The whistle blew. Possession seesawed back and forth for two minutes, then Johnson fouled Eagle, who swung at him with his mallet before the umpire warned him back. Burlingame was awarded possession and the referee threw the ball in at midfield. Petticlerq hit an aggressive back shot to Rodeen, who forwarded it to Fairbanks. Mack intercepted it, leaned in, and drove it toward his goal with a sloppy off-side back shot.

The ball bounced ahead of him to the right. Fairbanks seemed to like attacking from the near side. He came in that way again, behind Mack, galloping close. Mack turned his head slightly and saw the bobbing head of Fairbanks's pony.

The lawyer turned his pony into Mack's at precisely the right angle, and the pony's Pelham bit tore Mack's shirt and raked his back. Fairbanks laughed and pulled away, easily avoiding a spill. Mack rode the rest of the chukker with the hot warm feel of blood on the small of his back. It ran under the waist of his riding pants and over his buttocks.

"God, man, you're soaked with it," Eric Portfield said at the end of the scoreless chukker. Mack leaned over, hands on his knees, hurting.

"We'll put Jeremy in, old sport," Clive said.

"I'll finish the game," Mack said. "Tear up a shirt, a rag, anything to bind it up."

"But old fellow, no one will think the less of you if you quit. As it is, you'll likely bear a scar for months."

"Quit ragging him," Johnson snarled. "If he says he'll ride, he'll ride."

The others started to protest but something stopped them. Mack turned around. Against the sun's glare, he saw Fairbanks striding up to them. Mack couldn't believe the gall.

"Chance, I'm sorry the bit caught you that way. My horse turned into you by accident."

Mack wiped the sweat in his eyes. "Of course, Fairbanks. By accident."

"Get out of here, you jackleg," Johnson said.

Fairbanks stepped back, feigning aggrieved surprise, and left without another word.

In the fifth chukker, with the score still 1–1, Mack and Fairbanks again came together side by side. Fairbanks attempted a back shot, missed, and let his mallet deliberately overswing. Mack saw it coming and ducked, and the mallet hit his canvas helmet. The pain jarred him but at least he hadn't lost an eye.

Two minutes later, racing side by side, Mack and Eagle chased the ball toward the Burlingame goal. Both players raised their mallets high for the next shot. On Mack's near side, Eagle drifted back quickly and reached across to hook Mack's mallet with his.

Mack screamed a curse. Because of the wrist strap, he couldn't let go of the mallet. Eagle snorted and reined his pony to the left, pulling Mack's right arm and mallet over his head. Mack fell from the saddle and his pony, Royal, went down too.

Mack hit the ground in a cloud of dust and the impact sent fiery new pain up and down his bloodied back. Play halted. There were more oaths and recriminations, and another penalty against Burlingame. Mack no longer had any doubt about Fairbanks; there was one man, and only one, whom the lawyer wanted his teammates to foul.

Royal struggled to her feet lame, but it proved temporary. Mack swallowed dust, blistered out a few more profanities, and got up. The pain was excruciating.

Johnson trotted over. "Listen, you'd better stop before—"

"Umpire, I want a remount," Mack yelled, hoarse by now. A wide-shouldered shadow came between him and the white-hot sun.

"Sorry—I don't know how that happened," Eagle grunted, and rode off.

Before the last chukker, Fairbanks brazenly walked close enough to inspect the ponies saved for Riverside's final effort. Mack's Jubilee drew his eye particularly. Checking her saddle, Mack gave the lawyer a hard stare. He'd changed to a borrowed shirt but blood had soaked it too. Quickly Fairbanks finished his count of the Riverside ponies. The team had no extras. He hurried back to his men.

Fairbanks was tired and not a little desperate; he'd expected Burlingame to obliterate the opponents. Now he decided on his strategy. If he could put Mack out of the game, well and good. But if he couldn't, he'd remove that splendid pony from the field. Once Mack's mount was down, he'd be forced to finish the game on that blown-out plug from the first chukker. The advantage should be enough to allow a Burlingame score.

He called the other three to his side. "Gentlemen, let's be clear. Unless you pull this game out, you'll be off the payroll."

Petticlerq, swabbing his pocked face with his helmet, spat on the ground. "We're doing what we're paid to do, you high-assed son of a bitch."

"We're professionals," Rodeen growled.

"Then prove it. Or you're finished at Burlingame and everywhere else. I'll see to it."

The ball was tossed in for the last chukker. Fairbanks bided his time; he needed the perfect opportunity, nothing less. It didn't come until there were only two minutes remaining.

Clive Henley hit the ball, and Billy Rodeen chased and retrieved it with an expert tail shot, Mack and Johnson racing in pursuit. Hanging back, Fairbanks set himself up for the crucial play.

Rodeen's next shot angled the ball obliquely toward the goal. Fairbanks pursued it to the left of its line while Mack galloped in on his right to check the play. Fairbanks knew that aim was critical. Aim, and the appearance of an accident. He booted his pony pitilessly until the horse pulled slightly ahead of Mack's, then counted down in the enormous rushing silence of his brain; instinct and experience told him when to strike.

Savagely, he pulled off the line and delivered a hurtling full swing. It missed the ball and struck Jubilee's front tendon.

With a bellow, she went down, Mack tumbling again. Whistles blew, and the game clock was stopped. There was a sudden hush. Fairbanks reined in, then walked his horse toward Mack, who was running to Jubilee. The little Spanish horse was floundering on her side. Pleased, Fairbanks saw that he'd hit just right. Jubilee's playing days were finished.

Tan dust clouds drifted over the field. Mack knelt beside Jubilee, stroking her. She kept trying to raise herself and uttered great bellowing neighs of pain.

Fairbanks said, "Chance."

Hazel eyes seared his.

"It's turning into a bad-luck match," Fairbanks said. "I didn't see you behind me—"

"The shit you didn't. You destroyed this horse. Get away from me before I do the same to you."

Fairbanks started to reply, thought better, and shook his head in what he hoped was a sorrowful way. He swung his pony around and got a nasty shock. All of his men were staring at him with expressions that stunned him. Roscoe Eagle's was the worst; his brown eyes brimmed with loathing.

"I love horses. Any man who'd ruin one to win a game is scum."

"Shut up," Fairbanks whispered. "Shut up and earn your money or you'll be mucking stalls the rest of your life."

"I'd rather," Petticlerq said.

Billy Rodeen said, "So would I."

One by one they turned their mounts and walked them away.

Play stopped for ten minutes, as grooms rigged a canvas sling around Jubilee and dragged her off. The competitive joy had gone out of the game, and the spectators. Very little noise came from the canvas pavilions.

Mack trotted back on the field on Fireball. The three hired riders seemed to play more slowly now, even clumsily. Fairbanks shouted and hectored, but it did no good. With perhaps a minute left, a foul by Rodeen awarded the toss-in to Riverside. Eric Portfield took it but the ball was soon driven back into Riverside territory. Mack took it out of the pack. They needed 250 yards for a goal.

Mack shot it forward to Johnson, and the Texan slammed a beautiful shot of 150 yards. Fairbanks bent over his pony in wild pursuit, snapping a look over his shoulder. Petticlerq, Eagle, and Rodeen were all behind him, their refusal to help all too apparent.

Hell with them, Fairbanks thought, concentrating on the key shot on which everything depended—a back shot toward the sideline that would allow regrouping for an overtime.

He galloped up beside Hellburner Johnson, who gave him the most murderous look he'd ever seen from a human being. A lemon-colored bandanna streamed behind the sweaty Texan. Both of them jockeyed to hit but Johnson had lulled and fooled his opponent; instead of taking the shot, he leaned his horse into Fairbanks and bumped him out of play.

Fairbanks let out a raspy cry, unable to control his mount for a moment. Mack came up at full gallop and hit the ball resoundingly through the goal.

Before Fairbanks could rein in, the whistle blew.

Riverside 2, Burlingame 1.

Johnson trotted to Fairbanks, mopping his face with the soiled bandanna. "You're lucky you lost nothin' but the game, mister. I wouldn't stay in town after it gets dark."

In the canvas pavilions, the celebration was restrained, even somber. Champagne foamed, and there were expressions of pleasure at the victory, but they were half-hearted. The couples from Burlingame invented excuses for leaving immediately.

Walter Fairbanks didn't want to set foot in the crowd. But he reasoned that his best defense was a pretense that every serious foul and fall had been accidental. So he marched in and stared down all those who stared at him.

Tiny strain lines showed in the sunburn at the corners of his eyes. He felt a headache starting in his forehead, like an iron nail pounded there. Tomorrow morning he'd be too sick to eat. Defeat of any kind undid him; a major defeat rocked his life off the rails. He blamed Chance this time.

At least Carla didn't shun him. She was so flushed, and spoke so fast as she drew him aside, Fairbanks decided she was drunk, sexually aroused, or both. He remained rigid as a soldier, sipping champagne with one hand, plucking his sodden shirt from his skin with the other.

"You played splendidly, Walter."

"It got a little out of hand."

"Not your fault. Accidents happen. I'm very impressed."

She stepped closer, and he noticed the fresh stains of spilled champagne on her bodice. Her eyes had a hot bleary look.

"Please," she whispered, a gloved hand caressing his wrist. "When you have business in Los Angeles again, let me hear from you." Her eyes darted past him. "We'll visit somewhere that's more private."

The overture astonished him. Then, suddenly, it lifted the burden of defeat. Here was a way to win a more important game. He smiled, some of his charm and confidence restored, then he toasted her.

"Thank you for the invitation. I shall certainly try to accept."

She squeezed his wrist, then let go when she noticed Mavis Bunthorne watching.

The champagne refreshed Fairbanks. What did he care about these provincial parvenus, or their opinion of him? "Where is your husband, by the way?"

"He said he wouldn't be coming over. Jubilee's badly injured. I'm afraid Mack cares more about his damn polo ponies than he does about his wife—"

The pistol shot hit like a thunderclap. Conversation stopped, and a woman's gasp rolled through the tent while the echo rolled over the field. Long shadows of the pavilion stretched out on the parched and broken grass. Before dark, Fairbanks left Riverside on the Los Angeles local. He'd given the grooms pay envelopes for his men, who were nowhere to be seen.

MACK SPRAWLED NAKED ON THEIR BED. DOC MEL- **40**
linger had treated his back after the game, taking
two stitches and bandaging the wound. He was spent and wanted nothing more than to sleep and forget. The victory didn't have much savor, not with Jubilee destroyed.

He watched the movement of Carla's shoulders across the room. Wearing a satin gown, she sat in front of her makeup glass, rubbing at her cheeks. All evening, she had showed unusually high color, as if the game's excitement lingered long afterward. Damned odd.

"Carla?"

"What is it?" she replied without turning around, still rubbing her cheeks, rubbing out age lines she imagined she saw there. Her motions were jerky, nervous.

"Now that the game's over, I'm going to schedule a trip to New York later this fall."

"How long will you be gone?"

"I don't know . . . a week or two. I need to look at some irrigation equipment, and there's a firm of civil engineers I want to contact. Then I have to see about financing for those three ranches I'm buying up north."

She swung to face him. "California banks aren't satisfactory any longer?"

He couldn't imagine that she cared. But he answered politely, not wanting another fight. "You know I'm into a lot of ventures. Starting and expanding them takes capital. I should have credit established with the New York banks."

She began to brush out her long yellow hair. "Suit yourself. Just don't expect me to sit here idly and do nothing while you're gone."

With more candor than he intended, Mack said, "I don't expect anything from you anymore."

She threw the hairbrush down and they stared at each other without even minimal friendliness.

Angrily he said, "Good night," and rolled over on his belly to sleep.

41 SLUSH, SOOT, NOISE. THE ELEVATED ROARING. HORSE-drawn vehicles jammed hub to hub up and down Broadway, Fifth, the cross-town streets. Here and there a gasoline carriage, a rare sight. A boy herding pigs along Forty-second Street—not so rare. Telephone poles and water troughs beyond counting, and everywhere ripe brown manure, its smell perfuming the wintry air.

New York. After an hour there, Mack longed for the sunshine and uncluttered landscapes of California.

* * *

At the firm of Wardlow Brothers, Civil Engineers, he met the principals, twins born in Savannah. Each had a pink pate and a fringe of white hair like a friar's; they reminded Mack of Tenniel's drawing of Tweedledum and Tweedledee.

"Gentlemen," Mack said, "I've just visited Professor LeConte, who retired from his chair at Berkeley last year."

"Joe LeConte is a superb geologist and natural scientist," Clemons Wardlow said.

"A Christian and an eminent Georgian," said his brother Cole. "In younger days, we mustered with him against that devil Sherman."

"He recommended you two as the best hydraulic engineers in America. I want to hire you for an irrigation project. A new town."

"In California? We know nothing about California," Cole Wardlow said.

"A definite problem," put in his brother.

"I want you to come out there," Mack said, "for as long as it takes to study and understand the *ciénagas*, the canyon run-off system—the entire situation. Then I want your best recommendation, and I want you to build it."

Dubious, Clemons said, "That would require a considerable investment of time."

"A problem," Cole said.

"It's a system for a new town, you say? Challenging. Perhaps we could adjust our schedules. But Mr. Chance, have you considered the potential cost of our travel and consultation?"

"Another problem," Cole nodded. "Enormous."

Mack threw a banded packet of $100 bills on the desk. "No, that isn't a problem. I want you gentlemen to come to San Solaro, and I'll sit here till you say yes."

William Randolph Hearst roared into the office with his characteristic energy. "Mack! Nellie told me you were coming. She's in a meeting—she'll be here soon. What a sight you are. Hardly the penniless pilgrim who threw our girl into the Bay."

"True," Mack said with a smile. He'd dressed carefully, wanting to make a good impression. His overcoat was an expensive Chesterfield with a velvet collar, his hat a black homburg with a ribbon edge to the brim.

Hearst was in his thirties now, gangly and pop-eyed as ever. Seeing him brought good feelings of old times.

"How are you, Willie?"

"Never better. Welcome to the *Journal*. Morning, evening, and German-language editions." He thumped papers neatly

377

racked on a wall of Nellie's office. The office, on the third floor, overlooked Printing House Square at Park Row and Spruce Street. Down in the square, snow flurried around the noble bronze head of Ben Franklin's statue. It was three days after Christmas, 1897.

Hearst sprawled in a chair. "We're starting to run rings around Joe Pulitzer—can you imagine?"

"I can—knowing the kind of stories you like, and some of the reporters you hire."

Hearst grinned. "Willie's Yellow Fellows. I know it's meant to be an insult, but I like it. I never forget the man I first imagined as my typical reader back home. The gripman on one of the cable cars. Not much schooling, perhaps, but a lot of innate intelligence and curiosity. That man is bored during most of his waking hours. He wants excitement—" Hearst plucked a paper from Nellie's tidy desk. JOURNAL SOLVES GRISLY AX MURDER! He slapped the headline. "The gee-whiz feeling."

Footsteps in the hall quickened Mack's pulse, and then Nellie was in the doorway. "There you are," Hearst exclaimed. He went over and swept an affectionate arm around her. "Still one of my best, Mack."

Mack caught his breath. She looked trim and smart and very citified in a dark skirt and long-sleeved blouse the rich color of an acorn squash. But she'd lost her suntan; she was sallow, like most New Yorkers he'd seen. Into those pale cheeks color rushed now, and she gave him a swift, almost flustered look that was at odds with her sophisticated air. *It isn't all gone; she still feels something*, he thought exultantly.

She tossed sheets of copy on the desk and rushed to hug him.

"I heard you were in the building. I'm sorry I was so long—I was tied up with Mr. Brisbane."

Mack smiled and shook his head to say it didn't matter. His palms were warm, his mouth dry. Suddenly he wondered if he should have come. Seeing her again was painful.

Nellie moved toward the window. "We were expecting you long before Christmas."

"I know I said that in my letters. I had to postpone the trip three times. Press of business."

"Chance—the California millionaire." Hearst beamed. "You said you'd do it. You did."

At the window, Nellie watched the snow, as if reluctant to look at him too long. He felt a heartbreaking desire. Did it show?

"How is everyone? How's Bierce?"

"Still in Washington, slashing away." Hearst pulled another paper from the rack. A front-page cartoon caricatured old Huntington with dollar signs for eyes. He had his hands deep in the pockets of an oblivious Uncle Sam. "Just when we've got the old devil on the run—beaten on the debt issue—I'm going to lose the young woman whose copy helped turn the trick."

"You mean our Nell?"

"Now wait, it isn't definite—" she began.

"Yes," Hearst cut in. "Miss Ross may not realize that her departure is inevitable, not to say imminent, but I do. I've read her novel."

"A novel," Mack exclaimed. "You always said you'd write one."

"And it's damn good," Hearst said. "Nellie, take the day off. Show our California tycoon what a big city looks like."

"Yes, sir, gladly."

And she turned to look at Mack again, ravishingly beautiful to him as she stood before the window, New York's rooftops a winter quilt of black and white behind her. *What a special woman she is,* he thought. Her long-sleeved blouse with its full-flowing tie glowed like the California sun.

But not half so brightly as her eyes.

She showed him the sights, including one he especially wanted to see: Bartholdi's immense Statue of Liberty in the harbor. They gazed at it walking arm in arm through light snow in Battery Park.

They went next to Koster and Bial's Music Hall at Thirty-fourth, in Herald Square. In the darkened auditorium they watched flickering projections on a twenty-foot screen. Surf rolled in and crashed on the beach at Dover, England. An eccentric comedian danced and fell down. A woman with ringlets, sloe eyes, and gauze pantaloons swayed and twisted in a harem dance. Broadway stars May Irwin and John Rice indulged in a prolonged humorous kiss, his soup-strainer mustache tickling the lady's face. Despite the humorous tone, the kiss footage had aroused preachers and incited demands for "police interference."

The climax of the Vitascope show was film of a locomotive rushing down a track straight at the audience. Many at the matinee screamed, and Mack unconsciously grabbed Nellie's hand. Open-mouthed, he sat spellbound in darkness.

Afterward they ate at one of Nellie's favorite spots, the German Gardens, across Printing House Square and around the corner from City Hall. He told her about the New York bankers, about Wardlow Brothers and Professor LeConte at Berkeley. Nellie had studied with LeConte and admired him. "He was a charter member of John's Sierra Club."

She in turn told him stories about the paper.

Hearst had backed Bryan in the recent presidential campaign, and she'd trooped around the country with the candidate, one of the first women ever to report from the campaign trail. "You can't imagine the places I slept. Silver-tongued oratory all day, bedbugs all night."

Mr. Hearst continued to believe in the power of articles about pseudoscience and sex, so she wrote many of those (DO SEA MONSTERS THREATEN OUR SHORES?; REPUBLICANS CAUGHT IN LOVE NEST). The *Journal* still boosted its circulation with stunts, though some were now on a much broader scale, with international ramifications:

"Almost every day we print a dispatch about the Cuban rebellion: cruelty to prisoners in Spanish detention camps, priests beaten and burned alive, nuns raped and fed to the sharks in Havana harbor—I'm glad I'm not involved with our foreign news. Most of the stories are invented."

"Why?"

"Mr. Hearst wants war. Joe Pulitzer just up the street at the *World* wants war. They're trying to prove who wants it most."

"For principle, or circulation?"

"Not funny," she said, batting at his head. It was the spontaneity of old times. Her hand accidentally brushed his and she reacted with a start and a frown, then renewed concentration on her plate of schnitzel. Mack felt guilty about his own abrupt physical reaction, mercifully hidden by the red-and-white tablecloth.

Guilty, but not surprised. God, he loved her.

Nellie's studio flat overlooked the East River and Roebling's mammoth bridge to Brooklyn. It was not an untidy place; in fact the first impression was of spareness and space. Yet it had a bohemian quality, compounded by stacks of books and manuscripts, a guitar with colored ribbons hanging from the neck, the familiar pallets of fur, her silver samovar. Many mementos of California decorated the walls: bright Indian blankets, the photo of her relative in the round fur hat, a lithograph of the Bay that made him homesick.

As the dark came down and lights twinkled along the East River, the snow fell harder outside the three large arched windows. Glad to be inside, Mack sat reading Nellie's manuscript in front of an applewood fire. *A Daughter of California* dealt with the Anglo takeover of the state after the Gold Rush. It told the story of an affluent young woman, a Californio, who fell in love with a raffish American adventurer despite the warnings of her parents and friends. What the American really wanted was not the girl but the family's *rancho*. After he married her and took it away by means of the property laws and her inferior position under them, he threw her over. Her suicide in the ocean ended the short novel, which was part history, part treatise on women's rights. The prose was lean, like a news dispatch, though it was more emotional, bitter. He heard Bierce in it. The general style of the work was gritty and naturalistic. Because of the author's omniscient viewpoint, the reader was never deceived about the romance, as the heroine was.

The ring of Nellie's telephone had interrupted at one point. After the operator made the connection she spoke softly. "No, Frank. No, my dear, not this evening, I have company. Yes, Friday. As we planned. Yes, I do. Yes. Good night."

She hung up the earpiece and without comment busied herself in the open kitchen attached to the loft. So she wasn't lonely, nor living a spinster's life, pining for him. Why had he been conceited enough to think she might be? He hated the unseen Frank.

He squared up the pages after he finished the last chapter. "Nellie, I'm no critic, but I think Willie's right. It's powerful stuff."

"Thank you. I worship the work of Émile Zola: *The Dram Shop; Germinal.* Of course all you get in English are censored versions. But I hope I've paid him homage."

"I write a business letter—it creaks. You write without any sign of effort."

She laughed. "You can't imagine the hours and the agony it takes to achieve that effect." She carried plates to a small candle-lit table by the center window.

"It's going to be published, isn't it?"

"Yes, Appleton's. In the spring."

"That's grand. Congratulations."

She brought a green bottle to the table. "I've had this for weeks, anticipating your visit."

"Miraville Winery. Napa Chardonnay. What a treat."

He touched her hand at the same time as the label, standing close to her. A troubled look fleeted across her firelit face and she stepped away. The wind made the windows whine. He felt a chill off the glass, and another, different sort as they sat down.

"You really haven't told me much about yourself," Nellie said when they began eating.

"Not much to tell. I keep busy. I keep making money."

"Is your wife well?"

"Yes, Carla's all right." He snatched his wineglass and drank. The snow fell faster; he could scarcely see the bridge now, and the heights of Brooklyn not at all.

He watched the snow a while. "Last night, in that fine soft bed at the Astor House, the blizzard nightmare came back. When I walked outside this morning, there was the same snow. I know why I live in California." She smiled. He sampled the cold vegetable she'd prepared with a touch of vinaigrette. "These avocados are fine."

"They're from home. Like the oranges for dessert." She pointed to a bowl on the kitchen counter.

"Can you buy California navels here?"

"Yes, at the grocer's on the corner."

"Those oranges might well be mine, you know."

"There, you see? The railroad isn't all bad. Please don't tell Mr. Hearst I said that. Now I want to hear about this yacht you're buying."

"I haven't actually commissioned it. But I'm talking to designers, and I know what I want. Two hundred feet, minimum."

"Won't that require a huge crew?"

"I anticipate forty to fifty men. I can afford it. I told you I'd go back to San Francisco in style."

"And you're ready."

"Soon."

"It just delights me that you're doing so well. You must be very content."

"Content? I don't know—" He picked up the wineglass again, deeply chilled by the invisible breath of winter radiating from the windowpanes. He rose and walked to the fireplace. The applewood burned sweetly, its light burnishing the bowl of oranges so they glowed like spheres of gold. "There's always one more Klondike to explore, one more vein of gold to find. Sometimes I regret I'm too busy to chase off to Alaska and follow the new strike."

"But you are successful, and happy—?"

He turned around and laughed ruefully.

"Never ask that question of a married man."

"I didn't mean to pry, or—"

He startled her by striding to the table and setting his glass down firmly. He turned her in her chair, holding both her shoulders from above.

"No, I'm not happy. I tried to make it work with Carla but it hasn't."

"Mack, please . . ." She pried at his right hand, a curiously innocent, almost frightened expression on her face.

"It would be different with you," he went on. "That's the real reason I came to New York. To say that."

Deftly, she slipped away from him. Standing by the window nearest his chair, she said, "Carla struck me as an intelligent woman. I expect she knows how you feel."

His tooled boots rapped the floor as he followed her. He set the chair out of the way and caught her shoulders from behind. "Forget about Carla."

He kissed the back of her neck above her collar. The dark hairs were downy-warm. His mouth moved to the left, the curve to her shoulder, his right hand sliding around to find her breast.

She sagged and pressed back into him. "Oh dear God." She clasped both hands on top of his.

He released her long enough for her to turn, and she raised her arms around his neck and kissed him with her mouth opening a little, and her sweet tongue telling of memories of Yosemite, the falls' roar all about them, and this same fire licking up within them—

The moment broke when he started to pick her up in his arms.

"No, Mack." She was quiet but firm and pushed him away with a final, dogged "No."

"Why not? No one will know."

"We'll know."

"Nellie, I love you."

"I love you. That doesn't make any difference. An affair is never worth the turmoil and pain it causes. It hurts everyone, even those not directly involved."

Shocked, he realized she was admitting something. Anger found its way into his voice. "You're an expert, are you?"

She collected herself by the fire. "Yes, but never mind the circumstances; it's in the past. It happened soon after I came here. I think I was trying to get over you. Anyway—if we did what we'd both like, eventually we'd all suffer. You, and me—and your wife."

"I doubt she'd be overly concerned."

"I'm sorry, Mack. The answer's no."

She tucked her golden blouse into the waist of her skirt and smoothed it. He could almost see her walling up her emotions

383

with the cement of reason and will. "We must go on with our lives as they are. I have the novel to look forward to—you have San Francisco to conquer—another page to turn in that guide-book. Do you still have it?"

"On my desk in Riverside."

"Haines—that was the author. I still intend to look him up someday."

"You're changing the subject. I want to discuss—"

"No, it's settled. I'm glad you came to visit, very glad. But that's all it's going to be. A visit."

"Damn your fine high principles, Nellie—"

She stiffened and seemed to withdraw into herself as she hurried to the kitchen. "Will you be staying in New York a few more days?" she asked, returning with the bowl of oranges.

"Earlier this afternoon I thought so." He paused, his eyes bleak. "But I find there's nothing left to do. I'll catch a train tomorrow."

"Then you'll be traveling on New Year's Eve."

"Yes, I'll probably celebrate by watching the snowdrifts go by in some godforsaken place like Iowa or Nebraska. What does it matter?"

He was furious with her; he'd never loved anyone so much.

Nellie held out the bowl. "Would you care for an orange?"

"No thanks. I get all that I need back home."

Two hours after Mack left, the storm became a blizzard. Nellie heard the building creaking and stumbled from her hard narrow bed to peer out the window. She could barely see the bridge, or anything else, for the wind-driven whiteness.

She hadn't been sleeping. She felt wound tight inside and her feet were stiff with cold. She'd piled all the fur pallets onto the bed, but they didn't help. How she wished he were here for—

No, she mustn't think that. She had been so close to giving in tonight—too close. He was a married man now. But he was still a potent force in her life, she'd been stunned to discover when she first saw him with Mr. Hearst at the office. She hurried back to bed in the frigid darkness and shivered under the furs, remembering how he looked, how he touched her, all the small things he said to interest and secretly delight her—

Damn your fine high principles, Nellie. He said that, too.

"Oh God, yes, I wish I could. I wish I could," she murmured as she turned her tear-streaked face into the pillow.

* * *

On the last day of 1897, Carla went out to Pasadena on the Santa Fe. The train was packed with tourists, and she resented their noise and good cheer. She could only think of Mack and how he'd abandoned her a week before Christmas to travel to New York.

I'm the one who does the abandoning, my friend. You'll see.

"The Tournament of Roses" is a name well chosen to convey to the blizzard-bound sons and daughters of the East one of the sources of enjoyment of which we boast here in the Land of Perennial Sunshine.

So said the official parade program lying open on her lap. It was a splendid morning in the San Gabriel Valley, January 1, 1898. Carla was expensively, even extravagantly dressed. So were all the ladies crowding the veranda of this fine house on Orange Grove Avenue. It belonged to a vice president of the Bank of Pasadena, a dull little man who did business with Carla's father.

Since its inception on New Year's Day, 1890, the Tournament had become an important event on the Southern California calendar. A local traveler and promoter had persuaded the Valley Hunt Club to sponsor a parade of vehicles, followed by an afternoon of games and concerts. The promoter remembered colorful flower festivals he'd seen while traveling in the Mediterranean, and he suggested that parade entries carry floral decoration. The event was supposed to be an antidote to the low spirits that followed the bursting of the land bubble in '88. A corporation of private citizens ran the event now, and it attracted more tourists every year.

Precisely at ten-thirty the guests on the veranda heard music from Colorado Avenue, and they put aside their punch and champagne, their plates of fresh watermelon and strawberries in cream, and crowded to the rail to await the first units turning south on Orange Grove. Utterly bored, Carla nevertheless joined them, feigning enthusiasm.

Following the color guard came the City Band, blaring Sousa's "Thunderer March," then the gentlemen of the Valley Hunt Club, red boutonnieres in their lapels, red rosettes brightening the bridles of their thoroughbreds. There were marching units and bicycle units. A ten-man glee club rolled by on tandems, singing "My Old Kentucky Home." But the loudest applause was reserved for the vehicles artfully smothered with roses and geraniums, carnations and marigolds, sunflowers and chrysanthemums in blankets and garlands and sprays. Every wheel bore flowers, and every harness and headstall. Green chains of twining smilax complemented the flowers. Carla soon grew glassy-eyed at so much color.

Entries ranged from modest to magnificent, and were sorted into categories, starting with single Shetland-pony carts, tandem goat carts, and burro carts. Hotels and businesses entered huge gleaming four-in-hand and six-in-hand road coaches driven by professional whips. On top of these splendid equipages were giggling, waving girls, the prettiest to be found. Pennants of blue, yellow, and cardinal decorated the first-, second-, and third-prize entries in each category.

Professor Thaddeus Lowe, who had operated the Union balloon corps in the Civil War, was represented by six vehicles. Lowe and his family rode in the first one, a George IV phaeton. Something of a local celebrity, the professor operated a narrow-gauge scenic railway running to the summit of a peak named, predictably, Mount Lowe.

Carla's host and hostess sought her out.

"Enjoying yourself, my dear?" the banker's wife asked.

"Oh yes, it's beautiful." She hated it.

"After lunch we'll drive to the park," the banker said. "There are bicycle races, ring tournaments, burro races—it's thrilling."

Anyone thrilled by a burro race is an idiot, Carla thought. She smiled. "I certainly hope to go with you. But I seem to have developed a ferocious pain just here." She pressed a spot between her eyebrows. "I have it at certain times. It lasts for hours, sometimes a whole day."

They understood the feminine code, and withdrew graciously. At the conclusion of the parade, she pleaded indisposition and returned to her suite at the Green Park Hotel. She ordered a light lunch, ate it, bathed, and settled down to wait for him.

It was half past ten. They lay naked in the darkness beneath the crinkly sheet.

"I'm glad you telegraphed me, Mrs. Chance."

"And I'm so happy you could arrange to come down for the Tournament, Mr. Fairbanks."

"You're certain your husband is still in New York?"

"Yes. You'll be able to conduct all of your urgent business without interruption."

He laughed and seized her billowy breast. He was hasty, even a bit rough, but his muscles and his masculine smell aroused her. Her arm flew around his neck and, like a devouring animal, she opened her mouth. Soon he was jerking up and down deep inside her. She hung on his neck, imagining Mack's face if he could see this.

Then, overcome, she flung her head back and cried out.

Fairbanks took her three times in as many hours. After they slept, at her insistence, he came into her again. At half past four in the morning he crept out, shut the door, adjusted the DO NOT DISTURB tag, and returned to his own hotel.

ON FEBRUARY 15 THE BATTLESHIP *MAINE* BLEW UP **42** in Havana harbor. Of her crew of 350, 260 died.

Everyone suspected a Spanish mine, and war fever spread like an epidemic. A balky President McKinley backed step by step toward armed intervention, flogged by his Republican colleagues and the yellow press. Hearst and Pulitzer trumpeted their vindication and demanded military action: REMEMBER THE MAINE!

Villa Mediterranean seemed a long way from all that. A copy of *A Daughter of California* arrived, its flyleaf inscribed *Affectionately—N*. Mack decided not to show it to Carla.

Carla had been surprisingly pleasant, even ardent, when he came home. One evening early in April, they went driving down on the flats in their black trap with the elegant thin gold stripe on the side, taking a dirt road through the groves of ripening Valencias. The dark-green leaves rustled in a warm breeze and the perfume of the trees was thick and heady.

Carla asked him to stop the trap. Noticeably pale, she rubbed her arms. "I'm so glad spring's here."

"Are you feeling well? You seem to have lost color lately."

"Just a little faint now and then." She fixed her eyes on the multicolored clouds of evening, and it was hard to say whether she was disturbed or merely intent. "There's a reason for it, Mack," she said finally, resting her hand on his.

Mack snatched the receiver off the hook and racked the crank around twice. God, when would they get the new express phones that didn't require cranking?

"Central exchange."

"Harriet, this is Chance. Ring Doc Mellinger, please."

387

"Mr. Chance, it's five past eight. I was just about to close up and go home."

"Damn it, Harriet, this is an emergency. Ring him."

Dr. Gustav Mellinger answered in his perpetually grumpy Teutonic voice, and Mack barked, "Doc? Mack Chance. Will you come up here first thing in the morning? You need to see Carla. She's expecting again."

Later that night, they lay in each other's arms.

"It's wonderful news," he said. "But I'm not sure I know when we—"

"One of those nights right after you came home. The baby's due early in October, I think."

"Does it please you, Carla?"

She was silent a while. "I'll be honest. I never intended for it to happen again. Papa told you I'm not the domestic type. But I refuse to risk my life by going to one of those filthy midwives in some back alley in Los Angeles. I'll make the best of it."

"Yes, yes," he said, chafing her hand to warm it. "Things will be better from now on."

With a bitter little laugh, she patted his cheek. "You're always so optimistic."

"No, I feel it. I'm sure of it."

He wanted to be enthusiastic. Why was it so hard?

On April 19, Congress passed a resolution declaring that Cuba should be free of foreign domination. It empowered the President to so inform the Spanish government and intervene with appropriate force to bring it about. McKinley put his signature to the resolution next day.

At the end of the following week, Mack and Johnson took a Friday-night walk through the packing house down on the flats. Both of Mack's packing houses were showplaces because of the general cleanliness and electric lights.

The place was busy, and the spring crop looked exceptional. For this seasonal work, Mack employed mostly older men, married women, and young girls, at least a third of them Mexican. They worked in large interconnected rooms; the finishing lines ran straight through archways. Windows without glass admitted plenty of fresh air.

Mack and Johnson started their walk at the sorting conveyer. Oranges put onto the conveyer by hand had already been brushed, then washed. Farther down, men and women on either side of the conveyer plucked up the rolling oranges and sent them into three spillways, one for each grade. They worked quickly, their white cotton gloves darting and swooping like so many hungry birds.

Mack leaned over the shoulder of a stout woman and plucked an orange out of a channel. "That's a standard, not a fancy, Margarita." He gave her shoulder a forgiving squeeze, she returned an apologetic smile, and he and Johnson walked on.

Mack broke the skin of the orange with his thumbnails, then sucked the juice and some of the pulp. Johnson stared at the light fixtures. He had a distracted air this evening, and kept tugging at his sky-blue bandanna.

Something occurred to Mack. "I'm going to put stools in here. Convince the Exchange to do it everywhere."

"Why should the growers spend the money?"

"Why should these people stand up for nine hours and break their backs?"

As they passed into the next large room, Johnson's green eyes drifted back to the ceiling, or somewhere beyond. Mack said, "Where's your head tonight? It isn't here."

"Down in Texas, I reckon. That's where I'm goin'."

"Back home? Fort Worth?"

"Camp Wood, San Antonio. Leonard Wood and Roosevelt, that blue-blooded pup from the Navy Department, they're puttin' together the First Volunteer Cavalry Regiment. I read all about it. They want men who can handle a horse. Cowboys, polo players—I fit on both counts."

"Is the regiment supposed to fight?"

"Damn right. Chase those damn Spics out of Cuba."

"Hugh, forty-six is too old for that."

"I'm only forty-five. I'll shoe-black the gray in my hair and lie like hell. I seen a lot of sights and wonders, but never a war. I bought my train ticket this afternoon."

Depressed suddenly, Mack walked on. In this room the wide conveyer with its spillways branched into three separate packing lines. On each, women wrapped the fruit in pieces of bright-orange tissue. Farther down the line, other women—Mack's best, carefully chosen—speedily packed the fruit into two-compartment crates. A Calgold label with the old prospector covered one end of boxes containing the fancy-grade oranges. Less attractive labels, with different trade names, identified the lesser grades.

The packers chatted and laughed as they worked. Many had the tanned, coarse look of farm wives. This room was even noisier than the sorting room. As soon as a box was full, a packer yelled, "Box!" and a rustler ran up. Rustlers were always strong young boys, because it was the hardest work. A filled box weighed seventy pounds.

Mack noticed a boy's thumb bleeding as he raced by with his load. The box's coarse shook often ripped palms and fingers. Mack took a pencil and scrap of paper from his shirt pocket. "Got to tell Biggerstaff they need gloves in here." He put the paper against a pillar and scribbled.

"Listen, you got any objection to me traipsin' off?"

"No, I told you before—you can always leave whenever you want."

"If I go, I won't be around when your kid's born. I mean—in case you need help."

They walked out a side door into the warm breezy dark. "Isn't a hell of a lot you could do for me if you stayed."

"I'd cheer you up, if I could. You ain't exactly been clickin' your heels over the prospect of a youngster."

Electric light from the shed fell across Mack's bleak face. "I feel guilty about it. I don't know why this mood's on me. Maybe . . ." He shoved his hands in the back pockets of his jeans and gazed at the rustling trees. "Maybe it's because the whole marriage doesn't amount to much."

Johnson spilled pouch tobacco into a cigarette paper and rolled it. "Well, you was pretty impulsive about gettin' hitched. But then, bein' impulsive's one of your good traits too. Not like that stiff-collar lawyer Fairbanks, or some others I've met."

"I'm not sure Carla wants the baby."

"I don't 'spect she does, very much. She's a handsome woman, but she ain't cut out for home and hearth. Puts a double burden on you, 'f you want my opinion."

"I don't think so."

Johnson struck a match on his pants. "Too bad—you get it anyway."

He lit the cigarette dangling from his lip. "You clean forget about your wife sometimes. You're busy eighteen, twenty hours a day—you was in New York a mighty long time just for some business calls. That newspaper girl's in New York, ain't she? The one who wrote the book?"

"Forget about her. She has nothing to do with this."

Johnson didn't believe it, but he didn't argue. "All right. I'm just sayin' once again—don't nail Carla too hard if she gets the fidgets. You ain't exactly payin' court to her every minute of the day. Still, none of that matters a tad when it comes to this here youngster. You're the papa, so you got to do your part and maybe some of Carla's too, you want to raise the kid right."

"Do you think I'd want to do anything else? That baby will be cared for regardless of how Carla feels."

"Why, sure," Johnson said softly. "I was just remindin' you."

America fought her splendid little war on two fronts, and it lasted 105 days. In the Caribbean, General Shafter's expeditionary force whipped the imperialists on the island of Cuba, and General Miles whipped them on Puerto Rico. In the Philippines, Commodore Dewey, General Wesley Merritt, and Philippine rebels besieged the Manila garrison. On July 30, McKinley demanded Spain's surrender and dictated the terms. Spain capitulated during the second week of August, agreeing to cede Puerto Rico and Guam to the United States, and allow her to occupy Cuba and the Philippines. The victors counted about five thousand lives lost, 90 percent of them to yellow fever and dysentery.

In late August, Sergeant Hellburner Johnson came home from the war. About two dozen people gathered at the Riverside depot to meet his train an hour before dawn. Mack drove the black trap through a heavy wet mist that enfolded the town. The headlight of the local stabbed the fog and the train chugged in. As the conductor helped Johnson down the steps, the well-wishers clapped. Johnson shook his head, amazed. He picked up his portmanteau in his left hand, supporting his right side with a forearm crutch. His right foot, the one they'd replaced with cork, dragged over the wooden platform.

A Spanish sniper had hit him on July 1, during the advance on the hilltop village of El Caney. "Ain't nothin' like them Mauser bullets. You heard 'em comin' through the palmettos: *zzzzz*. If you heard 'em go *chug*, you knew they got somebody. I heard one go *chug* and looked down and it was me."

He'd recuperated in a Tampa hospital for a month. Considering his permanent injury, he was in good spirits. "Teach me to go sashayin' off to a war like it was a party. Well, I never was much for dancin' with the ladies. Rather get 'em into bed right off."

He was full of stories about his regiment: "Newspaper boys couldn't decide what to call it. Teddy's Terrors was one handle. Teddy's Gilded Gang—that was another. Finally a name stuck: Rough Riders."

Stories about the second-in-command: "Teddy really ran the

outfit. He's an all-right sort for a dude who wears little spectacles the size of dimes."

Stories about Nellie: "Colonel Roosevelt, he read her book. Dean, the Harvard football quarterback, he was carryin' it. So was Stephen Crane, a reporter fella. He said Nellie was famous."

"She's getting there," Mack agreed. "The book is selling fast. It'll be published in Europe this fall."

Johnson had questions, too.

"How's Carla gettin' on?"

"Physically she's fine. She's big now and she hates that. She stays in bed a lot. I sleep in another bedroom. She wants it that way."

On the night of September 27, ten days after Mack turned thirty without a celebration, Carla went into labor. Nearly twenty-four hours later, Dr. Gustav Mellinger stepped out of the master bedroom. Mack jumped up from a chair where he'd been dozing. Before Doc Mellinger shut the door, Mack heard a squall.

"Doc, is everything—"

"Fine, my boy. Your son is fine, your wife is doing well."

Mack slumped against the wall. He'd slept only lightly, sitting up, since the vigil had begun the previous night. His rumpled clothes had a stale odor, his skin a clammy feel. In spite of it all, his spirits lifted.

"Tell me about him."

"He weighs six and one half pounds. Very strong lungs. You can see him. Your wet nurse has already cleaned him up."

The old German stood aside with a gesture of permission. Mack tugged his vest down and tucked in his shirt. As he put his hand on the knob, Mellinger squeezed his shoulder and gave him a keen look he couldn't interpret. Congratulations? Or some kind of commiseration?

He heard his son's soft sucking cry before he saw him. The wet nurse held him in clean soft cotton blankets. Her name was Angelina Olivar. About thirty-five, she had only last month lost her first child, an infant son. Her shiftless husband had run off some months before. She had long braids, compassionate eyes, and a huge bosom contained in a tentlike blouse.

"Señor Chance, mire que magnífico se ve."

With a new father's trepidation, Mack lifted a corner of the outer blanket. He gasped at the strange sight of a little red head with a cap of blond fuzz, slitted eyes, puckish open mouth. He touched a tiny fist, still moist. Slowly, like a dawn, the miracle of birth lit Mack's face.

The boy-child started to cry again. Angelina Olivar jogged him in her fat arms and nodded Mack onward, toward the bed.

Doc Mellinger had chosen to deliver the baby under gaslight, keeping it trimmed low, and the dimness softened some of the harsh ancillaries of the birth: basins in a corner, still full of pink water, bloodied cloths.

In the rumpled bed, Carla sat with her unkempt hair spilling over the shoulders of her gown. Her dark-blue eyes looked huge as moons, and momentarily vacant. She was pale, sweaty, as unattractive as Mack had ever seen her. He took her hand. The line of her mouth remained downcast.

"The baby's fine."

"I know."

"Are you all right?"

"It hurt. My God, it hurt. I never felt anything so awful."

"What shall we name him? We talked about it but we never decided. I'd like to give him my father's name."

"Give him any name you want."

The bluntness stunned him, but he tried not to show it. Carla rolled her cheek onto the pillow, away from him. He felt suddenly helpless.

"Do you want to hold him again?"

"No. I did my part. Now you take care of him. Just like the rest of your property."

And so he did. He named his son James Ohio Chance II, and ordered special blankets from Los Angeles. On the corner of each, in handsome embroidery, the seamstress reproduced the familiar cartouche, but with the initials *JOC.*

IN THE LATE FALL, ENGINEERS FROM WARDLOW **43** Brothers established a field office at San Solaro. Mack hired a firm of land planners, and interviewed real estate men in Los Angeles. Before Christmas he signed an agreement with a successful broker named William Hazard. Hazard's Sundown Sea Realty Corporation would be the primary selling agent for the new town.

In January 1899, Cole and Clemons Wardlow stepped off the Southern Pacific in Los Angeles, and soon plunged into their studies and preparations for designing a water system. The brothers neither drank nor smoked. For relaxation they read the Scriptures. They worked six days a week, and as many nights. On Sundays they worshiped at a Baptist church.

Toward the end of the month, a wrinkled envelope without an address brought Mack a tear sheet from the Monarch of the Dailies. On January 15 the *Examiner* had published a poem called "The Man with the Hoe." The paper presented it in decorative type, with an ornamental border. Across the bottom Mack found a scrawled message: *A wonderful work of socialist conscience. The whirlwind is coming. Marquez.*

The poet, Edwin Markham, drew his inspiration from Millet's famous painting, now owned by the Crockers. The first lines captured the image in words.

> Bowed by the weight of centuries he leans
> Upon his hoe and gazes on the ground . . .

In the body of the poem Markham unleashed his wrath on the proprietors—the owners—who condemned the man with the hoe to a life of crushing labor.

> O masters, lords and rulers in all lands,
> Is this the handiwork you give to God,
> This monstrous thing distorted and soul-quencht?

The poem spread from paper to paper like a prairie fire. America embraced it as a literary sensation. Swampy Hellman didn't embrace it, however. On one of his weekend visits, he found the tear sheet and complained to Mack.

"This is garbage. This Markham, who is he? Some pink anarchist from New York?"

"A schoolteacher. Oakland, I think."

"They got lynch ropes in Oakland too. You know what Mr. Huntington said about this? He said any man should be grateful to have a hoe."

"Come on, Markham's right. Too many rich men exploit the poor. I like the poem."

"You like anything that's radical. You're a crazy person, a disgrace to your class. How you got such a fine son I don't know. Here, I got things for him. A toy pistol. Genuine Colt reproduction, bang, bang. Outside there's a little surrey you can hitch to a pony. He can ride around the estate.''

Mack laughed. ''When he can sit up. You'll spoil him, Swampy.''

''I got a right. I'm his grandpa.''

And a queer old bandit, Mack thought. Marquez wrote of the whirlwind of rising expectations among workingmen. What would Swampy do if that storm caught him? As a matter of fact, what would *he* do?

> How will it be with kingdoms and with kings—
> With those who shaped him to the thing he is—
> When this dumb Terror shall rise to judge the world,
> After the silence of the centuries?

By March 1899, the old depot office at San Solaro had been remodeled and expanded. Watercolor renderings and a plaster model of the new town, complete with blue water in the canal, offered prospects an attractive view of their future residence. Mack had written personal letters to all of the people who had closed on the earliest lots, describing the new water system and his plans for a real community and encouraging them to consider a home in San Solaro. He had three replies from couples near retirement who said they would enthusiastically consider it.

While the derricks pumped away, carpenters hammered up the framing for a row of four model cottages. They were done in Mission Revival, and were small neat homes of stucco with roofs of red tile and central patios to let in the sunshine and the fragrance of flowers. In his mind Mack defined the kind of future buyers he wanted in San Solaro: solid, settled middle-class folk eager to work or retire in Southern California. He didn't want a town of country-club types, or part-time residents.

He spent most of his weekdays in San Solaro while Johnson stayed in Arlington Heights to supervise the groves. The Texan had discarded his crutch and no longer limped so noticeably. Once a day he practiced walking in front of a mirror, balancing for minutes at a time on his cork foot or simply standing and watching the reflection, making sure his shoulders were level. ''Don't want the field hands callin' me a second-class man. Don't want to give up my glorious polo career neither. Those fellas on the club, they start thinkin' I'm a crip, they're liable to vote me off. Ain't fair, but that's how people treat somebody with a hurt like this.''

Mack returned to Villa Mediterranean every Friday and spent long hours with his son, whom he took to calling Little Jim. Carla usually wasn't home, and when she was, she showed no interest in the baby. Mack's interest, on the other hand, was boundless. Each new development—a gurgle that a proud father could misconstrue as speech, a bump on the gum that might be a tooth—was a source of wonder. Angelina Olivar tended the child well, and she never spoke a word against his mother.

In April, construction began on a breakwater at San Pedro. After years of advances and reverses, C. P. Huntington at last gave up the harbor fight. Mack tried to imagine Huntington's face—probably waxy and sullen with the rage of senility; he was almost eighty. Mack pictured Fairbanks too. It was shameful to be so vindictive, but he enjoyed it thoroughly.

A few days later the Sundown Sea Realty people began bringing prospects from Los Angeles. If Mack had a free hour, he showed them around the tract personally. He was with a couple from Michigan one Thursday afternoon, strolling by the canal.

". . . so if you build a home here, you can be assured of a permanent water supply. San Solaro Irrigation, the company set up to be owned by the residents, just completed negotiations for all the land between here and Cat Canyon. The canyon runoff will be a primary source of our water. Wardlow Brothers is designing a two-thousand-foot tunnel to trap and channel the flow in the underground gravel beds. We'll also have a diversion dam, and all the lines necessary to bring the water down here to a community reservoir. Pure, fresh water will be piped to every lot. It will fill this canal too, though the canal's function is largely ornamental. The Wardlows are the best in the nation. They're working this minute in those temporary offices you saw. As a general partner in San Solaro Irrigation, I'll finance the system and you'll vote ten shares of stock that accompany your building lot. Assuming, of course, that you decide to buy."

"I've decided," said the gentleman, a retired bank officer. "I like the layout. And I like your cut, Mr. Chance. Straightforward."

Mack thought of Wyatt Paul's hyperbole and smiled. "Well, I try to back up every promise."

"I do have a few more questions about—" The gentleman stopped, noticing a man from the Wardlow office hurrying toward them.

The man drew Mack aside. "Mrs. Olivar just got through

396

on the telephone. She asks that you come home right away. Your son has a bad fever—a hundred and three or four. He's had it since Monday night, and the doctor can't bring it down."

"What about Mrs. Chance? She's there, isn't she?"

The man replied with an embarrassed nod. "Yes, sir. But Mrs. Olivar said . . . uh . . . she said your wife refused to be bothered. She told Mrs. Olivar to call you."

Mack apologized to the retired couple and left immediately. He also lost the sale.

Riding the local trains, it took him most of the afternoon and part of the evening to get back, arriving at the Riverside station at half past nine. One of the housemen met him with a pair of saddle horses, and they galloped up to the heights. Mack was grimy from traveling and exhausted too; the hours en route had left him free to worry.

He dashed directly upstairs to the large nursery. Doc Mellinger met him with encouraging news: The fever had broken about six o'clock, and Little Jim was sleeping comfortably.

Carla was downstairs in the living room. Mack recognized the slurred speech and slightly foggy gaze. How long had she been at the liquor?

"Carla, Jim's your responsibility too. I can't be here all the time."

With an airy wave and an unsteady step, she started for the sideboard. "Then someone else will have to be. I went through the ordeal of having him. That was enough."

He placed himself between his wife and the liquor decanters and jerked the glass from her hand. "Listen. For six months you've hardly looked at that boy. You let another woman suckle him—"

"Yes." She shuddered. "The very idea's repulsive."

"—and you force Angelina to take care of him all day, every day, except when I can get home—"

She pushed his arm. "Get out of the way. I want a drink."

"Keep your voice down. You don't get another drink until I say so. I may never say so."

"Goddamn it, you run everything else—you're not going to run me." She struck at him with her fists. He dodged away, tossed the empty glass in a chair, and grasped her wrists, holding her easily. She tried to stamp his foot.

"Carla, calm down and listen to me. I'm telling you again, you have a responsibility to the boy."

"Why? I didn't want him. I don't love him."

Mack let her go then. He stepped back and stared at her. "That's the most obscene thing I've ever heard."

"It's the *truth*." She beat her leg with her fist and started to cry. "I warned you I couldn't handle marriage. Papa warned you. I was sick of it six months after the honeymoon. But I kept trying. I kept hoping it would be different with you. But it wasn't. It isn't."

"I don't give a damn—you have a duty to that child."

"Duty? Go to hell. I'm not cut out for *duty*. I'm good for drinking, and for screwing, and for being shown off to your friends like a piece you bought at an auction gallery. But no duty, Mack. Fuck your duty. Fuck it. Fuck it."

She ran past him to the liquor, and this time he let her.

He listened to the glassware clinking, and her crying, and tried to sort it all out. His emotions whipsawed back and forth between fury and compassion for her wretched state. How could he cope with this?

He had to start by calming her. Touching her shoulder, he said as gently as he could, "Let's go for a walk. It's a beautiful evening. We'll talk. We can work this out—"

She reacted like a wild thing. Whirling around and ducking free of his hand, she threw the contents of the full glass into his face. The bourbon stung his eyes, fumed up his nose, and dripped from his lip.

"We can work out nothing, Mack. Nothing!"

He listened to the retreating footfalls, a frantic staccato. A door slammed; a bolt shot into its socket. He closed his eyes.

Then he reached for the whiskey himself.

He woke with hot light striping his face.

He blinked several times while his brain slowly deciphered the meaning of the slanted sunshine. The light fell through the louvers of shutters left partly open in his office.

His mouth tasted like wool and dirt. He rolled over before he realized he was close to the edge of the leather couch, and he fell on the polished floor with a nasty jolt that woke him fully. The clock behind his desk showed ten-fifteen. Picking up the empty bottle from beneath the couch, he placed it on the desk near the guidebook.

His appearance in the crowded kitchen created a sudden hush.

"Angelina? Is Little Jim—"

"Fine, Señor Chance. The fever is gone. Imelda is with him

while I eat breakfast." Her brown hand hovered apologetically above a plate of corn cakes.

Mack watched the cooks bustling at the stove and chopping block. Rodolfo Armendariz, the elegant majordomo, sampled soup simmering on a hearth hook, avoiding the eyes of the master of Villa Mediterranean. Rodolfo's silver goatee matched the silver chasing of his short velvet jacket.

"Is Mrs. Chance downstairs?" Mack asked him.

The majordomo looked at him nervously, then handed the ladle to a cook's assistant.

"Rodolfo, what's wrong?"

The elderly Mexican gripped the lapels of his jacket and replied gravely. "Señor, your wife departed in her carriage shortly after daybreak. She drove herself, by her own request."

"To go where?"

"Señor, she did not tell us."

"Was she sober?"

The majordomo avoided his eye again. One of the cooks rattled her implements, which was answer enough. *Drunk and crazy out of her head. Damn her. Damn her.*

Wild-eyed, he ran up the staircase and flung open the doors of their bedroom suite. Empty drawers lay about, and the tall carved wardrobe stood open, everything removed. He walked toward it, feeling stupid and slow, as if someone had pounded him with heavy blows. He shut one door of the wardrobe, then the other. The mirrored front flashed an image of the unmade bed—and also of a folded note.

He snatched it off the pillow, knowing what it would say almost before he identified the sloppy hand:

Things are intolerable. I am leaving you.

C.

VI

POWER AND GLORY

1899–1903

At the end of the century, San Francisco was old enough to be recognized as a major city. Her population approached 350,000, and she ranked second only to New York as a trading port. She was old enough to replace her tumble-down buildings with splendid new architecture, even skyscrapers. Page Brown's new Ferry Building, with its 235-foot clock tower, loomed over the Embarcadero, and the new City Hall would be magnificent if they ever finished it.

San Francisco was also fully old enough for a tradition of personal feuds. This grew in the dark soil of politics, watered by the blood of slain men in a climate that tolerated old-fashioned American violence.

In 1859, U.S. Senator David Broderick, a Democrat, and Judge David Terry, also a Democrat, but of the hotly conservative "Chivalry" wing, exchanged insults, and Judge Terry challenged Broderick to a duel. They met on the shore of Lake Merced. Broderick was unfamiliar with dueling pistols, and his hair trigger discharged too soon. Given this advantage, Terry took careful aim and drilled Broderick's chest dead center.

New laws against dueling didn't stop the feuds, however. In 1879, editor Charley de Young of the Chronicle criticized a political candidate in print, and the candidate promptly announced publicly that "Mother de Young once ran a whore house." Charley de Young promptly shot him. The candidate lived, but his son entered the Chronicle offices one day in 1880 and shot Charley to death. Five years later, Mr. Adolph Spreckels, the sugar magnate, got so fed up with the paper's personal attacks on him that he entered the editorial rooms and shot Charley de Young's brother Mike, who was now in charge. A quick-witted bookkeeper in turn shot Mr. Spreckels. This time, both wounded men survived.

As fin-de-siècle San Francisco prepared to enter the new, presumably more enlightened century, one might assume such primitive frontier violence would end.

But no. It was by now a tradition, and there was much more to come.

44 ON A FALL DAY IN THAT SAME YEAR, 1899, MACK and Hellman met for a noon meal in Los Angeles. It was their third luncheon in as many weeks, Carla's departure having created a new bond between them. They were rather like foreign legionnaires who'd endured a forced march barefoot across miles of hot sand and lived to reminisce about it.

They dined until half past two. Hellman complained of gas so they took a stroll to work it off. Carla's father was in his middle-to-late sixties now; he was secretive about his age, though he insisted others celebrate his birthday. His hair no longer showed any trace of its original blond color and his paunch was huge and jiggly.

The old bandit wore a wrinkled suit of windowpane plaid, bilious yellow on brown. To adorn his summer shoes, white buckskin and brown leather, he'd donned yellow linen spats. The spats bore souvenirs of the street, his unbuttoned vest and shirt souvenirs of the meal. Mack, neat and proper in a summer wool, high collar, and four-in-hand, was always amused by Hellman's peacock wardrobe.

Hellman fanned himself with his straw hat as they strolled down South Spring Street. The mild breeze brought them the chug of oil wells pumping away. Mack decided it was time to give Hellman the news.

"Carla filed for divorce. I had a letter yesterday. She hired a San Francisco lawyer, a former partner of Walter Fairbanks."

"What grounds?"

"She's charged me with adultery."

Hellman blinked and almost stepped in a horse pie in the intersection. "With who?"

"A woman in New York. It isn't true."

"Then you got to contest it."

"No. She wants out of the marriage. And she'd be certain to win in court. My reputation's pretty bad. Consorting with defrocked priests. Hiring Chinese. Opposing General Otis . . ." Otis had commanded volunteers in the Philippines in the recent war; he'd received a brigadier's commission, and he let no one forget it.

Hellman shook his head. "That girl. She's something. You

should give yourself credit, Johnny. She stayed with you a long time. Longer than I expected, I can tell you now.''

Mack twirled his cane. Some of the shock and pain had burned itself from his system. He was sleeping soundly again, with only an occasional nightmare. ''Have you heard from her? I haven't, not directly, since she walked out.''

Hellman scratched his lumpy nose. ''I had a letter last month. She's in Europe. Carlsbad. Drinking champagne and bathing in the mineral springs. Be better if it was the other way around.'' He sniffed. ''I thought about cutting off her inheritance but that would just bring her back. Your son, Jim—he'll grow up better without her—now don't look at me like that. I told you plenty of times—I love Carla. But I know her inside and out—say, what's this crazy joint?''

Mack turned to a familiar storefront. Gaudy posters covered most of the glass; dark paint opaqued the rest. He knew the place, number 311 South Spring. He stopped in whenever he could. He pointed with his cane.

THOS. TALLY'S
PHONOGRAPH AND VITAGRAPH PARLOR
AMAZING NEW ''MUTOSCOPES''
&
EDISON ''KINETOSCOPES''
WHOLESOME—EDUCATIONAL—ENTIRELY SUITABLE FOR
FAMILIES!

Hellman scowled. ''Are these here the moving pictures I read about?''

''That's right. The Kinetoscope is a peep-show machine developed by Edison's laboratory in New Jersey. The Mutoscope is a competitor. In the back, Tally's got an Edison Vitascope. It projects the moving pictures on a large screen. Edison put his name on the projector, but I understand he doesn't think much of the process.''

''Smart man. Don't sound respectable to me.''

Mack opened the door and they peeked in. Peep-show machines lined both sides of a long aisle. There was one patron, a man in a cloth cap, crouched over the eyepiece of a Mutoscope. At the rear, a clerk on a stool lazily turned pages of a paper. The rear wall was divided between a curtained doorway and a partition of painted wood with seven peepholes sawed out. Chairs faced the three lower ones. A sign touted the MAMMOTH PROJECTING VITASCOPE.

"Don't look respectable, neither," Hellman said. "What kind of pictures do they show, the hootchy-kootch?"

The clerk recognized Mack and waved. "And other things. It's all pretty tame stuff, really. Fifteen cents a peep for the machines on the aisle. The film inside is fifty feet long. A small motor runs it in a continuous loop between the projection bulb and a revolving shutter—"

"You're really an expert on this stuff," Hellman said, taking the tone he might have if Mack had announced he favored dynamiting the presidential mansion in Washington.

"It's an exciting process. The back room's even better than the peep shows. There, you sit in the dark in front of a big screen, and the effect is—well, staggering. People won't go back there, though. Tally had to install those holes for looking through. Even with that, you can see how many customers he draws."

"Sure, you wouldn't catch decent people in there."

"If you mean families, you're right. I've never seen one."

"But you been inside."

"Often. Moving pictures are wonderful. Someone just needs to figure out how to use them right. Maybe to tell stories. Then they have to make them respectable."

Mack opened the door a little wider. "Come on—you can watch my friend Corbett lose to Fitzsimmons. They've been showing that film for two years."

"Go in there? No, sir. I got my principles."

Mack laughed, shrugged, and called in, "Sorry, Ned, another day." The clerk waved again without looking up.

Hellman stumped away quickly, as if escaping something pestilential. "How can you take up with such crazy newfangled ideas? They just upset the applecart."

"Swampy, things never improve unless new ways upset the old ones."

"Too much of that out here," the old man exclaimed. "Too damn much. More than anyplace I ever seen."

"That's one of the good and rare things about California—new ideas flourish; there aren't so many old restraints. People like that." He thought of Fairbanks, cold as some marble bust in a museum. "I take it back. Not everyone likes it. But I do."

"I keep saying it—you're the craziest rich man I ever met."

Mack held up on the corner. "I'll tell you something really crazy. I just bought a house on Nob Hill—three and a half stories and forty rooms. It takes up half a block on Sacramento and Clay, right behind Jim Flood's mansion. I bought it sight unseen."

Not much astounded old Hellman, but that did. Eyes popping, he said, "You mean you're finally going back?"

"It seemed a good time. I have the money, and there isn't a lot to hold me in Riverside. Billy Biggerstaff is a competent manager."

"What happened to your cowboy friend?"

"Sailed off to Alaska to see the territory and pan some gold."

Mack raised his cane and rested it on his shoulder, gripping it so hard his knuckles whitened. He stared into his father-in-law's pinkly sweating face.

"I'm going back and rub their noses in it, Swampy."

On December 1, Captain Piers Norheim docked the steam yacht off Catalina Island. She had come around Cape Horn from Long Island, where she had been delivered to her owner, Oswald Henry Langford III, only last spring.

Shortly after, Langford's wife had discovered her husband in a hotel tryst with his mistress, shot him, shot the music-hall girl, then shot herself. It was an enormous scandal, and it brought on the market Langford's splendid steam yacht, built at a cost of $850,000, which came complete with a master and a crew of forty-three, all temporarily out of work. Captain Norheim was sixty years old and vastly experienced; he'd been at sea almost continuously since shipping out of his native Copenhagen at age fourteen.

After exhaustive checks by marine brokers and insurers hired long distance, Mack bought the yacht. She was the equal of the vessels sailed by Morgan, Drexel, Whitney, the Vanderbilts—if not their superior. She was 250 feet long, with a low, lean hull and a clipper bow. A stack jutted amidships between two vestigial masts. Her interior was a luxurious maze of deeply carpeted staircases, carved balusters, coffered ceilings. Paneling and moldings changed from room to room, surprising and pleasing the eye with lavish variations of oak, cherry, maple, chestnut, of Chippendale, Empire, and Louis XV. A marble fireplace welcomed guests to the dining saloon. A smaller one cheered those who used her library. Some 790 separate lamps drew their illumination from an electric plant below. Her annual payroll ran $50,000, her annual operating cost $175,000; her appetite for coal was enormous. What of it? He was worth $9–$10 million, and the carefully managed wealth kept compounding. However, as Pierpont Morgan liked to say, if you had to ask the cost of running a yacht, you couldn't afford it.

407

Along the sleek bows, tasteful gilt letters proclaimed her name: QUEEN OF HAMPTON.

"Get rid of that," Mack said at his first meeting with the spare, frost-eyed Dane who skippered her.

"I will, sir. But what's the new name to be?"

"*California Chance.* I want owner's flags run up, using this design."

He tapped a drawing of the *JMC* cartouche.

"I want to see that above the door of every stateroom. I want to see it on the china and bed linens. I want to see it everywhere."

On the last day of the year, *California Chance* bore through a sunlit sea at fifteen knots as the hilly coastline, winter-brown, slipped by to starboard. Sunlight streamed down on Mack, and the wind and the salt smell invigorated him.

He watched the coast with a meditative look in his hazel eyes. Somewhere inland ran a road he'd stumbled down years ago, ignominiously escaping to the south. The yacht's clipper bow pointed north, and the sea crashed against it and broke in noisy celebration of his reversal of that old defeat. Spray landed on his face, and he tasted the brine triumphantly.

He stood with hands locked at the small of his back, behind Captain Norheim and the helmsman, under the quarter-deck awning. Signal pennants and the owner's flag streamed from the otherwise useless masts. The four-thousand-horsepower steam power plant seemed to shiver the teak deck and run its throbbing power up into his braced legs, renewing his hope, driving out bad memories of an ill-conceived and ruined marriage.

He recalled the old litany—*Never be poor again; never be cold again*—and added a line: *Never be a nobody again.*

He looked forward to establishing that fact in the communal consciousness of the City.

Mack had chosen his wardrobe carefully: white shoes, white flannel trousers, a navy blazer with the cartouche embroidered as a breast-pocket coat of arms. He wore a billed cap—again with the familiar emblem—and around his throat, a new style of scarf from England called an ascot. It, too, bore the initials. No one ever questioned the ceaseless replication of his identity on clothes and possessions and no one joked about it. Mack was a good-humored man generally, but some things were beyond the bounds of humor. Or discussion.

At his side, Angelina held James Ohio Chance in her strong arms to keep him from toddling into danger on the tilting deck.

408

The little boy wore a child's sailor suit, dark blue with white piping, that Mack had bought for him. He kept dragging off the cloth cap by yanking on its red pom-pom, and Angelina kept putting the cap back on. Finally she gave up, exclaiming, "Señor Chance, the wind is too strong. And he refuses to wear his hat."

Mack tousled his son's fair hair. "Never mind—the fresh air and sunshine are good for him. Besides, I want him with me when we sail into the Bay. How soon, Captain Norheim?"

The Dane with the marvelous chest-length white beard snapped open a brass telescope and raked it along the shore, where a few fishing boats bobbed in small inlets, and white cottages neat as cubed sugar perched on hillsides. Then he consulted a chart in the binnacle and spoke to the helmsman.

"I estimate the Bay in slightly over an hour."

"Splendid," Mack said with a hard shine in his sunlit eyes. The yacht lifted and fell and the motion of her passage stirred his pulses. He had no problem with nausea, not even in the worst swells. Norheim said he was a born yachtsman.

When it came to the child, however, Angelina was unimpressed by Mack's wealth, importance, or occasional ferocity. "That is too long," she announced. "I will take him below."

"Mind the clock and watch a porthole, then. Bring him up when we enter the Bay. When he's big, I want to tell him he was there when we came back."

She left the deck. *California Chance* sped north through a sea strewn with the flashing gold of the morning light.

MACK FOUND GREAT CHANGES IN SAN FRANCISCO. **45**
He found a new City landmark: the Ferry Building. Dominating the waterfront, its shining clock tower was a copy of an exquisite Moorish spire on the cathedral of Seville.

He found City Hall finished at the corner of Larkin and McAllister, after twenty-nine years of construction and expenditures of $8 million. Boosters said the French-Corinthian building with its high dome was beautiful. Cynics said so many corners had been cut, it would fall down if hit by a strong sneeze.

He found the town expanding relentlessly toward the ocean,

reclaiming the sandy wastes of the Western Addition for new homes.

He found the section south of Market—South of the Slot; a literal slot in the street for cable cars—much more congested and run down than he remembered.

He found a new mayor, Jim Phelan, in office. The eccentric populist Sutro was dead two years now, most of his reform schemes unfulfilled. Phelan was that rare bird, a rich Democrat. A grandee with a Jesuit education, he boasted idealistic visions and a frank loathing of the SP and municipal graft.

He found a burgeoning literary and art community whose movable party shifted back and forth between the City and windswept cottages at Carmel; Nellie had rented one there and would return to it soon. This news came in a letter from Rome. With great glee she reported that another San Franciscan, her friend Frank Norris—''cruelly handsome—alas, he's married''—was completing a railroad-bashing novel, a *roman à clef* based on the killings at Mussel Slough.

Mack found that youthful memories, good memories, of San Francisco almost balanced other memories: of Fairbanks; Bao Kee dead in the starlight; Huntington in his skullcap; Silver Tooth Coglan and that sour, damp room of pain and defeat. He found that, without realizing it, he had long ago given his heart to this shining pastel city on the Bay. When or where it happened, he couldn't say. But knowing it now filled him with a sweet sentimental satisfaction that he dared reveal to no one.

Mack lived quietly during the first months of 1900, attending to his various enterprises, hiring a staff, advertising for an assistant in Hearst's East and West Coast papers, buying more San Francisco real estate. He secured a local lawyer, Rhett Haverstick, Esq., a tall, regal man. An old-line City Democrat with family roots in South Carolina, Haverstick possessed the inbred good manners of Southerners, but none of their occasional arrogance.

Mack established substantial bank accounts at the Bank of California; he would have nothing to do with Fairbanks Trust. One of the bank officers proposed him for the Olympic Club and Haverstick seconded him. He was elected, though Haverstick told him Fairbanks later said he'd have tried to block the election, had not SP business kept him away from the City when the membership committee met.

Mack's turreted castle faced Sacramento Street and afforded splendid views of the Bay from the rear, the Clay Street side. He set masons to work building entrance pillars and casting a pair of cartouches in concrete, and hired a firm to furnish the house temporarily and plan a complete redecoration, starting with the ballroom. He decided to gut and remodel the entire top floor to create the largest, most lavish suite of private offices, conference and storage rooms the City had ever seen.

Gradually, the City's better element became aware of his presence. He knew the society leaders would consider him a parvenu, and prepared to overcome that by a simple method: He would buy his way into their favor.

Mrs. Jane Stanford was gray now, but energetic as ever. Her other guest was Dr. David Starr Jordan, the president of Stanford University. Jordan was about fifty and over six feet tall, with the ruddy look of a confirmed outdoorsman. He had been one of the first Americans to climb the Matterhorn.

Jordan declined Jane Stanford's offer of tea, slipping in a pointed little sermonette on the harmful effect of stimulants. Mack took tea, then presented the governor's widow with a draft for $100,000.

"This is most generous," Mrs. Stanford exclaimed with great emotion. "Most unexpected too."

"I believe in education. California's been good to me. And I've never forgotten that you and the governor gave me my first decent job." With disarming charm, he added, "I also hope this takes a little of the sting from the memory of the nickel ferry."

"How could it be otherwise, Mr. Chance? The university is my deepest concern—my only one, now that Leland's gone."

Jordan smiled. "She tends to our welfare as devotedly as Phoebe Hearst tends to that of the university at Berkeley." He examined the draft, obviously delighted. "Thanks to benefactors like you, the Stanford endowment continues to far exceed that of schools such as Columbia and Harvard. When I came here from the presidency of Indiana, members of the press predicted I'd have no operating funds, no faculty, and no students. They said I'd lecture all alone in empty marble halls for years—perhaps forever. We continue to give the lie to those nay-sayers. Thank you for helping us."

"Have another cup of tea, Mr. Chance," said Mrs. Stanford. "And should I not say welcome home?"

"We can put you up for the Bohemian Club, if you want," Rhett Haverstick told him. "When it was founded thirty years ago, it was just what the name suggests, a hangout for journalists and painters. Now it's the business and political crowd, the best and most powerful people. You might even make the summer encampment if things move speedily."

"Will they let me in?"

"Of course we must discount our friend Fairbanks again—"

"He belongs, does he?"

"I'm afraid so. As for the rest of the membership—I should think they'd be enthusiastic. You know what's being said about you around town."

"No, I don't."

" 'Chance is too rich to be ignored.' "

Mack smiled.

The decorators returned with an architect's scheme to knock out the foyer ceiling and the ceiling on the floor above. "What we propose is a dramatic three-story entrance roofed in Tiffany's finest multicolored glass."

Mack studied the plans a while. "How much?"

"Less than three hundred thousand dollars."

Again he was silent for a bit, turning the pages of the ledgers stored in his head and studying their numbers. Then:

"Go ahead."

The Bohemian Club admitted him, the only blackball Fairbanks's, and that was not sufficient to keep him out. He received an invitation to the Midsummer High Jinks, the annual retreat, to be held this year at the club's new campground in the Russian River redwoods.

As business took him around the City, he met more of its leaders. A few refused to associate with him—those connected with Fairbanks Trust and the high echelons of the Southern Pacific, and those connected with the *Examiner*'s arch competitor, the *Chronicle*. Publisher Mike de Young ruled his empire from a new ten-story skyscraper on Market Street. Though he was a stalwart of Mack's own Republican party, whenever the two met, he gave Mack a cool nod, no more; anyone known to be a friend of Hearst received the same treatment.

One man who should have been his enemy treated him cordially: Henry Huntington, the son of C.P.'s older brother Solon. Nephew Henry, nicknamed Ed, had taken a job with the SP back in '81. Now he managed the line's San Francisco streetcar subsidiary. He was a blunt man, about fifty, and perhaps he and Mack respected one another because they detected common traits, chief among them implacable ambition.

* * *

Weekends, Mack surrendered to his passion for the outdoors. He hiked down the wild Big Sur coast, and hunted quail, wolf, and wild goat in the Sierra foothills—but with nothing more lethal than one of Eastman's black-box Kodak cameras.

He devoured Clarence King's *Mountaineering in the Sierra Nevada* and took up the sport, climbing the wind-scoured volcanic heights of Shasta, and surveying the lush vineyards of Napa and Sonoma from the summit of Mount Saint Helena, named by the wife of a Russian governor-general. In Contra Costa County he climbed up through fields of wildflowers, then sycamore and pine, to the top of Mount Diablo. Nearly four thousand feet above the sea, he could see for almost a hundred miles in every direction sweeping vistas of the Pacific, the City, the North Coast, the Central Valley, and the far Sierras. On that peak on a summer afternoon, he was the king of California. The king of the world.

Whatever else he did, he devoted an hour every evening to Little Jim. The boy was going on two, toddling and using new words and pulling down any object not nailed in place. Little Jim's eyes had remained a deep blue—Carla's eyes—and a great lot of golden hair capped his head. Unquestionably, he favored his mother, Señora Olivar agreed.

Some weekends, Mack took his son walking in Golden Gate Park, or showed him the rocky coast at Bodega Bay from the deck of *California Chance*. The boy went on these excursions dutifully, but seemed uninterested.

"I cannot tell you why," Angelina Olivar said when Mack raised the question. "Perhaps, like his face, his disposition favors her."

God forbid, Mack thought with a shiver of dread.

The Grove, the Bohemian Club's newly acquired tract on the Russian River, hosted members for the first time that summer. An uncharacteristic shyness enveloped Mack as he carried his gear to his assigned cabin, where he met his camp-mates for the week of High Jinks: Hunter Vann, an important trial attorney; Oscar Himmel, a commission agent and warehouse owner; and Joe Snell, an official of the SP-controlled streetcar line. They greeted Mack with varying degrees of warmth; Himmel was too pompous and opinionated for real friendliness.

Joe Snell said he'd come up with his friend and fellow member Ed Huntington, and Mack said hello to old Collis's nephew at the first evening campfire. Like most of the others, Huntington wore boots and a lumberjack shirt. He shook Mack's hand warmly. Across the huge sparking blaze Mack saw someone watching them. It was Fairbanks, surrounded by cronies deep into their bourbon; the lawyer nodded to him.

Mack drank whiskey during the singing, as did everyone else. They locked arms and swayed to and fro under the gay Japanese lanterns, and generally acted like a lot of small boys suddenly relieved of daily cares.

Not everyone could leave everyday affairs behind, however. Huntington spoke of his love of books, and then about streetcars.

"I have a theory, Chance. Local transportation lines can do regionally what the Central and Southern Pacific did for this state. They can shape the future by shaping the way a city expands. Service must be fast, and clean—using overhead electric lines, perhaps. But I'm convinced the idea is sound. I'm going to test it out in Los Angeles one of these days."

Later, on a steep dirt trail back to his cabin, with the river purling nearby and insects harping in the dark, he met Fairbanks coming down, laughing with a friend. The trail wasn't wide enough for them to pass and one or the other had to step off.

Mack stopped under a paper lantern that cast feeble red light on the trail. Fairbanks stopped too.

"Well, Chance, I suppose I owe you a welcome to the Bohemians."

"You don't owe me a thing, Walter."

Fairbanks rubbed his mustache with his little finger. Sarcastically, he asked, "How's your stock in the People's Road?"

"I liquidated it after the sellout." It was a sore point. The San Francisco & San Joaquin had reached Bakersfield in '98, then, in a surprise move, the directors had negotiated and merged the line into the Santa Fe. Mack and some other substantial stockholders attempted to block the sale, charging the directors with fraud, but they lost.

"What a pity."

"We all lose some rounds, Walter. The harbor. The debt—"

Fairbanks didn't take the bait. "Neither of those detract from the company's strong position."

"Maybe not. But one of these days, Walter, you won't run California. One of these days the people will see to it. Good night."

Mack stepped forward so abruptly, Fairbanks was taken by surprise, and he stepped back. Then he realized what he'd done. The screwlike pain pierced his forehead.

"Who is that?" his friend asked as Mack disappeared up the trail.

"A son of a bitch I'll get rid of when the time is right."

They fished and sang and lazed away the bright summer hours. They celebrated the Cremation of Care in the traditional outdoor play written and performed by the members. Happy and relaxed, they returned to the City at the end of a week to be met with stunning news. C. P. Huntington had left his Fifth Avenue mansion for a vacation at his camp on Raquette Lake in the Adirondacks. There, in August heat, one year short of eighty, the old man had died.

The last of the Big Four was gone. RUTHLESS AS A CROCODILE, said the obituary in the Monarch of the Dailies. An era was over.

This was never more evident than at the funeral. One of the mourners was E. H. Harriman, a broker who'd found his métier in railroad speculation. From his position as chairman of the Union Pacific executive committee, Harriman was acquiring lines all over the country. "They say he's already negotiating for Ed Huntington's stock," a friend told Mack. "It's really the end."

"I don't think so. The Octopus is still choking the life out of this state."

Over the racket of tools and cursing workmen, Mack interviewed the seventeenth applicant for the job of assistant.

This young fellow struck him as just as unsatisfactory as the rest. He was small, no more than an inch or two over five feet, and had delicate hands and tiny feet. His hair was prematurely gray—he was perhaps twenty-eight or twenty-nine—and the thick lenses of his pince-nez only drew attention to his weak watery eyes. His skin was so white, it was doubtful that he ever saw sunshine. Two unnatural splotches of color crowned his cheeks.

He shook Mack's hand as if it were a pump handle. "How do you do, sir? My name is Alexander Muller. I am a Swiss. From the canton of Zurich. Traditionally, there is an umlaut over the *u* in *Muller*. I have dropped it. I want to be in all ways American."

Behind the young man's smile Mack sensed a driven person. Alexander Muller cocked his head well forward, like a bird ever alert for a tasty worm.

"You don't know a thing about my business, Muller. That's

415

the trouble I'm having with every candidate. No one knows my business like I do.''

"Perhaps you look for the wrong qualifications, sir.''

"Beg your pardon?''

"How can anyone know your affairs as well as you? In time—yes, perhaps. But it will require many years of industrious application. However, certain other qualities can recommend a candidate. A mathematical aptitude, for example. I clerked in a bank for three years. I am quick with numbers. I am industrious. I am dedicated to making my career in California.''

"Why is that? You're far from home.''

"Far from the banks of the river Limmat I roamed as a child—yes. But you see, sir—I can't lie if you are to employ me as a trustworthy person—I have been in a certain kind of hospital in the Alps for two years. When I was young, I was stricken with phthisis.''

"With what?''

"Pulmonary consumption, sir. It is in remission. It shall stay in remission, because I have come to the great hospital and sanitarium of the world, California.''

"You believe that?''

"Along with millions of other Europeans, I do, sir.''

A consumptive for an assistant? Mack didn't know if he liked that. But he liked this nervous, fragile, gray-haired man-boy quite a bit, he decided.

"Tell me more about yourself. Do you have a family?''

"No, sir. Parents deceased.''

"A wife?''

"No, sir.''

"A girlfriend?''

"No. My only mistress is my work.''

"Well, that's American, all right. You'd fit in well around here.''

Mack hired him.

In the summer Mack took up another old passion, cooking. With renovation of the foyer and ballroom on schedule, he decided to plan a gala party to celebrate the official start of the new century on New Year's Eve. A banquet would precede the dancing, and he'd prepare at least one main dish. But he was dissatisfied with the wine, and he and Alex Muller drove up into the country with a satchel of cash. At the end of three days, Mack owned the Sonoma Creek Winery.

* * *

Mack's busy life was not without its physical side. He was still young, and no anchorite, so when needs and stresses exerted themselves, he found a ready solution at hand: a visit to one of the so-called French restaurants.

The French restaurant was the City's own peculiar institution. There were two or three dozen of them, scattered in the shabbier districts, the earliest having sprung up during the Gold Rush. No one could say exactly why they were called French; the cuisine didn't qualify them for that description, being generally excellent but plain. Nor were the owners of French extraction. Perhaps the name had been given them because most Americans thought of the French as relatively relaxed regarding matters of sex, and sex was most definitely on the menu.

The first floor of every French restaurant was just that: a dining room, and a perfectly respectable one, often patronized by the most conservative and conventional of businessmen. On the second floor, however, you could take supper in a private dining room, either alone or in the company of a discreet female companion who resided on the premises. None of the rooms was without a comfortable couch large enough for two. For even longer periods of refreshment, there were small suites called supper bedrooms on the third floor; you rented those for the entire night.

Mack tried a couple of other French restaurants before he settled on a favorite, Maison Napoleon, tucked away on the north side of Mission, south of the Slot. During his second dinner there, he fell into conversation with the owner, who intrigued him because of her age—she was only in her early twenties—and her air of propriety. Her name was Margaret Emerson. He silently admired her enterprise and her obvious intelligence; no ordinary street trollop could have run a place so close to the edge of the law, yet so clearly successful. He and Margaret quickly became friends.

Margaret Emerson was a slightly built young woman with large brown eyes, auburn hair, and a dappling of freckles on her nose and cheeks. Her jaw was rather too long, and so was her neck. When she was on duty, acting as hostess for the dining room, she maintained a serious air and wore dark dresses befitting someone much older. She enhanced the effect by piling her hair high on her head in a dignified arrangement and covering her freckles with powder.

So long as she kept her mouth closed, Margaret resembled a maiden aunt, or the wife of a Presbyterian deacon. The moment she smiled, however, there was a marvelous transformation. She showed a mouthful of teeth, perfect white teeth.

That smile and her brown eyes banished any illusion of age and severity, and she became an ageless pixie, full of charm. But she carefully hid this side of herself from her dining-room customers, perhaps believing a respectable demeanor downstairs was absolutely necessary because of what went on upstairs.

Soon she and Mack were going on outings together. On sunny weekends, they rode wheels through Golden Gate Park, taking picnic baskets brought from the Maison's kitchen. Once he took her for an overnight cruise on *California Chance*. He had dozens of fresh flowers placed in the largest of the guest staterooms, and made a show of presenting her with the door key just as Captain Norheim's men were casting off. She gave him a swift look of comprehension. He wanted her company, but not in bed; that sort of companionship he could find on the Maison's upper floors. If there was a flicker of regret on her face just then, Mack didn't notice.

The offshore cruise, which lasted until late Sunday, was a splendid success, with past histories shared, and a great deal of laughter. By the time they docked, they were more than friends; they were confidants.

Mack had known Margaret for several months when it occurred to him that she would be an ideal guest and partner for New Year's Eve. That same evening, he dropped in and tendered the invitation. Her brown eyes showed her eagerness, but she didn't voice it. She said, "What if someone recognized me?"

"I doubt they will. But suppose they do. You keep telling me politicians and businessmen come in all the time."

"By the back door, usually. They'd never admit it. You're taking a risk."

"I need a hostess. I can't think of a prettier or more charming one."

"Very well. I accept the invitation."

On New Year's Eve, 1900, one hundred guests presented engraved cards in the three-story foyer roofed with Tiffany glass and lit from above by electric fixtures. An orchestra played in the ballroom while the ladies and gentlemen mingled for an hour in the public rooms. At half after nine everyone went into the immense dining hall.

Margaret sat at Mack's right, resplendent in a sapphire tiara he'd given her for Christmas. The great horseshoe table gleamed with white linen, glittered with silver cutlery, sparkled with fine crystal. He'd chosen low gaslight rather than the harsher glare of electrics. His boiled shirt shone like snow on a mountain when he rose to speak briefly before the meal.

"Ladies and gentlemen, welcome to my house and this celebration of the new century. I was not born in this state, but I am now a Californian to the bone." Some applause and murmurs greeted that; guests had been plied with unlimited amounts of Cresta Blanca champagne, the state's finest, before the banquet.

"Therefore, the dinner you're about to enjoy is a California dinner. Every dish is native to this state. You will be given a printed menu in a moment. Meanwhile, I hope you'll look with special favor on the stuffing and the glaze of the *caille rôti*— native quail from the San Joaquin. Cooking is a love of mine, and I prepared both the stuffing and the glaze. I confess I've never cooked for a hundred people before. That's a mighty lot of time in the kitchen."

Laughter.

"The wines, too, are Californian. Tonight we celebrate not only the New Year, and the twentieth century, but the state we love."

He lifted his brimming glass.

"To California. And your very good health."

The gentlemen rose for the toast, a long elegant line of black lapels and white ties. *I made it,* he thought, heady with wonder and pride.

Margaret took a symbolic sip of champagne and folded her white-gloved hands in her lap like the most proper of wives. By gaslight her eyes were enchanting, her face luminous as an affectionate child's.

Mack signaled to the column of waiters queued up in the passage to the kitchen.

"Menus, please. Let the festivities begin."

To start, *Les Huîtres de Tomales:* Tomales Bay oysters on the half-shell, each enclosed in a linen napkin intricately folded, a mignonette sauce served alongside.

Next, *Le Consommé de Hôte Palace:* clear chicken stock and abalone broth, placed in individual cups, napped with lightly salted whipped cream, dusted with nutmeg, and lightly glazed before serving.

Then, *Le Filet de Sole Sautée:* sand dabs, California's best fish, filleted, sauteed simply, and served with lemon wedges.

The quail followed, with Mack's own stuffing of brown rice, nuts, and dried apricots, the whole glazed with his marinade of orange juice and Sonoma Creek wine.

In the European style, the salad came after these entrees. *La Salade de Saison:* The Pasadena salad was a composition of greens, sections of grapefruit and orange—the oranges were Calgolds—and wedges of avocado. A slightly sweet vinaigrette flavored it.

Following *Le Plateau de Fromages Assortis*—Mack told guests seated nearby that very good French-style cheese had been made in Sonoma County for years—the waiters marched in with a triumph for dessert, *La Poire Conde:* whole cored pears from one of his Valley farms, poached in a sweetened wine collation and served on a bed of creamy sauce anglaise, the whole dripping with a dark-chocolate sauce and sprinkled with crushed almond macaroons.

To conclude—*Le Café Noir, Demi-tasse.*

At eleven-thirty, Mr. Joe Snell of the Bohemian Club proposed a toast of appreciation to their host.

Instead, someone started clapping. Astonished, Mack saw that it was the sob sister for de Young's *Chronicle.* He hadn't noticed her before, undoubtedly because he hadn't expected her to show up. He'd sent the invitation because de Young's paper was too important to ignore.

She jumped to her feet, breathy, tearful, and slightly drunk. She led the standing ovation.

They remembered that night long afterward in San Francisco. It was the start of a legend: the Chance banquets. Nothing like them in America, said those privileged to be invited, who didn't fail to brag pointedly to those who were not. Among the latter was Walter Fairbanks.

At half past three in the morning, Mack danced the last waltz with Margaret.

She was pliant and warm in his arms, and her small round breasts smelled of powder and perfume. She patted his shoulder gently as they danced on a floor strewn with confetti and pieces of streamer.

"A triumph. An absolute triumph, Mack."

"Yes, I think so—you helped immensely."

She squeezed him and risked criticism by resting her cheek on his. "I'd be happy to stay the night, if you'd like that," she said softly.

He thought of Nellie. Was she asleep now? Where? And with anyone?

"Thank you, but I'm tired. I'm sure you are too. Alex will drive you home."

She did her best to hide her disappointment.

HELLBURNER JOHNSON SWUNG DOWN FROM THE
cable car. It clanged on down California Street while
he paused on the corner, inhaling the spring breeze, which,
faintly fishy, blew from the Bay.

The sight of the Texan standing there turned heads in passing
carriages. A big muskrat cap with the earflaps tied up perched
on his head at a rakish tilt and he carried his arctic coat over
his arm. From a bulging canvas pack strapped to his back jutted a pair of snowshoes. In the pack, he'd stored his gun belt,
wrapped around a cash roll amounting to $4,500—the sum
received for the gold he'd panned standing in the sea off the
beach at Nome.

Johnson had never visited San Francisco, only seen it pass
to starboard as a coastal steamer bore him to Alaska. He had
strong memories of the last eighteen months: the onion-dome
churches of Sitka, the cold glassy gleam of Muir Glacier and
the caress of its icy breath as he walked on it. From Skagway
he'd trekked up to the Chilkoot Pass. He became part of a
human ascent chain fourteen miles long, sweating through his
red flannels one day, clinging to handholds in icy rock the next.
"Damnedest land in creation," he swore afterward. "Mosquitoes big as bullets, and mush ice in the creeks in August."

Dawson City was a dismal boomtown on a swamp, flooded
most of the time. He chewed onions from a carefully hoarded
sack to avoid scurvy, but he saw hundreds of victims, men
with joints swollen, teeth loosened, cheeks softened till a finger
could poke through the skin as if it were wet newsprint. On
the pier at Dawson, hundreds of new arrivals were soon lining
up to rush out again—all the way down the long snaky Yukon
River to the Bering Sea, and the new strike at Nome.

That was his last stop, Nome—a rowdy city of white tents
on a black sand beach. He'd survived two robbery attempts
there, and come back with more memories stored up. Also,
for once, he'd come back a little richer.

All that he'd seen tended to fade away as he walked up Nob
Hill. San Francisco was a mighty handsome town, with pretty
row houses decorating the hills, and her Bay shining blue out
yonder. But he was most impressed by the mansions of the
millionaires. When he turned right, then left again on Sacra-

mento Street, consulting an address on a paper, he found a house whose size and ornamentation overshadowed the rest.

Great pillars flanked the entrance, a foot-high cartouche of concrete adorning each. J. M. Chance had his brand on display. Johnson shook his head in amazement. He plucked his emerald-green bandanna out of his shirt to whisk away a tobacco fleck in the corner of his mouth, then opened the iron gate and went up the steps.

"Mr. Chance is occupied at the moment," said the stiff-necked butler. Johnson couldn't stop gawking at the sun-flooded Tiffany skylight, three stories above. "Please call again. In the rear. Tradesmen's entrance."

"You jackass, I'm his partner. Show me to his office, and right now, or I'll show you the business end of the Colt stashed in this here pack."

The alarmed butler led him up, and up, and up again, through a wonderland of carved banisters, potted greenery, sunlit carpet, to a double door on the top landing—again, the cartouche adorned each, hand-carved in a medallion of cherry wood— and these opened on a spectacular suite of rooms. Johnson walked through several, including one fitted out with twelve chairs around a long table. The last room was the largest, bigger and grander than the office in Riverside. Here Mack held forth at a mammoth desk. Behind him, a triptych of leaded windows spread the panorama of Russian Hill, the Bay, and Marin.

Mack was shaking a pencil at a tall, skinny chap with the sort of face Johnson considered suitable for an undertaker. Nearby hovered a young squirt with funny eyeglasses and the gray mane of a grandpa.

". . . and I won't go higher than sixty-five thousand on those blocks out by the Presidio—"

Johnson slung his pack to the carpet to make noise.

"Hellburner! My God. I thought you were going to stay in Alaska forever."

"Nearly did. Mighty beautiful place. Didn't mean to interrupt . . ."

Mack ran forward and embraced him. "No, no. We're almost finished for the morning. Sit down, sit down."

Mack was all smiles and energy, bounding back to his desk and rapidly shuffling papers.

He looked thinner, Johnson thought. Plenty of gray showing around the ears. How was he getting along without a woman?

422

he wondered. How was that sprout getting along without a mama?

Mack introduced him to the tall drink of water, Haverstick, a lawyer; and the funny little foreign dude, Alex Muller, who bustled around jerking open cabinets and consulting files from the desk like he owned the place. Haverstick, legs crossed, sat in a chair angled to provide a view of the entrance. All at once Haverstick nodded in that direction.

"Visitor, Mack."

Mack looked up and saw Little Jim. Mack's son was outfitted in a Norfolk jacket and tweed knickerbockers. His black stockings matched his shoes and his child's four-in-hand was perfectly tied. By someone else, Johnson figured. A perfect little dude. Was he ever allowed to get dirty?

The boy bore an unmistakable resemblance to Carla. He'd shed his baby fat, and he stood there observing his father with dark-blue eyes, earnest and maybe a bit scared. Or did Johnson just imagine that?

"There's my boy." Mack jumped up and hurried to him. "Two years old now, going on three," he said to the Texan. He swept his son off the floor and hugged him. "Jim, it's half past twelve. Time for dinner. Go find Angelina in the kitchen."

"You come, Pa."

"No, I can't."

"Pa, come on."

"I can't," Mack said in a harder voice. He set the boy down and patted the seat of his pants. "I'll see you later today."

Little Jim's mouth turned down, but he said nothing. With a last look at his father—Mack was already striding back to the desk—he walked out past the conference table and through the vast rooms beyond. Young as he was, there was definitely a sad air about him, Johnson decided. A lonely, abandoned air.

Like a dutiful little soldier, Mack's son marched straight through to the staircase, and Johnson watched his blond head sink from sight below the line of the floor.

Quickly Mack scanned the agenda Alex had prepared for the morning. "We're finished. The Presidio property was the last item—"

The wall telephone rang and Alex grabbed it. "Mr. Potter in Los Angeles," he said to Mack after a moment.

"Yes, Enrique," Mack said. He listened. "Absolutely not. No extension. We close on that Long Beach tract in thirty days or no deal. Tell them."

He hung up and scribbled a note on a pad. *Looks damn prosperous,* Johnson thought. A gold watch chain decorated the front of Mack's vest, and there was a gleam of the same metal inside his mouth. Nothing but the finest.

"That's it, gentlemen. Thanks to you both."

Rhett Haverstick closed the clasp on his legal case. "Mr. Johnson, welcome. It's a pleasure to meet you at last."

"There's a huge guest suite waiting for you on the second floor," Mack said.

Alex Muller snapped his pocket watch open. "Sir, you are due at the Olympic Club in fifteen minutes."

"Bankers," Mack said, giving his friend an apologetic smile and snatching his coat from a rack. "Call the carriage." Alex darted to the speaking tube in the wall.

Johnson licked a cigarette paper and pasted it shut. He stuck the cigarette in his lip and lit a match on his boot. "Olympic Club. Sounds pretty high-toned." He was beginning to feel out of place, about as comfortable as a minnow in the sea with a typhoon blowing.

"The best in the City, you'd have to say." Mack slipped into his coat. "Alex, what about the figures on the ranches in the Valley?"

The foreign squirt peered through his thick pince-nez. "On your desk, sir. Together with an estimate of the harvest at the winery."

"I'll go over them tonight."

Johnson's jaw dropped. "Winery?"

"Something else I picked up," Mack said with a grin. "In the country a few miles above Sonoma. I've started to throw supper parties. It's a hell of a lot cheaper if I serve my own vintages."

"I guess that's how the rich get richer," Johnson muttered. He slid lower in his chair and squinted through curling smoke while Mack whispered something to the squirt.

Then Mack waved to his friend. "Walk downstairs with me."

Johnson did, but he was feeling sour and didn't hide it. "This here all the time you can spare for conversation?"

"Look, I'm sorry. I'm glad you're back, but it's a busy day. They're all busy now. We'll eat supper tonight, catch up on things."

"This here's a palace, Mack."

"Too big for me. But it creates an impression. Helps with business." They clattered down the wide stairs and crossed the second-floor landing, which was big enough to park a covered wagon.

"What do you hear from Carla?"

"Nothing since the divorce."

"Your boy sure looks like her."

Colored lights from the Tiffany window patterned the marble floor of the foyer. The butler glided up in a spooky way and handed Mack his hat, gloves, and stick.

"Jim's a quiet one. I can't seem to talk to him very well."

"Takes time to raise a youngster." Mack shot him a look. *Shit, he can't stand criticism,* Johnson thought. He quickly added, "So I been told."

That mollified Mack. "Lord, I've missed your company. What have you been up to for so blasted long?"

"Chasin' after gold in the by-God frozen north. Some places, it's so cold even this damn cork foot got the frostbite. I met a young fella up there I think you'd like. Matter of fact, he's an Oakland boy. Your sort, in a way. A parlor socialist, don't y'know . . ."

Mack accepted that with a tolerant smile. The butler opened the front door, his expression indicating that Johnson was interfering with the orderly affairs of the house.

"He writes stories too—like Nellie. Name's Jack London. I got his address. I'll introduce you."

"Fair enough." Mack dashed down the steps to the waiting carriage, a double-suspension brougham with a shiny dark-green body and green morocco interior. The driver snapped the lacquered door shut after Mack. Sun flashed from the enameled *JMC* emblem. The driver scooted up the wheel to his seat and Mack leaned out. "And I'll introduce you to my new automobile."

"Your what?"

"*Automobile.* That's the name they've settled on for the horseless carriage. I bought a steamer. Eight hundred and fifty dollars."

The brougham pulled away. Johnson had a fleeting look at Mack leaning back and lighting a cigar. Johnson had seen him smoke cigars before—cheap stubby ones—but this monstrosity was green, and fully as long as the barrel of Johnson's Peacemaker.

The Texan tossed up his hands in dismay. *That's all; that's the end,* he thought. An airy wake of smoke followed the brougham as it left Nob Hill.

On Saturday, Mack, Johnson, and Jack London ate lunch in the tiny kitchen at the Sonoma Creek Winery.

London was eight years younger than Mack, a garrulous,

hard-talking towhead with thick knuckles and a burly build. Full of himself, he hardly gave the others time to speak. He informed them he knew everything important about the writings of Darwin, Huxley, Spencer. Karl Marx too.

"Don't know any of them boys," Johnson remarked. "I figure I get all the lies I need from the papers and ten-cent novels about Buffla Bill."

London's eyes flashed. "Those *boys* tell the truth. Like I do."

"Sure, Jack. Eat your lunch."

Halfway through, Mack jumped up and pulled on heavy driving gauntlets. He ran to the stove with a pair of tongs and gingerly opened the lower door, lifting out a *U*-shaped, glowing red steel pipe.

"What the devil's that?" London asked.

"The firing iron. To start the burner. Can't stop to talk. Have to keep it hot."

He ran out.

"He didn't answer my question," London said.

"The Locomobile don't run on gasoline. He has to get the steam up 'fore we drive. Takes about a half hour. That firing iron starts the burner."

"If I ever sell enough fiction to become a rotten capitalist, damned if I'll buy an auto that complicated."

"Me neither. Four legs an' a tail suits me."

In the yard they heard purple oaths. A moment later Mack walked in. The firing iron had turned gray.

"Not hot enough. Have to start over."

A thin fog settled in the afternoon. They didn't leave the winery till after three. But when they did, Johnson had to admit it was a sensational experience.

"Steam's up," Mack cried. "The water supply's good for twenty miles. Let's go."

The Locomobile Steam Runabout was a beauty, the best steam car offered by the factory in Watertown, Massachusetts. She carried a single wide passenger seat and a shining coat of red lacquer. On the front side of the dash panel Johnson discovered the *JMC*. Looking for it was getting to be tiresome, because you always found it.

Mack buttoned his tan duster, tugged down his goggles, and settled his stiff-billed canvas cap. He'd provided similar gear for his passengers. They squeezed into the seat and away they went, rolling down the hard dirt lane from the adobe-brick winery, past the arbors to the main road. The Locomobile didn't sputter, shake, knock, or generate any noise except a low hiss of escaping steam. Johnson and London hung on tight to the seat, while Mack handled the steering tiller. He was like a boy with a toy.

A ribbon of steam unfurled in the mist behind them as Mack steered expertly around a farmer's cart full of melons. The farmer cursed the steam car and calmed his frightened nag. They whisked through a cathedral arch of tall eucalyptus, Mack shouting, "I don't have to fool with a spark advance or gears. There's a lot to recommend steam."

"You're a demon driver," Johnson laughed. He enjoyed the reckless rush down the country road, and temporarily forgot his dislike of Mack's obsession with material things.

"I'm going to race one of these days," Mack promised.

Suddenly they found themselves in a flock of frightened doves, which flew in their faces and beat their wings against the tan dusters and the moving vehicle. Mack steered away from the birds, hit some weeds alongside a fence, jerked the tiller over, and brought them back to the road. Steaming and hissing, the Locomobile sped up a thirty-degree rise without a hesitation.

"She's a marvel climbing hills. No effort, notice?"

They drove on to the rugged terrain above Sonoma, the Valley of the Moon. "I'll have a house on one of those hilltops someday," London shouted.

"My friend Nellie Ross is making a lot of money from her book. No reason you can't," Mack shouted.

"She's a hell of a good writer," London shouted. "They call her the female Zola."

"I know," Mack shouted.

"Say, Mack," Johnson shouted, "what happens if something blows out the fire in this tin can?"

"We walk back."

Fifteen minutes later, they did.

Late one afternoon in May, Mack and Haverstick met for a drink at the Bank Exchange, a favorite watering spot of the City's rich and powerful. Haverstick ordered a martini, the gin-and-vermouth cocktail invented by the legendary bartender "Professor" Thomas of the Occidental Hotel, and Mack ordered a Blue Blazer. When Haverstick excused himself and squeezed through the crowd to speak to Hunter Vann, the trial attorney, Mack occupied himself watching Jerry mix the Scotch and a dash of sugar syrup, add boiling water, and touch a match to it. As the blue flame flickered, someone poked Mack's elbow.

"Hy Hazelton. President of Glacier Ice Company."

Mack regarded the sweating round face. Reluctantly he shook hands. "Macklin Chance."

"Oh, everybody knows who you are. I need to speak to you, one businessman to another. You own a large produce warehouse—"

"Three."

"That's a lot of drayage. Wagons in and out all the time." Hazelton's little eyes glistened.

Careful, here's another crusader. But for what?

"We don't need union draymen in San Francisco, Chance. We don't need union shops of any kind. We need a free labor market. The kind General Otis created down south. There's a new local organization of community leaders dedicated to that idea, the Employers Association. I want to personally invite you—"

"No thanks. I'm not interested in union-busting. Workingmen have a right to organize to protect themselves."

"That's a misguided attitude. Trade unionism's a cancer. We've let it grow too long in San Francisco."

"Hazelton, excuse me," Mack said with an ominous little smile. "I paid for this drink and I'd like to enjoy it."

Hy Hazelton the ice king sneered and waddled off. Jerry added a bit of lemon peel to the Blue Blazer, and Mack picked up the warm glass and sipped. When Haverstick came back Mack mentioned the conversation.

"I've heard about the Employers Association," Haverstick said. "You can't get a fix on who belongs—they're secretive—but there's talk on the street of the association forcing a confrontation this summer."

"What kind?"

"Against the union teamsters is what I'm hearing. With all your connections on the waterfront, you'll want to keep your eyes open."

"I can't tell you why they're called French restaurants," Mack said, in answer to Johnson's question. The two of them were walking down from Nob Hill in the purple dusk. Windows in electrified buildings twinkled along Market Street. The *wonk-wonk* of an auto's bulb horn sounded from a cross street. The changes, Mack thought. So many changes.

"Do any respectable people go to these joints?" Johnson

asked. He'd donned a new black suit, knotted up a string tie, and slicked his hair for the occasion.

"All the time. To the first floor." He explained what went on up above.

Brass electric fixtures and a painted tricolor plaque decorated the entrance of Maison Napoleon. Several couples and a large family were already seated in a dining room as conventional as any hotel's. A plaster bust of Bonaparte glowered from a corner pedestal and Empress Josephine's vapid face gazed down from a gilt frame. A small electric lamp with a fringed shade of translucent silk shed a peach-colored light on each table. The blue-rimmed bistro china was heavy and solid, and a thick carpet hushed the noise.

Johnson studied his menu, handwritten on parchment inside a leather cover stamped with fleur-de-lis. Mack lit one of his gun-barrel cigars and Johnson made a show of fanning away the smoke. Mack grinned and kept on puffing.

After a bald waiter took Mack's order for a bottle of cabernet, Johnson noted a stairway leading up from an alcove in back. "You been upstairs?"

"I've paid a couple of visits, yes. Mostly I just like the food here. And Margaret's company—there she is." He smiled and raised his hand as she came through the kitchen door. Johnson craned around to see a boyishly slim young woman, wearing a starched white shirtwaist with long sleeves and a white tie. Her navy skirt swished as she hurried to the table. She might have been running a bordello, but on any stage she could play a schoolmarm or someone's hymn-singing virgin cousin from Toledo. The disguise amused Johnson.

"Mack. Good evening."

He jumped up and kissed her cheek. She gave his arm a quick squeeze but he seemed not to notice. Then she smiled. *Lord, look at them teeth,* Johnson said to himself.

"Margaret Emerson, this is my friend and partner, H. B. Johnson."

They shook hands decorously.

"Welcome to Maison Napoleon, Mr. Johnson. Mack's said so much about you—"

"Nothin' good, I 'spect."

"To the contrary. Did Mack tell you about our two upper floors?"

" 'Deed he did. One flight up, as I get it, I can sit down an' eat dinner. Two flights up, I can lie down and have dessert."

Margaret laughed, though she darted a look at the family to see if anyone had overheard.

"Well put," she said. A bell above the door tinkled, and again she touched Mack's shoulder. "Enjoy yourselves, gentlemen. Please excuse me."

She hurried over to greet two men Mack recognized as City supervisors. Now her lips were pressed together almost primly. The pixie hid while the proprietress showed the gentlemen to a table.

"She's come a long way for a young woman," Mack said. "Her parents were pig farmers up in the Sacramento delta. Dirt poor. Our finer citizens call people like that Pikes, because a lot of them came here from Pike County, Missouri. Margaret's parents did. She ran away from home when she was twelve."

"Sounds like you know her pretty good."

"Not the way you mean. She's a smart girl, ambitious. I see a lot of myself in her. Maybe that's why I like her."

The bald waiter came back, and Mack ordered veal chops, Johnson a venison steak. "Seems like you always take a shine to hard-driving females," Johnson observed after he handed his menu away.

"I wouldn't say Carla fit that description."

"No, an' maybe that's why it didn't work out." Over Mack's shoulder he observed Margaret at the cashier's counter, pretending to check a customer's bill while darting looks at Mack. She caught Johnson watching, and as color rushed to her cheeks averted her head. The momentary loss of poise confirmed what he'd already decided: Margaret Emerson was interested in something a lot heavier than friendship.

Mack mused over his cigar, tapping it on the edge of the ashtray. "I suppose Margaret and Nellie are alike in some ways. I never thought of it before."

"Say, is Nellie back yet?"

"Week before last."

"She here? In town?"

"No, she moved right into the place she leased in Carmel. Wants to finish her new novel there."

"You seen her yet?"

Mack's hazel eyes shone in the light of the silk-shaded lamp. "Next week. We're going back to the mountains."

Johnson took one look at that lovelorn face, and then glanced at Margaret, who was busy now with a pen and a ledger.

Poor gal, he thought. *She can try till she's ninety and she won't get nowhere with him. Wonder if she knows it?*

THE PACK MULES PICKED THEIR WAY ALONG THE **47** bank of the Merced, with Mack riding a saddle horse at the rear of the string, Nellie in front. Yosemite Falls thundered in the forest to their left. If she reacted to memories of the falls, she gave no sign.

They stopped at Camp Curry, a well-kept enclave of twenty-five white tents at the foot of Glacier Point. A pair of young schoolteachers from Redwood City, David and Jennie Curry, had opened the camp in the summer of '99. Transplanted Hoosiers, the Currys were graduates of Indiana, where David Starr Jordan had inspired them with his love of the outdoors. Jordan had urged Mack to pay a call.

Over a hearty lunch prepared by Mrs. Bab, the camp cook, David and Jennie shared their pride in their new venture, the first commercial campground in a national park.

"They're grand people," Nellie said after they had said good-bye and started on toward their campsite. "I just don't like encouraging tourists. Too many of them will despoil this place."

"What do you propose to do, set up a board to evaluate virtue and intelligence, decide which tourists are fit to come in? You're dealing with one of the most beautiful spots in America. Everyone wants to see it."

"I don't know what I propose," Nellie said, irked. "I just know we have a problem here."

The valley rioted with springtime color. Woodpeckers hammered the trees, and floating clouds changed El Capitan from white to purple to white again. They made camp about three o'clock, Mack putting up the tents and Nellie gathering wood and laying the fire. The long trip from the coast had been friendly, even intimate, but without any physical contact except the most casual. They might have been a pair of brothers, he thought with extreme frustration.

He pounded in the last peg and lashed the corner of the tent. Nellie's tanned face turned up to the sky like a lodestone seeking the magnetic pole, and suddenly she ran from the glade into the meadow and danced with her back to him, her braided hair tossing around her shoulders. She was like an ingenuous child.

She ran back, flushed and excited. "Oh, Mack, I love this place so much."

"Had enough of German castles and Roman coliseums?"

"Enough for a lifetime. I'm back in California to stay."

She stood not two feet away, breathing out her palpable aura of warmth and strength. Sunlight through budding leaves laid a pattern on her scrubbed cheeks. *It's the right moment. Take hold of her—*

He hesitated too long. A rhythmic noise shattered the peace, and Nellie spun on her boot heel, shielded her eyes.

"There," Mack exclaimed. From the direction of Camp Curry, lurching along in a blue cloud, came an open auto carrying four passengers.

Goggles flashed and someone flourished a green bottle. The passenger in front threw something in the weeds. The auto resembled a horseless phaeton, and Mack recognized its design. "That's an imported Daimler, what they call the Siamese model because of the second seat behind the driver's."

The Daimler came down a curving road near them. From the backseat, the two ladies in picture hats tied with scarves hallooed and waved kerchiefs. The man at the tiller steered the chugging, rattling vehicle in and out of ruts. Nellie coughed hard—and somewhat artificially, Mack thought; the auto's blue smoke cloud was confined to the road.

"That isn't the first automobile in Yosemite," she said. "A few months ago I saw a photograph of a steam car up on Glacier Point. Now that the valley's a national park, John Muir wants the Interior Department to ban those metal monsters."

The Daimler passed on, laying down its trail of murk and noxious fumes. Now Mack got a whiff.

"I can see why," he said. He too started to cough.

Next day they hiked to the summit of Sentinel Dome. The last two hundred yards on the east shoulder required some hard climbing, and near the top Mack clasped Nellie's hand to help her over a rough place and she held tight for half a minute.

She looked trim and fit in miner's shirt and jeans. They clambered the rest of the way and then, in a cluster of scrawny pines on the escarpment, they stood silently in the wind, feasting on the spectacle of the valley.

Mack put his arm around her. The clasp of his hand while climbing up had pushed her close to the limit; this was too much. *Go on—don't stop there*, she thought. Then she cursed her own weakness, and controlled the faint trembling started by the feel of his strong arm holding her.

He felt her tension and frowned, but didn't say anything. Then, careful not to look at him, she pulled away.

They climbed the old Tioga Road with their mules. An abandoned mine road, it ran some fifteen miles to Tuolumne Meadows, high country Mack had never seen.

As they rode along, he felt the air growing cooler. Large patches of spring snow filled the washes and clung to sunless hillsides. Nellie pointed out cedars and ponderosa pines giving way to white fir, mountain pine, and tamaracks that showed the blazes of earlier trail makers. In dark shade away from the road, an occasional empty cabin with shattered windows spoke of some hope unrealized, some California dream abandoned.

In the meadows, the wind waved great fields of gentians and lavender daisies. Two black bears ambled in the distance. They crossed a hairpin bight of the purling Tuolumne River; Nellie said it ran twenty miles down to a valley called Hetch Hetchy. "I went there once with Muir. It's as lovely as Yosemite. And still pristine."

They chose a campsite in a grove of dead trees, mountain hemlocks blasted and burned by lightning. "Let's put up that piece of canvas for a windbreak," she said.

"Why? It's hot as the devil."

"You'll fight the black ants and the mosquitoes all day, but as soon as the sun's down you'll be freezing. We're at eighty-six hundred feet. I won't be responsible for death from pneumonia."

He laughed. "Where's the canvas?"

They set up their tents facing each other across a shallow pit dug for a fire. Mack's eye was repeatedly drawn to Nellie; if she was conscious of it, she gave no sign. She was a strong woman. She worked hard, sweating freely, and he discovered grace and loveliness in her swift, supple movements. The line of her throat, the light dew on her forehead—everything about her was special, and desirable.

Part of his desire was physical—he hadn't slept with a woman for a good while. But only part. What he felt—the love, the need—tugged on his heart and his mind as powerfully and insistently as it did upon his body.

He watched her raise and tie up the flaps of her tent while a doe and her fawn slowly, cautiously crossed the meadow near the dead trees. He longed for some way to catch and hold that fleeting image—Nellie, the deer, the meadows. Hold it forever.

Shadows stretched out, purple-blue and perceptibly colder. The thin air went whistling down into his lungs to produce a high mountain giddiness. Storm clouds blew up from the north, and the sunset disappeared in a sudden spring snowfall. To start the fire he had to dust a layer of white from the wood.

After dark they put on heavy coats. The fire generated a comforting warmth and light. Mack was famished: Slab pork, tinned beans, and hardtack tasted like a banquet at his mansion. He squatted with his fork and tin plate, his physical need strong again. Fortunately his coat hid that.

The snow diminished and the clouds passed, a quarter-moon visible now in the clear dark sky. When he couldn't stand the need any longer, he tossed his plate aside and reached for Nellie's hand.

"There's no way to say this but straight out—"

"Mack." It was half pleading, half warning.

"Come live with me. Marry me."

Her eyes grew larger and misted at the corners, as if she wanted what he wanted. He chafed her small hand between his harder ones. But she pulled away, and like the moment on Sentinel Dome, this one also passed.

"It's a lovely, flattering thought, Mack. I don't mean to dismiss or demean it when I tell you I can't do it."

"Why the hell not?"

"I have an agenda—just like you. Where is Mr. T. Fowler Haines, by the way? Still in Riverside?"

"Yes, that seems to be a good permanent home for him."

"I finally did some reading about that intrepid gentleman—"

"Don't change the subject. If you married me, you'd never have to work again."

The wind billowed sparks from the fire. Little ribbons of snow fluttered around the tents. Nellie's laugh rang in the frosty air.

"Am I really hearing this? Yes, I fear so. I have got to say this so you never misunderstand again. I care for you. I care for you very much. But I am not a Victorian woman. I am not dutiful, submissive, or a lot of other things I probably should be in the opinion of most men and far too many women. Well, too bad. I'm Nellie Ross, Natalia Rotchev, no one else. I have many more books to write, more than I can finish in a lifetime. I'll always work."

"But you're still a woman. There's absolutely no need for you to support yourself—"

She slapped her knees and stood. "You're impossible. Sometimes I think the word is *unredeemable*. Did you hear anything I said? One word?"

It was going wrong again. He didn't know what to do about it, and got angry. "Yes, but damn it, I don't understand. I never understood Carla. I don't understand you."

"Precisely, my dear." Her light tone didn't conceal a sudden bitterness. "Maybe that's the whole trouble. You don't try."

He gripped her shoulders. "I'm trying tonight."

Again she disengaged herself and he swore, his breath pluming out, a cloud tinted by the firelight. Shoving his hands in his pockets, he walked around the windbreak to the edge of the dead trees. With his back turned he said, "I'll sort out what we need for breakfast and hang it up so the bears can't reach it. That way we can get an early start down to the valley."

"Yes. That's best. It's turned cold up here."

He walked around the windbreak to the fire. She'd already gone in and laced the flaps of her tent.

Mack came into the billiard room buttoning his overcoat. Johnson sat on one end of the table, and at the side, standing on a stool, Little Jim leaned into the glow of electric light from fixtures with shades of green glass. Johnson rolled a red ball across the baize from his right hand to his left.

"One," the boy exclaimed.

Mack watched from the shadows. His son saw him and his face illuminated. Johnson whizzed a white ball to his left hand. Jim jumped up and down and clapped.

"Two."

Johnson ruffled Jim's blond hair. "This little sprout's mighty quick. He can count to ten easy, and up to twenty with a bit of cogitatin'." He ambled over to Mack. "You should stick around a little more and see."

The boy rolled balls across the table, all the while darting shy, affectionate looks at his father. Mack kept his voice down. "I give him all the time I can."

"An hour at the end of the day when he's tired ain't hardly enough. Not when he's nigh onto three and growin' and changin' so fast."

"What makes you such an expert on fatherhood?"

"I was a sprout once myself," Johnson said, just as testily. "A Comanche on a toot put a bullet in my pa, and I didn't

435

have him no more after age two. It hurts a youngster to grow up like that.''

"I do my best," Mack said. He crouched down and held out his arms. Little Jim ran to him. "Good night, son. Go to bed and get your rest." Mack hugged him and then left. The boy stared after him for a long moment.

He turned into the passage leading from Jessie Street. The fog rolled thick and white, muffling the hoot of a ferry in the Bay. Under a dim electric bulb on the rear stoop, Mack shot a look over his shoulder, then knocked. On the second knock someone unfastened the inner bolt.

"Mack," she said, stepping back.

"Evening, Margaret." He went into the dark little foyer that smelled of frying. Sounds of clinking dishes drifted from the far end of a hallway. "I felt in need of your hospitality tonight."

"You're going upstairs, then?"

"Yes, and I don't care to be seen."

That surprised her; always before, he'd used the front stairs, not the back door, which the girls and some of the customers jokingly called the husband's door. All at once his respectability was weighing on him—and evidently other things too. He looked tired, downright haggard. His voice had an uncharacteristic bite.

Margaret gestured to the stair, trying for a light tone. "We always protect the anonymity of our patrons. Go right ahead. We aren't busy tonight; you'll have your choice. I'll put it on your bill."

He nodded, went up quickly, and disappeared.

A girl with a peacock-green wrapper floating over her heavy white thighs crossed the landing smoking a cigarette. Faint laughter and thumping drifted down. Margaret pressed her closed hand to pale lips never touched up with color.

"Yes, go on," she said. "You could have any woman in the place if you only knew it."

IT WAS A SUMMER OF TROUBLE IN SAN FRANCISCO, **48**
the very trouble Haverstick had predicted.

The national convention of the Epworth League came to town in July, and the Employers Association, operating through its Drayman's Committee, secured the league's sizable baggage-handling contract for a nonunion firm. "So the association's first target is the teamsters," Haverstick said. The union was barely a year old, but already a strong member of the Labor Council.

The nonunion draymen found themselves unable to handle all the luggage of thousands of Epworth delegates and issued an emergency call for help. When union teamsters refused to respond, the Employers Association declared all union drivers locked out and further declared an end to the closed shop in the cartage business.

The union called a general strike on the waterfront. Along with the draymen, merchant seamen went out, longshoremen, warehouse workers—something like fifteen thousand men on both sides of the Bay. The commerce of the harbor came to a halt.

But produce from the Valley kept pouring into Oakland and rotting. Boxcars piled up in the rail yards and cargo ships rode at anchor, waiting to unload. Mack honored the strike, put his warehouse men on half-pay for the duration, and watched anger build on both sides.

Valley farmhands came over the Coast Range and started to handle the piled-up produce. Berkeley students were recruited as summer stevedores. The inevitable result was violence— scuffles, rock-throwing. Someone poured kerosene on two hundred crates of melons softening on a dock and set them afire. A warehouse belonging to Himmel, Mack's camp-mate at the Bohemian Grove, was vandalized at night.

Just a few defended the strikers. And just one newspaper, the *Examiner*. Hearst's editor Tom Williams wrote, "The attempt of the Employers Association to destroy the teamsters union is an act of criminal viciousness without parallel in the annals of the City."

Chief of Police Sullivan didn't see it that way. A colonel of militia in '94, Sullivan had moved ruthlessly against railroad strikers in Sacramento. Ordering his troops to fire, he had earned the nickname Shoot Low.

Shoot Low Sullivan said the nonunion teamsters would work, and the wagons would roll without hindrance. To ensure it he hired what he called special police. "Ex-convicts and Spanish-American veterans out of work," Mack fumed to Johnson. "They're registering their addresses in empty hotel rooms. You know who's supplying their pistols and clubs? The Employers Association."

Mayor Jim Phelan, whom Mack knew and admired, seemed to lose control of events. Pleading the need to maintain order, he approved the use of additional, specially deputized police officers. That infuriated the unions. Then he refused to call for state troops, and that enraged the businessmen. One of the City's best and most popular mayors suddenly found himself without a constituency.

The summer of trouble became a season of death. On September 6, at the Pan American Exposition in Buffalo, a deranged anarchist shot President William McKinley, who died eight days later. Johnson's commander in Cuba, Roosevelt, became the nation's twenty-fifth president, three weeks from his forty-third birthday.

"Teddy's all right," Johnson declared. "A mite green, but plenty of grit. You ever need help from Uncle Sam, I'll not hesitate to knock on his front door."

On September 29, several off-duty special policemen walked out of the Thalia, a dive on Kearney Street. They had been drinking for several hours. Some passersby recognized them as strikebreakers, and taunted them. Out of nowhere, other men came running with fists cocked and clubs raised, and the specials drew their pistols. The regular police refused to respond to the riot alarm.

Mack's face went white when he read the names of those killed and wounded. Knocked down with a bullet through his left leg was one Alonzo (Lon) Coglan, a special formerly employed as a San Francisco detective.

In answer to the Thalia riot, the union called a mass meeting at Metropolitan Hall. Four thousand chanting, shouting workingmen jammed every seat and squatted in the aisles. Mack donated half the rent on the hall, and watched the rally from backstage.

The young socialist writer London gave a fiery speech. Next

came Father Peter Yorke of the San Francisco Archdiocese. The priest was an Irishman from Galway and delivered his jeremiad in lilting English, pounding the podium repeatedly.

"They bring in university students and call it free enterprise. But they are rich men's sons, working not for themselves but against the common man . . ." There was cheering and foot-stomping. The floor shook and the gas mantles rattled.

Mack got a start. In the wings at the opposite side he recognized Diego Marquez, shabby and somewhat wild-eyed, Felicia clinging to his arm.

"What's he doing here?" Mack whispered to London.

"I'm told he's an old friend of Yorke. Wanted to speak but they wouldn't let him. Too extreme even for this crowd."

". . . a union of rich men attempting to crush the unions of poor men," Yorke thundered, waving his arms. "But they will fail. Because we are strong. We are steadfast. There will be no compromise. There will be no negotiations. There will be no retreat."

Every throat roared. Mack saw Diego Marquez staring at him and he lifted his hand to acknowledge him. Marquez hugged Felicia to his side, swaying back and forth. Drunk? His glassy stare met Mack's and slid away. Mack understood. Marquez was ashamed of being rejected.

A moment later, when Mack looked again, Marquez and the girl were gone.

Rain poured down on the sagging planks of the wharf, water streaming over the five-foot-high sign on the sloping roof above the loading dock.

CHANCE PRODUCE COMPANY
SAN FRANCISCO—SACRAMENTO—ODESTO—FRESNO

The warehouse sprawled along one side of a finger wharf jutting into the Bay. Only half the wharf frontage belonged to Mack, that nearer the Embarcadero. The warehouse at the outer end belonged to Oscar Himmel. To reach it, draymen had to drive past Mack's building.

In front of Mack's loading dock, blocking the wharf, half a dozen sodden pickets straggled around and around in a circle. Rain soaked and blurred their cardboard placards: WORKERS TOGETHER; NO SCAB LABOR; UNION STEVEDORES ON STRIKE.

Suddenly came the sound of iron wagon tires and hooves and a line of four wagons turned into the head of the wharf. A picket ran up the dock stairs, darted past some empty crates, and flung the door open.

"They're here, Mr. Chance."

It was two days after the Thalia bloodletting. Mack had heard through Haverstick that he was to be a target. He struggled into his coat and dashed outside, the Shopkeeper's Colt in its holster under his coattail.

He ran down onto the wet wharf as the first two-horse wagon approached. In addition to the driver it carried three passengers, tough-looking men in rain slickers and derbies. He recognized one, who stood directly back of the driver with the arrogance of a Roman charioteer. Buck Float was his name. He had worked for Mack for three months and was a Spanish-American War veteran; he'd complained of war nerves to justify frequent absences. He disappeared one Friday and never came back, though Mack had already decided to fire him. Buck Float was a heavy man with blond brows and a nose like a ripe beet. He wore a soiled duster and automobiling cap.

The creaking axles, grinding iron tires, hooves clopping on the planks, were the only sounds beside the rain. Mack saw no weapons but felt sure the specials had them.

He strode to the open side of the wharf. The water was greasy green, full of floating fruit rinds and paper trash. There was just enough room between this wharf and the next for a small vessel to dock. Way up at the head of the wharf Mack noticed someone watching, a small man in an overcoat and soft hat. Except for a brushy mustache, his face was a blur, but Mack thought he recognized him by his diminutive size. The man stepped into the lee of a shanty and from there continued to observe the advance of the wagons.

Mack moved between the worried pickets and the first wagon. The driver reined his horses and shoved the brake lever with his boot. Rain leaked off the hat brim of a special with his hand plunged under his gleaming slicker. Waiting. Just waiting . . .

"No traffic on the pier," Mack said. "We're honoring the strike."

"Get out of the way," Buck Float said. "These wagons belong to Oscar Himmel and we're going down to his warehouse to pick up a load. I'm deputized to protect Himmel's property."

"Doesn't matter. Turn around," Mack said. Rain ran down his face and collected in his hair, setting up a maddening itch. He wanted to glance up to the sign on the roof of the loading dock, but didn't dare.

The men with Buck Float stood up. Float's duster blew open and underneath it Mack saw a nickeled gun in an old holster. Buck Float tugged it to free it up.

"Chance, everybody knows you're in bed with these dirty communists. But Mr. Himmel won't allow you to infringe on his rights. We're duly deputized and we aim to see you don't."

"Don't push this, Buck. I've no quarrel with you anymore, or with any of these men, only with the people who hired you." Mack's palms prickled; fear made his belly hurt. "Leave peaceably. I don't want trouble."

"But you got it," Buck Float said with gleeful fervor. His hand flashed out with the nickeled pistol. Mack gestured upward to his right.

"Those men on the roof don't want trouble either, Buck."

The driver and specials turned as one. Two warehousemen with shotguns were balancing on the sloped roof at each end of the tall sign. They'd been hiding behind it.

The rain struck the roof and ran off, splashing the wharf and leaking through the cracks. A wagon horse busily dropped horse pies under his tail. Buck Float raised the nickeled gun to shoulder height, aiming at a man on the roof. Mack snatched his Colt out and steadied it with both hands.

"Don't."

Buck Float lowered his muzzle an inch or so, studying Mack over his gun arm. "I don't b'lieve you got the balls to pull that trigger, Chance."

"You try me, Buck. Come on."

"I'm turning around," the first driver blurted. "I ain't dyin' for Himmel or any other nabob. Sit down, Buck." Buck Float clenched his teeth. "Buck, damn you, I'm leavin'." Float delivered himself of some obscenities, and jerked the nickeled pistol down.

Mack lowered his revolver to waist level. The men on the roof held their positions as the driver executed a wide turn in Mack's loading bay and passed the other three wagons, which, one by one, turned around in the dock. Mack let his shoulders slump. His gut hurt fiercely.

He waved the men off the roof and trudged toward the door, his shoes squeaking and leaking water. He'd forgotten about the small man still standing in the lee of the shanty, watching.

"Quite a little stand-off," Johnson said early the next day. "All the papers got the story. Most ain't very complimentary about you."

"I'm used to that."

"I'd of been there with you 'f you hadn't been so damn secretive about it."

"I didn't want anyone hurt, least of all my friends."

"You don't seem too pleased about trouncin' that crowd."

"Nobody trounced anybody. We turned them back with loaded guns and an ambush. I had to do it, but I didn't like it. I'm guilty of using the same tactics as Shoot Low Sullivan. It solves nothing."

Johnson shrugged to say maybe, then tugged a scrap of paper from his vest. "Took a call on the downstairs phone while you was up with Alex. Gentleman named Roof. Asked you to meet him at the Pup. I wrote it down." He showed the scrap: *PUP— 7 PM—ROOF.*

"Ruef—that's who it was," Mack exclaimed.

"How's that?"

"There was a man watching down at the wharf yesterday. I thought I recognized him from a distance. Abe Ruef." He spelled the last name. "He's a lawyer. You don't follow local politics—"

"Hell no. A politician's just a road agent with a stiff collar an' a church membership."

"Something in that," Mack agreed. "Ruef cuts quite a figure. He's a Republican. Or was."

"One of you boys that's always suckin' hind tit, hey?"

That was true; San Francisco politics had been dominated for some years by Democrats and reform independents. Mack explained, "Ruef's worked in the party a long time. This spring he made a move to take control from Crimmins and Kelly and organized a splinter group, the Republican League. The league got whipped in the August primary. I voted against them because they struck me as a bunch of opportunists. Ruef immediately started promoting a new party. Which says to me he's chiefly interested in promoting himself."

"What kind of party?"

"Labor. Ruef and Izzy Less from the barbers' union are the organizers. They've already pulled in most of the waiters, hack drivers, cooks, and beer-bottlers. Ruef says they'll put up candidates in the fall election. He's a tough little bastard. Knows the town well—he grew up here. His father started the Meyer Ruef Dry Goods Company down on Market. Ruef went to Berkeley and Hastings Law College. I wonder what he wants out of me?"

"Y'don't suppose it could be money?" Johnson drawled.

* * *

The Pup was just up Stockton from Market. He walked in at ten past seven. The little restaurant was crowded and noisy. Electric light glared off white-tile walls and floor, and odors of cigar and fish floated in the hazy air. Waiters in long aprons shoved and blustered in and out of the kitchen with mountainous trays of dishes. Two huge silver coffee boilers behind the counter created a strange distorted mural of the scene.

Abraham Ruef spotted Mack from the rear corner table where he customarily held court. He dismissed the police sergeant seated there and then stood up as Mack approached. Ruef was about thirty-five. He wore a smart single-breasted suit and a dark striped four-in-hand. Several things about him struck Mack at once: his Gallic nose, his bouncy energy, the gleam of his bright brown eyes, shiny as sable fur. He was smaller than Mack remembered.

Ruef shot out his hand. He smelled of sweet cologne. "Mr. Chance. What a pleasure to see you again."

"Thanks. Mutual." Mack laid his stick and homburg on the table. He ordered black coffee, Ruef another slice of cherry pie.

The little pol gestured to the restaurant. "I hope the din doesn't annoy you. I like the energy in here. I do more business at this table than I do in my law offices."

Ruef's smile was cordial and winning. Mack could easily imagine him stepping right off of a Paris boulevard. Ruef's ancestors were in fact French. He enhanced the boulevardier look with a pink carnation in his lapel.

Ruef forked the pie with small, delicate motions, while Mack stirred coffee in a heavy white mug. "I watched the contretemps outside your warehouse yesterday," the pol said.

"I noticed."

"Everyone knew it was coming. I wanted to see how you handled it."

"And?"

"You handled it admirably. Still, you were interfering with the rights of Oscar Himmel."

"I was honoring the strike."

Ruef kept smiling, but he jabbed like a prosecutor. "Come, sir. The pier itself—the access road—you don't own those."

"Strikers have tied up other public thoroughfares."

"Breaking the law."

"To enforce a higher one: 'Thou shalt not squeeze blood out of thy weaker brethren.'"

"I like that. I was raised on the Hebrew Talmud—the patriarchs and the prophets. I admire men with a passion for justice. I was testing you with my questions."

443

"Cross-examining, I'd say."

Ruef laughed. His mention of religion struck Mack as calculated. The man was a manipulator.

"Down to cases, then. We've scarcely exchanged ten words at Republican functions. I thought we should have a chat because you endorse the strike. Not many men with your wealth and status would take that risk."

Mack kept stirring his coffee, waiting.

Ruef darted looks around, then leaned in. "I can tell you confidentially that Governor Gage intends to intervene to end the strike."

"That's bad news. Henry Gage is in the pocket of Walter Fairbanks, William Herrin, and the SP Political Bureau."

"Nevertheless, the unions simply can't win against hired strikebreakers and the police. I feel a settlement is inevitable, and I'm urging it, though it won't be favorable to our side."

So now it was *our side*. Mack's wariness grew.

"I like the situation as little as you do, Mr. Chance. But continuing the strike is foolhardy, as foolhardy as your confrontation with those thugs. What if there had been bloodshed? Bloodshed accomplishes nothing. We must take control of the machinery. Win the workingman's fight with votes."

"Are you talking about your new party?"

"That's right. The Union Labor party. Do you know Eugene Schmitz?"

"I've seen him conduct the orchestra at the Columbia Theatre."

"Another confidence, then. Schmitz will be our mayoral candidate."

Mack almost laughed. "He's a violin player. What does he know about running a city?"

Annoyed, Ruef said, "Everything. Because I'll teach him. Gene's an ideal candidate, German and Irish parents, Catholic, a family man. The musicians' union is less threatening than many others. And he'll look good on the platform—they don't call him Handsome Gene for nothing. He'll be the champion of the workingmen of San Francisco. He'll represent them in our halls of power. Just as Senator Abe Ruef of California will someday represent them in Washington. It took me years to understand that if you want to do good, the power to do it must come first. Power is the lever of Archimedes. Power is everything."

The electric lights glittered in Ruef's brown eyes, and he draped his arm over Mack's chair with a false bonhomie.

Dangerous man, Mack thought. "I hear what you're saying," he said out loud. "But I'm not sure why you wanted to meet."

"Because we share a common objective. We both want to build power for San Francisco's most important constituency."

"So you really have abandoned the Republicans?"

"I'll use them if I can. But most of them are entrenched plutocrats. Gutless. You're an exception. The Union Labor party is looking for exceptional men, men with the courage to support the candidacy of Gene Schmitz—with their ballots . . . and their checkbooks."

There it was. Mack leaned back. A waiter stormed by: "Goddamn it, coming through."

"I'm afraid I'm not your man. After your league lost the primary, you put your allegiance somewhere else. Overnight. I'm for supporting the workingman. I'm not interested in exploiting him."

The little pol's toothy smile turned cold. "That's a short-sighted view. Let me tell you what I foresee in San Francisco. I foresee a day when nothing moves on our docks—nothing happens in our government—without the sanction of the Union Labor party and its hand-picked mayor and supervisors. You may count on this, too. When we're in power, we'll assist our friends and remember those who disdained friendship."

I don't like this man, Mack thought. He drew himself up in his chair. "In other words, money up front will guarantee favors?"

Ruef flung down his napkin. "I don't think I care for that. I could name certain other intelligent, progressive gentlemen who don't take such a cynical view of friendship. They've donated to the party and, what's more, they've retained me on a regular basis to represent them in the future at City Hall."

Mack stood up. "Ruef, I don't pay extortion money. I especially don't pay it in advance."

The little pol's mustache quivered. His closely shaved cheeks were white as the china mugs. "That remark was a mistake, Mr. Chance."

"We'll see. Excuse me."

"Surely. We'll meet again."

His eyes promised it wouldn't be cordial.

With the intervention of Governor Gage, the strike ended, the terms of the settlement kept secret. The union drivers simply picked up and went back to work. Mack's warehouse men didn't want to talk about it, except to say the union shop was dead in San Francisco.

Abe Ruef personally wrote a basic five-minute speech for Handsome Gene Schmitz. He rehearsed the candidate, and Schmitz gave the speech everywhere, bringing to it a natural flamboyance from his theater work. Soon the women in his audience were sighing and wringing their hands while their husbands stamped and whistled for everyone's new idol.

The dismal conclusion of the strike had an effect on the campaign, driving union men to work hard for a political victory. They were helped by the lackluster candidates of the regular parties. The Republicans offered a hack, the city auditor. The Democrats put up Joe Tobin, a young supervisor with money; his chances were diminished by the widespread unpopularity of Mayor Phelan. The Monarch of the Dailies was unimpressed with the whole lot.

> The major candidates have been carefully picked over by representatives of the Southern Pacific, the Market Street Railway, and the Spring Valley Water Company. Those chosen are sure to carry out orders with a fearless disregard of the public good.

On the night of November 5, 1901, at Republican headquarters, Mack watched them chalk up the tally.

Tobin—12,000.

Wells—17,000.

Schmitz—21,000.

"Well," he remarked, "the wolf's in the fold."

49 ON A DRIZZLY NIGHT THAT WINTER, MACK WENT to Margaret's for dinner. While she cooked pork chops, and green beans spiced with ham chunks and brown sugar, he sliced golden bell peppers and artichokes brought from his own warehouse. She served a rich, almost syrupy merlot from someone else's winery; he made a comment about that.

Margaret had recently begun to fix dinner for them at least once a week when his schedule allowed. She lived in a flat next to the Maison Napoleon, but no connecting door breached the thick plaster wall between. It was as if she could shut out that part of her life by coming into these proper Victorian rooms furnished with the inevitable three-legged tables, potted greenery, old Rogers groups, and other assorted bric-a-brac.

Knife in his right hand, Mack pushed green beans onto the fork in his left. It was the European way; Margaret had taught him. His cravat was loosened, his collar unbuttoned, his vest open, his sleeves rolled up. Under the imitation Tiffany-glass electric, they sat together in a relaxed, almost domestic intimacy. While he finished eating she darned a tiny tear in a yellowed lace tablecloth. She never ate much—to preserve her figure, she said.

"I don't know a lot about Abe Ruef," Mack said after drinking some wine. "But I had a bad impression of him last fall, and it hasn't improved. I've never seen anyone move in so fast. They're paying court to him at the Pup until midnight or later, every night." Ruef's party had elected not only the mayor but three of its slate of eighteen supervisors. It was a strong start.

"I know him slightly. He dines next door about once a month. Always orders in French. He's proud of all the languages he speaks. He never goes upstairs. They say ambition leaves him no time for women."

"It's a fairly common disease," Mack said with a wry look. "Rhett Haverstick told me Ruef's picking up clients right and left: Pacific Telephone and Telegraph, Pat Calhoun's United Railroads. Rhett claims Ruef collects five hundred dollars a month from every one of them."

"What's going to happen?"

"While the voters let him get away with it, nothing. Schmitz is a lightweight, but he's a superb actor, and Ruef has a certain brassy charm. People like both of them."

He pushed his plate away, stretched, and patted his stomach. He felt the beginnings of a potbelly. "You're a fine cook."

"Anything for a friend." She applied herself to her needlework but promptly pricked her finger. Then, avoiding his eye, she asked, "Will you be going next door tonight?"

"No, I just want to relax. This is the best refuge in San Francisco. Better than my clubs. There, someone always wants something. Usually a donation."

He sighed, enjoying the rare contentment. A gold-plated clock on the parlor mantel chimed the quarter hour. He plucked a silver cigar case from his coat nearby.

"You said you were going south again—" she began.

"In a few days. I could stand some sunshine." He lit up and

447

puffed. Outside, rain fell harder, making their little island of light all the more cozy. "That's a lovely old tablecloth."

"Irish lace." She raised it to show the pattern. "It was my mother's only decent possession. I treasure it because it reminds me of her. It also reminds me that a person needn't stay in one place swilling pigs forever."

"Growing up was hard for you, wasn't it?"

She turned her head on that lovely long neck. A swan's neck, he called it in his thoughts. The face of a sad freckled child seemed to glimmer behind the face of the mature young woman. "The fine people of California, the ones who settled in the delta twenty years before my father, didn't exactly welcome dirt farmers. 'Pike' was not a name you called a friend."

"So you ran away. How did you ever get this place?"

"I worked for it." Watching for a reaction, she added, "In someone else's place. Resembling the rooms upstairs at the Maison. I'll tell you this: Mission Street won't be my last stop."

"What do you want from life, Margaret?"

The rain fell, beating on bay windows hidden by heavy velvet drapes. Far away, a trolley clanged on Market Street. She pressed the tablecloth into her lap, her thimble shining like a nugget of silver. The line of her slim bosom trembled with a noticeable tension.

"Something better. I want something much better than this."

Her eyes said the rest, and it made him uncomfortable. He put the burning cigar in a tray and stepped to her side, laying a paternal hand on her shoulder. She let out a breath, the tautness leaving her, and she averted her eyes to the precious tablecloth.

"I'd better start home."

"Walking?"

"I don't mind the rain. The air will do me good." He patted her. "I'll see you as soon as I come back. Meantime, thanks for the good meal."

"I don't have the budget for the kind of dinners you prepare. Or the talent."

He laughed and kissed her temple in a chaste way. Her high-piled auburn hair had a warm fresh smell. "You're a wonderful cook. A wonderful friend."

Her right hand swept up and across to press his. Standing behind her, he saw her pained face in the back mirror of a heavy old sideboard.

Quickly, she lightened the pressure of her hand. "Well, I'm grateful for that much, anyway."

After he went out, she locked the door, then leaned against it with the tablecloth held between her breasts. She closed her eyes and let the tears roll down.

He lay awake in the small hours. It happened more and more lately. Columns of numbers streamed through his head, lists of things to be done.

He kept a pad beside the great imperial bed with the *JMC* carved at the apex of the headboard. He was practiced at scribbling in the dark, though the notes were hell to read in the morning.

It stormed violently about 2 A.M., thunder bumping over the Bay, and the high dark house seemed to breathe and shudder. Margaret's face disturbed his rest. He knew what she wanted—what he could never give.

The stairs creaked. He opened his door and saw the glowing circles of Alex Muller's spectacles. The young man was going downstairs in his nightshirt, lamp held aloft. He coughed, a sound like shoes scuffing cement.

The light disappeared. Far below, Alex kept coughing. Mack wrote on the pad, then flung his hands under his head and shut his eyes.

No use. Too many worries, steady as the rain. Too many memories. Too much guilt . . .

Tonight, that involving Margaret dominated the rest.

As Mack strode into the sun-flooded office, Alex jumped up from his corner desk. "Ready, sir? So am I. All packed."

It was half past ten. Three tickers chattered and spewed tapes of the latest trades and postings from the stock exchanges—San Francisco, California, and Pacific. Mack had also installed a private telegraph wire and key, and a second telephone.

"I want to say good-bye to Jim. Is he outside?"

"No, sir, in the library."

"On a morning like this?"

He ran down three flights and flung open the library doors. Little Jim sat in a red velvet chair, his feet dangling above the floor. Johnson knelt beside him, watching the boy play with some kind of toy.

Mack stormed in. The dark room smelled of dust and leather bindings. "What the devil have you got there, Jim?"

His son held it up so he could see. It was a Chinese abacus, brightly finished in lacquer. On the frame, tiny hand-painted dragons chased each other, spurting fire from their jaws and smoke from their nostrils.

"Where did you get it?"

Johnson stood, his knee joints popping. "Kim Luck in the kitchen dug it up. Alex says Jim's a whizzer at ciphering. He's picked this up real quick. Jim, show your pa. How 'bout five hundred and seven?"

Little Jim studied the abacus a moment. Then his small hand pulled down a five-unit bead on the third wire from the right and clicked it against the dividing bar. He pulled down no beads on the second wire, a five-unit bead on the first wire, then pushed up two one-unit beads. Proudly he showed the abacus.

"Suan-pan," he said.

"That's the Chink name of the thing," Johnson said.

"Why are you fooling with that on a sunny day?" Mack grabbed it. "Go on outside and play."

"Don't want to, Pa. I want to do numbers." He reached for the abacus.

Mack kept it away from him. "I said go outside. Get some air."

Jim's small hands closed to fists. He jutted his jaw and held his breath, and turned red as he marched from the room. "Jim?" Mack called. "I'll see you in a week or two—"

In answer, a door slammed.

Mack threw the abacus on a table, then whipped the drapes open. Sunshine poured in. "This place is cheerful as a tomb."

"You ain't much better. You rag that boy too hard."

"I'm not going to raise a hothouse lily. I want him to enjoy the outdoors like everybody else in California."

"Maybe he don't take to it. Maybe ridin' and campin' and all the stuff you like ain't his style. He's a quiet one, but he's brainy. He can already pick out words in the newspaper."

"I want him outside, every day."

"Hell, he's only three. He don't have to climb Mount Shasta just yet—"

"Don't tell me how to raise my son." Mack walked out.

Johnson sighed. "And good-bye yourself," he muttered. "Jesus."

Mack found Little Jim walking along the Sacramento Street side of the house, dragging a stick across the uprights of the wrought-iron fence, *rat-tat-tat.*

"There you are. Give me a hug before I go."

The boy clutched the stick to his shirt.

"Come on, Jim. I didn't mean to yell. Fresh air's good for you."

And Little Jim was pale. Very pale from too much time indoors. The California climate had been good for Mack, and he wanted the same benefits for his son.

Stubbornly, he crouched down and held out his arms. Little Jim hesitated, snapped the stick in two, and edged sideways into Mack's embrace.

"I'll miss you," Mack said.

"Sure, Pa. Good-bye."

Mack felt the boy's stiffness. He was holding back, resenting him. *Damn.*

Alex drove around the corner with the buggy. Leaving, Mack watched Little Jim standing there without a smile. Joyless as a little old man in the California sunshine.

For the train trip, Alex carried a satchel of business papers and correspondence. Mack's valise held a similar stack, and some books: *The Octopus* by Nellie's friend Frank Norris, which he hadn't read; his marked copy of *The Conquest of Arid America* by William Smythe; and one he plunged into immediately, heedless of Alex's pleas that they work. Appleton's had published Nellie's new novel two weeks before. *Range of Light* was essentially another romance, but a somber, bitter one. Mack stayed awake most of the night in his berth, mesmerized by it.

The story involved a Yosemite hotel keeper seduced by greed and the blandishments of a San Francisco developer, who wanted to buy in and treble the size of the hotel. The hotelman, an older man, had previously brought a young wife to the valley. At first the natural beauty had diverted her from the loveless marriage. When Nellie introduced her, she was restless and discouraged.

A young Basque illegally herding sheep in the valley became her summer lover. In one scene they met secretly at Yosemite Falls. They soon saw themselves as allies in a war against the innkeeper's avarice and bourgeois mentality. Always, the Sierra range loomed as a presence, its light-flooded purity mocking their furtive love in the shadows on the valley floor.

Finally they decided to risk a meeting in full daylight. They would climb up together to taste the sun—once. The husband learned of their plan, followed, and shot them both during their tryst on Cloud's Rest, then accidentally fell to his death on the way down.

It made no difference in the hotel scheme. The developer took over the property, remodeled, and turned the hotel into an enormous success, bringing raucous crowds who sang and shouted all night long in the new saloon bar. In the final pages, a drunken guest kicked the bar's player piano. After the guests left, the piano kept playing "The Blue Danube" faster and faster, louder and louder. The piano started to shake itself to pieces, wires snapping and pinging, the music growing madder and uglier. It dinned from the open windows, drowned the voices of complaining guests, rolled down the valley. Nellie's last images seemed omens. Frightened deer fled along the banks of the dark river and wild birds flew frantically across the face of the full moon while the music of civilization played on.

He closed the book. Critics might never guess why the "female Zola" painted such a dark portrait of the lovers. He knew one possible answer.

Or was he flattering himself?

Not that it did any good. She was in Carmel—maybe with someone else—and he was here, in a stuffy berth, rattling through the California night, alone.

"Filth," editorialized the *Los Angeles Times*.

> We need no further outpourings of prurient prose and foreign ideology from Miss Ross, Mr. Norris, or any of their debased deviate cronies who purport to be artists and loyal Californians. Let them ply their trade in the sewers of corrupted Europe.

Despite this valiant crusade by General Otis to safeguard the morals of others, Californians bought every available copy of *Range of Light* within a week of publication.

It became a national best-seller. Every literate person in America knew the name Nellie Ross.

The wind raged. Yellow dust hid the mountains and attacked the eyes. Mack leaned into it, gritted his teeth, and held his hat, Alex staggering along behind. Mack had picked a devil of a day to trek out to Indio to reveal his latest scheme.

"Here's the marker. I bought a hundred acres. Fifty of it goes into date palms, the other fifty we'll turn into a camp."

"Camp, sir? What kind?"

"For consumptives. People who need the hot dry climate but can't afford to stay."

The blinding dust hid Alex's immediate reaction.

From an inner pocket Mack took a folded paper. The

screaming wind almost tore it away. "Here are the details and the numbers. We'll put up tents first, then build regular dormitories. We'll bring in cows and chickens. Invalids who can afford to pay something will be charged three dollars a week. If they're indigent, they'll pay nothing. We must hire at least one doctor, and a professional manager. We'll set it up on a nonprofit basis."

"Why are you doing this, sir?"

"Because I've taken a lot from California and I want to give some back. Thousands of people with tuberculosis come here with nothing but hope to sustain them. We can't help all of them, but we can help a few."

Alex's stalwart strength finally gave way. He wept.

"God bless you, Mr. Chance. You are a good man. Such a good man."

In Riverside, Mack inspected the groves and went over the books. He spent an evening with Billy Biggerstaff and the manager's wife and seven children, but their boisterous happiness made him melancholy.

He went up to Ventura for two days with Haven Ogg, then over to San Solaro, where the Wardlow brothers had completed the water system, and Hazard's realty company had already brought in twenty-three families. Cottages were under construction, clear water flowed in the canal, and the derricks continued to draw oil out of the earth.

Back at Villa Mediterranean, he and Alex met with Enrique Potter on a Saturday morning. The attorney, slightly stooped and paunchy now, presented a plat of the Los Angeles region with a webwork of red lines radiating from the center.

"Here are two more interurban lines Henry Huntington has announced. This one adjoins land that you own outside Redlands. This one cuts right through your property in Whittier. Pacific Electric's real estate department approached me last week."

Mack leaned back and tented his fingers. A warm spring breeze rustled papers on his desk. T. Fowler Haines occupied its customary corner.

"I bought some of this property because I was sure the city would expand," he explained to Alex. "You can only go so far west and then you're swimming. Ed Huntington talked about interurbans at the Bohemian Grove, and that's when I started buying more land. Since he incorporated P.E. last year, he's gone faster than I ever dreamed." Mack rubbed his chin. "Sometimes I feel guilty making money this way. Like one of the SP sharks, profiting from knowing ahead of time where the line will be built.''

''A quadruple increase in land values is damned good medicine for guilt,'' Potter said. ''Furthermore, Henry Huntington didn't coerce you into buying land; you did it on your own initiative. Spare me this Southern Pacific shark business.''

Mack laughed. ''All right. You know my bottom price in each case. Don't go below it.'' Potter checkmarked something on his legal pad. Mack shifted papers. ''What about that new acreage in the Cahuenga Valley?''

The attorney touched a folder. ''Here. They've accepted your offer. All the documents refer to the incorporated name, Hollywood.''

''Good work. You two handle the rest.'' Mack left the desk and plucked a fancy white felt Stetson from the rack.

''You're in a devil of a hurry,'' Potter said.

''There's a speed-driving exhibition down on the flats. I don't want to miss it.''

Henry Ford's 999 racer tore across the flat, leaving a rooster tail of dust. The noise was formidable. On a 109-inch wheelbase and a chassis painted rust red, the young automobile wizard from Detroit had created a brute machine and stripped it for speed. No bonnet protected the four-cylinder eighty-horsepower engine. The driver steered by tiller from a precarious seat only big enough for one.

A crowd of about three hundred lined both sides of the road west of Riverside. Some had taken the train from Los Angeles, some had driven carriages, and five had arrived in automobiles, two of them electrics. One gasoline auto belonged to Mack.

He liked the snappy little runabout with its steering tiller, three-gear lever (two forward, plus reverse), and its one-horsepower engine mounted behind the single seat. The auto, from the Olds Motor Works and thus named ''Oldsmobile,'' had a smart curved dash, a black lacquer finish, red trim, and rakish brass acetylene lamps. At a top speed of twenty miles per hour, it didn't go fast enough for him.

Spectators screamed and cheered as 999 turned around down the road and started back, accelerating for the test mile. Mack jumped up on the seat of Ransom Olds's little runabout and shouted with the rest.

The 999 howled across the finish line and the flagman whipped his green flag back and forth. Not the easiest car to steer, the 999 shot along the shoulder, slowing down. Rather than try another turn, the hired driver put on the brakes.

High on his wooden stand the timekeeper checked his clock. "Time for the measured mile—one minute, eleven and one fifth seconds. A new record for the Ford nine ninety-nine and its demon pilot from Toledo."

Pandemonium.

The driver stopped the racer, stripped off his goggles and leather helmet, and rushed back to the crowd surging to meet him. Only last year, young Barney Oldfield had been racing cycles in Ohio. He began working the crowd with a stubby cigar in his mouth, signing autographs, reveling in the attention.

Mack left the Olds runabout and spent a few minutes studying the 999. Ford had named the racer for the crack train of the New York Central. Fast driving excited Mack. He needed a faster and more powerful automobile to replace the Locomobile and the Olds. Not a steamer, or an electric; they were rapidly losing out to internal combustion. What should he buy? One of those German machines?

He was walking back along the dusty road pondering that when he noticed three people approaching: a man with a woman on each arm. The man's handsome face leaped out.

Mack had a strong urge to avoid them but he didn't, instead striding forward with forced good cheer.

"Wyatt. For God's sake."

Wyatt Paul stopped, his women obediently halting as well. Each held a sleeve of Wyatt's white linen suit, which was most peculiar, severely cut, with a white dickey and Episcopal collar and a white silk kerchief billowing from the breast pocket. Wyatt Paul looked like a photographic negative of a priest.

"By heaven. My partner."

Wyatt smiled, and the sun put that strange opal blaze in his eyes for a moment. Mack pulled his hand back, annoyed; Wyatt had blandly refused to take it.

They appraised each other. Wyatt's tan was darker than ever, yet he didn't look well. He was still dangerously thin, and white streaks like bird's wings swept back through the pomaded black hair above his ears. Curiously, his lips seemed fuller, red and womanly. It gave him a disturbing androgynous quality.

The two young women, both buxom, peered at Wyatt like children awaiting instructions, their high-collared dresses so tight, Mack could see the lines of stays beneath. Corsets cinched in their waists to the smallest possible measurement, which in turn put more emphasis on their breasts. Dust clung to chiffon veils tying down their huge velvet Gainsborough hats trimmed with ostrich plumes. Despite this altogether proper attire, they managed to look like whores.

"Ladies, this is my esteemed partner from San Solaro, James Macklin Chance. This is Deacon Martha. This is Deacon Mary. I remarked to the ladies that you lived near here."

"Arlington Heights," Mack nodded, vaguely uneasy; Wyatt kept track of him. "I presume the bank's getting your royalties to you regularly?"

"Indeed. My bookkeepers at the tabernacle post them and hand me a monthly report."

Mack swept off his Stetson and wiped his forehead. "Did you say *tabernacle*?"

"I did. The Tabernacle of the Sun Universal. We've just moved into our new sanctuary in the foothills near Pasadena. Ten acres, and a remarkable building. It's an octagon—many windows and very few walls. A man named Fowler built some octagonal houses around fifty years ago. He said there was something mystical and healing about the design. Of course it didn't catch on. He was ahead of his time, and dealing with the general public—and we know what *that* consists of," Wyatt said with a little smirk. "Dupes, village idiots, hymn singers—and worse. At any rate, an octagonal building is perfect for us. It fosters openness—the kind of freedom from conventionality that we endorse and encourage."

"So you're a preacher now?"

"I prefer 'teacher,' or 'spiritual leader.' " And Mack heard the old smooth gears mesh, the machinery of charm beginning to grind.

Wyatt brushed away the hands of his companions and let his own flutter and swoop as he spoke. "I founded what you might call a secular faith. We worship and study the natural forces symbolized by the sun."

"Health—healing—wholeness," Deacon Martha chirped with a vapid smile. Or was it Deacon Mary?

"We recognize the rightful supremacy of man's physical side," Wyatt said. "We cultivate its well-being. We maintain that robust health and completely free expression of biologic drives are the highest form of morality."

"That should make your church very popular."

The cynicism brought a scowl from Wyatt, but the other deacon chirped, "Oh, yes. We have more than nine hundred communicants already."

Mack slowly got over his surprise. Why should he be surprised at all? Wyatt had always been ambitious, amoral, and enormously persuasive. California was a seedbed for strange cults that appeared and vanished as regularly as the green hills of spring.

"Ladies, wait for me in the carriage," Wyatt said.

"But June—" one said.

"Do as you're told, sweet." He smiled and grasped her arm. Her knees buckled and Mack realized he'd hurt her. The other girl supported her as they hurried away, their fine dust ruffles dragging through dirt.

Still uneasy, Mack said, "If you're interested in autos, you must be prospering. I'm delighted."

"Are you. How generous. As a matter of fact, we're attracting a lot of rich communicants from Iowa and other states in the Midwest. They find the climate and our doctrine liberating."

Suddenly he stepped in close. The sun behind him put a halo around his head. "Is Carla with you?"

"No. We're divorced."

He stepped back. "You took her away from me, used her— then you disposed of her, is that it?"

"Come on, Wyatt. That happened years ago."

"Bad memories linger, my friend."

"We aren't friends, so stop pretending we are. Carla made her choice; I didn't force her. As for disposing of her later— she left me. Eagerly, I might say. That should make you feel good. I think we've said all we have to say."

He tipped his Stetson and walked off.

"Barney! Barney!" admirers were chanting back along the road as Oldfield posed for a cameraman who ducked under a black drape. *"Oldfield, hurrah!"*

The breeze snapped Wyatt's creased white trousers, soiled now with country dust. Naked hate disfigured his handsome face.

In the double bed at the hotel, Deacon Mary snored lightly with her cheek on his left arm. Deacon Martha worked diligently at his crotch. "Junie, don't you like this? Mmm, Junie. June?"

Indifferent, far away, he fondled her hair. Damn Mack for spoiling the day. Wyatt couldn't forgive him for stealing Carla.

Mack's success enraged him with jealousy. No—not so much Mack's success as his public personage. James Macklin Chance was a name often seen in the California dailies. J. M. Chance was not only a millionaire, he was a personality.

Well, goddamn it, Wyatt Junius Paul was on his way to that same pinnacle. He was mining gold from the fools who flocked

457

to the tabernacle. He was riding a cresting wave of his own ingenious devising. He was out in the sun again, after a long dark obscurity that he preferred to forget. *Couldn't* . . .

When he'd left San Solaro, he started to dip into his oil royalties. He could survive on them, but survival wasn't enough. He wanted spectacular wealth. Even more than that, he wanted to be known all over California.

Admired.

Loved . . .

How, though? For a long time, he couldn't find the answer. In San Diego, he met and married a tubercular widow. He was tipsy when he proposed, dead drunk when they stood before a justice of the peace. Wyatt helped the woman open a cheap sanitarium-hotel, one of hundreds in the state catering to the one-lung crowd. Her bad health, and the hotel, began to suggest a solution to his dilemma.

The woman died quickly, as he'd hoped, and he liquidated the hotel, using the capital to bottle the first thousand pints of Sunshine Health Syrup. Cripples and hypochondriacs who bought the slop claimed they were energized, pepped up. They fucking well should have been, considering the raw alcohol and cayenne in his recipe.

From this medicinal triumph he advanced to a more elaborate one. Living in a shore-side cottage in Santa Barbara, he built the first of his Alpine Inhalation Cabinets. Price: $1,000. He manufactured and sold eleven of them, making money, but he was still anonymous. He wanted the kind of notoriety and prestige J. M. Chance enjoyed.

One night, frozen from a long swim in the surf and running a fever, he fell asleep and dreamed of his mother in Osage, Kansas, her insane religious faith, her equally insane ideas about health. God, how he wanted to puke from all the oat gruel and graham crackers she forced into his mouth.

He woke before dawn, listening to the Pacific. His fever inflamed him. But so did a sudden idea, clean and simple and perfect for its purpose as a razor's sharp edge. Excited, he opened a hoarded brandy bottle. He was drunk by sunrise, drunk and ecstatic. He would combine his mother's two insane predilections into a single scheme superbly suited to the place, the time, the climate—and all the idiots who came over the mountains wheezing and spitting out bloody gobs from their lungs.

A church—not of the next world, but this. Headed not by some wild Jew claiming divinity but a man of superior intelligence. A church offering not some wispy chromo dream of an afterlife but the vibrant physical reality of longer, lustier life in this one. A *church* of *health*.

Goddamn Mack Chance for demeaning that vision today with his little looks and remarks. Goddamn him for turning his back, walking away, so respectable and superior in his fine suit and white landlord's hat.

And goddamn him most for stealing Carla.

"Bad memories linger. Oh yes they do."

"What did you say, Junie?"

"I said I love you, Deacon Martha."

"Junie," she giggled, "sometimes I think you're just crazy."

He yanked her hair.

"You pig-brained bitch. Put your head down and do your work."

IN THE SPRING OF 1903, MACK FELL INTO CONVER- **50** sation with Fremont Older at the Olympic Club. Older was managing editor of the San Francisco *Bulletin*. Ink for blood, they said of him. He'd risen through the ranks as a tramp printer and reporter, an admirer of Hearst and Hearst's sensational style. He was a huge man with a grenadier mustache and a passion for fine clothes and cigars, with eyes like searchlights and a lumpy bald pate. Wags around town said the lumps came from banging his head against the wall behind his desk. He banged his head over a weak headline or a grammatical gaffe. He banged his head over municipal corruption, which he abhorred. Sometimes he banged his head over things in general.

"I like your editorials about Schmitz," Mack said after he introduced himself.

"Thank you. Glad to hear it. Have a drink. Have a cigar." Mack took one and thanked him. Older then said, "So you agree this administration's rotten—"

"Ever since the Perkins election, you can hardly escape the stench." To return its tame dog George Perkins to the U.S. Senate, the SP Political Bureau had been forced to deal with Abe Ruef, who controlled four key votes in Sacramento necessary for Perkins's reappointment.

"That's only one symptom of the malady, one small symptom. There's an evil sickness spreading through this town, Mr.

Chance. I love San Francisco. I won't see it poisoned and left to die."

"Really that bad, Mr. Older?"

"I'll tell you how bad. Abe Ruef's turned City Hall into a mart in which everything's for sale: permits, votes, favors. Schmitz is a puppet, a nobody. Ruef runs things—from his law office, the Pup, his hip pocket. He throws the unions a bone now and then. Otherwise he ignores them. The corporations kiss his fundament and slip him a thousand or two every month to make sure they win franchises and municipal contracts. Now he's moving into the underworld."

"That I didn't know."

"The saloon owners put their advertising where he tells them to put it. They don't run it in the *Bulletin*, I assure you. He's making inroads in prostitution. It's all covert, hardly visible to the ordinary citizen, but it's poisonous."

"What are you going to do about it?"

"More of what I'm doing already—editorials, exposés. The facts are hard to dig out. Ruef chums around with important men, and I've been threatened. Our publisher Mr. Crothers has been threatened."

"Well, keep at it. I like what you're doing."

"Write us a letter and say so. Men of conscience are going to have to clean up this town. It's either that or let the barbarians reign."

The huge ornate fixture cast a circle of light on the green-covered table in the mansion's card room. On opposite sides, with cigars and mugs of steam beer, Mack and Hellman played two-handed euchre, ten points a game. The light isolated them in the midst of a great darkness.

Hellman had been staying with his son-in-law for the past week. He no longer seemed enthusiastic about his real estate and ranch holdings, which others managed for him. His hair was nearly gone, his eyes watered a lot, he was flatulent, and he climbed stairs with difficulty. It was melancholy to contemplate. It reminded Mack that he too was growing old.

Mack took the last trick with the ten of trumps, scoring a march. He'd euchred his opponent in hand after hand. "That's game, Swampy. Shuffle them."

The old man did so, but listlessly. "I got a new story. A visitor goes into the auto owners' ward at the nuthouse. He don't see nobody. 'What's the matter?' he says to the doc. 'Where are the patients?' 'Oh,' says the doc, 'they're all underneath the beds. Fixing the gears.'"

Mack finished his beer. It tasted stale.

"You didn't laugh," Hellman said. "You hear that one before?"

"Practically the first time I saw an auto."

Hellman shuffled the twenty-four-card deck, then suddenly put it down. "We been doing this four nights now. It gets boring."

Mack reached across to take the cards and shuffle. "You sound like your daughter."

"Did you know she's back from New York?"

"No."

"Well, I guess she wouldn't rush to tell you. She's running with that arty crowd down in Carmel. Painters, writers, socialists, free-love types. Rotten bunch."

The cards snapped and flowed together between Mack's hands. "Not all of them." He held out the deck. Hellman cut. "How is her—" He searched for a polite word. "Health?"

"You mean is she boozing herself to death? That's what I hear." He picked up his cigar and ash fell to the carpet. Ignoring it, he regarded his son-in-law gloomily. "You were the only good man Carla ever hooked up with."

"Oh, I don't know. There was her father."

They looked at one another. Shared affection relieved the boredom and their miserable loneliness. Johnson had left for South America a month before.

Mack dealt three cards for each of them, then two more, then the turn-up card. "Spades are trump."

The door opened, laying a rectangle of light on the rug, and Little Jim stood in the center, barefoot in his long nightshirt. His fair hair shone like a cap of gold.

"Come in, son."

"I came to say good-night, Pa."

Mack cupped the boy's chin. His hand was hard and brown, a contrast to the child's cheek. "Look at you. White as milk. You're still staying indoors too much."

Little Jim would be five in the fall. He was shooting up, slim and sturdy. "I like it indoors, Pa. I like sitting with a book or doing sums."

"Say, don't I know it," Hellman said, patting him. "Jim put on a real show for me this afternoon. With that Chinee thingamajig, my grandson can add numbers faster than I can say Kaiser Bill."

Frown lines cut in above Mack's nose. "I want you out of the house two or three hours every day, Jim. Tell you what— tomorrow we'll drive down to Stanford. The football team is

461

starting spring practice. We'll watch them scrimmage. Football's a hell—a devil of an exciting game. You'll like it."

Solemnly, Jim said, "I bet I won't."

"Come on," Mack said, trying not to show he was irked. "You're going to make a fine football player when you grow up."

"No."

Mack raised his hand. "Don't talk back to me—" He saw Hellman's disapproval. Then, lowering his hand, he said, "Go to bed."

Little Jim marched away like a soldier under orders. The door closed and darkness possessed the room again.

Mack sighed and scooted lower in his chair. "Lord, he's a difficult boy. Nothing I say seems to get through. Or maybe I don't know how to say it."

"He's growing up handsome, though. Don't look a thing like you. Looks like Carla. Acts like her too."

"That's what worries me."

"Deal the cards. Let's get this over with."

In the morning, Angelina Olivar said, "The boy can't go with you today, sir. He has a bad stomach ache."

"Is he faking?"

"Señor Chance. What a terrible suggestion. Of course not."

"All right, Angelina." He was unconvinced.

What am I doing wrong? he wondered as he hurried up the stairs to the day's important business.

On a fine April day, Walter Fairbanks parked his shiny Pope-Toledo in front of Mack's mansion. He enjoyed driving the powerful machine, which he'd bought after driving and comparing a Ben-Hur, a Luxor, and a Leland. The Pope-Toledo's black paint was suitably rich and conservative.

The sight of the *JMC* cartouche on the pillars disgusted him but he tried to rein in his emotions as he rang the bell. Fairbanks wasn't comfortable seeking favors in this house. This mission, however, transcended personal feelings.

A servant showed him to the third floor. Mack was, as usual, submerged in papers and memoranda. He felt as uncomfortable as his guest, whose secretary had telephoned for the appointment. Alex felt uncomfortable too, unconsciously twisting his swivel chair a few inches this way, a few inches the other way. He fully expected an explosion.

"To what do I owe the pleasure, Walter?"

Fairbanks laid his polished stick across his knees and gripped it tightly with his right hand. "As you may know, I'm on the committee handling arrangements for President Roosevelt's visit next month. Gene Schmitz is sponsoring the banquet on May twelfth. It's to be a celebration of San Francisco, and the Golden State. The Palace has promised us gold china, gold utensils, cloth of gold to cover the tables—"

"At a price of twenty dollars, gold, per plate. The invitation's around here somewhere."

Mack's casual hauteur infuriated Fairbanks. The worm of pain began to eat through the front of his skull. He'd argued long and hard in favor of sending someone else to plead with Mack Chance. But the harder he argued, the more the others insisted. Ruef wanted Chance at the banquet and he demanded that Fairbanks do the job.

"You've not sent it back?"

"I don't intend to."

"Mack, you're a prominent citizen. Please reconsider. The mayor is anxious that we demonstrate San Francisco's nonpartisan solidarity to the President."

"I'm a great admirer of Teddy Roosevelt. But I'm afraid my admiration isn't enough to overcome my dislike of your new friends."

"What are you talking about?"

"I'm talking about George Perkins going back to Washington. His reappointment was promoted by the SP and purchased with those four votes Ruef controls in the state senate. I'd say you now have an alliance with Boss Ruef, Walter."

"What has that to do with a banquet for the President of the United States?"

"Everything. One hand's washing the other. All very cozy. Well, there's an old saying: 'If you don't want to get covered with tar, stay away from tar barrels.' I wouldn't set foot in the Palace on the twelfth of May."

The tickers clicked and spat paper, and a gull swept past the sunlit window. Alex twisted in his chair some more.

"You're a fool to buck Abraham Ruef," Fairbanks said, small dots of red blooming in his cheeks. "His organization's already immensely powerful."

"I'm certainly aware of that. I'd like to see it destroyed before it destroys the City."

Fairbanks jumped up. "My God you're arrogant."

Mack parried with an icy smile. "Somehow you bring out the worst, Walter."

"You hold grudges—"

"You're right. You destroyed a fine horse down in Riverside.

You destroyed her so you could win your damn polo game. I despise any man who'd do a thing like that.''

Fairbanks trembled so hard he couldn't speak. Jamming his hat on his head, he rushed for the door, but not before his temper boiled over. He whirled around and shook his stick.

''You keep this up—this antagonism toward the people who run this town—every business you're involved in could suffer. You could be badly hurt.''

''Not by you, Walter. I beat you, remember? Show Mr. Fairbanks out, Alex.''

Six hundred guests attended the Gold Banquet at the Palace Hotel. President Roosevelt tactfully conversed with the mayor about music—nothing else.

The guests fretted as Eugene Schmitz rose to speak. They needn't have worried; Ruef had written the short address and Handsome Gene had dutifully memorized it. The applause at the end was loud and sincere. Everyone was glad Schmitz was through; he hadn't embarrassed himself, or the City.

Prominent men in the audience noted that James Macklin Chance had left town the day before, traveling down to the dedication of permanent dormitories at The Palms at Indio, his charity health camp.

A week before the November election, Mack wrote a letter that Fremont Older printed. It mentioned an increasing number of allegations of graft in the Schmitz administration and urged a vote against Schmitz's reelection, concluding that a vote for the incumbent was actually a vote for the Ruef machine.

After Abe Ruef read it, he was livid. ''Put the word out that this man's an anti-Semite, a Jew-baiter.''

''But Abe, he isn't.''

''What does that matter? Do it.''

When the rumor reached Mack, he immediately called on the rabbi of Temple Emanu-el on Sutter Street. ''I've never opposed any man for what he is, only what he does. How do I handle this?''

''Mr. Chance, calm yourself. I am not aware that the professed religion of Mr. Abe Ruef exerts one iota of positive influence on his character. I grant you the Jewish community holds a divided opinion of him. Many are pleased and proud to see him ascend to prominence. Others feel as you do. I am one—I dislike and distrust Mr. Ruef. Stick to your principles and follow them. Your friends won't believe any lies told about you. Those who believe them don't matter.''

Eugene Schmitz and his Union Labor ticket won reelection handily. Mack wrote a second letter, this one even more hostile toward Schmitz and Boss Ruef.

November 12 was a sparkling day, clear and cool. Mack felt refreshed and invigorated as he worked through the morning with frequent attention to the clock. Alex, however, seemed distraught. Mack finally pressed him for the reason.

"Sir, it's that most recent letter. The cousin of my friend Heidi Meyer clerks in the law offices of the Boss. I am told Ruef is furious with you."

"Are you surprised? He knows how I feel about him, and he's had a good six months to build up steam—ever since I boycotted the Gold Banquet and decided to put my feelings on record." Alex didn't look reassured. Mack rested a hand on his shoulder. "Look, let me worry about Abe Ruef. I honestly don't think it matters what I say or write. He isn't going to bother with me. He's too busy piling up two- and three-thousand-dollar retainers from people who want favors at City Hall."

"I hope that is the case. However—with respect, sir—I believe you underestimate your stature in San Francisco."

That surprised Mack, and amused him. "Do I, now?"

The office door opened.

"Pa? I don't feel so good—"

"Nonsense. It's a beautiful autumn day. Do you good to get out. Do us both good. Stanford against U.C. is the biggest game of the year." He snagged his coat and pushed Little Jim gently. "You can help me check out the auto before we go."

Alex followed. "I hear this is indeed a fierce rivalry. Very partisan crowds. Sometimes violent."

Mack grinned. "Right. So's the football."

He took his son's hand. The boy had already learned the futility of arguing with his father when he was in this kind of zestful, boisterous mood.

Alex left them at the upper landing. How sober the boy was. Except for his remarkable blue eyes. There, Alex saw the furious resentment.

51 MACK FOLDED BACK THE PANELS OF THE GARAGE door. Inside, his new 1903 Cadillac Runabout shone like a metal gem.

Jim peered at his reflection in the forest-green lacquer of the dash panel and stuck out his tongue. So did the reflection. Jim laughed, and a rush of hope buoyed Mack. It didn't last, though. Jim's smile faded and he eyed his father with an uneasy, almost distrustful look.

Mack began the ritual familiar to every prudent automobilist. He checked the grease cups, oilers, crankcase, radiator. He topped the tank from a special can of gas strained through chamois. Store-bought gas was often impure and full of bits of debris—even gas refined from Chance-Johnson Oil.

While he worked, he talked to his son, hoping to cheer him up. "It's a fine day. This will be an exciting game. They call it the Big Game. Stanford and Berkeley have played twelve times before—Stanford's won five games, lost four, and tied three. The coach, a man named Jim Lanagan, is new. Do you know what a coach does? He tells the team how to play, when to run the ball, when to pass, when to punt . . ." Mack demonstrated a punt. Jim watched, blank-faced. Mack put his hands on his hips. "Do you understand any of what I'm saying?"

Little Jim, five, shook his head.

It's your own fault. You're talking over his head. He isn't a little old man, he just behaves like one.

He checked the kerosene supply for the side lights, then inspected his toolbox, jack, air pump, tire iron, and extra tubes, and made sure he had all the supplies for patching stored in the bolted-on rear-entrance tonneau. He decided to leave the equipment for longer trips—the removable leather top, side curtains and storm apron, mud chains, shovel, block and tackle, rubber boots, canvas bucket, coils of rope and wire. On California's rutty and boulder-strewn roads, motoring was a pastime for pioneers.

From a department-store box he produced a child's cap and goggles. The boy reluctantly donned the cap and then played with the elastic of the goggles.

"Jim, put them on."

Mack heard his own sharpness and scored himself for it. He

466

knelt down. "Here, I'll help you. We're going to have a good time today."

Wearing the goggles, Little Jim resembled a mournful owl. His expression doggedly denied any possibility of a good time. Mack lifted him to the seat, and then he started the Cadillac. He liked the Runabout's sportiness but not its engine. The Leland and Faulconer "Little Hercules" lacked the power for racing. Mack was already thinking about other cars as he turned left out of the ground-floor garage, westbound on Clay.

A fat man studying a newspaper on the corner of Clay and Mason watched the Cadillac putter away in the autumn sunshine. The man wore a green plaid suit and a marble-sized paste pinky ring; he looked grossly out of place on Nob Hill.

He folded the paper and rushed south on Mason at what amounted to a fast waddle. Halfway down the block, two men waited in an old depot wagon with a flat top and the side curtains rolled up and tied. The vehicle, a poor man's carriage, was twenty years old. The original black color showed where patches of scabrous pea-green enamel had peeled off.

"He just left," the fat man said to the man in the rear seat. The man sat sideways, favoring a stiff left leg. "I don't know how you guessed it."

"Get your fat ass in that seat and shut up, Pinky. I don't indulge in guesswork. I spent eighteen years on the detective force. Macklin Chance gives a lot of money to Stanford. He loves the school. He loves the Cardinal team. Today's the Big Game. The conclusion's obvious. Slim, get going—I don't want to lose him."

"Yes, sir, Mr. Coglan."

Slim, a tough-eyed young man, whipped the horse and wheeled the wagon in a 180-degree arc, nearly knocking down a woman with a perambulator. Lon Coglan shifted his leg. The bullet wound from the Thalia throbbed a little. Even so, he was relaxed and confident. His collar-length hair was no longer the same bright silver as his right incisor, but white. Years of drinking had coarsened his nose even more. The pores were so large it resembled a red Swiss cheese.

"There he is," Pinky said as they turned onto Clay.

"Follow him, but not too close," Coglan said. "We want to earn our money but we don't want to go to the hoosegow. We'll move only if we get a good opportunity."

Nervously, Slim said, "I'd like to get this over with. I don't like daylight jobs."

Silver Tooth Coglan spread his arms against the seat cushions. "Daylight jobs are all right if you're smart. This one's going to be a pleasure."

Two blocks west of Lafayette Park, a loud explosion rocked the Cadillac and the left front end sank sharply. Mack swore and steered the machine to the curb. "It's a flat," he said. He was furious, because he'd put on the best tires he could buy, Goodyear pneumatics. But no tire lasted more than a thousand miles—with many a flat before that.

While Jim watched, he performed the herculean job familiar to anyone rich enough to own an auto and patient enough to put up with its vagaries. Demounting the punctured tire took ten minutes, the tire iron, and a lot of grunting and sweating. The tube was pierced but not torn.

"Blast it, Jim, we're going to be late."

"What do I do, Lon?" Slim exclaimed, panicky.

"Don't go past him, for Christ's sake. Turn left here. We can't take him on a busy street. Drive straight out to Richmond Field and we'll wait there. Maybe he'll arrive during play. Fifteen, twenty thousand people will be screaming their heads off. Could be a good distraction. I'd say things are breaking our way."

The November day remained cool, but Mack was awash with sweat when he finished roughening the tube with the grater, buffing the patch with emery cloth, and cementing it on. He waited ten minutes for the cement to set, then mounted tube and tire—more struggling, more muttering—and fell to with the hand pump. Once the tire was inflated, they got going again.

The puncture cost them forty-five minutes. Mack was in a temper by the time they bumped along Lake Street. Passing Fifth Avenue, they turned into the parking area adjoining Richmond Field at Sixth.

Through sunlit trees he saw the packed bleachers, the blue-and-gold pennants of California on the near side, the cardinal ones of Stanford on the other. An old man jumped up from a crate at the entrance to the parking area. "Five cents, please."

Mack stood up and stared over tops of horse-drawn vehicles and a scattering of autos. "Is there any room?"

"First lane in, turn left, go way down near them trees at the end."

"Do you know what's happened on the field?"

"Won't be the half for some minutes yet. Stanford's ahead six-zero."

"Who scored?"

"Dutch Bansbach, the quarterback. Faked a handoff up the middle, then cut around left end and went forty-five yards. Savage Dole kicked the conversion. My nephew Horace, he runs back from the stands and tells me if there's a score. Otherwise I wouldn't take this damn lonesome job—oh, excuse me, sonny."

Mack drove on. He made the suggested left turn and bumped toward a shady grove at the end of the lane of trampled grass.

Pinky stood watch on the top row of the bleachers, among rooters chanting for a California touchdown. He spied the Cadillac, whistled to someone below, then struggled down the steps.

Mack swung into the last space on his left and turned off the engine, still irked by the delay. Little Jim took off his cap and goggles. He looked tired and fretful. Mack patted him. "Come on, there's still plenty of action left."

He walked around to the passenger side. It was a beautiful crisp afternoon, with a few high clouds and the sharp, long shadows that decreed autumn. He smiled and raised his hands to help his son alight.

Behind him, the heads of three men appeared and disappeared among carriages and autos. They were walking fast but quietly. Silver Tooth Coglan's excitement anesthetized the ache of the bullet wound. He dipped his hand into his overcoat and caressed the metal knuckles.

Mack took Jim's hand and started toward the ticket booth near the U.C. bleachers. The blue-and-gold stands rocked with a chant: "Overall! Overall!" Overall was a fourth-year man, a star punter. Mack heard the *whap* of a well-kicked ball, and the punter's rooters jumped up with a thunderous shout while a brass band struck up a march.

"Chance."

Mack looked around. No one.

"This way."

They were off to his left, in the shady grove at the edge of the field. Three of them: a fat man wearing a garish suit and a flashing pinky ring, a younger one with the seedy air of a Barbary Coast hustler, and between them, smiling like an old friend, smiling and showing his gleaming silver tooth—

Mack's mouth turned to sand. Where had they come from?

469

Why? How had they known he'd be here? They must have guessed that he *might* be here—a Stanford partisan.

This was contrived, then, not accidental . . .

Jim squeezed his hand, unsure of what was happening, and Mack stepped around the boy to place him on his right side, away from the men. The sight of Coglan, aging but still exuding arrogance, unleashed all sorts of emotions. He fought them. The past didn't matter—only Jim.

Coglan fanned himself with his derby there in the shade. "You look a hell of a lot more prosperous than you did the last time. Come over here. I need to have a word with you."

Mack estimated the distance to the ticket booth. "Sorry, I'm late for the game." He nudged Jim, and they walked rapidly, straight ahead into the narrow space between parked buggies.

"Stop him!" Coglan yelled. The young one darted from the shade into the nearest rutted lane.

"Run for it, Jim."

Mack and Jim dashed across the next lane, squeezing between two more carriages. Slim chased them, coming from their left, weaving between vehicles like a backfield runner, Coglan and the ox with the pinky ring pursuing from the rear.

Mack and Jim made it across one more lane, horses picketed to iron pins shying from the commotion. As they ran between a carriage on the right and a trim imported Fiat on the left, Slim vaulted over the bonnet of the Fiat and came down like a swooping bird, blocking their way out. Coglan closed off the other end of the narrow space.

The detective strolled up with his right hand buried in his overcoat. Mack remembered the metal knuckles from the basement room where the water ran.

Coglan smiled, displaying the point of his silver incisor, while Mack held Jim tight against his waist, shielding him with crossed hands.

"What the devil do you want?"

"We're delivering a message. Some people around town don't like the things you've been writing in Older's rag. It'd be a good idea if you stopped it."

The bleachers roared, the brass blaring, snare drums beating. A cloud crossed the sun, putting them in shadow. Impulsively, Mack pushed his son to the ground. "Crawl under and run."

Scared, Jim didn't balk or argue, but dropped and crawled under the buggy. "Catch the kid," Coglan yelled to Pinky.

The fat man lumbered to the other side. "Come here, you little brat." He snatched Jim by the hair and dragged him out, yelping. As Coglan bent down to watch, Mack abandoned niceties and smashed his knee under Coglan's chin.

Coglan's head hit the side of the carriage and he let out a roar. Mack yanked Coglan's hand from his pocket, tore the metal knuckles off, and threw them away. Coglan came at him then with wild looping punches but Mack ducked and darted, to the left, to the right—

As Pinky pulled Jim toward the nearest lane, the boy managed to wrench free. Pinky charged and Jim put his head down and butted the man's groin.

Meanwhile Mack was weaving and feinting and trying to set up one good blow to Coglan's jaw. Suddenly he heard someone rushing up and, before he could pivot, a shot-loaded blackjack hit him behind the ear. As he fell against the low step of a buggy, Coglan kicked the small of his back.

"Help, somebody help us!" Jim cried.

"Shut up," Pinky said, holding him tightly with one hand and dragging him into the middle of the rutted lane, his other hand massaging his crotch. Pushing on the buggy step to regain his footing, Mack had a distorted view of Pinky's face, red with rage.

Slim rushed him but Mack tangled a foot between his legs and tripped him. He saw Lon Coglan on his knees now, hunting for his metal knucks. Mack jerked Coglan by his long hair and smashed his face against the big hub of the buggy wheel. The detective's nose cracked and spouted blood. He shrieked in a high, girlish way.

In the lane, Jim gamely kicked at his captor. Using both hands to seize Jim's legs, Pinky lifted the boy off the ground. Jim responded by attacking Pinky's face with his nails, raking an eye.

Pinky threw him down on his back. "You dirty little shit." He raised his high-top shoe. Hobnails studded the sole. He stomped on Jim's left foot, and the boy screamed.

Mack hammered backward with his elbow, catching Slim's ribs before the young thug could sap him again. Slim staggered away. Mack jumped up on the buggy, off the other side, and rushed at Pinky, too late. Pinky stomped Jim a second and third time.

At the ticket booth, several people saw the fighting and raised the alarm. Shortly a uniformed policeman appeared, his whistle punctuating another roar from the game. Slim waved frantically. "Coppers."

Mack lurched to his son, who was rolling on the ground. A

shadow flickered by—Pinky, his gut jiggling under his shirt as he fled to the grove.

Mack heard the police whistle again, and people running to help. Panting, he chased the fat man. Pinky looked around, his bloated face streaming with sweat. Mack's arms and legs pumped. Three more steps and he'd catch him, break his—

A tire rut caught his left foot and he sailed forward like a football tackler. The impact snapped his teeth shut on his tongue and blood spurted between his lips. He lay dazed while Pinky, Slim, and Coglan clambered all over each other like circus clowns, trying to be first into an old depot wagon parked in the shade. Coglan's face flowed with blood. He grabbed the reins from Slim and the wagon jolted away with Pinky hanging on the side, yelping as his hobnailed shoes dragged through the weeds.

"Oh dear God, the poor lad."

Mack got up, dizzy. He saw the policeman kneeling by Jim, gingerly lifting the boy's bloodied cuff. The shock hit him as he ran toward the policeman and the spectators crowding around. Blood soaked Jim's left shoe and trouser leg. Something white protruded.

"Jim, hold on!" He shouted at the crowd, "Get an ambulance!" A man ran.

Jim gulped and rolled his head from side to side in the brown grass. "Oh, Pa, it hurts. It hurts awful."

Mack knelt behind him and cradled his head. Hair hung in his eyes and sweat ran down his nose. Jim trembled and cried. Mack rubbed his son's shoulders, staring at sharp jutting splinters of bone that glistened in the sunshine.

Mack walked up and down, up and down outside the boy's room. A taped bandage covered the egg-sized lump behind his ear. Nuns in the habit of the Sisters of Mercy passed by with looks of sympathy or a murmured word for the distraught father. Mack wasn't Catholic, but that had no effect on compassion. One sister stopped to say, "Did anyone tell you about the game?"

"No, Sister."

"They tied, six points each."

"Thank you, Sister."

The teams could have sunk to hell for all he cared.

A horse-drawn ambulance had rushed Jim from Richmond Field to the hospital, St. Mary's on Rincon Hill. An examining doctor immediately urged telephoning a specialist, Dr. Theodore Steinmund. "Best orthopedic man on the Pacific Coast."

Steinmund had been inside with Little Jim for two hours. Mack kept walking up and down. After a while, spent and worried, he sought a bench nearby. He no sooner had sat down than the door finally opened. Dr. Steinmund came out with his vest and suit coat over his rolled-up sleeve. He shut the door and avoided Mack's eye. His professional reticence was infuriating, then alarming.

"I want to see him," Mack said, starting by.

The doctor's arm barred the way.

"Wait a moment. The sister is still with him. I must speak to you first."

BLOWING MIST HID GOLDEN GATE AND THE MARIN 52
shore. The December wind raked the Bay, heavy with dampness, and white water foamed on tall waves that broke and flooded the concrete esplanade.

The two men came out of the dark-green park at different points, walking toward one another on the esplanade like duelists. Mack had put on overshoes and a scarf and turned up his velvet coat collar. It did no good, though; the sea spray soaked his face and clothes. It was impossible to keep warm. He couldn't have gotten warm in 90-degree sunshine. He was cold in the bottom of his soul.

He was unable to sleep at night. Wherever he went during the day—his office, one of his clubs, one of his warehouses or ranches in the Valley—the scene kept flashing in his head, a jerky Kinetoscope with color. He saw the green of plants in the hospital alcove where he sat with Steinmund. He saw the red of Christ's bleeding heart in a chromo on the wall.

Mack and Abraham Ruef faced each other on the esplanade. Ruef cleared his throat. "I wasn't sure you received my letter asking for this meeting. You didn't favor me with a reply."

Mack stared at him.

"I'm grateful you chose to come. I must preface what I want to say by telling you this: It would not be to my advantage to be seen with you. If you ever discuss this meeting or repeat this conversation, I'll deny all of it. However . . ."

Mack stared. The waves broke loudly, and though the two of them stood at the esplanade's landward edge, water swirled

473

around their feet and the great windblown fans of water soaked them. Ruef mopped his face with a white linen handkerchief. He wore tight leather gloves. His fingers were small as a child's.

"However," he repeated after clearing his throat again, "I freely admit to you that one of my underlings, completely without my knowledge or authorization, sent those hoodlums to your home. On their own initiative they followed you to Richmond Field. It's well known that you are a fan of the Stanford eleven."

Mack had scarcely been outdoors since the accident. The tan was fading from his face. Now the color seemed to leach away completely. "I didn't come all the way out here for a little chat about football."

Ruef heard the suppressed rage and hastily raised his hand. "My apology. Please hear me out."

Mack heard instead the disjointed, dreadful phrases Steinmund spoke that afternoon. Phrases he didn't understand to this day. And understood too well.

. . . *midtarsal fracture dislocation. Midfoot and forefoot separated. Circulation embarrassment. Interference with dorsal and medial arteries* . . .

"Subsequent to the, ah, incident, I further discovered that the three men were ordered by my subordinate to give you a verbal warning, perhaps muss you up a bit. But nothing more. Absolutely nothing. I swear it. The attack on your son was spontaneous, accidental, and of course inexcusable."

Did he believe Ruef? What did it matter?

. . . *especially critical site. Every practitioner fears a fracture dislocation here* . . .

Ruef spoke with sincerity and passion, like a defense attorney summing up for the jury. "You and I have differences. No secret about that. But I deal fairly and openly with opponents—"

Damned liar. What did it matter?

"I do not—I will not condone violence in any form. Mr. Coglan and his fat associate departed some days ago on a passenger train from Oakland. They are residing in a remote part of the state. Neither man will be returning to San Francisco. Should they defy me and violate their exile, they'll be dealt with forcibly. I can do nothing about the third assailant, the young man. He disappeared on his own."

Ruef's persuasion couldn't breach the stony rage of his listener. The little pol applied the white handkerchief again, his own perspiration mingling with the wave spray. "For God's sake, Chance, I'm trying to tell you how sorry I am. I want to redeem the situation to the extent of my ability. Repay you in some measure for your boy's suffering."

. . . for the future, I cannot promise . . . I cannot guarantee that he . . .

Mack wondered if another dream had been layered over the memories of Steinmund and the hospital. He couldn't believe what he was seeing: Abraham Ruef with a tentative, unsure look on his face. Reaching into his overcoat. Pulling out money. A stack of it. Almost an inch thick, bound with a rubber band. On top was a $100 bill.

"Here. Take this. Perhaps it will help cover the medical—"

Mack shouted like a gored animal, and his balled fist knocked the money from Ruef's hand. The elastic broke and the packet sailed aloft, $100 bills whirling and sailing every which way. "You little bastard. You piece of scum. I'll see you in hell."

"Chance, Chance, I'm trying—"

"I'm going to ruin you, Ruef. You and your goddamned machine too." Terrified, Ruef retreated, but Mack was faster. He caught his overcoat lapels and dragged him up to tiptoe, screaming at him. "My son won't ever walk normally again. He's lame. He's in constant pain. For life."

Ruef could only whisper. "Oh my God. My God, no, I didn't know the full extent—"

Mack wanted to fling him off the esplanade, throw him under the white-topped waves and stand there till he drowned.

Trembling, he let go. "Get out of here before I kill you."

Ruef opened his mouth in one last attempt to persuade, ameliorate—

Mack's eyes convinced him he'd better not, and he bolted, flinging a scared look over his shoulder as he hurried down the flooded esplanade and disappeared in the dark pine trees. A few moments later a gasoline motor coughed, turned over, puttered, then gradually faded away.

Clouds of blowing mist streamed around Mack, the wind knifing his face. As breaking waves tossed wet money in the air with the spume, some fell on the esplanade and floated. Mack picked up seven $100 bills. He tore them up and threw the pieces in the Bay.

Johnson came back from a thousand-mile journey on the Amazon, through the rain forest.

"So you're goin' to get Ruef."

475

"I am."

"You blame him for Jim bein' crippled."

"Hell, yes. Who else?"

"Never mind—forget I asked."

VII

INTO THE
FIRE

1904–1906

The City grew up quickly, but not completely. She had a foot in the old century, and another planted in the new.

Solid commercial buildings proliferated; the plush elegance of her great hotels—the Palace, the Fairmont, the St. Francis— rivaled anything in New York or Europe. The enthusiasm of her civic leaders was equally impressive. Mayor Phelan had drawn important men together into the Association for Improvement and Adornment of San Francisco, and the group engaged Daniel Hudson Burnham, a celebrated architect, to draw up a comprehensive plan for the modern San Francisco, much as Baron Haussmann had ripped apart the old Paris and created the new for Emperor Napoleon III.

Burnham was to finish his work and present it to the supervisors in 1905 or 1906. Meanwhile, the City remained caught between the present and the past. In her slums and poor neighborhoods, there was no brick or fine granite. There were wooden row houses as congested, flimsy, and dirt-ridden as the ones that burned in the fire of December 1849—and five more times in the years after that. Progress vied with poverty. On Market Street there were people on foot or driving farm wagons; there were carriages, plain and elegant, horsecars shuttling up and down, cable cars riding the mechanized slot in the center. There were a few autos that now and then left all the rest behind.

Everyone was enthusiastic and confident; that was the tenor of the decade in the City that carelessly bestrode one of nature's most unpredictable and implacable forces: the cataclysmic power latent in the 650-mile San Andreas fault line.

53 EVENTS LARGE AND SMALL FILLED THE HOURS AND days of 1904, as they did every year. Mack took up a meerschaum he bought when he traveled to New York on business. While there, he discussed politics with Pierpont Morgan in Morgan's great marble library on Fifth Avenue, and he sat for studies by John Singer Sargent, who had sailed over from London for a month to accept Mack's commission.

Mack wore a black suit for the portrait. On the fingertips of his right hand, at waist height, he balanced an orange, as if he possessed and dwarfed the products of the earth. A dusky glint in the background suggested the dome of a stock ticker. Sargent would be many months completing the picture; when it was finished, Mack intended to hang it in the library at Sacramento Street.

He continued to tend all his enterprises dutifully, and none fulfilled him so much as The Palms at Indio. He remodeled the first dormitory and expanded the sanitarium on a cottage plan: fifty small private houses surrounding a large central building containing dining hall, sun room, offices, and a medical wing. He appointed Alex Muller executive director, with complete responsibility for the sanitarium, which now had a waiting list. This added a huge new work load to Alex's already considerable duties. But he didn't complain; if he worked the rest of his life without sleep or a day off, he still would not be working as hard as his employer.

For relaxation that year, Mack read Richard Harding Davis, and *The Call of the Wild*, a sensational literary hit written by Johnson's Alaska friend Jack London. He gave a banquet for the writer, and the "Kipling of the Klondike" attended without his new wife. Whenever he was introduced to someone, he said, "Call me Wolf." He frightened the guests with talk of the coming socialist revolution. After the first course he passed out, drunk.

In 1904 Mack's hair turned white. It was a thick, distinguished mane, but strangers guessed James Macklin Chance to be fifty years old, not thirty-six.

During the year, Señora Olivar learned mechanical sewing on an electric Singer machine Mack bought for her. She loved it, calling it a miracle of the new century. Alex had a new machine as well, a Blickensdorfer typewriter, on which he learned to write at great speed with very few mistakes. He hired a young female assistant to operate the machine part-time. She, too, was called a typewriter.

Nellie continued her writing, started smoking Turkish cigarettes, and actively worked for the suffragist movement. One day she went to the Roundhouse restaurant on Market Street and sat down and asked for a menu. They threw her out, reminding her that, like many establishments, they served men only. She returned the next night, this time refusing to leave. The police arrested her, and she stayed in jail till morning. Then she wrote an article, the *Examiner* providing the headline: PENNED UP WITH FELONS: HER NIGHT OF HORROR.

Hellburner Johnson spent the first five months of 1904 in Riverside, running the Calgold operation. Then he came back to San Francisco, joined a volunteer fire company, and spent hours at the Olympic Club with a guest card. "Till I took up polo I had no idea I was born to be a gent. I love that club. No women, dogs, or Democrats. Gives a man breathin' room."

Once back, he adopted Mack's son almost every way but legally. "I got an affliction similar to yours," he liked to remind Jim, tapping his cork foot. "It ain't so bad. You'll get along if you don't dwell on it."

Jim didn't seem to dwell on it. In fact an odd reversal took place, with him and with his father. Jim now wanted to be outdoors as much as possible, and Mack now wanted him indoors, sheltered.

Johnson ignored Mack's wishes, taking the boy hiking, sailing in the Bay, even climbing partway up Mount Diablo, though it was slow going because Jim's left foot dragged at every step.

Little Jim's new passion for the outdoors didn't lessen his passion for learning. The weakness of his foot made him keener to strengthen his mind. After he learned to read at age five, he read endlessly, and he ciphered like some kind of swift and amazing machine.

Mack hired one tutor after another but none satisfied him. Then, early in 1904, in answer to an advertisement there came Professor Lorenzo Love of Piedmont, Ohio. A small, ordinary, forgettable man when he kept his mouth shut, the moment Love spoke he controlled every listener, his voice pealing like a church organ.

He said he was a graduate of Oberlin College. He had no papers to prove it, but you didn't argue with that organ voice. He was full of enthusiasm for education, and full of maxims.

"The foundation of every state is the education of its youth, Mr. Chance. Enlighten the people, and tyranny of the mind and body will vanish like evil spirits at the dawn of day."

"Who said that?"

"I did, sir. Quoting Diogenes in the first place, and Thomas Jefferson in the second place."

Professor Love had fled "the boredom of Columbus, Ohio, and a certain female there bent on pressing me into marital servitude." He said a lifelong nasal condition had been cured the moment he set foot in California. He was a man obsessed with details.

"Mr. Oscar Wilde considers details vulgar, my boy. Not so. What separates those who fail in life from those who succeed? Attention to details. What is the bridge from the slough of commonality to the acme of accomplishment? Ask a rich man. Ask your father. Details, details, details. Tie your cravat again, please. It's a mess."

Lorenzo Love was a scold, and fussy. And Little Jim loved him.

In the summer of '04, there could be found in Mack's address ledger the names of 1,012 acquaintances in California. He added at least one name each week, the business address noted down in his careful hand, and the telephone if there was one. Sometimes he leafed through the book and gazed at all the names and realized he had but two male friends, Johnson and his father-in-law. Marquez, who might have been a friend in different circumstances, had disappeared in the Central Valley again.

Once a month Mack visited his ranches out there, giving him an excuse to look in on Hellman, who grew more feeble every day. The old man had moved into three rooms in a Sacramento boardinghouse.

Mack urged him to come to San Francisco. "You deserve better than this. You certainly can afford it. Let me hunt up a flat for you."

"Maybe sometime," Hellman said with a weary wave. "For now, I'm too tired."

Mack took his father-in-law for a drive in his open Cadillac. On the journey from San Francisco to Sacramento, the auto had broken down twice, about average.

They chugged along back roads of the delta. Mexicans knee-deep in bright water worked the rice fields. At a crossroads, they came upon two people different from any Mack had seen before, scrawny brown men in loose shirts and turbans who bowed respectfully to the auto, then hurried on as if afraid of being stopped and questioned.

"What kind of men are those, Swampy?"

"Those little brown buggers? Hindoos."

"In California?"

"Yah, I seen quite a few this year. They're coming down from Canada. Looking for field work, I guess."

"In Fresno, I ate dinner in a restaurant run by Armenians. The whole state's filling up with foreigners."

"You're starting to sound old, Johnny. You're starting to sound like Fairbanks or some other pure-bred snot-nosed native son."

"God forbid," Mack exclaimed. But he realized Hellman was right. It was something to guard against.

Late in the summer of '04 Mack finally saw *The Great Train Robbery*. Edwin Porter's little 740-foot moving picture had been released the preceding winter by Edison Films to instant acclaim. Mack paid his 5 cents and ducked inside Neville's Nickelodeon one afternoon between meetings.

The picture exploded in his mind. He'd never experienced anything like it. The last scene showed Barnes, the outlaw leader, in giant close-up. He aimed his revolver and fired point blank at the audience. Mack jumped in his seat. Two ladies swooned.

He ignored his schedule and sat through it four more times. "It has a story, a genuine story," he told Johnson that night. "If that idea catches on, the pictures could amount to something."

He took Johnson to see it. "Not bad for a bunch of dressed-up easterners playactin'," Johnson said afterward. "Jim might like it."

"No—too scary."

The trolley war started in 1904.

Mr. Patrick Calhoun, grandson of the famed South Carolina secessionist John C., owned United Railroads of San Francisco, and he decided it would be to his advantage to put all of his cars on overhead electric lines, doing away with the tangle of horse and cable systems on many streets. Calhoun promised improved service, while screaming opponents promised a new, incredibly ugly city choked with wires.

Calhoun wanted to electrify the Sutter Street system first. His men campaigned at City Hall, and it was no secret that he retained Abraham Ruef, Esq., for "municipal assistance and counsel."

Adolph Spreckels invited Mack to the Pacific Union Club for luncheon. Adolph was upright, bull-necked, about fifty, the second son of the ruthless old Prussian Claus Spreckels, who had created a sugar kingdom in the West. Claus had gone out to Hawaii, they said, and won vast cane fields from the king in a poker game.

Adolph ran the family business in the City. He had three brothers. John, older, lived down in San Diego, managing his holdings from there. Rudolph and Claus Augustus, called Gus, had chosen to strike out on their own after a bitter fight with the old man over disposition of some plantation land in Hawaii.

At lunch, Adolph politely muffled a cough with his starchy napkin. "This trolley business—"

"Your brother Rudolph's in the thick of it," Mack said.

"You know Rudolph, I take it."

"Yes. I've had dinner at his home a number of times. I was there when he first discussed a Sutter Street Improvement Club, to fight the overhead wires."

"Ruef, that little sheeny"—Mack winced—"is telling everyone Rudolph is against Calhoun because the Sutter Street line passes his front door."

"Every man has an ox to be gored, Adolph. It's still a worthy fight. I gave the club a thousand dollars to help with it."

Eyes darting, Adolph Spreckels leaned near, as if they were hatching a bomb plot. He drew a plain envelope from his coat. "I want to make a donation. Please take this cash and then write the draft in your name. My brother and I differ on so many things—he is an ardent, outspoken reformer, for example, while I prefer anonymity—I'm sure you understand."

Mack nodded, though he didn't. Feuds such as the legendary one that wracked the Spreckels family mystified him. Never mind; the money was good, and would be put to a good purpose. On a couple of occasions Mack had talked with Adolph's brother Rudy about the need for a serious reform movement in the City. That need seemed to grow more critical with every week that passed.

Every month or so Mack went down to call on Nellie at Carmel-by-the-Sea. She lived in a perfect little artist's bungalow, isolated among the pines but with a view of the windy blue bay. Mack never stayed overnight, and usually they argued—about graft, about the trolleys, about the City's water situation. To break the monopoly held by the Spring Valley Water Company, former Mayor Phelan had cast his eye on distant sources: Lake Tahoe, Shasta, the Sacramento River. Late in Phelan's administration, his water consultants recommended establishing a claim on behalf of the City to the Hetch Hetchy Valley.

Phelan had done so. Under the federal Right of Way Act, the City proposed to build a dam in the valley. The interior secretary blocked the proposal, and it had been tied up in litigation ever since.

"And a good thing too," Nellie said.

"Is that your opinion, or your friend Muir's?"

"What's the matter with you, Mack? If you dam that valley, you destroy it forever."

"What about the City's water supply? It's completely inadequate. Meanwhile the population keeps on growing."

"Not my fault. Put up barricades."

"Oh, the great democrat is suddenly the great exclusionist."

"No, I didn't mean—"

"Nellie, San Francisco has a major problem. But you and all the folks in the nature societies want to ignore it."

"Nature societies? Oh my God, that's so snide." She threw a book.

As a consequence of this kind of conversation, he had lately spent a lot of time with Margaret Emerson.

Mack forgave Nellie her short temper. Her San Francisco colleague Frank Norris had died suddenly and tragically two years before, of peritonitis, and with the permission of his widow she was attempting to write *The Wolf*, the last novel of his trilogy about wheat. She wasn't having any luck, and that roughened her disposition.

"I reread parts of *The Octopus* again last night," she told Mack. "Annixter seeing the wheat at dawn, the wonderful gangplow passage. In every sentence I hear the voice of a friend, but I can't imitate it. I try and I fail. I've never failed so miserably at anything before."

So Mack made an effort to excuse the quarrels, even to laugh about them. Underneath he was angry and bitterly frustrated because he couldn't move the relationship one way or the other.

Much the same kind of frustration bred of love spoiled his relationship with his son.

* * *

He found contentment in small things. California names. He loved them and, in a corner of his memory, he amassed a collection.

Pigeon Point, Calexico, El Dorado.

Fallen Leaf, Drakes Bay, Hurdygurdy.

Chinese Camp, Malibu, Likely. Pismo, Chowchilla, Havilah, Dinkey Creek. Rough and Ready, Sebastopol, Berryessa, Hobo Hot Springs.

Avalon, Ahwahnee, Fandango, San Juan Capistrano. Angels Camp, Coarsegold, You Bet. La Mirada, Yucaipa, Eureka, Glendora. Fiddletown, Modesto, Petaluma, Susanville.

Point Reyes, Death Valley, Malpaso Canyon, Mokelumne River, Mare Island, Signal Hill, Thousand Palms, Visitation, Hoopa, Tiburon, Portola, Calistoga, Ramona . . .

O California!

A year before, on the fifth floor of the Mills Building on Bush Street, Chance-Johnson Oil had opened an office. Mack's competitors at Union Oil occupied space two flights up. One day in the fall of 1904, Mack met there for three hours with Haven Ogg and two other geologists. After showing them out, he welcomed Fremont Older.

They lit cigars and relaxed by a window looking up Nob Hill. It was a cool and golden afternoon, one of those rare City days without a sea breeze. When there was no wind, the soft-coal haze from thousands of chimneys wrapped the rooftops and settled all the way to the streets. The haze was like a gray sea, with huge signs advertising oculists and beer swimming in it like painted fish.

"I have some word about the water situation," Older said. "The enlightened Mr. Ruef shares the view of the federal government. We must not dam Hetch Hetchy. At the same time, we must break the vile stranglehold of the Spring Valley Company."

"How will we do that?"

With a cynical smirk, Older said, "We'll bring in a competitor—Bay Cities."

"Bill Tevis's company."

"The same." Tevis, a San Franciscan, had inherited something like $20 million from his father, Lloyd, another of the state's nineteenth-century land and cattle barons. "The company has water rights up on the south fork of the American and the north fork of the Cosumnes. My moles who burrow around City Hall tell me the Boss is definitely leaning toward a franchise for Bay Cities."

"Is he a friend of Tevis?"

"No, but I understand someone in the Tevis organization has offered a little something to generate a friendship."

"What's a little something?"

"One million dollars."

"My God," Mack said. "It gets worse and worse."

"Indeed it does. There's hardly an honest man to be found at City Hall. They're all so hungry for boodle, they'll eat the paint off a house. We've got to unmask Ruef. Get him out, and his hirelings too."

"How, Fremont? Ruef's more popular than ever. So tell me how we do it."

Smoking their cigars, they stared at one another in the waning light of a coal-haze afternoon.

Mack, Johnson, and Little Jim went down to Fisherman's Wharf. It was a Saturday at twilight. Jim held tightly to his father's hand as they walked out on the long plain pier.

The trim little Monterey boats had come in for the night, their red sails furled, but the fishermen, dark weathered men who chattered and yelled in Italian and Portuguese, still had much work left to do. They hoisted baskets of wriggling halibut and sea crabs to the wharf, spread and hung their weighted nets on its rail. One of the young fishermen with a gold ring in his left ear tousled Jim's hair.

The three walked on out to the end. In the dusky bay, red and green running lights showed on small launches and an outbound Pacific steamer. Her great whistle bellowed and the boy watched her churning toward the sunset.

"Where's she going, Pa—China?"

"Good possibility of that."

"I'm going there one of these days."

"Sure. But right now we're going home. It's cold. Look at that fog rolling in." The bank lay just outside Golden Gate, the sun all at once swallowed by it.

"I want to stay a while."

"No, it's too chilly. I don't want you catching cold." Jim started to say something, but Mack patted his head. "Don't argue."

"Look," Johnson said to the boy, "they're bringin' in more live crabs."

That was enough to cue Jim to move away to see. Both men watched his tilting gait, heard the terrible slow scrape of his left foot. Johnson's bright-orange bandanna snapped in the wind.

"Listen here. You're treatin' that boy like the very kind of hothouse lily you said you wouldn't have."

"You're meddling again, Hugh."

"Well, I figure I better. He's your flesh and blood, but you don't have but a few scraps of time to give him. When you do take him out, you treat him like some little girl's china doll."

Mack held his temper. "What I wanted for Jim before and what I want for him now are different things. He's crippled."

"He ain't a freak. He's a healthy, growing young 'un. Every time you coddle him, you make him remember what's wrong with him, 'stead of what's right. He don't like that, and I don't blame him."

"He'll have to put up with it. I have only one son and I mean to take care of him."

"You ain't doin' it proper—"

"I don't need your advice and I don't want it."

Johnson pulled his Texas hat lower over his bushy gray brows and stomped back up the wharf. "Guess we got to go home now, Jim," he called. "Ain't my idea."

When Mack went to Jim's room to say good-night, the boy was quiet, almost sullen. Mack insisted on a hug, and Jim complied with a hooking motion of his small arm, a light, fast hug, to let Mack know he didn't like Mack's discipline.

Never mind. The boy was fragile. Look how easily he'd been injured at Richmond Field. Mack refused to risk it again. One of these days Jim would understand, and thank him.

As he went upstairs, a distant telephone rang. Alex Muller hurried to find him.

"Mr. Older is calling."

"What is it, Fremont?" Mack said when he answered.

The voice came over the wire faint and scratchy. "It appears the *Bulletin* has printed one too many stories about Abe Ruef and his cronies. About an hour ago, our publisher was attacked on the street by unknown assailants."

"Thieves?"

"They took nothing. They beat Crothers with lead pipes and ran away. It's doubtful that he'll live."

In November 1904 Mack voted for Theodore Roosevelt and argued with Nellie over the merits of national and local candidates. She was particularly strong for Judge Alton Parker, a Democrat Mack disliked. He said with some heat that she would probably vote Democratic if the party ran a name from a tombstone. She said, "Oh, enough. I'll be happy to discuss voting when you arrogant males condescend to permit me to do it.'' Which immediately ended the conversation.

R. A. Crothers of the *Bulletin* surprised everyone and survived his savage beating. The incident heightened tensions between the Ruef machine and the few who dared to speak against it or ignore its authority. As the year closed and the new year began, the struggle focused in the issue of the French restaurants.

Back in the spring of '04, Police Commissioner Hutton had launched a campaign against San Francisco's own peculiar institution, announcing that French restaurants were open houses of assignation and a menace to public morals, and proposing the revocation of their liquor permits.

For several months the other three members of the police commission board refused to go along; Hutton's brand of puritanism didn't fit the style of an easy-going port city. But things changed toward the end of '04. Members of the cooks and waiters' union tried to organize one of the largest of the restaurants, Tortoni's. Union business agents hired two men to eat supper there, then request introductions to the ladies working upstairs. Presented with depositions detailing what went on at Tortoni's, the members of the police commission board now were forced to act, and they refused to renew Tortoni's license. By early January 1905 the commission had refused to renew the license of a second French restaurant, Delmonico's.

"I had a call about it at six o'clock this morning,'' Margaret said to Mack. "From Pierre Priet of Marchand's. He's terrified we'll all be run out of business. The others are just as scared—Tony Blanco at the Poodle Dog, Jean Loupy at the Pup, Max Adler at the Bay State. They want to organize a French restaurant keepers' association. Each member will be assessed, and the association will hire a specialist to cure the illness.''

"A specialist? What are you talking about?'' Mack said. They were dining under the fake Tiffany electric in her quarters next to Maison Napoleon.

"I'm quoting Pierre. He was practically gibbering. We're all supposed to contribute enough to raise five thousand dollars immediately, and another five thousand for next year. To retain Dr. Ruef. That's what Pierre called him—*Doctor.*''

"Good God. What did you say?''

"I told Pierre to go to hell, I'd pay no graft for a legitimate liquor license.''

"That's a dangerous stance, Margaret.''

"I run a business patronized by some of the best men in San

Francisco. City officials eat here. They go upstairs with a wink and smile. Do you think I'm going to be threatened by a bunch of hypocrites who suddenly decide I'm a fine source of boodle? The answer's no. That's what I said in my letter.''

Mack's fork clattered on his plate.

"You wrote that in a letter? Let me see it.''

"I don't have it. I mailed it to the *Bulletin* this morning.''

"I'll call Fremont right awa—''

"Mack, sit down. I simply said City Hall was extorting money from businesspeople, and Ruef was behind it.''

"You don't say that kind of thing in San Francisco, Margaret. Not publicly. These people are powerful, and they're vindictive. Look what happened to my son. To Crothers—''

"I don't care, and furthermore it's too late. The letter's gone. I stand by it.''

"I admire that. But you're taking a hell of a risk.''

She patted his hand; her fingertips lingered. He was frowning, too worried to notice.

"You're kind and sweet to concern yourself,'' she said. "I think it's needless. They may harass me, but that's all. A woman is still safe in this town. Even a woman like me.''

54 ACETYLENE HEADLAMPS DUG TUNNELS OF LIGHT IN the evening fog as the Model A Ford putted around the corner onto Mission Street. The eight-horsepower car had a single seat under a folding top. Painted black, it resembled a motorized buggy. A second, identical Ford appeared. A man and woman crossing Mission to Maison Napoleon gawked at the autos, which were still not all that common.

The first Model A parked in front of Margaret Emerson's flat. The second stopped behind it. There were two men in each vehicle, men of some size, trying hard to fit in the single seats and present themselves as gents by wearing derbies and velvet-collared coats.

The passenger in the first Model A was in charge. He was a hulk with a huge mustache waxed in points. Jumping out, he signaled to the men in the other auto, then trotted up the steps to Margaret's door. He tested the handle, then signaled again. The two men from the second auto took up positions in front of the flat while the first man and his driver moved quickly to the entrance to the French restaurant.

The man in charge studied the foggy street. A horse-drawn cab passed with a clatter and glimmer of lamps. There was no other traffic.

"In we go," he said with a smirk that hid his state of nerves.

The little bell rang over the door. Margaret broke off her conversation with guests at a rear table and glided to the front, menus in hand. Only three tables were filled on this rather foul night; she was happy to see more customers, and showed it with her brilliant smile.

"Gentlemen, good evening. Table for two?"

The first man snatched off his derby. He was burly, with the sort of round face she associated with butchers or brewers. His dark eyes shone as brightly as his waxed mustache.

"We can take care of our business right here, Miss Emerson."

Margaret's palm prickled. The second man kept glancing at the front door. Fearful of interruption?

"You have the advantage of me, gentlemen. Would you be kind enough to tell me your names?"

The mustached man stepped close enough to brush the arm of her white shirtwaist. The touch felt unclean somehow, though the man's breath was heavily sweet from gin.

"Let's just say we represent the police commission."

Her heart raced. A waiter came from the kitchen with two dinners on a tray. Though she tried to warn him with her eyes, he devoted himself to his customers, bowing and smiling as he served the plates.

"May I see some credentials?"

"That isn't necessary," said the mustached man. "We want to inspect your liquor permit."

"You know I don't have one that's current. I told the last boodler who came in here that I'm not paying five hundred or a thousand dollars for a license."

"You can't operate without one.

"You mean I can't operate without kicking into a slush fund for Ruef. I work too hard for my money to throw it away on bribes."

"Bribe is a nasty word." He grabbed her wrist. "You used a lot of nasty words in that letter in the paper."

She wrenched away, and a couple seated nearby glanced up from their plates with worried looks. Softly, Margaret said, "Get out of my restaurant."

"You mean your whorehouse? You better pay what's asked, Miss Emerson, and you damn well better stop signing your name to letters full of lies."

Margaret felt a strange terrified flutter in her throat. The byplay about the license was a sham. These two had come for another purpose, and nothing she said or did would divert them. Panicky, she called to the waiter, now hurrying to the kitchen.

"Red, please step in the back and telephone—"

She stopped. *Telephone the police?* They'd never respond. Not in time. "No, never mind." The waiter hesitated, puzzled.

"I'm sorry about this, Miss Emerson; it's just orders," the mustached man said with a smarmy piety. He waved; she noticed for the first time that he wore tight gray leather gloves. "Bruno, go to work."

The other man pulled his right hand from his overcoat, and Margaret saw a flash of blue gun metal. "Be careful, everyone," she cried to the patrons.

The first man caught her arm and whipped it like a rope, throwing her into the wall. Josephine's framed portrait fell off and the glass broke. Then he pounded a fist in the small of her back, and Margaret dropped to her knees, gasping.

Bruno leveled his blue revolver. The waiter dropped his tray with an anvil clang while diners flung themselves from chairs, shouting and exclaiming. Holding his pistol in both hands, Bruno began to shoot out the lights over the tables.

Margaret's cheek scraped the wall, her head spinning. The pain from the blow to her back was brutal. She heard the little bell ring, then the mustached man's shout, "Give me that ax and get to work next door."

Next door . . . ?

Margaret bit her lip and pushed away from the wall, then fell back again dizzily. Bruno kept shooting. Glass showered the tables and the diners trying to crouch underneath. Someone passed a fire ax through the front door. The mustached man hacked the door until it splintered. Then, with a looping blow, he struck Napoleon from his pedestal, bursting the bust into hundreds of small pieces.

The waiter had darted into the kitchen, leaving the door ajar. There was plenty of light for the two men to do their work. Bruno reloaded and shot at the ceiling. A girl upstairs screamed. The mustached man attacked empty tables, shattering china and goblets and tabletops with the fire ax.

Next door, Margaret's mind cried out. She crawled toward the door, struggled to her feet, and pulled it open. The tiny bell rang again. Cold foggy air swept over her.

"The bitch ran out," Bruno shouted.

Panting, slipping, falling, and lurching up again, she managed to reach the little covered porch outside her flat. Electric light streamed through the open door. She heard them breaking things inside.

Earlier, anticipating a cozy end to the evening, Margaret had lit a small fire in her hearth, then carefully placed a screen in front of it. There were two other men in her flat, men wearing identical overcoats and derbies. They had flung the screen aside and one of them had a baseball bat.

She ran into the parlor just as he swung the bat and demolished her gold-plated mantel clock. Springs uncoiled with pinging sounds, parts flying everywhere.

"You bastard, leave my things alone." With both hands she grabbed the man's collar. He struck backward with the bat, hard. She clutched her knee through her skirt and fell in a chair, hair undone, tears of fury streaming from her eyes.

She was most conscious of the noise and their huge nightmare shadows. In the dining room, the second man overturned the table and then levered a leg back and forth until it loosened. He snapped it off, took a stance, made sure she saw, and used the leg to hit the fake Tiffany shade.

The electric bulbs survived the blow but pieces of colored glass fell, flicking specks of colored light across the walls. Twisted strands of lead hung from the fixture. A few more pieces of glass dropped, *plink, plunk.*

Looking for something else to destroy, the man reached under the table and pulled out the fine lace cloth, then ripped it in half like a rag.

Margaret's mind sank into incoherence. She struggled from the chair, hand raised. "Please, don't damage that, it was my mother's, I can sew it back together, just please don't—"

She sensed, heard, movement to her left. The man at the mantel swung the bat, the thick end smashing into her stomach. There was no corset beneath her skirt to protect her, and the pain was sudden, huge, felling. She flailed backward against her breakfront, her wildly swinging arms shattering the glass, spilling china. Glass cut her wrists as she went down again and blood ran over the buttoned white cuffs of her shirtwaist.

"Something special?" said the man in the dining room. He came into the parlor with the torn tablecloth in his fist. "Not no more."

He tossed it in the fireplace. Margaret screamed.

493

They finished quickly. Everything important or valuable in the parlor and dining room was ruined. She heard shoes scrape on the walk as they hurried away, then a chugging of autos.

In the hearth, the tablecloth caught fire.

On hands and knees, she crawled toward it. Glass littered the carpet. She was dizzy, disheveled, close to fainting, but kept crawling. She bit down on her lip and kept crawling, heedless of gashing her palms on glass.

It seemed a mile to the hearth. Glass tore her shirt and lacerated her knees. She left a bloody trail on the carpet, but at last she felt heat on her face. Closing her eyes, she wept against the coming pain, then plunged her hands into the grate, stifling a cry. She pulled out the burning tablecloth, smothered it against her filthy bloody shirtwaist, and fell on it to put out the flames.

She was found that way, unconscious.

At the hospital they treated and bandaged her. She had a broken kneecap. A great livid bruise marked her flat belly. The two physicians on call agreed that there might be serious internal injuries, but they couldn't tell as yet.

When she could speak, she asked for Mack. He rushed to her bedside and stayed twelve hours, leaving only to use the washroom or telephone the police department.

He telephoned nine times. Of course the detectives couldn't locate or even identify the perpetrators.

On a Saturday in March 1905, *California Chance* steamed out through Golden Gate. Following the owner's instructions, Captain Norheim set a course for ten miles offshore, and there cruised in a long continuous oval.

Under a white awning on the stern deck—an awning marked with the *JMC* cartouche—Mack's three Chinese stewards set out a buffet luncheon of oysters, paté, and other delicacies. It was a bright, invigorating day, a splendid day to cruise the ocean. None of the guests really cared.

Mack had invited three: Fremont Older, the former mayor Jim Phelan, and Rudolph Spreckels, four years younger than Mack himself. Rudolph was a tall, sturdy chap with a high forehead, the handsomest of the brothers. And he knew he was handsome; he bore himself with the unconscious arrogance of a prince, lounging in his canvas chair with his white flannel trouser legs crossed. Mack socialized with Rudolph but didn't especially care for him. He did respect Rudolph's wealth and his family name—and he could overlook almost any character flaw if the bearer hated the Ruef machine sufficiently.

"They wrecked everything," Mack said when the discussion began after lunch. *California Chance* left only a slight purling wake in the smooth sea. Shadows of gulls chased back and forth on the awning.

Older chewed his cigar. "I know that. I printed the story."

"You didn't print anything about her mother's tablecloth. Torn, burned—ruined."

"I'd say she was lucky to escape with her life and minor injuries," Rudolph remarked.

"Minor injuries?" Mack lit a cigar and snapped the match overside. "People are injured in different ways, Rudy. That piece of Irish lace meant more to Margaret than her own life nearly. I can help her rebuild her place; I will. But money won't restore that heirloom. Money won't erase her memories of what they did to her. We sit here fuming and arguing and meantime the machine hooligans do anything they damn please. They extort money from businessmen. They attack a decent woman—"

"Oh come, Mack," Rudolph Spreckels said. "A lot of people would question your use of the word *decent*."

"By God she is a decent person. They brutalized her. Don't be a fucking hypocrite. Have you never visited a prostitute?"

Rudolph turned away to study the sea.

"Now, now," Jim Phelan said. "We're not adversaries, we're in agreement. Seeking remedies here, in privacy."

"That's right—I'm sorry," Mack said.

"Yes," Rudolph muttered.

"The issue is, how do we get rid of this crowd?" Mack said. "There's hardly a thing they haven't touched or corrupted. The water situation, business permits—now the trolley mess—"

"It's a mess, all right," Rudolph said. "I'm told the Boss informed United Railroads that the regular monthly retainer of a thousand dollars was not enough to guarantee a favorable decision on the overhead lines. Pat Calhoun has to come up with a bonus."

Older bit on his cigar. "How much?"

"A quarter of a million. Cash."

"Christ," Phelan said. He stood up and gripped the stern rail. "Never had that sort of rot when I was mayor. I knew of small bribes, certainly. Ten dollars here and there under the table. But not this kind of cancer."

Older said, "I remind you, gentlemen: If you want to remove a cancer, you must handle sharp knives."

There was silence. The steam yacht slipped on through the water, trailing a thin plume from her big stack. The stewards refilled glasses, as soundless in their slippers as the gull shadows on the awning.

Mack leaned forward, hands spread. He'd let his beard grow again, though he kept it trimmed close. It was as white as his hair, which to his dismay was now starting to thin. "We've talked and talked about a reform movement. Talk must get it started, but we're long past that stage."

"At what stage are we, then?" Rudolph asked.

"We need a committed reform *organization*."

"We have the core of that here," Older said.

"Yes," Mack said. "So we have to address this question. Suppose we want to start gathering evidence on a serious and methodical basis. How do we do it? I'm not a professional detective and neither are any of you. We need one or two investigators who know what they're doing, and can't be bought. We need enough money to hire men like that."

He leaned back and sipped from his glass of steam beer. "We need a war chest."

Rudolph Spreckels studied Mack a moment, then languidly beckoned a steward to refill his glass. "I'll personally pledge two hundred and fifty thousand dollars."

Jim Phelan almost dropped an oyster over the side while Older clapped Rudolph on the back boisterously.

Then Mack spoke. "I'll go in for the same amount."

They were excited for just about a minute. Then Older finished his cigar and threw it in the ocean with a scowl. "All right, we've got money. With it we can probably hire investigators who can't be bribed. But we also need honest prosecutors, and judges. You won't get those in San Francisco unless you bring in the federal government."

"Then that's what we have to do," Mack said.

In the evening, *California Chance* bore east again toward the blue chalk smudge of the coast. The gentlemen had donned yacht caps provided by their host. All of them had drunk their share of champagne and wine, beer, or whiskey, but they were still relatively coherent about their purpose.

"I know one man we might enlist," Older said as they stood together companionably in the dusk. Even Rudolph's cloak of arrogant charm seemed happily misplaced. "Fran Heney. Francis Joseph. Born right south of the Slot. Hastings law de-

496

gree. He's in Washington as assistant attorney general and special federal prosecutor. He's only about this tall, and he parts his hair in the middle. He looks dull and harmless, but he bites in and hangs on and he gets convictions.''

"I know him well," Jim Phelan said. "An incorruptible man."

"Then he must have left town long ago," Rudolph said.

"Is he really tough?" Mack asked Older.

"Heney practiced law down in Arizona for a while. A man involved in one of his cases took a dislike to him and came after him with a weapon." Older's eyes turned to little ice chips. He cupped big hard hands around a match for a new cigar. "Fran shot the man in self-defense. They say he killed him without mussing his own cravat or disturbing a hair on his head. Is that tough enough for you, Mack?"

MACK BURST ONTO THE THIRD-FLOOR LANDING. **55**
"Nellie? I've got an important phone call. Two more minutes."

"The meeting starts in ten."

But he'd already disappeared.

Nellie paced the foyer. The young Japanese garage man ran in from Sacramento Street. The Cadillac had been at the curb for half an hour, he said. Did Mr. Chance still want it?

Nellie cradled her book against her bosom, her inscribed copy of John Muir's *Our National Parks*. "One never knows, Yosh. I trust the great man will enlighten us soon."

Yosh laughed and ran out.

Nellie walked around and around under the skylight. She'd lately celebrated her fortieth birthday, which sat on her much less easily than her fame. She looked smart and fresh, as always, with her hair worn longer and rolled over a rat into a pompadour. To complement her pleated plaid skirt and shirtwaist she'd put on a man's long-sleeved navy sweater. Her stockings were a misty pale blue and they nicely showed off her ankles above a pair of low-cut pumps with ribbon bows. Some considered the new shoe style too informal, even a mark of bad character.

Johnson strolled in with a billiard cue over his shoulder. "Mornin', Nellie. Beautiful cool day."

"Invigorating. I walked over from my flat." She'd taken a place on Russian Hill, though she still had the Carmel cottage.

Johnson's hair showed plenty of white now, almost as much as Mack's. The new century was rushing along, turning pages of the calendar faster than Nellie liked. The Norris sequel remained at a standstill, and her mirror revealed new lines in her tan face almost daily. She loved her independence but she hated sleeping alone. Trouble was, there was still only one man she wanted beside her at night. All in all, being forty depressed her.

Mack burst into sight again, jamming his arms into his jacket. He ran down to the second landing, plucked Jim from the protective arms of Señora Olivar, hugged him, and took his hand to bring him downstairs. Mack clearly wanted to rush, but Jim negotiated each riser slowly, cautiously, his body tilting, his hand jumping from baluster to baluster for support.

"The call was from Jesse Tarbox, one of my foremen," Mack explained. He snatched his hat from the stand. "Two of my laborers got the hell beat out of them in Fresno last night."

"Who did it?" Nellie asked.

"Some fine young white boys who don't think Mexicans deserve jobs."

"You know," she said with a sad air, "Henry Thoreau once observed that the experience of Americans coming to California meant nothing but getting three thousand miles closer to hell. Sometimes I do believe it."

He winced; it couldn't be called a smile. Then he took her arm. "Come on, let's see whether your friends can hold their tempers if I air my views."

"The question is can you hold yours?"

Jim limped over to stand by Johnson. The Texan put his arm around the boy.

"While you two palaver with the nature crowd, me and Jim thought we'd rent a couple of saddle horses and canter through Golden Gate Park."

"Make sure he gets a gentle horse. Go slowly. I don't want any falls. That foot can't take it."

"Yes it can, Pa. I'm strong. I want a horse with spunk."

"You let me decide that, young man."

"Just like you decide everything," Jim blurted.

Mack grabbed his son.

"Now, now," Johnson said. He laid his hand between them, pressing the edge of it against Mack's sleeve, and Mack backed off. Jim stepped closer to the big Texan. *How defiant he is,* Nellie thought. *When will Mack wake up and devote as much of himself to Jim as he devotes to his deals?* A month ago, in Carmel, she'd tried to say that to Mack. She'd never seen him so angry.

Drawn by voices, Professor Love bustled from the library. He flourished a mathematics text. "No skylarking with Mr. Johnson until we finish the morning lesson. The procrastinating man is ever struggling with ruin. Hesiod said that."

Johnson made a pistol of his hand and snapped down the hammer of his thumb. "Finish up quick, Jim."

"Yes, sir, H.B., right away." Jim went off with Love.

Johnson leaned his cue against the wall and walked out with Mack and Nellie. "The boy's right, Mack."

"Right to defy me? No."

"I keep tellin' you—you oughtn't coddle him so much."

Mack started to retort, but Johnson's green eyes caught the sunshine of the summer morning and held, unblinking. After a moment Mack looked away.

"Have a good meetin'," Johnson said with a chilly smile.

Shifting gears going downhill on Powell Street, Mack said, "Do you know what I read this morning? The army studied some automobiles and decided they have no use for them. Rich man's toys, they said. Horses and mules—that's all they need. Stupid bastards."

Mack sped around a dripping ice wagon, recklessly steering and braking and honking. Nellie held tight to the side rails of the seat.

"Why are you so angry again?"

"I can't get along with Jim. I try and I try but I always fail."

"Sounds like me and my novel."

"I'm in no mood to joke about it." He honked at an old Chinese gentleman with a laundry bundle crossing the street. The Chinese stumbled back and dropped the bundle in the water flowing in the gutter.

Nellie frowned. Mack was so irascible and dogmatic these days, she sometimes wondered why she continued to see him. Of course there was an answer, but she tried to keep it buried most of the time. At the moment, though, she was not only tired of his ideas, she was tired of him.

The Sierra Club met at eleven. The club had rooms on the third floor of the Mills Building. If Mack found any irony in the "nature crowd" meeting below the local offices of Chance-Johnson and Union Oil, he never commented.

About sixty people sat in rows of hard chairs in the plain,

drab room. Mack and Nellie were indeed late, and they drew stares as they took seats in the last row. The stares aimed at Mack were clearly hostile.

Under the club's banner on the platform, old John Muir held forth. He looked as wild and rustic as ever, with his long brambly hair and his beard flowing over a worn brown coat tightly belted above knickerbockers and high-top hiking boots. Nellie whispered that Muir had just come up from a ranch near Wilcox, Arizona, where he'd taken his beloved wife, Louie, desperately ill with pneumonia. What was his age now? Mack wondered. Almost seventy, surely.

What a wonderful face he had, though. Old as mountains; old as glaciers. Those sky-blue eyes had gazed on most of the world's natural wonders: the Himalayas, the Siberian steppe, the cataracts of the Nile . . .

The world knew him now, not just a few Californians, his articles appearing regularly in *The Atlantic* and other periodicals. He thundered in print, and he thundered in person. Camping with Teddy Roosevelt in Yosemite, he'd chastised the President for hunting and killing living creatures.

He was thundering this morning.

". . . the threat to Hetch Hetchy is still with us. Certain foolish men in that political quagmire known as our federal government continue to give consideration to the project. We must stand together, and never yield, because a Hetch Hetchy dam would be utter desecration of that pristine and lovely valley. It is not a civic need or a civic good, as some pretend. It is a scheme by developers and monopolists to exploit the wilderness for private gain."

Near the front, a man stood. "Mr. Muir, may I interrupt?"

"If you must, Mr. Phelan."

Mack whispered, "I didn't see Jim before."

"I feel compelled, Mr. Muir, because I don't agree with you at all. I admire your courage and idealism. I admire the zeal of the Sierra Club in protecting the forests and rivers of California. But in this case, with all due respect, you misstate the facts."

A displeased mutter ran through the audience.

"The proposal for Hetch Hetchy is not for anyone's private gain, but for the gain of all. Connected by an adequate pipeline, a reservoir in the Sierras will assure San Franciscans of clean, pure drinking water for years. The alternate proposal favored by the Schmitz administration—another franchise, to the Bay Cities company—is the monopolistic, exploitative proposal. The mayor and his supervisors stand with you against Hetch Hetchy because Bay Cities has bribed them to do so.''

Exclamations of "No" and "Sit down, Phelan" greeted that. Mack found his temper shorter than ever. He wanted to stand and argue.

"I don't accept those assertions," Muir retorted. "Once despoiled, a wilderness is gone. Whatever the rationale, you may keep your damnable dam scheme to yourself.''

Applause. Nellie joined in, sitting with her face straight to the front.

Mack jumped up. "John—ladies and gentlemen—Jim Phelan happens to be right.''

Flushed but pleased, Phelan yielded the floor and sat. Mack turned his hat brim in his hands. He fed all his nervousness into that movement, keeping his voice clear and loud. "San Francisco urgently needs a new and adequate water supply—''

"The supply is adequate now, laddie.''

"No, John, you're wrong. Before I offer some evidence, I want to say unequivocally that I love Yosemite and the high country as much as anyone in this hall—''

"How can you, sir? How can you when you talk like the worst sort of developer? We need none of your shoddy progress. We need no more sick starving immigrants crowding into the state—''

"I was under the impression that most Californians were sick or starving immigrants once, John.''

"—we need none of those, I say, if they put crushing demands upon our resources. We need no more savaging of God's natural wonders in the name of a few more hotel rooms, restaurants, souvenir shops that offer meretricious gewgaws to the shuffling hordes of tourists.''

"Growth isn't the issue, John. There I disagree with my friend Mayor Phelan.''

"Enough—sit down!" people yelled.

Mack's cheeks turned a dark choleric color. "I'll have my say.''

Old Muir held up a hand. "Yes, allow him that. Misguided as he is.''

"I am not misguided," Mack said. "The water situation in San Francisco is desperate. Over the weekend I read a copy of a report from the National Board of Fire Underwriters. It says that the thirty-six million gallons pumped every day isn't enough for a city this size. We need more water, new hydrants—a completely new system. What if we faced an emergency? One of those great raging fires that burned San Francisco six times in the fifties? Or a killer earthquake?"

"Persiflage," jeered a young woman with thick glasses. "We've not had a quake for decades."

"That's right."

"Yes."

"Not since '68."

"Shut him up."

"Listen to me," Mack said above the chorus. "Chief Sullivan runs the best fire department in the West. But what good is it without water? For years the chief's tried to build an emergency saltwater system or rebuild the old cisterns under the streets, but he can't get money for either. We're courting disaster here, and it scares me. I care about this city—"

"You care about your real estate."

"Who said that? I care about the lives of my son and my friends. I care about the truth. You people don't."

Someone shouted, "Liar!" A woman booed him. Mack felt he was laboring uphill foolishly. But there were great seas of anger churning in him, and they swept away all restraint and common sense.

"I've studied the philosophic base of this dispute and others like it. You claim to have all the right on your side. You don't. There's a well-regarded water doctrine called *conservation for public use*. A Hetch Hetchy dam fits comfortably within that policy."

Muir thumped the lectern. "That doctrine is not my doctrine, Chance. It is not our doctrine. So why are you here? Whose side are you on?"

"The side of reason, I hope. The side of compromise—"

"There will be no compromise. None."

Mack jammed his hat on his head. "Then I don't belong here."

Impulsively, he stepped into the aisle. In the heat of the argument, amid the shouts and finger-pointing, he expected Nellie to rise and follow. When she didn't, he reacted.

"We're leaving."

"Are you insane? Don't order me around."

Muir cried, "I say this to Mr. Chance, and his friends, and his dam. I say no. Eternally no. I say damn-dam-damnation!"

Wild applause. Club members jumped up. Nellie jumped up. Phelan slumped glumly.

Over the bedlam, Mack shouted, "You people don't have any answers. You have a single issue—and blinders—and no answers."

"That's it—that's the end," Nellie said.

He whirled on her, out of control. "It's true. You've got nothing but one narrow agenda and a talent for squealing like stuck pigs."

"You Republican capitalist bastard. Get out of here." She gestured to the door like an actress in a melodrama.

A man cheered, "Hurrah for Miss Ross," and led more applause.

"Get out." She was nearly incoherent. "Get out, get out of here, Mack. You're despicable—I don't want to see you. Get out."

"By God I will."

Jim Phelan shouldered through the crowded aisle. "So will I. Goddamned wildfowl sentimentalists . . ."

It was only a few steps to the anteroom, where Mack shut the double doors to mute the threats and catcalls. He leaned against the door, shaking.

"John Muir's right most of the time. But he isn't right all of the time."

"Totally unreasonable," Phelan agreed. "They'd rather see Frisco burn than damage a single tree."

Slowly Mack's brow cooled as the trembling worked itself out. He regretted the tone of his remarks, but not the content. Though he respected the Sierra Club, he did believe the members were wrong about the dam. He also realized he'd behaved abominably in Nellie's eyes. Phelan started to the stairs.

"Just a minute, Jim."

Mack opened the right-hand door. The meeting room had calmed down, and Muir was speaking quietly and patiently again, using a red wax crayon to mark a map of the Sierra range.

"Nellie?" Mack said in a stage whisper.

Still seated in the last row, she kept her eyes straight ahead. She was rigid.

He spoke her name again. When she finally turned and looked, her eyes said everything.

He shut the door and followed Phelan down the stairs.

During the afternoon and evening he telephoned her apartment on Russian Hill. The first time, she answered. He said hello and she hung up. The next ten times he listened to ringing. When the exchange closed, he went into the dark summer streets and walked for hours. He ended the night asleep in an armchair at Margaret's redecorated flat.

56ON THE NIGHT OF NOVEMBER 4, 1905, FRANCIS J. Heney addressed a campaign rally at the Mechanics' Pavilion. It was organized by the so-called fusion ticket, a coalition of Republican and Democratic candidates running against Schmitz and the hand-picked nonentities of the Union Labor slate. Heney had cleared his schedule and made the long trip from Washington to support the fusion group.

Mack and Fremont Older sat in the second row. From that low angle, they could barely see the little attorney behind the lectern. But they heard him:

"I personally know that Mr. Abraham Ruef is corrupt. I look forward to the time when I will be free to prove it in court, and I will do so gladly. If Eugene Schmitz and his crew of thieves are reelected for two more years, graft will become so intolerable that the people of San Francisco will beg me to come back and put them, and Mr. Ruef, in the penitentiary where they belong!"

On November 6, Boss Ruef published an open letter to Francis J. Heney, calling the lawyer's allegations lies and accusing him of a murder in Arizona. The next day, San Francisco voted.

Mack waited for the returns in Fremont Older's office at the *Bulletin*. The editor's wife, Cora, had come over from their rooms at the Palace. She knew what the election meant to her husband. A lovely, retiring woman whose shyness some mistook for snobbery, she and Mack tried polite conversation, but no subject lasted longer than a minute.

Outside Older's goldfish-bowl office on the second floor, reporters typed and shouted into telephones. Mack watched the city-room chalkboard, increasingly nervous about the numbers posted for the Union Labor candidates. At half past eight, Older poked his head in.

"I've been calling around. It looks bad all over town."

At a few minutes before ten, Mack was aware of a sudden lull in activity. Older walked in again. "Get your things, Cora. It's over."

Mack peered through the glass at the chalkboard. Until his

eyes focused he saw blurs instead of numbers. Damn it, on top of everything else, he needed glasses.

"Schmitz?" he said.

"Schmitz for the third time. Probably by more than forty thousand votes. That's the largest plurality he's ever received. As for his slate—just look. Every one of those eighteen toadies and charlatans elected to supervisor. What's wrong with this town? The people fall down and beg to be raped and plundered."

Cora Older helped her husband into his jacket, then put her arms around him and held him a moment. As Mack lifted his hat from the rack he heard noise in the street. He ran to the window.

"There's a mob coming."

They watched the first ranks surge around the corner, Ruef's cheering, chanting partisans filling the street from sidewalk to sidewalk. Their torches flung huge moving shadows on buildings.

A lot of them staggered drunkenly. They brandished bricks, bats, and four-sided box banners, and blew tin whistles and tin horns. They overturned a ragman's cart, blocked a horsecar heading for the barn, and rocked it. Some of them surrounded the downstairs doors of the *Bulletin*.

"We can't go back to the hotel now, Fremont," Cora said.

"Of course we can. I'll not let that riffraff interfere with us." Older put on his homburg while Mack was observing a new commotion below, a kind of human whirlpool spinning in the midst of the mob. At the center was Ruef, hatless, riding on shoulders.

Ruef shot his arms up in a great *V*. Someone spotted Mack and Older in the second-floor window and then someone else hurled a brick that fell short. A window shattered on the ground floor.

People threw more bricks and rocks and more ground-floor glass broke. Older grabbed his walking stick and ran out. Mack followed, trailed by a protesting Cora.

The editor stomped downstairs, kicking at broken glass littering the foyer. He went straight to the doors and flung them open, Mack beside him. People in the pushing, shoving mob threatened and cursed them, while the torches smoked, the box banners bobbed and turned, showing now a serious face of Ruef, now a smiling one.

Out there, above the crowd, the Boss suddenly sank from sight. Laughing, breathless, he was rescued and raised again. He spied the men in the newspaper door. Ruef pointed at them.

"There's Fremont Older. He isn't an editor; he's a raving anarchist."

The mob raged predictably, and Ruef's sweaty face glowed with excitement as they bore him on. A woman spat on Mack. He wiped it from his nose and cheek. Then a man darted at Older. "Who's that slut behind you?"

Older swung his stick at the man's head, narrowly missing. The man fled, jeering.

People in the mob lit Roman candles and shot their fizzing colored fireballs aloft. Others set off squibs and salutes in the middle of the crowd or heaved bricks at the last pieces of glass hanging in the ground-floor windows, knocking them out in a tinkly shower.

"Burn down the town while you're at it," Older snarled. "I'm going to the Palace and get drunk. Cora, take my arm."

"And mine on this side," Mack said.

With Cora between them, they stepped out on the firelit glass. The mob kept jeering and threatening them, but gradually flowed away, leaving room for them to walk.

Two blocks down Market Street, they found Walter Fairbanks watching the celebration. When he recognized Mack and the Olders, he smiled as if he were their warmest friend. Green and pink Roman candles fizzed in starry parabolas, coloring his gray eyes.

"Good evening, Fremont. Mrs. Older. Chance. This is one you lost."

"We lost the battle, not the war," Older said, not cordially.

"Still keeping score, Walter?" Mack said.

Fairbanks smoothed his thin mustache with his index finger in quick, agitated motions. "It's a habit I can't break. Good evening, all." He tipped his silk hat and turned up Mason, quickly gone in the glare of saloons and walk-up hotels.

Downtown San Francisco resounded with bells, horns, tin whistles, drunken singing. Someone fired a volley from a gun. Older seemed pale and spent all at once.

"I've decided something, Cora. In a few weeks I'm going to leave you for a while. It's time I bought a ticket to Washington. I've waited too long already."

"Buy two tickets," Mack said.

Phelan, Spreckels, Mack, and Older convened their reform committee in a private dining room of the University Club. Mack quickly voiced concern about Francis J. Heney. "He's the ideal man, but if we get him, we've got to recognize that the murder charge will be used against him."

506

"The case is fourteen years old," Older said. "I've had a man in Tucson investigating. Here's what happened. The wife of a certain doctor wanted a divorce. The doctor was a brute with a bad temper. He announced he'd shoot any lawyer who took his wife's case. Heney did, and the doctor attacked him in public. In the scuffle the gun went off and the doctor died. Heney was cleared immediately. Fifty people witnessed the shooting. My reporter brought back signed statements."

"One problem out of the way, then," Mack said.

"There's a bigger one," Phelan said. "You can't approach the federal government without evidence of a federal crime."

"I've been working on it," Older snapped. "You all know girls from the Orient are brought into the City for prostitution. They're sold in Chinatown for two to three thousand dollars a head. Two of my best men dug up something else about the trade. The girls are passing through immigration misrepresented as wives of American citizens of Chinese ancestry. The marriage papers are forged right on Grant Avenue. I secured two notarized affidavits citing names, dates, and circumstances." He leaned back. "We have a federal offense."

Spreckels was jubilant, but Mack less so. "Can you connect it to Ruef?"

"I suppose," Older said with a shrug. "He's mired in prostitution. At least his people are. I don't think it's necessary to prove a connection; we just use the evidence to get Heney here, get him appointed special prosecutor. Then he goes after Ruef on every front. Pack your bags, Mack. I bought our tickets this morning."

On December 3, 1905, President Theodore Roosevelt received them in his study, the remodeled Cabinet Room of the Executive Mansion.

A welcome fire blazed in the hearth. Outside, an unexpected snow fell, soft and wet, its fluffy three-inch icing decorating the bare trees. The storm had snarled wagon and horsecar traffic and brought chaos to the essentially southern town.

Mack thought the forty-seven-year-old Roosevelt resembled a thick oak tree growing in front of the fire. He was about five feet eight, with a bulging chest and thick midriff. The visitors felt his enormous energy, saw the flash of his blue-gray eyes behind his ribboned glasses. The President continually clenched his teeth, and he had huge teeth.

Roosevelt allowed five minutes for social talk. He presented them with inscribed copies of his memoir *The Rough Riders*, and showed them a prized photograph—a studio portrait of himself, much younger, in a grotesque cowboy costume, heroically posed with Winchester and scalp knife.

"Look at that dude," he said in his high-pitched voice. "Promotion photograph for *Hunting Trips of a Ranchman*. Ridiculous outfit. Putnam's insisted. Promotion—everything's promotion to those book fellows. I hope they get over it someday."

Mack mentioned that Johnson sent greetings to the President.

"Sergeant Hugh Johnson," Roosevelt responded. "Tall lanky fellow. Bully fighter, that Texan. Took a bad wound at El Caney. Convey my regards. Now—business."

Older summarized matters. Then he said, "Mr. President, San Francisco is a captive city. Abraham Ruef controls the mayor, the entire board of supervisors, and, for the moment, the district attorney's office. William Langdon, the new DA, is not so much corrupt as green. He used to be superintendent of schools. Ruef persuaded him to run after six experienced lawyers refused. The Boss will put pressure on him, that's certain. So what we have out there, sir—in addition to the federal immigration violations I have documented—is what amounts to a municipal bordello. Virtually every man in the government is for sale."

"I am aware of the corruption, sir. I was first made aware by certain gentlemen at the time of that grand golden banquet. Corruption on such a scale rots the moral fiber of California. Indeed, it taints the whole country."

Impressed by the man's aura and by the office he held, Mack nevertheless spoke calmly, with little nervousness. "Sir, our reform group can do nothing more—"

"You took a stand, Mr. Chance. You made a moral choice. I do not call that nothing."

"Thank you, Mr. President, but I'm referring to concrete steps. Legal action."

"Yes. Understand. Continue."

"We've escrowed nearly six hundred thousand dollars in a special fund for hiring detectives, renting offices—but that's as far as we can go. We need someone with the competence and authority to spend that money on investigation and prosecution."

"You have kept your activities largely covert?"

"Yes, sir. We didn't want to tip our hand until we had an attack plan."

"Oh, but they know who we are," Older said. "They know very well that we're after them. Mr. Chance here, Mayor Phelan, Spreckels—we're all watched from time to time. Mack and his son were brutally attacked."

"Yes, I'm aware. Very sorry about it. Go on, Mr. Chance."

"I suppose what's most galling is that we're all tarred as anti-Semites."

Roosevelt snatched off his pince-nez. "Is there any truth in that?"

"Absolutely none."

"It's a damned insult," Older said. "To us, and to honest Jews. That little bast— Mr. Ruef would be a crook if he were a Catholic, a Muslim, or a Hottentot."

Roosevelt locked his hands behind his cutaway and observed the falling snow a moment. Then he returned to his desk and showed them a sizable file.

"You have written me in some detail. I asked the Justice Department for a report on the authenticity of your allegations." He squeezed the file. "Most of what you say is corroborated. The matter of the Chinese women gives me grounds to act. I don't do so lightly, gentlemen. Never strike a blow if you can avoid it. But if you cannot, never strike softly. I offer you two of my best men."

"Two," Mack exclaimed.

"Yes, sir. Mr. Heney, whom you requested, and my chief of Treasury Secret Service, Bill Burns."

"William J. Burns, the detective?" Older asked.

"The same. Every prosecutor needs a smart investigator to ferret out evidence for indictments and trials. I've already asked both men to meet you tomorrow morning at Willard's Hotel."

Older's face shone. They hadn't expected this much largess. He jumped forward to pump the President's hand. "Sir, there aren't words to—"

"Wait, wait," Roosevelt said. "You may be less enthusiastic when I tell you that my order relieving Heney and Burns of current duties will take effect only when those duties are complete. Burns must clean up some cases. Francis Heney is still prosecuting Senator Mitchell and the others who stole our public lands in Oregon in order to strip them of timber."

Mack hid his disappointment. He was impatient. Every now and then when the tickers and telephones happened to fall silent, he would hear Little Jim moving through the great house on Sacramento Street, hear the scrape of the boy's ruined foot. At those moments he always imagined himself doing some kind of physical violence to Abe Ruef. The urge was even stronger, and darker, when he spent an hour with Jim and saw how much effort it cost the boy to walk, how he never complained. Those

509

occasions generated bloody fantasies: Ruef on a gallows with the trap springing, Ruef fatally shot, squirming in a pool of his own blood . . . Shameful images, people would say. The hell with them.

"It may be spring before Heney and Burns reach San Francisco," Roosevelt continued. "I assure you, the wait will be worth it. They'll take the stick to those looters and grafters. Yes, sir. The big stick."

He slapped their backs while firmly heading them out the door.

At Willard's on Pennsylvania, they met Burns and renewed their acquaintance with Francis Heney. Bill Burns was a Baltimore native and had a tough Irish charm. He'd fallen in love with police work when he was young, his father having been police commissioner of Columbus, Ohio.

"Here's the way I work a case," he told them. "Full tilt, and no questions asked. The man I'm after is guilty till he proves otherwise."

"That approach is efficient, but hardly legal," Heney said, amused.

"You handle the courtroom, Francis. Let me handle the rest. You don't catch crooks with parlor etiquette. Hard knuckles, that's what it takes. Hard knuckles and no sympathy for the bastards. We'll send this Ruef to San Quentin. Count on it."

In a westbound Pullman sleeper, Mack dreamed of drowning. He fell slowly through the clear cobalt water of a mountain lake, able neither to breathe nor to propel himself upward. He sank through sunlit depths in which dead things floated— drowned birds, foxes, a grizzly, a stag with a garland of dead wildflowers hanging from its antlers. There were hundreds of drowned things in the water with him. They moved gently, slowly, round and round in a noiseless sunlit dance.

He woke sweating, even though a prairie blizzard howled outside and chilled the rattling car. Except for the blizzard dream from boyhood, no nightmare ever terrified him so much or gripped him for so long afterward.

He thought he understood the dream, and he pondered what he ought to do. Once back in San Francisco, he dispatched a letter to John Muir at his ranch in Martinez. He said he'd changed his mind: The City remained in need of a new water supply, but he would back a search for alternatives; he would oppose the damming and flooding of Hetch Hetchy.

* * *

"When I'm here full-time in another month or two, I intend to open a law office," Francis Heney said to Mack and Older in the latter's office. "Take on a partner, Joe Dwyer. Tough man, and a fine lawyer. He's agreed to approach Langdon about putting me on as a special assistant district attorney."

Older leaned near the window above the street, puffing on his cigar. "Langdon's soft as cheese. Ruef will squeeze him to say no."

Heney allowed a tart little smile. "We'll squeeze harder with these." He tapped several files on Older's desk.

It was early April 1906, a Wednesday. Mack was impatient to end the meeting and get away on a short holiday.

"Burns is already gathering some astounding information." Heney selected a file from the stack. "The fight trust. A small group of promoters allegedly paid eighteen thousand dollars to ensure that they would be the only ones granted permits to stage prizefights. The informant said Ruef and Schmitz split the bribe."

Another file. "P.G. and E., our honorable utility. An alleged twenty thousand dollars to persuade the supervisors not to lower gas rates."

Another. "An alleged thirty-thousand-dollar legal retainer from Parkside Realty, Ruef to guarantee them the streetcar franchise they want on the west side—"

"My God, your informants are hardly reticent, are they?" Older said.

Mack shrugged. "They may be bragging, not squealing. They know the machine owns the police and the courts. They know Ruef and his pals won't be prosecuted."

Heney's mouth set. "They will be now." He scooped up the files. "Can either of you join me for dinner this evening? I'm meeting Hiram Johnson. I want to recruit him for our trial staff."

"You're pretty damned confident, Francis," Mack said.

"Totally confident. We're going to clean up San Francisco."

"Well, regarding dinner, I'm afraid—"

"God above," Older exclaimed, nearly biting his cigar in half. "I didn't believe the little thief would do it. Come here, quick."

Mack and Heney reached the window in time to see an open black touring car pass in the street. Abraham Ruef was enthroned behind his chauffeur, flanked on each side by several cardboard shirt boxes. Ruef basked in the sunshine, and the happy state of his world. Mack thought the Boss's eye roved upward to the *Bulletin* windows as he caressed the shirt boxes. The touring car chugged out of sight behind a horsecar.

"Do you know what's in those boxes?" Older asked. "Just fifty thousand dollars in cash, the first installment of Pat Calhoun's quarter-million bribe to get the overhead trolley lines. We got word of it day before yesterday. Someone in the East telegraphed the fifty thousand to the mint, and one of Calhoun's boys took delivery. He exchanged the gold for cash at Fairbanks Trust. Ruef bragged that he'd pick up the cash personally this morning."

"Pick it up where?" Heney asked.

"The offices of Calhoun's trolley company."

Mack's hazel eyes clouded. "Brazen son of a bitch."

"When a man becomes that powerful, he sometimes starts to believe he's invincible," Heney said. "It might make our task easier."

"Don't underestimate Abe," Older said. "He's a brainy little crook. In occasional moments of weakness, I admire him."

"Not I," Mack said with that cloudy look still in his eyes. Francis Heney squeezed his arm. "We'll put him away. It may take months, or years, but Abe Ruef's finished."

"I trust you, Francis. But I'll believe you when I watch them escort Ruef to San Quentin." Mack reached for his hat.

"Sure you can't join me to meet Hiram Johnson?"

"Not this time. I'm running down to Monterey for the rest of the week."

Older rolled his tongue in his cheek. "Nellie Ross lives down that way, doesn't she?"

"So I'm informed," Mack answered with a smile. "Actually the first purpose of the trip is to try out my new automobile."

Older snatched the cigar from his mouth. "You have another new one?"

"A beauty. She came off the boat from Liverpool Monday. I read a report on this model from the Olympia Auto Show over there. She cost me a thousand pounds at the curb in Manchester, and Lord knows how much to ship by sea. She shines like the morning. Henry Royce built her; he calls her a Silver Ghost."

Anticipation kept Mack tossing all night. At six he jumped out of bed. While he was shaving, Little Jim walked in. Father and son both wore nightshirts, but there the resemblance ended; Jim grew fairer, more like his mother, every year.

"Where are you going today, Pa?"

"Down the coast. I hope I'll see Nellie."

Jim thought about that. After a silence he said soberly, "Is Nellie a whore?"

Mack nicked his cheek and swore. He pressed a hot towel against the bleeding cut. "No, she is not. Who taught you that bad word?"

Jim examined his bare foot. "Oh, some boys."

"What boys?"

"Boys I met on the street."

"Well, stay away from them. And don't repeat that word, do you understand?"

Little Jim gave his father a sad, cold stare and left.

"He's hanging out with roughnecks," Mack protested to Johnson at breakfast. "The wrong kind of youngsters."

"What's he to do? Some of the right people ain't around most times. 'Sides, a little exposure to the streets won't hurt him none."

"The hell. He isn't eight years old yet."

"What of it? My friend Jack, when he was seven he was roughhousin' on the Oakland docks. Drinkin' hard liquor too."

"Jack London's a sot. Besides, he's a writer. You can't believe half of what a writer says. I'm going to order Angelina to restrain Jim. Forcibly, if need be."

"Oh, Mack, good God—"

"And you keep it in mind if you see him trying to leave the house. I won't have him roaming around San Francisco like some orphan."

"He's a smart boy. Tough, in his own way. He can take care of—"

"You heard me. If you're my friend, you'll go along."

Johnson regarded the man at the far end of the enormous dining table. "I'm your friend. But sometimes you make the job goddamn hard."

THE ONE-HUNDRED-MILE AUTO TRIP TOOK MOST OF **57** Thursday, but it was a joy rather than a trial, thanks to the great silver car. She measured fifteen feet, weighed thirty-three hundred pounds, developed between forty and fifty horsepower from her six-cylinder engine, and could carry seven. Her silver wheels were wooden, with pneumatic tires, and she had four forward gears plus reverse.

The car was operated from the right front seat, but Mack found that no great inconvenience once he got used to it. He was repeatedly thrilled by the feel of rumbling power coming through the steering shaft to the wheel rimmed in fine polished wood. The automobile lived up to all the manufacturer's claims; she was indeed quiet as an electric sewing machine or an eight-day clock.

At dusk on Thursday, he pulled up and parked in a rutted lane near Nellie's cottage. Whipping off his goggles and cap, he ran the rest of the way. He knocked on her door, tapping his foot.

The curtains were closed on the cottage windows. He knocked again, louder. After the fifth try, he circled the cottage on foot, then simply stood there, crestfallen.

Presently he tramped back to the Rolls-Royce. In the distance the surf boomed, a lonely sound. He was an idiot not to have written or contacted Nellie beforehand. He'd assumed she might say no to a visit announced in advance, and had relied on personal persuasion when he arrived on her doorstep. Now he faced a long trip back to the City, and he didn't look forward to it. He was tight with physical need again. He ought to get something more than this from his weekend.

Suddenly he recalled what was nearby: the Del Monte Hotel and Resort. What the hell—why not spend a few hours in the enemy's camp?

The Southern Pacific built the first Del Monte in 1880. Cholly Crocker was the guiding spirit, arguing that a society resort near the ocean in Monterey would fill up trains that were running nearly empty in those days. He was correct. In a parkland of 126 acres, artfully planted and enhanced by secluded paths and classical statuary, the Del Monte soon attracted the City's best crowd.

She was a wondrous three-story wedding-cake place, gleaming white with green shutters, winding exterior staircases, and turrets and spires crowned with American flags, California flags, and the railroad's own ensign. Actually this was the second Del Monte, a duplicate of the one that burned in '87. The owners had not tampered with success.

Mack put the Silver Ghost in the auto park, passing the attendant $20 to be sure no one touched it, and took a suite for three nights. The clerk didn't recognize him, which was good;

might be damned embarrassing to be seen enjoying himself on railroad property.

He was in a dismal mood, and warned himself against drinking too much. Changing to a blazer and white flannels, he stretched his solid-gold watch chain across his vest and fastened his cravat with a stick-pin diamond big as his thumb.

He ate lunch on the lawn, at a white iron table under an umbrella. The hotel was busy, crowded with cheerful, expensively dressed ladies and gentlemen. Having politely turned down an invitation to join a group for lawn bowling, he sat in a white wicker chair on the great veranda, where a unit of Ballenberg's Society Band played hits of the day: "Sweet Adeline," "In My Merry Oldsmobile," "Hello, Central, Give Me Heaven," Victor Herbert's "Toyland." The Herbert piece touched him with a sudden melancholy. What was he doing wasting his time among idlers?

Inside, at the arrangements desk, an officious gentleman booked carriage tours to the beach, the cypress groves, the Spanish mission ruins in Carmel. As Mack stood studying a leaflet on the seventeen-mile scenic drive, he fell into conversation with a plump blond woman who reminded him of Carla. She was a Miss Francie Howell of Denver, recently divorced. By five-thirty he and Miss Howell were sweatily making love in his suite.

After dining together that evening, they waltzed in the ballroom, again to the strains of Ballenberg's band, whose members had exchanged military tunics for tails. They met and chatted with three young naval officers in dress blues; their warship was anchored in the Bay.

That night they made love again. Next day, when they played croquet after breakfast, Mack discovered that Miss Howell was a determined competitor and expert shot. He had to fight hard to race through the wickets and beat her; losing to a woman was unthinkable.

He bought a bathing costume at the hotel shop. Miss Howell had brought hers, a very daring Parisian suit of striped tights, which elicited scandalized stares from some other guests when they went to bathe in one of the heated saltwater tanks. Proper female bathers wore modest blouses, ankle-length skirts, and stockings. Mack swam on one side of the soupy warm tank, Miss Howell on the other; a heavy net properly divided the sexes.

It proved to be a relaxing if inconsequential weekend. On Sunday morning, waking while his companion slept beside him, he decided he couldn't waste another hour, and would leave right after breakfast. The divorcée had been suitably ardent, but she wasn't Nellie. And San Francisco nagged him. There was always work.

There was always Jim.

He knew how to deal with the work; he understood less and less about how to cope with the boy. What he did with the best of intentions seemed to anger his son, and Jim's reactions and reticence angered him in turn. What was the answer?

He wouldn't find it lying in a bed owned by the Southern Pacific. He kissed Miss Howell's cheek and dressed.

Mack nosed the Silver Ghost down the winding drive. It was shaded by huge old cypress trees and the air smelled fresh and salty. A beam of sunlight between the cypresses flashed from the brass lamps of a massive dark-green auto coming up the drive. He identified a White steamer.

And then the driver. First by the tiny mustache below the goggles, then by the well-tanned features.

The driveway wasn't wide enough to accommodate both autos. Each gave way a little, and then halted side by side with right-hand tires off the road. The White hissed and trailed vapor; the Silver Ghost clicked like a loom shuttle quietly operating in the next room.

The automobilists leaned toward one another to speak, Mack at some disadvantage because he drove from the right. Fairbanks plucked off his stiff-billed cap and smoothed his auburn hair. "I heard you were in the hotel. The implacable reformer and railroad foe visits the Del Monte. Pity we didn't photograph it. What's this you're driving, a tin-plate bread box on wheels?"

"A new model Rolls-Royce."

"Ah. English. An American car isn't good enough for you? Looks slow as an elephant."

"Faster than that paraffin-burner, Walter."

"Would you like to put that to a test sometime?"

He snapped it out so fast and with such ferocity that Mack laughed. "Have you been lying in wait with that invitation? Yes, you have. Ever since the polo match. Or longer. Eh, Walter?"

Caught, Fairbanks thumped his steering wheel. "Yes or no?"

"Certainly. Anytime you say."

"Next Sunday. That's April fifteenth. I'll be down here again—"

"I can arrange it," Mack said. Maybe Nellie would be home.

"Just your auto and mine. My secretary will send particulars about place and time. Agreeable?"

"Sure." Mack leaned back, letting stray sunshine warm his brow. He felt fine suddenly, finer than he had all weekend. He couldn't help grinning, but it was done with a certain deliberation, because it goaded Fairbanks. "Delighted, in fact. Just prepare to get your ass whipped, Walter."

And, with a wave and a clashing of gears, away he went.

Fairbanks leaned over the back of his seat. Through a cloud of sunlit steam he watched Mack negotiate the next downward bend.

At the lower edge of the property the road narrowed to one lane on either side of a stone bridge that spanned an ornamental lagoon. Mack slipped the Silver Ghost through the tight space and accelerated on the straight road beyond. Fairbanks saw his dust. A sudden cramp in his gut brought a gasp of pain.

Friday afternoon: a sultry, overcast day. Mack switched on the electric lamps in the garage. He'd been at work on the Silver Ghost since 8 A.M.

Yoshimo Okada had demounted the spare tire that rode upright on the right running board. This allowed him to unlatch the toolbox built in beneath it. There was a similar toolbox on the left side, and Yosh had both lids raised and was checking the contents against a list. He'd taken off his shirt and singlet an hour ago. The garage smelled of grease and sweat.

Mack's forehead dripped. In the driver's seat, he was examining and testing every control. He pumped the clutch, then the foot-brake pedal that worked with the transmission to aid steering. A large lever on the outside right braked the rear wheels for stopping.

He reached for the gear lever, located outside between the door and the brake, and shifted from first back to second, over and down to third, up to fourth. He tested the magneto switch, even honked the bulb horn.

On his knees beside the left-hand toolbox, Yosh raised his head and grinned. He was tired, Mack could see. He decided they'd better close up and rest the remainder of the day; they'd be driving all day tomorrow, Yosh following in the Cadillac with extra tires, tools, and fuel tins. Already Mack felt a tightness in himself. He was putting more importance on the race than he should. Somehow he couldn't help it.

"Did you disconnect the governor, Yosh?"

"No, sir, I do that right before the race."

517

"Then that's about all we—"

He stopped, hearing a familiar sound on the back stair that came down from the floor above. Jim's left foot, scraping the risers.

The boy entered the garage and gazed at the great silver car with an expression of awe. "Hello, son." Jim responded with a small wave.

"Mist' Jim," Yosh said cheerily. He wiped his greasy hands on a cotton rag. "How you today?"

"All right, Yosh." The boy came a little farther into the garage. On the packed-dirt floor, his foot didn't scrape so loudly, but it left a trail where it dragged. From behind the wheel Mack stared at that. The sight of it hurt.

Jim sat down on a crate of spare spark plugs. "Pa, can I go with you down to Monterey?"

"No, I don't think so."

"I want to watch you race."

Mack opened the half-door and jumped down. The raised silver cartouche glinted under the tin-shaded lights.

"I'll be away a few days. After the race I'm going back to Carmel to visit Miss Ross. She wasn't home last week, and I'm really eager to see her." He reached for Jim's hair to ruffle it. "I promise you, this'll be the last trip for—"

Jim jerked his head away from Mack's hand, and Mack's face lost its look of good cheer. The boy darted behind the crate and then to the open door of the garage. He gazed at the dull sky, having taken himself as far from his father as he could without leaving.

Yosh's dark eyes jumped between Mack and the boy. With attention to the rag, he finished wiping his hands, cleared his throat. "I be back. Excuse me." He ran up the stairs into the mansion.

Jim stared at Mack with unhappy eyes.

"You don't care that I want to see you win the race."

"Of course I care, Jim." Mack picked up Yosh's rag and worked at some grease on his fingers. "But you've got to keep up with your studies with Professor Love. Angelina will take good care of you while I'm gone. She always does."

Doggedly, the boy said, "Why don't you ever want me with you, Pa?"

Mack wasn't prepared for such a direct question. He approached his son, watching closely for signs of temper or withdrawal. "Jim, I've explained before. I want the best for you—a good education at a fine college like Stanford. That means you just can't take time away from your lessons."

"I hate them."

"What? You used to like reading and doing math problems. What's changed?" He knew very well what the answer was; anything he liked, Jim disliked.

The boy was stubbornly silent.

"Well," Mack said, "regardless of how you feel about your studies, they're necessary."

He wasn't selling it. He saw it in Jim's angry pout, the sudden wetness of the deep-blue eyes. Westward, far away, thunder bumped.

"You just make all that up because you don't want me around."

"That's not true. And when it comes to your education, your future, I mean every—"

"Who's going with you to Monterey?"

"Yosh. To help me with the car."

"Is Miss Emerson going? That whore?"

Mack's hands dropped to his sides, clenched. "I've told you before. Don't use bad language. Especially a word like that."

"Miss Emerson's a whore."

"Jim, stop it. And stop crying. I'm tired of your sass and your constant rebellion. I won't have it anymore."

"That's all you care about, hanging around whores."

"You're making me angry."

He jutted his jaw. "Whore."

"Jim." Mack grabbed and shook him.

The boy danced up and down, pulling against Mack's hand, wrenching. "Whore, whore, whore, whore."

Mack let him go and slapped him.

Tumbling back against a wall stud, Jim smacked his head and almost sat down in the dirt. His tears seemed to dry up instantly. He clutched the stud, watching his father as if he couldn't believe, couldn't comprehend his cruelty.

Furious with himself, Mack stretched out his hands. "Come here. I didn't mean to blow up and—"

Jim ran under his hands as fast as he could with his dragging foot. Mack heard him on the stairs, struggling—fleeing.

Mack picked up a silver-plated wrench and twisted it. Suddenly he struck out. The blow left a deep dent in a stud.

He walked to the garage door to watch the storm gathering over the rooftops. The wind flung trash along the gutter. Yosh tiptoed in and they went to work, closing up, saying nothing.

Hellburner Johnson listened to the storm.

A single shaded electric light sharply defined a circle in the midst of his darkened sitting room. Johnson had slicked his crinkly gray hair with pomade and put on his best blue cotton traveling shirt and string tie. A folded coat, dark-blue cord, lay on his leather valise at the edge of the circle.

Things were in a fix in the household. Someone had spread the word about Mack hitting Jim; evidently Jim hadn't kept quiet about it. Meanwhile Mack had gone out in a fury. Johnson had been waiting for him in the rain-lashed house since dinnertime.

He sat by the light, trying once more to concentrate on the handwritten foolscap sheet given him by his friend London. Knowing Johnson's love of travel, the young writer had copied some thoughts he wanted to use in a future story.

> *Don't you sometimes feel you'd die if you didn't know what's beyond those hills, and what's beyond the other hills behind those hills? All the places of the Earth are just waiting for me to come and see them.*

That surely fit his own nature, and his present mood, Johnson reflected. He read the passage again. Lightning washed the windows. As the thunder quieted, he heard a familiar tread on the stair.

He folded the foolscap and tucked it in his shirt pocket to save. Then he reached for his cord coat and what lay under it.

"Jim?" Mack tapped softly. "Jim, answer me." He tapped again. Water oozed from the soles of his shoes and his cuffs were soggy. He'd wandered hatless, collar up, hands in pockets, bumping along in the downpour, trying to figure out how to correct his relationship with his son. That he had to correct it, and drastically, he no longer doubted.

The boy didn't answer the repeated knocks, so he tried the handle.

Locked.

A footstep startled him. Johnson ambled out of the shadow between little electric wall lamps. Their shades focused the light downward, leaving great dark spaces. Mack immediately noticed his partner's slicked hair, fresh shirt, black string tie.

"Leave him be, Mack."

Johnson's tone stunned him. "What?"

"I said leave the boy be until you can treat him right. I heard what you did, and I talked to Jim about it 'fore supper. Tried to make him feel better. Couldn't do it."

"I slapped him, I shouldn't have—"

"That's true, you shouldn't have. Tannin' a youngster's bottom is one thing. But what you did—that's downright mean. You better not do it again."

Mack stared into the leaf-green eyes and saw a clear reflection of how far he'd drifted. Putting an arm around Johnson, he drew him away from Jim's door. He felt weak and beaten. He was simply not used to feeling either way.

"What does he want from me, Hugh?"

"Ain't so hard to figure out. He just wants a father. One who ain't so damn busy all the time with his ranches and his oil and his real estate and his reform committees. And his women. *And* his personal feud with some snob lawyer. Are you and Fairbanks two snotty kids fightin' over the marbles in the schoolyard? You sure as shit act like it sometimes."

Mack stopped on the stair overlooking the hall. Above, sheets of rain battered the skylight. He felt a piercing guilt, a sense of being unmasked as a criminal. In a few plain words, Johnson had stripped down the long quarrel with Fairbanks and put it in a ridiculous light.

The right light.

He hated to admit that, and so he dodged around it. "You're all duded up."

"Goin' away again."

"You didn't tell me."

"Hell, Mack, you ain't around long enough for anybody to tell you anything. Wouldn't listen if they did. I'm catchin' the midnight for the East, then maybe a cattle boat to France. Lately, I don't like livin' here."

He stepped in front of his partner and jabbed him with a finger. "I'll tell you this much 'fore I go. You're still my friend, but in some ways you're sure-God messed up. You said some while back that you didn't want to raise no hothouse lily. Then you turned right around and started raisin' Jim exactly that way after he got hurt. Go off and get this damn stupid race out of your system—"

"I'll stay in San Francisco this weekend. I'll telephone Fairbanks that I can't—"

"Don't bother," Johnson said with a wave. "Jim don't want to talk to you right now. He'll cool down by the time you come back, I reckon. Then you can try to repair the damage. You better. You better start takin' good care of that fine, smart boy or you'll deal with me when I get back."

With an almost feminine delicacy, he touched and lifted the left side of his blue cord coat. The Peacemaker with the lone star embossed on the ivory grip jutted from his waistband. He dropped the coat again.

"You want to fight with somebody, I can make old Fairbanks look like a beginner. Don't ever give me cause. You got your work cut out around here. So long."

Little Jim heard the stutter of engines and flung himself out of bed. He'd hardly slept at all while the storm raged through the night. There was a worse one inside him.

He ran barefoot to the bay window. Dawn lit the lace curtains. He raised them and leaned on the sill. Under his dark-blue eyes his cheeks were puffed and raw from crying.

He watched the automobiles roll through the intersection of Sacramento and Mason, bound south. Four men with lunch pails pointed and commented from the curb. Pa drove the Silver Ghost, already mud-splashed. He'd raised the canvas top and Jim couldn't see his face, only the shoulder of his duster and his right gauntlet, working the brake and gearshift.

Emotions flew over the boy's face; resentment, and pain; anger, and resignation— Tears welled again. He hated them almost as much as he hated Pa.

The Cadillac followed the Silver Ghost through the intersection. Over San Francisco's sturdy downtown buildings, billowy clouds caught the pink light of morning on their eastern curves. What a beautiful day in spring.

A good day to do what he'd planned all night. Jim let the lace curtain fall. Head down, he stood motionless, then drew a deep breath, finding courage. He limped to the hulking mahogany chiffonier and opened a drawer, glancing briefly at the bolt on the hall door. Still secure—no one would bother him.

He pulled out a favorite shirt and threw it on the bed. Another. Then a belt. Jeans. From the wardrobe he fetched his heaviest shoes. Then he thought of something, hurried to his study desk, and rummaged under his schoolbooks. He caressed the lacquer of the abacus. He loved the parade of fire-breathing dragons chasing themselves around the frame. Clicking a couple of the red and yellow beads, he swallowed and then rubbed his cheeks. He'd show Pa.

He put the abacus with the clothes. Couldn't leave his favorite possession behind, could he?

STATELY EUCALYPTUS SHADED THE DRIVERS. THEY **58** had parked their automobiles in a grove on the east side of the Coast Road, some twenty yards separating them; they wanted to check and adjust their machines in privacy.

Fairbanks had brought the starter, an officious young man from the new City office of the fast-growing Automobile Club of Southern California. He was as dull as his brown suit, white shirt, detachable collar, and cuffs. He drove a dull brown Luverne.

Here, on this Sunday, the Coast Road below Point Lobos was deserted. Slightly inland from the Pacific and twisty and deeply rutted, it wound away south toward the Tehachapis, north toward Monterey and their chosen finish line. It was 11 A.M. on a fresh April day.

Mack sweated in his duster and driving cap. Yosh had the bonnet raised and was priming the induction pipe. "All right, Mist' Chance."

"Petrol tank air valve open." Mack liked to call out the steps in starting. It helped establish concentration. That was harder than usual today; all the way down from the City, his thoughts had repeatedly veered to Jim. And Johnson's warning.

He reached down for the hand pump and worked it vigorously, then watched the gauge needle rise. "Fuel pressure one p.s.i. One and a half p.s.i. Flooding carburetor now. Turn her over, Yosh."

The Japanese man slammed and latched the bonnet and grabbed the starting crank at the lower front end. He grunted as he revolved the crank, counting aloud. When he said, "Eight," Mack's gloved hands darted.

"Coil switched in. Magneto switched in. Advancing ignition."

The Silver Ghost had run a while this morning; she was warm, so advancing the ignition started her on the first try. He shivered and leaned back, ready.

The starter waved to the drivers. "Gentlemen, if you please. We're six and a half minutes late already."

Fairbanks shifted and drove his White steamer out of the grove, braking just this side of a line scribed across the road.

Mack pulled the Silver Ghost alongside the White on the left, acknowledging Fairbanks with a brusque nod. Fairbanks returned an unusual, almost smug smile and a little wave.

The starter held a blank cartridge pistol. "The rules of this contest are simple—"

"Just one moment," Fairbanks interrupted. "I'd like to wait for my rooting section. There."

Mack heard the auto approaching from the direction of Monterey. When it bounced over a low hill into view, he couldn't immediately identify the make or the two people riding in it. It was painted bright yellow, and it bounced and banged toward them with a tinny sound. A man in livery was driving. Beside him sat a woman in a beige duster, large gauntlets more suitable for a man, and a stiff-billed cap held on by a golden-yellow veil tied in a bow with its ends flying over her shoulder.

Can't possibly be. The little auto, which he recognized as a Buffalo, now puttered up to the starting line, and then there was no mistake; it was Carla.

She'd grown heavier, a half-moon of chin fat peeping from behind the veil bow, and her expression was bleary. The chauffeur pulled off the road, turned off the motor, and ran around to the passenger side. Carla put her yellow shoe on the running board and missed the edge. With a cry, she tumbled against the chauffeur. He wasn't quick enough to catch her, and she landed on her knees in the dirt.

The chauffeur babbled apologies while helping her up, but she wouldn't take his hand, waving at it as if it were a pesky fly. *Drunk. And this early. God help her.*

So far she hadn't glanced his way. Deliberate, he imagined. Fairbanks got out of his car, and Mack felt obliged to do the same. The dull young man with the pistol studied a pocket watch with affected concern.

Mack swept off his cap and goggles and, at that moment, Carla looked at him. "Good morning, Mack." A smile curved her rouged mouth. It was a self-satisfied smile, like that of Fairbanks a while ago. What kind of private joke were they sharing?

"Carla. This is a real surprise."

"I came all the way down from the hotel to wish you luck. But of course not as much as I'm wishing your opponent." She linked her arm with the lawyer's.

So that was it. A new liaison. He hadn't heard it mentioned in the City. But Swampy didn't keep track of his daughter, and Mack didn't keep track of Fairbanks's private life. Fairbanks had always wanted Carla, but Mack wondered if he really knew what he was getting. He was surprised to feel a genuine, if

524

brief, pang of sympathy for the lawyer. For himself, there was only a renewed relief, like that felt by an ex-prisoner whose freedom was all the sweeter because he could remember what it was like to be locked up.

Mack hid his feelings under a polite smile and tried to banter. "If you're cheering for Walter, you certainly don't owe me any good wishes."

"Oh, my dear, there's a lot that I owe you."

The hate in those deep-blue eyes chilled him. He put on his goggles and jumped up into the Silver Ghost. "Let's go."

Carla flung her gloved hand around Fairbanks's neck and kissed him. All the men saw her open her mouth. Fairbanks's embrace seemed stiff, and Mack caught the gleam of the rolling white of an eye. The man of propriety, worried about the brazen kiss.

Fairbanks extricated himself and turned away to shield a whispered conversation with Carla. Mack heard "my dear" and "at the hotel." Then Fairbanks strode around the bonnet of the steamer and vaulted up.

Carla stepped back and hit her heel on a half-buried stone. She'd have fallen again if the chauffeur hadn't caught her. She favored him with a slurred thank-you, not bothering to look at him.

The starter stepped in front of the auto bonnets shining in the sun. "You gentlemen are familiar with this road, I believe. A direct route running north and inland to the Del Monte. Total distance is ten miles. The first auto to reach the hotel and park in front wins. Drive off at the sound of my pistol. Do you have any questions?"

"No," Fairbanks said. He was driving bare-headed, with goggles. Carla blew him a kiss and waved with the energy of a sentimental schoolgirl. Fairbanks seemed to like that. He returned another jaunty wave, then began tapping his wheel with the fingers of both hands. It gave him a relaxed, almost playful air.

"Can we get on with this?" Mack blurted out. Carla's presence had unnerved him. He didn't love her, but she had once belonged to him. This new affair was a kind of violation of that intimacy.

He fiddled with his goggles. The elastic was too tight. Then he wiped a sweaty cheek. Yosh had been watching the byplay from the roadside. He knew the former Mrs. Chance by sight and reputation and he saw Mack's agitation; his face said he was worried.

A breeze ruffled Fairbanks's auburn hair. As the starter bustled to one side, Mack poised his hands on the wheel and the outside gear lever.

Then the pistol fired.

Fairbanks rammed the steamer across the starting line and immediately veered left. "For God's sake, Walter," Mack yelled. The steamer struck and glanced off the high forward end of the Ghost's front fender.

The White pulled back to the center of the road, accelerating. Mack coughed in the dust, then raised himself off the seat, inevitably losing speed as he surveyed the damage. The fender bent downward, inches from the Dunlop tire. Silver metal menaced the rubber like a knife.

So that was how Fairbanks wanted to play it. All right.

Mack twisted the levers that loosened the top half of the wind screen and slammed the top section down, striking the lower part so hard the glass cracked. His cap blew off, and wind and dust particles attacked his exposed face. Somehow it wakened him and fixed his concentration as nothing had before.

The great silver machine chased the green steamer through the empty countryside. The Monterey County highway hardly deserved the name. It twisted back and forth, and up and down like a corrugated washboard. Dust bathed the drivers and sweat on Mack's face turned it to a thin runny mud.

His speedometer showed thirty-nine miles per hour, the mileometer above it indicating that he'd gone two and a half miles. He roared along, one car length behind the steamer, the road too narrow for passing. Unexpected holes or shallow transverse ditches shook the cars and bounced the drivers like cowboys on wild broncs. Mack clenched his jaws so hard they hurt. Better that than an open mouth and a risk of broken teeth.

The road abruptly leveled between grape arbors, and some Mexicans pruning vines gaped at the roaring autos. Suddenly, a sharp report sent Mack's hand flying to the brake lever. The rear drums squealed and smoked. He narrowly avoided hitting the White as it careened off the road, its right rear tire punctured.

Walter Fairbanks spat profanity into the wind and dust as Mack roared by.

He settled back comfortably to cruise the rest of the way to the Del Monte. He could hardly believe he'd won so easily, but the flat would cost Fairbanks ten minutes, minimum, a loss impossible to make up.

He stopped for a minute at a rickety stand to buy a large green apple from an old woman. He was filthy with dust, his hair blown every which way, but the sudden easy victory left him famished.

The mileometer showed he'd raced six miles.

A half-mile farther on, he drove out of a grove of wind-blasted cypress into a long blind bend, and when he emerged from that, he suddenly confronted a wide pool of water in the road. If he slowed down to a safe speed, he'd lose momentum, but better that than breaking an axle. The decision was automatic. He braked and then hit the mud hole. He felt the engine strain, the front wheels spin—

The Silver Ghost lurched forward out of the hole. The rear wheels splashed in, spun, then sank back, mired.

Mack pounded the steering wheel. Why such a huge puddle? After the last storm, the whole route from the City to Monterey County had dried. Completely.

Then he noticed a man in scabrous overalls sitting in a rocker in front of a shanty set back from the road on the left.

The man wandered out to the Rolls-Royce, his eyes, little brown mud balls, assessing Mack with open amusement.

"Looks like you're stuck bad."

"Can you help me out? Have you got horses?"

"Two mules, yonder in that shed."

"I'll pay you."

"Sure," the man said. "A hundred dollars."

"I thought you were a farmer, not Black Bart," Mack snarled.

"Too high for you? Stay there," the man said with shrug. And Mack knew that Mother Nature wasn't the one who had flooded the hole in the road in order to trap the unwary automobilist out for a scenic drive. Mack had read about similar tricks aimed at the rich and their toys.

Seething, he said, "I've got the cash. Get the mules."

Hitching them took ten minutes. Bringing them to the road and attaching chains to the front axle took ten more. The farmer demanded his pay before he whipped up the team. Mack handed him a $100 note, and for the first time the farmer was impressed. He tucked the note in a dirty pocket of his overall and applied a quirt. "Giddap, General Grant. Giddap, General Lee."

Straddling the chains, Mack cranked the engine, then jumped in to restart it. With combined mule and horsepower, he surged the Ghost's rear wheels out of the mud. The auto's rear fenders were bent down as badly as the right front; now three twisted knives poised over the tires.

Mack jumped out again. The farmer gave him a witless grin, convinced he'd flummoxed the city gent neatly.

"That was a good job," Mack said. "I'll give you a little something extra."

"Why, that's real kind of you."

"Sure," Mack said, and blew him back with a fist in the face.

The farmer knew a lot of barnyard language, and he used it. Undeterred, Mack plucked the $100 note from the man's pocket, then rolled him into the mud hole headfirst.

He jumped back in the Ghost just as Fairbanks steamed out of the blind bend, yelling and gesturing. Fairbanks was coming out of the curve full speed. The farmer came up spluttering, saw the White looming, and jumped out of the mud hole with a shriek.

Fairbanks hit the brakes so hard they spewed smoke, and managed to stop a yard short of the mud hole. Screaming threats at the farmer, he ordered him to stay back. Accelerating the Rolls-Royce, Mack looked over his shoulder as Fairbanks roared to the mud hole. He was going faster than Mack had been; he was also luckier. The White plunged in, shuddered, started to settle, but then lurched out, muddy water streaming from the hubs. Mack was only narrowly in the lead.

The mileometer showed eight and a quarter miles now. The road widened and turned east, the ramshackle roofs of Monterey visible ahead. Coming out of the curve, Mack again saw the White over his left shoulder. Drawing up even where the road widened, Fairbanks suddenly wheeled over and rammed his auto into the Ghost.

The noisy collision sprang the Ghost's rear door. It clanged like a metal shutter in a hurricane. Fairbanks wrenched his wheel over a second time. This time Mack steered away, shooting across a shallow ditch and into weeds beside the road.

An enormous eucalyptus loomed straight ahead. As the hinges of the flying door broke and the door sailed away like a silver coin spun into the sky, Mack downshifted and steered around the tree, then left again toward the gray cloud behind the steamer. He smelled the Ghost's overheating rear brake, clutch, and motor.

Fairbanks hunched over his wheel like some maniacal goblin. Mack opened up the Ghost as far as he dared and chased Fairbanks in the dust.

Within a mile of the Del Monte, the road widened still more. Fairbanks nearly ran two excursion carriages into the underbrush as Mack gained steadily on the steamer, which was beginning to belch darker smoke. The Ghost shuddered and rattled as if about to fall apart, but the great engine kept her going, and shortly Mack pulled alongside the White.

Looking ahead now, he groaned; he'd forgotten the trap at the edge of the hotel property, the arched stone bridge over the decorative lagoon. Wide enough for one. Only one.

Side by side in boiling dust, the cars rattled and screamed toward the point where the road shrank to a single-lane bottleneck. Fairbanks swung over and rammed.

Mack hadn't expected that so late in the race. He'd unclenched his jaws. The impact jammed his teeth together on his tongue and blood spurted. But he held the wheel as if he were fused to it. There were carriages parked on the roadside beyond the bridge, spectators waving the racers on. Fat black clouds plumed behind the steamer and it coughed and bucked and Mack pulled slightly ahead.

The bottleneck rushed at them. Fairbanks sideswiped him again, and Mack's right-hand mirror snapped off while the front fender bent farther down and the edge sliced a thin shaving of rubber from the tire.

Fairbanks hit the Ghost a third time. Spectators jumped up and shouted, seeing the unsportsmanlike maneuver. Blood ran down Mack's chin and splashed his duster. The autos hurtled side by side toward the bottleneck and the bridge. Mack pressed his bloody lips together, put his head down, and steered arrow-straight. He could feel the White inches away, with the road narrowing thirty yards ahead.

Then twenty yards.

Ten—

Mack refused to give way, and finally Fairbanks's nerve broke. Mack heard a raging oath, howling tires. The White veered off.

Mack shot onto the bridge just as the bent fender carved through the tire and burst it. The Ghost banged into the stone rail on the right side. Mack fought to control the wheel as the twisted right fender raked the mortared stones, spewing up sparks and smoke. The spectators began to yell fearfully and jump from their vehicles.

The Silver Ghost roared off the bridge, hell to steer because of the burst tire. Mack flung a look over his shoulder and saw the White miss the bridge and shoot on, its front end lifting, sail over the narrow lagoon, and crash bonnet first in reeds on the other side.

Ducks fled with terrified honks as the steamer's rear wheels sank in shallow water scummed with green algae. The car bubbled and hissed, steam billowing out in enormous clouds. Fairbanks climbed groggily into the water, massaging his neck, then splashing to the reeds and ripping off his goggles.

Mack throttled down. Even so, the Ghost remained hard to drive. The wooden wheel rim was cracking and splintering.

He passed the applauding spectators and crept up the curving drive at two miles an hour, the Ghost straining and chugging on the grade. She almost didn't make it to the driveway in front of the hotel but Mack pleaded and coaxed, and she rolled to a stop at the extreme end of the veranda. There she seemed to sigh and settle on creaking springs.

Beneath her, like the flow from a fatal wound, hot oil spread on the sparkling driveway of crushed stone and oystershell.

Mack limped back down the drive to the bridge. Dust dyed his hair a curious tawny color, the blood on his duster and gauntlets already brown. He licked at his crusted mouth and wondered how Fairbanks felt, giving way at the last second.

Because he was on foot, he reached the bridge only moments before the Cadillac, the Luverne, and the gleaming yellow Buffalo drove into the bottleneck on the other side. Carla ordered her chauffeur to stop and park. She jumped out and splashed across the shallow lagoon, while, on the near bank, Fairbanks walked up and down with small agitated steps. An obese gentleman from a Packard landau pumped Mack's hand and congratulated him, and Mack's ghastly bloody face cracked in a poor imitation of a smile. Carla flung off her veil, her cap, her gauntlets, dropping them all in the green water. Fairbanks stepped down to examine the White, now settled hub-deep.

Carla reached him. "Darling, darling—are you all right?" Mack stood by the bridge rail where the Ghost had left a long scar, then sat down gratefully, exhausted. As usual, Carla wore a great number of rings—sapphires, emeralds, a huge oval-cut diamond—and Mack stared dully at the flash and dazzle as she caressed Fairbanks's face and shoulder. "Are you hurt, sweet?"

"I don't think so," Fairbanks answered. "The auto's a total loss."

"Don't worry, don't concern yourself, sweetheart." She kissed his dirty face. "I can buy you a new one. I can buy you ten new ones. It's the least I can do for my husband."

She knew Mack was resting on the bridge within earshot.

Fairbanks put his arm around her. They stood in the green water, smiling at him. Mack remembered how he'd felt in the room with Coglan, years ago, punched nearly senseless. He felt that way again. Fairbanks had won his victory before the race started.

"Congratulations, Chance," Fairbanks called.

"And to you and Carla. I didn't know you were married. When was the happy event?"

She smiled defiantly, letting her husband answer. "Two weeks ago. In Los Angeles. Very private."

"Yes. Well. Quite a surprise. All the best to you both."

With a weary, strangely queasy feeling, Mack walked back up the road past the silent spectators.

EXHAUSTION AND A DEEP UNHAPPINESS CONTINUED **59**
to grip Mack in the hours just after the race. He sent
Yosh back to the City with the Rolls-Royce, saying he wanted
a day or two by himself. He had no idea of where he was going,
but he promised to telephone Alex Muller next day. Driving
the Cadillac, he found a small, quiet country inn as dusk was
coming down.

On Monday, from the Monterey central telephone office, he placed a call to Sacramento Street. There was some kind of trouble on the line; the operator couldn't get the call through. After the third attempt, he gave up. No real harm done; his various enterprises would survive for a bit without him.

On Tuesday he drove to Carmel. Nellie served him lunch of fish chowder and beer. It was a dark day, and she'd lit kerosene lamps inside the snug redwood cottage. She had neither electricity nor a telephone.

The solitude didn't seem to sit well on her. Her outdoor color had faded; she was pale as a piece of china. Strain marked her eyes with charcoal smudges. She was humorless, ate almost nothing, smoked one Turkish cigarette after another.

He said he'd changed his thinking about Hetch Hetchy. Said he'd written Muir. He expected an enthusiastic response, questions. She said, "That's good" in a distracted way. That was all.

In silence they cleared the table, and then she put on a sweater and led him over a winding path to the white dunes. The fog hid all but fifty yards of gray-green sea. Huge pieces of driftwood lay about in tortured shapes. One reminded Mack of a hunchback kneeling to pray.

They walked in the cold murk, careful not to touch. Sandpipers fled from them. A man with a fan beard, dim as a ghost, hailed Nellie from a quarter-mile away. He was hurrying off the beach with his easel and paint box. Nellie returned his wave listlessly.

He told her about the race, and some of the events that led up to it. The news of the wedding surprised her. "Did you see any more of them?"

"No, they checked out right away. It was so damn strange, Nellie—once the race was over, I found I didn't care about it anymore. There wasn't any satisfaction in beating him. We were acting just the way Johnson said—like a couple of eight-year-olds in a schoolyard."

Head down, hands in the pocket of her skirt, she said, "Sometimes grown men play those games all their lives. They call it business, politics, sports. You can feel good that you're outgrowing it."

The surf rolled foamy white and glassy green from the enveloping fogbank, and a ship's horn uttered its lonely plea far to the west. Mack's white hair blew in the dank wind. He wanted to hold and comfort her.

"Time to talk about you," he said. "You don't look well."

"Oh—physically I'm all right. It's the depression. The fog lifts, but the feeling doesn't. I've never been so low. Not in my whole life."

"Are you writing?"

"No, I don't even pick up the pen. I kept hitting my head against Frank's book until I couldn't stand it. So I quit. Now I read, I'm a beachcomber—I failed, Mack. I just failed."

"It's allowed, you know."

A wry smile came and went in a moment. "Do I hear the great J. M. Chance admitting human beings can be less than perfect?"

He laughed. "You can't get my goat with that. You want to discuss failure? I'll tell you about failure."

He told her about Jim.

At the end he said, "Johnson's right about that too."

It seemed to draw her out of herself. They sat on a driftwood log, staring into the mist. Sandpipers kept marching through the shallows in quick-step.

The wind blew her hair and she brushed at flying strands. "You're amazingly frank about yourself."

"I told you, a lot of things came clear at the hotel. But what good is that? I don't know what to do."

"Why, H.B. had one of the answers. Forget business for a while. Concentrate on Jim. Give him more of yourself. No matter how awkward it seems at first, or how difficult . . ." She watched the fog. "You don't want to make the same mistake you made with Mr. Fairbanks's new wife."

"Now listen. About Carla. When we were married, I tried—"

At that point he cut it off. It was bluster, an automatic defense. He no longer believed it; why should others? "No, you're right," he said finally. "I neglected her. She drew away, so I neglected her more. The pattern's repeating with Jim. I began to recognize that yesterday, dimly. You've seen it clearly, I guess. You're a smart woman."

"Oh, yes. Expert with everyone's problems but my own." She scooped up sand and flung it angrily.

Then she rose and wandered down to the water with a hopelessness that alarmed him, and he hurried after her. He touched her shoulders and turned her. The wind blew her hair forward on either side of her face, teasing his skin like unseen hands.

"I hate to see you feeling so bad."

"I hate it too. Where's all that California hope? God, I need a little." She averted her face, eyes shut, crying now.

Mack embraced her, felt her shuddering against his wrinkled motoring coat. She crept her arms around him and clung to his back.

They held each other a while. Then she pulled her head back to gaze up at him. Her mouth was pale as ivory. He kissed her and tasted salty tears.

Her hair blew against his closed eyes, and he put his mouth to her ear. "Nobody else keeps me straight like you. I wander off the path and you kick me back. Stay with me. I love you—"

She kissed him with enormous ardor, twisting her head back and forth, finding his tongue. He rubbed his palms up and down the back of her sweater and felt her legs brace against his. He kissed her throat.

"Let's go back," he said.

"No. I can't." Her voice strengthened. "Not when I'm in this state. I've got to straighten myself out. Then—we'll see."

"Damn it, Nellie, I want you so damn bad—"

She pushed against his chest—not hard, but firmly. "Your son needs you. If you're serious about him, now's the time to show it."

"I can't get back to San Francisco tonight."

"Start now, you'll be there in the morning."

"Let me stay."

"God, I'm tempted. But—no."

He kissed her ear, her eyelids. "You want what I want. I know it."

"Please, Mack. Go on. You don't know how weak I am. If you stay the night, I'll beg you to stay a week. A year. Forever. I'd hate myself if I kept you from Jim one hour longer than necessary."

"That's very selfless."

"Oh, don't be bitter."

"What the hell do you expect? You're turning me away. Again."

"You're losing your temper again. When you get over it, you'll see I'm right about—"

"Very selfless, and it makes me feel like hell."

"Well, I don't feel much better. Not about you, myself, anything. Go. Go. Go."

She ran off over the dune. He stood there, a study in despair, while the surf rushed and the hidden foghorn mourned.

Damn woman—stubborn as ever. He went straight back to the Cadillac and drove off without knocking on her door.

60

THE SEEDY LITTLE BUILDING OVERLOOKED HALF Moon Bay. Bilious tan paint was peeling from the siding and a weak electric bulb lit the sign over the doorway: SHORE CAFÉ   WINES BEERS LIQUORS.

Mack peered at the sign through the dust rising around the acetylene headlights. He shut everything off and walked to the café. Behind him, in the black abyss of the ocean, he heard gulls. He was spent. He'd been driving steadily, stopping only for gasoline.

The owner, the only person in the place, was cleaning up.

He was a burly thick-necked man in a shirt with vertical blue stripes. A single shaded lamp threw light on the back bar, where three plates were propped on a narrow shelf above the bottles, souvenir plates, painted in gaudy enamels. One showed Cliff House, another the Ferris wheel at the 1894 Midwinter Fair in Golden Gate Park, and the third depicted angelic tourists in the Japanese Tea Garden.

The snap of his rag indicated that the owner didn't like Mack's rumpled clothes and general air of raffishness. "Closed up," he said. "See the clock? Half past ten."

"I want some whiskey." Mack dug in his pocket. "You can take time to sell me a pint of whiskey, for Christ's sake. You can take time to sell me some gas."

The man studied the bill on the bar. Then he laughed, a hog snuffling. "Twenty dollars? For that I can. For that I'll set you up in style." He gestured to the deal table under porthole windows made nearly opaque by smoke and cooking grease.

"If you want to go to bed, go on," Mack said. "Just fill the car and leave the whiskey."

"How many pints?"

"How many have you got?"

Lifting his head, Mack winced and groaned.

His mouth tasted of the risen bile of his belly. He ground the butts of his palms in his eye sockets. Three pints of whiskey stood in front of him, one empty, on its side, one a quarter full, one unopened.

"God," he groaned, "what time is it?" He dropped his pocket watch, fumbled for it under the table, snapped it open. A few minutes past five.

In the morning?

There, outside the greasy portholes, the Cadillac glistened with dampness. Beyond it, Half Moon Bay spread gray and flat, though there were touches of pink brightening it. Three little fishing smacks were raising sail.

"In the morning," he said with a sorry shake of his head. He'd let Nellie's rejection get the best of him, had drunk the café's bad whiskey till he passed out or fell asleep.

Probably just as well, though. He'd pushed himself to exhaustion yesterday. Couldn't have driven any farther. He felt a little better in spite of his excess; his head was clearing. He'd work things out with Jim, then he'd work things out with Nellie—in that order. Mustn't forget the lesson of T. Fowler Haines: There was always hope.

He pushed away from the table, anxious to get out in the air and watch the dawn break. As he started for the door, though, the floor seemed to shiver. He heard a rumbling, as of distant detonations. Plaster dust sifted from the ceiling, powdering his shoulders.

Then there was a thump upstairs, and oaths. The floor shook steadily. Bottles on the back bar clinked, danced merrily to the edge, fell, and broke. An ornamental plate plummeted off the shelf and demolished the tourists in the Tea Garden; the Cliff House crashed; the Ferris wheel fell and exploded.

Mack heard a grinding and watched in amazement as a fissure shot across the stained ceiling, then branched into fingers . . .

Then silence. The floor had stopped shaking finally; it had lasted thirty seconds or so, he judged. In the distance, someone rang a fire bell. A door slammed open upstairs, and the owner stumbled to the landing, his red flannels unbuttoned over a hairy navel. He rubbed his morning beard. "Jesus, I fell out of bed. It woke me up."

"What the hell was it? An earthquake?"

"Yeah. Felt like a bad one."

"Well, at least it didn't last long—"

The floor swayed and shook again, and suddenly the ceiling opened and the light fixture dropped, along with crumbling plaster and lath. Mack kicked the door and dove outside just as the Shore Café fell down on its owner.

Little Jim woke up about the same time as his father.

He smelled the raw odor of garbage. Above a milk wagon at the end of the alley where he'd taken shelter for the night a streetlamp went dark.

Jim sat against the building, stiff and cold, clutching his tramp's bundle against his chest. He'd left Sacramento Street at dusk on Sunday. It took him that long to find his opportunity. Alex, Señora Olivar, and Professor Love were all out of the house finally, and the servants busy.

I'm going home, he said to himself now as he shook off sleep. Three nights on his own had weakened any desire to run away. Sunday and Monday he'd slept in Golden Gate Park. Freezing. Eating the last of the apples and bread filched from the kitchen. On Monday night an unkempt man approached him, unbuttoned his pants, and showed his thing. Jim fled while the man shouted dirty invitations.

Last night, after wandering all over, he found this narrow, trash-strewn passage. He'd slept against the wall of the four-story Valencia Street Hotel, a cheap place just below Market.

Pa didn't like him. Pa was a stranger. But he'd had enough of defiant adventuring by himself. He was stiff, cold, starving. Home was better than this, even with Pa to put up with . . .

A sound distracted him, and he turned to the other end of the alley, the end away from the street, and saw a man's silhouette against the breaking light, the rooftops. He was a tall man in a queer, ankle-length garment, a patchwork coat of quilt and carpet squares. The man wore woolen gloves without fingers.

For a second Jim thought it was the terrifying stranger from Golden Gate Park. But it wasn't; this one had wild locks straggling to his shoulders. Water trickled. The man was relieving himself.

At the nearer end of the passage, Valencia Street, the milk-wagon horse began to toss its head and stamp. Then it neighed, as if it sensed or saw something frightening.

I want to go home. Right now.

Little Jim scrambled up. "Hey, who's that?" the shadow-man called out. He slipped along the alley, toward Jim.

Jim ran the other way. Half a dozen steps and he reached Valencia Street. The milk-wagon horse flung itself against the traces and stamped, its wild neigh signaling something awful but still unseen.

A rumbling filled the air then, a sound like a rushing train. Jim shot looks left and right but couldn't find the source. A few early workers trudging along stopped and looked around. Then the street was rippling like a shaken carpet. Jim's mouth fell open. The roar grew louder, mingled with creakings and grindings and crunchings of the rickety frame buildings crowded around. Upstairs in the Valencia Hotel, guests woke, crying out, and suddenly it seemed as if every church bell in San Francisco started to ring. They pealed and clanged without rhythm or melody, wild bells filling the air.

A huge cornice hurtled down in front of Jim like a meteor, exploding as it hit the street. With a cry he leaped back and put his face against the hotel, fragments of the cornice stinging his cheek and ear. One nicked his eyelid.

A gloved hand grasped his shoulder. "Boy, what's happening?"

Jim screamed. Saw a stranger's face above him—long locks. It was the man in the carpet-square coat.

"Let me pass, youngster. Let old Jocker see—"

A guest from the hotel ran into the street as the wagon horse whinnied and bucked. A chimney on a two-story frame house across Valencia ripped apart on the mortar lines and collapsed, a dozen of its bricks striking the milkman; the wire carrier dropped from his hand, corks popping out, and he rolled on the sidewalk, his blood flowing into the milk.

Roofs tore open, a second chimney sheared in half, and sparks spun upward, a whirlpool of fiery dots. The street waved and rippled like the ocean. Jim was stricken with terror, held fast by the dirty tall man.

"Jesus God, judgment day," the man cried.

After what seemed like forever, the tremor stopped.

"It's an earthquake," the man panted.

People ran out of the flimsy houses and the Valencia Street Hotel. A long tongue of fire rose from a broken chimney, then fell back, and black smoke rolled behind some windows down the block. The bells still rang across the sky, but the tolling slowed somewhat. For approximately ten seconds the morning seemed fresh and sweet and still again, the heavens sun-brightened, though hazed with drifting dust from wrecked buildings. Down toward Market, Jim heard a rush of water and saw a great foamy geyser spurt up two stories, a burst hydrant. Then he saw another.

Jim ducked and pulled against the tall man's hand. Then the next tremor hit. The street began rippling again. Halfway down the block, ten yards of pavement bulged up and formed a hill. The Valencia Street Hotel tilted forward, and across the way, three abutting houses leaned south, tipped to an angle of forty-five degrees in the space of a breath.

A grinding, shuddering roar filled Jim's ears again. Lumber fell on him.

"Here, boy, watch out," the man cried, throwing himself on Jim to shield him moments before the entire Valencia Street Hotel fell apart, fell on top of them, raining debris and human bodies.

Mack drove the Cadillac north like a man demented.

Rocks ticked and snicked against the wind screen. His white hair blew and the sleeves of the filthy duster flapped. Practically leaning on the wheel, he tried to force more power, more speed from the sputtering overheated machine.

Behind him, Half Moon Bay lay ruined. Nearly all of its frame buildings and piers were down. An aftershock about half past five leveled the few structures that had survived the initial quake. By six-thirty Mack and some neighbors had cleared a small mountain of wreckage and rescued the café owner, who was still alive. They stretched the man on blankets by the gas pump.

Ahead of him, filling the horizon, extending to the Pacific on his left and across the peninsula on his right, a billowing, boiling rampart of cloud showed the enormous sweep of the earthquake.

On his left, toward the sea, he saw half a mile of railway line sunk out of sight.

On his right, a man waved his arms in front of a collapsed pile of lumber. On it lay a ripped-down sign: ARTICHOKES! AVOCADOS! FRESH!

"Stop, turn back," the man yelled, waving. "Everything's down, telephone's out, I was calling Palo Alto—the university's in ruins—"

The man and the wreckage blurred away behind.

Mack squinted. In the rampart of dust and smoke a mile high, there were new flashing colors: reds, yellows, pinks.

He couldn't see the City, only its southern approaches, its outlying hills. But he could tell from the color-shot clouds that the quake four hours ago had done more, much more, than demolish property.

"Jim." He beat on the wheel. *"Jim."*

At nine-fifteen in the morning, April 18, 1906, Mack Chance drove into San Francisco.

San Francisco was burning.

"SPECIAL POLICE," THE CIVILIAN SAID. **61**

He stood in front of the stopped Cadillac at the intersection of Tenth and Bryant and stretched his arm over the bonnet, his big blue Colt pointed at Mack's forehead.

Smoke drifted in the intersection. Directly east, south of Market Street, huge clouds boiled skyward, flashing orange within. Every few seconds Mack heard windows blowing out.

"Who deputized you?"

"Mayor Schmitz. Me and a thousand others."

"Where are your credentials?"

"In the cylinder of this gun."

"Get out of my way. I live on Nob Hill. My name's Macklin Chance."

"Oh. Mr. Chance. Yes, sir. Didn't recognize you right off. I've seen your photo many times—" He stepped away from the front of the auto. "Go on, but be careful. And pay attention to this." He pulled a handbill from his pocket. Meantime Mack's eye fixed on a corner hydrant. It was open, its base surrounded by a slime of mud.

"What's wrong with the water?"

"Isn't any. Just a muddy trickle all over town."

"The underground mains broke?"

"That's what they think. Listen, it's bad on Market Street. Rubberneckers, pickpockets, people hauling out what they can save—it's a damn madhouse. Don't make any suspicious moves. This paper means what it says."

Mack looked at the proclamation. Signed by the mayor, its boldfaced words leaped out.

KILL any and all persons engaged in looting or the commission of any other crime.

"Kill people with no questions asked? How can Schmitz order that?"

"How can something like this happen?"

The special waved him on.

He drove around a big brick pile, a chimney that had tumbled into the street. In the ruins of a house, a blue gas flame hissed from a twisted pipe. Up on Market, a steam pumper raced east, the manes of its horses flying. What good was fire equipment without water?

A spindly man in a long flannel gown ran alongside, begging a ride.

"I was recuperating in the Central Emergency Hospital. It fell down around us. I've got to find my wife—I'm afraid she's left our flat in North Beach."

"Get in. I'll take you up to Market Street."

As Mack drove, the spindly man babbled. "It's terrible, it's so terrible. The Hearst building is burned. The Opera House is gone, and all the Met scenery, eight freight cars of it. Caruso sang Don José last night, you know. He stayed in one of the hotels. They say he's dead. Oh, God, I'm so worried about my wife."

"Where do you think she's gone?"

"To the Moon. All of my wife's relatives live on the Moon."

Mack stopped just short of Market Street. "Good luck." The man thanked him and got out. Mack shook his head in wonderment. The Central Emergency Hospital had disgorged all of its patients. Including the lunatics.

* * *

Astonishing sights assaulted him as he turned right on Market Street.

The City Hall dome was a mere skeleton now, dangerously canted.

Soldiers were everywhere. Soldiers from Fort Mason, the Presidio, the Pine Street cavalry barracks, mounted soldiers and foot soldiers. All were armed, some with bayonets.

Ahead, looking eastward, buildings were burning in several blocks immediately south of Market. North of Market, in what appeared to be the waterfront area, a second great cloud arose. That was the wholesale produce district. Heavy smoke rolled over Market Street, sometimes hiding most of the taller structures like the eighteen-story *Call* building on the south side at Third Street. The *Call* was still untouched.

Down that way too, he saw huge crowds of people milling around—men in business suits and derbies, women with parasols. They were sightseeing. Incredible . . .

He nosed the Cadillac ahead slowly. It was a small metal boat in a human tide flowing the other way. Hundreds of San Franciscans were fleeing west, toward the parks and ocean beaches. They dragged steamer trunks. They pushed lawn mowers and sewing machines piled high with goods. They carried belongings in suitcases and pillowcases. Two men went by rolling an upright piano stuffed with clothes, a moose head, a banjo, a dress form.

The pervasive smoke began to sting Mack's eyes, and he coughed repeatedly. He noticed more and more long blue coats, more and more tall helmets. Along with the soldiers and the specials, every policeman in Chief Drinan's six-hundred-man force must have been called out for duty.

"Clear away." A mounted army captain in a khaki campaign hat waved his crop and rammed his horse through the fleeing people. "Squad, follow me." Six foot soldiers with bayonets double-timed behind. The captain and his men surrounded the Cadillac.

"We're taking this auto."

"Just a minute, Captain—"

"Get out. That's an order."

Angrily, Mack flung himself to the street. "I thought the army had no use for rich men's toys."

"I don't know what you're talking about. We're moving the dead and wounded in autos. Commandeering every one. Nothing else can get through these streets. Private Allen—drive."

He signaled to the east with his crop. Mack stood amid the

541

flowing crowds and watched a grinning twenty-year-old in khaki depart with his automobile.

He trudged on. Down side streets, he saw dead horses. Pavements were awash with the flood from burst mains. Every saloon was closed. BY ORDER OF THE MAYOR, signs said. Clouds from the two fires above and below Market rolled higher into the sky. Mack could no longer see the sun.

A woman lay in a Market Street doorway with her skirt hoisted, both her hands clutching the door frame above her. She heaved up and down and screamed like a hurt child as a man and another woman crouched on the sidewalk in front of her. Mack saw them pull a bloody newborn baby from between her parted legs.

Half a dozen men overtook him from behind, three pushing wheelbarrows full of canvas sacks stenciled FAIRBANKS TRUST. The other three carried pump shotguns.

"What have you got there?" Mack asked, stepping toward the nearest barrow.

"A million dollars in bearer bonds," one of the armed men said, taking aim. "You want a close look? It'll be your last."

"No thanks, I believe you."

Mack stood aside and they rushed on down Market with their barrows. Going where? The Ferry Building? Oakland? Were the ferries still running?

He recognized a police sergeant who was trying to direct traffic and asked him for details.

"Oh, Mr. Chance, it's a catastrophe," the policeman said in his lovely Irish brogue. "There's no water except what can be pumped from the cisterns and the Bay. None of the fire alarms worked. All the battery jars at the Chinatown alarm station broke in the quake. Poor Dennis Sullivan was mortally injured when headquarters came down . . ." Sullivan was fire chief, a twenty-six-year veteran, and the man who'd pleaded for money to improve the water system. ". . . and there's nobody as keen and sharp as him to direct the firemen. We got a third blaze, a bad one, back there in Hayes Valley." He pointed over Mack's shoulder. "Some damn fool woman tried to cook breakfast with a damaged flue. It's God's judgment, I think. 'Tis a sinful town, this one. Whores and sodomites. Sodomites and whores—"

"How's Nob Hill?"

"Safe so far. Who knows for how long?"

Mack watched the apocalyptic clouds. The *Call* building jutted like an iceberg in a smoky sea.

Who knows for how long?

He fought on to within a block of the *Call*. The crowds were heaviest here; thousands packed Market Street from curb to curb, asking questions, offering opinions. They weren't typical sightseers, Mack realized when he was among them. They weren't lighthearted; they were worried.

"Think the *Call* will go?"

"Not on your life. The building's fireproof."

"The Crocker building was fireproof. It's gutted."

"The Palace is standing. See her flag flying down there?"

"Hurrah for the old Palace . . ."

Some of them applauded.

The general noise level was incredible, the roar of the south-of-Market fire background for horses trotting, windows bursting, soldiers and police yelling, children crying, autos honking as they wove reckless paths through the crowds with cargoes of bodies or the wounded. Unseen buildings continued to crash down.

Mack pulled out his watch. Almost noon. A cry went up and a plume of smoke was visible spewing from a window on the *Call*'s top floor. Windows began to explode, a torrent of glass falling toward the street. People around Mack pushed and screamed and ran. A triangle of flying glass slashed the back of his neck.

The policeman had used the right word: *catastrophe*. The heart of San Francisco was not yet gone, but it was going.

He turned up Grant, then west again for a quick look at Union Square. It was packed with people, and so far unscathed. On the edge of the square he bumped into a man he knew from the Bohemian Club.

"Chance. You're on the Committee of Safety—do you know that?"

"No, I don't, I just got back—what's the committee? What's it for?"

"The mayor organized it to run the fire fighting, the emergency hospitals—everything. Fifty of the City's best. Jim Phelan's chairman. They've sent appeals to Mayor Mott in Oakland and Governor Pardee in Sacramento. I saw your name when they posted the committee list at ten. They're supposed to be in session right now."

"Where?"

"Not sure. I heard they left the Hall of Justice for the new Fairmont . . ."

"Thanks," he said, pushing and shoving his way onward toward the Dewey Monument with the Winged Victory figure crowning it. On the Geary Street side of the square, a man was shouting and waving. "Get away to Oakland. Launches to Oakland, Pier Thirteen."

"How much?" someone yelled.

"Fifty cents."

"That's thievery."

But twenty other people rushed after the tout.

Mack kept squeezing and pushing forward, toward Post Street on the square's north side. Another mass outcry turned him around suddenly. Four upper floors of the *Call* were ablaze. Behind it, the fire clouds rose two miles or more, darkening the sky. To the southwest, similar clouds indicated that the Hayes Valley fire, the fire from the woman's breakfast, was spreading. The constant crash of collapsing buildings made it sound like wartime.

Mack crossed Post on his way back to Powell. Suddenly he spied Alex Muller over near the entrance of the St. Francis. Hatless and coatless, Alex dove across Post into the square Mack had just left. Mack recrossed the street and chased him.

"Alex," he yelled, waving as he swam through the human sea. Alex heard his name, turned, and peered through the dull daylight.

"Mr. Chance." The sight of his employer seemed to upset him.

Alex's sweaty shirt was smudged with dirt. He'd rolled up his cuffs to a point just below his black sleeve garters. Alex never showed his sleeve garters, or went out with soiled linen.

"Sir—I didn't know where you were, or when to expect you. The mayor's committee—"

"Yes, I heard. Are you out for some sightseeing like everyone else?"

"No, sir. I am here in hopes of—that is—sir—have you been home?"

"Not yet."

"You don't know about your son?"

In the palpable heat of the infernos to the south and east, Mack grew cold.

"Is Jim hurt?"

"Sir, not exactly. On Sunday evening, the professor, Angelina Olivar, and I were all out of the house, for various reasons, for a period of several hours. I was the first to come back, at approximately a quarter past ten. Since Angelina was not due to return until early Monday, I checked Jim's room to see that all was well. I couldn't find him. Apparently he slipped away sometime during the evening."

"What the hell do you mean, 'slipped away'?"

"Excuse me, sir, I'm sorry—" With a guilty look he blurted, "Ran off."

"Oh, Jesus. No."

"We tried to contact you, sir. We didn't know precisely where you were. The Del Monte said you had left. Yosh told us to expect a call on Monday, but it never came. Belatedly, then—Monday evening—we asked the local authorities to attempt to contact other law-enforcement agencies south of here. I must say candidly, when your name was mentioned, we did not get the best cooperation . . ." Mack was too stunned to react to that. Alex continued, "I have been out all morning. Ever since the earthquake woke the household. I hoped I might spot Little Jim somewhere. There are so many people abroad, and I feel he must still be in the City—"

"Are you sure he ran away?"

"He removed many of his things from his room. The bed was still made—"

"Did you call the police on Sunday night?"

"Naturally. At once. We gave them a full description of Jim."

"Damn it, can a seven-year-old boy with a limp be that hard to find?"

"No, sir. Last night a foot patrolman saw him on Market Street. He lost him in the crowds. This morning—well. You see for yourself. The police have no time."

Somewhere another building came down in thundering ruin. Mack scanned the sky, Union Square, the crowds. Tears of rage and guilt began to run. He fought them.

"God, where is he?"

A detonation, louder, different, shook the pavement. People screamed and pushed, flinging their arms over their heads.

"It's another quake—"

"No, no—they're dynamiting. The army's dynamiting. Firebreaks—"

A second detonation followed, and a third. "Sir," Alex began, "if I might suggest—"

Mack whirled away, shoving a man crowding next to him. He didn't think coherently, just ran.

He hurried up the steep slope of Powell Street. Behind him,

the fire south of the Slot was burning along a mile-and-a-half front, from the Bay all the way to Sixth Street, and from Folsom to Market. Fire was gutting the entire *Call* building at Third and surging on toward the Palace Hotel at Montgomery. The produce-district fire was advancing as well, and the Hayes Valley fire was spreading in the direction of Mechanics' Pavilion and City Hall. It was a panorama worthy of Hell.

Mack ran away from it, up Powell toward home.

He passed a small pigtailed girl wandering with a rag doll.

He passed an old Chinese woman sitting in a doorway, her cheeks shiny with tears. A white bone poked through a torn black trouser leg. "Broke," she said to Mack as he ran by. "Oh, broke."

He passed an Italian with a pushcart full of sheet music.

He passed a coffeehouse where two special policemen had cornered a looter. One pulled silverware from the man's coat pockets; the other beat the thief with a truncheon.

Mack struggled up the hill to California Street, an awl of pain turned deep in his chest. The hours of hunger, shock, and exertion finally took their toll. He leaned his forehead against the cold granite of the new, but still unopened Fairmont Hotel. Unexpectedly, he thought of Margaret, her place on Mission Street. Destroyed, surely. Was she all right?

He raised his head, his white hair blowing in the hot breeze. He was so tired he wanted to drop. But he had to go on. To the mansion—

But why was he hurrying? What could be done if Jim was gone? Who could find a lone boy among so many thousands in flight?

And there was the committee . . .

He identified himself to a guard and walked into the Fairmont Hotel.

Former Mayor Jim Phelan noticed when Mack entered through a rear door of the parlor, which still smelled of fresh paint. From a draped table up in front, he said, "Mack. Welcome. You're a sight."

"Drove up from Carmel. The quake caught me at Half Moon Bay."

"We're trying to decide how to save this town," Rudolph Spreckels said. He was seated among the committee members.

"It's too late." The voice belonged to Fairbanks.

His remark angered Phelan. "Don't talk that way. San Franciscans may be guilty of a lot of things, but they aren't quitters.

546

They don't sit down and cry. Shall we get back to work, gentlemen?''

Fires burning at 2,000 degrees and higher rapidly consumed entire blocks. Granite pillars melted, shrank, and cooled as misshapen rocks. Steel beams bent like sticks of macaroni in hot water. Iron folded like shirt cardboard, sandstone cracked like window glass, concrete crumbled into sand.

At 1 P.M. the army began dynamiting north of Market Street. The produce-district fire was sweeping west.

At 3 P.M. the flag on the Palace Hotel vanished in the smoke, and the great old hostelry waited for the end.

By 8 P.M., with the sun down, an eerie false daylight illuminated the City. Frantic fire fighters watched the westward advance of the produce-district blaze, then reorganized to hold the line at Powell Street.

The south-of-Market fire crossed Eighth Street.

The third fire, the one started by the unknown woman at breakfast, raged on from Mechanics' Pavilion toward City Hall. Someone had christened it the Ham and Eggs fire. It jumped Market Street at Ninth, mating with the south fire to create a new one—bigger, deadlier, a huge hot hurricane of flame. The fire rushed west toward the Mission District.

At the Fairmont, as everywhere else, telephone lines were dead, and commandeered autos came and went with messages, orders, reports on the position of the fires. The Committee of Safety rushed available supplies to Golden Gate Park, facing a possible one hundred thousand people homeless for the night. A messenger from Oakland said an emergency train was already en route from Los Angeles with doctors, nurses, food, medical supplies.

By 11 P.M. it became certain that Chinatown was going. All of its ten thousand residents were flung from their homes and shops into streets already overflowing with refugees.

Mack worked through the night with only a cup of cold tea and half a stale roll to sustain him. Shortly before 3 A.M. he heard running in the corridor outside the parlor.

"We have to evacuate the hotel," someone cried. "The fire's jumped to this side of Powell."

"Mack, you'd better go home," Phelan said. "Save what you can."

The official fire-defense line moved west to Van Ness. The produce-district fire burned along Bush Street and Pine Street, taking a building, heating the next till it ignited, taking that one, and heating the one beyond. The fiery dominoes fell one by one, randomness injected only by shifts of the breeze.

After the fire took the first blocks of Bush and Pine west of Powell, the wind turned it north on Mason, toward the wooden gingerbread palaces of the rail and silver kings.

The mansion on Sacramento Street had sustained severe quake damage. The great Tiffany skylight was gone, its remains littering the foyer three stories down. The floor of Mack's bedroom canted at a thirty-degree angle.

In his office, he packed a Calgold orange crate with ledgers and papers. At 3:40 A.M., the exodus from the house began. Señora Olivar carried out a precious painted Madonna. Professor Love carried out his Bartlett's and some other books. The servants carried gladstones, teapots, Bibles, photograph albums.

Yosh drove around the corner in the Silver Ghost, her acetylene lights poking through the smoke. She lacked her ruined fenders and spare tire and was dented, but she was oddly grand, bright as an ingot. Yosh parked her at the gate, pointing west.

Coatless now, Mack struggled down the steps with the orange crate. He was beaten to exhaustion, to a kind of numbed somnambulism. But he kept moving. One foot ahead of the other. The servants were watching him with concern.

In the confusion of firelight and shadow, he bumped into Alex, who was carrying the large Sargent painting on his shoulder.

"Leave that."

"Sir, it's a valuable piece of art."

"I'd rather have my son."

"I know, sir. This is my choice to save."

He slipped out the gate with the portrait of Mack still balanced on his shoulder.

All of them but Alex and Mack piled into the Rolls-Royce, crowding in like comedians in a nickelodeon picture, eleven people in an auto built for seven. She sagged but her springs held.

Mack turned for a last look. He saw for the first time the crack in the left-hand pillar. It ran down through the cartouche, cleaving his initials.

It's God's judgment, I think . . .

The fire swirled above the roof of the Fairmont and danced behind its windows. Yosh watched anxiously. "Mr. Chance?"

What arrogance, Mack thought, staring at the pillar. *What stupidity.* This was his punishment.

Jim was his punishment . . .

"Please hurry, sir," Alex said.

Mack's face convulsed. With a great heave he threw the orange crate back through the gates. Papers scattered; ledgers flew. Overhead, wind gusts whirled flaming sticks and debris. Some landed on the mansion's highest cupola, and a little white thread of smoke unraveled.

"Burn, goddamn you."

He turned around and walked away.

Standing in front of the Silver Ghost, between the acetylene lights, he had a pale, wild, almost demented look. He flung off his torn vest and threw it in the street. Those in the car saw the Shopkeeper's Colt riding in its holster on his right hip.

"Follow me, Yosh."

He started walking. The car crept forward, Alex walking behind. On his shoulder, Mack's painted eyes stoically watched the Fairmont burn.

The false sun heated the back of Mack's neck. The false noonday lit the way ahead. He led the slow burdened auto down from Nob Hill, leaving the hill to its conqueror.

VIII

RUINS

1906–1908

While the fires raged, the City was on her knees. They burned all through Wednesday and Thursday. On the western fire line at Van Ness Avenue, soldiers spread and lit kerosene to burn houses and create firebreaks. More dynamiting made plenty of noise but experts later said it did little or no good.

The price of holding the Van Ness line was high. With manpower concentrated there, the fire to the northeast jumped Washington Street and consumed parts of Russian Hill and North Beach. To the east, the fire burned to Columbus Avenue, then on toward the waterfront.

On Friday, the fire storms spent themselves and the fire fighters began to win. Fireboats helped save most of the piers on the Bay. The western fire jumped across Van Ness, but there the breaks held. Then, on Saturday, it rained, and the reckoning began.

The death toll approached five hundred. No one could be sure how many had been lost in collapsed buildings that later burned. Fires had razed over 2,800 acres, wiping out 490 city blocks and 250,000 dwellings. They had destroyed six times as much land and property as the London fire of 1666. Even the Chicago fire of 1871 was but two thirds the size.

The great landmark buildings, the banks and theaters, were gone. All the records in City Hall, the books in the public libraries, the Nob Hill mansions of the Big Four, gone. The ferries had never stopped running, but the cable cars were out of service indefinitely.

San Franciscans responded with astounding pluck and heart. They had beaten disasters before, and they would beat this one. The Committee of Safety immediately opened 150 relief stations to distribute survival portions of food and water. Distant towns and states loaded food and blankets into boxcars and sped them west.

Schoolchildren took up collections. Foreign nations sent money, the Japanese alone giving almost a quarter of a million dollars. In all, $9 million in relief aid poured into San Francisco to house and feed its homeless in the enormous tent camps erected on every available square foot of green space and ocean beach.

Less generous were some of the companies that had smilingly

insured San Francisco's goods and real estate when the skies were blue. Now, with smoke hanging in the air, some of them reneged. Claims ran to over $500 million, and many honest firms pledged to pay in full. Twelve American companies did so and went bankrupt, but several European insurers either discounted claims as much as 25 percent, or welshed altogether.

The mind-numbing proportions of the disaster slowly emerged. San Francisco was far from the sole casualty. To the north and south, the quake had buckled the earth for a distance of two hundred miles in a path up to forty miles wide. North to Fort Bragg and south to Salinas, railroad tracks had softened like taffy, risen and frozen into roller-coaster hills. Eyewitnesses said sidewalks shot up and stopped like elevators arriving at the second floor. Earth along the opened fault line moved as much as twenty-one feet. In Sonoma County, downtown Santa Rosa was leveled. At Palo Alto, on the peninsula, the university sustained massive damage. Large sections of San Jose were rubble.

Looked at one way, it was an unspeakable nightmare, but in another, it became an achievement. Who else but Californians could survive a mammoth quake and the worst fire in man's history, yet exhibit such courage, spirit, and resilience? In this mood, the City began to shrug off her shock and despair and was soon displaying the charming cockiness that had always made her special. Handsome Gene Schmitz proclaimed, "Our fair city lies in ruins. But as your mayor I say—these are the damnedest, finest ruins ever seen on the face of the Earth."

Cleanup began. Soldiers patrolled with bayonets to keep order. City government resumed its operations in the Whitcomb Hotel on Market Street. Architects declared their intention to implement the Burnham plan at last. God had already cleared the land for them.

People shared living space, food, memories of good times and of narrow escapes as they ate their rations shipped over the rails from Chicago or Denver or Jersey City. For a while, everyone forgot to hate the SP.

Within three years, virtually every block of the City's commercial heart, her downtown, was rebuilt as if there had never been an earthquake, never been a fire. The alchemy of time was already turning the base metal of disaster into the gold of legend. Years afterward, San Franciscans still boasted of "the damnedest, finest ruins ever seen."

EVEN BEFORE THE FIRES WENT OUT, MACK WAS **62** moving—roaming through the parks and along the ocean beaches. He showed his pass signed by Governor Pardee. Over and over, to the camp commandants, soldiers with bayonets, refugees, he said:

"My son is seven, going on eight. His most noticeable feature is a limp; his left foot is crippled. He's tall, and mature for his age. He's fair-haired, with dark-blue eyes. I don't have a picture of him, but he looks exactly like the woman in this photo from the *Oakland Tribune*. Have you seen him?"

On Saturday, the day it rained, he went to the temporary police headquarters, the park station out on Stanyan Street. The place was bedlam, officers coming and going, distraught relatives shouting and weeping. Mack's name got him into the office of Chief Drinan immediately. Drinan knew about the disappearance, but had nothing new to report. He muttered a few words of sympathy that Mack found perfunctory, and sent him to see Detective Mulvihill.

"Ike Mulvihill," the detective said, giving Mack a damp handshake. His desk looked like someone had emptied several wastebaskets on it. "Sit down, sit down." Mulvihill gestured to a flimsy chair. He was a spindly, gray-haired old-timer with bags under his eyes, a shirt that gave off a stale odor, and a tie on which he'd spilled innumerable cups of coffee and mugs of beer.

"I suppose it's about your son," Mulvihill began, shuffling some papers aimlessly. "We have the description, but he hasn't been seen. Under the circumstances, it isn't surprising. Hundreds of persons are still missing. I mean literally hundreds. But I'm telling you, sir, you're making our job harder because you can't provide a photograph of this boy."

"I had two of them. Both burned along with the house. I was interested in getting my people out, rather than personal effects. I trust that won't hamper you from working on the case." Mack was growing sarcastic.

"When we have the time and can spare the manpower," Mulvihill said. Perhaps he was tired—worn out—but he too seemed unsympathetic, and he shrugged in a way that snapped Mack's temper.

Mack hammered his desk. "The time is now, detective, not next week or next month."

"Don't yell at me, Mr. Chance. Don't you come in here and yell. I've got my hands full."

"Haven't we all. I want you to *do* something."

"Don't take that tone with me. Remember who you're speaking to—"

"You do the same, goddamn it. I'm a taxpayer—"

"But no friend of the government of this city," Mulvihill exploded, shooting him a look. He began shuffling and arranging papers again, rapidly now, his eyes fixed on them. "I'm busy, Mr. Chance, you can see all these cases of people missing just like your boy. We'll do our utmost, as we would for any citizen. If we come up with something, we'll inform you right away. Where are you living?"

"We're camping in the panhandle of Golden Gate Park."

"Fine. Good day," Mulvihill said, not looking up. On his way out Mack slammed the door. It made him feel no better.

Leaving the station, a new thought struck him. Considering Mulvihill's age, he was undoubtedly a colleague of Lon Coglan. Maybe even a friend. God; what a situation.

Among the forty thousand camped in the park, Mack and the others from the mansion had set up their own little community in a double row of white tents. They took turns standing in the food and water lines. For the first few days all the water came across from Oakland, transferred from barges to tank wagons that traveled through the ruined city under heavy guard.

Their tent community grew quickly. Rhett Haverstick found them, with his wife and five children. Margaret found them, along with two of her waiters and a shy black whore, Gisella. Maison Napoleon was completely gone. She had operated it with a few girls, without dining-room service, in the months since her release from the hospital. Though she'd confessed to Mack that she didn't have much heart for the business anymore, she'd have to reopen eventually because it was the only trade she knew.

Margaret's waiters brought an upright piano with them. No one asked them where they got it. In the evening, everyone would gather around to enjoy it. Gisella played and sang; she had a lovely soprano voice. Their favorite was the song people had adopted after the quake and fire, "There'll Be a Hot Time in the Old Town Tonight." Gisella performed it with a hard rocking beat. Sometimes, though, she sang it slowly, like an elegy. Then all the women wept.

He went downtown on Sunday after the fires went out, describing Jim to strangers, showing Carla's photo. Hundreds were roaming in the sunshine, sightseeing. There wasn't much to do yet but that. Steam rose from the rain-soaked ruins. Young men in khaki, with rifles, guarded every block, watching for looters. Matterhorns and Shastas of abandoned goods loomed at the street corners, piled there as part of the cleanup. Touring cars painted with red crosses chugged by with food, blankets, clothing. Walls of burned buildings cast long shadows, like cemetery monuments. Row houses spared by the fire leaned over sidewalks at crazy angles, thrown out of plumb but not thrown down.

Perceptions were distorted. Landmarks had vanished, and the skyline was lower, or seemed lower. The City appeared smaller, and downtown intersections revealed vistas of a wasteland. You walked what appeared to be three blocks and found it to be a mile.

While Mack was standing outside the gutted Hearst building, a sad expression on his face, a small round Chinese gentleman came up to him. He gave Mack a smile and a pat on the shoulder and said, "Don't worry—by and by, we build all new."

Mack showed him the photograph from the *Oakland Tribune*, to no avail.

On another corner, a rumpled man on a soapbox waved a Bible at half a dozen mildly curious listeners. "Babylon is fallen—Babylon the sinful is fallen! God struck at her painted whores and her prancing deviates. God leveled her dramshops and her play shops. God scourged her thousands of complacent sinners for tolerating such evil . . ." Mack shook his head; many a zealous preacher was blaming all the devastation on the City's tradition of easy morality. The preachers never mentioned an inadequate water system.

Near the Ferry Building, Mack ran into Jack London. London's reputation as a writer and lecturer was solid now, but tainted by sex scandals and his socialist politics. The author wore a baggy blue suit and a Baden-Powell hat. He told Mack that he'd come down from his ranch at Glen Ellen and was writing up his impressions.

Mack went through the ritual of describing his son. London shook his head. Then he said, "I tell you, I've never seen San Franciscans so kind and courteous. In this kind of catastrophe, I thought the social classes would turn on each other. I thought we'd have war."

"You sound a little disappointed."

London gave him a level stare. "No. Touched. But mark

557

this, my friend. The old Frisco—the city of the nabobs—is gone. The new San Francisco will belong to the people south of the Slot. Factory people, poor people. Look, nothing personal. I hope you find your son." Touching the brim of his big hat, London moved on.

Bitter about the near-insult, Mack wondered why, if London was so touched and moved by City poverty, he had promptly moved to the country when he made some money.

In conversation later, Professor Love said he thought London's social theories were balmy, but his stories were original and thrilling, and he was right about the disaster bringing out the best. "*Animus tamen omnia vincit.* 'Courage conquers all things'—Ovid."

Money bought nothing; there was nothing to buy. Mack stood in the long food lines with lawyers, bankers, society matrons, maids, bricklayers, hod carriers, reporters, milliners, pickpockets.

He swung a shovel with the rest of the men in their encampment, digging their latrines, then emptying them. He soon got used to the stench. It was, after all, a stench of life.

People communicated by scrawled notes or chalked signs on special outdoor bulletin boards: MRS. J. FOX IS SAFE IN OAKLAND; ANGELO FANUCCI, FIND YOUR FAMILY IN CAMP NUMBER 2; RELATIVES OF BABY BOY SEELIGSON CONTACT CITY MORGUE; MALCOLM, MEET HERE FRIDAY NOON IF YOU SEE THIS, NORA. Mack almost wrote one of his own. JIM—WHERE ARE YOU? PA.

Some were quick to take advantage of San Francisco's misfortune. One day Mack accompanied Rhett Haverstick to the post-office substation in the park. The post office had established tent substations almost as soon as the fires went out.

Mack had no mail, but the attorney got an outrageous postcard from a cousin in Los Angeles, who was a realtor. In a huge bold hand, for all to read, he'd written: OUR REGION WAS TOTALLY UNAFFECTED BY THE EARTHQUAKES. IN THE FUTURE WHY DON'T YOU CONSIDER LOS ANGELES—OR RECOMMEND IT TO FRIENDS? MANY EXCELLENT BUYS ARE AVAILABLE. REGARDS, PHIL.

James Phelan addressed members of the Committee of Safety at an open-air meeting. "We were right about the water supply. The critical shortage, and the state of the system during the fire, proves the urgent need for the Hetch Hetchy dam and aqueduct. We must keep pressure on the federal government to approve the project. We must not be further deterred by the sentimentalists in the nature societies."

At an outdoor Catholic mass, Alex Muller met Sophia Carminelli, a frail, plain, but intelligent girl. She introduced the young Swiss to her parents and eight brothers. Two weeks later, Alex looked for Mack during one of the evening song sessions. As usual, Mack was seated on a crate by his tent. He never sang with the others, just sat listening with a dead look in his eyes.

Alex told his employer that he'd proposed and Sophia Carminelli had accepted and they would be married as soon as conditions were normal again.

On a bright sunny Saturday, a distinguished silver-haired businessman addressed a crowd in the refugee camp.

"My fellow citizens, you all know who I am, Patrick Calhoun, president of United Railroads, your trolley company. I am carrying word from camp to camp that I have pledged to earthquake relief, personally and on behalf of my firm, the sum of one hundred thousand dollars."

There was long, loud applause. Standing at the back, under a great shady cypress, Fremont Older said to Mack, "And don't you suppose the city fathers will be moved by Patrick's humanitarianism and let him put up his wires?"

On May 14, Boss Ruef's captive supervisors approved the overhead trolley ordinance.

Mack spent hours with the newly incorporated Relief Committee, which handled distribution of the carloads of food, bedding, clothing, and horse fodder pouring into Oakland from all over the United States.

To everyone who asked, needing encouragement, Mack would say, "Of course we'll rebuild San Francisco." It sounded like his first priority. But his first priority was really the one he seldom discussed: Jim.

He went back to police headquarters six times in the first three weeks after the fires went out, but each visit was more discouraging than the last. It was always the same answer: nothing new; no one had seen his son. Mulvihill was off the case, hospitalized with a stroke brought on by overwork, and the new man, a detective with a flip manner, young, seemed even less interested than Mulvihill.

Indoor cooking was banned indefinitely in all structures still standing. When the residents of Mack's tent community could obtain some beef by standing in line, they liked to cook it outdoors, on a large square of salvaged sheet iron propped on bricks. Haverstick, an excellent cook, called the outdoor stove a "barbeque." He said barbequing was catching on all over town, and predicted other Californians would take to it.

Street and sidewalk kitchens sprang up everywhere. Some were established with relief funds, and these served meals in the open air at long trestle tables, often right in the middle of enormous ruins. For breakfast the relief kitchens served mush, milk, and bread. For dinner, hash, vegetables, and bread. For supper, soup, stew, and bread. No one complained. Those with money paid 15 cents. Those who couldn't pay got the meal free with a ticket from the Red Cross.

Individual entrepreneurs set up shop too, offering a more varied fare. One afternoon Mack returned from a relief meeting across the Bay and went to his warehouse. Water pumped from the Bay had saved the Chance Produce Company. A block from it he was surprised to see a new corner kitchen—a booth and a barbeque—with ROSS CAFÉ chalked on the booth.

"Nellie."

She looked up from a pot of stew simmering on the sheet metal. Two bearded men waited patiently. She had good color again. After serving the customers, she wiped her hands on her apron and led him around to the other side of the booth. There she'd chalked the menu for the day, and a slogan: EAT DRINK & BE MERRY, FOR TOMORROW WE MAY HAVE TO GO TO OAKLAND.

"I couldn't sit in Carmel and do nothing."

"How long have you been here?"

"Five days. It's broken the logjam in my brain. Night before last, I started writing a story."

"Did your flat on Russian Hill survive?"

"Yes, the fire missed it. How are you?"

When he told her about Jim, she cried. He found himself struggling to be unemotional, if only to restore her calm. Then he told her something almost as unpleasant.

"I changed my mind again. If no acceptable alternative can be found, I'll back the Hetch Hetchy dam."

Nellie's novella *The Fire Zone* was bought later in the year by *The Saturday Evening Post*, the editor declaring that she had never done better work. William Randolph Hearst heard of it and wrote a personal note from New York to congratulate her.

Growing desperate about Jim, Mack hired one of the first job printers who reopened after the fire to print up a flyer he had drafted; the headline was LARGE REWARD FOR INFORMA-

TION. In a long block of text, he drew the best word-picture of Jim that he could. Fremont Older helped him change and refine it, and suggested insertion of a line meant to trick opportunists into revealing themselves. The reward itself, boldfaced at the bottom, was $25,000 cash, but Mack was prepared to double or quadruple that if necessary. The address for forwarding information was the post box Haverstick was using for his law office.

Mack ordered twenty thousand copies of the flyer and had them shipped in batches to his various managers, with orders that they be distributed to newspapers and police and sheriff's departments, and posted on public notice boards and even telegraph poles in the most populous regions of the state. He told his managers in a letter that distribution of the flyer was their first priority in the coming weeks, and he wanted no slacking. Poor execution of the job would be cause for dismissal.

On a balmy night toward the end of May, Mack and Margaret ate together, sitting some distance from the others. Mack had cooked the dry stringy roast beef and green beans; those in their little community took turns.

"The meat's tasty," Margaret said.

"I scorched the beans."

"I watched you at the barbeque, scowling, muttering—you don't enjoy cooking under these conditions, do you?"

"I don't enjoy anything under these conditions."

After a minute she said, "I've decided to rebuild the restaurant."

"Oh. I wondered if you would. I'll loan you whatever you need."

"You're very generous. Did your banks move their cash and records in time?"

"Some did. For instance I had forty thousand dollars in Pete Giannini's Bank of Italy. Pete put his cash and ledgers in a wagon and personally drove them to San Mateo. The banks whose cash burned up are handing out certified chits. You take a chit to the mint for the equivalent in gold coin; the gold in the mint got through all right."

Margaret took another bite. Mack was sitting and staring at his plate on his knee.

"Mack, you don't look well. Is it Jim?"

"Yes, I suppose. I don't know." He let down. "I sleep for eight, nine, ten hours and wake up exhausted. I get pains in my head, pains so bad I can barely see, just here—" He rubbed his forehead close to his brows. "They start, they stop—no pattern, no reason. I spend a lot of time wondering why the hell I bother to take another breath."

She thought a moment. "You feel sad much of the time? Despondent?"

He nodded. "It has to be Jim."

"Perhaps not altogether. I've heard the same complaints from other people in the camps. One of them said her preacher told her it's remorse."

"What?"

"Remorse. Because we came through but so many others didn't."

"We're guilty about that?"

"I think so. You sleep for hours, but I have trouble sleeping at all. And I only lost some property, not a son."

Mack's face twisted. "Do any of these acquaintances of yours say how long the feelings will last?"

"No, I haven't heard that."

"Well, I'll tell you how long I expect mine to last. Forever."

She wanted to reprove him for the gush of self-pity, but his eyes were so vacant, his face so white and saggy that she didn't have the heart. He put his plate aside. He'd eaten only two or three bites of the stringy beef.

Touching his sleeve, she spoke hesitantly.

"Mack, you shouldn't feel—"

"Yes, I should. My son ran away. I'm responsible. I'm tired, Margaret. I think I'll go to bed."

He went into the tent he shared with Alex and Professor Love, but he couldn't sleep. The pain came at the bridge of his nose, and spread to either side in a moment. Old litanies chanted in his head.

Never be poor again.

Never be cold again . . .

He remembered coming down out of the Sierras into the California spring, full of hope. Where was the hope now in this accursed place?

Firelight glowed on the tent canvas. He flung a forearm over his eyes to try to ease the red pain in his head. He despised his weakness. He'd always been strong and confident before, able to overcome setbacks and sorrows.

Not this time.

In the first ten days after distribution of the flyer began, Haverstick received nine letters and two telegraph messages, all from claimants "certain" they knew Jim's whereabouts.

"Six of these are obvious frauds," he declared when he and Mack discussed the matter. He waved one of the letters. "All six people identified the boy by his limp, and by the small birthmark on his right cheek, shaped like a butterfly."

Mack gave him a bleak nod; the birthmark was the item inserted to trap cheats. "I guess the flier was a bad idea."

"Not necessarily, but even the promising replies must be checked into. You can't do it all yourself—"

"The police sure as hell won't do it," Mack said. "They're sitting on their hands."

"Perhaps you should hire a private detective bureau. Why don't you talk to Bill Burns?"

Mack's head snapped up, his expression animated. "I will."

Burns recommended a Los Angeles detective, a Pinkerton and former bull on the Great Northern Line, Wild Bill Flyshack.

"I think he gave himself the name because he's anything but," Burns said. "Wild Bill's a plodder. Reliable, but a plodder. Also, his real name is Selwyn. I'd call myself something else if my folks named me Selwyn Flyshack."

Mack wired Flyshack, who promised to come north for an interview as soon as he finished his present case.

May blurred into June. Between them, Mack and Haverstick looked into the apparently honest replies to the reward flyer. By a combination of short trips and telegraph messages, they satisfied themselves that all of the replies identified the wrong boy. One reply, from Santa Barbara, was a lucid letter from a woman who guaranteed that Mack's son was living next door. The crippled "boy" turned out to be thirty-seven years old; the woman had been in and out of asylums for years. "We're getting too much of that," Haverstick sighed as he finally disposed of the letter. "Problem is, I don't know how to stop it." Mack was too despondent to comment.

He attended more meetings than he liked, but they were necessary. He joined the new Committee of Forty for the Reconstruction of San Francisco. When he had a free hour, he still roamed the camps, asking his questions, though by now they were hollow in his mouth. Too much time had passed, and no one seemed to give his inquiry more than a moment's thought. There had been too much loss, too great a drain of emotion in the weeks since the quake and fire. And everyone had a life to rebuild in some fashion. Still, in the face of all of it, Mack kept on.

Walking down the lane of tents in Golden Gate Park one evening, he encountered Alex with a set of plans rolled up under his arm. Alex knew his employer's state of mind, and he struggled to hide or at least mute his own happy state. It was hard, given his love for Sophia.

"Any news, sir?"

"Same as yesterday. And the day before. And last week. No one's seen him."

Alex cleared his throat. Two boys ran by rolling hoops. "Yes, sir . . . Well. I've been waiting anxiously for you to return." They continued a slow walk down the trampled lane between the tents. Three were empty. Mack had let most of the servants go; he wouldn't need them in a new place, and they had left to find other jobs. He'd paid each of them six months' wages.

Alex pointed to the tent established as a temporary office. "Mr. Haverstick has an agenda of urgent matters needing your attention. Particularly the insurance claims."

"Rhett knows my feeling. If those companies try to discount my claims so much as one percent, I'll take them to court for eternity. People in San Francisco paid premiums for years in good faith. Now some of these crooks turn around and chisel."

"Yes, sir, there is a problem in that regard. Our claims with Aetna of Hartford are in fine shape. But Hamburg-Bremen Insurance is reneging."

"Sue the bastards," Mack said darkly, thrusting his hands in his pockets. "Hire the best lawyers in Germany. I can afford to fight those welshers for all the people who can't. What else have you got?"

"These, sir."

He displayed the roll of plans hesitantly. "Mr. Starr dropped these by this morning."

"Who the hell's Mr. Starr?"

"Mr. Kingsley Starr, sir. Of the firm of Starr and Meldrum. Original architects of your house."

"The mansion?"

"Yes, sir. Mr. Starr assumed that with rebuilding starting up all over town at such incredible speed, you would want to . . ." Mack's tired dead eyes bored into him, making him falter. "He—uh—brought the original plans, together with sketches of some suggested modifications."

Mack kept staring. Alex cleared his throat once again.

"Of course, sir, the architect knew nothing about your son being missing. He only meant to be helpful."

Mack's truculent expression softened, and he extended his hand. Relieved, Alex gave him the plans.

"Tell Rhett I'll see him tomorrow or the next day," Mack said. "I'm going to nap for an hour. Then I'm going to the camp at Harbor View. I haven't asked there for a week."

"Yes, sir."

Mack started away, then noticed Alex on tiptoe.

"Something else?"

"Only, sir, that—may I say—we all remain deeply grieved by your loss. But we're confident Jim will be found alive."

"Thanks, Alex. I'm sure too. It can't come out any other way."

In his dark tent, with a bright swathe of pale sun and leaf shadow on the canvas, Mack stared at the plans. Rebuild that place? Now? He wanted to laugh. Or burn the plans in the barbeque, which Angelina Olivar tended in her role as housekeeper. Instead, he tossed the plans under his cot and lay down. He slept and dreamed of Jim and the blizzard again, waking abruptly in the midst of a hard rain and howling wind that nearly knocked the tent down. His cheeks were wet with tears of fright and, soon, fresh tears of guilt.

Wild Bill Flyshack was not a pleasant man. Slovenly and crude, he spoke with a constant leavening of sarcasm. He chewed rather than smoked cigars, and was always spitting out specks of green wrapper.

"Pinkerton's will need a photograph of your son, Mr. Chance."

Mack explained why he had none.

Flyshack spat. "You mean to say you had two pictures and you didn't even save one? You saved an oil portrait of yourself, I notice."

"I wasn't the one who— Never mind. Do you want to discuss my deficiencies, or this case? All you need is a photograph of my former wife. There are plenty of those. Jim looks exactly like her."

"Nobody looks exactly like anybody," said Wild Bill Flyshack.

"For Christ's sake, will you try to find him or not?"

"For the retainer you're paying, we'll hunt for St. Peter and all the archangels and throw in Judas."

"I'll pay a substantial bonus over and above the reward when you locate him."

"*If*, Mr. Chance, *if*. I courted my wife for sixteen years. I pursued her, I pleaded with her, I beggared myself buying her presents. On my forty-third birthday she said yes. On our second day at our honeymoon cabin, lightning hit the outhouse and fried her. Nothing in this world is guaranteed—especially not the life of a boy gone this long under these circumstances."

565

SLOWLY A SEMBLANCE OF NORMAL LIFE RETURNED, **63**
and the municipal government began to function
again. Inevitably, the truce of good will between the
Ruef machine and its enemies, the truce that prevailed in those
first days when the priorities were cooperation and survival—inevitably that truce was forgotten. Burns set operatives to digging.
Through the influential men who backed him, Francis Heney exerted pressure on District Attorney Langdon and Langdon agreed
to make Heney an assistant DA at the appropriate time.

Mack decided he couldn't live and conduct his business in
the park forever, and began to search for a large flat to rent.
He quickly found there was no rental space to be had, so he
bought a two-floor building on Greenwich Street, on the Bay
side of Russian Hill, which the fire had spared. The earthquake
had demolished the owner's brewery. His wife, a spiritualist,
earnestly explained to Mack that the dead striving to escape
from the earth had broken it open along the fault line and
caused the quake. Husband and wife wanted no more of San
Francisco. For cash they closed the sale of the duplex and
moved out the same day.

The building was frame, with large bay windows in front.
Mack set up offices in the lower apartment and lived above.
The house was identified by its number; there was no name
outside, no initials.

Alex hung the Sargent behind Mack's desk. Mack didn't want
it there, or anywhere about him, but somehow Alex considered
it important to hang the portrait, so he didn't press the issue.

Mack chose to live alone. Señora Olivar came in from 7 A.M.
to 7 P.M. each day to cook and clean. He found her a small
house on a sandy windswept street out near the ocean. Alex
Muller lived in a rooming house and applied for housing in
one of the fifty-six hundred refugee cottages being pounded
together in the parks. Winter would come soon, winter and its
rain, and tents wouldn't serve. The hideous little houses stood
in dreary rows with scarcely a foot between them. Some had
two rooms, some three. Alex and Sophia planned to be married
before Christmas, and as a family, they were eligible to rent
one of the cottages.

Professor Lorenzo Love lived in a rooming house too. There
was nothing for him to do. Mack knew it was foolish to keep

paying the tutor's salary, but he did so out of a superstitious belief that as long as Love was kept on, Jim would be found.

Mack shaved his beard and he finally bought spectacles, round with steel wire frames. Having sold the Silver Ghost, he bought a small black Oldsmobile. He didn't mark it with the familiar cartouche; nothing bore that insignia anymore.

One day in late July, Haverstick telephoned Mack with great excitement. "There's a letter that you should see. The signature's unreadable, and the sender doesn't mention the reward, only the flyer. But the description fits. I mean it fits perfectly."

Mack nearly wrecked his auto driving over to the reopened law offices. He slammed open the gate in the waiting-room rail, brought a shriek from a stenographer just backing out of a supply closet, and practically tore the crudely written envelope from the hand of his attorney. It bore a blurred address in Visalia, in the Central Valley.

Person you seek resides with Randolph
family, Wild Horse Road, Visalia . . .

There followed a perfect description, without mention of the false birthmark. Mack couldn't help feeling an enormous surge of hope. "Did you call Flyshack?"

"No, he's down below the border in Ensenada, checking out another lead."

"Good, I'll go to Visalia myself."

"Oh, I wouldn't do that, Mack. You can't be sure this isn't another—"

"This time I feel it. I *feel* it. It's Jim. I'm going."

He spent a sleepless night staring out the window of a sooty railroad car, and late the next afternoon, in blistering heat typical of the Valley at that time of year, he stopped his hired buggy on a dusty yellow side road identified back at the turnoff as Wild Horse Road. The side road had become too narrow for the buggy, so he hiked the last quarter-mile between broad flat fields, sweat soaking him under his duster.

His hope sagged a little when he saw the pitiful plank shanty at the end of the dirt track. A sickly rooster scratched in the dust and ran off as he approached, and he smelled pigs in a pen. He remembered Haverstick's skeptical expression when he said he'd make the trip personally, and he began to have a feeling that he'd let his emotions run away with him. And yet if there were the slightest possibility . . .

He knocked on the ramshackle door, his heart hammering.

An old gray-haired woman in a faded and patched print dress opened the door. Her skin was blue-black.

"Yes?"

Mack's heart was heavy as a rock then. With sweating hands he fumbled the letter and a flyer from an inside pocket. "Is this— That is, I'm looking for Randolph—"

"Yes, this is the Randolphs."

"I'm from San Francisco. I received this letter saying—that is, there's a young man missing, you see. A white boy, with blond hair and a bad limp. He's my son. The letter says he's living here."

Her eyes suddenly sad with sympathy, she opened the door wide. "Mister, I can't read that letter, nor write, but the only lame boy here is my grandson Lester. Yonder." Mack saw a black boy about Jim's age, standing with a homemade crutch under his left arm.

"Jesus," Mack said, unable to stop the tears welling. "Jesus, why would someone write a letter like this?"

"You got somebody that don't like you?" the woman said softly. "There's a lot of cruel-hearted people out in the world. I'm mighty sorry if one of 'em tried to hurt you."

Who? he thought. Carla? No—ridiculous—she wasn't that depraved. Fairbanks, then? Or someone in the San Francisco Police Department with relatives in Visalia? Someone who'd found out about the false birthmark reference, and thought he'd play a fine joke with just a letter and a stamp? Mack knew he'd never learn the answer. *Jesus God, she's right—what kind of despicable scum is out there?* he thought, shaking his head to fight back the hot tears.

The woman was watching him, concerned. He collected himself and gently squeezed her arm. "I'm sorry I disturbed you. I'm very sorry . . ." He turned and stumbled away, hearing the door close behind him.

He was still churning with fury and disappointment, but he had enough presence of mind to leave a $100 bill under a stone, but visible, in the center of the yard. Then he walked on toward the buggy, his face dead and expressionless.

Back in the City, Haverstick was sympathetic about the incident, but candid too. "You've got to expect that sort of thing."

"That kind of viciousness?"

"Yes. Look how Jim was crippled in the first place. You're neither bland nor uncontroversial, Mack. You've made enemies. It happens to anyone who accomplishes anything. And you've accomplished a great deal. I'm sorry, but that's the truth."

For days afterward, Mack still felt numb. It was then, for the first time, that he began to admit to himself, in the deep privacy of his heart, that Flyshack's warnings about the difficulties of finding Jim, especially as more time passed, might—just might—be right.

That summer saw the resumption of politics as usual in San Francisco. The SP didn't like the incumbent governor, George Pardee, feeling that he was not quite friendly enough, cooperative enough. Through its spokesmen, Herrin and Fairbanks, the railroad announced support of James Gillett, congressman from the First District, as the Republican candidate. He was the personal choice of the SP's president, Mr. Harriman.

The party's nominating convention was to be held in Santa Cruz in the first week of September. Abe Ruef controlled all the members of the San Francisco delegation, and they in turn could tip a nomination one way or another by voting as a bloc, according to the Boss's directions. It was assumed that Ruef would endorse Gillett, but he surprised everyone by letting it slip before the convention opened that he wanted the nomination for J. O. Hayes, publisher of the *San Jose Mercury.*

"What a stupid choice, even for a grafter like Ruef," Mack said. "Hayes is a complete nonentity."

"Calm down," Fremont Older said. "Ruef isn't serious about Hayes; he's just playing a game. You know as well as I do that the Boss wants an appointment to the U.S. Senate one of these days. Who can arrange that for him? The men who control the votes up in Sacramento. Walter Fairbanks. Bill Herrin. The gentlemen of the SP. So I predict a great ray of light will fall from heaven, the Boss will suddenly change his mind and generously swing his delegation behind the railroad's candidate. Wait and see."

At the Sea Beach Hotel in Santa Cruz, the Boss did indeed have an amazing change of heart, and the votes of the San Francisco delegation delivered the nomination to James Gillett.

That night, state committee chairman Frank McLaughlin threw a dinner party at his seaside home, his honored guests Gillett and Ruef. It occurred to McLaughlin that all those attending might like a souvenir of the evening, a memento of the triumphant alliance of the San Francisco machine and the greatest, most powerful corporation in the state, the West—perhaps the whole country. He brought in a photographer. The important guests, having imbibed heavily, saw nothing wrong. Little Abe sat in the middle, like the kingmaker he was. Gillett stood behind him, a comradely hand resting on Ruef's shoulder. Posed on either side, in various stages of inebriation, were

Porter, the SP's choice for lieutenant governor; Fairbanks and McKinley of the railroad law department; two judges; and assorted political operatives of the corporation, including its chief lobbyist, George S. Patton, Sr.

Everyone had a grand time making the photograph. No one saw anything wrong with handing around copies to friends later. Ruef inscribed several for favor-seekers.

Then the opposition papers got hold of it. The Monarch of the Dailies captioned it HARRIMAN'S CABINET. Fremont Older called it THE SHAME OF CALIFORNIA. It was perhaps the single most famous political photograph in the state's history. And it was a match thrown on the carefully gathered kindling of the reform campaign, kindling that had been piled up at some cost, then almost forgotten in the aftermath of the quake.

The Republican convention and "The Shame of California" shocked the reformers into action. On Sunday, October 21, 1906, District Attorney Langdon went public in the city papers, announcing the graft investigation and identifying Francis Heney and William Burns. He stated that special detectives had been shadowing Ruef and others for months, collecting evidence, and he promised indictments. Later that same week, selection of a new grand jury began.

Like a trapped ferret, Ruef bit at his attackers. His captive supervisors issued an order suspending Langdon and appointing counselor Abraham Ruef as DA. The opposition immediately filed a restraining order, arguing that the district attorney was a county, not a city official, and therefore not subject to removal by the Board of Supervisors. Superior Court upheld Langdon in his job. The ferret was in the corner.

Jim flailed and fought his way through the blizzard. Snowflakes melted on his eyelids. He was freezing.

He dropped to hands and knees in a huge drift and dug down to find the path. As soon as he dug the hole, the storm filled it. The strange snow was as fluid as running water.

Some distance away, hatless, Mack floundered toward him. He knew Jim was somewhere ahead but couldn't seem to reach him. The howling wind kept battering him back, blinding him with flying pellets of ice.

"Jim? It's Pa. I'm coming. Hang on—"

Mack saw dark shapes towering in gaps in the flying snow—shanties on the hillsides, the superstructures of mine heads. He knew this place. Why couldn't he find the path?

Suddenly, another rip in the snow veil revealed his son digging frantically. Mack threw himself forward and shouted Jim's name again. The boy raised his head. His skin was gray, his mouth blue.

"Pa? Pa, here I am. . . ."

Mack laughed triumphantly. Only twenty or thirty feet more, and he'd swoop the boy up in his arms and take him home . . .

A grinding in the earth made him look down. The snowdrift shuddered and split open, and underneath, a great crevasse of ice appeared; it was half a mile deep.

Snow crumbled under Mack's feet. As the crevasse widened, Jim reached toward his father with pleading arms . . .

Their fingers almost touched. Then Mack fell into the blue depths of the ice gorge, and landed hard on his back.

On the carpet at Greenwich Street.

Weak autumn sunshine filtering through the lace curtains patterned his face. Mack rubbed his head and yanked at the silk dressing gown binding him around the legs. Blinking and straightening his spectacles, which had slipped off his left ear, he climbed to his feet amidst the litter of last night's newspapers. He remembered now: He'd drunk two bottles of wine, then lain down to nap.

Someone was knocking. He stumbled to the parlor door. On the landing, Señora Olivar gasped with relief.

"Señor Chance, are you all right? I heard a great thump."

"I was asleep on the couch. I fell off."

Angelina Olivar twisted her apron. "I was so worried. For two hours and more, I have been thinking I must wake you."

Mack turned his stubbled face toward the soft light at the windows. "How late is it?"

"Sir—it's half past ten."

Mack groaned and rubbed his temples. Sleeping late was becoming a habit. An escape.

Noisy wagons passed in the street. Municipal crews worked all day and all night. Older said they were cleaning up something like six or seven million bricks.

Señora Olivar was still standing at the door. "Yes?" Mack said. "What else?"

"A gentleman is downstairs. An old friend who has come home again."

"Hellburner?"

"Yes, Señor. The same."

"Warm the coffeepot. I'll throw some water on my face and be right down."

He vanished in the hall leading to rooms in the back. Angelina Olivar took note of his step. For once her employer was not moving like a tortoise. Ah, but behind his hazel eyes—there, she saw no change. Behind his eyes, he was dead.

The parlor on the floor below had been converted into Mack's office. It was dark and fusty as the rooms above, but crowded with cabinets and work tables.

Mack came shuffling in. Johnson stood next to his valise, turning his wide-brimmed hat in his hands. He wore a sheepman's coat and the inevitable bandanna, this one black. His fingers constricted on the hat brim.

"Lord God. I heard you wasn't doin' so well. Looks like that ain't the half of it."

"Hello, Hugh. Welcome back."

Mack moved slowly to his desk, flattening his uncombed hair with his palm. Angelina Olivar served mugs of coffee on a tray and quickly retired. Mack sat and eyed his partner.

"If you're really back," he added.

"Yep." Johnson sailed the tall white hat onto a black horse-hair sofa. The muffling drapes were black too. Johnson shucked off his coat and dropped it, then dropped himself into a chair and reached for coffee. "Back for a spell, anyway."

"I live upstairs. There are three empty bedrooms. You can take your pick."

Johnson nodded to acknowledge the offer. "I sure don't recognize the town after what happened." He blew steam off the coffee. "You know I'm not so good with words. But I want to tell you how sorry—"

"Don't bother. Jim's alive—somewhere."

Mack left his desk and drifted across the room to a closet. "There's whiskey in here if you want to lace that."

Johnson covered the mug with his other hand. "My Lord, never this early."

"You don't mind if I do."

He opened the closet. Johnson saw decanters and bottles and bottles of Sonoma Creek Vineyard wine. Mack rummaged a glass from a shelf and filled it with red wine from an open bottle. Then he knocked it back like a couple of swallows of water.

"What about the place on Nob Hill?" Johnson asked. "I didn't go by there—"

"Burned to the ground."

"Gonna rebuild, aren't you?"

Mack refilled his glass and shut the closet. He picked up a roll of plans from a bookshelf. "Starr, the original architect, thinks I should. Margaret thinks I should. Everyone thinks I should." He threw the plans back on the shelf. "Except me."

He drank a second glass of wine in quick gulps, then shuffled back for more. Johnson sipped coffee and unhappily watched his friend pour his third drink. He didn't know how to help Mack. Maybe no one could help him in this state.

ON A TUESDAY IN EARLY NOVEMBER, MACK RE-**64** turned to the apartment on Greenwich Street at half past three in the afternoon. Three men on scaffolds were brushing gray paint on the frame of the bay window next door, and someone was hammering in the tobacco shop on the corner. Hammers could be heard all over San Francisco.

Mack wore a brown derby, a suit with a brown stripe, and a short, solid-brown topcoat. The suit and outer coat were London-made, but it was a conventional, not to say drab outfit. It discouraged attention rather than inviting it.

Mack hooked his cane on his arm and unlocked the front door. Alex sprang out of the parlor, red-cheeked and eager; he still had not come down from his romantic cloud. He touched a stack of folders on a marble-topped table. "A messenger from the Haverstick office brought these. Mr. Haverstick himself telephoned five minutes ago to remind you that the oil leases require attention immediately."

Mack dropped his cane into a ceramic stand. "They'll wait."

Alex stepped back, thwarted by his employer's curt, almost defiant answer. He indicated the office door. "You also have a caller—Mr. Marquez."

Mack's stoic face suddenly became animated. Stepping inside, he found Diego Marquez sitting with Johnson. Although the heavy drapes on the bay windows were open and tied back, it was fall, and afternoon, and the parlor seemed dimmer than usual. Dusty too.

Marquez heaved up from the horsehair sofa. He was almost grossly fat, and shabbier than ever. His beard hung to the middle of his chest, gray and patriarchal. He walked to Mack with an odd rocking gait, like a man hurting. Piles, Mack suspected. Piles or some other malady of age.

"Diego." Mack held out his hand. "Welcome. Is Felicia with you?"

"No, Felicia left me. Pregnant by a rancher's son. That's an irony, eh?" A sad little shrug. Then he said, "It was inevitable, I decided. To be poor all the time, despised, constantly threatened—it's no life for a young girl. And idealism melts in the acid juices of an empty belly. No need to discuss it further. Let me instead express my profound regret about the loss of your son."

"Temporary. Just temporary, Diego. We quarreled—he ran away—he'll be back. I've hired Pinkerton's to find him. Sit down. Do you want some whiskey? Some wine?"

He didn't. Mack helped himself. "What can I do for you?"

Marquez ordered his thoughts before speaking. "I have been working in the Central Valley. Quite near your ranch below Fresno."

"Working with the stoop labor?"

"Yes. They must be helped constantly. They must be educated so they can speak up for their rights. Not only a fair wage—adequate food, decent quarters. Do you know that some of the owners will not provide even one toilet for a hundred men and their women and babies? That is not the case on your property, I'm happy to say."

"Then what do you want from me?"

Johnson crossed his legs and scowled over the abruptness of Mack's question. Marquez frowned too. It wasn't going well.

"I am here to speak for a certain group of workers no one will hire—just as the ranch owners once refused to hire my people, or the Japanese and Chinese. There are several hundred of these men presently in the vicinity of Fresno—"

"Who are you talking about?"

"The Hindustani."

"Ah, the Indians. I've seen them."

"They come principally from the Punjab, in India's northwest. They are expert agriculturists, skilled in the cultivation of cotton, melons, figs, corn. But they can't find work—not even at the meanest, lowest wage."

"Why not, if they're so good?" Johnson asked.

"Because they are too dark. Very different. We like to boast that California is a golden door of opportunity standing open for all. Unfortunately, if you don't have white skin, that is usually untrue."

Mack regarded him with lifeless eyes. Marquez leaned forward. "I personally know of seven Hindustani who are starving. If you would lead the way—hire some of them, if only for a trial period—"

"I'm a businessman, not a social pioneer. Hiring is my foreman's responsibility."

"Mack—I am asking you in the name of friendship."

574

Mack grabbed the upright telephone. He seemed put upon, annoyed. "I'll speak to the foreman, but it's his decision."

In the Valley, it was still 87 degrees, and hot harsh light flooded Jesse Tarbox's office. Outside his dusty windows bright fans of water rained on the low short-pruned arbors of raisin grapes.

Tarbox was a lean, pale man who tended to redden with sunburn. For clothes, he preferred what he was wearing—tan jodhpurs, brown cavalry boots, a khaki shirt. He sweated heavily and changed shirts two or three times a day. His wife sometimes complained, but one or two strokes of the cane shut her up.

A Hoosier, Tarbox had been run out of a private academy after teaching for sixteen years. His abusive disposition undid him; he caned one pupil too many, and the young man's broken forearm didn't set properly. After that, he drifted through Kansas and Colorado, learning farm work, gaining experience. Finally, at fifty-seven, he had a position he liked. Here he could cane with impunity.

The wall telephone rang and Tarbox sprang to answer. Fresno central connected him with San Francisco. "Tarbox speaking," he said nervously. His employer was a hard man—moody these days, and unpredictable.

Tarbox listened. "All right, sir, you want my opinion, here it is. Don't hire rag-heads. Absolutely not. They look like niggers—in town, just walking around, they scare the womenfolk half to death. Some ranchers claim they're good workers, but I don't believe it. I say they're not worth the trouble."

"Thanks, Jesse. Everything all right?"

"Fine, sir."

Mack said good-bye and rang off. Tarbox hung the earpiece on the prongs. Out in the arbors, the pumps hissed and clicked, brushing the air with the great golden fans of water that sprinkled the Alexandria muscat vines and left them gleaming.

The foreman stared at the telephone in a fixed way. Macklin Chance paid well, but Jesse Tarbox didn't like him. Tarbox hated all those he perceived as his betters, and he loathed his inferiors. Which left damn few worthy white men on his own level.

The door flew open and a runty Mexican rushed in, clasping his straw hat to his sweat-soaked blouse. *"Señor, la tubería de la estación de bombeo se rompió y se está inundando."*

A burst line in the pump house was a problem. But Tarbox perceived a bigger one. In Spanish, he said, "Aguilar, I've told you and told you, never come in here without knocking first. I'll have to remind you in some way you'll remember."

Smiling, he reached for his cane.

575

Mack pushed the phone back to its corner of the desk.

"My foreman says no. The local people don't like the Hindus."

Abruptly, wrathfully, Marquez rose. "That's your answer?"

"That's right."

"I think the man I met some years ago would have answered differently. He would have decided for himself. I heard it said that the loss of your son changed you. I did not understand how completely."

"Diego, I don't need your moralizing."

"I'm sorry, Mack. If you're the enemy of those I help, you are my enemy also."

Mack shrugged. "Whatever you say." He turned away, as if interested in the dusty heaps of correspondence around him.

Johnson and the burly man exchanged sympathetic looks. Then Marquez picked up a battered straw hat like those worn by his migrants, and without a backward glance, left.

The moment the door shut, Johnson whistled.

"You're pretty rough on an old friend."

"That's your opinion."

"No opinion. Fact." Johnson shook his hand-rolled cigarette at Mack. "Time was, you'd of jumped to help any underdog in sight."

"Christ, you sound like Diego. Is he giving you lessons for the priesthood?"

"Don't you get snotty with me. If Nellie was here, that'd be three of us tellin' you to head in."

"Well, Nellie's on her way back to Europe to write a new novel. You probably passed her on the cattle boat coming home. Stand on your own feet."

Johnson planted them in front of the desk. "I surely will. I got somethin' to say."

"As usual. I don't want to hear it." He opened a folder of sales and construction reports from San Solaro. The summary sheet said permanent population had reached 1,003.

Johnson snatched the folder and flung it, spilling paper. "Listen here, Mack. I know you're hurtin' bad inside. I'm sorry about that. But it don't give you leave to act like a son of a bitch."

Mack hurled out of the chair and began picking up the papers as if they were treasures. "I think we've had this conversation before. I didn't like it then and I don't like it now. If you object to the way things are, Hugh, the door's right there. Always open.''

The Texan drew a long soft breath. "I think I'll take advantage. Pack my valise and light out for good. Reckon I was a damn fool to come back at all. You can stay here with the curtains shut—pityin' yourself—pickin' at your own misery and swillin' wine and snarlin' like a rabid dog, but I don't have to sit around like I think it's a whole lot of fun. Like I approve."

He walked out and shut the door so hard a picture fell off the wall, a framed photograph of the iron gateway arch at San Solaro. The glass cracked and the photo leaned crazily against the baseboard. Mack left it there.

Ten minutes later he heard the irregular rhythm of Johnson's boots on the stairs. Bang, went his crippled right foot, and a couple of moments later, bang again. He listened to the street door close, then the crown of Johnson's tall hat sailed past the bay window.

Mack rubbed his flushed face. He hated the self-righteous Texan. He hated him for his arrogance, and he hated him even more because Johnson knew the truth—that his rich shiny world was falling apart.

He tried to forget that by opening another Sonoma Creek red.

Out in the Valley, Hellman tripped on the stair at the boardinghouse and wrenched his leg. His landlady said he fell because he was old, couldn't see, yet was too vain to wear glasses. Mack heard that and laughed in a chilly way; he understood perfectly.

He drove to Sacramento and found his father-in-law confined to bed for a month. The sight of the old man saddened Mack. Hellman swore he was as hale and vigorous as ever, then fell asleep with a sentence unfinished, dribbling out the last words as slowly as the drool in the corner of his mouth.

"He's too old to live alone," Mack said to Alex when he returned to the City. "Find him a place. I'll move him bodily if need be.''

Mission Street smelled of mud and new lumber. Mack and Margaret stood on the corner of a vacant lot on the south side. Two muddy men worked on a broken main in a deep ditch bisecting the lot. A donkey engine chugged, pumping water out of the ditch.

Mack and Margaret were watching the lot across the street.

577

There, carpenters were hammering in the first-floor framing of a new building. The sunshine flattered Margaret, accentuating the red in her auburn hair. She was elegant in wine velvet, lace gloves, an immense picture hat. In the shadow of its brim, her marvelous smile shone out. She was as delighted as a child.

Mack smoked a cigar with scarcely a change of expression.

She took his arm and they resumed their walk. "I'll be open by March. The contractor told me yesterday."

"Good," he said. His hazel eyes got lost somewhere above a windowless brick wall, somewhere up in the fat breeze-driven clouds.

She stopped and touched his chin. "When will you ever get out of this misery?"

"When the police or the Pinkertons find my son."

"Is there anything . . . ?"

"Nothing."

They walked on, alternately in sun and shadow as the autumn clouds sailed over. At the corner, two dray horses lay stiffly in a lake of congealed blood. Horses dropped in their tracks every day, worked so hard in the cleanup that their hearts burst. Crews hauled them away at night.

Margaret choked at the odor, then apologized self-consciously. "Pigs smell worse. Now you know why I ran away from the farm."

They went up toward Market Street. A wrecker's ball crashed against a wall somewhere. In the middle of Market, a small SP switch engine pulled three gondolas piled with rubble. The temporary railroad tracks were new, for the cleanup.

A newsboy's shrill cry sounded before the wrecking ball crashed again. "Something about Ruef," Mack said, livelier suddenly. "I can't quite hear—"

They hurried and found a small crowd around a boy hawking early editions of the *Examiner*. Hearst had ordered new presses for a new building, but even so, the paper would have to be made up and printed in Oakland for months yet.

"Paper here, latest paper. Abe Ruef and Mayor Schmitz charged with crime."

Mack pushed through. He and a sallow man reached for the last paper. Mack was faster. He showed Margaret the twenty-four-point screamer: RUEF, SCHMITZ INDICTED!

It was the news the reform group had awaited from the grand jury for weeks. "Five counts of extortion," Margaret exclaimed, scanning quickly. "The Poodle Dog—Delmonico's—Marchand's—Mack, they've got the evidence. Amounts, dates paid—"

"Burns and his detectives are doing a fine job. The French restaurant case is just the start."

She clapped her hands. "Oh, my. At last. Isn't this something?"

Something, he thought. *But not enough.*

Bitter Bierce sent him a note from Washington.

Nellie's earthquake tale is published in *The S. E. Post.* Envy rages in my ink-stained bosom. She continues to achieve, while I hack on for the Great Wm. R. Hooey, whose cheap yellow journalism I hate, but whose pay checks somehow retain their power to enthrall.

On December 6, Fremont Older arranged press credentials for Mack, and the two squeezed into the crowd at the Ruef-Schmitz arraignment. Courtroom space was still limited because of the destruction. Mack thought it a fine irony that this proceeding was held in a room customarily used for Sabbath school at Temple Israel.

During the reading of the first indictment, Handsome Gene Schmitz stood before the bench, fidgeting. The Boss remained seated, legs crossed, gazing at the ceiling with affable unconcern.

It was too much for Judge Dunne. "Defendants will stand for arraignment. No one receives special treatment in this court. The clerk will start over."

Ruef snapped to his feet, genuinely shaken.

Wild Bill Flyshack visited Greenwich Street a week before Christmas. Darkness was settling outside. His report was succinct.

"Still no sign of him."

"Have the flyers produced anything?"

"Five more leads, all bad."

Mack hit the desk. "Flyshack, I'm not paying you to take the train up here and recite your failures. Put more men on the case."

"Mr. Chance, just a minute. We're already using every available—"

"Then find him. Pinkerton's is supposed to be the best bureau in the country."

Flyshack jammed his cigar into a glass tray, splitting the cigar and ruining it. "I'll stake my personal reputation on

Pinkerton's any day of the week. You're just not facing certain facts.''

Mack snapped on a dim electric light, brass with a green shade, and its glare washed over Flyshack's pocked face. Mack gave him a hard stare. ''Such as?''

''Pinkerton's is a private bureau. We don't have the full resources of police departments. Not that they're giving us any help, especially here. You aren't popular with the city government, Mr. Chance.''

''You think I don't know that? What the hell does it have to do with this?''

''Plenty,'' Flyshack shot back. ''Most of the cops in this town hate you, or at least they won't go out of their way to help you. It's more than your opposition to Ruef; it goes all the way back to Lon Coglan. He was a stalwart on the detective squad for many years.''

''Get to the point. What's the connection?''

Flyshack didn't like being tongue-lashed. He reacted with high color, hovering on the edge of rebellion. His voice actually shook. ''I didn't like the cooperation we were getting from the cops, statewide, so I put an informant into the department here. Low-level, but he sees and hears plenty. I understand there have been some telephone calls made about your flyer to other major departments in the state. San Diego, Los Angeles, the Valley . . . nothing clearly illegal, you understand. Just a slow-down. Flyers pulled off station bulletin boards, inquiries from my operatives lost or misfiled—nothing big, nothing noisy. But it has an effect, like a stone thrown in a pond.''

''Did Abe Ruef instigate this? Do you mean to tell me he'd get even at the expense of my son?''

''I'm not saying Ruef directly. Friends of Ruef. Associates of Ruef, in the city government. They have connections all around California, and a big dislike of you and your reform crowd. It's all kind of like moonlight. You can't take it into a court as evidence, but it's there. It's real.''

''And that's why Jim hasn't been found?''

''It's one reason, yes.''

''You're giving me excuses.''

Flyshack jumped up. ''I'm giving you what I see. I can also give you my notice, right now.''

The harshness sobered Mack abruptly. ''No, no, I'm sorry. I believe what you say. I want you to stay on the case. Sit down.''

With an air of reluctance, perhaps exaggerated, Flyshack did. He examined the ruined cigar, grumbled, and lit another. ''Mr.

Chance, I'd like to give you soothing words and promises, but frankly, I'm beginning to think we're pissing uphill. All this underground stuff I mentioned, it contributes, but it's secondary to something else: It's December already. You've ragged the police, you've nailed up thousands of flyers, and after eight months, your son is still missing. We must at least recognize that the boy may have died in the quake, or the fire afterward."

"No. He didn't. You find him."

"California's a huge state. An enormous amount of territory to comb for one boy who may be lying low—"

"Find him."

Flyshack glared, then contained it. With a flicking motion he drew a paper from an inner pocket of his chalk-stripe suit.

"I have this month's bill. Do you want me to give it to Mr. Muller?"

"Mr. Muller is on his honeymoon. Leave it."

The detective slapped the paper on the desk, then picked up his travel bag. "As a client, I won't say you're easy, Mr. Chance."

"No, but the money is—right?"

Flyshack managed a grudging laugh, and Mack walked with him to the foyer; their tempers were settling down.

Flyshack looked around. "You've no Christmas decorations."

"Is there reason for any?"

"Well—I don't suppose—" Flyshack's shoulders drooped noticeably. "I see your point. Merry Christmas anyway." He tipped his derby, and as he went out into the dark Mack slammed the door behind him.

IN 1907, THE UNITED STATES PLUNGED INTO AN-other financial panic. Stock prices fell, banks failed, **65** unemployment rose. Pierpont Morgan telegraphed capitalists around the country to secure private loans to shore up the shaky bank and credit system. Mack pledged $7 million of his personal fortune.

Aeronautics and airplanes crept into the news. The Wrights had flown at Kitty Hawk in '03, but respectable, conservative people hooted at flying as they'd hooted at autos in the 1890s.

They believed that anyone seriously interested in flying belonged to the lunatic fringe. Mack qualified.

Nellie wrote from Florence, Italy, to say she had nearly finished her novel, squeezing it out nine hundred words a day, in pencil, on lined copy paper. She said the book was "sure to make me hated by Collis Huntington's heirs and appointees. Those of Uncle Mark Hopkins too."

Mack traveled to New York on business, and returned to California via a steamer for Colón, Panama. He crossed the Isthmus and inspected the great raw wounds in the earth where thousands of workers were digging and blasting Teddy's Big Ditch, the canal to join the oceans. On the coastal ship for San Francisco he read *The Jungle* by Upton Sinclair.

Vacationing in California, Willie Hearst took Mack horseback riding at his Piedra Blanca ranch, a vast property in San Luis Obispo County. Willie's father, the senator, had bought up the original forty-five thousand acres of Spanish land grant back in '65. Willie was married now, and the father of three sons, and he was serving a second term as a U.S. Congressman from New York City. But he spoke little of Washington or his family. Instead, as he and Mack galloped along the wild coast above the Pacific, he talked nostalgically about the beauty of California, and particularly this site. Here, he said, he would build his dream castle someday.

Mack began to hear of a new and radical labor organization, International Workers of the World. Wobblies, some called them. In public statements, they said their aim was to educate "the oppressed working classes" as a prelude to "world-wide revolution." In a news article listing IWW men arrested for street-corner speeches in Visalia, he saw the name D. Marquez.

Mack moved his father-in-law from Sacramento to a pleasant house far out on Lombard Street, within earshot of the Bay, and hired a nurse and a cook. Hellman was sickly, suffering from angina and enlarged veins in his legs, and his memory was failing. He denied he needed help from anyone, though he relied on Mack.

Professor Lorenzo Love had enough of waiting for his pupil to be found and accepted a post at a female academy in Bakersfield. When he said good-bye, he told Mack he prayed for Jim's return someday. But if it was not to be, he knew Mack would survive. "Lear said, 'I am tied to the stake, and I must stand the course.' Longfellow wrote that it is sublime to suffer and be strong."

"Lorenzo, that's bullshit and you know it."

The men embraced. "Bring back that boy, Mr. Chance. Bring back that fine boy."

Flyshack reported regularly, though there was nothing new. One night toward the end of 1907, sleepless, Mack rolled over and stared into the dark and let the cool dispassionate truth take hold of him.

There wasn't any hope. Jim was gone.

Meanwhile, the graft prosecutions moved forward. In March 1907 the grand jury had returned sixty-five indictments of bribery and fraud in the fight-trust case, seventeen in the gas-rates case, thirteen in a telephone franchise case, seventeen in the United Railroads trolley-line case. Special prosecutor Heney locked Ruef in a secure house at 2849 Fillmore Street and negotiated with him. The Boss agreed to testify for the prosecution in return for limited immunity.

In June, Ruef had testified against his crony Schmitz in the French restaurant case. The jury's verdict: guilty of extortion. Schmitz was at last removed from office and sentenced to five years in San Quentin.

The year was not without its perils for friends of the prosecution. Mack received three anonymous death threats in the mail, and Rudolph Spreckels took a telephone call late one night warning that his home would be dynamited. While Fremont Older was on a trip to Southern California, three men attempted to kidnap him when his train was stopped at a station. The men were armed and carried a warrant for Older's arrest, but Older shouted that it was a forgery, and station employees and passengers helped him drive off the would-be kidnappers.

At least once a week in 1907 and early 1908, Mack drove to Lombard Street, picked up Hellman, and took him to the courtroom for the day. Hellman reveled in the dishonesty of his fellow man. Mack supposed he liked to know that others were as crooked as he'd been.

The Parkside Realty case came up for trial early in April of '08. Parkside was a development firm, and one of its principals was William Crocker, president of the Crocker Bank and son of Cholly, of the Big Four. Parkside had schemed to spur sales of an oceanside tract with a new trolley line. A trolley line required a franchise. A franchise meant a bribe paid to Ruef. The trial was bound to be complex, because Ruef himself had helped secure the indictments against Parkside's officers, testifying before the grand jury in return for limited immunity. Between that time and the start of the trial, Ruef and the prosecutors had quarreled repeatedly; Heney wanted Ruef to testify to more than he was willing to say. As a result, the immunity arrangement had broken down, and Heney and his staff were once again after the Boss on every front.

"They're having trouble finding jurors now," Mack said as he helped his father-in-law down the steps at Lombard Street. Hellman labored across the unpaved sidewalk to the Oldsmobile.

"Is that what's on today, more jury-picking?"

Mack nodded. "The dynamiting of Gallagher's house threw the graft trials back on the front page in a very lurid and emotional way. It'll be damn hard to get jurors who are objective."

He was referring to an event two nights before. Dynamite had blown out the front of the residence of former supervisor James Gallagher. Under immunity, Gallagher was giving evidence in the trial of Tirey Ford, an official of United Railroads; Gallagher had been a go-between for Ruef, carrying Ford's bribe offers to City Hall. Gallagher and his family had miraculously survived the dynamite attack.

Hellman wheezed and grimaced as Mack helped him into the auto. "Thanks, Johnny. I ain't so spry anymore." Mack walked around the hood. "What d'you hear about Hetch Hetchy these days?"

"Dragging on," Mack said as he climbed in. "No decision yet."

When he reached for the brake release, the old man grasped his sleeve. Hellman's hand was red and flaking; he had a vile skin rash, and smelled heavily of tar-based ointment. "Listen, I never been good with compliments. But I got to tell you I appreciate all you done for me. Finding me this place. That dandy little nurse with the round bottom. Coming out here and taking me to court every week when you're so busy—"

"That's a real carnival downtown. I know you love it."

"Watching them fry those crooks is more fun than watching bare-assed girlies dance the hoochy-kootch. It is at my age, anyhow."

Hellman's smile was sad somehow, the smile of a man keenly aware of his own mortality. Mack felt old himself.

"It's nothing," Mack said finally.

"Hell it isn't. Ever since the ranches got too much for me to manage and I moved into that boardinghouse, Carla stopped coming around much. Now she don't come around at all."

"I know that."

"And you know why. She's getting long in the tooth, like the rest of us. She ain't helping matters, drinking and carousing with those nancy-boy artists she runs with. But her pa—oh, no, she don't want to look at him; he'll show her that old age is real. She don't want to be reminded." He squinted into the sunshine, his eyes gleaming as though they were watering. "I'll always love that girl, Johnny. But I don't like her very much."

Mack was silent; he shared the feeling.

Francis J. Heney approached the bench. In the witness chair sat a man recalled from the panel of provisional jurors, a man with unruly yellow-gray hair, a big mustache, and a wall eye that gave him a slightly mad air. There were about thirty people scattered in the spectator section of the courtroom. Three of Abraham Ruef's four expensive defense lawyers—Shortridge, Ach, and Fairall—conferred behind their hands while the judge said:

"Morris Haas was accepted yesterday as a juror in the Parkside bribery trial. You now wish to challenge that, Mr. Heney?"

"I do, your honor." Heney handed up a sheet of stiff paper. "This evidence is new. Unearthed by our staff."

Morris Haas sweated and squirmed while the judge studied the photograph.

Heney said, "I'd like permission to present the evidence to Mr. Haas."

"Proceed," the judge said, nodding.

Heney marched to the witness box. "Mr. Haas, I show you this twenty-year-old photograph from the Department of Prisons. A photograph of a man with a shaven head, a man wearing convict stripes."

Haas's eyes bulged and sweat streamed down his yeasty face.

"Are you not the man pictured? Were you not at the time serving a term in San Quentin prison for embezzlement?"

In the second row, his favorite place, Hellman leaned over to whisper, "That Heney's a tough little apple. I wouldn't want to get him interested in what I done fifteen or twenty years ago." He rolled his eyes.

Heney pounded the witness box. "Mr. Haas. If you please."

"The governor granted me a pardon," Haas exclaimed. "Restored me to full citizenship—"

"Then you don't deny the evidence?"

"No, I don't deny it. How can I? There it is. But I paid my debt. I came back to San Francisco, married, and raised four children. You didn't have to rake it all up again."

Heney was icy. "I beg to differ. Your Honor, the prosecution

585

cannot accept a juror susceptible to undue pressure, for whatever reason. A concealed criminal record certainly makes a man a potential target of extreme pressure. Our investigators unearthed these facts about Mr. Haas, and I regret having to bring them forward. But I must ask that he be stricken as—"

"Damn you, Heney," Haas yelled, jumping up. He was a small man, five feet six at most.

The judge gaveled him silent. "Mr. Haas, step down. You're dismissed."

Haas lunged at Heney, who had already turned his back, but a deputy sheriff strong-armed Haas away from the prosecutor, and Foley, the prosecutor's bodyguard, rousted him out through the gate in the rail separating lawyers from spectators. A massive woman with a dark mustache rushed to Haas in tears.

"I won't let this pass," Haas yelled as the bailiff and the woman pushed him toward the courtroom doors. "You've ruined me in San Francisco—you'll pay . . . "

"Crazy man," Hellman said with a shiver. Mack was about to comment when the hall guard slipped into the vacant seat beside him.

"There's a gentleman hunting for you, Mr. Chance. He went to your house and your assistant sent him here."

He handed Mack an engraved card. Intrigued, Mack studied it, then, noticing Hellman craning to see, gave him the card. "Can you read it?"

"Sure I can read it." Hellman was defensive about his afflictions. He held the card three inches from his nose. "Shit. What's it say?"

"Gilbert M. Anderson. Essanay Manufacturing Company, Argyle Street, Chicago."

"Never heard of him. Go on, go see him. I'll be fine."

Mack hurried down the aisle. For the first time in a long time, there was a sparkle of interest in his hazel eyes, inspired by a decorative device on the card: a crudely drawn strip of movie film.

In the New Golconda Saloon and Grill two blocks from court, Mack ordered schooners of beer. Gilbert Anderson was a thickly built, rather plain young man. About thirty, Mack guessed. He had soft luminous brown eyes and a magnificent nose that would suit a statesman. He was dressed as drably as a bank officer.

"Essanay"—he pointed to the card lying between them—"that's *S* for George Spoor, my partner, and *A* for Anderson.

George handles our business affairs. I'm in charge of production."

"You're talking about moving pictures."

"Yes, sir. I appreciate your taking time to discuss the subject. I was told you're an investor who isn't afraid of new ideas."

Mack packed tobacco into his meerschaum. Was he wasting his time? There was nothing dynamic or forceful about Anderson. He seemed, instead, rather shy. Yet that very lack of sophistication, that sincerity, was curiously winning. Mack nodded to indicate that he should go ahead.

"I'm a stage actor," Anderson began. "That is, originally—"

"From New York?"

"Yes, but born in Pine Bluff, Arkansas." He studied Mack and seemed to decide that he could trust him. "Gilbert Anderson's the name I adopted for the theater. It's more—ah—acceptable than Max Aronson. Some producers don't like Jewish actors. Some theatrical boardinghouses won't rent to Jews."

"The world is full of stupid people, Mr. Anderson. Do I understand that you quit the stage for moving pictures?"

"That's right. I've been roaming all over the West shooting one-reelers for Essanay. I even shot two down in Westlake Park in Los Angeles. But we need a permanent base out here. I want to buy land, establish a studio to take full advantage of the constant sunshine. Unfortunately every cent of Essanay profit goes into operating the Chicago studio. I have to find supplementary capital."

"What kind of pictures do you want to produce?"

"Pictures that make money."

Mack laughed. "The best kind."

"You like pictures?"

"I love them."

Anderson leaned in, so eager he nearly upset his beer. "Actually, I'm most interested in pictures about the West. The old West is practically gone. Autos, interurbans, modern roads—and all those midwesterners coming in with their real estate offices and tourist cabins—they buried it."

"I have a partner who'd agree with you." *Or do I?* Johnson had disappeared as completely as Mack's son, his oil royalties continuing to pile up in his account in Los Angeles, untouched.

With enthusiasm, Anderson said, "People still love the West, Mr. Chance. Partly because it's vanished, but also because it's simple, open—honest. And mighty exciting too. Did you see Porter's *Great Train Robbery*?"

"Many times."

"I was in it. I was a passenger at the mercy of the outlaws."

"Well." Mack puffed his pipe and tried to be tactful. "I certainly saw you. But I didn't know you then."

Despite the gentle letdown, Anderson was wounded. Typical actor, Mack thought, amused. He liked this fellow who loved the West, though he hardly looked like a westerner. Anderson had unbuttoned his cheap plain jacket; a sizable belly roll showed.

"I was just an extra," Anderson admitted. "I was hired to play one of the train robbers. But Porter happened to ask whether I could ride a horse, and I couldn't lie to him. Matter of fact, I was sick of New York and ready to give up acting when I got that job. Porter's film changed my life. It changed movies too."

"Because it had a story."

"You're right. That little movie contained just fourteen scenes. When we shot it in the wilds of New Jersey, I didn't think much of it at all. Then I went to see the finished film projected. I stood in the dark at Eden's on Fourteenth Street—it was astounding. When the outlaws robbed the train, people jumped up and shouted, 'Catch them.' When it was over, they yelled, 'Run it again, run it again.' The picture was also playing uptown, at Hammerstein's, on Broadway. I couldn't believe the reaction at Eden's, so I went to Hammerstein's, figuring the audience would be highbrow, cold. Know what happened?"

"Did they shout 'Run it again'?"

"Exactly!" Anderson quickly drank some beer and forgot to dab the foam off his lip. "They couldn't get enough. I said to myself, Anderson, that's it. It's the picture business for you."

"And now you want to produce Westerns."

"A series, featuring one character, a sort of good-hearted bad man. I'll play the part to save money for us."

A wry look fleeted over Mack's face. He was sure economy wasn't the primary reason Anderson wanted the role. But the man's enthusiasm excused his ego.

"Have you found property for your studio?"

"Yes, sir, out in the East Bay—Niles Canyon. Well away from the worst of the fog."

"Here's the important question: Have you learned to ride a horse?"

Anderson burst out laughing. "Tolerably. If I fall off, we can always do a second take. That's the beauty of movies."

Smoke rose from Mack's pipe, and he gazed at it thoughtfully. Conservative men would have nothing to do with a scheme like this. Never mind. He had a hunch, an impulse. He'd bet on similar feelings before—and won. Folding your hand, you won nothing.

To his surprise, he realized something remarkable had happened. Here in this drab saloon smelling of sawdust, a stranger had lifted him a little way out of his despond. It was a refreshing feeling.

"I must get back to court, Mr. Anderson. Send me a proposal. Tell me how much you need."

THE PARKSIDE TRIAL ENDED IN A HUNG JURY. THE **66** prosecution pressed forward with the trial of Boss Ruef himself, on charges that he bribed supervisors, specifically Supervisor J. J. Furey on behalf of United Railroads. Furey would testify under immunity, as would Gallagher, Ruef's alleged go-between.

This time it was even harder to seat an unbiased jury, and the process took seventy-two days. Ruef's chief counsel, Henry Ach, hurled challenges like rice at a wedding. He dismissed any veniremen who read the *Call*. He dismissed any veniremen who subscribed to the *Bulletin*.

"Pretty soon he'll be dismissing them if they take a piss first thing in the morning," Hellman grouched.

Henry Ach continued to strike names, object, and stall, until more than fourteen hundred jurymen had been screened.

Meantime, on November 3, the nation voted. Mack cast his presidential ballot for Secretary of War William Howard Taft, personally picked by Roosevelt to be his successor. It was a victory for the Republicans, a humiliating defeat for the tired old populist William Jennings Bryan, whom the Democrats had dragged out a third time in desperation.

On November 6, the United Railroads jury was finally sworn and the trial began.

Late in the afternoon of November 13—Friday the thirteenth—Judge William Lawlor announced a short recess. The courtroom in Carpenter's Hall was filled to the limit—two hundred people or more. They jammed the balconies along the sides of the drafty hall and packed the seats behind the press tables on the main floor. Mack and Hellman sat on the aisle, second row, main floor. They'd been listening to defense attorney Ach cross-examine James Gallagher, the prosecution's star witness.

As the gavel fell and people left their seats, Mack heard snoring. Hellman's round dimpled chin rested on his shirt front. His yellow-and-brown plaid suit, an offense to taste, was spotted with red clam sauce from their noon meal. Better take him home soon, Mack thought as he stood up.

A small man bumped him. Mack had seen him before but couldn't recall where. The man was visibly agitated and pushed through the crowd toward the attorneys' tables.

A hubbub of conversation filled the court. Anxious for some air, Mack shoved his way toward doors at the back. Suddenly his neck prickled. He remembered that the man who'd bumped him had a bad eye. A wall eye—

"What's he doing? What is that man doing? Oh my God, he's got a pistol!"

The woman's voice escalated to a shriek. Mack spun around with a feeling of dread. It had all been there on the face of the wall-eyed man. Hatred—and the intent. He just hadn't paid attention.

More outcries. Then a shot.

Mack jumped up on a chair. Forever afterward, he could recall the scene exactly. Francis Heney fallen facedown on the prosecution table, blood running from a wound in front of his right ear. The juror in his dirty overcoat standing with the small blue pistol smoking in his hand.

In the second row, Hellman woke up and wobbled to his feet. Except for the screaming woman, the courtroom was dead silent. Then everyone yelled at once.

A deputy sheriff and Foley, Heney's bodyguard, rushed Morris Haas, and Haas retreated. Excited and confused, Hellman stumbled into the aisle four feet behind Haas.

It was Hellman's style to bellow when he didn't understand something. He bellowed now, at Haas.

"What's going on, mister? What the hell's that gun for?"

"Stay away from me," Haas cried, though Hellman wasn't moving, and then fired two more shots. Huge clam-sauce splotches appeared on Hellman's gaudy jacket, and he fell forward in the aisle.

"Swampy," Mack shouted, jumping down. He flung people out of his way while the deputy snatched the pistol and beat Haas to the floor.

* * *

"How is he?" Bill Burns said on the telephone the next night around eleven o'clock.

"Bad," Mack said.

"In the hospital?"

"No. He wanted his own bed. I've been sitting with him all evening. How's Heney?"

"Damnedest thing. He's going to live. The docs think he had his mouth open, maybe laughing, when the bullet hit. The slug went into the jaw muscle under his left ear. Another quarter-inch and he'd be gone. He'll be down a long while— that's a setback—but he'll recover, and they don't think he'll lose his voice."

"Well, good," Mack said in a tired way.

"Actually, I called with news about Haas. He's dead."

"How?"

"Suicide."

"In jail?"

"Right. They found a derringer in his hand. He did it lying on his cot, under a blanket. That gun wasn't on him when they locked him up, that's certain. Someone smuggled it in."

A chilly shiver worked down Mack's back. "Bill, I don't like to see conspiracies all over the place. But this makes me wonder. Haas was clearly a nerve case. Maybe someone banked on that."

"Who do you mean?"

"Someone who set him up to kill Heney."

"You think he was set up?"

"It's a possibility. They used dynamite, why not an assassin? Maybe they figured Haas was crazy enough to do them a favor afterward. I mean do away with himself, out of fear or despondency. Provided he had a gun."

After a silence Burns said, "Interesting theory. We'll never know, will we?"

He broke the connection.

HEADLIGHTS PIERCED THE DARK OF LOMBARD **67** Street. The long gleaming Pope-Toledo parked and the chauffeur opened the passenger door. At the front window, drawn by the sound of the motor, Mack watched Carla stumble out.

Her evening wrap brushed the dusty sidewalk. It was mauve velvet, ornamented with a black velvet collar and an excess of passementerie—golden gimps, cords, and tassels.

He opened the door. He was in shirtsleeves, old trousers, and suspenders. His face was grim. "About time. I've left messages at your house in Burlingame for three days."

Carla regarded him with bleary nervousness. How round, white, and matronly her face had become. It was caked with powder and rouge tonight, and smears of lash blacking stained the hollows under her eyes.

"Walter's in Washington. I was in Carmel. The servants didn't know where to reach me."

Shutting the door behind her, he detected a stronger, sweeter odor beneath her perfume.

She dropped her wrap on the parlor rug. She'd come from a party, and was in a gold satin evening gown. Its bertha of black lace was sheer enough to show her ballooning cleavage. She wore a wide dog-collar choker, solid with diamonds all the way around that splashed the walls and ceiling with sparkling reflections of the dim electric lights.

"Don't you read the papers, Carla?"

"Not in Carmel. There was a weekend party—"

"Where did they hold it, the bottom of a barrel of gin?"

She raised a fist. "You bastard. You're so unkind."

He pushed her hand aside. "I'm feeling unkind. They took out one bullet but they can't reach the other. He's dying. You should have been here sooner."

They walked the long hall. It was black as a mine shaft, with only a slim band of light showing under the door at the end. Mack opened it a few inches, and Carla clutched him. "Oh my God."

The electric lights were off in Hellman's bedroom. But there was a glow, the glow of an altar. On tables and taborets crowded on both sides of the headboard, votive candles burned—perhaps a hundred, flickering and smoking in small red and blue glasses.

Hellman lay with his eyes shut, his cheek resting on the round bolster. He wore a nightshirt of gray flannel and his hands clasped a rough wood crucifix.

A broad-shouldered nurse sat on a chair near the bed.

Mack said, "He asked for the candles and the cross the first time he regained consciousness. I never knew he was Catholic."

"Papa was born Catholic. He was unruly growing up, and

592

he said the German nuns beat him unmercifully for it. He abandoned the church when he was sixteen. He always told people we were Protestants.''

Mack opened the door fully. Carla searched his face. No sympathy there. She drew a breath and stepped inside. Her ankle wobbled, her foot coming out of her beaded slipper. Mack jumped and saved her from a fall. "For God's sake, stand up.''

The nurse gave them an angry look. The noise roused Hellman. "Who is it?'' His eyes opened. Filmy eyes, seeing little but moving shadows at first. Then they fixed on the shimmer of gold at the bedside. "Carla? My baby. Carla.''

Mack shut the door and leaned against it. The room needed airing. There were smells of stale bandages and the chamber pot. Smells of death.

"Papa.'' Carla uttered it in a broken voice, dropping to her knees at the bedside and putting her face down on the blanket. Her shoulders heaved. "Papa. Oh, Papa.''

Hellman's nose looked like a radish. Someone—the nurse?—had center-parted and combed his thin white hair. He looked waxy and neat as a corpse just attended by morticians. His hand groped and found his daughter's head, then stroked the spun-gold hair.

"My little Carla. God above. You smell like a saloon.'' He said it lovingly, stroking.

"You'll be all right, Papa.'' She sounded like a child. "We'll get you the best care we can.''

"I got the best. The finest doctors in—'' A wheezy cough shook him. "In California.'' He pressed the crucifix against the bosom of the nightshirt. Obviously it cost him effort to talk, effort and pain.

He kept stroking Carla's bowed head. "I got my son-in-law taking care of me. Your new husband, what's his name? The stuffed shirt. Maybe he's a go-getter. But Mack now, he—''

More coughing. Sudden sweat glistened all over his face. The nurse stepped in to pat his brow with a hand towel, dab away a bit of green phlegm from his lip. Hellman looked at her like she was a viper, and she retreated.

"Mack's the best man who ever loved you. You didn't pay any attention. You had everything and you just threw it away. You were a damn fool.'' He was drowsy, mumbling. "A damn fool to leave him.''

Carla raised her head. Lights from the votive candles shone in her eyes. Her mascara ran, streaking her powder. She looked at Mack.

"I know, Papa."

"Such a fool . . . but a beautiful girl. *Schönes Mädchen*. Just like your mama—she was beautiful too . . ." Hellman sighed. He closed his eyes.

"Papa?"

The nurse felt Hellman's pulse, then his brow. "Nothing to be alarmed about, Mrs. Fairbanks. He's asleep again, that's all. Please let him rest."

Carla stumbled to the hallway. Mack closed the door on an image of Hellman sleeping with the crucifix and the nurse holding his wrist.

She slumped against the wall. "I thought he was—"

"Not yet. The doctors say it's a matter of a day, maybe two, at the most. There's bleeding internally. They can't stop it."

"Oh, Mack." She fell forward against him, shuddering, then stole one arm around his neck. Mack smelled her perfumed hair, felt the warmth and bulk of her body. Over her shoulder he stared at the wallpaper, examining the pattern. She said, "I need a drink. Please don't criticize, just give it to me."

"A little brandy. That's all. In the parlor."

He pried her arm off and walked down the black hall.

In the parlor he shut the drapes on the street side. No need for the chauffeur to watch Mrs. Fairbanks and her former husband.

He put a measured half-inch of Napoleon brandy in a snifter. She consumed it in two swallows, then held the snifter out. He shook his head.

"Swampy and I talked about his will," Mack told her. "You inherit half of everything. The other half's in trust for our son when he's found."

She gave him a peculiar coquettish smile. It startled and sickened him. Was she blind drunk already? They did say that some drunkards needed only a sip to lose control.

"Papa was right, I was crazy to think I'd ever find someone better. You were the best in every way. In bed you were the best, too."

"This isn't a very appropriate time to talk about that."

"Why not? We were married—there's no pretense between us." She slid the bolt on the hall door, then caressed the gleaming wood in a slow, sensual way, smiling.

His stomach turned over.

She ran her hand over the black bertha, rubbing the curve of her bosom. "You were the best. Sometimes I forget." She took a lurching step. "I'd like to remember. I'd like to be reminded—"

"Carla, for Christ's sake—"

She snatched his hand and rubbed his palm with her thumb. He stepped back but she followed, arm sliding around his neck again. Her tongue licked his cheek, then his ear. The round breasts mashed his chest. He felt stays.

"Do you know what I'm wearing underneath this? A corset from Paris. Brocaded satin and lace. Ribbon garters. Wouldn't you like to see?"

He threw her arm down. "Stop it."

"I love you, Mack. I've always been in love with you. I ran away because I couldn't control you, make you do what I wanted. I didn't like that. But I didn't stop loving you."

"As I recall, you didn't want the responsibility for Jim, either."

"That was a mistake. Leaving was a mistake. We were good lovers." She reached for his waist. "Remind me."

He caught her wrist and held her hand away.

"No thanks. The only time I was entitled to that was when we were married. I despise your husband but I'll be damned if I'll cuckold him."

"Mack—why not?" She held out her arms, begging, swaying back and forth, weaving, starting to simper at him. "Why not, lover? Why not?"

"You'd better go. I'll telephone Burlingame when there's a change in your father's—"

"Mack—"

"Leave."

The rebuff was quiet, hard, final. She lowered her arms, trembling.

"You prig. You arrogant self-righteous son of a bitch. I've had better than you dozens of times. Bigger and better. Even when we were married, you weren't good enough. I had lovers. More than one."

He walked away, supremely tired. "It doesn't surprise me. I think you're drunk, Carla. Drunk, or unhinged by all this. Go sleep it off." He picked up her evening wrap to lay it around her shoulders.

"Don't tell me what to do." She threw the tasseled wrap halfway across the parlor. "You think you're so superior. Always in charge. I'll tell you one time you weren't in charge. New Year's Day, 1898. You were in New York seeing that bitch who writes books. Do you remember where I was?"

A cold rock of dread fell to the bottom of his belly. "Pasadena."

"That's right. But I wasn't alone. Walter was there. I had Walter in Pasadena. I had him in here, Mack. Right in here, are you looking? He got in me New Year's Day, and more than once. He loved getting back at you that way. So did I."

She was leaning toward him, so overwrought that she could smile while tears streamed from her eyes.

Mack flung the evening wrap at her. "Get out."

But she had the knife in him. "Not till I tell you something else. You thought Jim was a month early. No. I was full term when he was born. I was already pregnant when you came back from New York. Jim isn't your son; Jim is Walter's son."

"You're a liar."

Carla flung her head back and laughed at him. "Hurts, doesn't it. Good. Good! There's no mistake. Walter was my lover when you were away. You raised his son. And Papa called me the fool."

"You goddamn liar." He backhanded her mouth.

Carla cried out and spilled sideways, hitting the sofa with her head. Mack stared at his right hand as though it belonged to someone else—a leper, a Jack the Ripper. He'd struck Jim, and now he'd struck a woman—

"You cowardly bastard," she said as he circled, hand outstretched to help her rise. "Don't touch me, don't you touch me or I'll have the police on you, you fucking woman-beating *monster*."

He reached again. "Carla, I'm sorry, I didn't mean—"

Carla shoved him and ran past to the foyer door. She breathed hard, yellow hair coming undone and tumbling to her shoulders. The diamond dog collar studded Mack's face with light points as she gripped the edge of the door.

"I'm glad I told you. Let it hurt, you cruel shit. I hope it hurts till the day you die."

She left, spraying diamond points of light on the walls, the ceiling, comets and stars flying in some great stellar cataclysm. The street door slammed and the crazed heavens became a plastered ceiling again.

The young Lutheran pastor was red-faced in the November cold. He nevertheless prayed with passion.

"Lord God, we now commend Thy servant Otto Adolphus Hellman to Thy eternal care."

Gray mist from the ocean blew across Redeemer Cemetery and wet the gravestones and the brown grass.

"Thou shalt in time redeem all of mankind soul by soul, as Thou hast redeemed him."

Mack stood at the foot of the open grave, his sad gaze on the bronzed metal casket. Yesterday the monument company had raised the obelisk, a tall shaft of pink marble surmounted by a Prussian eagle, with HELLMAN in relief on the base, ten inches high. Hellman's dates were a quarter of the size.

"Thou hast cleansed him till he is innocent as a child, his soul bright and pure as dawn, his heart prepared, ready for Thy everlasting care."

Fourteen mourners ringed the grave. All but Mack were connected with Hellman's various real estate enterprises, managers, foremen, bankers, insurance brokers. All men; neither Carla nor her husband was present. They were represented instead by a five-foot floral tribute already wilting and browning.

"Receive him now, Almighty Father, now and forever—amen and amen."

After an appropriate silence, the pastor's glance signaled that the service was over, and the mourners dispersed quietly. Mack put on his derby, shook the pastor's hand, and gave him an envelope containing his fee. Two bored cemetery workers turned cranks to lower the casket on straps.

The mist was turning to rain. Mack walked quickly up the slope, speaking to no one. At the summit, several black automobiles waited in a line. He was startled when a woman in a black wool coat and large black hat stepped from behind a stone angel.

"I thought you might need company afterward," Margaret said, taking his arm. "You've been so grim since he died—it must have hit you terribly hard."

Mack said nothing. His expression never changed. She thought he'd reached bottom when his son disappeared but it was worse now. Mack's skin was yellowing, and huge dark rings showed under his eyes. James Macklin Chance, age forty, looked like an invalid.

Near the parked autos, a man in a cloth cap adjusted a box camera on a tripod. He uncapped the lens and raised his holder of flash powder. "Mr. Chance? This way, if you don't mind."

Mack ran at him, kicked his tripod, and rubbed dirt on the lens. He and Margaret sped off in the black Olds.

68 "ABRAHAM RUEF, YOU HAVE HEARD THE VERDICT of the jury in this case. You are hereby sentenced to confinement in the state prison at San Quentin for the maximum term specified for the crime of bribery, fourteen years."

Judge Lawlor rapped the gavel once.

The Boss grabbed the arm of Henry Ach, his defense attorney. The trial had ended two weeks ago. Gallagher's testimony had established Ruef's guilt beyond question.

"It's an outrage—we'll appeal," Ach shouted. Reporters broke for the rear of the courtroom like track sprinters, several jostling Mack as he left his aisle seat. An exuberant Fremont Older pummeled his shoulder. "Got him, by God. Told you we would."

Hiram Johnson, the stout and florid Sacramento lawyer who'd taken over for Heney, began to gather and stack his various notes and depositions with neat, crisp motions. People pumped his hand. Three men in blue surrounded Boss Ruef and swept him toward a side door. Ruef traveled to and from jail under heavy police guard.

Mack put on his derby. The Boss spied him and stopped. One of the policemen ordered him on. Ruef ignored him, quickly walking over to lean across an empty press table. His eyes were moist and shiny. "Well, are we quits?"

"I'd give you a hundred years if it were up to me."

Ruef looked affronted. Then the police dragged him away.

Mack walked down the stairs at Greenwich Street. He'd packed one old leather valise. Señora Olivar stood just inside the parlor, tensely twisting and squeezing her apron. She watched Mack's face, hunting for some sign of a reprieve.

Instead, he pressed an envelope into her hand. "That's for Christmas. Alex will send your wages every week, as usual." Alex and his wife had left for Riverside three days before.

"When will you be back, Señor?"

"I don't know. I'm sick of this town."

Under a winter half-moon, Mack drove through the outskirts of San Jose. A couple of revelers lurching from a roadside tavern waved and shouted, "Merry Christmas, Merry Christmas,'' but Mack didn't return the greeting. He drove on past the little island of red and green lights. Christmas night was nothing special. Just a night to put more miles behind his car. A night to drive the bumpy roads as long as he could before pulling over to sleep with his hand on the Shopkeeper's Colt in his overcoat pocket.

On New Year's Day, after two road breakdowns, Mack's mud-spattered Oldsmobile coughed and strained up the last few hundred yards of winding road to Villa Mediterranean.

The servants tried to greet him cheerily, but the unspoken reaction was shock and dismay; their employer was haggard and sallow.

Mack handed over his valise and opened the office. Alex had been in, obviously. Papers and files were stacked and marked with notes written in his small, precise hand, indicating the priority of each batch.

He unlatched shutters. Shafts of winter light touched the desk, and *The Emigrant's Guide to California & Its Gold Fields.* Mack picked it up and blew on the cover. A little puff of dust arose. Suddenly he hurled it against the wall.

He dragged a chair to the window and sat in the sunshine, staring out. Staring inward, at his confrontation with Carla.

The scene played and then repeated, like a film loop on a nickelodeon screen inside his head. Sometimes he stopped the image, froze it, to better examine Carla's face at the moment she told him. He wanted to discover little signs of deception, falsehood. But he'd lived with her; he could tell—there were no such signs. He saw instead hysteria, and raw spite. She wasn't lying about Jim. She'd picked her longest, sharpest knife and put it in his vitals to the hilt. He could feel it there. He'd never get it out.

IX

SMASHING THE MACHINE

1909–1910

The movies fled west. They fled from the wilds of New Jersey, and grubby studios like Biograph's in a converted piano show-room on Fourteenth Street, New York. They fled the confine-ment of winter weather, endless days and weeks without sunshine, and they fled with even greater alacrity from the wrath of Thomas Edison, his writs, and his lawyers.

Edison had little to do with the invention of motion-picture cameras and projectors, generally scorning them as trivialities. But he was a canny businessman, always willing to lend his name to inventions that might make money, and when produc-ers of silent movies began copying the design of Edison equip-ment and constructing duplicates, even selling the clones as their own, the inventor went into a frenzy. He claimed his mo-tor design and the film-loop design were stolen. He couldn't claim the film—that was made by Eastman—but he insisted the sprocket holes were patented.

In 1907, a federal court in Chicago held that independent producer William Selig had violated Edison camera patents. Like many of the early producers, "Colonel" Selig was a brawler, not inclined to shrug and accept defeat. He organized a production unit and sent it where he thought no Edison law-yers would pursue: over the Rockies to California.

Other independents read the lesson of the Selig case. If they bucked Edison, they foresaw endless harassment—endless in-terference with production and profits. Led by the powerful Biograph, seven of them amalgamated to make peace with the famous inventor. They would pay him royalties and, in return, would be the exclusive licensees of his equipment. Producers who weren't members of their little club were forbidden to use the equipment under any circumstances.

Thus was born the Motion Picture Patents Company, a mo-nopoly, soon to be nicknamed "the Patents Trust." Its ap-pearance in 1908 sent a horde of independents westward, where Selig had gone. But Patents Company goons scouted out their secret locations in California and the Southwest and interfered with production; they liked to pump bullets into the camera, just to make sure the picture was never finished.

Eventually, the Patents Company perished, trust-busting un-der the Sherman Act hammering some of the nails into its cof-

fin. But in its day, the Patents Company drove many a moviemaker to California, while others such as Biograph and Essanay, Vitagraph and Kalem, comfortably established as members of the trust, went west for the greater productivity afforded by good weather year-round. The various producing companies were so delighted with results that wintering in California became an annual rite.

By the 1920s, Southern California had become the industry's permanent home. The movies, too, had struck a vein of California gold.

ON A BRIGHT, BRISK MORNING IN NOVEMBER 1909, **69** Mack and Alex Muller cantered down the foothill drive on saddle horses.

Mack wore jeans and a faded denim shirt, red neckerchief, and leather vest. The months in Southern California had restored his color. He enjoyed these morning meetings on horseback. Alex didn't; as usual, he looked fretful on his piebald. He also looked peculiar, sitting in his saddle in suit, waistcoat, and cravat.

Behind them, Villa Mediterranean presented a changed appearance. Ironworkers had torn out the *JMC* cartouche in the gate and filled the gap, and masons had chiseled the cartouches from the house, then repaired and painted the stucco.

Ahead, the luminous light of early morning lay on the orange groves, pencil lines of smoke showing just above the treetops; the previous night, when an early frost threatened, the burners had been set out. Now Mack's white and Mexican laborers were sleepily piling the burners back into wagons.

"What's first?"

Alex pulled out his neatly written agenda for the horseback meeting. These days he lived in a cottage at the foot of Mount Rubidoux, the proud if somewhat exhausted father of twin boys.

"We had a letter from Mr. Flintman, the bookkeeper at the tabernacle. He questioned the sum on our last oil royalty. I went over the statements. He was simply misreading one figure, so I telephoned and corrected him. He was extremely agitated over the mistake. To me he sounded like a man who suffers if he misplaces three pennies."

Mack laughed. "How are the sun worshipers doing? I don't keep track."

"The tabernacle is the largest nondenominational church in all of Southern California, I understand."

"Don't call it a church. It's a cult, a damned fraud. Someday they'll catch up to Wyatt."

"Meantime, it's said that he lives like a rajah."

"He would. What's next?"

They walked their mounts into a lane between the trees. The manager, Billy Biggerstaff, and two Mexicans called to them and waved. Mack returned the greeting while Alex bent over his paper, which kept him from hitting his head on a branch six inches above. He never saw it.

"Captain Norheim requests severance if you have no plans to take the yacht out of dry dock."

"I don't. Let him go. Pay him generously."

"Very good, I'll take care of it. Mr. Anderson writes, asking that you visit the new studio at your early convenience."

Mack had put $50,000 into the Essanay studio in the East Bay. He'd also shared the opportunity with Giannini at the Bank of Italy. The shrewd little banker had interviewed Anderson, then put in $15,000. Giannini's enthusiasm for movies matched Mack's.

"I'll see it when I go north again. Or *if*."

"You are a major stockholder, sir. Shouldn't you inspect your property?"

"I trust Anderson. I liked the scenario for the one-reeler that he sent last week. He's calling his Western character Broncho Billy."

Alex missed that. He was preoccupied, not to say bug-eyed behind his pince-nez. A green snake was wriggling along between the horses. Alex loved California, but he preferred to enjoy its natural aspects indoors, with his eyes jammed to a stereopticon.

Again he consulted the paper. "Wardlow Brothers. On Monday they will have final schematics and cost estimates for the new irrigation system at Fresno."

Mack pondered. "I suppose I'll go ahead. It's a big outlay, though. New reservoirs and canals and dikes and spillways—"

"But the system will make the ranch a showplace for the Valley."

Mack's voice hardened. "Who am I going to show it to?"

Chastised, Alex lowered his head over the paper. "Selwyn Flyshack's assistant telephoned from the Pinkerton office in Los Angeles."

"And?"

"Nothing to report. It was just the required weekly call."

Mack no longer took the calls himself. In August, Flyshack had delegated them to an underling. The Pinkertons had almost relegated the case to inactive status. Who could blame them? No one liked failure.

"One bit of good news," Alex said in a hopeful way. "Miss Emerson telegraphed last night. She will arrive on vacation shortly after the first of the year."

That seemed to restore Mack's spirits somewhat. "I've been inviting her all year. I'll be glad to see her. Are we finished?"

"Yes, sir. Except for a reminder of your appointment at two this afternoon. The gentlemen from the Lincoln-Roosevelt league."

"Hell. I forgot. I don't want to see them. I only let them come for the sake of politeness."

The three visitors were white, Republican, and prosperously dressed. Their spats, cravats, and buttoned waistcoats didn't fit the Italian-Spanish atmosphere of the living room, and clashed strongly with the attire of their host, who looked like a seedy cowhand.

Dorian Stimson, young and earnest, was a Harvard-educated lawyer Mack knew slightly through Enrique Potter. They'd talked at some length when Mack was a guest and Stimson the speaker at a meeting of the Christian Socialist Economic League, the Los Angeles organization of Dr. John Randolph Haynes. Haynes was a remarkable, complex man Mack admired because he somehow balanced passionate Fabian socialism with a lucrative surgical practice and great success as a real estate speculator.

The second visitor, Max Margolis, was a dry-goods magnate with seventeen stores from Ventura to San Diego, and a power in the Los Angeles Good Government Group. The third man, Randall Noone, edited the *Modesto Annunciator.*

After Mack served whiskey and they took care of pleasantries—what fine orange groves; what a magnificent house; what an interesting train ride out to Riverside—Stimson spoke for the visitors.

"You know that Republicans have organized a League of Lincoln-Roosevelt Clubs throughout California, Mr. Chance."

"I do," Mack said.

"We have done so for one purpose. A year from this very month, we must return our state to the people. We must do it by instituting reforms, and by once and for all defeating every candidate promoted by the SP."

"Most important, we must elect a governor," Noone said.

Stimson walked back and forth in front of the vast hearth, clearly confident of his own persuasive powers. "Hiram Johnson has agreed to run. He did a superb job standing in for Francis Heney while Heney recuperated from his bullet wound. Johnson will likely be the prosecutor given the credit when Boss Ruef finally goes to San Quentin."

Margolis said, "And it's a damn rotten shame that he hasn't."

A shaft of sun from a high window lit Mack's white hair as he leaned against the tan wall. "There are a lot of good lawyers in California."

"You have a right to be sardonic," Stimson said. "The delays and maneuverings are scandalous. But it's due process, and when it has run its course, Ruef will fall. Ruef will go to prison, I guarantee it. Back to the point, if we may. Hiram Johnson. He's an ideal candidate. He's state vice president of our league. A tough, experienced man."

Randall Noone said, "You can measure the depth of Hiram's commitment by understanding the personal cost of his decision. You know his father, Grove, has a big law practice in Sacramento, and he's pro-railroad. Grove is furious with his son. But Hiram is still willing to go ahead."

"So are we all," Stimson said. "Last year, for six months, we pleaded and argued and lobbied in Sacramento, and the legislature finally, reluctantly enacted the direct primary system into law. Primaries will take the nomination process out of the hands of the corrupt state conventions, which the SP usually dominates. That's step one. Step two is this: Win the 1910 elections. That requires candidates, and good men standing behind them. We're here to recruit you as one of the latter, Mr. Chance. We need you in the Lincoln-Roosevelt league. We particularly need your influence up in San Francisco. And— I'll be frank—we need your money."

"But I'm living in Southern California. I have no plans to go back."

Stimson squared off in front of Mack like a debater. "Enrique Potter said I'd have a hard time selling you. But please consider carefully before you refuse. A decade ago, the citizens of California won significant victories over the SP—the Los Angeles harbor decision, the defeat of Huntington's scheme to cancel the debt. But the Octopus is still huge—and powerful."

"Damned arrogant too," Margolis said. "They slung most of the mud at the Good Government Group. Sneered and called us the Goo-Goos—"

"It's intolerable," Stimson said. "And we won't tolerate it. Not any longer."

"Mr. Stimson—gentlemen—I admire your zeal. And I don't disagree. I believe every word. But you must also believe me. I've fought enough battles. I'm tired of fighting."

Dismayed, the three proper Republicans exchanged looks.

Noone, the editor, said, "Your friend Rudolph Spreckels is one of us. Jim Phelan too."

"I admire them for it. It doesn't change anything."

With sharply reduced enthusiasm, Stimson said, "Do I understand that you're saying no?"

"That's exactly what I'm saying. Have a pleasant trip back to Los Angeles, gentlemen."

MARGARET EMERSON ARRIVED ON THE SLEEPER **70** from San Francisco. Stepping down into sunshine and billowing steam, she was the very picture of Parisian style. Her travel suit was dark-brown wool, and a beige blouse with a jabot and a tight high collar enhanced the long graceful line of her neck. Brown gloves, brown silk parasol, brown straw hat with brown plumes—everything matched.

She threw herself into Mack's arms for a long hug. "It's so wonderful to see you."

"I thought you'd never take me up on my invitation. I'm glad you did."

"How are you?"

"About the same. This way."

They passed from under the eaves of the platform and she watched sunlight strike him. Physically he looked much improved, but those eyes were still dead. Margaret's bubbling excitement turned to pain.

He stowed her suitcases in the rear of his newest automobile, a four-wheeled yacht of a car, a Packard landau, brilliant yellow, with black fenders and trim and Packard's stylish hex-shaped hubcaps. "I thought we'd spend the day sightseeing, then drive to Redondo Beach for the night. I reserved two suites," he added in an offhand way. She got the point.

Mack sped the open Packard away from the SP depot. Minutes later, he was weaving through downtown traffic. He shot around one of the big red cars of the Pacific Electric interurban system, and the motorman clanged his bell defensively. Margaret hung on to her hat and her seat cushion, gasping.

"You're a demon. What's the speed limit?"

"Six miles an hour downtown, thirty everywhere else. I can't stand to go that slowly."

The Packard threaded through openings Margaret thought impossible. Mack was a fine driver, and never endangered pedestrians. Still, he hunched at the big wheel as if he had some unseen presence on his shoulder.

"This is my first visit to Los Angeles," she said. "It's huge. I pictured adobes, and cows wandering the streets."

"I saw it that way in the eighties. There are three hundred and fifty thousand people, maybe more. We get a dozen or so off the trains every day." He motored past the *Times*, now headquartered in a massive dark-red building crowned by brick turrets and battlements. "The unofficial capital of Otistown. The general's commission in the Philippines went to his head. Notice the sentry box at the front door? He calls this place the Fortress. His home's the Bivouac. Inside, they keep fifty or sixty high-power rifles."

"Whatever for?"

"For the day the mad anarchist trade-union dogs rise up and attack," Mack said with a wink.

He drove through streets of small neat homes with derricks pumping noisily in backyards. He showed her the well he'd dug for Doheny, "one of the richest men in the state now." Next he pointed out some of his own wells. In the late forenoon, he took her by Echo Park Lake. Sunshine painted rainbows on the heavy oil slick. "Someday all that seepage will catch fire."

He showed her Angel's Flight, the cable railway that ascended Bunker Hill. When he offered to take her to the Alligator Farm on the east side, she declined.

"All right, but you can't experience Southern California fully unless you see something bizarre. Tell you what. Before you leave, we'll go to Pasadena and I'll show you the headquarters of a cult. I've told you about my old partner, haven't I?"

They ate pork loin, vegetables, potatoes, and gravy at Brown's Union Square Cafeteria, a new kind of restaurant without table service. They pushed their trays along a shelf in front of neatly cased displays of food, selecting only what they wanted, and paid the cashier at the end of the line.

"Another new California idea," he said. It was hard to make himself heard. The Michigan Society was holding a meeting at several nearby tables. The Grand Wolverine, as his satin sash proclaimed him, extolled the state from which he and all his listeners had fled. At every mention of Michigan, the audience stamped, clapped, and clanged silverware against water glasses.

"I guess they love snow now that they don't have to shovel it," Mack said.

They drove out to Washington and Grand. "Biograph is filming there. They've sent a whole crew from New York for the winter, to take advantage of our sunshine. The picture they're doing is called *In Old California*. They want to shoot at the San Gabriel mission, and on some property I own in the Hollywood hills."

Mack didn't mention that most of Riverside considered him crazy for putting money in moving pictures, or having anything to do with them. "Still a novelty, and a trashy one," Clive Henley said. "It's a business run by a lot of ghetto Jews from New York.. Glove merchants. Rag pickers. Dirty little sheenies, the lot of them."

"Your bigotry and snobbery are showing, Clive," Mack said in reply. "Also the moss on your back."

Clive sniffed. "If you want to chum around with Jews and low-life actresses, don't come to me complaining you've caught some disease."

Clive was trying to be humorous, but he came through as merely crude. Mack didn't like him very much anymore. Nor did he like the constant attacks by the solid men of Riverside, the badgering he took because he held strong opinions and refused to run with the herd. He'd resigned from the polo club because of it.

They found the Biograph Company working on a wooden-walled stage on a lot next to a lumberyard. There seemed to be a great deal of commotion. Actors and actresses rushed back and forth from four wooden huts to the stage, costumed as señoritas, friars, Spanish dons. Mack handed Margaret a business card.

"That's the man I have to see. Mike Sinnott."

"This says Mack Sennett."

"They all have professional names. Sinnott's an assistant to the director. Also a bit player and scenario writer. So he said on the telephone, anyway."

They stepped onto the stage, suddenly immersed in the noise of many conversations and the rapping hammers of carpenters finishing a row of flats. The flats represented an *hacienda* interior. The roof of the stage was open to the sun, but hung with long linen battens to diffuse the light.

"Sinnott?" Mack said to a girl rushing by with an armload of monk's habits. She pointed to a burly bare-headed man with long, simian arms and rough features. He was talking to a little

611

man with a cap and a tall, beak-nosed fellow of thirty-five or so. Striking rather than handsome, the tall man drew the eye because he wore a suit, cravat, and straw hat. Everyone else was in old clothes or costumed for the picture.

The gent in the straw hat leaned an elbow on the great box of the camera, puffing a cigarette and gesturing like some languid dandy. Those around him hung on his words. "Must be the director," Mack said.

The conference ended and Sinnott broke away. Mack introduced himself and pulled a document from his coat. "My lawyer, Mr. Potter, made one or two small changes in the location contract. I initialed them and signed it. I'll expect the hundred-dollar fee by the end of the week."

"Right you are, Mr. Chance. Would you and the lady like to meet our principals?"

He introduced them to a handsome young actor named Jack Pickford, and his sister Mary, an ingenue of striking beauty, who was perhaps fifteen or sixteen. Then he presented them to the little man in the cap, the cameraman, Bitzer, and the director, Mr. Griffith. "Welcome to the Biograph lot, Mr. Chance, Miss Emerson." Mack heard the South in Griffith's voice.

"We're all set with that fine location in Hollywood," Sinnott advised his boss. "Mr. Chance and I struck a deal in ten minutes."

"Two Macks certainly ought to get along, don't you think? Where are you from, sir?"

"At the moment, Riverside. You?"

"I was born on a plantation in Oldham County, Kentucky, about twenty miles from Louisville. I'm proud to say the blood of the old Confederacy flows in my veins. My father fought for the white race in the First Kentucky Cavalry. He rode for Bedford Forrest and Joe Wheeler. What about you, Miss Emerson?"

"Northern California."

The director fondled Margaret's chin in a familiar way. It annoyed Mack, and made Miss Pickford pout like a jealous lover. "What a smile you have," Griffith said. "If you'd like to go waltzing some evening, leave a message at the Alexandria Hotel down on Spring Street."

It was lighthearted, superficially a joking invitation. But Griffith's eye feasted on Margaret. Mary Pickford said sweetly, "Will Mrs. Griffith let you out, D.W.?"

Griffith shot her a look. "I love you too, Mary," he said,

turning his back on the little girl with curls. Jack Pickford pulled at his sweaty monk's habit and snickered.

All charm again, Griffith shook Mack's hand and smiled at Margaret. "Guard her, Mr. Chance. If you don't, someone will steal her."

He kissed her hand, about-faced smartly, and clapped three times. "All right, ladies and gentlemen. Jack, Mary, Wally—rehearsal, please."

They watched for an hour. Margaret was fascinated by the actors, the orderly disorder, the hand-cranked camera, and Griffith's absolute command of every detail. The director deliberated before each shot. He argued with Bitzer but seldom gave in. A general in charge of a raffish army, when he worked he was blunt, even biting if something went wrong, quite different from the courtly Southerner who'd tipped his hat and flattered Margaret.

"What an attractive man," she said as they left the stage.

"I didn't like his crack about defending the white race."

"No. But did you notice that lovely Pickford girl? She's mad for him."

"She and three or four others I saw mooning over him. Marriage doesn't seem to keep his eye from roving."

"You sound like a grumpy old prude. Marriage doesn't interfere with my customers at the Maison either. They come in spite of it."

"Or because of it."

She laughed, but he didn't.

The January afternoon grew cool, the shadows long and sharp, the light a deepening gold, and melancholy. On the way out to the ocean, he pulled to the roadside near a large colorful billboard. While he raised the folding top and latched it to the wind screen, Margaret studied the board. Painted aircraft filled a painted sky—fanciful dirigibles, balloons with gondolas, monoplanes and biplanes with translucent ribbed wings.

FIRST IN AMERICA!
AVIATION MEET
LOS ANGELES   JANUARY 10–20

"What's an aviation meet?" she asked as they started up.

"A big exhibition with races, demonstrations, time trials, that sort of thing. The Hearst paper in Los Angeles is sponsoring it. Glenn Curtiss is bringing a replica of the *Golden*

613

Flyer, the plane he flew to win the Gordon Bennett Cup at Rheims. Louis Paulhan's coming from France. It's shaping up to be quite an event."

"I've read a lot about flying machines. I'd never want to ride in one but I'd love to see them. Could we go?"

"I suppose. We might as well. I've no family to entertain you while you're here. Nor any close friends, for that matter."

"Have you heard from H.B.?"

"Not since he left."

Mack sped the Packard down the dirt highway. He caught up with a bicyclist and honked him out of the way. Margaret frowned and held on, and soon she was gasping again, clutching any available handhold while her cheeks paled and her heart raced. She exclaimed over the noise, "It'll be a wonderful vacation if I live through it."

The clerk at the Redondo Lodge showed them to adjoining suites without comment. Mack immediately noticed a connecting door.

They unpacked, changed from their dusty clothes, and walked down to the shore of Santa Monica Bay. An orange winter sky reflected in the silver water and high waves broke and roared toward the wet shingle. Two young men in tight striped bathing costumes balanced precariously on prow-shaped boards atop the rushing waves.

"What on earth are they doing?"

"It's something called surf riding. Brand new. There's always something new out here."

They watched the spray-soaked surf riders on the crests of their waves, tilting from side to side with arms out for balance, laughing in their strength and their youth. Margaret slipped her arm through Mack's, and he could feel the roundness of her breast touching him. He didn't pull away.

They ate in the cozy wood-paneled dining room of the lodge. Mack was surprised to find Sonoma Creek cabernet listed among the offerings of the small cellar. They drank one bottle with their abalone steaks, and then a second, and both of them were weaving a little as they went up to bed. Margaret gave him a polite good-night kiss on the cheek and went to her door with her own key.

He'd drunk too much. He fell asleep facedown on the bed, still in his clothes. Sometime later he heard tapping on the connecting door. Opening it, he saw Margaret with the small bedside candle in its brass holder; the lodge was not electrified.

Her nightgown was white as a bride's, her nipples dark and large as dollar pieces beneath.

"Margaret—"

She put her palm on his mouth.

When she was sure she'd quieted him, she kissed him, and he could smell her hair and her skin. He flung off his clothes. She blew out the candle, and soon she was astride him.

They slept a while. When they woke he held her in his arms.

"Margaret."

"Yes?"

"We mustn't do that again. Ever."

"No. But I had to do it once."

She kissed him, her auburn hair tumbling down on his naked shoulders. "Thank you, my love."

She left the warm tangled bed, and a moment later the connecting door closed. In the morning she was refreshed, humming as they walked down to breakfast.

"What a lovely dream I had, Mack. I dreamed you and I made love. We made a little bargain beforehand too. I'd sleep with you if you would take me to see the airplanes. Yesterday, you didn't sound at all enthusiastic. I thought you loved new inventions."

"I do," he said with surprising vigor. He'd shaved clean and close, put on fresh linen. Despite the wine he had no hangover. For the first time in months, he felt better.

"Good, it's settled." To the waiter she said, "A table in the sunshine, please."

A THREE-CAR PACIFIC ELECTRIC SPECIAL ARRIVED AT **71** Dominguez Junction every 120 seconds. From there it was a half-mile hike up a muddy road to the flat summit of Dominguez Hill. Promoters of the air meet had constructed a grandstand to hold twenty-six thousand, a three-mile wire fence to protect spectators from taxiing aircraft, and an area of large exhibition tents behind the stands. Special telephone lines linked the site to the city room of the *Los Angeles Examiner*. Concession booths lined both sides of the auto road leading to the hilltop. The promoters christened it Aviation Park.

From a modest twenty thousand or so on opening day, attendance jumped to forty thousand a day by the end of the first week. On Sunday, a boy and an older man squeezed in with many others aboard one of the P.E. specials from downtown. The boy's left shoulder dipped noticeably each time he put his weight on his left foot. The man used a cane and moved stiffly because of arthritis. He was tall, and so was the eleven-year-old with the handsome face, blond hair, and dark-blue eyes. Both seemed to be crippled. People took them for relatives.

The boy went by the name Jim David, the first name that had come into his head when the older man asked what to call him. The man was called Jocker Sprue, though that wasn't his real first name. "I was named for various thimble-riggers, money-grubbers, and whited sepulchers among my ancestors in the tidewater of Virginia. My full name, I regret to say, is Arlington Arvide Murtha Sprue," he said once, when Jim asked the question. "Is that a mother's triple sin against her offspring, or isn't it?"

Jocker was the tall man who had created such an impression of terror in those vividly remembered moments just before the Valencia Street Hotel collapsed and a wall came down on them in the alley. Jocker had flung himself on top of Jim instinctively, and being more agile then, and powerfully strong from living a rough life in hobo jungles, he protected Jim in those moments when lath and plaster, siding and flooring and roofing and even a bed fell and buried them.

Jim had been knocked out for a while, waking to darkness, choking dust, and the weight of Jocker and the rubble on top of him.

"Shout, boy," came Jocker's hoarse voice in the dark. "Shout and pray to God somebody pays attention. It's an earthquake, and a bad one."

They yelled, "Help, under here, somebody help," for what seemed like hours, meantime listening to a growing cacophony of sounds: fires crackling, injured or dying hotel guests moaning and pleading, people running and yelling in fear. Finally Jim felt he could yell no more and, in a gasp, said so. The unseen man whose weight was grinding down on him managed to grasp his shoulder and squeeze it—an excruciating pain.

"Don't you say that, don't you give up on me, you yell your throat raw, you yell till you pass out from yelling, or we won't get out of here."

Jim yelled.

Finally, ready to weep with exhaustion, he heard the tall man exclaim, "Somebody's out there." And then he heard a second, more distant voice:

"No, Harry, back here, under that bedstead in the alley. I distinctly heard a voice."

Two dusty, sweaty San Francisco policemen dug them out with the help of another man. Jocker said his back was sprained, but he straightened up readily enough when the police asked his name. "Arthur Jones. We're grateful to you, officers," he said, dragging Jim away.

They emerged into the nightmare of Market Street with the great fire burning immediately to the south, and other fires over by the Bay. But they were alive, and Jim was too frightened and grateful to disobey the tall man with the long locks when he whispered, "You take my hand, boy. Jocker's got you now, and he'll look after you. Don't you question me, or so much as look cross-eyed, because I've got to pick some pockets so we can get enough money for two ferry passages to Oakland. I hope to God the ferry's running, because this side of the Bay looks like an inferno. Doomed."

On Market Street, in the milling crowds, Jim thought he saw his father at one point. He almost called out, but the crowd shifted so fast that he couldn't be sure it was Mack, and he wasn't certain whether he wanted to be back with him now that he was alive, albeit bruised and gashed from his stay under the rubble. Besides, Jocker had one fingerless glove wrapped around his hand tight as a vise, to be sure they wouldn't be separated in the confusion.

On Market Street that morning, Jim was introduced to one of the hobo's unusual skills. Jocker successfully filched $5— from the purse of a sightseeing woman, no less—without detection, and they escaped to Oakland on a noon ferry.

It was on the ferry ride that Jocker asked his name, and he invented Jim David. He told Jocker that his folks were dead.

"If you say so," Jocker replied with a snaggly smile; his teeth were white—later Jim learned he brushed them once a day, even if he had to use a twig and water—but he was missing a couple in front. "If you were a street boy, your face'd be weathered and your hands'd be callused. Which they aren't. All right with me, though, if you ran away. We won't go into it. I did the same thing when I was just a mite older than you. Oil and water don't mix, and I determined at a pretty early age that Sprue and responsibility of any sort would never mix either."

He leaned on the rail among the horrified crowds and watched the smoke and flame above the receding city.

"I've ridden the rods with a couple of boys, but neither was

617

as quick and sturdy as you seem to be. So here's the arrangement. You try to run off, I'll catch you and whip you. You stick by me, I'll take good care of you. I've never seriously hurt one of my boys, or harmed 'em in a nasty bodily way. Never touched one, in fact, unless it was to give a little discipline—or maybe a little necessary affection,'' he added, slipping the arm of his queer patchwork coat around Jim's shoulder. ''Sort of like a father, don't you know.'' He said that so softly, Jim almost didn't hear it above the slap of the waves and the churn of the engines.

''I think we'll get along fine,'' Jocker decided then. ''You'll have to fetch and carry for me—I'm not getting any younger, and this blasted arthritis is cruel—but you'll eat more or less regularly, and you'll sleep safe, out of the weather most of the time, and you'll be safe from some of the less savory brethren we'll bump into in the hobo jungles. Old Jocker, he'll see to it, Jim David.''

He squeezed the boy again. His sleeve was coated with dust from the Valencia Street wreckage, and it left a white mark all across Jim's shoulders, like a brand. But Jim didn't see it, and he was not at all unhappy to have fallen into the company of the peculiar, untidy, but oddly likable old tramp.

They lived for two weeks in the vicinity of the Oakland rail yards, and for five nights actually had a splendid warm residence inside an empty boxcar that bore a painted legend on its sides.

TO THE CALIFORNIA SUFFERERS FROM THE PEOPLES OF IOWA

Finally, though, Jocker declared that they must move on. ''Thought we'd find some nice pickings after the quake, but there's too many soldier boys all over the place. Time we went where it's warmer. My arthritis craves the sunshine.''

And so they began to move eastward. It was exciting to travel the way Jocker did, but it was dangerous too. The old tramp taught Jim how to swing aboard a freight when it was moving slowly—not as easy as it looked; the first time Jim tried it, it wrenched his arm sockets so badly, he almost fell beneath the wheels of the boxcar. Hanging in the door, Jocker pulled him up one-handed.

Jocker taught him how to ride the rods, down between the bottom of a locked car and the track speeding beneath, and do it without falling to your death. He taught Jim how to pluck a stolen chicken, cook hobo stew, and dodge the railroad bulls who always wanted to roust you, and sometimes beat you half to death, in the yards. Jim learned fast—it was that or perish— and he tried doubly hard to master the old tramp's lessons because he fancied himself a drag on their progress; his crippled foot naturally made him slower and more awkward than Jocker. Jocker never complained, though, only encouraged and occasionally corrected him.

They went all the way down to the Gulf near the Mexican border, then east again through the Texas cattle ranges and cotton fields, and on across Louisiana and the rural South, into Florida. They roamed the pristine Atlantic beaches for a while, swimming and rollicking in the surf and catching and picking big Atlantic blue crabs for supper. Wherever they went, they lived off the land, stealing when they had to—"Man should only resort to stealing out of necessity, Jim, never for the sport of it"—and Jocker was good as his word, protecting Jim from the occasional advances of some unsavory love-starved hobo in the camps along the railway lines.

Jocker was an entertaining companion, Jim found, and a smart one too, despite his lack of formal education. He read any old newspaper he could find, every word—"the poor man's university, don't you forget it"—and he knew a little about every part of America, it seemed. At least he always had a comment when some hobo spun a story by a flickering fire about some town he'd visited. "Buffalo, you say? I was there with a couple of gents called Captain Silverheels and the Gray Spats Kid. Wouldn't give you a plug nickel for Buffalo—too cold. They don't like us knights of the road there either. That famous writer Jack London, he was in jail in Buffalo a whole month. He was a road boy like Jim here. He saw how bad the jail cons were treated in Buffalo and it turned on a light in his head, they say. Ever after, he championed poor folks."

Finally they grew tired of road life, and decided between themselves that they should settle down again. They chose California, and specifically Los Angeles, because of the climate. By now Jim was growing taller, and there was very little of master and slave left in their relationship. They were friends, partners, surrogate father and son.

In Los Angeles, Jim found this or that job to help pay rent and buy food. He was industrious and smart, and he seldom lacked for work. Jocker worked when he could, but his arthritis was beginning to cripple him badly, so Jim worked that much harder. He was hugely fond of Jocker now; except for the fact that Jocker wasn't his real father, Jim loved the old tramp almost as much as he'd loved Mack before Mack turned on him.

Of his mother, Jim thought very little; he had seen newspaper photographs of her, he knew she was beautiful, a society lady, and was still living somewhere in California. But Mack had made clear that Jim's mother had abandoned them for her own pursuits, and her own reasons, and to Jim, she was a remote, cold being, almost like a marble statue in a museum. That was mostly imagination, of course, because he'd never been inside a museum, only read of them; Jocker preferred pool parlors.

Occasionally too, in the papers, Jim spied his father's name. The sight of it filled him with much more sadness and anger than did any photo of his mother. Why had his father hated him? Because of failings in himself? He felt that was true, though he was still too young to puzzle out the nature of those failings and try to change them. But it hardly mattered. He had a new life, a free life. He had long ago decided he'd never go back to the old one.

Now, on the day the P.E. special bore them to the aviation fair, Jim and Jocker both had good jobs in suburban Pasadena. Jim loved being out in the sunshine, learning about and working with the exotic trees and shrubs and flowers of Southern California. Finally, he felt, life was going in the right direction for him. He'd be twelve in the autumn, but he looked two or three years older because of his height and the maturity of his features, and he was starting to get interested stares from young girls. He wasn't quite old enough to like girls, but he was surprised and vaguely flattered by their new reaction. When he discussed it with Jocker, the old tramp chuckled and said, "Yes, I know you aren't altogether keen for it now, but wait a while—you'll be crazy about it. Trust old Jocker."

"You know I do," Jim grinned, squeezing his gnarled hand.

The P.E. interurban slid into the two-hundred-foot platform specially built for the air show. Jim took Jocker's hand and helped him off, elbowing and pushing when necessary. The crowd was boisterous and impatient, and there was a lot of buffeting. Jim felt obliged to protect Jocker, because any rough contact made his joints hurt.

It was a cool, windy morning. Jim shielded his eyes, then pointed toward the hilltop. "Look, Jocker, some of the balloons are up. Don't you think it's grand?"

"I think I want to get this over with," the old tramp said. Jim had trimmed Jocker's hair for the outing, and Jocker had donned his only suit. But it was shiny at the knees and elbows, and he still looked seedy. "God didn't mean for Jocker Sprue to leave the ground in a basket dangling from a gas bag. Nor in anything similar. Got me?''

Laughing, Jim clasped his hand tightly and pulled him away from the platform. With whistles and bells, a special train was chugging into a siding, a locomotive and six flatcars carrying shiny autos chained down. Smartly dressed men and women sat in the autos. A banner on one flatcar said SAN DIEGO AERO-SHOW TRAIN. The gentlemen who owned the autos began to loosen the chains before the train stopped, excited about the air show.

Well, so was he. So was all of Los Angeles. Flying fever, people called it. In the comics that Jim read faithfully, his favorite, Little Nemo, was zooming through the sky in his own dirigible. On their way to change interurbans they'd passed a saloon advertising Aviation Highballs: TRY ONE—HAVE A MEN-TAL ASCENSION.

Strung tight with anticipation, young James Ohio Chance II—now Jim David—pulled the old man along the muddy road to the hilltop, ignoring his complaints.

It was hard going on the road. For one thing, recent winter rains had muddied it. For another, autos in a long line were attempting the ascent and having difficulty because of the mud. Three men with teams of mules worked the roadside, selling their services.

People on foot and on bicycles added to the congestion. Along both shoulders, hawkers shouted and beckoned from canvas booths, You could buy coffee and doughnuts, cheap field glasses, sunglasses, auto radiator caps shaped like airplanes. Jim wasn't tempted. He'd carefully saved money from his wages to pay their admissions—$1 would take them both into the grandstand—and buy a 10-cent program.

"Take heed," cried a man temporarily established on a soapbox. "The coming of the airplane will drive the birds from the skies. All species will become extinct because of this mechanical plague."

"Are the Wrights here?" a man in a mired auto asked. His companion said no, they had refused to attend.

Jim pulled Jocker faster than he wanted to go. A gluey brown mud covered their shoes. At the sound of distant staccato explosions, Jim jumped up and down and squeezed Jocker's misshapen hand.

"Those are engines, they're starting engines—we've got to hurry."

"I was happier riding the rods," Jocker said. But he labored to keep up with the boy.

Tons of sawdust had been thrown on the mud of the exhibit area. Tents sheltered the aircraft on display, and special policemen stood guard to prevent vandalism.

Glenn Curtiss had brought four of his biplanes, and there were three Bleriot monoplanes from France, as well as two Farman biplanes. One tent housed a balloon-gas plant, a mysterious and intricate tangle of tanks, pumps, and pipes. On open ground nearby, an eager young man lectured about his ornithopter, which resembled a unicycle with ribbed wings attached. The young man cleared the crowd away, slipped his arms into straps on the wings, and mounted the cycle seat. He started to flap the wings, and the ornithopter rolled forward perhaps two feet, then crashed sideways.

"See, Jim? Man was never meant to fly. Trains are perfectly good enough."

"Oh, come on," the boy said, grinning. "Let's pay and find a seat. I don't want to miss Curtiss."

Mack fought the Packard up the muddy auto road and paid $1 to park. You could watch the air demonstrations from your car but he'd bought a front-row grandstand box for $2. About half past twelve, he ushered Margaret into the box and opened a hamper in which the servants had packed a luncheon and two pair of German field glasses.

The speed course was hexagonal. One straightaway lay close and parallel to the wire fence, the other on the opposite side of the field. Ten-foot towers topped with snapping flags marked the course, and at the foot of each, a deputy with pistol and rifle sat on horseback. A youngster ran onto the field, and one of the deputies galloped to intercept him. The boy darted beneath the deputy's horse, thumbed his nose, and dug his way under the fence to safety before the deputy could dismount. Margaret laughed and the crowd applauded and whistled.

A lumbering three-hundred-pound man approached the fence and cupped his hands around his mouth.

"Mr. Horton of Long Beach," Mack said. "They call him the Human Megaphone."

"Ladies and gentlemen," the Human Megaphone boomed, "I direct your attention to the flying field. In the replica of his famous *Golden Flyer* air racer, Mr. Glenn H. Curtiss will attempt a new speed record around the course."

The stands roared. A biplane sheathed in khaki cloth taxied

622

onto the field, its sixty-horse engine chattering and stuttering. The plane, little more than a skeleton of wings and ribs and struts, had a box tail, tricycle gear, and a control wheel. There was no protection for the aviator, merely a small seat attached to the biplane's lower wing, behind a control wheel. Curtiss sat in the open, his feet braced against pedals. Swathed in a leather coat, scarf, and goggles, he controlled the biplane's elevator and rudder with the wheel, the brakes and oil pump with the pedals, the wingtip ailerons by means of a shoulder harness worn over his coat.

Mack adjusted his motoring cap to keep the winter sun out of his eyes. Curtiss waved to the crowd, then revved the engine; the biplane bumped and bounced over the ground, and lurched into the air.

Pandemonium. A woman in a nearby box fainted, and Mack's arms prickled with goose bumps. It was a thrilling sight. He pictured Southern California as he'd first seen it: rural, dusty, a frontier. Now autos and electric interurbans and flying machines were thrusting California, and the world, farther and farther from that lost past of memory.

Curtiss's biplane climbed above the towers and began to fly the course. When the biplane swooped over the closer straightaway, even sturdy men ducked. The motor roared and the great shadow flickered over upturned faces, the harbinger of the new world coming.

Curtiss failed to set a record that afternoon but he received a standing ovation anyway. When he landed, Mack stood and clapped till his palms ached.

Louis Paulhan took off next. Paulhan was a former circus tightrope walker and mechanic at the Voison airplane works in Paris. A year ago, he'd set a stunning distance and endurance mark, flying eighty-four miles in two hours, forty-four minutes.

Paulhan's Farman biplane was even more ungainly than Curtiss's, its wings and tail resembling gray-white box kites, its undercarriage consisting of wheels plus skids. A fifty-horsepower air-cooled Gnome engine powered it. And today, Paulhan carried a passenger. The Human Megaphone stepped forward.

"Riding with Mr. Paulhan is Lieutenant Finger of the United States Army. They will present a demonstration of the potential of airplane warfare."

The crowd quieted. A man in khaki strapped himself to the wing next to the aviator, his legs dangling over the leading edge.

"I wonder if Paulhan would take me up," Mack said.

"Would you really want to risk it?"

"Sure. Airplanes aren't a fad; they're here for good. We'll all go up regularly one day."

He could tell from Margaret's expression that she doubted it—and feared it if it were true.

The Farman rumbled out and took off, climbing over the field and then circling back on a course between and parallel to the straightaways. Lieutenant Finger leaned over and dropped a paper bag. It hit the ground and burst, shooting out a great cloud of white chalk dust.

"A simulation of dropping high explosives," explained the Human Megaphone. "Mr. Paulhan confirms that his aircraft can carry up to three hundred pounds of explosives." The crowd gasped.

The Farman banked and returned. Finger threw out three more paper bags, and they hit one after another, laying down overlapping circles of white. The crowd hushed again. Wind blew some of the dust, which covered an enormous area. Mack realized that if the plane had dropped bombs instead of chalk, there would be little left of anything at the point of impact.

"Fifty dollars?" Mack said.

"One hundred," said Paulhan. He was a cheerful young man of twenty-five or so with lively dark eyes and a perfect Gallic mustache waxed to points. His buxom wife, Celeste, and his mechanics, Didier and Edouard, hovered behind him.

"Done." Mack began to count out bills.

"Are you sure this is safe?" Margaret said.

"Why, I took Monsieur Hearst aloft yesterday; he is still alive," Paulhan said. "Strap yourself in place, Monsieur Chance."

Everything happened too hurriedly for Mack to be frightened. He left his cap with Margaret but kept his goggles. The mechanics spun the propeller, the Gnome motor made his eardrums throb, and he gripped the struts of the fragile wing as the ground raced by underneath. Cold wind beat his face. Paulhan lifted the Farman skyward and Mack's stomach dipped and churned.

He watched the grandstand swoop away and diminish and fields shrink to patterned squares. Paulhan turned west toward the ocean. Mack held tight with both hands, the fear waning. *What an incredible feeling. Angels must feel this way.*

They passed over farmhouses, arbors, the interurban line, racing toward the glittering ocean at incredible speed. Mack saw the land and sea from a perspective altogether new, but there was so much moment-by-moment excitement—the motor's roar, the battering wind, the constant dips and bumps of the biplane—he had no time to consciously examine sensations, only experience them.

"Two thousand feet," Paulhan shouted over the wind. The struts cut into Mack's white-knuckled hands. As the Farman shot away from the shoreline like a slingshot stone, he looked down with a new, dizzying feeling. Water—nothing but the herringbone wave pattern of dark-blue water beneath . . .

Paulhan banked south and pointed at a small fishing smack plowing to sea, then he sank the Farman, and Mack's belly with it. They flew fifty feet above the fishing boat, the fishermen waved, and Paulhan wagged his wings. Then the aircraft banked again, and Mack confronted the panorama of the California coast: surf, shore, green land, toy buildings, the distant mountains. It reminded him of the moment he came down from the Sierras. It was a magnificent, exalting sight.

Paulhan took note of his passenger's rapt expression and concentrated on flying.

"It's the most incredible experience I've ever had, Margaret." Mack was walking through the crowd with his arm around her. Utterly chilled after the flight, he'd dragged her off to search for a coffee booth.

"Didn't you think you'd fall off or crash?"

"Of course. Every minute. But I didn't care—"

Suddenly, in the aisle between concession tents, Mack dropped his arm from her waist. He was staring down the lane.

"What is it?"

"Someone who looks familiar." He bolted forward. "Wait right there."

He worked his way through the crowd, shoving, turning sideways, his eye fixed on the tall boy studying a display of souvenir pennants. Sunshine lit the boy's face like a medallion. The boy was fair, handsome, and browner than Carla had ever been. But her features were unmistakable.

"Jim?" Mack shouted, his heart pounding.

The boy turned and saw him. There was a rush of emotions Mack couldn't quite read—surprise, confusion, fear, perhaps.

"Jim— Damn it, out of my way." Mack manhandled a portly gentlemen eating cotton candy, and the man stumbled against him, smearing him with the sticky stuff and delaying him for ten seconds. Finally Mack got around him and ran up to the pennant display.

"Where'd that boy go? The one who was standing here?"

The concessionaire pointed down the lane between his booth and the next.

The lane was empty.

Panting, Jim limped along as fast as he could beneath the grandstand. He kept flinging looks over his shoulder, his deep-blue eyes full of panic. "Look out—one side—let me through."

He wasn't sure; he wasn't sure at all. He'd seen the face only as the briefest of blurs. Then the white-haired man called him by name. Of course there were a lot of Jims in the world. But he wasn't going to stand around and wait for the man to catch him. If it was his father, he wanted nothing to do with him.

Out of breath, he burst into the sunshine and raced up the grandstand steps. He grabbed the old tramp's hand, twisted as some root freshly dug from the ground.

"Jocker, let's go."

"What? What are you saying?"

"Come on, Jocker, right now. I'm sick to my stomach. I've got this fearful bellyache. So bad I'm like to die. Let's catch a train. I want to go back to Pasadena."

Jocker didn't object. They escaped on an empty P.E. red car without seeing the white-haired man again.

The fair was spoiled for Mack. Once Margaret understood what had happened, she readily consented to leave. "I'll drop you at a hotel for an hour," Mack said. "I'm going to the authorities before we drive back to Riverside. I *know* it was my son." He pounded the steering wheel and never thought twice about his choice of words. He'd accepted that quite probably Fairbanks was Jim's real father. But Jim remained his son.

The drowsy sheriff's deputy he spoke with late in the afternoon woke up when he heard Mack's name. The man was much less hostile than the San Francisco police crowd, but he wasn't encouraging:

"Yes, I grant you, a limp is a noticeable trait. But we can't send people house to house, Mr. Chance. So if the boy doesn't *want* to be found—if he's law-abiding, and doesn't attract attention—he may not be. We'll do our best, but please don't expect any miracles."

Refusing to be discouraged so easily, he called Pinkerton's and left a message for Flyshack with the man on duty. Then he telegraphed Alex Muller and ordered an updated reprinting of ten thousand copies of the old reward flyer.

A HAMMERED BRASS SUNBURST WITH RADIANT ARMS **72**
crowned the arch of the padlocked iron gate, and
sunlight slanting into Pasadena Canyon lit the device to shimmering brilliance.

Outside the gate, Mack and Margaret were tucked under a lap robe in Mack's smart Studebaker trap, the four shiny bay horses blowing out their breath in pale plumes. The long iron fence and meandering dirt road were in shadow. Even as they watched, the sun's angle changed and the sunburst darkened.

"The Tabernacle of the Sun Universal." Mack didn't hide his distaste. He touched the padlock with his long buggy whip. "Evidently not everyone is welcome."

"That's odd for a church."

"It isn't a real church. They do conduct weekly services, I understand. Up there, in that octagonal building." Still in the sunlight, the building shone on a terrace cut from the hill. The trim was white, the siding a soft butter yellow—sunny outdoor colors.

The tabernacle was reached by a dirt road that curved up the grassy slope from the gate. Windows ran around the building on both floors, flashing back the sun like signal mirrors. Two women in white robes, tiny as miniature dolls, emerged from the house and took a path to a cluster of cottages even more remote. The property was heavily treed and well tended. Six gardeners were visible pruning stands of white azalea and weeding flower beds.

"But they sell merchandise too," Mack went on. "Nostrums. Health gadgets. Quack stuff. They collect thousands of dollars from newcomers bedazzled by the sunshine and the rhetoric of my former partner. He runs the whole thing. Calls himself Brother Paul. He stole that sunburst from our San Solaro tract."

"Obviously you don't think he's sincere about what he does."

"Oh, yes. If there's one thing Wyatt is sincere about, it's making money."

"What I meant was, you don't believe there's anything to this cult."

"Sunshine does make people feel better. Sometimes it actually promotes recovery from illness. Should you have to pay someone to tell you that—as though it's some new gospel? I don't think so. Wyatt's a con artist, a crook." He picked up the reins. "Seen enough?"

"Yes, certainly."

Mack whistled to the four bays and the trap went briskly down the road, scattering gravel and tan dust behind it.

On the hillside near the octagonal house, the young gardener heard the noise of the trap and horses. He was kneeling on a walk of blue slate, weeding a bed where gardenias would bloom in warm weather.

Jim raised his head and studied the departing sightseers. A man and woman, that was all he could tell. Nothing unusual; they got plenty of rubberneckers up here. People showing Pasadena to visitors always included a drive past the tabernacle.

He watched the trap disappear on its way down to the main canyon road. Then he spent ten minutes finishing his chore. After the narrow escape from Dominguez Hill, things had settled down again. Jim had a calm, sequestered existence, and he liked it. He worked at educating himself by reading books from the public library, and he seldom saw people outside the tabernacle. He and Jocker went into Pasadena once every three or four weeks, and that was enough. Life at the tabernacle was a soothing respite from the storms he remembered from his father's house.

The sun set behind the canyon, shooting rays of light upward behind it, and the hillside shade had a wintry tang suddenly. He shivered as he stuffed his cotton work gloves in his jeans pocket and walked up the path to the cottages.

There were fourteen cottages scattered through a large eucalyptus grove. Beyond them lay the stable, storage buildings, and a small dining hall. Workers lived in the cottages and ate in the hall. The cook fixed real food. That was noteworthy in light of a pamphlet authored by the founder of the tabernacle and foisted on its members. In *A California Sunshine Diet*, Brother Paul's recommendation for a proper breakfast was a bowl of cornmeal mush and chilled spring or well water. For dinner and supper, Valley fruits and vegetables, more water, and as a special treat, an orange or grapefruit. Jim liked oranges, all right. But the mere thought of the rest of the diet almost made him puke. In the dining hall—behind the scenes, so to speak—he got more solid fare: panfried steak and breaded cutlets, eggs cooked hard as leather, and biscuits as heavy as a handful of fishing sinkers. Normal, healthy food.

The tabernacle's founder occupied the entire top floor of the octagonal house. Often at night, the whole floor glowed with electric lights. Once, unable to sleep, Jim had seen the lights burning at half past four in the morning. He'd walked up near the house and listened. Behind the closed drapes, he heard the squeals of women and the rowdy laughter of men.

He was pretty sure of what was going on; he'd learned a lot, very early, traveling with Jocker. He wondered if that sort of behavior was not a little improper for a church. But if it didn't bother all the red-faced worshipers who drove out to the tabernacle once a week, why should it bother him?

Jim's familiarity with the octagonal house was limited to the first floor; he had never been upstairs. Nor did he care to go. Brother Paul was a moody, bad-tempered man. Jocker had several times spoken of the founder's humidor of Canton opium. "Smokes it in his pipe. Don't you ever take a puff if he offers. Kill you quicker'n the syph, that stuff." So long as Brother Paul paid decent wages, Jim figured the founder could do anything he wanted.

A meeting hall took up half of the first floor of the house, offices of Brother Paul and his part-time lay staff filling the rest. One of those offices belonged to Elihu Flintman, a queer old bird who lived near Covina, came to the tabernacle because his wife insisted, and kept the books on a volunteer basis. Flintman was on the board of elders that ran the tabernacle. He complained that the board had no power.

Flintman's wife raised roses. Jim had done a little part-time work in her garden. He'd gotten acquainted with Flintman—more accurately, had been watched by him; Flintman wanted blood for every dollar—and thus the bookkeeper had learned that Jim had a passion for ciphering. When Flintman was especially busy at the tabernacle, he'd bring Jim into his office for a few hours to run sums and double-check ledger figures. Jim enjoyed it, though he found Flintman fussy and inclined to be difficult.

Moving up the path, he saw Jocker picking up small branches around one of the cottages. Jocker wasn't a very efficient gardener; he moved too slowly and couldn't bend over easily. Jim ended up doing a lot of his work, but he didn't mind.

Jocker straightened up with a melodramatic groan, then leaned his rake against a eucalyptus tree. "Tired."

"Let's wash up and get ready for supper. Here, lean on me."

Jim put Jocker's arm over his shoulder and helped him up the path toward the cottages.

The following Saturday, Jim and Jocker hitched up the horses and drove into Pasadena to buy sacks of fertilizer. Jim took the occasion to dash to the public library. Waiting for him while the wagon was being loaded, Jocker happened to stroll past a flyer tacked to a telegraph pole, the word REWARD leaping out at him. He paused to read it.

Ashen, he looked one way, then the other, along the dusty street. A dairy wagon creaked past. As soon as it vanished around a corner, Jocker tore the flyer down.

On the way back to the tabernacle, Jim drove the wagon. There were books on the floor: by Mark Twain, Dickens, James Fenimore Cooper. Jocker hummed to himself, then cleared his throat several times before he finally said, "Look here. I found something on a telegraph pole you ought to see." He pulled out the flyer.

"I don't know why they put in that birthmark," he said while Jim read the flyer. "Otherwise it's you, to perfection. Isn't it?"

Jim crushed the paper into a ball, threw it away, and concentrated on the road ahead, both hands gripping the reins so tightly, his fingers turned white.

Jocker observed him for a moment or so, then said, "You haven't told me everything, have you? Somebody's after you. Somebody you don't want to see."

Jim didn't answer.

Suddenly Jocker's eyes opened wider. "Say. I'll bet you saw that somebody at the air show. I'll bet you didn't have a bellyache after all."

"Jocker," Jim exclaimed in a warning tone.

"Who is it, Jim, folks?" the old man persisted. "Is that it, you really do have folks somewhere—just like I always suspected?"

"Don't ask," Jim whispered, staring straight ahead. "If you're my friend, Jocker, just don't ask."

Jocker reflected, wiggling his tongue in one of the gaps where teeth were missing. "I am, so I won't. I had a funny idea you might say something like this." He pulled a wad of paper from another pocket—two more flyers. "That's why I tore down all the others I could find before you got back from the library."

* * *

On the depot platform, Margaret gave Mack a big hug. "I've had a glorious vacation. Thank you." The back of her glove rested on his cheek. "Especially for the first night."

He looked away.

Saddened, she said, "You were so cheerful for a day or two. Then—"

"Then I saw my son. I saw him, and I lost him, and even though the Pinkertons have redoubled their efforts, still nobody can find him . . ."

"Get aboard, miss, if you please," said the conductor on the steps of the car.

"Yes, in a moment. Mack—won't you come north for a visit sometime soon?"

"I told Older I would when Ruef went to San Quentin."

"Wait for that and you may wait years. Don't you need to see Mr. Anderson out at Niles?"

"I suppose," he said with another of those vague shrugs. He gave her a brotherly kiss on the cheek. "I'll think about it."

She searched his face. Lifeless again. Then she squeezed his arm. "I really don't care what reason you come up with—I just think seeing the City might be a good change. You can't spend your whole life dwelling on mistakes."

"You can if they're big enough."

The conductor harrumphed and insisted she board. Margaret flung an arm around his neck and hugged him again, tears glistening on the lashes of her closed eyes. She held him, and shared his pain, then let him go.

As the Daylight Limited pulled out, she gazed at him from the window of her seat in the parlor car. Mack stood motionless in the steam, right hand raised. Slowly he disappeared. But the image of his haunted face remained with her.

THE GIRL IN JEANS AND RED GINGHAM SHIRT BOOTED **73** her stallion harder, ducking at the sound of cracking gunshots from her pursuers. She flung a look of terror over her shoulder. There they came, eight hard-riding outlaws. The leader was a lanky desperado in a cowboy hat with a Montana peak, its wide brim hiding the upper part of his face, a leaf-green bandanna concealing the lower part. He rode at the head of his band of scruffy hard cases, each of whom had a brace of pistols.

The outlaws chased the girl down a country road at the base of steep tree-clad hills. The leader held the reins in his teeth, controlling his black mare with his knees, and fired shot after shot from a pair of silver-plated Smith & Wesson American .44's. The other outlaws shot too, white smoke puffing from their gun muzzles.

Miraculously, though, the fusillade didn't harm the girl on horseback. Eyes round with fright, she urged her horse to go faster, but now the outlaw in the Montana peak hat galloped to within twenty feet of her, firing relentlessly, apparently never exhausting his ammunition.

Suddenly, on the crest of the hill to the right, the girl spied a lone rider in sheepskin batwing chaps, tall hat, cowboy vest, flowing bandanna. Sizing up the situation, he snatched out his Colt Peacemaker.

The girl waved and wailed, "Oh, Billy—help me, help me."

The lone rider gritted his teeth and spurred his horse down the brushy embankment. With his reins in his teeth like the outlaw chief, he snatched a second Peacemaker from a holster, firing while his horse slid down the hillside. He knocked his hat back with a pistol barrel and the sun bathed his face. His jutting jaw said he was fighting mad.

The endangered damsel, her pursuers, and her savior all raced toward a grove of arching trees at a bend in the road. The lone rider picked off one outlaw, then a second, each malefactor falling with an elaborate toss of his weapon, a great clutch of his shirt bosom, a piercing cry. The outlaw leader flashed furious looks at his weakling assistants lying shot at the roadside. One of them sat up, dusted himself off, and grinned.

The chase thundered toward the trees. In the dappled shadows, a couple of dozen men and women shouted and waved, urging the riders on. Directly beneath a limb that overhung the road, the cameraman, his cloth cap reversed, crouched behind the big boxy Mutograph camera, cranking furiously. The Mutograph's gears were noisy; it sounded like a defective meat grinder. The camera punched sprocket holes as it filmed, and the little squares of film spewed from a tube in the bottom.

A man in riding breeches and puttees bellowed through a megaphone. "Pour it on, Dora. Your face lights with hope. Billy's coming to your rescue—"

Dora lashed her horse with the reins as Broncho Billy reached the bottom of the slope, raising dust and blazing away with his Peacemakers. Another outlaw dropped from the saddle, but landed hard, cursing.

The director waved his megaphone. "Nobody look back—he's all right—keep coming." In the shade, Mack jumped up on the high stool on which he'd been seated and clutched the limb above his head, able to see better now.

"Looking good," the director cried as the horses galloped into the last eighth of a mile before the grove. Halfway up the slope on Mack's right, a second cameraman had stopped cranking, the action having passed him. People on the crew shouted excitedly. It was a perfect take.

Twenty yards from the camera, Dora's stallion suddenly stumbled, letting out a shrill neigh and somersaulting forward. Dora sailed over the animal's head and landed in high underbrush across the road. Broncho Billy was still firing, facing the other way.

The director danced in the dusty road. "Oh Jesus Christ, cut it, cut the action. Billy, Dora's down."

The remaining outlaws reined their mounts. Gilbert Anderson responded to the director's call by trotting his horse toward the fallen actress. Makeup girls, scene shifters, the cameraman, and the director all ran after him.

Mack took off his glasses and hurried that way too. He had a fierce, almost blinding headache, brought on by Flyshack's latest report, again entirely negative. He didn't notice when the leader of the outlaw gang abruptly stopped his horse in the middle of the road. Under the brim of the Montana peak hat, startled eyes took note of the visitor, the only man on the site wearing a suit.

Mack and the others reached Dora in the high weeds. Holstering the silver-plated revolvers, whose supply of blanks he'd exhausted, the outlaw leader turned his black mare and trotted away up the road.

Dora sat up, wincing and clutching her leg. Anderson pulled her boot off and gently probed her ankle. Then, with a great sigh of disgust, he stood up.

"I'm sorry you got hurt. Should have put a double on that cayuse."

"I can keep going—"

"Not a chance. You rest."

Anderson slapped his big Stetson against his sheepskin chaps. "Buster, get the buggy. Ride into Niles for Doc Clabaugh.

633

Some of you rig a lean-to so Dora doesn't have to lie in the sun. Hop to it.''

The Essanay company was filming *Broncho Billy's Pursuit* on a deserted road off Niles Canyon two miles from the studio, which was in turn four miles beyond the town. It was a morning in March 1910. Mack had returned to the apartment on Greenwich Street the previous week, and driven out to Niles, a trip of over an hour, starting at sunrise.

Together, he and Anderson walked back toward the trees. "Devil of a way to greet an investor on his first visit," Anderson said.

"What are you going to do, Billy?" Everyone called him that, Anderson having submerged himself in his cowboy character. His first three Broncho Billy one-reelers had been hits, and exchanges around the country were yelling for more.

"Close down until we find out whether Dora can work. I don't think she can. I think her leg's broken.''

In the early afternoon, his head still aching, Mack waited for the verdict in Anderson's office at Essanay. The studio layout was efficient but primitive, with a single large wooden stage, the roof glassed in, in the middle of an abandoned alfalfa field. A number of California-style bungalows surrounded the stage, the largest of which, cheaply and sparsely furnished, housed the office and Anderson's living quarters. From the window, Mack could see three cows grazing in a pasture fenced with barbwire.

Still in cowboy costume, Anderson walked in and sat down heavily. "It's broken. She's out. What the devil am I going to do? We have to keep finishing these pictures on schedule, one every three days. If I don't bring this one in by Friday, George Spoor will be telegraphing for my scalp.''

"Can't you replace the girl?"

"Sure, next week. I need her replaced tomorrow morning.''

Mack tapped the brim of his homburg on his knee. "Is it necessary that a new girl be experienced?''

"If she's breathing and she can smile while hanging on to a California saddle, that's all I need. We can double her when we reshoot the end of the chase, and double her in the saloon brawl too.''

"I know a girl in San Francisco. She's not an actress, but she's a pretty thing. Smiles like an angel. A Biograph director in Los Angeles thought she was a stunner.''

"Who was the director?"

Mack struggled to remember. "Griffith.''

"Hell, D.W. is a connoisseur of the ladies. If he approves, she must be a peach. Can you have her here tomorrow morning?"

"I can try."

"The call is for seven thirty."

"Billy, it's a long drive. She won't get much sleep."

"Does she want to be in pictures or doesn't she? Half past seven, sharp."

Hellburner Johnson sat against the side of the stage in the middle of the overgrown alfalfa field. In his lap lay the silver-plated S&W Americans, a type of revolver he loathed. His legs stuck out in the sunshine, a cabbage butterfly examining the toes of his boots.

There was a lot of thumping and shouting on the other side of the wall. A comedian with whom Essanay had struck a deal was filming *His Night Out*, a one-reeler about a drunk doing the town, and the drunk was taking pratfalls.

Johnson opened a cardboard box of blanks and thumbed cartridges into the cylinder of the first revolver. Silent pictures amused him. As the outlaw leader, he'd probably fired thirty-five or forty rounds from each piece during the chase.

He was glad to sit a spell. Fifty-seven now, riding that hard damn near killed him. He felt almost as weak as he had when he recuperated in the hospital in Panama after a fever that turned his bowels to water for three weeks and gave him evil dreams to boot.

Talk about evil dreams. Working for Gil Anderson out here in the country, he sure as hell never expected to bump into his partner.

Hearing an auto on the road at the edge of the field, he became still, his hat brim slanted far down so that it touched his nose. When the sound of the Packard's engine faded, he pushed the hat back up. Fortunately, Mack had lit out in a hurry, giving him some breathing space. Did he want to meet up with Mack again or not?

The side door of the stage opened and the comedian popped out, a small, dark-eyed young man with curls.

"Ben Turpin?"

"Not out here," Johnson said.

"Miss Purviance?"

"Haven't seen her."

The comedian gave a funny rabbity wiggle to his nose. "Sunstroke, Mr. Johnson?"

"Sore ass, Mr. Chaplin."

"Yes. Well. Carry on." Another wiggle. He shut the door.

Snotty little Brit. Music-hall fella. Thought he was a sketch. He'd never amount to beans. With that thought, Johnson returned to loading his revolvers.

The Packard swayed and bumped on the road from Hayward to Niles. A jackrabbit sprang across in front of the auto, and Mack sawed the wheel wildly. Margaret uttered   cry, then leaned back, shaken.

"A few more thrills like that and I'll faint before we get there."

Gritty-eyed and grim, Mack didn't reply. There was a pale glow above the hills, and birds were waking in the woods. He'd been up most of the night, persuading Margaret to do it. As soon as she agreed, he bundled her into the car. They'd left San Francisco long before daylight.

"Mack, I'm so nervous—"

"Calm down. Anderson will coach you. This isn't high art— it's a one-reel action picture. You keep saying you don't want to run a French restaurant all your life. I took you seriously."

"All right, I'll do my best." She patted her hair with nervous motions. "At least you seem interested in something again."

He steered the Packard around a curve. "Damned if I don't." He smiled. "It sneaked up on me." Margaret screamed. Mack yanked the wheel hard to the left, just missing a red cow chewing its cud in the road.

Margaret had composed herself by the time they reached Niles. She stepped from the Packard with the cool elegance of a princess and extended her hand to have it shaken by the excitable director, Van Zant Morgan. ("Not his real name," Mack had told her earlier. "His real name's Sid Morgenstern.") She gave him one of her incredible smiles.

"Oh my God, perfect," Morgan cried, clasping his hands in a prayerful way.

At half past seven, a buckboard rushed Margaret to a glade near the alfalfa field. Carpenters and painters were finishing a wilderness cabin that consisted of a front and side wall and half of a roof, all of it canvas and lath. It stood on the bank of a rushing woodland creek sparkling with reflections.

The camera crew set up the huge Mutograph as Morgan strutted around eyeing the sun and changing the position of gauze diffusers mounted on tripods. Margaret fidgeted in a canvas chair while a makeup woman patted powder on her face. She'd been put into a gingham dress with puff sleeves and a properly high neck. Standing off to one side, Mack and Anderson watched the makeup girl pin a huge schoolgirl bow in Margaret's auburn hair. Anderson wore his Broncho Billy vest, sheepskin batwing chaps, and six-guns.

"I'm in your debt, Mack. That's one pretty girl. There's a freshness about her that's just remarkable. What does she do for a living?"

Mack polished his spectacles with a white handkerchief. "Runs a small family business."

"I hope there's someone to manage it. I may use her again."

"You haven't seen her act, Billy."

"I've seen her smile. Hey, Morgan—there's too much sun reflecting from the creek . . ." Off he went, boot heels digging the leafy compost on the ground, paunch jiggling under his cowboy vest. Amazingly, this ordinary man with the hook nose and rather bovine eyes had become a movie idol in a matter of months.

Mack pulled out his meerschaum and tobacco pouch. His neck started to itch, and he looked around to see if someone was watching him. His gaze collided with that of an actor leaning against a tree in the cool morning shade.

Several things registered at once. The lime-colored bandanna, the green of his unblinking eyes, the crinkly gray hair—

"Good God. Hugh?"

The men met in a patch of misty sunlight. Showing no emotion, Johnson extended his hand.

"How are you, Mack?"

They shook and Mack stepped back, still astonished. "What in the world are you doing here?"

"Tryin' to keep the wolf away."

"Come on. You don't need money."

"Tryin' to fill the hours, then. Playactin' parts I used to play for real in Texas."

"How'd you get here?"

"Answered an advertisement. You seen much of our outlaw gang? It's mighty strange. Jesperson yonder, he's a genuine hard case. Two terms in Arizona state prison for train robbery. Then we got that pair." He meant two cowboy actors standing close and whispering like lovers. One fondled the other's hand. "Beats all, don't it? I grew up in the West and this is all that's left of it. Playactors dressin' up to get their pictures on little bitty strips of nitrate film. Funny how things work out."

"You look fit, H.B."

"Wasn't for a while there. One of them tropic diseases nearly kilt me down in Panama." In a few sentences he described his experience swinging a shovel on a canal work gang. "You're healthier than you was the last time I saw you. Did the police or the Pinkertons find Jim?''

''Not yet. But he's alive. I saw him.'' Mack told him about it.

''I'm right sorry, Mack. Even sorrier that I blew up and walked out. Got a fearful bad disposition sometimes. Lived by myself too long. Guess I need a wife to learn me manners.''

Mack heard the forgiveness in that, and he relaxed. Hunkering in the shade of a budding sycamore, he filled and tamped his pipe. ''I think I'm the one who should apologize. I was acting rotten that day.''

''Well, you was hurt bad.''

''No excuse. I'm surprised you'd even speak to me again.''

''Hell, we're more'n partners. We're friends. A friend's like this here bum foot of mine. It pains the shit out of you more than it ought. But you'd never take an ax and lop it off.''

''Couldn't have said it better. What do you think of our actress?''

''Plain gorgeous,'' Johnson declared. ''This work's more respectable than what she's been doin'. But not much.''

Mack grinned. ''Look here. I'm back at the apartment in San Francisco for a while. Come visit when Anderson wraps up on Friday.''

Hellburner Johnson rolled his tongue in his weather-reddened cheek. ''Why, I just might. Yes, sir. Thanks.'' His laconic answer couldn't quite hide his pleasure.

A week later, at twilight, Mack and Johnson walked out of the Fairmont Hotel. Mack savored the Bay breeze, salty, fresh, and cool. He felt fine. Two schooners of beer in the gents' bar, plus some raw oysters, helped, as did the presence of his friend.

They dodged a long black DeLannay Belleville touring car with blazing headlights, which was turning into the hotel's half-circle drive. The Fairmont's granite exterior had withstood the fire, the interior had been rebuilt with red-plush opulence, and the hotel had opened officially in the spring of 1907.

They strolled north, toward Sacramento Street. Johnson wore a proper city suit, but he wouldn't sacrifice his bandanna. White silk, it looked incongruous. His crippled right foot dragged only slightly.

''Any word from Nellie?''

''She's due home from Europe next month. Her third novel's just been issued by her new publisher, Scribner's.''

''Didn't know that. Got to read it.''

''You'll find it different from her others. Funny, but in a

638

savage way—like Mark Twain. One of the critics called her an authentic American genius. I hear Walter Fairbanks and his crowd want to crucify her."

"My, my. She's come a far piece, our Nell. But she's still a little girl with a big case for you."

Turning down Sacramento they soon stood before the rubble of the mansion. Red light from the west lit it like the midden of a forgotten race. Johnson picked his way into what had been the front yard and turned over a chunk of stone. A brown rat leaped over his boots and ran.

"You ever gonna rebuild this mess?"

"The architects brought me plans right after the earthquake." San Franciscans had a simple new calendar by which they kept track of the past. An event happened before the earthquake, or it happened after. Mack picked up the stone Johnson had moved and threw it on a larger pile, a puff of dust blowing away in the cold breeze. "I put them in the closet."

"Maybe you should get 'em out. Place looks like a damn trash dump."

"I've had any number of letters from neighbors expressing the same thought."

Johnson brushed off a fallen slab of marble and sat. He started to roll a cigarette. "I'm glad you got Margaret that part with Broncho Billy. It ain't only good for her—it's good for you. Margaret said it shows you're comin' back to the real world. You been away in those dark pits too long. Can't say's I blame you, but you got too much to offer—you can't hide down there the rest of your life."

With a somber expression, Mack sat down too. For once he didn't rebel at Johnson's gratuitous advice. Maybe it was a certain tiredness, a resignation, after all the shocks of recent times.

Johnson scraped a match on his pants and lit his twisty handrolled cigarette. "I can understand why you was hit so hard. If I'd ever found the right woman, and had me a son, I'd love him as much as you loved your Jim."

"Jim isn't—"

The wind whispered over broken stones. Electric lights warmed the windows of rebuilt homes on Nob Hill. Faint scurryings told of rats running beneath the rubble.

"Isn't what? Isn't coming back?"

"I've accepted that as a possibility. No, more than that. You see, I'm absolutely convinced I saw Jim at the air meet, and that means . . ." Mack faltered, rubbing hard at a spot in the center of his forehead that pained him suddenly. "Hugh, it means he's turned his back on me completely. He ran from me that day. He doesn't want to be found, and probably wouldn't come back if he were.''

Johnson saw his friend's pain, and he too faltered: "Well—don't give up. Maybe there'll be some good luck after so much bad . . .''

Mack shook his head. "Look at the search that's been conducted. Law officers, Pinkertons, thousands and thousands of flyers—and over forty false leads at last count. And nothing else. What's more, come the twenty-eighth of September, Jim will be twelve years old. Grown up. Changed a lot since he ran off. Suppose he's really going out of his way to hide? Suppose he works hard at leading a quiet, ordinary life? Suppose he's taken a different name? That would blur the trail almost completely. Only his limp would be left as solid, conclusive identification, and maybe he's even learned to walk a little straighter. You did.'' He slapped his knees. "What difference does it make, all the theorizing? This is the sum of it. I'll probably never see him again.''

Johnson was silent a while. Then he sighed. "Guess you're right. It's a real possibility, and mighty hard to bear. You can't dwell on it, though. You got work to do in this world.''

Mack's hazel eyes challenged him. "What work?''

"For one thing, the 'lections this fall. That lawyer Hiram Johnson—fine name—he looks like the one the reform crowd's gonna run for governor.''

"Not exactly news.''

"No, but what I seen in today's *Examiner* may be. The SP says it's goin' all out to stop these here Progressives from electin' Johnson. The railroad's puttin' its whole damn machine to work, and today they announced the name of the man headin' up the effort.'' He pursed his lips and let smoke trickle from his nose. "Your pal Walter.''

"He's in charge?''

"Yes, sir.'' Johnson chuckled. "Thought that'd stir you some. It's gonna be a mean, raw fight, you ask me. The state of California's suffered with that blasted railroad near onto forty years, and a lot of folks are plain sick of it. The *Examiner* said the railroad'll be fightin' for its life. Everything on the line.''

Now the red light had leached from the sky. Mack walked out to the ruined gate pillars and stared off toward the bright windows of the hotel. Cold wind blew his hair and Johnson's cowboy scarf about. Mack felt a curious stirring, as though he'd just awakened from heavy sleep.

"Maybe you're right, Hugh. Maybe I should crawl out of

the cellar and do what I can to nail Walter and those bastards he works for."

"Thought you might see it like that." Johnson stepped up beside Mack and rested an arm on his shoulder. "Nothin' like good clean hate to stir a man's blood."

At Greenwich Street, Mack took a hot bath, put on his dressing gown, and turned on a light beside his favorite chair in the room he used for a library. At half past three in the morning, he finished reading Nellie's novel for the second time.

Huntworthy's Millions, or, an Honest Dollar was a raucous, outrageous tale, cruelly unforgiving in its portrait of Clemons Parsifal Huntworthy, founder and chief thief of an unnamed railroad in an unnamed western state bordering the Pacific.

Nellie had divided her picaresque story in two. In the first section, in order to build his line, Huntworthy lied, stole, and swindled everyone from his trusting partner to President Lincoln. Established as a power in his state, he then bought himself a United States Senate seat. The night before leaving for Washington, he had another of his poisonous and profane arguments with his wife, Asphodel.

Asphodel Huntworthy was an illiterate shrew, a Mother Lode laundress who'd washed Huntworthy's long underwear when he was too poor to pay a Chinese to do it. The quarrel was monumental, which Nellie suggested by using dashes for omitted obscenities, and it built over two and a half pages, with the last half-page little more than quote marks around dashes. At the end, severely tried, Huntworthy dropped dead of a heart spasm.

The second half of the novel dealt with vain and conceited Asphodel, her pretensions to social eminence in San Francisco, and her marriage to a slim, cultivated young decorator from New York City. Wallis Flummerfelt was twenty-eight years younger than Asphodel. At her invitation, he traveled west to refurbish her palatial residence. A Dartmouth man, he was charming and affectionate—until he got the ring on Asphodel's finger. Then he showed himself to be fully as dishonest as her first husband, maneuvering behind her back, and ended up owning the railroad. She ended up as she began, arms in harsh hot water in a laundry tub in the failed mining town of Try Again, California.

Ed Huntington loathed the novel, and wrote Mack a boiling letter to say so. It was likewise hated by anyone with a fond memory of Uncle Mark Hopkins, whose widow had married her antique dealer.

Mack loved it, absolutely awed by Nellie's savage wit. He badly wanted to see her and tell her.

He wanted to tell her how he really felt about his son, down underneath the show of hope he still maintained for others: Jim was alive somewhere, but almost surely lost to him now. He wanted to tell her he was taking a first step back into the world in spite of everything. And he wanted to tell her he loved her. That, of all his wants, was somehow the hardest to satisfy.

74

IN A PRIVATE ROOM AT THE OLYMPIC CLUB, THE four men dined one Thursday in April: Mack, Rudolph Spreckels, Fremont Older, and Dorian Stimson, who had traveled up from Los Angeles. Stimson nearly spilled his soup when Mack told him why he'd invited them.

"Mr. Chance—Mack—that's wonderful news. I'm pleased beyond words that you'll join us. We're going to put forward a splendid slate of candidates with Hiram Johnson at the top. The Progressive platform is simple and unequivocal. *Kick the railroad out of politics.*"

Spreckels applauded. Mack said, "I certainly agree with a program like that. I'll give you as much money as I can."

"How about your personal involvement?" Older asked.

"That too."

"Best news of all," the editor declared. "We need you. We need every hand. The campaign will be rough. The railroad knows what we're up to . . ."

"The railroad is desperate," Dorian Stimson said.

The Southern Pacific boardroom was sequestered on the third floor of the temporary general offices at Market and Powell. There were plans for an entirely new and opulent headquarters building, but construction had not yet begun.

A life-sized portrait of Collis Huntington dominated the room. The old bandit's painted eyes stared down at dusty sunbeams playing on the burnished wood paneling of the long table. Eighteen men sat around the table, eighteen proper, sober company men. All of them, including the executive at the head, concentrated on the man seated by himself at the other end: Walter Fairbanks.

The meeting's chairman was William Herrin, the only attorney in the Southern Pacific with more authority than Fairbanks. Herrin was a bland sort, deceptively innocent. He didn't smile, but neither was he unfriendly—merely direct and a bit formal.

"Walter, I speak for the entire board when I say that we respect you as a colleague and treasure you as a friend. You've directed and coordinated the state and local efforts of our political bureau almost since you joined the company. Your level of effort and accomplishment is high. But I'm afraid that does not and cannot carry weight in this situation. We are plunged into a desperate struggle for leadership in our state. The SP has been good for California—good for industry, good for agriculture, good for the common citizen in a thousand hamlets that might have moldered and vanished had we not favored them with our right-of-way. But there is a certain element—foreigners, Jews, jackleg journalists, rich men who are traitors to their class—a certain crazed element dedicated to ignoring the facts. Dedicated to pushing us out of the counsels of power and shutting the door. We are faced with a fight for our political survival. So, then, by extension, are you."

Fairbanks's gray-metal eyes blinked twice. He was not a man easily disturbed, but this disturbed him. Deep in his gut, he felt a sudden stab of pain.

"I understand, Bill."

"Let's hope so. The executive committee can't and won't excuse failure in this crisis. But we have enormous confidence in you."

Enormous confidence. Unless I fail, in which case you'll spit me and roast me alive. I know how this company works.

"You are challenged to attack and rout Hiram Johnson and the whole pack of lying Progressives. Johnson is an evil man. He represented the dregs of the trade unionists, the San Francisco teamsters, for eight years. He convicted Ruef. He's a ruthless opportunist, and his backers are waiting at the door with a portfolio of socialistic legislation. You're familiar with the man the Democrats are putting up, Theodore Bell of Napa. He says he's a Woodrow Wilson Democrat and a reformer in his own right. We don't like him, but we'll back him in preference to Johnson. That, in essence, is our program. We want you to implement it as if your job and future depended on it. Which, in fact, Walter, they do."

"Bill, are you saying—"

"Johnson and his crowd must lose in November. *Must.* Nothing else is acceptable."

75 A PROCESSION OF LIMOUSINES ROLLED INTO THE court entrance of the rebuilt Palace Hotel. Press hounds with cameras and flashlight powder photographed the notables arriving for the ball. It was September.

Mack drove in at half past eight. He didn't want to attend but the cause was too worthy to be ignored. As he alighted from his hired chauffeured car, he scowled at the photographers. It didn't stop them.

He was turned out in a formal evening suit of black worsted with silk braid down the sides of the trousers, his waistcoat and cravat a fine white pique. Pearl studs gleamed on his cuffs and starched shirt bosom, and his black patent-leather pumps and tall opera hat shone. He carried a cane and white kid gloves and wore a white silk scarf draped over his shoulders. With his white hair and round spectacles he cut a striking figure. He felt like a fool.

"Be here at eleven. I'll be ready," he said to the chauffeur, and the car rolled off.

Behind him a middle-aged man and his wife stepped out of their limousine. It was Mike de Young, the publisher of the *Chronicle*. He was a capable, feisty man of Dutch-Jewish extraction, a power in the City, though still not one of Mack's intimates. These days the publisher treated Mack more cordially than he had in the past. Although Willie Hearst's paper was still very much a part of the City, Willie himself was long gone, and that, plus a general mellowing perhaps brought on by age, seemed to have cooled de Young's anger toward Hearst's friends. He spoke to Mack in a way that recognized him as a member of the City's small and exclusive club of the very wealthy.

"Good of you to come out for this benefit," he said now. Wax on his handlebar mustache glistened under the lights.

"The De Young Art Museum deserves everyone's support, Mike."

He greeted de Young's wife and the three of them started into the hotel. "I'm glad you feel that way, because we desperately need a new building," de Young said. "That brick heap left over from the Midwinter Fair has outgrown the collection. Until we get a new museum, the operating budget for the old place must be raised every year. With all those needs, we'll even accept donations from friends of Hearst."

"None of that, Mike. I read your paper right along with the *Examiner*. I figure the old saying's true: two sides to every story—"

De Young sent his wife along to the cloakroom. "What about the state election? Two sides to that?"

"No. There's only one right side. The Progressive side."

"On that we agree." De Young squeezed his arm. "Glad you're with us. Thanks for coming."

The music of a Ballenberg orchestra, a jaunty rendition of "Shine On, Harvest Moon," drifted from the ballroom. Mack crossed the foyer to the cloakroom and handed the attendant his opera hat, stick, and gloves. As he slipped the check in his pocket he noticed a couple coming down the staircase from the floor above.

Walter and Carla. She wore an ermine wrap over a peach satin gown with matching gloves and a lace décolletage. Tiny satin bows on the lace seemed too girlish for someone her age. White aigrettes bobbed in her hair, and Mack wondered how many water birds had died to decorate her for this affair.

Carla groped her way down the stairs, one glove never leaving the banister. Her husband's eyes darted over the foyer crowd, then back to her. *Deathly afraid she'll make a gaffe.*

She almost did when her silver pump slipped off a riser; she would have fallen, but for Fairbanks's sudden lunge. They exchanged words. Carla was flushed and shook her head vehemently, then flung off Fairbanks's hand and descended the last several steps by herself.

"Walter—Carla—good evening. I heard you were living in the hotel."

Fairbanks brushed at his little mustache. "When we're not in Burlingame." He shot looks over Mack's shoulder. Taut as a wire, Mack thought. It pleased him in a perverse way.

Carla swam in perfume. She started to speak but a matron with a battleship bosom grabbed her. "Carla dearest, do come here and meet Cloudsley Ballantyne, the painter." Carla lurched away to be presented to a young man with a fey face and center-parted brown hair combed down into horns on his temples. He'd pinned a golden California poppy to his lapel with a pearl pin.

"I'm surprised to see you, Walter," Mack said affably. "I thought you might be out of town, turning up the heat under your county political bureaus. The election's not far off."

Sliding a silver case from an inside pocket, Fairbanks took out a cigarette and tapped it on the case longer than necessary. A pallor had replaced his usual ruddy color.

"Everybody deserves a night off. We'll have no trouble beating your crowd."

There it was again, the old smug condescension. God, how Mack despised him. He gave in to the impulse to hit back. "Don't get overconfident. Remember how the polo match came out. And the race."

Fairbanks snapped the wooden match he was lifting to his cigarette and the burning head fell to the carpet. He stamped on it, then lowered his voice. "You arrogant bastard. Haven't changed, have you? You're trash. That first day, by the creek, Hellman should have put a bullet in you."

Mack smiled too, a broad smile, but hard. "What the hell do you want from me, Walter? No fight at all? No competition—so you never have to risk losing? Well, I'm afraid not. Especially not this time. This is the big one. And you're going to lose. Again."

Livid, Fairbanks struck another match. Deep in his eyes something new lurked, or so Mack thought—fear that Mack might be right.

What an ass you are to goad him. Only makes him hate you more.

Carla flung herself between them. "Such an elegant young man. So talented. Well." She blinked and touched Mack's sleeve. "This is charming. My present husband and my former one. Hello, former."

She made a little lunge at Mack, enveloping him in flesh and the overwhelming scent of her perfume. Had she bathed in it?

Fairbanks bit out a complaint, but she was already draped on Mack and twining her arms around his neck. She found his mouth and opened hers. He smelled and tasted whiskey, strong whiskey.

He tried to step away and Fairbanks dragged Carla off by seizing her wrist. "For God's sake, don't make a fool of yourself."

"Darling, I was only greeting my ex—"

He showed what he thought of that by forcing her to take his arm. Then he pivoted her toward the ballroom. The little scene had played to one side of the foyer, but Mack saw a number of couples shooting sly glances at Mr. and Mrs. Fairbanks. The damage was done, and Fairbanks knew it. He yanked her against his side and marched her toward the high gilt doors.

She turned once, quickly. What Mack saw in that blurred

glance surprised and saddened him. He saw longing, the same longing he'd seen the night Swampy lay dying.

He drifted among the tables ranged around the dance floor, stopping first by a large table hosted by Adolph Spreckels and his wife, Alma. Rudy's older brother was still too proper and starchy for Mack's taste, but Mack genuinely liked Alma, a handsome, breezy, full-figured woman twenty-four years younger than her husband. Until she married Adolph in 1907, when he was fifty, she had been plain Alma de Bretteville, an artist's model of uncertain background (she claimed her ancestors were French and Danish nobility). She said openly that she'd been deflowered at a tender age by a Klondike miner, but had taken the son of a bitch to court for a settlement of $10,000. Everyone said she was the model for the Winged Victory atop the monument in Union Square, and she didn't deny it.

Marriage to Adolph Spreckels had raised her overnight to social eminence. She was the City's youngest *grande dame*, lunching at the St. Francis every Tuesday with her own chosen circle. She involved herself in cultural affairs, notably the planning of another art museum, in direct competition with Mike de Young. The rivalry was a sharp one; the Spreckels table was as far as possible from that of the de Youngs tonight.

Mack had known Alma casually before her marriage, and in some ways, respectability had changed her not at all. She still had a foghorn voice, a salty vocabulary, and few pretenses or inhibitions. "For Christ's sake, Mack, aren't you going to ask me to dance?" she said as he stood by the table.

He grinned. "I'd better, or you're liable to cuss me out." The guests laughed politely, but Alma brayed. Adolph pursed his lips, his version of hilarity.

Mack extended his hand. "Thank you, darling," Alma said loudly as he led her to the floor to waltz. "Some of those friends of Ade's are fucking cadavers." Heads turned; she was unperturbed. She fitted nicely into his arms; she had the kind of ample figure men called Junoesque. "Tell me, darling, why didn't you bring a companion this evening?"

"I wanted to ask Margaret, but she's filming another Broncho Billy picture."

"I'm sure there are any number of ladies present who'd happily share their dance programs and their tarnished virtue. I certainly would if I weren't married and loyal to dear Ade."

There was a stifled cry and then commotion. The music scraped and squeaked to silence. Alma stretched on tiptoe. "Oh my God, Carla Fairbanks fell down."

Mack saw her floundering on her side, callously revealed by couples who had quickly stepped away. Her long skirt was hiked over her knees, and garters and a white satin petticoat were exposed. Her partner, Cloudsley Ballantyne, fluttered his hands and dithered.

"Help her, for heaven's sake," a portly man growled at the painter.

Carla gripped Ballantyne's pasty fingers and pulled herself halfway up, then lost control and sat down on her round bottom with a thump. Mack wanted to hide. Such an ordinary thing, sitting down like that. But you didn't do it in the middle of this crowd.

"Oh my God, how embarrassing," Alma said in her brassy voice. "Drunk again."

Fairbanks stormed through the hotel suite, snapping on electric lights in a pair of bordeaux lamps with cut-glass grapes decorating the globes. Carla limped from the foyer and threw her fur carelessly. A claw-foot gold clock on the mantel showed ten past three.

Fairbanks tore off his coat, then his white tie. Unfastening his waistcoat, he broke button thread, and two buttons spun through the light and bounced on the Oriental rug. Carla wandered past him, opened the bedroom door, and turned on the light.

Fairbanks's hands shook as he tried to open the silver cigarette case. Hearing a cabinet door, then glass rattling, he hurled the case down, spilling cigarettes, and ran into the bedroom.

Pushing Carla, he banged the cabinet shut with his knee. "You've had absolutely your last drink of the night."

"Get out of my way."

"Carla, you've had enough."

"Enough of you."

She feinted left, but he wasn't fooled, and, blocking the cabinet with his body, seized her wrists. Her lipstick was smeared again; a hook of red decorated her cheek. She'd repaired her makeup twice during the evening—twice that he knew about.

"Sit down," he said, shoving her.

Off balance, she backed into the double bed and went down with a little gasp. Fairbanks stood over her like a wrathful father. "I have had my fill of this kind of behavior. You spent the whole damned evening fawning over that flaming queer who couldn't even keep you upright on the dance floor."

Carla leaned back on both hands. "He's more of a man than you."

"Speaking from firsthand experience, are you?"

"You have a spiteful rotten temper, darling. Go fuck yourself. You bore me."

She rolled sideways off the bed and lurched back to the parlor. Fairbanks noticed stain rings on the peach satin. What had she spilled all over herself? And in front of whom? He ran after her. Hearing him behind her, she snatched off one silver pump and tried to clout him with the heel. He grabbed the shoe and threw it, breaking the pane of a window overlooking Market Street. The velvet portiere ropes swung to and fro. His head was buzzing.

"Pay attention, Carla. No, damn it, don't sneer and turn your back. I am not going to be fobbed off one more time with your spoiled arrogance. You made a spectacle of yourself downstairs. You started with Chance, but he was only the first. There were important people at the ball, people who must be influenced in this election. It's the last time you're going to embarrass me. For the duration of the campaign, it is—the—last—time."

"My. Oh my." She giggled. "I've seldom seen you so passionate. Certainly never in bed."

He pushed her again, dropping her on a sofa of Turkish leather. To his amazement, she laughed, turned her smeared face upward and *laughed*. The buzzing in his head grew louder.

"Carla, I mean this warning. You'd better not do anything to embarrass me from now until November or you'll pay for it."

"Oh, is he scared? I believe he is. Dear little Walter, the uncrowned prince of California, is scared—"

"My future rides on this campaign," he shouted. "Not only my job, but my reputation."

She laughed and knifed him again. "Why are you so scared, sweetheart? Because you're pitted against Mack Chance?"

A sudden, awful, total silence. An auto honked down on Market. Distantly, in the Bay, a ferry bell rang. Fairbanks admonished her with a shake of his finger, but it was feeble, without heart.

"You'd just better heed what I said. If you don't, you'll regret it."

"If I'm still here." She flounced over and picked up her ermine.

"Where are you going? Back to him?"

"Maybe. Why not? He's a better man than you'll ever be. He's beaten you at every turn. He even raised your son."

"My—?"

His mouth hung open, and his sleek hair, shiny as his dancing pumps, straggled over his forehead. At that moment he resembled nothing so much as a child lost in a dark wood.

Carla leaned against the brightly papered wall, hands behind the small of her back. Her round breasts moved up and down, the only sign of her excitement. She placed the next knife gently, almost tenderly.

"Yes, I said *son*. Mack isn't Jim's father. It was you. That New Year's in Pasadena. I worked out the dates. I'm positive about it." Venom flowed into her smile. "But you see, I wanted Mack to raise him. I knew he'd be a better father."

"Better? Mack's boy ran off, for God's sake. The whole town knows it."

"Well, yes—things went wrong. Doesn't change anything. I was his mother, and I had a choice to make. I made it. Just one more little contest that you lost to the best man, Walter."

"You slut." He shook her by the shoulders. "You dirty vindictive slut." He bounced her against the wall and she fell, crying out.

Seeing Fairbanks curl his hands into fists, Carla groped for a hold on the drop front of a writing desk. It pivoted down and her weight pulled the desk over. Ink gushed from the well; steel-nib pens flew; creamy Palace letterheads and envelopes sailed like seabirds.

"I'd kill you, but you're not worth it," Fairbanks said in a breaking voice. He gathered a homburg and overcoat, and a moment later the door slammed. Carla bent her back and shut her eyes and laid her cheek on the overturned writing desk.

At half past four the next afternoon, Gaspar Ludlow knocked softly on the door of the sanctum.

Ludlow was assistant chief clerk of the legal department. A smarmy young man, always smiling to please, he'd graduated from the business course at U.C. Berkeley and been employed by the SP for three years. The previous Thanksgiving, he'd created a vacancy by planting a Lincoln Steffens book on the desk of his immediate superior. The man was fired and he was promoted.

"Come."

Fairbanks was at work in shirtsleeves, writing on a ruled sheet of yellow legal paper. The clerk wasn't accustomed to seeing the general counsel without his coat, or doing anything so mundane as using a lead pencil. Fairbanks hadn't come in until half past nine. Ludlow was on another floor at the time. When he got back to the department, others whispered about it. Walter Fairbanks III was a punctual man; it was part of his perfectionism.

Several clerks told Ludlow his chief looked ill, and he did. His face pale as a bowl of cold oats and haggard, he handed Ludlow the yellow sheet.

"That is a description of a runaway boy—all of the description I can provide, anyhow. I don't know what name the boy may be using, but he bears a strong resemblance to Mrs. Fairbanks. His left foot is crippled, and he limps. He would be about twelve years old now. It's presumed that he ran away from San Francisco just prior to the earthquake. He may be dead. He may have left the state. If neither is true, I must locate him—for personal reasons. Transmit the description to every California sheriff and police department friendly to us."

Ludlow immediately characterized it as a futile assignment. However, one didn't get ahead in the SP by disagreeing with superiors. "We've paid enough money over the years to make certain there are plenty of those, sir. I'm sure we'll have some good results promptly."

Fairbanks stared at him with a sick expression, as if he were sure of nothing any longer.

IT WAS A THURSDAY IN THE LAST WEEK OF SEPTEMBER, a stiflingly hot day. Elihu Flintman drove over **76** from Covina in his buggy—not for him these newfangled autos, or any other creation of a dubious modernism. Despite the heat, he wore his heaviest suit, single-breasted and black, together with a black bow tie and fedora. He looked more like a preacher than most preachers.

Like thousands of others, Flintman had migrated to California from the Midwest. After his heart attack he had retired as vice chairman of the Merchants and Farmers Bank of Xenia, Ohio. Because of his heavy brows and big fan beard, he bore a strong physical resemblance to Charles Dickens, especially those stiff frontispiece portraits. Spiritually he was kin to Mr. Scrooge.

A visitor's buggy was tied outside the octagonal house. Flintman pulled in beside it and noted, as usual, the platoon of gardeners busy on the grounds. Flintman despised the Tabernacle of the Sun Universal, particularly because of its extravagances and pretenses, including the abundance of white flowers and shrubs and the cheery yellow and white paint adorning its headquarters.

Flintman's wife, Winona, worshiped the place, however. She worshiped the founder, whom Flintman considered no better than a crook, and perhaps a lunatic. Elihu Flintman yielded to the authority of no man, but with Winona it was different; he did what she told him, sometimes resentfully, but he did it. He'd volunteered to keep the tabernacle's books because she wanted him involved.

Flintman was the tabernacle's first trained bookkeeper. Brother Paul didn't want him, but the elected board of elders decided it was a good idea, and insisted. Previously, the founder kept the books. Flintman's exposure to the grossly inexact records, full of smudges, blots, and strikeovers, led him to launch a kind of secret crusade. Certain the founder stole a lot of the money the communicants paid into the tabernacle, Flintman was searching for hard evidence he could present to the elders, and particularly to Winona.

He crossed the airy veranda to the frosted-glass front door. The pie-wedge rooms of the octagonal house were all connected to a central foyer, which you reached by walking straight back from the entrance. The tabernacle was decorated in typical late-Victorian style, with heavy furniture, palms in pots, and every spare inch filled with something. For the walls the founder had commissioned some unknown hack to paint a series of sunlit California landscapes. These cheap works hung everywhere, along with small versions of the tabernacle's metal sunburst.

The door of a counseling room off the foyer stood ajar, and through the opening Flintman saw buxom Deacon Rowena at her desk. She had prospects: two retirees, dressed in their shabby best, their hope-filled faces craggy with age. Flintman pitied them, for Deacon Rowena, young and sun-browned, was spreading before them a segmented belt of canvas about five inches high.

"This is the solar longevity belt. The founder himself developed and approved it. You'll note the eight segments, corresponding to the octagon shape of the tabernacle. Each segment collects and stores the healing energy of the sun in special honeycomb cells. The cells disperse the energy into the body gradually and pleasantly. I think you'll agree that the price we ask—three hundred dollars—is remarkably low when I tell you this: Combined with Brother Paul's principles of good health and sunlight therapy, the belt is effective against many forms of malignant tumor. We've printed this little brochure with testimonials of Californians who have been completely cured.''

Old veined hands reached eagerly for the pamphlet. Deacon Rowena's eyes flicked to the door, sensing someone there, and Flintman hurried on. He was no scientist, but he presumed the belt was worthless, and the testimonials fraudulent.

The bookkeeper opened the door of his office. His occasional assistant was seated at the left half of a partner's desk. Sunlight falling through a window lit his hair like a great nugget of gold. He was a handsome lad, and tall. In front of him lay invoices, ledgers, his Chinese abacus with its lacquered dragons racing around the edge.

"Good morning, Jim David."

"Good morning, Mr. Flintman."

The bookkeeper hung his fedora on a peg. Suddenly he spied something peeping from beneath an account book. Jim blushed, discovered. Flintman pulled out three dime novels with lurid covers, issues of *Pluck and Luck* and *Work and Win*, and one of *Motor Stories*.

"Not in this office, Jim David," Flintman said, throwing the dime novels into a waste can.

"Those are good stories—" the boy began.

"They are trash. Especially those ridiculous tales of boys who earn millions after a stranger's plug hat is blown off on Fifth Avenue and they retrieve it and discover he's the richest man in New York, childless, and possessed of a completely unmotivated urge to share his moneymaking secrets with an adolescent. Trash," Flintman repeated, and sat down. "What have you been doing this morning?"

"Checking the bank deposits. I found another mistake."

"Show me, show me."

Jim gave him the open ledger. "An extra zero on the weekly deposit to Brother Paul's account. Instead of eighteen hundred dollars, it's eighteen thousand."

"That's the second such error in as many months." Flintman snapped the ledger shut. "I'll call it to his attention. Is he here?"

"No, sir. He went to the horse races. He'll be back late in the afternoon, Deacon Beatrice said. You could wait and visit him upstairs."

"Can't do it this evening. Busy. Besides, I never go upstairs.

I am his bookkeeper, not his crony." The tabernacle seethed with gossip about the activities up in the founder's rooms. Flintman had never ventured there, but now he thought perhaps he should. Perhaps he ought to search for evidence to confirm the rumors. Especially with Winona babbling about rewriting their wills to include a large bequest to the tabernacle.

"I'll confront him in due course, my boy. But it won't do any good. He'll laugh and say it's an oversight, just another oversight. A lot of honest and sincere people in this tabernacle are getting mighty tired of Brother Paul's oversights." He set his lips primly. "You're smart with figures, Jim David. A good worker too. I'm glad I was able to steal you from Mr. Sprue once a week."

"Yes, sir."

The bookkeeper's righteous face softened a little. "Is Sprue your stepfather?"

"No, he just looks after me."

"Have you no family in California? No mother?"

"I never knew her."

"A father?"

Jim's eye quickly shifted to the trashed dime novels. He stared at them, struggling to hide his pain.

"Once. But not anymore."

He bent his head and went back to work.

At four-thirty on the afternoon of October 1, a long curtained touring sedan drove through the tabernacle gate. As the black auto glided up the hill, a pearl-gray glove drew aside one of the rear curtains.

Walter Fairbanks leaned near the window, studying the yellow-and-white octagonal house on the terraced hill. He'd heard a lot about the place, and the sight of it sent a guilty thrill chasing through him.

The chauffeur halted the car. "I don't know how long I'll be, Sanchez. Pull over there and wait."

The chauffeur said, "Yes, sir," and opened the door for his passenger. After a quick, nervous look around—he saw a few gardeners, many plantings, some distant bungalows—Fairbanks darted up the steps and inside.

He expected exotic furnishings; he found conventional ones. But the young woman who took his card was anything but conventional—muscular and deeply browned, with huge round breasts. She carried the card upstairs. Within minutes, Wyatt Paul came down.

His linen suit and clerical dickey shone with a snowy brilliance, and the hand he extended to Fairbanks was brown and manicured. The white streaks in his hair were dominant, sweeping back from his temples like horns on a Viking helmet. His clear blue eyes looked feverish.

"Mr. Fairbanks. Pleased to make your acquaintance. Good of you to come all the way out to Pasadena."

"On the telephone, Mr. Paul, you insisted."

"It's a substantial donation. I thought I was entitled to hand it personally to the top man in the campaign."

"Yes, perfectly reasonable," Fairbanks said quickly. He didn't dare lose a donation so large.

"By the way. Communicants here call me Brother, not Mister." Wyatt caressed the arm of the buxom girl. "Thank you, Deacon Helen. I'll call you if our guest needs anything."

Fairbanks was put off by the smoky glance the young woman gave him as she left. It seemed to say, however briefly, that if the guest wanted her favors, she would readily oblige.

"Come along and see our sanctuary. I must say, Mr. Fairbanks, you look like you've had a difficult day."

"I was meeting with the M and M at breakfast—the Merchants and Manufacturers Association—when we got word of the disaster."

"Disaster?"

"You don't know? The *Times* building was dynamited early this morning. Sixty or seventy sticks were planted in an alley on the Broadway side. They've no idea how many are dead. At least twenty. Blown up—burned alive—"

"Terrible. Who did it?"

"General Otis has accused the striking metalworkers."

"I didn't realize there was a strike."

"Largest in the city's history. Fifteen hundred men have been out since June."

"I'm afraid I'm not good about keeping track of mundane matters."

"It isn't mundane to those of us in commerce," Fairbanks said a bit testily. "It's life and death for the open shop here. The San Francisco trade locals poured in money and professional agitators. This is the result—anarchy and murder. Otis calls it the crime of the century. He swears he'll have the culprits in front of a firing squad."

"I certainly hope he's successful. This way, please."

Soothed by Wyatt's charm, Fairbanks followed him across the round central foyer. Wyatt slid back carved doors and they walked out on a dais to a pulpit that faced semicircular rows

655

of pews. Fairbanks glanced around, noting another great metal sunburst suspended on wires above him.

"This is where I lecture on the principles of solar medicine, physical and emotional health. By the way, you'll stay the night, won't you? I have a spacious guest room in my quarters upstairs."

"No, I'm afraid I can't, Mr.—Brother Paul."

"You're turning me down?" Wyatt's clear blue eyes showed a curious opal blaze. "It's late in the day, and a long drive back to the city—"

"But there's a rally for Hiram Johnson downtown. Nell Ross, the radical writer, is speaking. I must listen to her. Find out what sort of lies she's spreading about Bell and his slate, so we can counter them. I'm sorry—it's a duty I can't avoid."

Obviously irked, Wyatt said, "Pity. My evening—ah—socials with some of the deacons are quite special." A pause. "Quite private too, if that's a concern."

Fairbanks understood what Brother Paul was suggesting, and it weakened his knees. He could certainly use a little discreet companionship after all these weeks of riding the SP from town to town, meeting with grubby merchants and farmers, speaking to groups, and begging money until he was glassy-eyed. But he couldn't rest or let down until it was over. Until they won.

"Thank you, Brother Paul. I really must go back. Miss Ross is scheduled for half past eight."

"The check won't be ready until nine." Wyatt said it sharply; Fairbanks had overstepped. "If you want it, call Los Angeles and get someone else to spy on the woman."

"Certainly. Of course."

Brother Paul was pleased again. He draped his white sleeve over Fairbanks's shoulder a little too intimately for the lawyer's taste. "Good. We can at least have a drink in my rooms. Perhaps you'd like a rest and brushup first?"

Fairbanks felt dizzy. What if he'd lost the donation and the board had found out? He felt like a man on a precipice these days. That was why he drove himself through the tank towns, repeated the same dreary speech at local chamber-of-commerce dinners, survived on three or four hours' sleep a night and meals of hard rolls and acidic black coffee that destroyed the stomach. He had to win. You either made a perfect mark, or you didn't. There was no middle ground. There had seldom been any in his life, and there was absolutely none this time.

Brother Paul was staring again. Fairbanks fumbled out his reply.

"I'm sorry—yes—kind of you. I'll make the telephone call. Then I'll rest. It has been a trying day."

To his astonishment, Fairbanks napped, for a long while. When he woke, fully dressed, on the large bed in the Victorian bedroom on the second floor, he checked his watch hastily. Five minutes past nine. His eye leaped to the windows. It was dark.

In front of the mirror he smoothed his hair and straightened his cravat. He heard distant music, a woman singing in a slightly tinny voice, as though she sang inside some huge re-sounding sewer pipe.

The tabernacle rooms were equipped with old gas mantles as well as newer electrics, and the gas had been lit and trimmed low. Fairbanks followed the music to double doors at the back of the house, directly above the sanctuary, and knocked. Wyatt's cheerful voice bade him walk in.

Fairbanks felt the hot guilty thrill again. His palms were perspiring. He slid the doors open and tried not to let his eyes bug.

Wyatt's quarters were spacious, but crowded with dark fur-niture. He was relaxing on a leather lounge, wearing only his white trousers. His hairless chest was hard, flat, sun-browned. Beside him sat Deacon Helen, a peculiar dreamy look in her eyes. She'd changed her dress for a white dressing gown, and Wyatt had his hand inserted under one lapel, idly teasing and pinching her great sagging breast.

"Good evening, Fairbanks." Wyatt had to speak loudly to be heard. On a stand, an enormous Victrola poured music out of its fluted horn. The needle scratched on the Red Seal disc and the singer reached for the sweet aching high notes of "*Un bel dì.*" Fairbanks counted four dark-green wine bottles on a white rug, two of them empty. "Do come in and have a drink," Wyatt went on. "Is it nine o'clock already?"

"Just past." Fairbanks stepped onto the white rug and started. His foot had come down on the stuffed head of a polar bear, its huge fanged jaws open and glass eyes shining.

Wyatt laughed over his discomfort. "You're still tense. I don't think you relaxed properly. Some of this wine will help."

Fairbanks noted other details: the butts of fat green cigars in a cut-glass tray, the remains of a meal on a taboret, gnawed beefsteak bones strewn on a platter of bloody juice. He was cynically amused; before napping, he'd skimmed a copy of *A California Sunshine Diet* in the guest room.

A curtain parted in the shadows and another young woman

walked into the room rubbing her eyes. She was short, with blond ringlets, and was even more stupendously endowed than Deacon Helen. Her robe was carelessly open, exposing her bobbling breasts and pubic mound. Fairbanks almost strangled getting his breath.

Amused, Wyatt used a waiter's corkscrew to open a new bottle of wine, then filled a clean silver cup. "This is very special."

Fairbanks drank, expecting some ordinary vintage. Sweet fumes floated up his nose. The red wine was heavy, with a curious undertaste. "Remarkable. What is it?" Perhaps it was his imagination, but he felt the soothing effects at once.

"Vin Mariani. It contains a specially prepared extract of cocoa leaves. A young Corsican developed it and ships it all around the world. He has endorsements from H. G. Wells, Rodin, the czar, the Prince of Wales—the pope even awarded him a gold medal for it." Wyatt splashed wine into cups for the two deacons, and the new girl seized hers in both hands and drank noisily.

It wasn't an ordinary wine, then. It contained a drug. Fairbanks perched on the edge of a plush chair, rolling the silver cup between his palms. He wanted to run to the new girl, so voluptuous and vacant, and throw her down and rut on her. The moment he imagined it, guilt stabbed him. Not because he was married—fidelity to Carla hardly mattered anymore—but simply because a part of him wanted to succumb so badly. Only proles and degenerates behaved that way. His bowels began to grumble and pain him.

"Brother Paul, I really don't want to be an ungracious guest—"

"But you must go. Until you came in I didn't realize it was past the appointed hour. Time tends to lose meaning when one is surrounded by charming diversions." He parted Deacon Helen's robe below her waist. Fairbanks saw her tanned strong legs. He saw everything.

"Look at their bodies, Mr. Fairbanks. Golden bodies. California bodies. Strengthened and made vital by the mystic healing sunshine."

A cold little knot wound up inside Fairbanks's head, and he was suddenly fearful of this dim room, the sweet rich wine, these strange, dreamy-eyed people. The evil part of him wanted to sink into this world and drown in it, forget all the responsibility crushing down. But a larger, dominant part knew that it was imperative he leave. The pupils of Brother Paul's eyes were huge as a cat's at night. Fairbanks could deal with ordinary people, but this man wasn't ordinary; this man was not right in the head.

Steering the conversation clumsily, he said, "I do appreciate your willingness to donate to our campaign—"

"It's the right side," Wyatt exclaimed. "The side of free commerce, which is the genius of California. Those Progressives would have us saddled by all sorts of restrictive laws to make us our brother's keeper. Well . . ." He drank from his silver cup and the Vin Mariani ran down his chin. "I am my own keeper. And sometimes my sister's."

He reached up between Deacon Helen's spread legs and fondled. She giggled and held out her cup. The other girl, unwanted, lifted the needle scratching at the end of the record, then disappeared.

Fairbanks stood up, his pulse loud and fast in his inner ear. The wine had set him afloat. "Brother Paul—"

"Oh, all right. But you're a spoilsport." Wyatt opened the door of a small drum table next to the lounge and rummaged inside. A news clipping fell out, then a bank check. He picked up both, handing Fairbanks the check.

Damn him, he probably had it ready this afternoon. Had to show his power by making me wait.

"Thirty thousand dollars from my personal funds," Wyatt said. "But it's anonymous. You understand that?"

"Perfectly." Fairbanks folded and pocketed the check as if it might melt. "It will be of enormous help."

"Better be." Wyatt sounded drunk. He waved the clipping. "I don't want any of this bastard's candidates to win so much as one damn vote."

Fairbanks took up the invitation to examine the clipping. At the head of the column, Mack and Hiram Johnson peered out of a photograph. It was an unflattering, grainy picture of both.
J. M. CHANCE STUMPS VALLEY WITH PROGRESSIVE CANDIDATE.

Fairbanks's palm grew moist again. "You know Macklin Chance?"

"Too well. Twenty years ago he defrauded me of oil rights to land we owned jointly. And he stole something else that was mine. A woman." Wyatt wiped a shiny dab of drool in the corner of his mouth.

Fairbanks's neck itched, and the constrictions in his middle worsened the moment the awful suspicion occurred to him. "Would I know this woman?"

Wyatt was staring at him, but now looked away with a shrug. "Oh, I don't think so." A little smile played on his mouth a moment. "She's prominent, but—no, I don't think so. Her name

659

isn't important. What's important is how I felt about her. I wanted to fuck her for the rest of my life. He took her, and that's why I'd like to put Mr. Macklin Chance into permanent retirement. Unfortunately there are laws against murder, so I'm reduced to fighting him with money."

Fairbanks switched to his careful courtroom mode. "Chance has a great many enemies in California, I find."

Wyatt rubbed Deacon Helen's exposed thigh. "But none like me, Mr. Fairbanks. Absolutely none like me."

Fairbanks could fairly feel the poison. Remarkable to find someone who hated Mack even more than he did. Hated him to the point of wanting to kill him.

"Brother Paul, thank you again for your hospitality."

Wyatt shrugged. "Didn't avail yourself of much. Shame to be so tight all the time, so scheduled—"

"We must win this election."

"That we must. Can you see yourself out?"

"Certainly."

After Fairbanks rolled the doors shut, he started at the unexpected sight of a man half visible at the head of the stairs, a bearded man with papers in his hand.

The man looked stunned and angry, but Fairbanks supposed it had nothing to do with him. Then he realized that the man might have glimpsed Brother Paul without his shirt and Deacon Helen beside him, glimpsed them just as he came up, when Fairbanks opened the doors to leave.

The man shot him a suspicious look, turned, and hurried down the stairs. When Fairbanks reached the first floor, the central foyer was empty.

Outside, he woke the chauffeur, who was snoring in the front seat. Faintly, through muffling layers of glass and velvet, the soprano sang *"Un bel dí."* The aria was masked suddenly by another woman's shrieking laugh. Walter Fairbanks dove into the backseat.

"Get away from here, Sanchez—fast."

THE MUTOGRAPH CAMERA WHIRRED AND CLACKED. **77**
A slim rider on a palomino galloped along the Niles
Canyon road, skirt hiked above the stirrups, auburn hair
streaming. Suddenly the long hair lifted and sailed into the
roadside weeds.

"Cut it, cut," Van Zant Morgan screamed, throwing his
tropical helmet on the ground. "Makeup, damn it, can't you
secure that wig?"

The chagrined young man in the dress reined the palomino.
Anderson, who was to ride into the shot at the last moment,
trotted his white horse forward and commiserated with the stunt
player. Anderson didn't seem too disturbed, but the director
acted like a child robbed of his candy.

In the shade, Mack sat on a wooden box next to Margaret,
whose chair had white letters on the canvas back that said MAR-
GARET LESLIE. Her dress, a plain cotton befitting a frontier
woman, matched that of the rider who was pulling burrs from
the auburn wig.

"How is the campaign going, Mack?"

"We look stronger south of the Tehachapi than we do in the
north. I expect it's because the Progressives are basically Republican and Protestant, and those are the kind of people who
predominate down south. San Francisco is more cosmopolitan.
We're drawing good demonstrative crowds in the Valley. I predict a big win."

"You've been out with Hiram Johnson, haven't you?"

"Yes, and I'll start again tomorrow. I came down on a boat
from Sacramento to take care of some business with Haverstick. I had a free afternoon so I decided to look in on my
investment and my favorite actress. How is she?"

"She's in bed in her bungalow by eight every night. This is
hard work."

Mack tapped the white lettering on her chair. "This is new."

"Billy's idea. He picked the name."

"I like it."

"So do I. Miss Leslie will be billed in the titles when the
new Broncho Billy is released next week. Billy keeps assuring
me Miss Leslie will have a long career."

"I think so."

He said it quietly, reflectively. A sadness gripped him. Perhaps it was the season—late October—or the nearness to sunset. Van Zant Morgan took note as well, clapping. "Hurry up, hurry up—we'll be chasing our tails in the dark before long."

Mack was staring fixedly at the homburg held between his knees, and Margaret made up her mind to speak.

"I finished Nellie Ross's novel last night. It's wonderful."

"The railroad doesn't think so." The mention of Nellie perked him up noticeably.

"Where is she, still campaigning?"

"She's largely finished, I think. She's back in Carmel."

"Have you seen her?"

"I've thought of it. Quite a lot. Haven't done anything about it."

"But you should." She laid her hand on his. "Let me confide in you, Mr. Chance. I knew the very moment I fell in love with you—" His head snapped up. "—I knew I might as well fall right out, because there was no other woman in your world, only Nellie."

"That's quite an admission."

"Not really surprising, is it? You've known how I felt for years."

"Yes." He seemed embarrassed. "But if what you say is true, I've certainly done my best to keep Nellie out of my world for a long time."

"Do you know why?"

"Oh—many reasons. Different ideas, for one. We're never able to agree on major things. And she accused me more than once of overweening ambition. I could say the same about her."

"That sounds like male pride speaking."

"Now wait—"

"Please let me finish. Pride is deadly, Mack. It injures all of us. We shouldn't allow it. Time is too precious. Look at this lovely day—it's almost over, and so is another year. Autumn weather reminds me that I'm not as young as I once was. Neither are you, my dear. Don't waste the rest of your life because of pride."

"Margaret, I have a lot of bull-headed notions, I admit it. I've been wrong plenty of times, especially in the way I've expressed certain things to Nellie. About her work—I do respect and admire, but I'm not sure a woman should spend her entire life at a writing table."

"In preference to what? Childbearing? I don't understand. You don't find a career acceptable for her, but you encouraged me in this one. Why two standards? Because you decided Nellie should marry you?"

Mack turned scarlet, then slid past the accusation. "I encouraged you on an impulse. I have money in Essanay—Anderson needed an actress on short notice."

"And that's how lives change forever? As a result of an impulse? How disillusioning." A mocking sigh. Then: "Don't take that seriously. I'm not unhappy."

"I hope not. Everything's going splendidly for you."

"Yes. Billy has almost convinced me it's safe to sell the Maison. But we're discussing J. M. Chance." She clasped his hand. "Forget the arguments with Nellie, your differences. Soften your stand. Lower the righteous male fist you shake at everything not quite in tune with your views. Go to her."

"She'd probably turn me down again."

"She might not."

His expression was skeptical, but he wanted to believe it.

"Mack, you've changed a lot in the time I've known you. You're willing to examine your ideas about most anything else. To try the new—jettison the old—can't you do it with her? And has it never occurred to you that Nellie may have changed too? You should find out. Take the first step. If you're too proud to do that much, and you lose her permanently—"

"Ready, please, Miss Leslie," Morgan's assistant shouted through a megaphone.

Mack stared at the woman who'd admitted her love as calmly, as casually, as someone might express a taste for black coffee. She had never said it straight out before, not even during their night at the Redondo Lodge. Her admission sharpened a new guilt in him. Margaret was special, and she needed someone equally so, a man who'd devote his life to her. He couldn't be that man. She knew it, and in her generosity she was sending him where she knew he wanted to go.

Golden light slanted past the hills, thin and pale as the day waned. Anderson walked toward them, leading his white horse. His bulky shadow fell across Margaret's skirt. He'd seen the earnest conversation and spoke now in an apologetic way.

"We're ready."

Margaret stood and touched Mack's cheek. "Perhaps you did drive her away long ago. But that's past. Remedy it, Mack. Change. If you can't change for the person you love, then you're a bigger fool than you were in the first place. I'd change for you if you so much as lifted an eyebrow. I'd wear rags for you. I'd climb Mount Shasta in a blizzard. I'd do anything. That's what love's about."

She kissed him almost chastely on the mouth, then gathered up her skirts in both hands and ran to her puzzled employer.

They crossed the San Joaquin, and soon the red Locomobile chugged into Manteca. If Mack remembered correctly, the SP had established this depot and named it after a creamery in the neighborhood.

At the edge of town they passed a billboard, an enormous photo enlargement of "The Shame of California," captioned VOTE PROGRESSIVE. The Johnson campaign had spread this board all over the state.

Open to the heat and dust, the Locomobile left its passengers sweaty and dirty after a short time on the road. Neither Mack nor Hiram Johnson nor the driver minded, because there was a sense of great forward momentum in the campaign, a presentiment of victory, and it energized them.

In Manteca's dusty downtown, they parked and followed the established routine. Mack and the driver walked along different streets, ringing cowbells.

"Come hear Hiram Johnson, the Teddy Roosevelt of the West—your next governor. Hear the Progressive candidate in ten minutes. Look for the big red Locomobile parked in front of the hardware store."

Forty-four years old, energetic, and enormously ambitious, the corpulent Johnson put on the same show at every stop. He doffed his coat and wire spectacles, loosened his tie, rolled up his shirtsleeves, and jumped on the rear seat of the open auto. From there he lit into the opposition, whether he had an audience of two or two hundred. He was a splendid, polished orator with a vibrant voice.

Today he gathered about thirty-five people. Mack sat on a shaded bench in front of Person's Hardware, paging through the previous day's *Stockton Trumpet*. He knew Johnson's stump speech by heart.

"My friends, we are going to reclaim California for honest government. We are going to drive the money changers out of the temple of the people. We are going to do it by electing trustworthy officials and enacting three important reforms."

Unexpectedly, Mack saw someone familiar at the back of the crowd: Diego Marquez.

"One, we will enact the initiative provision in the state constitution and local charters. This will put legislative power directly into your hands. You will be able to band together to initiate new laws or modify bad ones. No legislator in Sacramento wiggling in the hip pocket of the SP will be able to stop you in this exercise of your rightful power."

A couple of farmers clapped, but Mack's eyes were riveted on Marquez. His spectacles were thicker. His beard hung almost to his enormous belly and he hadn't cut his hair in a long while. Large bruises discolored his forehead and left cheek; someone else had taken exception to his opinions.

Mack folded the paper and stared at the ex-priest. He was sure Marquez had seen him, but was refusing to make eye contact.

"Two, the referendum. This reform will allow citizens of California to step to the ballot box and veto any corrupt or wrongful legislation. It will send a powerful message to Sacramento, and foil those lawmakers who consistently and shamelessly serve special interests instead of the common good. Third, and finally, the recall. If all else fails—if the toadies of the Southern Pacific and the other power barons fail to heed the will of the people—your will, my friends—they can be removed from office. Those are the three strongest planks in the Progressive platform. I ask you to vote for them—for me—and for a new era of decent government in California."

Johnson's fiery finish stirred them: Everyone clapped long and hard. After looking at the candidate for several moments, Mack glanced into the crowd again. Marquez was gone. He'd have liked to talk to the ex-priest, whether Marquez wanted it or not, but there was no time to search for him. They had one more stop before sunset, down the road in Salida.

The crowd broke up, and Johnson jumped out of the car to shake hands, while Mack leafed quickly through the rest of the paper. A boxed advertisement for a San Francisco rally caught his attention; Nellie's name was prominent. He checked the date.

"Hiram, I'm leaving you for a couple of days," he said when they were rolling down the dirt highway. "I have to go back to the City. It's important."

He couldn't find a seat—hundreds packed the hall and squatted in the aisles and leaned against the side walls—so he stood in the dark at the rear. Under a huge portrait of Johnson, photographed triumphantly with his arms upraised, Nellie spoke passionately to the throng.

"During the administration of Abraham Lincoln, the first secretary of war, before Mr. Stanton, was named Simon Cameron. Cameron was a powerful, some say venal political boss from Pennsylvania—he ran the state machine. On one occasion

665

someone asked him for his definition of an honest politician. 'That's easy,' Cameron replied. 'Once he's bought, he stays bought.' "

Laughter. When it quieted, she went on. "My friends, California has suffered for several decades with a plague of 'honest' politicians. The Progressives intend to change that with the initiative, the referendum, and the recall—three checks upon the outrageous cupidity of some of our elected officials. Further, our party is pledged to work for social good. For conservation of our forests. Hospital and prison reform. A curb on illegal child labor and on the unregulated urban saloons. We want direct election of United States senators, instead of nomination by political cronies—or secret ballot in the SP boardroom. We demand a minimum wage for working women. A public utilities board with real power, beholden to none. A railroad commission that will set fair rates, and then enforce them—a commission that is not a puppet or a propaganda bureau for those it is meant to regulate."

On the huge stage, dwarfed by the great portrait, she still held every listener's attention.

"As a woman, I am forbidden to vote for Hiram Johnson or any other Progressive candidate. That in itself is a crime and a scandal." In the orchestra and gallery, men booed. Nellie's eyes flayed the great dark pit of the audience. "I repeat: a crime and a scandal. But we'll win that battle someday."

A man in a front row snickered. The sound fell into a moment of silence, and mass laughter erupted. Nellie slapped the podium. It was loud as a shot, and her subsequent words carried to the farthest rows.

"Yes, we'll win that battle—gentlemen—and write our suffrage doctrine into the Constitution, whether you approve or not. Our first priority, however, is to win on the eighth of November. So I say: Down with the railroad and its political captives. Down with 'honest' politicians who warp the truth, scoff at morality, and manipulate our legislatures and our courts for profit. Now, after forty years and more, that kind of despotic rule is over. On the day after the election, California will once again belong to you, to me, and to all of her people. Thank God, I say. Thank God. Thank you, and good night."

Nellie's face was turned up to catch the stage lights. For a moment that face, a shining cameo of bravery, maintained the silence. Then the first rows came up stomping and cheering, and like a breaking wave, the ovation spread. Mack clapped till his hands hurt. In the anonymous dark at the back of the hall, his face glowed with pride and love.

For nearly five minutes, pols and well-wishers milled around her. Then the chairman gaveled the hall to order and introduced two local candidates, each of whom spoke well, but it was anticlimactic. Mack fidgeted, eager for the rally to end so he could find Nellie. It was time to mend things, start over.

After the concluding speech, the pit orchestra struck up a march. Mack fought his way down the aisle, against the noisy enthusiasts coming the other way, and ran up the steps at stage right.

He saw her in the wings, in her evening wrap. She dashed up to a portly and genial-looking stranger in a tuxedo. The man was older, bald, deeply tanned, and wore an expensive silk scarf draped around the collar of his jacket; it was as white as his huge drooping mustache.

Her eyes shining, Nellie threw her arms around the man's neck and kissed and hugged him. They walked out arm in arm, laughing and chatting like intimates. Stunned, Mack turned and left the stage.

On November 5, the Saturday before the election, Wyatt faced the tabernacle's board of elders.

The special meeting was convened with a day's notice, and the elders had invited all communicants, Elihu Flintman personally spreading the word by telephone to a network of callers. At 10 A.M., Wyatt confronted all of the elders and some 270 tabernacle members in the sanctuary.

Wyatt sat in a tall chair behind the pulpit, stiff and affronted. Dust-moted sunbeams lanced down from high windows. He let his eye rove over the congregation. What a shabby, ignorant lot, he thought. Indiana farmers newly come to California and still raw red from the sun. Stiff-necked ugly women with dried-up dugs, wrinkles, and righteous expressions. How he hated them—all the more because they were so gullible.

This morning, though, he noted a difference in the faces of these small-towners come to live out their last years in cheap bungalows. Where he had previously seen earnest sympathy and affection for him, he now saw dislike, even outright hate. It was the hate of infantile minds coming sluggishly to an awareness that they had been deceived . . .

Flintman stepped up and took charge, clearly savoring the opportunity. He was prosecutorial with the bank check, which he flourished like a dead fish left in the sun too long.

"I call your attention to this thirty-thousand-dollar donation, Mr. Paul."

"Brother Paul, if you don't mind."

Flintman glared right back. "You donated this money to the Democratic campaign of Theodore Bell. I show you the name of the state campaign organization on the face, and the endorsement on the back. The bank that cleared the check called the irregularity to my attention."

"What irregularity, for God's sake?"

"We'll come to that."

"They had no right, Flintman. Bank transactions are private."

"Yes, the bank violated confidentiality. But its officers obeyed a higher law—"

"What shit," Wyatt said under his breath. A woman in the third row heard, but he stared her down.

"They called attention to the donation because it was not permissible."

Wyatt shot out of his chair. "What do you mean, not permissible?" He was loud, belligerent. There was no trace of his customary charm. Flintman had first shown him the canceled check at 4 P.M. the day before, and he hadn't slept all night. "Why not, I ask you. That money came from my personal account."

"That is not true. That is a flagrant lie. The account on which this check is written is not your personal account, it is the general tabernacle account. That is why the bank took notice. I charge that you diverted tabernacle funds for a private purpose. That is serious malfeasance. Not all of us here wish to see the SP candidates elected."

Cries of, "No!" and, "They're crooks!" filled the hall. Christ, how those smug stupid faces disgusted him. He saw Winona Flintman in the second pew, looking at him as if he were vermin. He wished he had a pistol to blow her eyes out.

Wyatt stormed to the pulpit; Flintman retreated a step. "You're telling me to whom I can and cannot make political donations?" He tried to be scornful, to brand the thought ludicrous. But Flintman stood up to him:

"In this case, yes. What misguided thinking prompted you, I don't know. Nor do I care. I am merely stating irrefutable fact. You gave tabernacle funds to a personal cause."

"I *am* the tabernacle. The rest of you are ciphers. Dung. Nothing!" He yelled it, pushed beyond reason.

Outraged stares and exclamations showed the dreadful miscalculation. He dug his nails into his hands, the pain helping him regain control.

Flintman was pleased by Wyatt's outburst and now regaled the founder with a pious smile. "Your opinions are immaterial at this stage, sir. You are not the supreme authority here. You are not a dictator, though perhaps through benign neglect and tolerance we have given you that illusion. You have broken faith with the members and the ruling elders of this congregation."

And then Wyatt knew, truly knew, how bad this was. The bearded old bastard was going for a kill. A great vomitous feeling overwhelmed him. Of course he wouldn't allow them to win. He would *not*. He went on the attack, seizing hold of the pulpit and startling Flintman into another retreat. With his aggressive stance and his fierce gaze, Wyatt defied all the set mouths, the vicious pig eyes, the puny minds in front of him.

"Ruling elders? What have the ruling elders got to do with it? Who do you think coined the term *ruling elders*, for Christ's sake? I did. I wrote the articles of organization—me, personally. They were meaningless then and they're meaningless now."

"No, sir. Lawyers have examined them. Advised us they are enforceable and urged us to act upon them. We are specifically enforcing the clause which states that all members of the tabernacle shall be of high moral character, beyond reproach. You have cheated us, Mr. Paul. You have falsified other financial records. You have engaged in acts of moral turpitude which I personally witnessed."

Wyatt's smile went on like an electric light. "Elihu. Friend. Let's not air these ridiculous—"

"You are a disgrace, sir." Flintman pointed at him with a trembling hand. "A whoremaster, a deceiver—a monumental fraud."

Winona Flintman sagged forward, sobbing into her gloved hands as angry mutters ran around the hall. Wyatt stood slack-mouthed again. His attack had failed, hadn't intimidated them even slightly. A queer ringing filled his ears, and he saw double images of Flintman.

"Effective at noon tomorrow," Flintman said, "the board of elders relieves you of all authority in the tabernacle. You have no followers, no church—and with the cooperation of the bank we have seen to it that tabernacle accounts are beyond your reach. You'll steal no more of our money, Mr. Paul."

Wyatt jumped him. "I'll break your fucking neck."

Flintman yelled and pulled at Wyatt's hands on his throat, then lunged sideways. He missed the edge of the platform, fell, and landed hard in front of the first pew. Everyone heard his head knock the pew seat. Winona Flintman shrieked and threw herself over the back of the pew. "My husband has a weak heart."

Men from the congregation ran to the platform and surrounded Wyatt. He spat and snarled and rammed his elbows in their bellies. "Hold him, for God's sake." They were older, less strong, but his violence drew them out of the audience in large numbers, and in a few moments, he was wedged inside a mass of bodies. He cursed and kicked until a louder voice overrode him—that of another elder.

"Let him go. Jephtha, Donald, Cleve—stand away from him. He's whipped."

Panting, Wyatt shoved his tangled hair off his forehead. They'd rumpled and soiled his white suit, ripped off his clerical collar and trampled it.

Elihu Flintman stood up groggily. His cheeks had a blue tinge and he was bleeding from a forehead cut, but he had the strength of righteousness. He swayed forward to the platform and pointed.

"Noon tomorrow. Twenty-four hours. Be out of your quarters and off these premises, taking nothing but your clothing. Otherwise there will be a sheriff's warrant for your arrest."

On Sunday, Elihu Flintman and Jim worked in the bookkeeping office from one o'clock until dark, pulling and listing every ledger and record of the tabernacle in preparation for turning the lot over to the attorneys. Flintman dictated the descriptions and Jim wrote them down with a steel nib in his fine large hand.

Flintman was smugly exultant, though his good feeling was blunted by occasional severe angina, and by worry about Winona. After the frightful session the day before, from which Wyatt had stalked screaming the vilest obscenities, Winona Flintman had collapsed. Flintman rushed her to Pasadena Hospital, where she was sedated for nervous prostration.

Jim worked quietly, following instructions, asking no questions. He hadn't been allowed to attend the meeting, but he knew that a group of elders and a sheriff's deputy had escorted Brother Paul off the grounds at five past twelve. Jim was relieved that the founder was gone; Brother Paul had always frightened him a little. He just hoped he and Jocker would continue to have jobs.

Around eight o'clock, just as he was starting to yawn behind his hand and wonder if he dared ask Flintman about supper, he heard someone cross the veranda with a soft tread. Then faint clicks signaled the opening and closing of the front door. Immersed in canceled checks, Flintman didn't look up.

"See who's there, Jim David."

Dutifully Jim left the office. Deacon Rowena, Deacon Helen, and the others had packed up and departed sometime Saturday night. Could it be one of them coming back for something? He limped from the central foyer past the staircase and caught his breath. Brother Paul was halfway up the stairs.

"Mr. Flintman," Jim shouted.

"You little prick." Brother Paul lunged at him, shooting his hands over the banister. Jim jumped back, but his bad foot twisted, and Brother Paul's fingers brushed his throat.

Elihu Flintman lumbered from the office. "Here, what are you doing? Come to add thievery to your mischief?" Flintman rushed up the staircase, though he slowed noticeably on the last few steps. He grabbed Wyatt's arm. "Get off these premises. Jim, telephone the sheriff."

Brother Paul bashed him with an elbow and Flintman staggered down three steps, sucking air, his eyes bulging. Jim struggled up past the bookkeeper as fast as he could. "You hurt him," he yelled, throwing himself at Wyatt. He got one hand around Wyatt's arm and then Wyatt punched his jaw.

Jim's teeth cut the lining of his mouth. He spat bloody saliva. A few drops splattered Wyatt's sweater, and it seemed to drive the man wild. He grabbed Jim's blond hair and kicked him between the legs, then flung him bodily down the stairs.

Jim landed hard, skidding. As Wyatt ran down, Flintman clutched at him. "You—monster—" Wyatt pivoted and threw a brutal blow into Flintman's abdomen. The bookkeeper collapsed, grasping for the banister and choking. His eyes rolled up in his head. Then he flopped like a rag doll.

Wyatt's head was afire with rage and the lovely unexpected satisfaction of dealing with these two. He darted the rest of the way down and paused over Jim's prostrate body.

If he had ever seen the boy before, it hadn't made an impression. They said everyone in the world had a twin; this boy was Carla's. Uncanny. How like a beautiful sleeping seraph he was . . .

Wyatt's dreamy smile vanished, and he kicked Jim's head viciously. The boy's head snapped over. Wyatt heard his weak cry as he ran to a bay window. Grinning, Wyatt tore draperies from their rings, and then he held one edge up to the gas until it flamed.

Jocker Sprue was sitting in the cool darkness outside his cottage when he saw the rose-pink light in the octagonal house. He shouted until he roused two other gardeners who could run faster than an arthritic old man. They reached the tabernacle

671

as the fire spread out of the foyer. Flintman was found with his legs still on the stairs and his mussed gray hair resting on the polished floor. The gardeners dragged his lifeless body outside, then rescued Jim from the puddle of blood where his head lay.

By nine o'clock the fire had gutted the tabernacle. By half past, the last beams crumbled in shining waterfalls of sparks. Old Jocker shivered in the night air and thoughtlessly remarked that the fire was bright as the sun.

78 CARLA LEFT THE PARTY AT HALF PAST ONE.

Party? It was a funeral. She'd consumed two full bottles of champagne and half of a third. She was still depressed, and wanted more.

After eleven o'clock Walter barely said a word to her, just sat there watching the numbers going up on the chalkboard, sat there with a full glass and a sick-dog expression as the telephone lines brought the totals into the St. Francis. Around twelve-thirty she slipped into a cloakroom with a randy little ward captain. He bolted the door and she screwed him standing up. When she came back, Johnson still held his twenty-thousand-vote lead. Walter didn't know she'd been gone.

She staggered out the Post Street entrance, taken aback by the sound of rain. It was pouring, sluicing off the canopy and flooding the sidewalk underneath. To her left, headlamps came on, and Walter's newest Pope-Toledo, black as usual, glided out of its space and pulled in near the canopy. Carla's fox fur dragged in the water as she crossed the sidewalk.

After he had gotten Carla in, the chauffeur U-turned, heading west on Post, then south on Mason. The rain hammered the metal roof and rushed under the car like Niagara. Carla leaned back and shut her eyes. Walter had failed the SP. God. What next?

The car slowed for the O'Farrell intersection, and she opened her eyes. On a brick wall ahead she saw two big posters washed by the rain. One advertised a motion picture with a large, heroic illustration of a cowboy firing spitting six-guns. An oval inset showed a young woman with auburn hair and a pretty smile.

But what drew Carla's attention was the other poster: ELECT HIRAM JOHNSON. Someone who didn't like the suggestion had torn a long strip from the center of the new governor's photograph.

"Stop, Haines."

"Mrs. Fairbanks—"

"I said stop right here."

"Ma'am, I got orders from your husband to take you straight from the party to the Palace."

"Screw you." She struggled with the door handle. "Some party. A fucking wake for the political dead—" Unexpectedly, her weight hurled the door open and she almost pitched into the gutter. A silver flask fell out of her beaded bag and lay in the rushing water like a silver fish, her fur piling on top. She staggered to the posters, rain soaking her gown, matting her tangled hair, and dissolving her makeup. Weaving back and forth in front of Hiram Johnson's portrait, she spat on him, then attacked him with her nails. "Piss on you, Johnson—goddamn pious hypocrite—piss on you and your whole pack of righteous—"

"Here, stop that." The voice came from the corner. A second later the chauffeur called a warning. He was crouched in the beams of the headlights, his fine uniform soaked.

Carla heeded neither voice, tearing at the picture savagely. A fingernail broke, then another, but she kept on cursing and shredding the paper face. Suddenly a bright beam blinded her.

"Take that fucking light out of my eyes."

A young policeman in a slicker and bill cap strode up. "Ma'am, I don't know who you are, but it's illegal to deface political posters—even after the election. I'll have to take you in and—"

Carla spat in his face.

The cop blinked and wiped his chin with his sleeve, then grabbed Carla's arm. "Listen here, lady." With her other hand she raked his jaw, three bloody nail tracks. He cursed and blew his whistle, and that enraged her more.

The chauffeur pleaded and tried to wedge between them, but the cop was angry and she was out of her head, battering the cop, kicking and gouging him. Suddenly there were running footsteps, splashing in the rain. The struggling cop heard them and, holding Carla at bay with a palm against her chin, called, "Frank, for God's sake, help me with this bitch."

The second cop, older, and burly, wrestled Carla against the brick wall. She spat on him too, then tried to kick his testicles. He whacked her with a hard backhand; it was done neatly and professionally, with no animosity. Her eyes lost focus and she started to slide down the wall. There was a flash of plated metal and then something snapped shut.

Carla braced her legs and opened her eyes. Dragging her forearm forward into the glow of the headlights, she saw the diamonds dazzling on her wrist bracelet, but the links of the handcuff chain were almost as bright. The chain connected to another cuff on the wrist of the older cop.

"I know who this is, Tommy," he said. "We'll take her in, then I'll telephone around to find her husband."

Sobriety came like a thunderclap. Carla stared at the policemen with the wild look of a trapped animal.

At 3:20 A.M. Fairbanks pushed open the doors of police headquarters at Fillmore and Bush. He practically dragged Carla down the steps in the pelting rain.

He started when he saw two black Fords parked one behind the other at the curb, then put on a show of calm as he descended the last three steps.

Two men leaped from the Ford in front, another from the second car. The fastest, wearing a fedora and belted coat, shot up to Fairbanks with a reporter's pad poised.

"Reeves of the *Examiner*, Mr. Fairbanks. I'd like to ask—"

Fairbanks smashed him down against the running board of the Ford with a roundhouse punch.

Fairbanks walked out of the opulent bathroom of their suite at the Palace. Clouds of steam from the hot tub dulled the luster of the gold faucets. He tried not to think of his loss of temper outside headquarters.

He crossed the bedroom to the parlor. Carla sat drowsily in her muddy finery, rolling her head from side to side. Open-mouthed, she hummed a tuneless little song.

"Get up." He could barely keep from striking her, and she seemed to realize it; she didn't resist. Fairbanks dragged her back through the bedroom like a chattel, then shoved her roughly into the billowing steam.

"Take your clothes off and sober up, goddamn you."

Carla gave him a sad, searching look. Her eyes were stained black from all the running makeup, and she looked like a tawdry circus clown. Bowing her head, she shut the bathroom door.

Rain rushed down the window, throwing a mottled pattern on his face. In the next bed, Carla slept restlessly, muttering. Fairbanks was sitting up, arms crossed over his starched pajama jacket.

With his eye fixed on some remote point of the dark, he tried to chart the probable course of his future. He didn't know the exact time—four-thirty or five in the morning. He couldn't sleep; his stomach was tearing him up with pain.

Carla pushed at her pillow and muttered something. Fairbanks regarded her with loathing. She rolled her head from side to side, then spoke the word again.

"What did you say?"

She repeated it. He swung his legs out of bed, stepped over, and leaned down. She rolled from her shoulder to her back, fretting in her dream, then pushed the sheet down off her satin nightgown. This time he heard it clearly: "Mack, Mack."

Carla's tongue crept out and slid across her lower lip. Her hips arched a little and her hands found the roll of her fat stomach. She held herself as if suppressing pain or some other sensation, and moaned again. Fairbanks hardly had to speculate about the dream.

He walked barefoot to the window. There he gazed down at the rainy bleakness of a deserted Market Street. He heard Carla tossing and grumbling, her hips heaving up and down. Fairbanks watched, contemplating murder.

Hiram Johnson carried the state 177,000 to 155,000, rolling up his greatest margin in Protestant Southern California.

At the San Francisco celebration, Mack drank and danced with Margaret until it was light, then drove her up Nob Hill. He showed her the site of the old house. It was cleared now, sodded, and planted with a few skimpy trees.

"But I have no plans to rebuild."

At Greenwich Street he cooked breakfast. She asked whether he'd seen Nellie and he told her Nellie had a new lover.

"Are you sure?"

"I saw him. Do you want champagne with your eggs?"

Fairbanks, like a man under a death sentence, was allowed to dangle the rest of the week. Then he was summoned to the boardroom at ten o'clock on the Monday following the Progressives' statewide sweep.

It was a gray, foggy morning in the City, and the drab light made Fairbanks's face all the more mealy and ghastly.

"Walter, I deeply regret this—" Herrin began.

"Spare me, Bill. I know you need a goat to sacrifice."

Displeased, another executive said, "There's no need for emotional rhetoric, Walter. We explained the consequences of a loss very clearly beforehand."

Herrin regained control of the meeting by clearing his throat. "Your wife's arrest and all the attendant publicity make a decision not only more unpalatable, but, I'm sorry to say, even more necessary."

Fairbanks's gray eyes had a destitute look. Wearily, but doing his best to square his shoulders and maintain good posture, he stood up. "Is there really any need to prolong this? I'll give you my letter of resignation by the close of business."

"In that case . . ." Herrin spoke with surprising kindness. "No, there is no need to prolong it. Thank you for being understanding, Walter."

"Of course," Fairbanks said, bitter suddenly.

He marched out like a good soldier, though not under the best of control; he slammed the door.

Once outside the room, he bowed his head and covered his eyes. He heard the rustling skirts of a secretary walking along the hall. She passed him and saw his shame and disarray. He was surprised at how little he cared.

Gaspar Ludlow found his chief at his desk with his head in his hands.

"The word's all over the building, sir. Speaking for everyone in the legal department, it's damned unfair."

Fairbanks pulled his hands down slowly. "What a consolation." He knew the little rodent was probably scurrying around kissing the asses of all those presumed to be in line for his job.

Ludlow nervously offered a yellow flimsy. "At least I have one piece of good news."

Fairbanks looked at the clerk blankly.

"One of those queer cults down south threw out its leader over the weekend. The man returned and burned the headquarters. A bookkeeper died of a heart seizure trying to prevent the arson, and a young gardener named Jim David received a head injury. The gardener is recuperating in a local hospital. We received all the details from the Pasadena police. They

676

were interviewing the gardener, and one of the officers recalled the description we circulated. It was still lying on his desk . . ."

Fairbanks continued to stare at him. Ludlow desperately rattled the flimsy.

"Sir, the young man in the hospital fits the description. Blond hair, blue eyes, a crippled left foot—he fits it exactly."

Fairbanks sat motionless for some fifteen seconds, then snatched the flimsy and smoothed it with both hands. He read it twice. Grabbing the telephone, he clicked the hook up and down. "Eunice? Eunice? Dammit, answer."

He kept clicking the hook. Ludlow almost interrupted to add something else Pasadena had told him on the telephone, when he called to verify after receiving the hospital's address. Pasadena told him that the officer who made the connection between the boy and the SP description also recalled a similar inquiry, and a similar description, from Pinkerton's detective agency, months before. But the point didn't seem that significant, so he decided to drop it.

"Eunice? Where the devil were you? This is Mr. Fairbanks. Telephone the main ticket office. I want a reservation on the Daylight Limited to Los Angeles tomorrow."

The coastal range shone blue and white to the west of the speeding Limited. Fairbanks leaned his forehead against the cool glass and watched the mountains. Long ago, he'd studied Darwin, and more recently, the superman theories of the socialist Jack London. Out of such reading, his upbringing, and his long association with important and powerful Californians, he'd evolved a theory of how he should live and behave. This place, California, called on a man to dominate it. The sheer overwhelming natural beauty inspired some, but others, like him, it taunted. Its very bigness challenged him to a contest for mastery. He understood a man like Cholly Crocker, who had torn down trees, plowed up the earth, drilled and blasted through mountain rock to build the CP line and prove to everyone that he was mightier than God's own handiwork. Fairbanks shared Crocker's need to prove he was the master of his time, his place. But in that effort, he had lately failed on a scale unimaginable in any previous season of his life. He'd failed and been kicked aside like a street cur. Dreaming in the sunshine, his brow on the cool glass, Fairbanks felt he had but one great opportunity left, one opportunity to recoup the enormous loss, vindicate himself, win.

One opportunity.

79 "THERE, SIR."

The matron pointed down the aisle of the sunny ward to the farthest bed on the right. Fairbanks tipped his hat and walked quickly. Although the walls were whitewashed and large arched windows admitted fresh air, he disliked the odors: the staleness of dressings, blood, strong cleaning solution.

He stopped suddenly, and an orderly with a tray of medicine cups almost ran into him. Muttering an apology, Fairbanks thought he'd lost his mind.

It was Carla in the last bed. A younger Carla, with less flesh on the face, but the same features, the same cap of bright-gold hair.

From a high window opposite his bed, sunlight fell on the boy, and the gently moving shadow of a palm. The boy was supposed to be twelve, but the size of his shoulders and the maturity of his face suggested fourteen or fifteen. A bandage bulged on the back of his head, fastened with sticking plaster, the hair around it shaved.

Fairbanks tapped his gold-headed stick on the bed's metal foot rail. "Good morning. You're Jim David, aren't you?"

The boy put down his dime novel and pulled the sheet higher over his coarse cotton gown. His eyes were large, and as blue as Carla's. Fairbanks was unmanned by emotion. In a rush of excitement before leaving the City, he'd told Carla the boy's assumed name and mentioned Pasadena. To his astonishment, Carla broke down completely. Crying, she begged him to telephone the moment he found out whether or not it was their son. This touched him in a way he'd not been touched for a long time. He patted and soothed her, and promised he'd call.

The boy didn't directly answer the question. "Who are you?"

"Allow me to introduce myself. Walter Fairbanks the Third. I'm an attorney." The identification was automatic; he was incomplete without it. "I came down from San Francisco to see you on a personal matter." He pointed his stick at a stool pushed under the bed. "Might I sit down?"

Jim remained suspicious. "I guess."

The stool was low and Fairbanks felt awkward, less authoritative, on it. His eye was on a level with the boy's hip.

A patient in another bed called plaintively, "Matron. Matron, may I have the—ah—receptacle? Hurry please, matron."

Fairbanks concentrated on his son. "I'm familiar in a general way with the tabernacle in Pasadena, the fire set by the man who ran it. I'm sorry you were injured—"

Jim shrugged it away. "My head hurt like the devil for three days. It doesn't now. They'll take the stitching out Monday, they said. Then I can go home with Jocker."

"Who's Jocker?"

"A friend. He takes care of me, like." Jim stared at the visitor, awaiting some better explanation than he'd received so far.

The boy's deep-blue eyes fascinated Fairbanks. They were a man's eyes, experienced, wary. How remarkable—and strange—that this was the offspring of his own loins.

"The admitting records show your name is James David, but it isn't, is it? You're really James O. Chance."

A curtain closed behind the boy's eyes. "Who are you? What's this about?"

"Please, it . . ." Fairbanks extended a gray-gloved hand, a supplicant. Tiny sapphires of sweat popped out in his trimmed mustache. "It's very hard for me to answer that. You see . . ." He faltered again. He had no skill in personal dealings, no charm like that bastard Chance had. He felt especially inadequate dealing with a son.

All at once Jim's face showed hostility. "Then just answer."

"I am . . ." Fairbanks cleared his throat like a public speaker. "I'm your real father."

There was a long, long silence.

"Oh, matron. I'm finished with the—ah—receptacle."

Jim rolled up the dime novel and held it in both hands, his knuckles white. "What are you saying to me?"

"I know it's probably difficult for you to comprehend that assertion . . ."

Angry tears appeared. "Use words I can understand, will you?"

"Sorry, I'm sorry," Fairbanks blurted, his voice pitching high. He made nervous gestures, little quirky attempts at a smile. "I'm a lawyer, you see—accustomed to a certain formal—" *Christ, I'm botching it.* "Yes. Well. What I said is true. I'll take all the time necessary to explain the circumstances, but I'm telling you the truth. Please believe me. Your mother is Carla Hellman. When you were born, she was married to James Macklin Chance of San Francisco and Riverside. But Chance is not really—that is . . ." Jim's incredulous expression undermined him and he faltered again, his voice weakening. "Please give me the opportunity to prove what I'm saying. Can you get out of bed? Walk down to the superintendent's office with me? I'll telephone your mother. You can speak to her and she'll corroborate everything . . ."

That sentence died too. It was no good. The boy stared at him with open disbelief, and even fright. Fairbanks reached out to touch him.

"Jim, you're my son—"

Jim pulled away from the pleading hand. "I don't understand this. But I don't think I want to, mister." Fairbanks heard something new in the boy's voice—a deep underground river of emotion rushing to the surface. "My father is the man who brought me up, J. M. Chance. He was rotten to me sometimes, but he's my father. I can't change that, and you can't either."

Fairbanks jumped up so fast the stool fell over. A man with his foot in traction called, "I'm trying to rest here."

"You ran away from him, Jim."

"What's that to you? Maybe there were reasons."

"But you've never gone back to him—" Fairbanks grabbed his wrist. "You're *my* son. Macklin Chance has beaten me every other way—he isn't going to beat me with my own flesh and—"

"Let go. Get away."

Fairbanks held on, control crumbling. The boy twisted his strong tanned wrist but Fairbanks held on.

"Dammit, let go, mister—you're crazy."

The lawyer's gray-metal eyes had a strange frantic light in them. "Oh, Jim, I beg you—"

"Matron?" Jim shouted over Fairbanks's shoulder. "Matron!"

My own son's frightened of me. Look at him, terrified. Chance did this.

Fairbanks let go of Jim's wrist and stepped back all the way to the aisle. His hand flew to his cravat. It didn't need straightening but he straightened it. A swift look revealed the matron bearing down, skirts flying, a bull-necked orderly close behind.

"Sir, you are not permitted to come in here and disrupt—"

"Excuse me," Walter Fairbanks said. He shoved the matron, then rushed by her, avoiding the orderly's grasping hand, and ran out of the ward.

He ran down the noisy wooden stairs, the heat of humiliation fevering his face. He ran past puzzled employees peering from doorways and a cashier's wicket. He ran out of the hospital, beaten.

THREE NIGHTS LATER, AT DARK, FAIRBANKS WALKED **80** into Three Dog Alley in the squalid Chinese section on upper Broadway.

Fairbanks was usually a controlled man, but for three days and nights he'd been out of control, drinking recklessly, yet staying sober enough to, first, conceive the idea and, second, make his inquiries. He'd cashed a large draft at a correspondent bank of Fairbanks Trust, and with that money he loosened tongues.

Yes, one saloon keeper said, that man had been seen around town. Another informant said the man had a liking for the poppy. A third sent him to a tea parlor controlled by the Hong Chow Company, the largest criminal tong in Los Angeles. An enormous oily Chinese with a dropsical eyelid and a diamond-studded ring in his left ear grinned and wriggled his fingers for more money—$50 wasn't enough. He pocketed another $50, shrugged, and said Fairbanks might try Mr. Tom Sun Luck's in Three Dog Alley. No guarantees.

Sometime during this rolling binge, Fairbanks remembered his wife's plea and telephoned San Francisco. He didn't reveal any details of his defeat at the hospital, but simply told Carla the boy had a new life in Southern California and didn't want to return to his old one.

"Oh, tell me—how did he look?" she asked.

"Fine," he said, and hung up. He leaned his head against the wall by the telephone. "Goddamn you, Chance."

So he'd not told his wife everything. Not said a word about his drunken binge—a necessary purging of his pain, and a purifying and focusing of his intent. He certainly would never utter a word about this expedition into a filthy little corner of hell called Three Dog Alley.

Though it was warm in Los Angeles, he'd put on his overcoat to hide his fine clothes. You didn't advertise your station or prosperity in this kind of criminous sewer. Strange foreign eyes blinked at him from windows in dim hovels. By the light of pretty paper lanterns on a porch, a girl of twelve or thirteen opened her blouse and showed him breasts like small pears. An old woman with an idiot grin and no teeth fondled his arm. "You like a boy, gen'man?"

Fairbanks walked on. A short-haired dog with scaly flanks squatted in front of him, shitting. Fairbanks kicked at the dog and it snapped back at him.

He walked perhaps a block but it seemed like miles. Finally, following the directions on a crumpled scrap, he located the establishment of Mr. Tom Sun Luck by means of Arabic numerals painted under Chinese characters on the door post.

Mr. Tom Sun Luck was a curious hybrid: white skin, Oriental features. Quite old, he was unctuously accommodating. In his round cap and threadbare silk gown, he conducted Fairbanks to his cellar, a dirt-floored corridor with curtained doorways on both sides. Heavy white smoke with a fruity odor drifted the length of it. Mr. Tom Sun Luck led him to a beaded curtain at the end, which he rattled by brushing it with his four-inch fingernails.

"Right there. You pay me now."

Fairbanks jammed $10 into the queer creature's hand and the fingers shut like a spring trap.

"Leave me alone with him."

"Sure, OK, mister bigshot." Tom Sun Luck shuffled away into the dark.

Fairbanks parted the curtain and stepped through. A wick shimmered in a small shallow bowl of oil standing on a crate. It was the only illumination in the dirt-walled cubicle.

Eyes closed, Wyatt lay on his side in a wood bunk covered with sheets of a Chinese newspaper. He wore a filthy dark sweater and pants. His right hand dangled over the edge of the bunk, near a crate littered with paraphernalia: a small clam shell that held a long steel needle and a small brown ball of opium; a spirit lamp, extinguished at the moment; a pipe with an ivory-banded bamboo stem, ivory mouthpiece, and large four-sided Happiness bowl.

He approached the foul bunk, his soles crunching on something that might have been dried rodent droppings. Wyatt's eyes opened.

"Hello, Brother Paul. Do you remember me?"

Wyatt's white-spiked hair had a dull greasy shine and his once-handsome face was dirty and wasted. Blinking, he lifted his head a few inches. "I remember." Grunting, he worked his left elbow under his side and raised himself a little higher. "No more donations. I'm not Brother Paul now."

What a pathetic joke. What a pathetic man. "I know. It took

me a long time to find you in this hole. I imagine you're extremely short on money."

Wyatt's enlarged eyes showed a sleepy interest. "I have money. Money comes in. But it isn't enough anymore. Never enough."

"I'm prepared to pay you a very considerable sum in return for . . ." Fairbanks licked his lips. "A service."

"That's nice. How much?"

"Enough to buy a lot of these." Fairbanks indicated the pipe. "For a long time to come."

"That's nice," Wyatt murmured again. "What do you want?"

"I want someone . . ."

As he'd done at the hospital, he faltered. The magnitude of the step brought to mind the platitudinous pronouncements of his law-school professors. It gave him pause, until he remembered all the wrongs done to him.

"I want someone—taken out. Is that the phrase? Removed. Is that clearer?"

Wyatt swung his legs off the bunk and sat up. He pushed his fingers through his white-winged hair, smoothing it back from his temples. Sickle moons of dirt showed under his fingernails. Now that Fairbanks had adjusted to the cellar's pervasive opium smell, he could pick up another, more offensive one. Wyatt's clothing was foul as a privy.

"You mean killed."

Fairbanks swallowed. "Yes."

"Lovely. Why not?"

Quickly Fairbanks parted the rattling bead curtain. The dark cellar was still empty. He went back to the bunk.

"If you do the service, my name must never be connected with it. Never."

"It's possible," Wyatt said. "Anything's possible for a price." He smiled at his caller. "Who is it?"

If he answered, he couldn't go back. Well, what of it? The deed first contemplated in anger could be done handily, because this piece of human refuse was desperate, and there would be no witnesses to a bargain. The morality of it didn't trouble Fairbanks, only personal safety after the fact.

"I said, who is it?"

"I'll tell you. When you hear, I believe you'll be eager to help me."

X

CALIFORNIA GOLD

1911

In 1905, in Chicago, a new and different kind of labor union arose. The old A.F. of L. was an alliance of craft workers, men who clung to their pride and skills and wanted no part of common, untrained laborers. But Eugene Debs, "Big Bill" Haywood, and other socialists decided that exclusionary pride was dangerous and wrong. Trade unionism, and the new century, demanded something better, the International Workers of the World.

The new union planned to organize the skilled and unskilled alike, industry by industry, not craft by craft. The IWW pushed first into the lumbering regions of the Pacific Northwest. Soon, shocked citizens and outraged owners were hearing a new rhetoric, one that called for the "pie in the sky" of a worker's paradise, brought about, if need be, through sabotage and the revolutionary overthrow of capitalism.

Reaction was predictable. General Otis called IWW men "criminal syndicalist scum," and sneered at them as "Wobblies." The name caught on.

As the first decade of the century ended, the Wobblies eyed the golden fields of California, the Valley towns, where rich crops were harvested and large migrant populations could be recruited for the union. From Missoula, Spokane, Denver, and elsewhere, Wobblies began riding the rods into the Valley. They jumped off at places like Bakersfield, Brawley, Stockton, and Visalia.

Always their technique was the same: agitate, heighten class awareness, promote worker solidarity through mass meetings and street-corner oratory. Rarely did they talk specifically of union organization. Instead, they railed against local "bourgeois" agents who manipulated and cheated field-workers through their "slave labor marts." Of course the unspoken antidote was organization, but in the Wobbly master plan that came later.

To make sure they wouldn't be run out of a town too soon, the Wobblies raised a second cry—"Free speech!" It was a shrewd strategy, because free speech was exactly what the Wobbly-hating authorities had to suppress in order to suppress the union. The harder that police and civil authorities pushed on this issue, however, the harder the Wobblies fought back.

Every time they were seriously threatened they sent pleas to union members around the nation.

In the fall of 1910, Wobblies were riding west in response to the latest war cry in their newspaper: FREE SPEECH FIGHT IS ON!

And so it was. The Wobblies were campaigning in Fresno. For a couple of months, the police there merely harassed them sporadically, but then, in December, the town stepped up the fight. The Fresno board of trustees unanimously passed an ordinance that said in part:

> *It shall be and is hereby made unlawful for any person to hold, conduct, or address any assemblage, meeting or gathering of persons, or to make or deliver any public speech, lecture, discourse, or to conduct or take part in any public debate, in or upon any public park, public street or alley within the 48-block area bounded by Tuolumne, M, Inyo and D Streets.*

This was, of course, an abrogation of the First Amendment to the Constitution. The Wobblies advertised again: FREE SPEECH FIGHT NEEDS YOUR HELP! RALLY AROUND! ALL ABOARD FOR FRESNO!

WINTER RAINS. ALL DAY AND ALL NIGHT, THEY **81** poured over the red tiles of Villa Mediterranean. Mack heard them in his dreams.

The days of January marched by in gray procession. He tired of working an hour after he began, and his hands hurt constantly. He spread them on his desk. The knuckles were enlarged—the hands of an old man. In every mirror, that old man mocked him: white hair, lackluster eyes behind the round schoolmaster glasses. Something had died—maybe just the energy to pursue dreams.

T. Fowler Haines remained on his corner of the desk. One afternoon, Mack idly opened to the Foreword: "I have never beheld a place where I would so gladly fix my permanent abode as in this Paradise of sunshine."

"Liar," Mack sighed, and shut the guidebook. The rains of January 1911 poured down. He was forty-two years old.

The detective Bill Burns called at Riverside.

"The mayor of the city of Los Angeles hired me for the *Times* case. We're going to unravel it and hang those dynamiters. I'll tell you where I'm looking, Mack: Indianapolis, Indiana. It's the home office of the Bridge and Structural Iron Workers Union. I know you feel strongly for union men—well, not union men who do murder; I'd not accuse you of that—but you're partial to the movement as a whole, you can't deny it. That's why I wanted to be square with you. Square and in the open. We're on opposite sides this time, boyo."

They shook hands and Mack wished Bill Burns well.

On a blowy day of large clouds and cool sunshine, there came to the pretty little town of San Solaro one Yacob Steinweis of the Kalem Studios (for the founders Kleine, Long, and Marion) of Twenty-first Street, New York. He found Mack examining some construction blueprints in the cool shade of the bandstand in San Solaro Park.

Steinweis introduced himself with a business card instead of verbally. He was, at best, twenty-five years old, a studious but starved-looking fellow with a lot of white teeth and a smile of radiant innocence. Mack presumed you didn't get by in the

picture business, as you didn't get by in any other, on innocence. Steinweis had to have something more.

One readily apparent trait was enthusiasm. He shook his
head when Mack offered him a seat on a bandstand bench,
bobbing up and down on his brown calfskin shoes. Though he
probably couldn't afford it, Steinweis dressed himself like an
Englishman, in a walking suit of tan worsted, a figured brown
four-in-hand, tan derby, gloves, and spats. Somehow his energy amused Mack, while saddening him a little too. He remembered when he'd felt the same way about opportunities.

"Sir," Steinweis began, "I am quite experienced in moving
pictures—three years as Sid Olcott's right hand. I worked on
many Westerns shot on the Jersey Palisades. I was Sid's assistant director on the one-reel—" He stopped, unable to continue; no sound came from his mouth.

"Mr. Steinweis, what's wrong?"

The young man reddened, seeming to tense and tremble all
over. He made queer gargling sounds. At last he burst out,
"N-nothing." The color rushed from his face. "I have a certain slight problem with—" Another long choked silence.
"Stammering. The p-picture to which I referred is—" Finally
the name exploded. *"Ben-Hur."*

"I saw that," Mack told him. "It was good."

Steinweis slumped, too overcome with embarrassment to
care about the compliment. Mack liked him for admitting his
problem. He asked him again to be seated and, this time,
Steinweis sank gratefully onto a bench.

"It isn't easy being a moving-picture man, and a—" Another painful pause. "A Jew, and a stammerer too. Three
strikes, as the ballplayers say. On the other hand, the more
obstacles a man confronts, the more he's challenged to stretch
himself and achieve, wouldn't you say?"

"Yes, definitely. But what brings you here?"

"I came to California originally because I saw more—
opportunity. But I refuse to work for others the rest of my life.
I am looking for—property, land on which to start the Emory
Stone Studio. A more euphonious name than Steinweis, don't
you think?" He was relaxed now, and having less trouble with
his speech. "I have the promise of a loan if I locate s-suitable
land. I found a hundred acres in the foothills of Hollywood.
Ideal. Please sell them to me, Mr. Chance."

"What property is it, exactly?"

"Here, I'll show you, I brought along a surveyor's drawing." Steinweis unfolded it and Mack put on his spectacles.
"I have studied you, Mr. Chance. For weeks now I have been

doing it. You have huge holdings. You'll never miss this hundred acres. Please, set any fair price and I'll pay it. Just sell me the land for my studio. Give me my dream in—'' After the strained silence: "California."

Mack ended the meeting without committing himself. "I'll think about it and let you know," he said. Steinweis smiled, shook his hand, and uttered a perfectly articulated thank-you. But he looked heartbroken.

A week later, two gentlemen from the town of Hollywood arranged an appointment through Alex, and visited Mack in San Solaro. They represented something called the Committee of Conscientious Citizens. They were pale, forgettable sorts. Mr. Silas Ribner didn't mention his occupation; Mr. Joe Hughes sold real estate.

"We're Christians and Protestants, Mr. Chance," said Hughes. "We understand you are too. Hollywood is a Christian community—up-and-coming, full of boosters. But we don't like this movie crowd from the East. We don't like them renting rooms, and we especially don't want them settling permanently. That's why we organized. Our committee got wind of this little New York Jew who wants to buy a piece of your land. We ask you to help us keep Hollywood a safe, clean residential community of Christian people. Don't sell to him."

"You came all the way out here to speak against a man because he's a Jew?"

Mr. Ribner's ire was roused. "A motion-picture Jew. Doubly undesirable. You can see that, surely."

"I can see that you're a pair of bigots."

"Mr. Chance," cried Hughes, jumping up.

"Out of this house before I throw you down the stairs myself."

They left in a huff.

Two nights later, at half past eleven, Mack received a telephone call from Alex down in Riverside.

"I was just contacted by the authorities in Hollywood. You know the old abandoned barn on the property Steinweis wants to buy? Someone torched it this afternoon."

The next night, after supper, Mack took another call.

"Jew lover," said a distant unfamiliar voice, and hung up.

"God, I don't need this," Mack said.

In other days, in better times, he would have leaped into a fight with Hughes, Ribner, and the Hollywood burghers they represented. He loathed such men. They reminded him of Fairbanks, and of all the others who wanted to slam doors when he first trudged down from the mountains in '87.

Now, though, things were different. His mood had been darkened by recent events, and the winter, and a persistent sense of failure. He'd lost Jim, he'd lost Nellie long ago—he seemed to have lost his grip on life itself. Were it not for the stewardship of good trustworthy helpers like Alex Muller, Enrique Potter, and Rhett Haverstick, God knew that he might have lost his millions too.

Steinweis telephoned at least once a day, pressing for a decision. As Mack stared at the little message chits, his antagonism focused on Steinweis rather than the self-professed Hollywood Christians. *Get out of California, Steinweis. Go home. I don't need your money. I don't need your trouble.*

The short letter that went to Steinweis early in February said in part:

> I have considered your offer. I can't at this time see my way clear . . .

One gray afternoon in the February of what seemed an endless winter, Mack quit work at two-thirty and went for a drive alone. The Packard bumped down the foothill drive, which the rains had rutted badly. At the bottom, turning into the main road to Riverside, he heard a loud report.

Backfire, he thought. But he'd felt the left side of the auto vibrate. He parked and got out to study the Packard's yellow paint. What he saw made the hair on the back of his neck crawl. Round and black, a hole was punched through the passenger door.

Scanning the groves across the road, he saw some men at work, but they were too far away to be clearly visible. He also heard a horseman somewhere but couldn't see him.

He stuck his finger in the hole, all the way through to the inside of the auto. Then he spied something gray and flat on the floor rug: the spent bullet.

He thought of the Committee of Conscientious Citizens from Hollywood. "My God, surely not."

"But what other explanation is there?" he said to Hellburner Johnson at supper that evening. Johnson had stepped off the 5 P.M. local. He had a week's vacation from Essanay while Anderson rushed to Chicago to confer with Spoor about broadening distribution of the stupendously successful Broncho Billy

692

pictures. In the next, Johnson was to be promoted to town marshal, a major character part.

"Dunno, Mack," Johnson said. "You've made a passel of enemies in your time. Could be any one of 'em. Does it make a hell of a lot of difference who's on the givin' end, so long as you don't get caught receivin'?"

Mack retrieved his .45 Shopkeeper's Colt from its peg in the office closet. He oiled it and wore it wherever he went now, with spare ammunition weighing down a coat pocket. Sometimes the chopped-off Peacemaker reassured him. Other times, he was more realistic. Lot of good a holstered revolver would do if some crazy Californian wanted to blow him down from ambush.

Carla saw him quite suddenly, his face bright as a coin, lit by winter sunshine. He was up on a ladder, spraying some chemical on a Valencia orange tree.

"Pull over, park here," she said, tapping the chauffeur. He steered the touring sedan to the shoulder. "Not so far," she exclaimed as the bonnet nosed up beside a tall billboard that trumpeted REDLANDS CITRUS COOPERATIVE. The chauffeur braked, the rear end of the auto stopping clear of the board.

Carla had badgered her husband until he'd revealed where he had seen the boy. He would say no more than "Pasadena," so she resorted to using her own money to hire a private inquiry bureau. "Don't bother me with a lot of details, just come back to me when you know where he is."

It took them seven weeks, starting at the Pasadena Police Department. Her son had been a witness to some crime, and though the perpetrator had disappeared, the boy had been required to leave a forwarding address, in case the man was caught and indicted. The address was no longer good when the detectives got there, but the landlord said he'd put Jim and his companion or guardian in touch with a relative, a grower in Redlands who always needed good workers. Her son was working in the groves and living with the older man in a shanty in the country outside Redlands. He was apparently making no effort to conceal his whereabouts. Well, why should he?

Weak yellow sunshine bathed the car and reflected from its windows. The chauffeur lit a cigarette. Carla cranked her window down a few inches.

Several of the workers had noticed the long dark car and were staring, but Jim had given it a glance and gone back to work. Even so, Carla drew back into the shadow of the tonneau—as if anyone could see her, heavily veiled as she was.

The veil was golden silk, thin as a membrane of some shining insect. It hid the unbidden tears on her cheeks.

What a handsome boy he was. Darkened by weather, slim, and strong-looking in his denim pants and old shirt. Flesh of her flesh. The sight of him made her feel soft and full of a diffuse love. She wanted to know that he was all right. She wanted to know that he could care for himself. He certainly looked capable of it—tall, hardy, and capable. A young man . . .

"Mrs. Fairbanks?" said the chauffeur, finishing his cigarette.

"Not yet. In a moment."

"Water," Jocker said as he pulled the hand cart through the grove. "Water here, my lads." When the orchard workers surrounded his cart, he handed out dippers filled from two casks. The owner of this orchard was a decent man, took care of his help. That's why Jim insisted they stay on.

The winter afternoon had a muted pastel quality. Spears of misty sunshine thrust between the trees and the earth and the air smelled sweet and damp. A speeding train whistled in the distance, but the real world seemed remote. Jocker picked up the cart handles and trudged along to the end of the row. Jim was just coming down the ladder with his sprayer.

"Hello, Jocker," Jim said. "Hand me some water, will you? It's stinking work spraying this stuff."

Jocker couldn't work on the trees because of his arthritis, but he could do odd jobs like pulling the water cart. Together, he and Jim made enough to live decently, and drifted through the days with no ambition but to get their food and sleep and an occasional growler of beer. That was fine with Jim after the ordeal with Brother Paul at the tabernacle.

Jocker passed out dippers to three other men, then filled one for Jim. Jocker wore a regular jeans coat and pants now—no more peculiar tramp costumes. A Redlands barber cut his hair once a month for 10 cents; Jim insisted. As he handed the boy the dipper he spied an auto partly hidden by the co-op's billboard at the edge of the grove.

"Did you see that car?" Jocker said. Jim nodded. "Someone inside is lamping us pretty hard."

Jim turned and saw a woman in a huge hat and golden veil. She saw him look and drew back from the window.

"Just some tourist," he said with a shrug.

The auto started its engine and pulled away in a cloud of exhaust.

Carla clasped her hands tightly in her lap. She was thankful for the veil; the chauffeur wouldn't see her tears. She struggled to keep them silent.

What a handsome lad, her son. He favored her, resembled her unmistakably. She hoped he didn't resemble her emotionally or psychologically; that would ruin him.

For a moment back there, she'd wanted to step out, run to him, and clasp him to her. "Hello, Jim—I'm your mother."

Ridiculous. She knew what she was. Why spoil his life?

The auto bumped on down the country road toward Redlands.

In the last week of February, Margaret motored from the City to the Monterey peninsula, a five-shot pistol under her seat in case of trouble. No one molested her, though she had to change a tire and later stop overnight. In Carmel, she asked directions to Nellie's cottage by the sea.

She found Nellie in disarray, the sleeves of her shirtwaist blouse rolled up, the tie collar undone, the bosom smudged all over with lead pencil. Margaret was beautifully and expensively dressed. She gave Nellie her hand in a mauve glove.

"I do hope you'll forgive the unannounced call. You've no telephone here, so I couldn't contact you in advance."

For a moment, opening the door, Nellie had looked annoyed. But it had passed now, and she was gracious. "Come in, please, Miss Leslie. I know your face. I saw your last picture, *Broncho Billy and the Orphan*. You were very good."

"Thank you, that's very kind of you."

"The films are enormously popular—"

"America loves Billy."

The cottage smelled of fresh coffee. Nellie showed Margaret a sunlit writing table and many discarded sheets of foolscap. "I've been drafting an article for William R. Hearst. I don't do many of them anymore, but he'll take any that I finish. His editors send me pleading letters regularly. They'd like me to cover news stories again. I do that only once in a great while."

"You certainly don't need to—you're a very famous and successful writer. I admired *Huntworthy's Millions* more than I can say."

"Thank you." Nellie cleared some pillows from a sofa. "Would you care to sit down?" The initial pleasantries were running to their end and Nellie's dark eyes fixed on her visitor curiously.

"Might we walk down to the beach?" Margaret said then.

"I hear it's lovely. I've never been fortunate enough to visit in Carmel before."

"Then this is a special occasion." Nellie reached for a shawl. "But I'm really not sure why you're paying this call, Miss Leslie."

"To speak to you about a man who matters to both of us. Mack Chance."

They crossed the dune to the same shore Mack and Nellie had walked before. This afternoon the vista was considerably more beautiful: Long white combers rolled in, and the ocean, dark as navy cloth, sparkled in the sunshine. The cloudless air made for superb visibility. The horizon seemed to be a hundred miles away.

After they talked a while, Nellie sat down on a driftwood log. She planted her chin in the palms of her hands and stared out to sea, the salty wind tossing her straight dark hair. Today she was the hoyden, while Margaret—swan-necked Margaret with her smart clothes and aristocratic features—might have come from a society luncheon at the St. Francis. Margaret had a courtly air; it befitted a member of America's new, slightly scandalous, but vastly admired moving-picture royalty.

"It's all very well to say these things, Miss Leslie—how I ought to think differently about Mack because he's changed—"

"But he has, in certain important ways. Let me repeat what I said as we walked down here. Mack encouraged me in my career with Essanay. He never once discouraged me because I was female."

Nellie made a cynical little moue. "Apparently he has different rules for different people."

"Well, I'm sure there are special ones for you. You're the only one he truly cares for, other than his son, who's gone."

"Why are you doing this? Crusading for him?"

"Because I love him."

"You—"

"Love him. Probably as much as you do."

"See here, I'm not absolutely sure that I—"

She stopped, an elbow on her knee, the back of her wrist to her forehead. "Hell. That's a lie. Of course I do."

Margaret smiled, then said in a gentle and sympathetic way, "You've also cleared up one terrible, ridiculous misunderstanding."

"Mack never asked me about my visitor from Northern California. I never even saw him that night. He just went off with his assumptions and sulked."

"He's an impulsive man. He can be frightfully wrong-headed. Does that mean you should reject him forever? If you do, you're not the intelligent woman whose mind shines through in her books."

"You're certainly forthright." Nellie pressed her lips together. "Sorry. I am too. When forthrightness is applied to oneself, it can sting badly."

"To be sure," Margaret agreed. She found Nellie both too defensive and too uncertain, and she decided a jolt was needed.

"I must be leaving soon. Please understand one more thing before I go. I'm no altruist. I'd take Mack Chance away from you in a trice if I had the slightest hope of doing so. I don't. He doesn't return my affection. I've accepted that. I have my own life and I intend to get on. Mack feels strongly about you. Two people who care for each other shouldn't be kept apart by trivialities."

"That sounds perfectly reasonable. But I'll tell you, it isn't easy for me to admit past mistakes."

"He said the same thing."

"There you are." Nellie made a helpless little gesture. "Impasse."

"If you choose."

"If *I* choose?"

"Yes, I think so. It's 1911, Miss Ross. A lot of time has passed since you and Mack first met. He's a wonderful brave man in spite of his shortcomings, which I don't minimize for one moment. However, no man like Mack will spend the rest of his life alone. Eventually he'll find another woman. More likely, she'll find him. She'll be enthusiastic about his virtues, and quite willing to forgive his worst faults. And he'll respond. One of these days, when he's tired of being alone, he'll respond to that woman. If she's someone other than you, it would be a tragedy."

"What can I do?" Nellie exclaimed. "I'm what I am."

"I grew up poor, Miss Ross. But we had a neighbor, a farmer, who was prosperous. He planted many willow trees on his property. I loved them. I noticed that even if there was a fierce storm, they survived. They bent, but didn't break. And after the storm they kept their same beauty, their same shape—their same character."

Nellie stared at her. Margaret smiled again. She held out her mauve glove and Nellie grasped it, looking a bit dazed.

"Thank you for your courtesy, Miss Ross. I hope I've not offended you with my candor."

"No," Nellie said, though there was a strange, distracted light in her eyes. She gazed at the ocean, the combers, the wheeling gulls. "No," she said again, sounding unsure.

Margaret went over the dune and left her.

Nellie sat a long time, her head in her hands. It was a defeated posture, not characteristic of her. But the visitor had shattered her defenses with her unexpected candor.

She's right, Nellie thought. *I've done so many things wrong. My ambition was proper, his wasn't. I have a lot to make up for . . .*

To Mack in Riverside, Margaret wrote:

Her "lover" is her favorite cousin, Tomás—the one she accompanied to Yosemite Valley when she was small. She said she told you about him years ago. You're an idiot, Chance. I forgive you because idiocy is inevitable—you're a man.

Love,
M.

82 THEY ATE THEIR LUNCH AT AN ARMENIAN restaurant. The proprietor was friendly to the movement, so no one caused them trouble.

There was little conversation. The Fresno campaign had begun with enthusiasm in August, but since then enthusiasm had waned. The campaign had gotten rough, and the number of men willing to risk themselves was shrinking. Today they were down to three.

Now they left the restaurant silently, Marquez carrying the soapbox, Frank Little, the tough bantam-sized leader of Local 66, the flag. Gopal Mukerji trailed along with copies of *The Industrial Worker* for distribution to listeners—if they managed to collect any listeners on this weekday in late February . . .

Mukerji was a slight, sinewy brown man, twenty-two years old. His eyes were small and bright, his face dark and finely featured. He came from a village near Jullundur, in the Punjab, and had crossed the Canadian border and worked his way down to California when he was nineteen. He read English passably, and had a large fund of off-color stories that he was fond of relating, in Hindi, to other workers from his part of the world.

They set up on the usual corner, Mariposa and I streets. Marquez placed the soapbox. He lived up to the name *Wobbly*; a fever was consuming him. After three days in solitary and a night of the water cure in the Fresno jail, he'd taken sick. It was the third time he'd been locked up since the campaign started.

Frank Little unfurled the red flag, then slipped the staff into a hole in a corner of the box. His good eye raked the streets; the other eye was milky and useless. As he seated the staff, the side of his coat lifted to reveal the walnut butt of a revolver stuffed in his pants. Many of the Wobblies practiced what they called passive resistance; Frank Little thought it not only cowardly but stupid.

Gopal Mukerji placed himself next to the box, an engaging smile on his face. He wore secondhand pants, a much-washed blue cotton shirt, and a spotless white turban—his treasure. A well-dressed gentleman in a bowler paused to spit a cigar cutting at his feet, and Mukerji smiled and offered a copy of his paper. The gentleman hit it with his walking stick and strode away, muttering about anarchy. Mukerji kept on smiling.

A trolley passed, bell ringing. I and Mariposa was a busy downtown intersection in the city of twenty-five thousand. There were buildings of Victorian gingerbread on the corners, trolley tracks, trolley wires, and modern autos along with farm wagons, pedestrians, and horsemen. The Wobblies were by now a familiar sight in town; what little attention they generated was mostly silent, mostly hostile.

Marquez put a foot on the soapbox. The toe of his shoe was split, showing a dirty sock. His stained and wrinkled black suit resembled a priest's, but his shirt was red silk. Mukerji found Marquez's seediness quite distasteful. Like most Hindustanis, he bathed every day if it was possible, and considered personal hygiene almost as important as one's religion.

"Sure you're up to this, Diego?" Frank Little asked. His good eye shifted here and there, searching out potential danger.

"Certainly. If not me, who else?" Marquez said. Above his long beard his cheeks glistened as if they were greased.

Sometimes Marquez felt a vast futility about this campaign. A lot of comrades had come to Fresno in the fall, riding the rods from Denver, Salt Lake, Chicago. But a lot of them were gone now, scared out by the billy clubs of Chief Shaw's police, the midnight torchings of Wobbly tents out at the western city limits, the screaming editorials in the *Morning Republican* and the *Sacramento Bee*, the vagrancy arrests, the militant patriotic wrath of sentencing judges, the brutal jail with its bread-and-water diet and its water cure. A lot of the comrades had worked off their sentences with leaf rakes in Courthouse Park, then fled. Others had pleaded guilty and been paroled on condition that they leave town.

Still, Marquez refused to quit. On the twentieth of December last, the Fresno trustees had unanimously passed the anti-speaking ordinance. Marquez was determined to test it and test it until they smashed it, or the campaign smashed him.

Which, given his bleary head and burning skin, it might.

He stepped up on the box. The intersection tilted forty-five degrees and swam out of focus, and his gut fluttered. Then the intersection slowly tilted back to horizontal, and forty-five degrees the other way. Finally it settled to normal. A light breeze fluttered the red banner.

"Ladies and gentlemen, I address you once more on the subject of free speech, which is guaranteed to us by the United States Constitution."

The ex-priest's audience consisted of his two comrades and a painted wooden Indian chief outside a tobacco shop. Gopal Mukerji, smiling and earnest, offered his papers to the empty air. Marquez swung into his standard oration.

"The war we are waging is being fought all across California. International Workers of the World campaigns for freedom of speech in San Francisco, Bakersfield, Brawley, and many other places."

He eulogized the First Amendment and damned the Fresno authorities for abridging it. It was part of the IWW strategy not to speak directly to labor issues in these soapbox addresses, but to stand instead as defenders of fundamental rights, of keeping the streets open for free expression. Which of course included keeping the parks and plazas open for rallies to organize the railroad and field-workers of the Valley towns. Both the IWW and its enemies understood the scenario, though most street-corner listeners did not.

Marquez spoke passionately for five minutes, flailing away at the air with flamboyant gestures. He collected an audience of three: a coarse-faced farm woman with her adolescent son, and a dandy in a checked vest who cleaned his teeth with a gold pick while he listened. Marquez then heard the siren. Distant, but coming fast.

Gopal Mukerji's brown eyes darted to Frank Little, who fanned back his coat and unbuttoned his vest, leaving the pistol butt in the clear.

The eyes of the young Hindustani grew round, and his smile wavered. He'd been in Fresno, taking part in the campaign, only for a week. He had not been rousted from the streets before.

The gent with the gold toothpick darted into a dry-goods store. The farm lady said, "We're late, Rupert," and hurried the gawky lad away, just as the police sedan careened into sight behind a hay wagon on I Street.

Marquez rubbed his eyes with the tips of his fingers, trying to clear his vision. "Remember, Gopal—fall down limp if they seize you."

"I remember, Diego," Mukerji said with a fervent nod. He spoke English with the clipped upper-class accents of his white schoolmasters in the Jullundur district.

"You won't catch me falling down," Little said. "I ain't going back in the tank one more time."

Marquez shrugged. "As you wish." He stayed on the box by the fluttering banner. The black police sedan, its canvas top down, screamed in to the curb. A small crowd gathered across the street.

Five Fresno policemen in brass buttons and blue serge piled out like cops in a one-reel chase comedy. Marquez's heartbeat sped. There was nothing funny about these men with their tall hats, soup-strainer mustaches, and billy clubs. He'd met all but one of them before.

"Get down from there, Marquez," said the sergeant, brandishing his billy. "You're in violation of the anti-speaking ordinance, same as you were last Tuesday, and the week before, and the week previous to that."

Marquez stayed on the box. "Sergeant Lummis, I'm exercising my right of free speech. I refuse to be moved."

Lummis was a big, hearty man with a good-natured face, everyone's uncle. He sighed. "You're under arrest."

Gopal Mukerji spoke up politely and seriously. "Sergeant, if I may point out something—"

"Oh, we got a new Wobbly here," another policeman said. "A rag-head."

"For Christ's sake, Gopal," Frank Little whispered.

Mukerji wouldn't be deterred. "Sirs, the Constitution of this great republic guarantees to all men the right of expression without interference."

"Is that a fact, sir?" Sergeant Lummis said, edging up to

him. "I didn't realize I was in the presence of such a distinguished and informed person as yourself. A regular street lawyer, is that what we have here?"

"No, sir," Mukerji said, misunderstanding the sarcasm as sincerity. "I am Mr. Gopal Mukerji, a field-worker. It is kind of you to allow me to state my view."

"Jesus," Frank Little groaned, slipping back into shadows by the store fronts.

Lummis grinned. "Why, sure, rag-head. Just any time." His arm flew up and his billy smashed across Mukerji's nose. The Indian screamed as blood spurted out. Sergeant Lummis was quick for a man of his age and bulk, sidestepping so Mukerji's blood splattered Marquez's trousers. A cop swung his billy into Marquez's spine, and he was pitched off the soapbox.

Two policemen caught Marquez and began to pound him with their clubs, while two others seized Mukerji and worked on him. The corner of I and Mariposa resounded with the whap and crunch of billies. A gentleman in the small crowd of spectators applauded.

"Don't fight them," Marquez shouted, hanging limp in the hands of a cop. He shielded his head with his arms but otherwise offered no resistance. Blue legs and backs hid him from Mukerji, who was himself surrounded. Lummis kicked Mukerji's ribs repeatedly. In the shade by the store front, Frank Little drew his revolver partway, then gave up and fled down the street. Mukerji's cries and the pulpy sound of billies followed him as he ran.

The booking officer asked their names. Mukerji had been coached. He smiled politely.

"John Doe, sir."

Asked his name, Marquez said, "Harrison Gray Otis."

"I'll kill one of these fuckers someday," Sergeant Lummis muttered behind them.

The police threw them in a cell with three other Wobblies, previously identified on the blotter as Woodrow Wilson, Leland Stanford, and John L. Sullivan. Because Marquez was obviously ill, the Wobblies made room for him on the only bunk.

Mukerji sat down in the corner with a forlorn air. Messrs. Wilson, Stanford, and Sullivan were in good fettle considering their ragged state, their two-day incarceration, and the general hostility of their jailers. They immediately tried to buck up the new prisoners by singing "The Red Flag," a Wobbly anthem.

702

Then raise the scarlet standard high,
Beneath its folds, we'll live and die.
Though cowards flinch and traitors sneer,
We'll keep the red flag flying—

"Shut your mouths in there," boomed the voice of Sergeant Lummis. He came stumping along the aisle, peeled down to his singlet and chewing a cigar. He looked less like a kindly uncle, more like everyone's bad relative.

Lummis raked his billy along the bars. "Welcome to Fresno jail, boys. Four of you been here before, but we got a new one with us today. Come up here, Mr. Rag-Head."

Mukerji obeyed warily. Blood had dried brown under his bruised nose and a large purple-yellow ring was forming around his right eye.

"Sir, that is an offensive term," he said, staying out of reach of Lummis's billy. "We demand our rights. Also the presence of an attorney."

The sergeant furiously chewed the end of his cigar and whacked the bars with the billy. "Oh, you demand, do you? Well, Mr. Rag-Head, I'll tell you what we do with hotheads who demand things in Fresno. We cool 'em down with a little something called the water cure."

The scarecrow calling himself Woodrow Wilson stepped forward. "Lummis, Father Marquez is desperately sick. If you turn more water on him—"

"He ain't no father, he's a goddamn communist agitator," Lummis interrupted. "The water it is."

Woodrow Wilson grabbed the bars. "You're liable to kill him."

Lummis put his palm over Woodrow Wilson's face and shoved. "Good. That'll be one less Wobbly. Elmer? Let's unroll that fire hose in here. Get a couple more of the boys. Time to give Mr. Rag-Head a Fresno jail welcome."

The fire hose snaked all the way into the cell area from a hydrant outside the jail's back door. A jailer turned on the hydrant and the cannon blast of water blew the unsuspecting Mukerji off his feet. The other three prisoners crouched around Marquez, trying to shield him. In the long run it helped not at all.

The Wobblies were sprayed for fifteen minutes, then given a half hour's respite and sprayed again. Lummis and the jailers kept at it throughout the afternoon. Other cops drifted in from time to time, most of them wearing black rubber waders; the jail cells were not designed for drainage. By 7 P.M. the corridors and all the cells were a foot deep in water.

At half past eight Sergeant Lummis excused himself; his wife and six children were waiting supper. Going out, he called, "Keep it up, boys. The longer the better."

Gopal Mukerji crouched in the water. He'd removed his turban and slipped it under his shirt in an effort to save it. Strings of hair hung over his brown forehead and his face had lost its cheery innocence. He gazed at the jail corridor with shocked rage. How could human beings retaliate so cruelly for the mere exercise of a right guaranteed to all citizens of this beautiful state?

The jailer named Elmer opened three high windows at the end of the corridor and chilly night air swept in. Soaked, Gopal Mukerji began to shiver, his teeth chattering uncontrollably. Behind him, Marquez raved on the bunk, barely conscious.

A cop thrust the fire hose through the bars. "Another bath, you lice. Before we're done we'll clean you up real good." Water shot from the nozzle and hit Gopal Mukerji with enough force to stagger him. In one corner, Woodrow Wilson, Leland Stanford, and John L. Sullivan groveled against the wall.

"Stop it. I had enough," Leland Stanford wailed as the stream beat and bruised him. Gopal Mukerji glared at him through the roaring spray. He wouldn't be so cowardly. He would fight this outrageous cruelty. And not in the passive way that had proved itself futile.

The dirt road ran east and west, baking in the sunshine. To the east lay Bowles, to the west the hamlet of Raisin. Arbors stretched north and south into the hazy distance. Men in straw hats and loose white clothes worked among the vines.

Gopal Mukerji staggered along, supporting Marquez. The former priest's black suit was incredibly filthy, and Mukerji wasn't much cleaner. Sweat streamed down Marquez's face, his purblind eyes slitted against the sun's glare. Sergeant Lummis had personally broken Marquez's eyeglasses and thrown away the frames.

Suddenly Marquez's legs gave out. "Oh dear me," Mukerji exclaimed, struggling. The weight was too much, and Marquez tumbled in the dust, rolling halfway down the side of a roadside ditch.

Frightened, Mukerji knelt beside his fallen comrade. Unfastening the end of his soiled turban, he unwound it until it was long enough to reach Marquez's face, then blotted the perspiration. He could feel the heat of his comrade's sickness.

Mukerji rocked back on his haunches, casting a forlorn eye at the flat valley and endless arbors. Silent workers saw the pair but made no move to aid them. Gopal Mukerji felt a renewed rage and sorrow. He was alone and lost in this cruel land he'd entered with such soaring hope. He didn't know what to do . . .

A shadow fell over Marquez's greasy cheek. The man who stood there was about seventy, small and wiry, with a dark leathery face and big work-hardened hands. He removed his straw hat and regarded the fallen man and Mukerji.

"Buenos días, señor. Soy Ramón Obregón."

"Please, I don't understand. Only English."

"I said I am Ramón Obregón. In charge of these men." He gave a nod at the nearby field-workers. "What happened to this man?"

"He was speaking in Fresno. They locked us in jail and gave us their water cure. They let us out two days ago."

"Two days, and you're only this far south of Fresno? It isn't even ten miles."

"I know, but he can't go fast. Just a few steps, then he falters. The fever and now the belly sickness—they're eating him away."

"Yes, I can smell the result of the belly sickness."

Ramón Obregón crouched down, waving his straw hat gently between his knees and watching the hot silver sky. "Not good for workingmen to speak in this part of the Valley. Not unless they confine themselves to saying, 'Yes, sir.' "

"So I am learning."

Obregón touched Marquez's forehead. "Christ save us. It's like a hot coal."

"Yes, sir. I fear that if he doesn't have a doctor, and medicine, he'll die."

"You are right, I think." Again the elderly Mexican scanned the hazy flatland. "The *padrón* of my ranch would not summon a doctor for him, that much I know. But we can make a place for him in our barracks. It's better than most. You get on that side and help me lift him."

The frame barracks, occupying one side of a large treeless yard a mile from the Bowles-Raisin road, baked in the hot sun. Dragging Marquez between them, Obregón and Mukerji crossed the yard, passing a water trough with an upright spigot at the end. Obregón's eyes moved back and forth watchfully.

In the distance, bright fans of water churned from noisy pumps, irrigating the arbors. Farther away, a huge chugging

Hart-Parr tractor plowed a fallow field, its great steel tires giving off occasional flashes in the sun. Marquez's eyelids fluttered. Sensing that someone was helping him, he tried to move his feet and slipped from Mukerji's grasp, dropping on his side in the yellow dust.

"Pick him up—quickly," Obregón whispered. "The *padrón* rides the property every day about this hour. He mustn't see this man. You either. He'd turn you out."

"No," Mukerji said.

"What's that?"

"I said, no, he won't turn us out."

"You're sure, are you?" Obregón said crossly.

"Yes, I am sure. You see, this man was once a Roman Catholic priest. A holy man, full of Christian love. He taught the Wobblies to be passive and not fight back when attacked. I learned quickly that he was wrong. Before we left Fresno, I went to our friend Mr. Frank Little. He gave me something."

Gopal Mukerji undid two buttons of his sweat-soaked shirt. The astonished Obregón saw a small revolver concealed against the man's belly.

"I have bullets too," Mukerji said. "No one will move Diego until he's better."

Obregón stared at the Hindustani with a keen new appreciation. Then the sight of a dust plume down a side road roused him. "It's the *padrón,* Tarbox. Let's get him inside; we can argue later."

They dragged Diego Marquez to the barracks stoop, where a stout black-haired woman and two barefoot children regarded the activity with mild surprise. Obregón gestured for her to open the heavy door. As the sound of a horse grew audible, they hauled Marquez from the blinding sunlight through the shade of the stoop to the cool dark of the interior. The woman closed the door from outside, leaning against the whitewashed siding and the painted wooden sign, which said CUARTEL beneath a faded *JMC* cartouche.

83

ON MARCH 6, FREMONT OLDER CALLED AT GREENwich Street. Mack had come north at the end of February. Now he received his friend in the first-floor office.

"No more stays. No more appeals. Tomorrow's the day," Older said. "Abe Ruef finally goes to San Quentin."

"It's taken long enough."

"I grant you that. I thought you'd like to come down to the county jail to watch the transfer. The caravan leaves at half past twelve."

"What do you mean, *caravan*?"

"It's turning into a blasted carnival. Reporters cordially invited. Honest Abe is the biggest and most celebrated con ever to be locked up in Q. His cell mates can't wait to meet him. He's already lined up a cushy job in the jute mill."

"I'll be there if I can." Mack jotted a note. In the next room, a telephone rang. Alex Muller's muffled voice could be heard answering.

Older tapped the arm of the visitor's chair. "The transfer isn't the only reason I came by. I want to be open with you and Rudy and everyone else in the reform group—"

"Open about what?"

"Ruef's fourteen-year sentence will net down to nine years with good behavior. The present rule states that a prisoner isn't eligible for parole until half the sentence is served. I intend to campaign to get that rule set aside. I'm going to use the full resources of the *Bulletin*."

Mack leaned back. "I don't believe I'm hearing this."

"Abe Ruef has been tried and convicted. He's a ruined man. His political apparatus is destroyed—he'll never wield power again. Why humiliate him?"

"Because he's a damn crook who bled this city for years."

"And we drew his blood too. We needn't wallow in it." From a card case Older brought a folded sheet of paper, which he gave to Mack.

"What's this?"

"Notes for an editorial."

Mack deciphered Older's hand with difficulty.

One needs a strong sense of self-righteousness to hold the key to another man's cell. One should be very sure of his own rectitude before he feels a pharisaical gladness over the humiliation of Abe Ruef.

"Fremont, what is this? What's going on?"

"Business, Mack. Business is what's going on. I went to Ruef's cell yesterday and arranged a deal with him. As soon as he's settled in prison, he'll start drafting his memoirs. To be published exclusively in the *Bulletin*."

Mack's mouth dropped. First came a searing anger, and he was about to remind Older that Ruef's hirelings had lamed Jim. Then a sad and cynical resignation sapped the impulse; Jim was gone.

"What's your angle?" he said instead. " 'Confessions of a repentant boss'?"

Older ignored the sarcasm. "Exactly."

"Good Lord." Mack shook his head. Alex Muller banged the door back in his haste to enter the room.

"Sir? It's Jesse Tarbox on the wire. Extremely urgent."

"Excuse me a minute." After Mack left, Fremont Older took the opportunity to slip out the front way with scarcely a sound.

"Found them this morning," Jesse Tarbox said. His sinewy face was red and sun-blistered, his khaki shirt sweated through at the armpits and across the back. He rapped his riding crop on his thigh. "Two of them. Wobblies run out of Fresno. One's a crazy rag-head, the other a Spic named Marquez. The rag-head's packing a pistol."

He listened.

"Actually it was my *segundo* Mr. Keeter who found them." Over by the office door, Homer Keeter stood idly scratching his crotch. He was a sandy-haired lout with a broom straw in the corner of his mouth.

"We're trying to keep it quiet—Christ knows what some of the hotheads around here would do if they found out." *Tar and feather me first, probably.* "The problem is the rag-head's got that gun, and he says I can't touch the Spic because he's bad sick. On top of that, he's a priest. Or he used to be. Can you feature that, a Wobbly priest?"

He listened.

"That's right—Marquez."

He listened.

"No, sir, I can't just order them out. I tried." Homer Keeter snorted; he'd been the one sent into the barracks with orders for the Wobblies to vacate.

Tarbox listened.

"Goddamn it, Mr. Chance, that isn't fair. I didn't just let it happen. My best foreman, Obregón, he picked them up and took them in. I'd like to flay the hide off Obregón but he's got eighteen relatives in that barracks." *And I'm scared of every one of them.*

He listened.

"I know it's my responsibility but I don't know what the hell to do," he shouted. "That's why I called."

He listened, slapping his crop against his riding breeches.

"All right, sir. Yes, sir. I'll sit tight until you get here but please make it fast. Yes, *sir.*"

Jesse Tarbox hung up the earpiece carelessly, and it fell off the hook, banging the wall at the end of its cord. When he tried to hang it up again, he broke the hook. Swearing, he let the earpiece dangle.

"I don't know why I work for that snotty son of a bitch."

"Because he pays top dollar, that's why."

"He's coming down here personally."

"I gathered."

"Be here sometime tomorrow."

"Well, he better hurry, because we got fifty greasers in that barracks, and you can't count on all of 'em keeping their mouths shut. Any of our neighbors find out we're hidin' two Wobblies on this ranch, we are in trouble."

"Shit, that's what I told him," Jesse Tarbox said. He hit his crop on the desk so hard, Homer Keeter jumped.

Mack checked the timetables. All the trains in the next few hours were locals, so he decided it would be faster to drive the Packard. He made good time for a while, but south of Stockton, just across the Stanislaus County line, a tire blew out. The Packard's headlamps veered wildly toward the left, and as the auto bounded for the shoulder, Mack hauled on the wheel to keep it out of the ditch. The rear end slewed. He tramped on the brake and killed the engine.

The Packard shook once and settled, an enormous cloud of tan dust slowly ascending into the purple twilight. He heard coyotes barking in the distance. He'd sure as hell guessed wrong about taking the car. He could either change the tire and keep driving, or hike to the nearest depot and wait. He certainly wasn't going to hike and wait.

Mack threw his fedora on the seat next to him and leaned his forehead on the wheel. The cool evening air laved his face. He felt grubby from hours of driving, and hungry, but he'd brought no food. There was a dairy barn about half a mile on, and he wondered if he could cadge a drink of milk or a butt of bread.

But first he had to change the tire. He climbed out, shed his coat, and undid his cravat. The western light winked on the blued metal of his Shopkeeper's Colt. The delay didn't improve his mood.

709

Repeatedly, the wrench or the wheel nuts slipped from his arthritic hands. All in all it took him over half an hour. When he finally got to the dairy farm, he paid for a quart of milk and half a loaf of bread and was allowed to crawl up in the haymow for an hour. Then he drove on through the vast star-strewn night. He had a powerful sense of a tide flowing against him.

At the Merced River crossing in Merced County, he found the bridge blocked by carpenters repairing sections of bridge floor that had collapsed under a wagonload of quarry stone. Mack swore and drove miles out of his way, up to Snelling. There he drove onto a barge that ferried him over the river.

It was 12:30 P.M. and too hot for March. The gritty wind had a parched smell, as if it were August. He sweated and drove without rest, without food, steadily south.

Above Chowchilla, a Madera County deputy on horseback came galloping from a side road, firing shots in the air. Mack stopped and the deputy arrested him for reckless speeding.

Mack showed identification, then named his companies and some of his connections in the state—it meant nothing. The rural magistrate and the deputy had never heard of him.

He thought of Abe Ruef. How would he handle this? He offered the magistrate and deputy bribes of $100 each, and they suddenly became cordial and helpful, the deputy directing him to a decent café, the magistrate inviting him to relax in the swing on his front porch. Mack stifled his sulfurous rage and said no. At half past three, on the raw edge of exhaustion, he continued south.

The Packard roared into the dusty yard in the red sundown. With the day's field work finished, families were together, barefoot children chasing each other around the trough and pump, a naked infant crawling to and fro, an imposing rooster pecking at nothing, a wiry yellow hound chasing its tail and yapping. The air smelled of warm earth and spicy cooking.

The picture of dishevelment, Mack flung himself out of the Packard and strode inside the barracks. A majority of the field-workers recognized him, the women smiling shyly and the men knuckling their foreheads. Mack fumed; he assumed Tarbox was responsible for the subservience.

The building consisted of clean, spartan living spaces off a hall that ran down its length. Some of the living spaces consisted of three rooms, some, for the bachelors, only one. Everything was freshly whitewashed, and ceiling fixtures provided electric light. The second floor was identical.

Up there, halfway down the corridor, Mack spied a young man in a turban standing in a doorway. He was brown, but not a Mexican. Mack went straight past him, noticing his wary look, and into the two-room space. The sight of Diego Marquez was a shock. He lay on a bunk, fat, sallow, and sick. Mack smelled the sweat soaking his cotton nightshirt.

He knelt by his old acquaintance and rested his palm on Marquez's forehead. An elderly Mexican appeared at the door and stepped in.

"Soy Ramón Obregón. Buenas tardes, señor."

"Chance."

"Ya sé—lo he visto en fotografías."

They shook hands, the young Indian peeking over Obregón's shoulder. Marquez snorted and rolled his head back and forth. Then he calmed and began to snore with his mouth open.

Continuing in Spanish, Mack said, "His fever must be a hundred and four."

"It has been thus for several days," Obregón said. "I expected him to die. He refuses. He is a big man. Powerful, like a bull."

"But he can't last like this. I'll get a doctor out here."

"That is good," said Mukerji in such perfect English that Mack was startled. "Diego is an excellent man. But they hate him very much in Fresno. Almost as much as they hate all Hindustani."

"You're the one who brought him here?"

"I am, sir."

"How did he get this way?"

"He was arrested for speaking. They sprayed us with the cold water hose all night in the Fresno jail. Diego had suffered it once before. He was already sick. I brought him out of town."

"I found them on the main road and took them in," Obregón explained.

"You had no business doing that, no authority to do that." Mack said it sharply, out of both weariness and a desire that this problem would just vanish.

Visible disappointment clouded Obregón's face; he had heard better of J. M. Chance. "No authority, perhaps," he replied quietly. "But a duty." The old man's eyes showed no subservience, no intimidation.

Mack retreated. "All right, I'll accept that. No authority to do it, but every reason. I'll drive up to Tarbox's office and phone for a doctor. Let's just keep this quiet. I don't need any grief from the other ranchers. They think I'm too radical as it is."

That brought a wearied smile from Obregón. "I understand. It is radical to build this barracks with proper wood floors instead of dirt. Radical to provide decent privies instead of open trenches, or nothing. It is radical to house your people here, instead of crowding them in the usual tents and hovels. Radical indeed, sir."

Mack and the old Mexican eyed one another, silently making peace.

Marquez groaned in his sleep. The red of sunset faded away outside the window. Mukerji reached up to the cord of the tin-shaded electric bulb and snapped it on.

Mack walked downstairs and into the yard, all dusky now. He wrinkled his nose at the odors of dirt and sweat left on him by the long journey. Things were still all wrong. He didn't like harboring Wobblies, no matter who they were.

His body felt heavy as granite as he dragged to the water trough. He turned the spigot, stood away from the splash, and filled the dipper. The water was cool and sweet. He tilted the dipper and ran some over his chin, then spilled more over his forehead, licking it as it dripped from his nose.

When he opened his eyes, he saw the Indian on the stoop under an electric light. The man walked over quickly.

"Mr. Chance, sir. One moment please before you leave. I am Mr. Gopal Mukerji, sir. In my home village, Chandpur, in the Punjab, I learned to be a number-one first-rate farmer. I sailed by steerage to Canada, where I harvested wheat. Then I traveled down to California, where others from my region work also. I like it so much, despite the hatred I found in Fresno, I will be a Californian now."

Tired and annoyed all over again, Mack didn't know what to make of this foreigner. "I can't talk now," he said.

"Just please one more moment, sir. I am a very good, hard worker. An absolute top man with crops of all sorts, including muscat and muscatel raisin grapes, which I see you grow in quantity."

"For God's sake, Mukerji, this is no time—"

"Why not, sir? I am eager, industrious, honest. Give me a job, sir."

Mack leaned on the pump. "Look. They don't like your kind in the Valley. Didn't Fresno teach you that? They also don't like anyone who hires Indians. I said inside and I'll repeat it—

I don't need more grief; I have plenty. You'll have to go somewhere else."

"But sir, I guarantee, you will find me a most capable number-one man. Working hard for you on this ranch, any long hours you ask, I could save enough to bring my prospective wife from Chandpur. I have great hope that we could prosper here in California."

"You'll have to go somewhere else. Now get inside, out of sight."

"Sir . . ."

Mack clanged the dipper on the pump. "No job."

The Indian stared at Mack as he hung up the dipper and turned toward the Packard. Then Mukerji plucked the dipper off the hook and twisted the spigot. Somehow that was too much. Mack spun around and knocked the dipper out of Mukerji's hand. The tinned metal flashed as the dipper landed in dust.

"Goddamn it, I told you—get inside."

"Sir. Not even a drink of water first?"

An enormous stillness seemed to descend on the yard. The two of them stood well away from the stoop, in the dark, barely touched by the electric light. A narrow luminous aura of yellow and white defined the peaks of the coast mountains.

Mack saw nothing of the surroundings, only a hopeful young wanderer at a meandering brown stream. He saw Swampy Hellman on horseback, denying the interloper a simple necessity and comfort . . .

"Sir?"

Mack rubbed his mouth, then walked over and picked up the fallen dipper. With an unconscious solemnity, he handed it to Gopal Mukerji.

The two men stared at one another.

Gopal Mukerji turned on the spigot.

What the hell have I become? How is it that I've forgotten so much? Is it age? Money? Frustration? Sorrow? Whatever it was, Mack was ashamed.

While water splashed in the trough, Jesse Tarbox galloped along a dirt track into the yard. Red and excited, he waved his riding crop over his head as he reined. "Homer Keeter saw you drive in, Mr. Chance. There's headlights on the main road. Whole damn bunch of cars."

Mack sprinted to the Packard and jumped on the rear bumper, then the trunk. From that height he could see across

713

the field to the Bowles-Raisin road. Sure enough, bobbing and flashing, headlights stabbed the roiling dust. Mack counted five, six, seven pairs of lights coming in a column from the east. From the Fresno pike.

Tarbox pranced his nervous mare toward the auto. "Whoa, Sal. Calm down, blast you." The foreman slapped the mare savagely with his reins, drawing blood.

"Why are we suddenly entertaining visitors, Jesse?"

"Somebody must have talked in town."

Gopal Mukerji ran to the Packard and, without invitation, stood on the bumper. He said to Mack, "I will not be moved, sir. Not until my friend and companion is well." He yanked his shirt out of his pants and palmed a small pistol.

God almighty, everything is falling apart.

Tarbox sounded close to hysterical when he said, "Seven cars means a lot of men. They might burn us out. Kill people. Why don't you hand over those two?"

Mack was tempted. He wished the burden would pass, but it wouldn't.

"Why don't you shut your mouth, Jesse? Ride to the office and get me the shotgun."

He jumped back down off the car, throwing off his coat and pulling the Shopkeeper's Colt off his hip. After opening the cylinder to check the loads, Mack jumped back up on the Packard's front bumper. Now he heard as well as saw the caravan. Snarling and roaring, the autos turned one by one into the lane leading to the heart of his property.

Mack waited at the water trough. He'd sent Jesse Tarbox back to the office again, with orders to stand by the telephone. He tugged the holster around to his right hip, where he could reach it quickly. In the crook of his arm rested the ranch shotgun, an eight-gauge Ithaca with a modified choke on both barrels.

The single line of autos came on toward the yard, their headlights stabbing through boiling dust clouds. To Mack, in his tired state, they sounded like hungry, evil-tempered mountain cats.

The lights of the first car blinded him a moment. Four or five men were packed into the black Ford T-model. It veered left into the yard, then right again, its lights splashing the front of the barracks as it stopped.

One by one the other six cars pulled up alongside each other. Mack was staring at fourteen headlights. He locked his knees so his legs wouldn't shake; he didn't want them to see how frightened he was.

Doors on the cars sprang open and men in overalls and cheap suits piled out—stringy redneck Fresno County farmers and town merchants with derbies and high collars. Mack knew most of them, including Sergeant Phil Lummis from the police department—out of uniform—and the man who stepped out in front as if he were the leader, a bald and paunchy wheat rancher named Peter Sledgeman.

Sledgeman walked to the water trough with a wary eye on Mack, the others forming up behind him. Mack's quick count came to twenty-three. Work-gnarled hands clutched ax handles and two-by-fours. He saw no guns.

Mack nodded to acknowledge the spokesman. "Pete."

"Mack."

"What can I do for you?"

"I expect you know. You're harboring two men we want."

Mack's round eyeglasses flashed in the headlight glare, his hair shining white as new cotton. Sibilant Spanish was audible in the barracks. He'd ordered everyone inside, away from the open windows, and he hoped to heaven they'd obeyed.

"I said you've got two men we—"

"Calm down, Pete, I heard you. Is it them you want, or me?"

Sledgeman smiled coldly. "Well, yes—there's that. You never have run with the crowd around here. Always made your neighbors look bad, out of step. Take this blasted barracks. Tents aren't good enough for your stoop labor—"

"That's right. Not good enough. What else, Pete?"

"Those two reds. Hand 'em over and we'll have no trouble."

"Hand them over? What for? Another water cure at the jailhouse? Or is it a lynch rope this time?"

"Don't stall us, Mack. We know they're inside. One of Ramón Obregón's cousins swallowed a lot of tequila in town and shot off his mouth."

"I'm not denying they're here. But you can't take them. I gave them shelter and you boys are the reason why. I'll thank you to remember this is my property, Pete. I want you to vacate it, right now. Go home. Cool off."

Another farmer, Carl Cass, stepped in front of the lights of his Reo. Cass's neck was genuinely red from working his melon fields. He chewed tobacco; stains showed all over his overall bib. Mack had once loaned Cass $500 for emergency medical bills for his little girl Clarice. There was no memory of that in Cass's snake-mean stare, nor any when he shouted.

"You're crazy, Chance. Why are you protectin' a couple of damn reds who'd just as soon steal all your money and your land too?"

Some in the crowd muttered and said, "Yes," or "Tell him, Cass."

"Listen, Carl," Mack said, "I like the Wobblies about as much as you do. Which is not very much. But speechmaking never hurt anybody. Something reminds me that American people are allowed to make speeches anywhere they please, on just about any subject. If that argument doesn't move you, try this one. I know one of the two men from way back. He's wasting away with fever and probably pneumonia, liable to die if I don't get a doctor in here. A human life's more important than money or land."

A farmer leaning on a shiny green fender snickered. "Since when?"

"Might as well forget about calling a doctor or anybody else," Sledgeman said. "We stopped half a mile up the road and Len Sudder shinnied up the phone pole and cut the line. We also sent one more car down the back road with its lights out. There's a few good boys in the field behind this place, in case anybody gets a notion to run that way."

A knife twisted in Mack's middle and his mouth turned dry and juiceless.

Sledgeman ran his tongue over horsy yellow teeth, then settled his frayed old straw hat a little more firmly. "I think you just better let us have those two, Mack." He walked around the trough, headed for the stoop.

Mack lined up the shotgun on Sledgeman's gut. Sledgeman stopped, and so did the muttering from the others.

"Pete, I don't want to fire this, but I will if you push. You want those men, you'll have to take me first. I guarantee I'll take some of you with me."

Sledgeman chewed his lower lip and eyed Mack up and down, gauging his determination. Finally the farmer leaned over and expelled a big shiny blob of spit right into the dust in front of Mack's shoes.

"You're violating the law, Mack."

"What the hell do you mean?"

Carl Cass shouted the answer. "Sheriff Chittenden deputized us. Every man-jack."

"Except me—I already got a badge," Sergeant Lummis said to general laughter.

Mack rubbed an index finger over his chin. He could hear the rasp of his beard, growing out dark as a twilight shadow; he hadn't touched a razor since leaving the City.

"So you see, Mack—"

"Nothing, Pete. I see nothing."

"If we want those two, we got the authority."

"I'd like to see a warrant. Some legal paper." Men shifted their feet and muttered again. "This deputy talk is bullshit, Pete, and we both know it. But I really don't care one way or another. You'll bleed just as much deputized as not." He held the double-barrel Ithaca a little higher, the blued metal shining in the headlights.

Sledgeman finally answered him with a shrug. "We can wait you out. We can wait all night. We can wait a week. We're gonna make an example of that greaser and the rag-head. Examples for the whole damn valley."

"The whole state," an Armenian farmer named Pazian yelled, drawing a lot of noisy approval from the others.

Sledgeman turned around and trudged back to the autos. Lummis and a few others huddled around him, whispering.

Mack walked backward to the dim pool of electric light on the stoop. "Anyone there?"

From the darkness of the hall came the reply. "I, sir. Mr. Mukerji."

"Try the telephone on the wall. Let me know if it's working."

Mack waited.

"No, sir, I do not think so."

Swearing, Mack sat down on the stoop and leaned back against the siding. "Turn out this light."

Mukerji snapped it off. Mack watched the farmers and townsmen gesturing and arguing in front of the parked automobiles. He'd never been one to waste his money on gambling. But if this were poker, it was a pretty sure bet that he held the losing hand.

Ticking. A steady ticking . . .

His head jerked up. He'd dozed off.

A cock crowed somewhere. Clouds like white veils trailed across the stars. The ticking kept on. He remembered where he was and wished he hadn't. Hours ago, he'd put on his suit coat for warmth, but he was freezing, his hands raw and cold. When he exhaled he could see his breath faintly.

The Ithaca rested on his knees. The ticking, he realized now, came from his twenty-four-karat-gold pocket watch. Bought

717

and engraved before the earthquake, it bore the *JMC* crest on the lid.

The barracks faced north. To the east, light was breaking over the valley floor. Mack picked up the watch and tilted it to put some light on the dial. Half past five.

He yawned and wiggled his stiff legs. The auto lamps had been turned off long ago and the men had piled into the cars to doze, or had curled up on the ground. As the light brightened, Mack saw an arm stretched out here, heard a yawn there; they were rousing.

Behind the barracks, a sudden explosive hiss signaled the start of another irrigation cycle. Jesse Tarbox had thrown the switch in the office three quarters of a mile away. It might as well have been in China.

Slowly the men in the mob woke up and greeted each other. Someone's muffled words were answered with a laugh. That commonplace sound made Mack feel even more alone.

He heard a rustling behind him, inside, the creak of a stool being moved. Mukerji had sat there all night, sharing the vigil like a servant attending his master. With his pistol, it was a total of two handguns and a shotgun against twenty-three.

Not good enough.

Lummis gathered Cass and Sledgeman and five others and once again made a show of conferring. They stood in front of the Model T, where Mack could see them clearly—which was their intent. All night, he'd cudgeled his mind for a way out of this, a way to forestall violence. He considered Tarbox worthless in this kind of emergency, and Homer Keeter too. Mukerji had volunteered to try a dash through the fields for help, but Mack had vetoed it. To whom could they appeal? Maybe the Fresno city and county authorities hadn't encouraged this marauding, but they'd surely look the other way, whatever happened. No other help was available.

Sledgeman seemed to be talking loudest in the group by the Model T. He smacked a fist in his palm. "No, right now." Lummis shrugged, and after some more argument, Sledgeman put on his straw hat and stumped out to the water trough.

"Chance?"

"Yes."

"You listen. We played your game all night, but the boys are hungry and cold and they want to get this over with. You aren't going to be reasonable; we aren't either. We brung some spare tins of gas with us. If you won't deliver those two, we'll punish them right here. Fry their hides inside the barracks. Cook 'em alive, and your Mex help in the bargain."

"Pete, there are women in the barracks."

"I know that."

"Youngsters—"

"Mack, it's your choice. If they die, the guilt's on your head."

"You'll have to get up close to start a fire."

"We will. You can put some shot in some of us, but not all of us."

A vein in Mack's forehead stood out like blue string. He didn't want to contemplate how bad, how truly bad this could be if they carried out the threat.

"Mukerji?" he said over his shoulder.

"Sir?"

"Are they still watching the back too?"

"Yes, sir, I looked not ten minutes ago."

Mack stood up, shivering, but not from the chill. With his knee joints cracking and popping, he walked rapidly to the corner of the barracks and looked down the wall to the arbors. There he discerned three men, widely spaced, about fifty yards beyond the barracks. One carried a piece of bar iron.

Mack heard the slosh of liquid. Across the yard, Cass was lugging a five-gallon gas can out in front of the parked autos; a second man behind him had another. Mack ran back to the stoop, his palms slippery on the shotgun.

Sergeant Phil Lummis found an ax handle. Someone else produced a rag. Lummis tied the rag around one end of the handle and Cass poured gas over it.

Lummis stepped well away from the gas containers, holding the ax handle at arm's length and averting his face. A man struck a match and threw it, and the rag ignited with a whoosh and gush of flame.

After the flame settled, Lummis hoisted the improvised torch and started on a path to the water trough. Inside the barracks, a woman pleaded in Spanish for her children to gather close and hold on to her.

Mack cocked the shotgun. "Far enough, Phil."

"No, sir, I got police authority. You pull a trigger on me, you'll hang."

Lummis kept walking.

"Phil," Mack said in a raw voice.

Cass shouted, "Don't worry, Phil, he ain't got the balls to kill you cold."

Bastards. *Bastards.* They knew him.

They started to edge forward, all of them, all across the row

719

of parked autos. The sun was coming up. It promised to be a mild, sweet California day.

"One last time, Phil. Stay back. This is senseless. A lot of people will be hurt for nothing."

Sledgeman yelled, "I don't think keeping the radical unions out of California is nothing, you cocksucker."

There were shouts: "Right, by God"; "Kill him"; "And ever last one of his greasers—"

Mack wanted to weep with rage. He never imagined it would degenerate to this. But Lummis kept walking, straight on past the water trough.

Mack rammed the shotgun against his shoulder, taking aim. Lummis stared him in the eye from fifteen paces away. Mack fancied he could feel the heat of the burning rag.

Then only ten paces . . .

Do it. Shoot him.

And seven . . .

And five . . .

SHOOT HIM.

Lummis broke into a wide grin. "You're a stinking yella coward, Chance."

Lummis wound up to throw the flaming ax handle through a window. Mack hardened his heart and touched the trigger.

Another sound ruptured the silence, a sound louder than the sprayers in the arbors.

"Reinforcements!" somebody yelled.

"Shit, no—we rounded up everybody who wanted to come," Sledgeman said.

Mack's crooked finger caressed the trigger. Then, squinting, he saw something unbelievable. Lummis turned around and saw it too. It was as if a little Essanay film of the previous night was playing on a screen. Five autos in a line roared down the Bowles-Raisin road and turned left into the property with headlights blazing.

"What the hell's going on?" Lummis shouted. The fiery ax handle burned too close to his hand and he threw it in the trough. There was a fierce hiss, and a squiggle of smoke in the air, and then nothing but the snarl and growl of the autos coming on through the dust clouds.

A gilt star decorated the side of the first auto, along with the word SHERIFF. Looks of panic spread on the faces of the farmers and townsmen as the big black Stoddard-Dayton slewed around the parked cars and braked in front of them. The four other vehicles pulled up behind, blocking the road. Men jumped out, talking, yelling questions—city men, from the cut of their clothes.

The sheriff heaved himself out of his car, tugging up his pistol belt against his sizable belly. He was bowlegged and walked as though his boots pinched. Gray hair showed beneath a creamy Montana peak hat. He spoke with the aggrieved air of a schoolmaster in a room of rowdies.

"Everybody put down those clubs. Chance, put away that shotgun. Lummis, what the devil is an officer of the law doing mixed up in this?"

"They said you deputized them, Chittenden," Mack said.

Sheriff Chittenden looked even more aggravated. "They're damn liars. They'd say anything to get their licks at you, I expect."

The men fingered their ax handles and two-by-fours. Sledgeman narrowed his eyes as Mukerji peered cautiously from the doorway, his pistol in hand.

Sheriff Chittenden dragged out his revolver, a homely old .44-40 Colt Frontier model, and fired a shot over his head. The echo rolled away above the sunlit arbors. "I said, put everything down. That's an order. Barney, Al—if they won't, arrest them."

"You heard him, gents," said a voice. The speaker was the first of a pair of deputies, younger men with boyish faces, who had slipped between the parked autos. One carried an old Winchester Express, the other a later-model .30-30. After the deputies grabbed a couple of baseball bats and tossed them, the rest of the men pitched their weapons down voluntarily. Pazian and a few others looked relieved in a guilty sort of way.

The city men moved nearer the farmers and townsmen. Mack saw checkered suits, spats, fancy watch chains. Sledgeman swatted his leg with his straw hat. "Chittenden, who the hell are these dudes?" From the pads and pencils in evidence, Mack knew.

"San Francisco *reporters*, Pete," Sheriff Chittenden said. Sledgeman failed to understand the warning. "Came in on a special train at half past four this morning."

"How the hell did they find out about it?" an angry farmer demanded.

A reporter with a waxed mustache and a radish of a nose marched right up to him. "Well, I'll explain that, ruben—"

"Listen here," the farmer sputtered.

"One of your loquacious country cousins must have mouthed it around town, because somebody sent a telegram from the depot, maybe somebody who thinks this sort of sport is pretty barbaric. The message flashed from Sacramento to San Francisco, and my city editor dragged me out of Shay's Market Street Saloon and said there was likely to be a shootout or a lynching here in the sticks. The *Examiner* hired a special train within the hour. That's it in a nutshell, ruben."

The farmer glared. "You goddamn city wiseacre, my name ain't *Ruben.*"

"Well—whatever," the reporter said with a shrug. "Sounds like it's a crackerjack story you've got here. Wobblies besieged! King Mob and Prime Minister Arson reign in Fresno County! Yes, sir—could be bigger than Mussel Slough."

Sledgeman stumped over to Mack and leaned close. "Hadn't of been for you, we'd have those two. Nobody'll forget this."

"I hope you're right."

Sheriff Chittenden brandished his Colt. "Now I'm going to say this just once and everybody better listen. All you boys from around here, you climb in your cars and vamoose. Some of the rest of you, move those cars in the lane so they can leave. Collect the bunch out back, too. This party's over."

"Sheriff, we came a devil of a long way. We've got to talk to these people," a reporter said.

Chittenden considered that. "All right. Five minutes. That's all."

The new arrivals went shooting among the locals like pool balls ricocheting after a break. One farmer took a swing at a reporter; a couple of others couldn't wait to start telling their side.

"These are newspaper journalists?" Gopal Mukerji asked Mack.

"That's right. From San Francisco."

The Indian thrust his pistol into his pants, grinned, and dashed for the nearest of them.

Tension drained out of Mack's hands and shoulders, leaving him spent and fighting a yawn. He laid the Ithaca shotgun beside the trough and leaned forward to dip his face in the water, which rippled with highlights from the morning sun.

After immersing his face, he straightened up and shook like a puppy coming out of a creek. Then, opening his eyes, he saw a reporter in a skirt and shirtwaist stepping around the hood of the parked Model T.

"Nellie."

He was so astonished, he couldn't move, just stood there with water dripping from his cheeks and chin.

Her face was pale and puffy from lack of sleep and her hair

showed more gray than he remembered. She watched him with a strange, tremulous, almost tearful expression.

Gopal Mukerji plunged among the reporters, aggressively shaking hands. "How do you do, sirs? I am Mr. Gopal Mukerji, a very good number-one agriculturist and Californian. I wish to say that were it not for that gentleman, Mr. Chance, we would certainly all be dead—or worse. He is a very brave gentleman for whom I hope to work for many years to come."

"You work for him now, is that it?"

Gopal Mukerji swiftly looked at Mack.

Mack called, "Yes."

Mukerji's grin shone like the sun. Mack ran to Nellie and flung his arms around her.

"Mack—good Lord." She gasped and struggled; he had a strong grip on her waist. Her slim body felt wonderful under his hands, wonderful and right. "I have a dispatch to write and file—"

He paid no attention, forcing her to the side of the Model T and kissing her. Though the kiss lasted only seconds, by the end of it she relaxed in his arms.

"What are you doing here?" He felt giddy as a schoolboy, miraculously reprieved from exhaustion.

"You heard what Kipper Harkness said a minute ago. This story got on the wire from Fresno. I was in the City last night, ready to sit down to dinner with old friends from the *Examiner*. They got a telephone call from the city room and you were mentioned. Within twenty minutes the paper decided to hire a train. I had to come along."

She studied the barracks. Workers and their wives and children crowded the stoop and upstairs windows. "You're defending Indian labor now? That's a whole new side of you."

"I don't think so. You know I've always had a passion for underdogs. That young man Mukerji is one. He was treated brutally in Fresno. Marquez too. Mukerji brought Marquez here."

"Diego Marquez?"

"That's right. He's inside." Mack leaned against the Ford's fender. "Before you go to work, I want to tell you something. I'm worn out from dealing with all this by myself. All these people and their problems." He rubbed at his damp face and decided to take the risk. He tried to couch it lightly, though he suspected she could see how tense he was. She could probably hear his heart beating.

"I wouldn't mind laying back for a while, Nellie. I mean a

good, long while. I wouldn't mind having a wife who could support me with her writing."

"A—?" Nellie formed the *w* with her lips. Then astonishment silenced her.

"*Wife*, Nellie. Wife."

"Damn you." Her eyes filled with tears. She caressed his cheek, not caring who saw. "Damn you, Mack Chance. How am I supposed to write a coherent sentence when you come at me with a statement like that?"

"I don't know. I just had to say it. I'm tired of living without you. I was proud for too long, ambitious for too long, and thick-headed and a lot of other things. I've never loved any woman but you and you know it. I'll take the blame for keeping us apart."

"My." She rocked back. "You have changed."

"I don't know," he repeated with a shrug. "I'm willing to try, though."

With a little laugh, she leaned her head on his shoulder. "I've changed too. Look at all this gray in my hair."

"It's becoming."

"Nonsense. I'm not young any longer. I'm not sure of myself, the way I was when I was twenty. It's a penalty of age. I'll tell you another: I get cold in bed at night. Books won't keep a body warm. I think a husband would be . . . very desirable."

"The right husband."

"There's only one, Mack." Unable to hold back, she clung to his neck and cried. Peter Sledgeman walked near the auto and gave the lovers a look of hatred.

"No, there's never been any other." She kissed his dry, cracked mouth.

He hugged her there in the morning sunshine, ready to faint from excitement and exhaustion. But he had things to do. "I have to drag Tarbox out of whatever hole he's hiding in," Mack said then, "and send him to Fresno for a doctor."

"I must get busy too," Nellie said. She found her reporter's pad and set her sights on Sheriff Chittenden. Moving away, she closed her eyes and said, "Margaret, bless you."

"What did you say?" Mack called from six feet behind her.

"Nothing, darling, nothing."

Nine days later, Diego Marquez was well enough to leave the barracks. Mack drove him into Fresno to catch the Southern Pacific.

As he walked with Marquez to the platform, he wondered

724

what would become of the ex-priest. He looked grossly fat, and still showed poor color even though he'd quite recovered from the dangerous fever and pneumonia.

"Good-bye, Mack. Thank you for what you did."

"*De nada*. It was the only right thing. I wish we could be real friends again."

With a weary wryness, Marquez said, "A long time ago you suggested I was a conscience. Self-appointed. Can you tell me the name of any man who is friendly with his conscience?"

"I'm serious, Diego."

"What you propose is not possible."

"It was possible once."

"All greedy men despise a liberal spirit. Are you such a rare exception?"

"If that's what you think about me, it makes me angry. You don't know me anymore."

"I know myself. I know what I believe and preach. The Church constrained me to walk a narrow road. Then I left her to walk another, steeper one, strewn with thorns and traps and almost sure to lead to darkness. It's the familiar road of fools and martyrs—those who willingly let their bodies be crushed because they are so presumptuous as to think their ideas must prevail. We are on different sides."

"Different armies. The same side."

Marquez looked doubtful as they shook hands and he put his foot on the step of the southbound Pullman car. For a moment his eyes lost focus and he swayed. The black porter caught Marquez quickly and steadied him until he recovered his balance.

Mack shook his head. What a pair they were, he and Marquez. Two California outcasts. After a moment Marquez said, "Thank you again."

"You're entirely welcome."

Marquez made the sign of the cross. "God protect you." The porter helped him up the steps.

It was slow going, and Marquez frequently uttered little gasps. He acted like a man beset by everything from piles to the white Christian Republican wrath of General Otis. Well, that too was California. Mack was consumed by an enormous sadness as the southbound express pulled out in a cloud of steam.

That night he had a strange dream. It began with the blizzard but soon shifted to California, to scenes of himself with Swampy, the old German refusing him water. Then Mack saw himself refusing it to Gopal Mukerji in the yard of the ranch.

Waking about 3 A.M., he thought he knew what it meant. He'd come perilously close to becoming a Walter Fairbanks, a man who claimed his gold and then denied others the right to look for theirs.

In the morning, using the repaired telephone line at the ranch, he contacted Alex Muller on Greenwich Street.

"Dig out the address for Yacob Steinweis. Telegraph him and tell him I'll sell him the land."

84 AT NOON ON THE THIRD FRIDAY IN AUGUST, 1911, James Macklin Chance married the former Natalia Rotchev in a parlor of the Hollywood Hotel, a justice performing the civil ceremony. William R. Hearst gave the bride away and Johnson came down from Niles to stand up for Mack. The moment the Texan stomped across the veranda of the rambling frame hotel, two bellhops recognized him and one asked him to sign a baggage check. Such was the escalating fame of Broncho Billy, his pictures, and his stock company.

There was a lively reception following, attended by a raffish crowd of journalists and some of Mack's associates—Alex and his wife, Sophia; Billy Biggerstaff, his manager in Riverside, and Mrs. Biggerstaff; Haven Ogg of the oil company, with his wife and all twelve children; Enrique Potter, a widower now. At about seven, Mack and Nellie bid the guests good-evening and retired to the bedroom of the hotel's largest suite. There was none of the shyness or hurried clumsiness of lovers new to one another; rather, a comfortable quality, like a reunion of longtime sweethearts.

After, they talked a while of the convoluted road each had traveled to this intersection of their lives that they'd almost passed by. Nellie had a strong point to make to her new husband.

"If I give up some of myself, I expect the same of you. I won't be ignored—jobbed aside—the way Carla was."

"I understand." He reached out. "What time is it?" He knocked his pocket watch off the side table and crawled out of bed naked and knelt over it, squinting. "Half past ten. I have to go."

726

"Now? Where?"

"Downstairs. The chef promised me the kitchen as soon as the dining room closed."

"Why on earth—"

"Be patient. It's a surprise."

He kissed her ardently, jumped into his trousers and a shirt, and left her in the dark. He didn't come back until after midnight.

At Hollywood and Highland, on the corner opposite the hotel, a man watched the high cupola of the wedding suite.

The night air had a stale, dusty smell, the smell of drought, relieved only a little by the faded scent of withering rosebushes. But the man, whose age and features the darkness concealed, was immune to the subtle odors. All he fixed on was the flash of electric light in the cupola, the figure moving in silhouette, then the light blinking off again.

Good. They were still there. He could safely sleep till morning in some out-of-the-way corner of this proper, righteous suburban community of thirty-five hundred souls.

He wandered for several blocks until he found a nook between two alley trash boxes, next to a fence with a sign reading NO DOGS—NO JEWS—NO ACTORS.

Trembling, Wyatt crouched down between the trash boxes. His tongue felt huge and heavy. A thousand little insects crawled over his scalp, in his ears, under his arms, up his groin. He fumbled in the pocket of his rancid coat, a stolen coat two sizes too large, then nearly broke the needle giving himself the desperately craved injection.

In the morning, Mack loaded two wicker hampers on top of other gear in a rented surrey. Soon after, Mr. and Mrs. J. M. Chance went clipping along westward on Sunset Boulevard, a broad dirt avenue with P.E. rails in the center and telephone and telegraph wires straggling overhead. Hollywood was a drowsy little town of checkerboard lots, dull midwestern bungalows, and the occasional interruption of a showy Cape Cod manse. Nellie clung to his arm and smiled and sang to herself. After Mack came back to bed smelling of flour, spices, and other kitchen scents, they'd scarcely slept. She was tired, but she felt delicious.

"Saddle horse," Wyatt said to the youngster on duty at Knarr's Sunset Livery. He'd watched the isolated building about twenty minutes until he was sure there was but one person inside.

"Here's a nice fast mare. Rosabelle. Need her one day, or more?"

"One day." The boy reached for a saddle blanket without great haste. "Hurry up about it."

When Rosabelle was saddled, the boy had second thoughts about this stranger. The man's nondescript suit bore all sorts of foul-looking stains, a shiny, weeping sore marked the corner of his mouth, and his hair was long, spiky, and dulled by dirt; even the white streaks had a gray cast. The boy decided on his own initiative to discourage the customer by doubling the price.

"Six dollars."

The livery was dark and smelled of straw and manure. Wyatt kept shooting glances at the burning sunshine outside the double doors. The boy held out his hand for payment, hoping the man wouldn't have it. Definitely something wrong about him.

Turned away from the youngster, Wyatt suddenly swung back with his hands clasped together, a hammer of flesh. He bashed the boy's head, staggering him, then pounded him a second and third time.

The horses began to stamp and whinny and kick their stalls. Wyatt slapped a hand over the youngster's mouth and dragged him into an empty stall. Gripping the sides of the stall, he watched the double doors while he stamped the youngster's head, neck, and chest with his hobnailed shoe.

He left the youngster dead and, after locking up the stables, mounted Rosabelle and trotted into Sunset Boulevard, immediately turning west and galloping ahead of a big red interurban car.

It was another hot, hazy morning, and Mack soon shed his jacket. The foothills of the Santa Monicas had a sere yellow look. A sultry breeze came up, raising dust.

He turned the surrey toward the foot of Coldwater Canyon. At the last farm they passed, the householder, up on a ladder repairing his windmill, shouted to them.

"You goin' up yonder?"

"Yes, sir, I own some property. We're going to hike in and camp."

"Careful with your campfire—this drought's bad, and everything's tinder dry."

"Appreciate the warning." Mack shook the reins and drove on.

* * *

At dusk, Wyatt stole into a grove a few hundred yards above the twisting Coldwater Canyon road. Dust blew over the ground; the wind was stronger. But there'd be no rain tonight. The evening sky was yellow-white, like firelit brass.

Chilly and shaking, Wyatt staggered behind a tree for the last of his syringes. He dropped it when he finished, needle and barrel catching the light.

Mack had unhitched the surrey and tethered the horse with a large nose bag. Now, smelling Wyatt, the horse whinnied. Wyatt sidled up to the fretful horse and began to smile and stroke and charm the animal to silence while his eyes searched the hills above. A mile or so up, on a folded edge of ridge, a smudge of red located the campsite. The hot, still air and the dust of the countryside made him feel excruciatingly dirty, and so did his four-day stubble of beard. He hated that soiled, gritty feel of his skin; it was the feel of poverty. Failure . . .

Well, things would improve when he finished this. That lawyer would deposit the agreed-upon sum into the separate bank account he had set up, and he could move forward again. Of course to clear his trail he had to dispose of Nellie along with Mack, but that didn't bother him, not for a moment.

He continued petting and whispering to the horse until it was quiet. Then he stole out of the purpling shadow of the grove and began to climb a narrow foot trail.

In a clearing on the brown ridge, Mack had set up the double tent. As he started a small fire for the evening, Nellie cast an apprehensive eye at the sere hilltops. "Mack, it's a tinderbox up here. Should we really be doing that?"

He cast his eye around too, but said, "I'll take extra care, douse it thoroughly when we're ready for bed. I can do this, too." With his big clasp knife he traced a safety trench all the way around the fire, then spent a few minutes deepening it with a stick.

He next unfolded a little picnic stool—canvas between crossed legs. From one hamper he brought two bottles of Sonoma Creek zinfandel, his vineyard's best. From the other he took his waiter's corkscrew, silver, plates, napkins, and goblets.

Then he produced the delicacies.

First, a *pâté en croûte* of veal and pork, mushrooms and brandy, the crust glazed with egg before he baked it. Next, some Hass avocados, halved, with fresh lemons to squeeze over them. His main offering was *matambre,* a dish he'd learned from the Argentinian woman who now cooked in Riverside.

729

To make it he'd butterflied flank steaks and filled them with spinach leaves, thinly sliced onion rings, carrots, peppers, olives, and hard-boiled eggs, then rolled up the steaks, tied them, poached them in red wine and broth, and baked them. He took the result from a box of ice already melted into cold water, unwrapping the protective oilskin and slicing the cold meat into round sections. There were grapes and Calgold oranges for dessert. He rocked back on his boot heels and grinned.

"Your wedding supper, Mrs. C."

"It looks heavenly. I'll have to hire a cook; I can't match you in the kitchen."

"I confess I didn't do it all. The hotel chef helped with preparations."

"No false modesty now. You have a wonderful touch."

"I miss doing those big dinners. I've started to miss my polo ponies, and a lot of other things I enjoyed before it all went wrong." He knelt beside her and kissed her cheek. "You'll put everything right."

"I'll try."

They sat on the ground with their plates and wineglasses, the little camp stool serving as their table. The darkening sky was vast and hot, the stars blurred. Far down below, lights twinkled in farmhouses and a few imposing homes. To the south, they could just see the lighted oil derricks on the flat open land along Wilshire Boulevard. The tent flap snapped and crackled in the wind.

After they ate, pleasurably sipping their way through one bottle of the zinfandel, Mack went to the tent for the plans he'd brought along. They studied and discussed them for a while by the fire.

"The design is still very good," Nellie said finally.

"I agree. It's time we built a new house on Nob Hill."

The wind blew bits of parched brown grass into the fire, igniting and whirling them upward on the air currents. Mack hadn't hiked in the hills for years, and he felt renewed and refreshed.

"You're smiling," Nellie said.

"I'm happy. I wish Jim were still with me, but he isn't, so I'll settle for what I have." He leaned over to plant a light kiss. "Which I like very much, Mrs. Chance."

She caressed his cheek, but her eyes were momentarily troubled. "Do you really think he's gone for good?"

"Yes. I feel sure he's alive, but I know now that he doesn't want any part of me. Maybe I don't want to find him anymore—"

"Oh, Mack, no."

"It's true. Maybe I can't stand to face him and hear what he thinks of me. I do know that lately I haven't kept after the Pinkertons quite so hard as I once did."

"But if you think there's still any chance of finding him, you mustn't give up. You simply mustn't. Not while you can draw a breath. He's your boy."

"Nellie, Nellie . . ." He tousled her hair, his face lined by pain. "I know. Do you think I don't know? God, there's hardly an hour that I don't feel it."

And she was right, absolutely right, about pressing the search till the day he died. Yet deep within, he was apprehensive. He'd probed for the truth about Jim's feelings, and found it, and he feared it.

The canvas of the tent snapped again, and wind blowing over the mountain summit streamed into the fire, causing them to hitch back away from it. Scattering sparks fell among the tall weeds to one side of the clearing. Mack scanned the sky.

"Wind's changed direction. *Santan* coming. Guess we'd better think about going home in the morning. I've things to do in Riverside."

Drowsily, lovingly, Nellie caressed the curve of his chin. "All right. But we still have the night." She gave him a lingering kiss. "Oh, my, I do wonder why it took me so long to come to my senses."

"Both of us, Nellie. I had some pretty wrong-headed ideas about women."

"I had some pretty wrong-headed ideas of my own. Long ago, I should have gotten over being scornful of the way you set your sights for the top of a mountain, and then got there. I really do admire you for all you've accomplished—and especially the way you've put all your success to so many good uses."

He kissed her chin, smiling again. "Are you trying to soften me up so I'll take you on a better honeymoon someday?"

"This has been the best honeymoon I've ever had. And the only one I want."

She kissed him.

The *santan* blew.

Higher up, in deep weeds so dry they snapped at the touch, Wyatt watched the embracing couple in the penumbra of light. The climb up the hills, well away from the foot trail, had been long and arduous, but worth it; he'd cornered them. And the

731

shift of the wind gave him an extra benefit he hadn't antici-
pated.

He rummaged in his pocket for his last scrap of bread, then
stuffed it into his mouth. He probed the pocket again. The
matchbox was safe, but he should hold off until they were
sleeping soundly in the tent before he set the fire. So he hunkered down to wait. In ten minutes he was perspiring. In thirty
his palms crawled and silent screams filled his head. If he
didn't get back to Los Angeles soon, didn't get a pipe of opium
or a syringe of morphine, he'd die. He couldn't wait hours and
hours.

He pulled out the box of matches and sat there cross-legged
in the parched weeds, tossing the matches up and down, up
and down, listening to them rattle.

The wind ripped down over the Santa Monicas, blowing
harder.

Mack leaned on his elbows, musing.

"I've made so much money in California—more than I ever
dreamed of making—and I built such a wall of property, and
propriety, around myself, I didn't understand what it had done
to me till the moment that Hindustani fellow stood there with
the dipper and I told him to put it down. I had a dream that
told me I was doing exactly what Swampy and Fairbanks did
to me. I almost shut the door on Steinweis too. 'I've got mine,
you stay out, so I can keep more for myself . . .' "

"There's a lot of that in California," Nellie said.

"There's a lot of it in human nature."

With an enormous whoosh, the wind blew a cloud of sparks
off the fire. They momentarily swirled in the air, then settled.
Not three yards from where Mack and Nellie stretched out on
a blanket, the knee-high grass smoked and caught fire. Mack
ran over and stamped it out.

"That farmer was right. These hills are tinder."

Creeping down on them, Wyatt heard.
And smiled.
And struck a sulfur match on his boot heel and touched it
to the brush.

Nellie saw the sudden blaze above them and scrambled to
her feet.

"Mack, I saw someone on the hill up there."

"Are you sure?"

"Yes, I saw a man. Someone started that fire."

* * *

Chuckling to himself, Wyatt ran stealthily through the brush. He slipped and stumbled across the ridge and struck another match and tossed it, then ran the other way, starting a third blaze. All three leaped high and quickly began to spread. Wyatt bobbed up and down on his toes, tapping his palms together like a gleeful child.

"I saw him too," Mack yelled over the roar of wind and the crackle of fire. It leaped down the dry slope, devouring brush, growing hotter and higher every moment.

"Come on, Nellie, we're going down."

"What about the tent? Our things—"

"The hell with *things*. Hurry."

He caught her hand, the hand with the plain circlet of gold on the fourth finger. They started for the winding foot trail to the glade where they'd left the surrey. Above them, the fire raised a red wall with flags of smoke blowing on top. After running twenty yards down the trail, they looked back. A long finger of fire poked their tent and then the canvas smoked, blackened, and burst into flame.

Mack shielded her with his arm, the wind snapping his shirt-sleeves and tossing her cap of graying hair. Stumbling, sliding, they ran on with the whole ridge starting to burn behind them.

Through rents in the wall of flame, Wyatt watched. A sudden enraged confusion swept over him. He'd made a mistake by not waiting; they were escaping.

No, he said to himself. And aloud, "No."

He skidded down a slope, around the left edge of the fire. It was traveling down the ridge with incredible speed, having already consumed the tent and engulfed the campsite.

The *santán* gusted suddenly and fire billowed at Wyatt from the right. His sleeve caught.

He shrieked in a high girlish voice, pounding his arm against his thigh until he beat the fire out. Then, careless of his footing, he stumbled and fell, bouncing, rolling, turning over and over, dry brush whipping his cheeks, small stones raking and drawing blood. He rolled into a shallow gully that braked his descent abruptly.

His left leg was bent beneath him. As he started to roll over and straighten it, he knew something was wrong. *Christ—the pain* . . .

He screamed, and then he felt intense heat. Twisting onto the other shoulder, he saw the fire directly above, racing down.

He screamed words this time.

"Mack! Mack, help me!"

On the foot trail, running and jumping and at the same time steadying Nellie, Mack heard the cry. He dug in his heels, and Nellie exclaimed and crashed into him, rattling his teeth. He bit his tongue and tasted blood.

He stroked her hair while he stared upward at the rampart of fire, not believing what he'd heard, yet almost certain he wasn't mistaken.

"Mack!"

"That man's hurt."

"The one who set the fire?"

"God help me, Nellie—I know who it is," he said, pulling away.

"You can't go back up there."

He ran up the trail.

Mack climbed the ridge through the raging wind, choking smoke, furious heat.

Wyatt lay on his side in the shallow gully, in excruciating pain. On the back of his unwashed neck he felt the fire coming closer. His confused thoughts sorted themselves with a speed and clarity unknown to him since well before the tabernacle failed. He stretched a hand downward.

"Hurry, Mack."

"Wyatt? Is it you?"

In his dementia, Wyatt started to weep. "I didn't want to kill you," he sobbed. "But Fairbanks promised me a lot of money . . ."

Running, climbing, pain beginning to bore into his chest from the exertion, Mack shouted the name he thought he'd heard. "Fairbanks?"

"Fairbanks," Wyatt cried, so clearly there was no possibility of misunderstanding. Mack was fifty feet below Wyatt, but the fire was scarcely twenty above the fallen man. The heat began to parch Mack's exposed skin, and he flung up a forearm. The hillside was bright as noon, the *santan* and the fire singing an evil duet, soprano and bass.

"Mack, hurry, I'm hurt, I can't move—"

"Hold on," Mack shouted, now within twenty feet of him. A blast of fire leaped over the gully, almost into Mack's face. The smoke blinded him and set him coughing.

Go on.

He ran at the fire with every intention of doing so, but

734

stopped when the flames shot over his head. Through a rent in the smoke he had a glimpse of Wyatt's trousers burning, and then his hair. A hand with spread fingers groped for the sky. Flame ran up Wyatt's sleeve . . .

The fire wall battered Mack backward, and the gap closed.

Mack held Nellie in his arms a half-mile down the trail. Above, the fire was jumping to a second ridge, and very faintly, on the dark flatlands below, alarm bells pealed.

"I couldn't get him," Mack said, his eyes full of angry tears. "Not without dying myself, and I wasn't willing. God, that's shameful."

"How can you say that? He came up here to kill you."

"He must have gone crazy. Poor Wyatt. Poor Wyatt."

Wyatt the failed dreamer.

California had given Mack everything. For Wyatt, everything was too much. The freedom was too much. And it had killed him.

THE OPERA WAS *Trovatore*. AT THE FIRST INTERVAL, **85** Mr. and Mrs. James Macklin Chance and their guests, the Essanay star Margaret Leslie and the character player H. B. Johnson, left the Chance box for the lobby.

It was autumn, the season's gala opening, and everyone was in finery. The circle foyer was packed, and so was the magnificent marble stair leading down. Some crushed their way up; some crushed their way in the opposite direction. The foursome were among the latter, and Margaret excited comment and drew stares because her face was widely known. Johnson beamed; the old cowboy looked almost respectable in white tie and tails.

"Do you like it?" Margaret asked as they squeezed and pushed on the stair.

"Not much. I don't know Eyetalian and I don't know what they're carryin' on about," Johnson complained.

Margaret patted him soothingly. "You'll understand in the next act."

"But I won't like it."

She patted again. Under the great crystal chandelier, a diamond bracelet worn outside her white glove winked with starry light. Anderson had given her the bracelet when he decided the public loved her.

A few steps below, Nellie and Mack came upon a familiar couple.

"Governor. Mrs. Johnson," Mack said. He shook hands with Hiram Johnson while Nellie exchanged greetings with the first lady.

Hiram Johnson drew Mack to the balustrade and whispered a word or two in his ear.

"Consider it done, sir."

The governor and his wife then pressed on upward. Near the bottom of the stairs, Mack paled suddenly. Nellie said, "Darling, what—?" and then saw a couple breaking away from a group.

Walter Fairbanks III. And his wife.

Mack's head whirled in a red fury. He'd not seen Fairbanks since Wyatt died in the Hollywood foothills, his body consumed and never found. Mack thought Wyatt had probably been responsible for the bullet fired into his car in Riverside too. Nellie wondered how her husband would react, given the name Wyatt had shouted just before the end. She watched Mack with a grave air, knowing that in the old days, the old California, a man like Mack, meeting a man like Fairbanks, would have drawn a pistol and shot him.

Now, looking trim and altogether proper in his tails, Mack simply stood by the balustrade, defying the lawyer to come up.

Fairbanks didn't avoid his eye—Mack had to give him that much. He held Carla's elbow to steady her on the steps. Mack tried to imagine what Fairbanks would say, and how he should answer.

It was an unnecessary effort; Fairbanks cut him, walking right by and waving at an acquaintance at the head of the stairs. Over her shoulder, Carla gave Mack a blurred smile of apology.

Then, a step above Mack and a step behind her husband, she stumbled. Mack shot his hand out to prevent a fall, and her face came into focus. There was still something youthful and cornflower-pretty about her blue eyes, but the rest was wasted, ruined by drink, age, and weight. Carla Hellman Chance Fairbanks wore Parisian clothes, an amber satin gown with a dolman wrap of black-and-gold brocade, a white fox fur edging the wrap; some creature was always dying for Carla, he thought cynically. She was opulent, but fat, every pound an unhappiness. He felt sorry for her.

"Thank you, Mack. Thank you so much." She pressed his hand with her glove and gave him an intense look. He thought he detected a certain confusion or doubt in her eyes, but then it dissolved.

A glance up the stairs showed her husband occupied with his acquaintance. "Please telephone me Monday," she whispered. "Walter will be in Sacramento arguing an appeal. There's something I want to tell you before I go away. It's important. Please call."

Fairbanks was glaring down at her, and now she signaled that she was coming. Under her perfume Mack smelled whiskey. She tottered up the stairs.

With Nellie's permission, he telephoned Carla as requested.

She arranged to meet him at two o'clock at virtually the same place he'd confronted Abe Ruef. Today the weather was different. Marin's gentle hills were sharply defined in the crystalline sunlight, and the sparkling Golden Gate teemed with inbound and outbound marine traffic.

Mack paced up and down, consulting his watch. Carla was late. For a moment he wondered if Fairbanks had found out about the meeting. Possible, but not likely, he decided. Carla's husband was busy with many other things these days, domestic matters the least of them. Only a week ago, over highballs at the Olympic Club, Rhett Haverstick had told him a story about the lawyer.

"I have a colleague who's wild for Charles Dickens. He came up with this wonderful Dickensian name for Walter, and every other attorney in the City—at least the ones who despise Walter, and that's a majority—is using the name behind his back. They call him Mr. Oldefood."

"Mr. what?"

Haverstick repeated and spelled it.

"I don't understand."

"Simple enough," Haverstick said. "Walter has a practice, all right: real estate contracts, society divorces. Hardly sufficient to keep him in his customary style, but of course that doesn't matter with the income from all his Fairbanks Trust stock. However, there is a man's money, and then there is his self-respect. The only legal work that enables Fairbanks to call himself a real attorney—keep a staff of clerks and typewriters—is the work from the people who cast him off, like the SP legal department. They throw him crusts and bones. Hence Mr. Oldefood. Esquire." Haverstick chuckled. "If he ever heard the name it would kill him."

So Mack had won a victory of sorts. But it gave him no satisfaction.

Carla's chauffeured auto arrived at twenty past two. She stumbled toward him along the esplanade.

"I can't stay but a moment, my dear. I'm leaving in the morning."

"Yes, I recall you made some reference to that. Another trip?"

"Not one I care to take. Walter's sending me away. All the way to New York—Saratoga Springs, a health spa. Actually it's a sanitarium for drunkards."

"God, Carla." He shook his head.

"Oh, perhaps it'll do me good," she said with an airy, empty laugh. "We're not here to discuss my woes. We haven't for years, have we?"

Thinking of her husband, he said impulsively, "Will you answer one question for me?"

"I'll try, sweet."

"What the hell has Walter wanted all these years? From me, I mean? Just my life? My complete total capitulation?"

"You mean you have no idea?"

"Would I ask if I did?"

"To be like you."

"Like—"

"You. He's wanted to be like you from that first day Papa refused you a drink and you stood up to him. You're what Californians used to be . . . and Walter never was."

She touched his face with an elegant glove. "Oh, Mack. So much trouble between us. So much terrible trouble . . . I hated you, a lot of times I wanted to hurt you, but I was never bored. Never with you; Papa was wrong about that. You're the only man who never bored me for a single minute. I was afraid of you most of the time. I was afraid you'd see all of my bad side, and then start thinking about it . . . I was afraid, and frightened people are angry people. That's why I drank so much around you. I knew you hated it. And then I walked out on you and the baby when I was drunk and crazy and . . . well, you know. Papa was absolutely right about one thing. You are the best man I ever loved. If you want to know the truth—the only one."

Mack turned red.

Bright tracks of tears showed on her pouchy cheeks. "I want to tell you something in absolute confidence," she went on. "Something you deserve to know. You mustn't ask how I come

738

by the information, just take me at my word when I say it's true. Promise?"

"All right, yes."

A long beat of silence.

"Our son is alive. Walter saw him in Pasadena and I saw him in Redlands this spring. He's taken another name. He wanted no part of Walter. He said you were his father."

Mack wondered if he'd been hurled back to the moment when the great quake rocked the earth. He felt so.

"Now I hope you believe I love you."

Slowly, tenderly, Carla leaned forward and gave his cheek a wet, mussy kiss. She left lip rouge like a bloodstain.

Looking his face up and down, she caressed it once. Then, with the stiff, stately elegance sometimes achieved by the inebriated, she walked down the esplanade. A floating cloud covered her with shadow.

"THE LAME BOY? JIM DAVID?" The manager of the Redlands Citrus Cooperative pointed into the sunshine.

86

"Should find him right out there somewheres."

Mack turned his homburg around and around in his nervous, sweating hands.

"Jim David? Hello. Do you know who I am?"

His face said he did.

"I guess you also know that I'm not your father. But I've come here to say I want to be if you'll have me."

On the ladder, Jim David stared at the well-dressed white-haired man, so out of place in the sunny orange grove.

CODA

EL DORADO

1921

THE PAINTED SIGN ATOP THE HUGE HANGAR ANNOUNCED ITS owner.

CALROSS AVIATION
LONG BEACH • LONG ISLAND CITY
LONDON • PARIS

The hangar doors were open, and a trim racing biplane stood on the sunlit tarmac, its colors gold and black.

Mack walked out of the hangar in a leather coat, helmet, goggles, and a too-flamboyant white scarf. He was portly now, his face heavily lined.

Nellie followed, along with Jim, limping as always, but tall and smart in his business suit. He was twenty-three years old this twenty-eighth day of September, and while he couldn't whirl a girl on the dance floor, he was one of the most sought-after bachelors in Southern California.

Johnson emerged from the hangar pushing Jocker in a bright chrome wheelchair. Mack's chauffeur had fetched the old man from a home for the elderly, where he was maintained in good style at Mack's expense. Jocker was snowy-haired. His hands rested on the blue tartan coverlet wrapped around his legs; they were grotesquely misshapen. But his eyes were sharp and alert, and his smile was genuine. He understood the significance of the occasion.

Proudly, Mack indicated the Calross Special standing on the chocks. "There she is, Jim, with the new Swiss racing engine that's going to help us whip the Curtiss R-One."

Jim smiled but said nothing. He wasn't sure Mack had finished speaking. People were obliged to listen attentively to J. M. Chance; he was that kind of man.

Nellie watched her husband with loving tolerance. Nearly as gray as Mack now, she wore a two-piece country suit of tweed, complemented by a white ascot and a black silk sailor—all bought in Paris on Mack's last business trip.

Nellie hadn't published a novel since *Huntworthy's Millions*. She hadn't abandoned writing—she did it regularly, three or four mornings a week—but had moved to nonfiction. She had nearly finished a work closely related to her early career, a candid memoir of her days on the *Examiner*. She called it *We Made the News*. It was doubtful that Mr. Hearst would care for it.

"We're going to race her," Mack said. "The Pulitzer Trophy this fall—hell, I may even put floats on her and send her to Europe for the Schneider Cup. She's yours."

"Sir? I believe I misunderstood—"

"No you didn't. The Special is yours. Happy birthday, my boy."

Mack hugged him. "Don't look so startled. Why shouldn't I give my son a plane if I want? You're an excellent pilot, and you're doing a first-class job managing the finances of Calross. And all the other companies."

"Thank you, Pa. It's a labor of love. You know that. Have you flown her?"

"Not this version. The privilege of the first flight belongs to the owner. You."

With a teasing smile, Jim said, "I know it isn't politic to disagree with the founder of the firm, but the first flight has to be yours. With my compliments."

"No, no, I couldn't—"

"Pa, I insist. If it wasn't for you, the Special would be just another dream on a designer's drawing board. Please—take her up."

"Well," Mack muttered, abashed and touched. "Well—all right. Thank you, son." He started fitting on his leather flying gloves tucked into the belt of his coat. Jim and his stepmother exchanged amused glances.

"Ah, wait, I almost forgot," Mack said abruptly. He reached into the pocket of his leather coat for something flat wrapped in butcher paper. "Small. But important. With my love."

Jim unwrapped the butcher paper and then looked wonderingly at his father. "Your book."

"That's right. T. Fowler Haines. The original. I thought it was time I passed it on. That book taught me a lot, my boy. It taught me about the real treasure of California. It isn't oil, or oranges, or real estate—or even the gold people are still panning for up in the Mother Lode country. It isn't the sunshine or the Sierras that make this state so special. It's hope. That's the real gold of California, Jim—hope. Not a human being on God's earth who doesn't need hope." He squeezed his son's shoulder. "I want you to have the book. I wish I could get rid of that damn blizzard dream as easily."

Jim flung his arms around his father. Jocker chortled.

744

A moment later, Nellie took Mack's arm. "I'll walk out to the plane with you."

Surprised, he said, "Why, certainly, come along." Jim stayed with Johnson and Jocker, thumbing the pages of *The Emigrant's Guide to California & Its Gold Fields*.

As they walked, Nellie said, "I don't know whether this is the appropriate time . . ."

"Time for what? You sound positively ominous."

"Time to tell you a secret I've harbored for years. Sometimes I've quite forgotten it. The book reminded me. I didn't know you were going to give it to him."

"What is this, Nell? What secret are you talking about? You're too old to be pregnant."

She laughed. "The book—T. Fowler Haines."

"Yes? What about it?"

Glancing back at their son, she stepped near the plane. She kissed his cheek and by means of that, contrived to whisper, "It's a fake."

"I beg your pardon?"

"Mack, don't be angry. You've always respected the truth. This is the truth. T. Fowler Haines never traveled west of his birthplace on the Passaic River in New Jersey. Remember, years ago, I said I intended to look him up? I did. I discovered a whole literature of scholarship about Gold Rush guidebooks, chiefly centered on exposing the fakery of most of them. In '49, publishers were no different than they are today. They seized on every trend. And the Gold Rush was the biggest event of its time. Eastern publishers rushed to hire any available hack, and Haines was one, a journalist for the penny papers. He died at thirty-six of a liver ailment, one year after he wrote his guide in a loft near Printing House Square. He was no worse than a lot of others."

"Why didn't you tell me before?"

"Many a time when we fought, I came close."

"But you held back."

"Some knives are just too sharp to be used."

"Well."

Mack rested a hand on the rim of the cockpit of the Calross Special and studied the sky with a vaguely wounded air. "Well," he said again. "Haines may have been a fraud, but he was right about California. Dead right." His mouth set. "I refuse to tell Jim."

She touched him affectionately.

"That was my idea too."

* * *

The mechanic ran out of the hangar and Mack lowered himself in the cockpit. A moment later the hornet snarl of the water-cooled aluminum-block Hisso engine deafened the observers. Mack showed a thumbs-up above the cockpit. The mechanic jerked the chocks. Then the Calross Special rushed down the sunlit runway.

Suddenly airborne, the racing plane rose through the splendor of the morning, mothlike against the panorama of the California mountains, the California sky.

Holding her black sailor hat, Nellie murmured, "I've seen that same look on his face as long as I've known him."

"So've I," Johnson said. "He's goin' prospectin'."

"He'll never stop," Jim said. He put an arm around his stepmother's waist and his other hand on Jocker's shoulder, and they watched the Calross Special shrink to a dot above the blue Pacific. Flying due west.

> The real Eldorado is still further on.
> —Peck's 1837 New Guide to the West

AFTERWORD

It is hard to believe in this fair young land . . . because
there has always been something about it that has incited
hyperbole, that has made for exaggeration. . . . For there
is a golden haze over the land—the dust of gold is in the
air—and the atmosphere is magical and mirrors many
tricks, deceptions, and wondrous visions.

CAREY MCWILLIAMS
California: The Great Exception

California is quintessentially American. Yet it is also a universal symbol, exerting a universal appeal with its visions of sunshine and surf, palm trees and movie glamour, indolence and
escape and renewal. California is the world's paradigm of hope
and opportunity.

Why this is so, and how it came about, are subjects I have
long wanted to explore in a novel, together with some of the
flavorful and exciting history of the state as it changed from
the old frontier to a modern society. On my shelves of California reference works I can immediately locate the first one I
bought, a general history of the state by Warren Beck and
David Williams. I bought it in a chain bookstore a couple of
blocks from the Beverly-Wilshire Hotel, where I was staying
on a book promotion tour. On the flyleaf I inked the year,
1979. I wanted to write about California before I finished *The
Kent Family Chronicles*, or undertook *The North and South
Trilogy*.

A decade later, *California Gold* is the realization of that
dream.

The late John Dickson Carr wrote a number of vivid and entertaining mystery novels with historical settings. At the end of each one, Carr always added a section to footnote certain events in the story or explain any small liberties taken with the factual record. These he called "Notes for the Curious." I have borrowed his apt phrase for the same purpose. Before each note, I have given the section and chapter most appropriate.

I.5 and *ff*. My portrayal of the railroad, its methods and influence, is consistent with the attitude of a great majority of Californians at the time. They feared and loathed "the Octopus." In the early decades of the twentieth century, this highly negative slant was almost universal among scholarly and popular historians. Today, however, the early, traditional view is considered one-sided and unfair, and is being challenged by scholars. The revisionist view is that the railroad empire created by the Big Four not only united the nation, but was a major force in the growth of California; in short, the SP was not the absolutely malign power it was perceived to be in the late nineteenth and early twentieth centuries. I am aware of at least one scholar who is working on a new, more balanced history of the SP, and there may be others.

I.5 Pope Leo XIII published the Encyclical *Rerum Novarum (On the Condition of Labor)* in May 1891, later than indicated in the story. This remarkable letter is "a comprehensive analysis of the world labor problem," and a far-seeing humane plan to alleviate it.

II.13 and *ff*. Bao Kee's nickel ferry is based on John L. Davie's larger, and later, effort to make a success of such a service. He had a thriving business for a short time, but ultimately the competitive muscle of the SP was just too strong, and Davie's ferry line shut down.

III.16 Health claims in Wyatt's literature are taken from promotional literature of the day. Truth in advertising did not exist.

III.21 The Los Angeles typographers' strike actually took place in 1890. In 1888, however, Harrison Gray Otis was already campaigning against the open shop.

IV.27 Johnson's oil burner was actually invented by Lyman Stewart of Hardison & Stewart, the forerunner of Union Oil (now Unocal). The present-day corporation cannot turn up a detailed description or picture of the burner. If there are any oil historians out there who can, I would be grateful to know;

this remains one of a few loose ends of historical research that I could not tie up to my satisfaction.

IV.31 Some details of the railway accident are taken from the January 1883 wreck of the Overland Express at Tehachapi Summit. It was a famous tragedy of the period; fifteen people died.

V.34 and *ff.* Chinese laborers were driven from the orange groves when the panic of '93 sent thousands of unemployed whites onto the roads of California seeking work. There is a great dark vein of bigotry running through California history. Driving around Riverside on March 15, 1988, I saw the following spray-painted on a large water tank: ALL NIPS MUST DIE. CALIFORNIA NATIVES RULE.

V.41 The lovely phrase "spellbound in darkness" is the title of a work on silent pictures by the late George Pratt, a distinguished film historian.

VI.44 An immigrant from Britain, W. K. L. Dickson, invented the Kinetograph at the Edison laboratory in 1888. Later, Edison lent his name to the Vitascope projection system of Thomas and J. Hunter Arant of East Orange, New Jersey, because it was superior to the projection system he was developing. As stated in Part IX, Edison was not always enthusiastic about moving pictures, but he was a keen promoter, and took more credit for creating the movies than he deserves.

VI.49 I have advanced the date of Barney Oldfield's driving exhibition in Riverside by some months. The speed record was actually set in December 1902, and it was broken six months later, again by Oldfield.

VII.56 Abe Ruef drove through San Francisco with $50,000 in shirt boxes one month after the earthquake, not before.

VII.56 and *ff.* I arbitrarily advanced the commercial introduction of the Rolls-Royce Silver Ghost by one year because I wanted Mack to drive one of these great cars.

VII.61 Despite the devastation and tragedy, there are occasional flashes of humor in the aftermath of the 1906 earthquake. While the story may be apocryphal, Caruso is said to have been awakened when part of the ceiling of his room in the Palace Hotel fell on him; he reportedly dashed into the street in his nightshirt, clutching a towel and an autographed photo of President Roosevelt and exclaiming, " 'ell of a place. Give me Vesuvius!'' From the same fount of legends comes the story of a young actor on tour, John Barrymore, who, in characteristic fashion, was too busy to get up when the commotion started; he was in bed at the St. Francis with someone else's fiancée.

VIII.62 Like Jim Chance, and at roughly the same age, Jack London was a hobo on the road. Later in life, in very euphemistic and unrevealing language, he wrote about his experiences with "jockers"—older tramps who kept young road boys as "slaveys"; the inference is that while many of the men used their young companions sexually, London escaped this fate.

VIII.62 Nellie's outdoor café—and the slogan on it, deriding Oakland, are taken from a postquake photo showing those very things. Jokes about Oakland were common even then.

VIII.66 On November 13, 1908, the rejected juror Morris Haas shot Francis J. Heney, as described. Of course he did not shoot any fictional characters.

IX.73 Young Charlie Chaplin filmed four short comedies at the Essanay studio out in Niles. However, he found the facilities too primitive and, with Anderson's consent, moved on to Los Angeles.

IX.76 The bombing of the *Los Angeles Times* ultimately dealt a severe blow to organized labor. In April 1911, after a sensational nationwide manhunt, detective William J. Burns (of the San Francisco graft investigation) arrested one Ortie McManigal, characterized as a "professional dynamiter." McManigal in turn implicated John McNamara, secretary of the International Association of Bridge and Structural Iron Workers, and his brother Jim. Labor leaders staged parades and gave speeches protesting a "frame-up," and Clarence Darrow was retained to defend the trio. Then McManigal struck a deal to become a state's witness. In the face of conclusive testimony, the McNamaras stunned their fellow trade unionists by confessing that they had indeed planned the crime. Darrow counseled them to plead guilty to avoid execution, which they did. The muckraking journalist Lincoln Steffens, a Californian from Sacramento, helped arrange the plea bargain; General Otis was understandably the hardest to persuade.

X.81 The "Committee of Conscientious Citizens" did exist for a short time in rural, largely Protestant Hollywood. The committee circulated petitions urging that movie actors be kept out of the community at all costs.

X.82 and *ff.* Indian migrant workers began coming down from Canada in the first decade of this century, bringing to the fields a high level of agricultural skill, like the Japanese and Chinese before them. The landmark book on this subject, *Factories in the Field* by Carey McWilliams (1939), estimates that by 1915, the peak year, there were ten thousand Indians at work in the state. Two of them wrote fascinating personal memoirs of their experiences.

Coda *The Emigrant's Guide* by T. Fowler Haines is an invention of the author, but is based on many other Gold Rush guidebooks compiled by eastern journalists who never set foot in the West. Among the most famous are those of Joseph Ware (a best-seller), Henry Simpson, and J. Tyrwhitt Brooks (real name: Vizitelly).

Finally, here are a few brief notes on people and stories touched on in the novel.

William Randolph Hearst lived until 1951; the publishing empire he founded of course exists to this day. Hearst's long and flamboyant career included attempts to be elected mayor of New York and governor of the state, and heavy-handed efforts to influence America's public policy (he was notably successful at whipping up fervor for the Spanish-American War). Hearst had a mistress for many years, the former Ziegfeld Follies girl Marion Davies, whose film career he promoted and financed. For the two of them, he constructed his fabulous coastal retreat in Big Sur, San Simeon, a tourist landmark. Late in his life he used the full power of his empire to condemn and try to suppress Orson Welles's classic *Citizen Kane,* whose central character is clearly Hearst.

James J. Corbett lived until 1933, and earned money on the stage in a play specially written for him. According to the record, he was a creditable actor.

Jack London died young, at age forty, in 1916. He was world famous, but had been broken physically by alcohol and diseases contracted in his travels.

John Muir's remarkable life ended in 1914. To the last, he crusaded against damming the Hetch Hetchy Valley, but it was a losing fight, and the struggle weakened and saddened him. President Wilson and his secretary of the interior eventually cleared the way for the project, and the dam was completed in 1923. (It's difficult to know whether the 1988 Reagan-administration proposal to destroy the dam, drain the valley, and create a second tourist destination like Yosemite was a serious idea or just more bureaucratic maundering.) Regarding Muir, the great naturalist and conservationist, James D. Hart closes the Muir entry in *A Companion to California* with these words: "More sites in California have been named for him than for any other person." Dr. Hart's volume is available, and indispensable to any serious student of California history.

In 1914, Ambrose "Bitter" Bierce went to Mexico on a journalistic expedition in search of the guerrilla Pancho Villa. He disappeared and is presumed to have been killed, though no one knows the circumstances.

As noted above, Lyman Stewart's little oil company was the forerunner of one of the world's largest, Union Oil. Ed Doheny's street well in Los Angeles was the foundation of a dynasty of California oil and money. Doheny was implicated in the Teapot Dome scandal during the administration of Warren Harding.

Abraham Ruef was paroled from prison in August 1915, and received a pardon in 1920. He dealt in real estate until the end of his life in 1936, and died bankrupt.

History has a way of turning bandits into benefactors. Henry (Ed) Huntington, one of the heirs of the rapacious Big Four, was a passionate book collector whose agents sought out and bought whole libraries around the world. He created the Henry E. Huntington Library and Art Gallery in San Marino, one of the great historical repositories of this or any other continent. Some of the important research material used in this novel came from the Huntington.

Acknowledgments

Quite a few people have contributed time and knowledge to this novel. I want to thank them publicly. Whatever the contribution—a letter, a bibliographic reference, the vetting of some copy, just general support and encouragement—it must be made clear that none of them should be held responsible for errors of fact or judgment in the text. The sole responsibility is mine.

During my research, I collected a great many books on California, among them some handsome first editions. To gather them, I had the help of three California bookmen: Jim Chapman of Barry Cassidy Rare Books, Sacramento; Michael Dawson of Dawson's, Los Angeles; and Richard Hilkert of Richard Hilkert, Bookseller, San Francisco. Many thanks, gentlemen.

The following people also deserve special appreciation: John and Val Curry of Hilton Head Island (John's grandparents founded Camp Curry at Yosemite, and for some years John himself managed the Ahwahnee Hotel); Merry Franzen, docent of Heritage Square, Los Angeles; Ed Hardy, president of Yosemite Park and Curry Company; Dr. Gerald Haslam; Michael T. Hogelund of Unocal Corporation; Andrew Jameson, librarian-historiographer of the Bohemian Club, San Francisco; Rainer Heumann; Beverly Rae Kimes; Peter LaMotte, M.D.; Harry Lawton of the University of California at Riverside; Kim Miller, librarian of the Antique Automobile Club of America; Vince Moses, curator of history at the Riverside Municipal Museum; my friend Jay Mundhenk, an expert historian as well as veteran of the California food-and-wine business (and also a descendant of the Berryessa family); Elizabeth Young Newsom, curator of the Waring Historical Library, Medical University of South Carolina; Andrew Nurnberg; Bill Roe, an expert polo player and friend (who promised to keep his weight down so he could play the villainous Billy Rodeen in any film version of this book), and Bill's good wife, Nancy, who raises horses and is encyclopedic about polo in her own right; Dick Schaap; Charles Silver of the Film Study Center, Museum of Modern Art, New York City; Monsignor Francis J. Weber, archivist of the Diocese of Los Angeles; and Jim Young, assistant sports-information director of the University of California at Berkeley.

In preparation for writing, I read literally hundreds of articles, monographs, diaries, news clippings, statistical studies, and books—mountains of books. Almost all were useful, and a great many were memorable. Two, however, deserve special mention because of the intellectual debt I owe to them. *Americans and the California Dream, 1850–1915* and *Inventing the Dream: California Through the Progressive Era*, both by Dr. Kevin Starr, are seminal works. Starr chronicles and explains the great political and social themes and movements of California history. Scholarly, yet written with felicitous style, these are challenging books packed with detail. They richly reward the patient and inquiring reader.

I have saved the best, and most important, for last.

I traveled extensively in California before I sat down to plan and write the book. But my two home bases are on the East Coast, so I decided, for the first time, that I needed an on-site representative. I was miraculously blessed with a recommendation that I contact Melissa Totten of Los Angeles.

For over a year, Melissa served as my research associate in California. She found invaluable documents in all the great libraries, checked obscure points, provided me with the addresses of experts, and generally performed herculean labors of scholarship with unfailing accuracy and good humor.

I am, quite literally, old enough to be Melissa's father, and whenever I grow despondent about some of the sluggards who pass for young people these days—sluggards who think success ought to come without effort; who consider that a half-baked job is good enough because who really cares anyway?—I have only to think of Melissa, and be encouraged by the realization that there must be others like her (but not many!). She was a good right hand in the West, and a good companion on field trips. I thank her heartily. Like me, I think she will be a graduate student all her life—no matter what her "real" profession. She also knows the single most important thing about using California's great scholarly libraries: how to find a parking place.

This novel marks the start of what I trust will be a long and happy relationship with my new publisher, Random House. I am particularly pleased to be with Random House because they publish two of the absolute giants among historical novelists, James Michener and Gore Vidal. It's appropriate, then, that I acknowledge the ongoing support and encouragement of four Random House people: Bob Bernstein, Joni Evans, Susan Petersen, and Bob Wyatt. I also send thanks to Howard Kaminsky, who was with Random House when I came aboard.

I am grateful to Amy Edelman for her intelligent and skilled copy editing (and for pointing out several blunders by our forgetful author—the kind of blunders that are perhaps inevitable in a twelve-hundred-page manuscript but that nevertheless cause red faces if they see print). My editor, too, aided the project all along the way with his invaluable thoughts, expertise, and general good cheer. He won't be named here; he knows who he is.

My good friend and counselor, attorney Frank Curtis, has guided this work from its inception. My debt to him is much too large ever to be repaid.

And my wife, Rachel, as always, has been there from the beginning, with her steadfast encouragement and unfailing love.

Final Thoughts

California author Gerald Haslam writes of "redskins" (native-born regionalists) and "palefaces" (literary carpetbaggers from outside the Golden State)—and I am unmistakably one of the latter. Perhaps I'll never understand California as thoroughly or deeply as a writer born there; still, I have formed some strong views.

For example, the general level of travel writing about California is, in a word, pitiful. When I began to build my library of California books, I bought up all the standard travel guides that I could find. I opened them when my wife and I started planning our first research jaunt, and was horrified to discover, in such a purported industry "standard" as *Fodor's California*, that the whole central part of California is ignored. One finds something about the Mother Lode country, and of course a little chapter on Yosemite, but there is just one skimpy mention of the vast agricultural basin that now supplies 25 percent of U.S. food crops. It hardly exists; it is a *non*-place. The editors of the volume assumed that visitors would never want to go there—even though the Central Valley is not only essential California, but fascinating in its own right. Unfortunately, most California travel books share this kind of shortcoming: Their California consists of San Francisco, the redwoods, Big Sur, Los Angeles, Disneyland, Universal City Studios, San Diego, Yosemite, and the casinos and resorts at Tahoe.

Moreover, the universe of California historical scholarship is finite and surprisingly small. Books that should exist simply don't. A new scholarly history of the building of the Central Pacific is badly needed; *The Big Four* by Oscar Lewis has been the standard work since the 1930s, and while it's good as far as it goes, it's thin. There is an apologist biography of C. P. Huntington, but no balanced and readable one. There is no full biography of Ed Doheny that I could locate. There is no biography-filmography of Broncho Billy Anderson, our first Western movie star, who was as big as or bigger than William S. Hart, Tom Mix, or John Wayne. These and other gaps await some new and talented Ph.D. candidates in history.

In the late winter of 1988, as Melissa Totten and I were driving up to Riverside on a sunny but smoggy morning, she laughed and said, ''When they ask you about the hardest part of studying California, you can tell them it was finding it in the pollution.'' Right. There is a particular sadness in looking at present-day California, and then reading the descriptions of its clean, pristine beauty in works such as Nordhoff's from the late nineteenth century. If California is quintessentially American, it is also the exemplar of the quintessential American ruin—the destruction of a place of God-given beauty, chiefly by the automobile, its manufacturers, sellers, and users. If I were to put a slogan on a bumper sticker, it would be this: SAVE YOUR STATE BEFORE IT'S TOO LATE. Maybe it already is.

There was a kind of accidental symbolism in an event that occurred in March 1988, a few weeks before I wrote the first chapter: My fifth grandchild, Duncan, was born in Santa Rosa, California. My own roots go back to a farmer named John Downs, who fought in the Virginia Continental Line throughout most of the Revolution. My people, descended from Downs, who, as a veteran, was granted land by Congress, are mostly midwesterners. Duncan is the first native Californian in my family. It seemed a fitting and propitious omen.

To close, I present this novel to the diverse people of modern

California, a gift in appreciation of what has been a wonderful learning experience.

—John Jakes

Greenwich, Connecticut
San Francisco, Santa Rosa,
    Sonoma, Modesto, Yosemite,
    Bakersfield, Riverside,
    Los Angeles, California
Hilton Head Island, South Carolina

January 4, 1988–January 24, 1989

#1 *NEW YORK TIMES* BESTSELLERS BY

J O H N
J A K E S

THE BELOVED
NORTH AND SOUTH
TRILOGY...

❏ **North and South**   0-451-20081-0/$7.99

❏ **Love and War**   0-451-20082-9/$7.99

❏ **Heaven and Hell**   0-451-20083-7/$7.99

"An entertaining...authentic dramatization of American history." —*New York Times*

Classic John Jakes...
The New York Times *bestselling*
Crown Family Saga

❏ **Homeland**   **0-451-19842-5/$8.50**

"A powerful tour de force, a rich, sweeping story of America as only Jakes can tell it. *Homeland*...is a marvelous blend of fact and fiction, the stuff of great historical novels."

—Nelson DeMille

❏ **American Dreams**   **0-451-19701-1/$7.99**

"Exhilarating...*American Dreams* allows readers to vicariously experience a time and place far removed from their own... Top-notch."

—*Chattanooga Times*